Cynthia Harrod-Eagles grew up in Shepherd's Bush, attended Edinburgh University and University College London, and had a variety of jobs in the commercial world, from junior cashier at Woolworth's to Pensions Officer at the BBC. She won the Young Writers' Award in 1973, and became a full-time writer in 1978. She is the author of over seventy successful novels to date, including thirty-one volumes of the Morland Dynasty series.

Visit the author's website at www.cynthiaharrodeagles.com

CYNTHIA HARROD-EAGLES

The Fourth Bill Slider Omnibus

Gone Tomorrow
Dear Departed

sphere

SPHERE

This omnibus edition first published in Great Britain
in 2009 by Sphere

The Fourth Bill Slider Omnibus
Copyright © Cynthia Harrod-Eagles 2009

Gone Tomorrow Copyright © 2001 Cynthia Harrod-Eagles
Dear Departed Copyright © 2004 Cynthia Harrod-Eagles

The moral right of the author has been asserted.

A CIP catalogue record for this book
is available from the British Library.

ISBN 978-0-7515-3998-1

Typeset in Amasis by Palimpsest Book Production Limited
Grangemouth, Stirlingshire
Printed and bound in Great Britain by Clays, St Ives plc

Papers used by Sphere are natural, renewable and recyclable
products sourced from well-managed forests and certified
in accordance with the rules of the Forest Stewardship Council.

Mixed Sources
Product group from well-managed
forests and other controlled sources
www.fsc.org   Cert no. SGS-COC-004081
© 1996 Forest Stewardship Council

Sphere
An imprint of
Little, Brown Book Group
100 Victoria Embankment
London EC4Y 0DY

An Hachette UK Company
www.hachette.co.uk

www.littlebrown.co.uk

Contents

Gone Tomorrow

Author's Note

Shepherd's Bush and White City are real places, of course, but this *is* a work of fiction, so if certain liberties have been taken with the geography, please don't write and complain. None of the characters is based on a real person; and though there is a police station at Shepherd's Bush, my Shepherd's Bush nick is a made-up one, as are the Phoenix and the Dog and Sportsman pubs; which have no relation to any hostelry living or dead.

CHAPTER ONE

Too Much Like Aardvark

By the time Detective Inspector Bill Slider got to the scene, the rest of the circus was already there: the area had been closed off with what always struck him as inappropriately festive blue-and-white tape, the screens were erected, and uniform had got the crowd under control and space cleared for official cars.

Detective Sergeant Hollis held his car door open for him.

'You're very kind,' said Slider, climbing out.

'I used to get hit if I wasn't,' Hollis said. He was a scanty-haired beanpole of a Mancunian with a laconical delivery.

'Atherton not in yet?' DS Atherton, Slider's bagman, was due back from holiday that morning.

'Not when I left.'

Slider nodded towards the screens. 'Who is it?'

'Dunno, guv. He's not saying much. Large bloke, no ID. I don't recognise him.'

'Who found him?'

'Parkie. He doesn't know him either.'

Hammersmith Park was a long, narrow piece of land which lay between the White City estate and Shepherd's Bush. It had a gate at either end. One was in South Africa Road – home to the stadium of Queen's Park Rangers football team, known locally, for their horizontally striped shirts, as *ve 'oops* (or, if they had been having a successful run, *superoops*). The other gate was in Frithville Gardens, a cul-de-sac turning off the main Uxbridge Road which also led to the back door of the BBC Television Centre. Between the two lay the moderately land-scaped green space of lawns and trees, with a sinuous path from gate to gate which was used as a cut-through for estate dwellers to and from the Bush.

Slider had been called to the South Africa Road gate. Just inside it, to the left, was a children's playground, whose amenity had been much reduced over the years in the retreat before vandalism. There was a paddling pool with no water, a sandpit with no sand, two rocking horses which, in the interests of safety, had been bolted to the ground and no longer rocked, and two sets of swings, one for babies and one for children.

Between the playground and the road was a small two-storey building which had once been an office and residence for a park keeper. It was now unused and all its orifices had been sealed up with breeze-block – the only way these days to keep out vandals, who had the tenacity of termites and would set fire to their own left legs in pursuit of a thrill. The only purpose of the building now, Slider noted a little glumly, seemed to be to conceal activity in the playground from anyone passing by in the street.

The body was on one of the children's swings. Slider passed through the screens to take a look. The swings were of a simple, municipally sturdy design, suspended from a framework made of scaffolding poles by chains thick and heavy enough to have towed a ship. The seats were made from short, thick chunks of wood that might have been chopped from railway sleepers, and the one was bolted to the other with sufficient determination to have resisted mindless destruction.

Deceased was seated, slumped forward, head and arms hanging, legs bent back and feet resting pigeon-toed on the ground. He had been a large, muscular man, otherwise he would probably have slipped off; as it was, he was kept in place by his own weight pressing against the chains, the bulge of the deltoids to one side and the pectorals to the other making a sort of channel for each chain to lie in snugly.

Hollis ranged up silently beside Slider.

'When was he found?' Slider asked.

'Park keeper came to open up at half seven. The gates are open between seven-thirty in the morning and dusk,' he added, anticipating Slider's question. 'Dusk is a bit of a movable feast, o' course. Sunset's around nine o'clock, give or take, this time o' year. But in practice the parkie shuts up when he feels like it, or when he remembers.'

Slider grunted, staring at the body. It was a fit-looking man, probably in his thirties, dressed in an expensive leather blouson-type jacket and a thin black roll-neck tucked into tight blue jeans, Italian leather casuals and a gold chain round his neck.

'The Milk Tray man's uniform,' Slider commented.

'He looks like an up-market bouncer,' Hollis agreed.

The hair was light brown and cut very short, the face was Torremolinos tanned, and he had a gold earring in the top of his left ear, small and quite discreet, the sort that said *okay, I'm cool, but I'm also tough.*

It was strangely hard to tell with corpses, when the face was without expression and the eyes closed, but this man probably would have been quite good-looking in life, of the sort a certain kind of woman fell for. Only his hands let him down: they were ugly, with badly bitten nails and deep nicotine stains. He wore a heavy gold signet ring, unengraved, on the middle finger of the right hand – the place fighters wore it, where it would do most damage.

Hollis reached out with a Biro and delicately lifted aside one side of the jacket to show Slider the stab wound below the left breast. 'Single blow, right where he lived. The only one as far as I can see, without moving him.'

'Not much staining,' Slider said. There was a stiff little patch around the wound, but nothing had gushed or dripped. 'Probably killed him instantly. If the heart had gone on pumping for any length of time there'd've been a lot more blood.'

'That's what I thought. Professional?' Hollis suggested.

Slider did not commit himself. 'No sign of the weapon?'

'Not so far.'

'And no ID?'

'Nothing in the jacket or the back trouser pocket. I've not gone in the front trouser pockets, o' course, but they feel empty.'

'Those jeans are so tight there can't be room down there for much more than his giblets,' Slider observed.

'Anyroad, all I found was money and fags.'

'Oh well, there might be something more when we can strip him off. Doctor been yet?'

'No, guv. Held up in traffic.'

Slider stepped back out to look around. What had brought this man here to his death? A meeting? Or perhaps he had been killed elsewhere and left here on the swing as a nasty kind of

joke? At all events, it was a fairly private place, hidden from
the road by the bulk of the defunct building. The park was overlooked only from the right-hand side by the upper floors of the
flats in Batman Close, and then only in winter. At this time of
year the foliage on the well-grown trees baffled any view of
the ground. Yes, provided a person could get into the park in
the first place without attracting attention, the spot was well
chosen.

Beyond the park railings a small murmuring crowd had now
collected, the usual mix of the idle, the elderly, and truanting
kids. Slider scanned them automatically, but he didn't recognise anyone except Blind Bernie and Mad Sam, a well-known
couple round the Bush. Mad Sam was Blind Bernie's son, and
was not mad, only mentally retarded, a round-faced, smiling
child of forty. He was Bernie's guide, and Bernie looked after
him. They each kept the other out of A Home, the thing both
dreaded with Victorian horror. Slider could see Sam's lips moving
as he told Bernie what he could see, and Bernie's as he translated what Sam told him. Now he came to think of it, they lived
in Frithville Gardens, so they naturally would be interested in
something that happened in what was virtually their front garden.

Along the roof of the disused keeper's house a row of sea-
gulls sat, shuffling their wings in the small breeze and turning
their heads back and forth to see if all the unusual activity
portended food. Once, they had come up into the estate from
the Thames only in bad weather, to shelter, but now they seemed
to live here all the time. Probably the large area of high buildings reminded them of cliffs; and there was plenty of rubbish
for them to pick over. They had forgotten the sea; but on a
quiet day their raucous squabbling cries brought it near in
Slider's mind.

It was quiet here today, with the road temporarily closed to
traffic. Somewhere out of sight a car horn broke the gentle
background wash of distant city sounds, a composite murmur
like the 'white noise' of silence; a crow cawed in one of the
park trees, a fork-lift truck whined briefly behind the wall of
the TVC, and far above a jumbo growled its way to Heathrow,
flashing back the sun as it crawled between clouds.

All around, for miles and miles in every direction, in streets
and shops and houses, real life was going on, oblivious; but

here a dead man sat, the full stop at the end of his own sentence, with a little still pocket of attention focused fiercely and minutely on him. Why him? And why here? Slider felt the questions attaching themselves to him like shackles, chaining him to this scene, to a well-known process of effort, worry and responsibility.

He had a moment's revulsion for it all, for the blank stupidity of death, and longed to be anywhere but here, and to have any job but this. And then the doctor and the meat wagon arrived simultaneously, one of the uniforms asked him about press access, the police photographer came to him for instructions, and one of his own DCs, Mackay, turned up with the firm's Polaroid. Extraneous feelings fled as the job in hand claimed him, with a familiarity, at least, that was comfortable.

Detective Superintendent Fred 'The Syrup' Porson looked exhausted. He'd had this nasty 'summer flu' that was going around – seemed to have been having it for months – and his face looked grey and chipped. The rosy tint to his pouched eyes and abraded beak was the only touch of colour in the granite façade.

The HAT car (Homicide Advice Team) had been and gone, assessing the murder.

'We're keeping it,' Porson told Slider.

'The playground murder?'

'What did you think I meant?' Porson snapped irritably. 'Queen Victoria's birthday? And you don't know it's a murder yet.'

'Single stab wound to the heart and no weapon on the scene,' Slider mentioned.

'When you've been in the Job as long as I have, you'll take nothing for guaranteed,' Porson said darkly.

Slider almost had been, but he let it pass. The old boy was irritable with suffering.

'Anyway, it's ours,' Porson repeated.

'The SCG doesn't want it?' Slider asked.

The SCG was the Serious Crime Group, which had replaced the old Area Major Incident Pool, or AMIP. No doubt the change had brought joy to some desk-bound pillock's heart, and SCG was one letter shorter than AMIP which must be a great saving on ink; but since the personnel in the one were the exact same as had been in t'other, Slider couldn't see the point. It was hard for a bloke at the fuzzy end to get excited about a new acronym, especially one that did not trip off the tongue.

'SCG's got its plate taken up with the Fulham multiple,' Porson answered. 'Plus the Brooke Green terrorist bomb factory – to say nothing of being short-handed, *and* having four blokes on the sicker.'

Slider met The Syrup's eyes and refrained from reminding him that they too were short-handed. What with chronic under-recruitment, secondment to the National Crime Squad – not to mention to the SCG itself – plus absence on Roll-out Programmes and the usual attrition of epidemic colds, IBS and back problems – the ongoing response of over-stretched men to a stressful job – there could hardly be a unit of any sort in the Met that was up to strength. But Porson knew all that as well as he did. The SCG were supposed to take the major crimes, which these days generally meant all murders apart from straightforward domestics, but the fact of the matter was that Peter Judson, the head fromage of their own particular SCG, was a cherry-picking bastard who had obviously logged this case as entailing more graft than glory and tossed it back whence it came.

'After all,' Porson went on, trying to put a gloss on it, 'when push comes to shovel, it's a testament to your firm's record of success that they want to bung it onto us.'

'Yes, sir,' Slider said neutrally.

'You ought to've got a commendation last time, laddie, over that Agnew business. It was pure political bullshine that shot our fox before we could bring it home to roost. So here's your chance to do yourself a bit of bon. Brace up, knuckle down, and I'll make sure you get your dues this time, even if I have to stir up puddles till the cows come home.'

The allegories along Porson's Nile were more than usually deformed this morning, Slider thought, which was generally a sign of emotion or more than usual stress in the old boy. But he knew what he meant. He meant that Slider should put his nose to the wheel and his shoulder to the grindstone, a posture which inevitably left his arse in the right position to be hung out to dry if necessary; and Slider had a feeling, from the preliminary look of the thing, that this one was going to be a long, hard slog.

When he got back to the office, Atherton was there, looking bronzed, fit, rested and generally full of marrowbone jelly. Slider felt a quiet relief at the sight of him. Atherton had been through some tough times recently, including a near nervous breakdown, and there had been moments when Slider had feared to lose him altogether. He'd had other bagmen in a long career, but none that he would have also called his friend.

Atherton did not immediately look up, being engaged with the *Guardian* crossword. DC McLaren was hanging over his shoulder, a drippy bacon sandwich suspended perilously on the way to his mouth.

'I can't read your writing,' McLaren complained. 'What's that?'

'Aardvark.'

'With two a's?' McLaren objected.

'It's a name it made up for itself when it heard Noah was boarding the ark in alphabetical order,' Atherton explained kindly. 'The zebras were exceptionally pissed off, I can tell you. That's why they turned up in their pyjamas – as a kind of protest.'

'Now I know you're back,' Slider said. Atherton looked up, and McLaren straightened just in time for the melted butter to drip onto his front – which was used to it – instead of Atherton's back. Atherton was a classy dresser, and it would have been an act of vandalism akin to gobbing on the Mona Lisa.

'No need to ask if you had a good time,' Slider said. 'You're looking disgustingly pleased with yourself.'

'Why not?' Atherton agreed. 'A fortnight of sunshine and unfeasibly energetic sexual activity. And now a nice meaty corpse to get our teeth into.'

'Some people have strange tastes. How did you know, anyway?'

'Bad news has wings. Maurice was talking to Paul Beynon from the SCG while you were upstairs.'

'I knew him at Kensington,' McLaren said. 'He rung to give me the gen.' His time at Kensington was his Golden Age, source of all legend. Amazingly, it seemed he had been popular there. At all events, they were always ringing him up for a bunny, and vice versa.

'So it seems I just got back in time,' Atherton said.

'Yeah, from what you said, another day'd've killed you,' McLaren said lubriciously.

'How's Sue?' Slider asked.

Atherton smiled. 'You'll never know.'

McLaren pricked up his ears. 'Oh, is that who you were with? That short bird I saw you with that time? Blimey, you still going with her?'

His surprise was understandable, if tactless, for Atherton had always demanded supermodel looks as basic minimum, and Sue – a colleague of Joanna's – was neither willowy nor drop-dead gorgeous. She had something, however, that melted Atherton's collar studs. But he didn't rise to McLaren. He merely looked sidelong and said, 'You know the old saying, Maurice: better to have loved a short girl than never to have loved a tall.'

'Right, shall we get on with it?' Slider interposed. The rest of his team, bar Hollis and Mackay who were still at the scene, had come in behind him. 'With no identification on the corpse, we've got more work even than usual ahead of us. In fact, I expected to find you all hard at it already,' he complained.

'We have been. Hive of activity, guv,' McLaren said smartly. 'Just waiting for you to get back to see how you wanted it set up.'

'Never mind that Tottenham. When did I ever want it set up any differently? Here's the Polaroids from the scene. And I shall want a sketch map of the immediate area up on the wall. Get on with it, Leonardo.'

McLaren stuffed the last of the sandwich in his mouth. 'Right, guv,' he said indistinctly. 'Get you a cuppa first?'

'From the canteen? Yes, all right, might as well. It'll be a long day.'

'Get me one too, Maurice,' Anderson said.

'Slice cake with it?'

Anderson boggled. 'You what? Turn you stone blind.'

McLaren shrugged and hurried off.

Atherton shoved the newspaper into his drawer and unfurled his elegant height to the vertical. 'He probably thought you meant DiCaprio,' he observed to Slider.

The park keeper, Ken Whalley, was in the interview room, his hands wrapped round a mug of tea as if warming them on a cold winter's day. He had a surprisingly pale face for an outdoor worker, pudgy and nondescript, with strangely formless features, as if he had been fashioned by an eager child out of pastry but not yet cooked. Two minutes after turning your back on him it would be impossible to remember what he looked like. Perhaps to give himself some distinction he had grown his fuzzy brown hair down to his collar where it nestled weakly, having let go the top of his head as an unequal struggle.

He looked desperately upset, which perhaps was not surprising. However un-mangled this particular corpse was, it was one more than most people ever saw in a lifetime, and finding it must have been unsettling.

Slider, sitting opposite, made himself as unthreatening as possible. 'So, tell me about this morning. What time did you arrive at the park?'

Whalley looked up over the rim of the mug like a victim. He had those drooping lower lids, like a bloodhound, that showed the red, which made him look more than ever pathetic. 'I've already told the other bloke all about it,' he complained. 'Back at the park. I told the copper first, and then I had to tell that plain-clothes bloke an' all.'

'I know, it's a pain the way you'll have to keep repeating the story,' Slider sympathised, 'but I'm afraid that's the way it goes. This is a murder investigation, you know.' Whalley flinched at the 'M' word and offered no more protest. 'What time did you arrive?'

Whalley sighed and yielded. 'Just before a'pass seven. I'm supposed to open up at a'pass.'

'At the South Africa Road end?' A nod. 'And what time did you leave home?'

He seemed to find this question surprising. At last he said, as if Slider ought to have known, 'But I only live across the road. I got a flat in Davis House. Goes with the job.'

'I see. All right, when you got there, were the gates open or shut?'

'Shut. They was shut,' he said quickly.

'And locked? How do you lock them?'

'With a chain and padlock.'

'And were the chain and padlock still in place, and locked?'

'Yeah, course they were,' Whalley said defensively.

'And what about the Frithville Gardens end?'

'I never went down there. Once I saw that bloke in the playground I just rang you lot, and then I never went nowhere else.' He looked nervously from Slider to Atherton and back. 'Look, I know what you're thinking. You're thinking I never locked up properly last night.'

'I didn't say that.'

'Well I did. I done everything right, same as always. It's not my bleedin' fault 'e got done!'

'All right, calm down. Nobody's accusing you of anything,' Atherton said. 'We just need to get it all straight, that's all. Once we've got your statement written down we probably won't need to bother you again.'

Whalley seemed reassured by this. 'All right,' he said at last, putting the mug down and wiping his lips on the back of his sleeve. 'What j'wanna know?'

'Tell me about locking up last night,' Slider said. 'What time it was, and exactly what you did.'

'Well, it was about a'pass nine. I'm s'pose to lock up at dusk, which is generally about arf hour after sunset, but it's up to me. I generally lock up earlier in winter, 'cause there's not so many people about. It's a cut-through, but there's no lights in the park, so we can't leave it open after dark. Course, people still want to take the short cut, and they used to bunk over the gate, so we had them new gates put on down the Frithville end, with all the pointy stuff on top.'

Slider had seen them: irregular metal extrusions, vaguely flame-shaped, topped the high gates, looking as if they were meant for decoration but in fact a fairly good deterrent. Of course, a really determined person could climb over anything, but the flames prevented 'bunking' – hitching oneself up onto one's stomach and then swinging the legs over – which would deter the casual cutter-through.

Whalley went on, 'But in summer it stays light longer and it depends what I'm doing what time I shut up. But anyway, I went over a'pass nine with the chains and padlocks. What I do, I shut the South Africa gate but I don't lock it, then I walk through telling everyone it's closing. Then I lock the Frithville gate, and walk back, make sure everyone's out, then lock the South Africa gates.'

'And that's what you did last night?'

There were beads of sweat on Whalley's upper lip. 'That's what I'm telling you, inni? I did everything just like normal and then I went home.'

'Have you ever seen deceased before?'

'No, I never seen him before in me life,' Whalley said emphatically. 'I don't know who he is, and that's the truth.' He wiped his lips again.

'Did you see him in the park anywhere before you locked up?'

'What, j'fink I wouldn't a noticed a bleedin' dead body?' Whalley said indignantly.

'No, I meant did you see him alive? Was he hanging around, perhaps?'

'I dunno. No, I never.'

'Was there anyone in the park who took your notice? Anyone unusual or suspicious-looking?'

Whalley drew up his shoulders and spread his hands defensively. 'Look, I don't go checking up on people,' he whined. 'It's not my job. I just go through telling 'em it's closing. Everyone was out before I locked up, that's all I know. You can't put it on me. F' cryin' out loud!'

'It's just,' Slider said gently, 'that you said you didn't go down to the Frithville gate this morning, but when one of our constables went down there, there was no padlock and chain. The gates were shut, but they weren't locked.'

Whalley stared a long time, his lips moving as if rehearsing his answer. Then at last he licked them and said, 'Someone must've took 'em.' Slider waited in silence. Whalley looked suddenly relieved. 'Yeah, someone must've cut through 'em. You could cut that chain all right with heavy bolt-cutters.'

Walking away from the interview room, Atherton eyed his boss's thoughtful frown and said, 'Well?'

'Well?' Slider countered. 'How did you like Mr Whalley?'

'Thick as a whale sandwich, and more chicken than the Colonel. What did you think of him?'

'I don't like it when they start supplying answers to questions they've no business answering,' Slider said.

'That stuff about bolt-cutters?'

'If you were breaking into the park for nefarious purposes, would you bother to take the padlock and chain away with you? Or having cut through them, would you just leave them lying where they fell?'

'I see what you mean. So you think Whalley's lying? He's nervous enough.'

'In his position I'd be nervous, whether I was lying or not. When a corpse is found on your watch it doesn't bode well even if you're innocent. It's possible he merely forgot to lock the gates, and doesn't want to admit it in view of the consequences.'

'Point.'

'The other possibility is that he's in on it in some way. But what "it" is, we can't know until we can find out who deceased is.'

'Well, I can't see Whalley as a criminal conspirator,' Atherton said. 'He's a pathetic little runt.'

'I expect you're right. It's just the padlock and chain not being there that bothers me. Our corpse was too nattily dressed for climbing over gates. Especially gates with pointy bits on the top.'

'You think he had an appointment in the park?'

Slider shrugged. 'Whatever he went there for, he went there. Alive or dead, he went through one of the gates or over it, and I can't make myself believe in over.'

CHAPTER TWO

Opening the Male

In the post-mortem room of the hospital's pathology department, Freddie Cameron, the forensic pathologist, presented to
the world an appearance as smooth as a racehorse's ear. It was
his response to the unpleasantness of much of his work to culti-
vate an outward perfection. His suiting was point-device, his
linen immaculate; his waistcoat was a poem of nicely calculated audacity and his bow-tie *du jour* was crimson with an old
gold spot.

All this loveliness, of course, was concealed as soon as he
put on the protective clothing, but still he was positively jaunty
as he shaped up to the corpse.

'Anything's better than facing another pair of congested lungs,
old bean,' he said when Slider queried his pleasure. 'I'm even
beginning to eye my bath sponge askance. This flu epidemic
seems to have gone on for ever. Good to see you back,' he
added to Atherton. 'Good holiday? You're looking very juven-
ile and jolly.'

'Fully functioning on all circuits,' Atherton admitted.

'So, you've no ID on our friend here?' Cameron asked.

'Not so far,' Slider said.

'Well, I'll take the fingerprints for you, and a blood sample.
Chap looks a bit tasty, to my view.'

'I agree. Everything about him suggests there's a good chance
he'll feature somewhere in our hall of fame.'

'Right. Well, as soon as my assistant arrives, we'll begin. Ah,
here she is. Sandra, this is my old friend Bill Slider. Sandra
Whitty.'

Slider shook hands. She was an attractive young woman, sensa-
tionally busted under her lab coat. Her lovely profile preceded

her into a little pool of held breath which had gathered round the table; broken a moment later as McLaren muttered fervently, 'Blimey, she takes up a lot of room!'

Why is it we're all so childish about bosoms, Slider wondered. He wasn't immune himself. Charlie Dimmock had a lot to answer for. He met Miss Whitty's eye apologetically. 'Excuse the reptile.'

Fortunately, she only looked amused. 'That's all right, I keep pets myself.'

She obviously knew what she was doing, and handled the body with an easy strength as she and Freddie removed the clothing and put it into the bags McLaren held out. There was nothing in any of the pockets to identify the deceased. One jacket pocket yielded cigarettes – Gitanes, a rather surprising choice – and a throwaway lighter. The other contained a quantity of change and a crumpled but clean handkerchief. The inside jacket pocket contained a fold of notes held with an elastic band. When McLaren unfolded and counted them, it came to over a thousand pounds, in fifties, twenties and tens.

'Now there's a thing you don't see every day,' Freddie said. He breathed in deeply. 'Ah, money! I can almost smell the mint.'

'Evidently robbery from the person was not a factor,' Atherton said.

'But there's no wallet, driving licence, credit card, or any of the gubbins a man carries about,' Slider said. 'Was he unusually self-effacing, or did the murderer cop the lot?'

'If he did, why wouldn't he take the money?' Freddie added. 'Only fair, after taking the trouble to kill the chappie.'

'I'd have taken the jacket,' Atherton said. 'It's a lovely piece of leather. I wonder where he got it?' He looked at the label sewn inside just under the collar. '"Emporio Firenze",' he read. 'Never heard of them. Still, it's very nice.'

'Nice watch, too,' Sandra said.

'Is that a Rolex?' Atherton asked, leaning forward.

'It only thinks it is,' she said succinctly. 'Good fake, though. Date, phases of the moon, two different time zones, alarm, stopwatch function and integral microwave oven and waffle maker. Not cheap.'

'How do you know so much about men's watches?'

'I've handled a few,' she said. Slider could see Atherton working it out and felt a mild urge to kick him. When it came to women he had all the self-restraint of an Alsatian puppy on a bowling green.

'Look here, Bill,' Freddie said a moment later. 'Someone has been into the pockets. You see here, the left inside pocket is stained with blood where it rested against the wound. Now, over here, a tiny smear of blood on the *right* inside pocket. Someone's checked the contents of the left pocket and then transferred the blood on his fingers to the right.'

'While looking for something,' said Slider.

'Which presumably he found,' Atherton added. 'Any chance of a fingerprint?'

'I'll have a look under the microscope, but I wouldn't hold my breath,' Freddie advised. 'It's a very tiny smear.'

When the jumper was removed, it revealed a tattoo on the right forearm.

'Nice,' Sandra commented tartly. It portrayed a plump red heart with a steel-blue dagger thrust through it. There was a realistic drip of blood falling from the tip of the dagger, and around the heart was wrapped one of those heraldic ribbon scrolls bearing the word 'Mary'. It was an unpleasant and disturbing combination of sentiment and violence. 'Mary's a lucky girl,' Sandra said.

'It may help to identify him,' Slider said.

Atherton was not impressed. 'He could have got it done anywhere, any time.'

'Not any time,' Cameron said. 'I'd say it was quite recent – within the last couple of years.'

'All right, but anywhere. If we've got to start trawling the tattoo parlours of the world—'

'It's better than nothing,' Slider said.

'Not by much.'

Slider knew what he meant. A tattoo was a bit like finger-prints – good for confirming an identity when you already knew who you had; but for plucking an identity out of the void, it was as useful as a fishing net on a stick for retrieving a ring you'd dropped over the side of the cross-Channel ferry.

When the body was naked, Cameron made his external examination, reporting as he went. There was a little click every time he activated the tape recorder by means of the foot button; that and his cultured voice were the only sounds that disturbed the hum of the air conditioning. Slider thought it was a bit like being in his office, with the coo of a pigeon on the windowsill and the murmur of traffic outside. Strangely soporific. He found himself drifting a little.

'Deceased is male Caucasian, height five feet eleven, age apparently mid-thirties. He appears to be well nourished and in good health. Good musculature. No skin lesions, no surgical scars. No sign of any drugs usage.'

He measured and described the knife wound in the chest, and continued, 'No other visible wounds. Some evidence of bruising on the left side of the jaw, on the left upper arm and to the knuckles of the right hand. Bruising is not fully developed, suggesting that it was inflicted a short time before death.'

Slider jerked back to the present. 'What sort of bruising?' he asked when the recorder clicked off.

'Looks as if he was in a scrap of some sort. This one on the arm, you see, shows the shape of knuckles: one, two, three lobes and a fainter fourth, the little finger, which has less impact because of the curve of the fist. A right-handed punch, delivered with great force.'

Slider looked, recreating it. 'Probably turning away slightly, fielding it on his arm instead of his face.'

'Well, that should help us identify him,' McLaren said. 'A man with a tattoo who was in a fight.'

'Narrows the field wonderfully,' Atherton agreed.

'Right,' said Cameron, 'let's open him up. Mints, Sandra.'

Sandra Whitty pulled out of her pocket the obligatory tube of Trebor and passed them round. Reaching for his long scalpel, Cameron began to whistle softly, a habit he hardly knew he had. The tune, Atherton recognised after a moment, was 'Some Enchanted Evening'. Whistling, he slipped in the blade and opened the body like a man opening his mail.

A post-mortem is not a pleasant thing to witness, and it was good to have something else to focus on at particular moments. Slider found the lyricism of Miss Whitty's moving torso very soothing. It was plain to Slider that she was quite well aware of the effect she was having. He liked a woman to enjoy her own prowess – why not? – but he couldn't help thinking that it was not the best thing for a newly revitalised Atherton to be exposed to. *One* of them ought to have his mind on the job.

'Well, what can I tell you?' Freddie Cameron said at last, with a certain sympathy in his eye.

'Some good news,' Slider said.

'If I had any of that, I'd open a shop,' Cameron said. 'Deceased died from a single stab wound from a double-edged, narrow blade, about five inches long, maybe longer – there's always a certain amount of compression – which penetrated the heart. There's no sign of any chronic disease or any other contributory cause.'

'And there wouldn't have needed to be?'

'Oh, no. That wound is quite sufficient. Death would have been instantaneous.'

'There's no reason to think he was poisoned or drugged, is there?'

'Nothing in the pathology. The stomach contents are well digested. It looks as if he hadn't eaten for several hours, though I fancy he had a pint not too long before death. Do you want them analysed?'

'Not at the moment. There's the budget to think about, and we might have to have the DNA analysed. Any way of telling whether he was killed where we found him or moved after death?'

'Not really. The hypostasis is consistent with the way he was found, but as you know it can be two or three hours before it settles, and even if the body is moved after it appears, it may well slip down to the new position anyway.'

'And the time of death?'

'Well, old dear,' Freddie said cheerfully, 'I can give you an educated guess. Based on the temperature, I'd say anything up to eight hours before I first saw him.'

'That means some time after midnight,' Slider said. 'I could have told you that.'

'But it could have been earlier,' Freddie went on, ever more cheerfully. 'He was a muscular chap, and it wasn't a cold night; and if he'd been kept bundled up or in a sheltered position – indoors, or in the boot of a car, for instance – he wouldn't have cooled so quickly.'

'I can't think,' Slider said with dignity, 'why they call it forensic *science.*'

'Ah, if only I were a fictional character,' Freddie said, 'I could take one squint and tell you he died at exactly twenty to three on Tuesday-was-a-week.'

'If *he* were a fictional character,' Slider capped him, 'his watch would have stopped at the moment of death and I wouldn't have had to ask you.'

Freddie took pity on him. 'Absolutely best guess, between four and eight hours. But don't quote me. And if you finally discover he was done at eleven pm or five am, don't come crying foul to me.'

'King Death hath ass's ears,' Slider said.

'Sounds like one of those tongue twisters. "The Leith poleeth dismisses us." Not easy to say with a mint in your mouth.'

'Well, guys and gals, the bad news is that the fingerprints have come up with no match. Our deceased friend has no previous.'

There was a murmur. Atherton, sitting on a desk contemplating his shoes, said, 'I must say that does surprise me. He looked like a villain.'

'Maybe he was a successful villain,' said DC Swilley. Her given name was Kathleen, but for phonetic reasons, as well as her ability to look after herself, she had always been known as Norma. For as long as Slider had known her she had been engaged to a man called Tony whom no-one had ever met. Swilley had always been reticent about him to the point of mystery; some – generally those who had tried to make her and failed – had even said he did not exist. Then a couple of months ago she had electrified the department by actually getting married. Tony's surname turned out to be Allnutt, and it had not taken much agonising for Swilley to decide to keep her maiden name while she was in the job. Life was hard enough, even for a tall, Baywatch blonde like her, without adding unnecessary problems.

Atherton for some reason had been very upset about Swilley getting married. He had told Slider he couldn't bear to think of any man defiling her. Slider had pointed out that Mr Allnutt had of a certainty been defiling her for years, but Atherton claimed illogically that she was different since the wedding: less unattainably godlike, somehow diminished. Annoyingly, Slider knew what he meant. There was a strange ordinariness to Mrs Allnutt, a glow of domestic contentment, which was like polished pewter to her previous burnished silver. He didn't, however, go as far as Atherton and blame her for it.

So when Swilley said, 'Maybe he was a successful villain,' Atherton immediately contradicted her.

'There's no such thing.'

'Don't be such a dick,' Swilley said impatiently. 'Of course there is.'

'Criminals are basically stupid. They always give themselves away in the end. We'd have had him through our hands.'

'Yes, and if we'd had to let him go for lack of evidence or whatever, he wouldn't have a record and the prints would've been destroyed,' Swilley pointed out.

'Well, if that's what you call successful—'

'Children, can you wait until playtime if you want to quarrel,' Slider said. 'Now, I must say I was rather counting on a record to identify him. What we're left with is a blood sample which we could have checked against the DNA database, but that's expensive and—?' He looked round like a friendly lecturer.

'If he's got no fingerprint record, there'll be no DNA record,' Mackay filled in obligingly.

'Give that man a coconut. If all else fails we may have to fall back on his dental profile—'

'God forbid,' Atherton said. 'He was pre-fluoride. The bastard had teeth like Madeira cake.'

'It can take months to get a match on dental,' Mackay said.

'Exactly. So before we tread that despairing route, there are other things to do.'

'Mispers,' McLaren suggested.

'It's probably a bit early for that, but check it anyway. And meanwhile, we do it the hard way. Knock on doors, show his face and the tattoo, until we find someone who recognises him.' There was a composite moan. 'Start with the flats and houses nearest the two park gates and work outwards. You know and I know that it's twelve to seven he wasn't from outer space or the Outer Hebrides. He'll have been a local, and chances are he's used the park before for whatever he was using it for.'

'What if he was dumped there dead?' Anderson said.

'Well, that's probably even better from our point of view. It's impossible to move a large dead body around without some-body noticing something. But it's my belief he went to the park alive and was killed on the spot – for the same reason, that it would be a ludicrously difficult place to dump him without being seen.'

'Guv,' said McLaren, 'he was stabbed, had all his ID lifted, but his money left, and no attempt made to conceal the body. That looks like a punishment thing, dunnit? Or a gang thing. He was involved in something and they caught up with him, sorted him, and left him there as an example.'

'That's one theory.'

'I just can't see why they didn't take the wonga,' McLaren urged. 'Who's gonna leave well over a K in folding when it's sitting up and begging to be took?'

Mackay agreed. 'We've got Doc Cameron's evidence that his pockets were gone through, so it can't just be they missed it. But if it was a punishment thing, why not take it anyway?'

'To make it scarier,' Atherton said.

'What?' Swilley challenged derisively.

He shrugged. 'A villain who's not interested in money? It scares the shit out of me.'

'All right, let's get on with it,' Slider intervened. 'While we've got all the uniform help with the doorstepping, I'd like you people to try for a short cut. That's pubs, clubs, cafés, anywhere you can think of on our ground that the lowlife gather – remembering that he might only have been a fringe player. Don't forget your snouts – they're probably the likeliest to know him. Swilley, get the pictures off to the other boroughs. Most likely he's local but he might have strayed at some time or other: it's not as if we've got border control. McLaren, check Mispers. Atherton, have a go at our own dear Criminal Intelligence System to see if there are any matches on single stab wounds to the heart or anything connected with the park. And,' he added through the scrape and rustle of troops rising, 'let's not forget the obvious. Show the pictures to our own. Who's on downstairs?'

'Paxman,' someone said.

'Oh, well, he knows everyone who's ever lived. I think I'll pop down and have a word with him myself.'

Sergeant Paxman was a great solid bull of a man, his curly poll growing a little grizzled now, like an elderly Hereford. He had a bull's massive stillness too, a complete lack of fidget, which spread out around him in waves. It made him invaluable when they brought in belligerent drunks or drug addicts with the screaming abdabs: in a room full of thrashing arms and legs he was a kinetic black hole.

His relationship with Slider had sometimes been uneasy. Paxman was a devout Methodist and disliked any form of moral laxity, particularly in policemen, who he felt ought to set an example to society at large. PCs on his relief tended to find themselves getting married to the people they were living with almost without their own volition. His current favourite in the Department was Norma, whom he favoured, when she passed him, with his rare smile.

Slider had once been one of Paxman's okays, but he had fallen from grace when his marriage to Irene broke up and he went to live with Joanna, who had been a witness in one of his cases. Paxman would never say anything, of course, but his disapproval of hanky-panky spread around him in the same palpable ripples as his stillness. However, Irene had remarried, and Joanna had gone abroad. She was a professional violinist and had been offered a lucrative and prestigious position in an orchestra based in Amsterdam. With work so scarce at home, she had felt she had to take it. Slider missed her with a horrible hollow sucking emptiness; but at least now that he was living alone, hankiless and without a shadow of panky, he thought he had detected a breath of rehabilitation with Paxman.

Paxman stared at the photographs for a long time, stationary as a ton of paper. Slider waited, feeling the dust of aeons sifting down on him, soft and implacable. Then at last the sergeant lifted his head and said, 'No. I don't know him. Not been through my hands. But you said he'd been in a barney?'

'Apparently. He was sporting some knuckle bruises.'

'Hm. Well, there was a bit of a frackarse last night down at the Phoenix.'

'Really?' This was the pub in South Africa Road, a little way along from the park gates. 'Who went down there?'

'Oh, we weren't called,' Paxman said. 'It wasn't anything major. Just a bit of a barney. Two blokes throwing punches. Over before it started sort o' thing. Dunno if it's anything to do with your bloke.'

Slider wondered, if the police weren't called, how Paxman

knew about it; but the question would probably only be answered with a shrug, so he didn't ask it. Sometimes he thought even Paxman didn't know how he knew things. Osmosis, probably.

'Well, thanks, Arthur,' he said. 'It might well be something. I'll point one of my lads at it.'

'Right,' said Paxman. He laid an enormous hand over the photos. 'I'll keep these, show 'em around. You never know.'

You never did, Slider agreed. 'And pass them on when the relief changes? Thanks.'

In the event, Slider went down to the Phoenix himself. He wanted another look at the immediate surroundings. The White City was a large estate of five-storey blocks of council flats, built in the thirties. It had originally been created to be a complete community, with its own shops, park, playground and public house, the General Smuts. However in the sixties there had been a small expansion on its south-eastern border, where the new park had been opened; and there an infant school, another row of shops and a second pub had been added.

Created in that unloved period of architecture, the Phoenix was everything a pub didn't ought to be, a featureless pale-brick box with picture windows. It inspired no affection or loyalty as a local, and almost from the beginning the rougher types had been tempted there. Now most of the picture windows had been bricked up to avoid temptation, and the interior was as dark as an American bar – so dark the security cameras Slider noted at the angles of the ceiling must have worked on infra-red. The prevailing design motif was the avoidance of anything that could be picked up and thrown. The bar stools and tables were bolted to the floor and the only other seating was the banquettes round the walls, covered in red leatherette gaping open to its foam filling in numerous wounds. The brewery that owned it had recently yielded to this fashion trend and restocked with plastic beer glasses. It was that sort of pub.

On this sunny day, however, it was peaceful. The door was standing open to let some light into the interior, and the three customers it could boast were sitting up at the bar over their pints not bothering anyone. The landlord was a moody-looking bald man with a glass eye. He looked about fifty, but was mega fit for it, with a weightlifter's vast shoulders and nipped-in waist, which he emphasised by wearing a clinging black teeshirt and jeans with a heavy leather belt cinched tight in between. The fact that he was only five foot six somehow made him seem more, rather than less, dangerous, as a terrier is more unnerving than a Great Dane.

His name, according to the licence notice over the door, was Colin Collins – which Slider reckoned was enough to jaundice a man from earliest childhood – but he was always known as Sonny. Slider assumed it was spelt with an 'o': a 'u' would have been too needlessly cynical. He had old, faded tattoos on his forearms and left biceps; and at some, presumably drunken, point in his merry life he had had a dotted line tattooed right round the base of his neck. In the gloom of the far reaches of the bar his black-clad torso was almost invisible, and his pale throat and gleaming ivory head floated eerily above the dotted line as if someone had already obeyed the implicit instruction to cut along it.

Slider introduced himself and passed the photographs over the bar. Collins looked down at them with his good eye, while the glass one continued to stare furiously at Slider. It must be something that came in handy when dealing with the obstreperous, Slider thought, and was briefly beguiled by the memory of a story Tufty Arceneaux, the forensic haematologist, had told him about his time in Africa. It was about an up-country estate boss Tufty had frequently drunk with, who had a glass eye. When he couldn't be in two places at once the bloke used to take the eye out and leave it to supervise, the natives believing that he could thus see what was going on *in absentia*. Once a man had been brought to him for discipline, but he had been called away urgently in the middle of the interview, so he had left his glass eye on the desk and told the man to stay put. In dealing with the emergency he had forgotten to go back, and the miscreant had sat in the office facing the eye for four days. His relatives had taken turns bringing him food and water.

Sonny Collins didn't take four days about it, but it seemed to Slider an uncomfortably long time to wait under the basilisk gaze. 'I understand there was a bit of a barney outside last night,' he prompted. 'Two men throwing punches. I wondered if this was one of the men.'

'Might be,' Sonny vouchsafed at last.

'Can you tell me about it,' Slider asked patiently.

'About what?'

'About the fight.'

Sonny shrugged, and his massive muscles manoeuvred about under his skin like Volkswagen Beetles trying to pass in an alley. 'Not much to tell. Two blokes started arguing.' He closed his mouth tightly after each sentence like someone switching off unnecessary lights to save electricity. 'One's throwing his lip. Effing and blinding. Told 'em to take it outside.'

'And they went.'

'In my pub,' Sonny Collins said, suddenly expansive, 'when I say take it outside, outside it goes.'

'I believe you,' Slider said, trying a bit of flattery. It melted Collins in the same way a one-bar electric fire melts a block of granite. Both eyes were as yielding as marbles as they stared at Slider. 'What time was this?' he asked, humbled.

'About closing time.'

'And what happened outside?'

'Didn't see it. Heard about it. Not much of a fight. Couple o' punches thrown. Then it all goes quiet.'

'And who were the two men? You think this was one of them? What's his name?'

Sonny Collins stared as if Slider were being irrational. '*I* don't know,' he said impatiently. 'He's not a regular.'

Slider picked up an inference Collins perhaps didn't intend him to. 'But the other man *is* a regular,' he said, not making it too much of a question. 'What's his name?'

Collins seemed to weigh the pros and cons of co-operation. At last he said, 'Eddie.'

'Eddie what?'

The impatience again. 'You don't ask surnames,' he said. 'Pub like this, you don't ask names at all. Heard him called Eddie, that's all. Lives local. Comes in two, three times a week. That's it. That's all I can tell you.'

'And this other bloke,' Slider said, gesturing to the photograph, 'had you seen him before?'

Collins shrugged. 'May have. He looks a bit familiar. That's all I can tell you.'

'Can you describe this Eddie?'

'Tall, dark hair. Fancies himself. Always talking about how many women he's had.' Collins grew impatient. 'Is that it? Only I can't stand chatting to you all day. I got customers to serve.'

None of the other three people in the pub had moved a muscle since Slider had entered. They hunched over their half-empty glasses like three Mystic Megs staring into their crystal balls. Slider thought Collins knew more than he was telling, but he knew he wouldn't get any more out of him now, and if he pushed him it would spoil the chances of getting more next time. With naturally irritable people like him, going against their grain could be counter-productive.

CHAPTER THREE

A Load of Crystal Balls

'You should have let me go,' Atherton said.

'He wouldn't have told you even as much as he told me,' Slider said.

'Why not?' asked Atherton, ready to be offended.

'Because you're tall and he's short. That's psychology,' Slider added kindly. 'So we've got our man having a fist fight outside the pub some time after eleven, and being stabbed in the park a few dozen yards away at any time between then and seven-thirty the next morning.'

'The obvious inference is that they took the quarrel, whatever it was, into the park, and it turned to murder.'

'Hmm. But I always like to resist the obvious,' Slider said. 'And it wasn't the South Africa gate that was unlocked, it was the Frithville gate.'

'That could be nothing to do with it. You said yourself Ken Whalley might just have forgotten to lock up.'

'Yes, and that's more likely than that someone cut through the lock and chain and then carried them away,' Slider said.

'I wish you wouldn't always argue both sides at once,' Atherton complained. 'Still, the simplest solution is that Eddie and deceased had a row, deceased maybe got scared and legged it, nipped over the gate into the park, Eddie followed, caught him up in the playground, and stabbed him.'

'Except that with that gate, you wouldn't be doing any nipping. Climbing carefully would be the order of the day. And if he was running away from a homicidal Eddie he'd make better time sprinting along the road. Eddie must have been right behind him, and he'd have been able to grab him before he got over the gate.'

'You don't know that. Anyway, fear lends wings. Stuffed full of adrenalin, he might have nipped.'

'Fear would have had to lend him a lot of luck, too, not to have torn his clothes on those pointy bits. Anyway, if he did climb over the gate he will have left his fingermarks on it somewhere, so we'll soon know.'

'As will Eddie. Unless they were wearing gloves.'

'Yes, a wise man always puts gloves on to have a fight outside a pub.'

'I get the feeling,' Atherton said with dignity, 'that you aren't taking my suggestions seriously.'

'Oh, did you mean me to?' McLaren appeared in the doorway. 'Yes, what is it?'

McLaren looked pleased with himself. 'Guv, I've had a nibble!'

'Must we discuss your sex life?'

'The betting shop just up the road – corner of Loftus and Uxbridge Road. They recognised the mugshot *and* the tattoo.'

'Betting shop? That was a good idea of yours. What made you think of it?'

McLaren writhed slightly. 'Well, I didn't exactly – I was just passing and I thought—'

'All right,' Slider said hastily. If McLaren had gone in to place a bet while on duty Slider didn't want to have to know about it just now. Later, when all this was over . . . 'So they recognised him.'

'Yeah, they said he used to be a heavy punter until about a year ago. In every day, got through a shitload o' money. Then he just stopped coming. They reckoned he either gave it up or went elsewhere.'

'It took brains to work that out,' Atherton commented.

'Did they give him a name?' Slider asked.

'Said his name was Lenny. They called him Unlucky Lenny. Said he was so unlucky, if Liz Hurley had triplets, he'd be the one on the bottle. He was a foul-mouthed, violent bastard an' all, they said, but he lost so much money with 'em he was worth keeping. When he stopped coming in they didn't know whether to be glad or sorry.'

'Lenny what?'

'Dunno, guv. That's all they knew, Lenny. But they said he was local – lived somewhere local.'

'All right, it's a start, I suppose. You'd better get someone to go round all the other betting shops in the area, see if he changed allegiance.'

'I can do it,' McLaren offered.

'I wouldn't put you in temptation's way,' Slider said kindly. 'Tell Anderson, will you? He's a steady chap.'

'As long as you don't send him to B&Q,' McLaren said darkly, departing.

'So now we've got two people to look for,' Atherton said. 'The pony-mad Lenny and the woman-mad Eddie. Both local and neither with a surname.'

'Sonny Collins said Eddie was a regular. I think there's a case for someone going into the Phoenix tonight to see if he comes in. No, not you,' he anticipated. 'It's got to be someone who fits in at a dump like that. Better be Mackay, I suppose.'

'I won't tell him you said that.'

The full report came in from Freddie Cameron, but he had nothing to add to what had been said at the post-mortem. 'The weapon was a two-edged, non-serrated blade, about five inches long and not more than three-quarters of an inch wide, and with very little taper. The blow was given with sufficient *force* to leave bruising where the hilt or cross-guard struck the skin. However, it does not follow that great *strength* was needed: if the point of the weapon were sharp enough it would penetrate the skin relatively easily and the rest of the blade would follow without effort. I would estimate from the clean edges of the wound that the point in this case was sharp.'

Slider put down the report and imagined the blade. Straight and double-edged like a dagger, but only three-quarters of an inch wide. It sounded like a flick-knife. Add that to the pockets being searched and the money left and it began to sound very much like a gang or professional killing. And if there was one thing that depressed Slider more than another it was gang killings.

He read on. The blood smear on the right inside pocket. No hope of anything from that, it was too small for a fingerprint. Inkstain on the inside bottom of the same pocket. Well, people did carry Biros about, though none was found on the body.

The phone rang.

'Hullo,' said Joanna. 'I've been ringing you at home. Wasted calls are expensive from Frankfurt, you know. What are you still doing there?'

'We've had a murder.'

'Oh dear. I'm sorry to hear that.'

'You sound as if I said I'd got a headache.'

'I should think you have, figuratively.'

'Especially as the corpse is still unidentified. It's hard to find out who dunnit when you don't know who they dunnit to.'

'Still, you oughtn't still to be there. It's a quarter to nine, you know.'

'I've got a man out in a pub, trying to track down a drinker who was seen with deceased. It's a rough pub and I want to be on hand if he gets into trouble.'

'You're a loony,' she said affectionately. 'What're you going to do if he does, rush round and punch noses? That's a job for uniform.'

'I suppose so,' he said reluctantly, and then, 'I do miss you!'

'Me too,' she said briefly.

There was a silence, through which he heard a distant clash of voices. 'Where are you?'

'Backstage. We've just finished the first half. Beethoven fourth piano concerto. Sigmund Manteufel.'

'First half? You make it sound like a football match.'

'With a soloist like him it was like a football match.'

'What was the score?' he asked.

'Beethoven four, Manteufel nil. So now it's the interval. Wolfie's getting me a drink. I wish you were here. Even gin and tonic loses its savour.'

'How d'you think I feel? Going home to that empty flat—'

'Ah, now I know the real reason you're still there at this hour. Are Jim and Sue back?'

'Just. I spent the night there once while they were away,' he confessed. 'On the sofa with the cats. Couldn't face going home to that big empty bed.'

He heard her sigh. 'Bill, you don't make this easy for me.'

'Who said I wanted to?' he answered, but he put a smile in his voice, not to pressure her too much.

'I'd better go,' she said. 'There's a queue waiting for the phone, and the interval's only twenty minutes. You do know why concert intervals are only twenty minutes, don't you?'

'Tell me, tell me,' he said obediently.

'So you don't have to retrain the violas.'

'I love you,' he said.

'I love you too.'

'Phone me tomorrow.'

'If I can get to a phone.'

'And watch out for that Wolf person.'

'Don't worry, Wolfie's not that sort of girl.'

'Ha!' he said. 'You forget, I've met him.'

It wasn't really, he thought as he put the phone down, that he was jealous or didn't trust her. His fear was that she could live without him much more easily than he could without her; and that if she got used to being away from him, she might eventually fall for someone else, especially if someone else was a musician. It was a thing that happened all too easily among people whose jobs isolated them from the rest of humanity, like musicians and policemen. You fell for someone you worked with, however unsuitable they were in every other respect, because they understood your way of life. They knew what you were talking about.

This job Joanna had taken with the Orchestra of the Age of the Renaissance was a permanent position, though she had taken it for the moment on a six-month trial. It was a very good job for her, too good to have turned it down – and not just from the money point of view: it was prestigious, and artistically satisfying as well. But could they continue their relationship on the basis of seeing each other once a month? Could that even be said to be a relationship?

He suddenly realised that he was very hungry – absolutely ravishing, as Porson might say – and that he was doing no-one any good sitting here by the phone, Mackay least of all. Nicholls, who was the uniformed sergeant in charge of the night relief, knew all about it and could be trusted to send in the infantry if there was any trouble – and why should there be, after all?

There was an all-night café under the railway arch next to Goldhawk Road Station where the taxi drivers noshed. Taxi drivers always knew the good places. He had a sudden, golden vision of sausage, egg, chips and beans, tea and a slice, and his mouth watered. Atherton would shudder with horror at the thought, but Atherton had Sue. A man whose love was in

Frankfurt needed the comfort only a greasy fry-up could provide.

Morning brought disappointment. Mackay had manfully done his duty and consumed four pints of deeply indifferent beer, but no-one who might be Eddie had shown up, and the other drinkers with whom he had managed to scrape up a conversation had shown blank incomprehension when presented with the names Eddie and Lenny or the suggestion that there had been a fight.

'I don't know whether they clocked me for a copper and that shut 'em up, or they're just naturally stupid,' he said. 'Bit of both, I expect. I couldn't push it too hard or ask too directly or the barman would've clocked me and that would've been that. Maybe if I went in a few more times, built up a pattern, they might open up.'

'I hate to put anyone's innards through that punishment, but it might be necessary,' Slider said. 'Hold yourself in readiness. Anything from anyone else?'

It all added up to a big, fat zero. 'Nobody jumped at the mugshot or the tattoo,' Norma summed up. 'And my snouts deny all knowledge.'

'Tattoo parlours in the area turn up blank,' said Hollis, 'but that's not surprising. There's no reason it had to be done locally. He could have had it done in Brighton on a day trip for all we know.'

'Nothing from the other betting shops in the area,' Anderson reported.

'Don't you think that *is* surprising?' Atherton said. 'Does a betting man just give up like that? McLaren's source seemed to be suggesting he was a heavy and regular punter.'

'Smokers give up. Alcoholics even. Why not a gambler?' Swilley said.

'I know it's possible,' Atherton countered, 'but is it likely?'

'There's offshore betting these days on the Internet,' McLaren put forward.

'Bit sophisticated for Laddo?' Atherton suggested.

'We don't know how sophisticated he was,' said Swilley.

'He had that swanky watch and that expensive jacket,' Hollis put in.

'Yes, what about that jacket?' Slider said. 'Any chance of tracing it to its source?' He looked at Atherton. 'You're the one who knows about clothes.'

'I don't recognise that brand name,' Atherton said. 'I doubt whether it was from this country, and if it was sourced abroad we'd never track it.'

'Have another look at it,' Slider said, 'and see what you can do. What else?'

'The door-to-door has come up with nothing so far,' Hollis said. His was the unenviable task of overseeing the reports. 'The usual crop of mysterious strangers but nothing that looks like our man. Trouble is, that park isn't overlooked from anywhere in summer, when the trees are covered with leaves.'

'Except from the BBC building,' Swilley said.

'Only from the very top, which is a long way off for recognising anyone, even say someone was bothered looking; and even then, you can't see into the playground.' He met Swilley's raised eyebrows and added, 'Yes, I did go in and try. What did you think I was doing down there all day?'

'So our hope really is from someone who happened to be passing when Lenny went into the park,' she said.

'Or when – to stretch a point – someone carried his body in there,' Atherton added. 'What about the people living in Frithville Gardens?'

'Nothing so far,' Hollis said, 'though there's still some doors to knock on. Trouble is, it was late and most people are in bed by half past eleven.'

'What an indictment of the most exciting, frenetic, cosmo-politan city in the world,' said Atherton.

'Did you turn up anything on the CrimInt?' Slider asked him.

'Nothing to put in the diary.'

Slider rubbed his hair up the wrong way in frustration. 'I can't believe this bloke's never been in trouble before. Maybe we'll get a nibble from one of the other boroughs. Meanwhile, everybody keep asking around. Not just your snouts, but anyone you've ever had contact with who's local, or knows the area. Don't forget that the park is less than half a mile away, and Frithville Gardens is the next road along from here. It won't take the press long to start asking why we can't get a handle on a murder right in our own back yard.'

'I don't see why that's supposed to make it easier,' Swilley said indignantly.

'Police-bashing is their favourite sport,' Slider said. 'When has logic ever come into it?'

It was time, Slider thought, to follow his own advice and talk to a few of his contacts. It was something he had to do in person. In the Job, a man's snouts are sacrosanct; generally they would not talk to anyone else in any case. He had already tried a few phone calls to his usual informants, with no result. Now it was time to spread the net wider.

He bethought himself of One-Eyed Billy, a small-time thief who had latterly managed to pull himself together and go straight. He lived in one of the tiny Victorian terraces in Ethelden Road, but this time of day he ought to be at work; or rather – he checked his watch and registered with routine surprise that it was lunchtime already – in the British Queen having a pint of Bass and a pork pie. This, indeed, was exactly where Slider found him, sitting up at the bar with the paper folded open at the racing pages, pie and pickle part consumed, pint glass usefully almost empty, down to a golden half inch at the bottom and a white line like soapsuds marking the level before his last swig.

'Hello, Billy. What is it?'

He looked up sharply, registered Slider's presence and the absence of anyone at his shoulder, and answered the nod in the direction of his glass. 'My usual, ta very much. Pint o' Bass.'

Slider gestured to George the barman and did the honours. One-Eyed Billy watched him with slight reserve but no hostility. He had two perfectly good eyes to do it with. His name did not denote any ocular deficiency, but was a sort of patronymic, his father having been known as One-Eyed Harry, a well-known local trader with a pie-and-eel shop in Goldhawk Road. Harry had lost an eye in Korea, having been too young, to his intense regret, to be called up for the Second World War – 'the real war', he called it. 'Korea was a bloody mess,' he used to say, 'but dooty is dooty, and I'm proud to have served my Queen and country.' He always kept a framed picture of 'Her Maj' prominently on the wall of his shop and Mrs One-Eye had a large scrapbook of royal family cuttings; they prided themselves

on being old-fashioned honest traders and had given generously to various charitable efforts got up by the police.

So it had been a dreadful shock to them when their youngest
son, Billy, had turned out bad. Harry often said they must have
dropped him on his head when he was a baby; Mrs One-Eye
blamed the sixties. 'What a world for a lad to grow up in!'
However it happened, Billy had early refused to show any
interest in the family business, and had ducked out of helping
in the shop. Harry had stopped his pocket money as a quid pro
quo – 'You don't get anything in this world without working for
it, my lad!' – to which challenge Billy had risen by stealing the
sweets and comics he could not now buy.

The dropped-on-head theory gained ground with the gathering evidence that Billy was not just a thief, he was a very bad
thief. His career developed, if that was the right word, into a
succession of easy cops for the police; his villainy was so petty,
so inept and so plain daft it was hard for them to take him seriously, and he was slapped on the wrist more times than was
good for him. Slider well remembered the occasion when One-
Eyed Harry came, in agony of soul, to ask them not to let Billy
off any more. 'I reckon if he doesn't get a shock and see where
it all leads, he'll be past hope. Me and Gladys are very grateful
for what you've tried to do for our boy, but he's got to learn,
the hard way if necessary. He's bringing shame on the whole
family.'

So when Billy stole a Magimix from Curry's for his mum's
birthday and was caught because he took it back to complain
that one of the fixtures was missing, the boom was lowered on
him, and he went down. The lesson did not immediately strike
home. It took several more years, and sentences to a progressively longer spell in jug, before the shock of his mother's death
(hastened by shame, his brothers said) changed his ways.

He was now employed by an uncle who had a greengrocer's
stall in the Shepherd's Bush market, and was working off his
forgiveness in this world by hard labour and co-operation, when
it was asked for, with the police. His quick guilty glance beyond
Slider's shoulder suggested that he was still up to something,
but Slider thought it was probably something very mild and on
the fringe, like illegal betting or buying hookey fags, which was
best left alone. It was not so much turning a blind eye to crime,

but the necessary price that had to be paid to have Billy just on the sticky side of the line that divided the real world from the criminal world, where he could be useful.

The pints came. Billy said, 'Cheese mite,' and drank off a good quarter, and Slider said, 'Well, Billy, how are you keeping?'

'Straight, Mr Slider,' Billy answered quickly. 'Straight as a die, I promise you. Uncle Sam'd kill me if I wasn't.'

Slider smiled. The guilty man, etc. 'I didn't mean that. Are you well?'

'Gawd, yes. Never been ill in me life.' He was perhaps a little undersized, but stocky enough, with a curiously young face, given that he must be forty by now. It was smooth, almost unlined; small-featured, and pleasant enough under bristle-cut light brown hair, only a little vacuous, and with eyes that were just too far apart, which gave him a slightly glassy look, like a stuffed toy. 'Yourself?' he returned politely.

'Oh, I'm fine. Busy as always.'

'Yeah. This murder up the New Park.' This was what locals had always called it – to distinguish it, of course, from the old park, Wormholt. 'I've been reading about it.' He gestured vaguely towards the newspaper.

Slider saw that it was the *Daily Mail*. 'Bit up-market for you, isn't it?'

Billy smirked. 'I got this young lady now,' he said. 'Bit of a looker, she is, if I say it myself. She's dead posh. Works in that hairdressers on the Green, The Cut Above, it's called. Qualified and everything.'

'Good for you,' Slider said. 'Thinking of settling down?'

'Maybe,' he admitted. 'Anyway, she wants me to better meself, so she's started me reading this instead've the *Sun*.' He looked at the paper a bit hopelessly, and then said, 'Well, I never was one for reading. It's got the racing in it all right, though.'

'I didn't know you were a betting man,' Slider said. 'Fond of the ponies?'

'Oh, I always done a bit. It's an interest more than anything. Me mum didn't approve of betting, but she liked watching the races on the telly. Liked the horses. Same with me, really. Me uncle Sam what I work for now had a horse and cart when I was a kid, did a round on the White City estate. I used to like helping round the stable an' that.'

Slider took a leisurely drink of his pint, feeling Billy relax at this reassuring lack of hustle. 'Funny thing,' he said, 'this bloke that got murdered in the park, he was a betting man. I wonder if you've come across him any time. Unlucky Lenny, they called him.'

Billy chuckled. 'Unlucky Lenny? Gawd, yes! I've heard about him all right. Is that who it was?'

'Seems so.'

'Gaw, what a mug! Talk about good money after bad! Always picked the long odds, daft outsiders, mug doubles, you name it. And if he ever did pick a good 'un, it got scratched or fouled or fell down. He 'adn't got,' Billy added instructively, 'no science. If you're gonna bet on the ponies, you gotter have luck or you gotter have science, one or the other. He didn't have neither.'

'And what have you got?'

'Me? I don't do much, just a bob or two. It's more an interest, like I said. What I got is a sort of instinct. It comes over me every now and then, almost like I can see into the future. I look at a certain horse, and I just know. Then I stick a tenner on its nose and sit back. You'd be surprised how often it comes off.'

Slider would have been surprised. It sounded like crystal balls. In his experience betting men forgot their losses almost instantaneously, but remembered their wins for ever – a function which greatly improved their overall statistics and the bookies' profits. He took another drink and said casually, 'So about this Lenny – what was his surname?'

Billy shook his head. 'Now that I can't tell you. Never knew him personal. Everyone just called him Unlucky Lenny. He used to punt at the shop on the corner o' Loftus Road. Just up the road from you,' he added on an afterthought.

'Yes, I know,' Slider said. 'Know anything else about him? What was he up to, Billy? He looked a bit tasty to me.'

'I dunno exactly, but he was up to something all right,' Billy said, flattered by the assumption of his omniscience. He desperately wanted to give value for money, and Slider could almost hear his brain creak as he strained to remember something worth delivering. 'I see him around the estate a bit,' he said at last.

'Is that where he lived?'

'I reckon he did. I dunno for sure.' A light went on inside his head. 'What I *do* know,' he said triumphantly, 'was he lived with a tom. What was her name? Tanya or Terry or something like that. No, Tina, that was it. Definitely. I heard some geezers talking about her.'

'She was a prostitute?'

'Oh yeah, she was definitely on the game. Lenny knew all about it.'

'Was he her pimp?'

'I dunno. Maybe. He wasn't a professional pimp, I don't mean that. He didn't have no other girls. I reckon he just lived with her. Maybe he like organised it for her. And got it for free himself – you know. They say she's a bit of a sort an' all. A cracker. Goes like a train.' He dropped a man-to-man wink. 'So maybe old Lenny wasn't so unlucky after all, eh?'

CHAPTER FOUR

Tart with a Heart

The tailor's shop was just off Shepherd's Bush Green – a few yards down a side turning, Caxton Street, which made all the difference to the rent and rates. It also made all the difference to the drop-in trade, but one glance at the window showed that drop-in was not the mainstay of this emporium.

Over the window was the name *Henry Samson* in chipped gold-painted plastic letters screwed to a black fascia. The window was exceedingly dirty and contained no display, only some bales of cloth wrapped in brown paper, a couple of old biscuit tins full of odds and ends, and three plastic roses in a vase *circa* 1973.

Atherton pushed the door open, and an old-fashioned bell on a strap tinkled pleasantly. It was dim inside after the sunshine in the street. The shop was tiny, and most of the space was taken up with the shelving round the walls on which bales of cloth were stored. A wooden counter with a glass front was covered in professional litter: scissors, tape measures, boxes of pins and a neglected sea of invoices, orders, correspondence and – probably – final demands from utility companies. The display element of the counter contained cardboard boxes of buttons and zip-fasteners. The tiny unused space in the middle of the floor revealed bare, dusty floorboards and a small square of old carpet on which the customer might stand to view himself in the cheval mirror which stood beside the curtain into the back shop.

The curtain moved now, and the proprietor poked his head out like a stage manager checking the House. The broad, fat, wrinkled old face creased into a smile of welcome, revealing the porcelain uniformity of the National Health's finest.

'Mr Atherton! Welcome, welcome! Just one moment and I'll be with you!'

The curtain dropped, there was a sitcom rustling and thumping of hasty activity, and then it was thrust aside with a rattle of curtain rings, and the tailor came out. His head had first come through the curtain at Atherton's level, but that was because he did his sewing in the back room sitting on a table (which kept the cloth off the dusty floor). Now he was on his own two legs his head was hardly more than five feet from the ground; but what he lacked in height he made up for in girth. He was wide all the way round, with tiny feet and quick, pudgy hands; rimless half-glasses poised halfway down his nose; surprisingly fine eyebrows, and a scantling of hair combed carefully over his bald top and dyed soot black with a tailor's vanity. He wore old-fashioned striped morning trousers with a black waistcoat over a white shirt with the sleeves rolled up. The waistcoat glittered with the needles and pins thrust into both fronts, and a tape measure hung round his neck like a garland of honour.

He advanced, beaming, on Atherton, his hand out, and when Atherton gave his, enfolded it in both his own and pumped it up and down rhythmically as if he hoped for water. 'Good to see you! Good to see you! Are you well? You look well.'

'I'm in the pink, thank you,' Atherton said. 'I don't need to ask you how you are.'

'Never better!' the tailor cried boastfully. 'I'm never ill, you know. Hard work is the best medicine.'

His name was James Mason ('No relation!' he cried gaily on first introduction) but since he had escaped with an older sister from Germany during the war, that almost certainly was not his real name. He admitted to seventy-five, but Atherton would not have been surprised to discover he was eighty-five. With the wrinkles, the vitality and the swift, plump movements it was impossible to tell.

'So what does my favourite customer want this morning?' Mr Mason asked, relinquishing Atherton's hand and drawing the tape measure off his neck with anticipatory relish. 'Favourite customer' was less of a hyperbole than usual with such titles. There was a small group of cognoscenti who treasured Mr Mason as he should be treasured, but he eked out a living with alterations and repairs to clothes it pained him to handle. 'You've come at just the right time, as it happens. I have some cloth here – come, come and see. Let me show you. Just came in this morning, and I thought of you right away.'

He twinkled over to the window and heaved a wrapped bale, with astonishing strength given that it was nearly as tall as him, off the stack and over to the counter, dumping it on top of the clutter with a fine disregard for administration. Quickly he unfolded the brown paper and drew out a length of the cloth. 'Look, look how beautiful. Feel. Lovely, isn't it? I wish I could get more of it, but I thought of you first. I said to myself, "Mr Atherton must have a suit out of this. A pair of trousers, at the very least."'

Atherton stepped forward to finger the cloth. It was charcoal grey with a faint stripe which was not colour but merely in the weave. Mason gazed up into his face, nodding and beaming.

'Yes? Beautiful, isn't it?'

'What is it?'

'You tell me.'

'It's very soft,' Atherton suggested.

'But very hard-wearing. It's a mixture, of course. Wool, cashmere – mostly cashmere – and just a little mink.'

'Mink?' Atherton said, bemused.

'I joke you not. Very hard, mink hair. Cashmere alone would not cope with all the sitting. But mink—!' His eyes screwed up with anticipation of a coming jest. 'When did you ever see a ferret with a bald patch?'

Atherton laughed dutifully, and prepared to break his tailor's heart. 'It's very nice, but I'm afraid I didn't come here for anything to wear.'

Mason took it well. He knew Atherton's calling. He spread his hands a little and said, 'Sandwiches I don't do, it must be information.'

'That's right.' He brought the leather jacket out of the bag he had carried it in, and held it out. 'I hoped you could tell me where this came from.'

Mason looked serious. 'Leather? Leather is something else. I am not an expert on leather.' But he took it anyway, his fingers seeming to do their own examination, separately from his eyes. 'Nice, nice quality skin. Off the shelf, of course, but the tailoring not bad, all the same. An expensive piece, I would say.' He turned to the inside. 'Good-quality wool lining.' It was tartan, but of no clan or sept known to Scotland: a mixture of caramel, cream and milk-chocolate shades. Subtle and attractive.

Mason examined the label, and snorted. 'Not Italian, of course! All the world wants Italian this, Italian that. Why? I can't tell you. Italian food, Italian wine, yes, but when did you ever hear of an Italian tailor? Mean jackets, tight trousers, shoes too narrow – you want to look like a barrow boy? So choose Italian. You want to look like a gentleman . . .' He left a space there for his most generous shrug.

'If not Italian, what is it?' Atherton asked patiently.

'American,' Mason said promptly. 'The cut, the quality of the stitching. And the name I've heard of before.' He examined the two tiny tags sewn into the seams near the bottom. 'North-east America. These code numbers you get in New England, stock control. Not for export.'

'So it was probably bought over there?'

'Yes, but they sell such things also in PX stores. That's export as far as we're concerned, but to an American the PX is United States soil.'

'I see. Well, thank you. I knew you'd be able to pin it down for me.'

'Does it help?' The bright eyes scanned his face keenly.

'I don't know that it does,' Atherton said. Purely in the name of thoroughness he drew out the photographs and showed them to the tailor.

'He's dead, nuh?' Mason said, looking closely at the mugshot. 'It was him who wore the jacket? No, I don't know him. And the tattoo – very few people with tattoos come to me. Or at least, not tattoos of that sort.'

'Ah well, I didn't think you would know him. Thanks anyway. At least I know he got the jacket from America.'

'Or maybe an American gave it to him,' Mason cautioned. 'In payment for a debt, maybe. He doesn't look the kind to get birthday presents. And now, from business to pleasure,' he went on beguilingly, displaying the cloth again. 'A pair of trousers, what do you say?'

'That's business, surely?'

'To make trousers for you is a pleasure,' Mason said seriously. 'I tell you no lie. A pure pleasure, Mr Atherton.'

* * *

'Getting information on this case is like pulling teeth,' Slider grumbled. 'Now we know that Lenny lived with Tina, but not where, and no surnames for any of the blasted crew. And an American jacket. Where does that get us?'

'Nowhere,' Atherton acknowledged. 'We don't know that they were never imported. Or he could have gone on holiday to America and brought it back. People do, all the time.'

'Or bought it in a pub from an American,' Norma added. She was leaning against the door-jamb of Slider's office, her arms folded across her chest like a housewife. Marriage had really changed her, Atherton thought. Any minute now she'd be getting a perm. 'Or from someone who nicked it from an American – that's more likely. So what now, boss?'

'We try and find a tom called Tina,' said Slider.

'Needle in haystack time,' Atherton commented.

'If this were Ruislip it might be worth investigating a possible American connection, but there are no bases near here,' Slider sighed.

'What about the cultural legation or whatever it's called in Holland Park?' Swilley said. 'That's only just up the road.'

'Culture?' Atherton said. 'A bloke called Unlucky Lenny who lives with a tom?'

'Maybe he provided a service of some kind. Even an embassy needs cleaners and dustbin men.'

'That's very profound, Norma.'

'All right, you can look into it,' Slider told Atherton. 'I don't suppose it's anything, but it's better to leave no stone unturned. Meanwhile, it's on with the clubs, pubs and especially door-knockers. If Lenny lived on the estate, he must have been someone's neighbour.'

'Have you any idea how many flats there are on the estate?' Norma said with horror.

'I daresay in a couple of weeks you'll be able to tell me exactly,' said Slider.

Porson was sitting down – in itself an unusual thing. His usual torrent of restless energy seemed to have been staunched. He sat at his desk reading, looking grey and old. Even his wig seemed limp and spiritless. Normally Slider's fascinated fear was that it would go flying off with one of the old boy's rapid changes of direction, but today it seemed to huddle close to the bony pate for comfort like a dog sensing disaster. Slider would have liked to ask if he was all right, but sympathy was not a thing you could show to The Syrup.

'So,' he said, looking up at last, planting a finger to mark where he had stopped reading. He had big, knuckly hands with an old man's chalky, ridged nails, but they pinned down the paper firmly, just as, however random his vocabulary, his mind would pin down the facts of an investigation. 'What have you got?'

'More reports than a balloon-popping contest,' Slider said, 'but nothing to go on yet. We've got a first name, but no surname or address. An informant says deceased lived with a prostitute, but we've only got a first name for her as well, and of course there's no knowing it was her real name anyway.'

Porson looked at him steadily from under eyebrows so bushy they always made him appear to be frowning. 'You know we're going to be under the microscope from the press with regard to this one? Our own back yard, and et cetera?'

'We're doing all we can, sir,' Slider said.

'I know, laddie,' Porson said, unexpectedly kindly. 'But I think we'd better go public all the same. Can't do much investigating if you don't even know who he was, can you?'

'When, sir?' Slider said, with a shrug in his voice. Going public was always a two-edged sword. It might bring in information, but it also warned people you might hope to take by surprise; and it spread knowledge of your weakness across the widest audience.

'Too late today. I'll talk to Mr Wetherspoon, get something in the morning papers, and arrange an item on the early evening news tomorrow. The local.'

'Yes, sir.'

'What d'you feel about doing it?' Porson asked unexpectedly.

'Doing it?'

'The broadcast. I know we've got a press officer, but the journos always want to talk to a warm body. A real copper. Plays better in the one-and-nines.'

'Me, sir?' Slider looked his horror. 'But you always do the broadcasts. I'm not – I've never liked cameras.'

Porson looked annoyed. 'Do you think any of us do it for fun?'

'I always thought you looked such a natural, sir.'

'What, seeing myself plastered all over the screen like a blasted Spice Girl? I shake like an aspirin, every damn time! But needs must, laddie. Only this time, what with this cold and—' He paused. 'Other considerations – I'm not really up to it. You've got a nice, friendly face. You'll look good on camera. You might find you like it – being the sinecure of all eyes.'

'Atherton's a handsome chap—' Slider tried in a last-ditch defence.

'No bon. You know it's got to be a DI or better. No, you're it, Slider.'

'Is it an order, sir?' Slider asked.

'No, it's not an order, it's a request,' Porson said, growing impatient. 'But if you refuse a perfectly reasonable request from your senior officer, I'll have to make it an order, won't I?'

'In that case, I'll do it,' Slider said glumly. As long as I know where I stand. I never craved the limelight, the fierce doo-dah that beats upon the thingummy, but if that's the way the runes fall, it is a far, far better thing and so on. Joanna always said he ought to go on the box; and the children would be thrilled. They were of the generation that felt nothing was real until the TV validated it. But he had never wanted anything about himself to be public property. To him it was a violation. He didn't even like to see his name in the telephone directory. And anonymity was not just a personal preference, it was one of the tools of his trade. He was the Alec Guinness of Shepherd's Bush Nick.

'Brace up, laddie,' Porson said, reading his face. 'Most people gape at the telly with their mouths open and their brains in neuter. You'll slip in one side and out the other. It's deceased they'll be interested in, if at all.'

True, thought Slider, but not much comfort to the reluctant performer.

Atherton put his head round Slider's door. 'Anything else before I go?'

Slider came back from a long distance. 'Are you off?'

'It's after seven.'

'Is it? Blimey, doesn't time fly when you're having fun?'

'Everyone else has gone. Why not have an early night? You look tired.'

Slider shrugged. 'I don't sleep well in that bed when Joanna's away. It needs a new mattress. It's like the slopes of Mount Etna. Strange, though, somehow I never notice the lumps when she's there.'

'Sleep on the sofa,' Atherton suggested. Slider got the impression he wasn't taking his plight seriously.

'What are you doing this evening?' He didn't like to ask, but if Atherton invited him back for a meal he wouldn't say no.

But Atherton said breezily, 'Oh, I've got plans. Well, if there's nothing more, I'll be off. Night!'

'Goodnight,' Slider said, concealing his disappointment as Atherton whisked away. He stared at the empty doorway a moment, and then turned to look out of the window. A warm, slightly hazy evening was spreading its buttery light over the streets, quiet in this time between commuting home and going out on the town. In the old days, he and Atherton would have gone for a pint in a pub with a garden, and maybe for a curry afterwards. Now women had come between them; which was fair enough when the women were all present and correct. But all that beckoned him now from his desk was an empty flat and, he was pretty sure, an empty fridge.

Oh, well, he thought, there are plenty of restaurants in Chiswick. He pictured them – a long and varied row, French, Italian, Chinese, Indian, Thai, Black Tie, new British, Old Greek, Middle Eastern – and wondered what he fancied, trying to whip up some enthusiasm for the notion of a meal out alone. Or he could take fish and chips home and eat in front of the telly like a sad divorcé. He so rarely watched it, he hadn't the faintest idea what was on. And if he had known it wouldn't have helped much. All television was a bit like a serial, he thought; or like science fiction, based on the assumptions of everything that had gone before. If you didn't keep up with it, you couldn't understand what they were on about, and lost interest.

And then the thing that had been bothering the back of his mind swam to the forefront. Atherton had said, 'I've got plans.' Not, 'We've got plans.' He wondered if it meant anything, or if it was only a slip of the tongue. He hoped the lad wasn't up to something.

When he got outside, he thought better of the whole idea of going home. He left his car where it was and walked up Abdale

Road. The air was warm and still, and there was a smell to it, not entirely unpleasant, but a little used and smeary, like the smell of one's own bedsheets after they'd been slept in. The houses in Abdale Road were terraced cottages, two storeys with the tiniest front gardens – you could have leaned across from the street and knocked on the window. They had been built for Victorian workmen but owing to the increasing desirability of Shepherd's Bush they were being gentrified out of all recognition. You could tell the ones that were now in middle-class hands: they had freshly painted front doors, lots of pot plants, and no net curtains.

Round the corner in Loftus Road the houses were much bigger, three storeys plus a basement, with steps going up to the front door over a wide, well-lit 'area'. By an odd reversal of fortunes these houses, which had been built for the servant-employing class, were now on the whole occupied by people lower down the social scale than were the tiny cottages in Abdale. They were mostly split up into flats and bedsitters, and were shabby and peeling. One or two, however, had been spotted for their potential by the newly affluent and were being done up regardless. Skips, scaffolding and contractors' vans marked them out for work in progress.

There was one, towards the end of the road, in which the process was complete. Its sooty brick had been cleaned back to the original pleasing London yellow; new double-glazed sash windows, new paint, new roof slates, even new railings proclaimed its status as a beloved object. The time-nibbled edges of the steps up to the front door had been repaired so that they were as sharp as the day they were born, like a freshly unwrapped bar of chocolate; the area had been paved with expensive Italian tiles. Slider slowed his pace so that he could look appreciatively as he passed. It was a pleasure to see an old house properly taken care of, and it just showed what good houses these could be. The Victorians knew how to build all right. Someone had sunk a lot of dosh into this one, but they had got a fine and very large property out of it, which would probably have cost them three times as much in Fulham or Notting Hill.

Loftus Road was a cul-de-sac, but there was a cut-through into South Africa Road through the courtyards of Batman Close – one of the later additions coeval with the Phoenix. It was very quiet everywhere. Hardly anyone was about. The door of the pub was open, and the subaural thump of its background music issued forth like a dragon's heartbeat. In the small flight of shops the newsagent was still open and a couple of kids on bikes were hanging around the door, evidently the best use they felt they could make of the golden hours of childhood. Two men were in the launderette, reading newspapers at opposite ends of the bench before the row of machines; and there was a queue of three in the fish-and-chipper. The smell of frying, sharpened with vinegar, drifted out on the warm air. Slider's stomach growled a warning. He hadn't eaten since a meagre egg-and-cress sandwich Anderson had brought him in at lunchtime. He felt grubby from the day's work, and his feet felt the pavement too keenly, as though his shoe soles had got radically thinner since this morning.

He was heading for Buller Close – all the blocks of flats were named after Heroes of the Empire, the estate having been built on the site of the old Commonwealth Exhibition. Who was Buller, he wondered as he trod the chewing-gum-pocked pavement, trawling his schoolboy history lessons. The name Redvers Buller sprang to mind, but it came with no information attached and pretty soon sprang out again.

The flat was on the first floor. There was a long pause after he had knocked on the door, and he turned his back to it and leaned on the balcony wall, staring down at the yard and wondering where all the children were. It was the great advantage of the estate that it was ideal for 'playing out' – enclosed yards, large greens, no through-traffic, and the blocks were low-rise enough for even a top-floor mum to shout down to her children and be heard. But the yards and greens were deserted. All indoors watching telly, he supposed sadly.

Behind him there was a sound, and he turned quickly to find an eye peering at him through the merest thread of a crack. At the sight of his face, the crack widened enough to reveal most of a face and a hand clutching a pink dressing-gown at the neck.

'Hullo, Nichola,' he said. 'It's all right, it's not trouble. I'm alone.'

Nichola Finch opened the door fully. Her face looked puffy and creased as if she had been asleep, but otherwise she was a pretty girl, wafer-slim, with full lips, big brown eyes and thick, curly dark hair. With her smallness and slimness she looked at first glance almost like a child, but on closer inspection – at least in daylight and without make-up – the ravages of time were apparent. As far as Slider knew, she was in her late twenties or perhaps early thirties. She admitted to nineteen; but that was not surprising in a person who spelled her name Nikki on her calling-cards. He thought she had probably admitted to nineteen since she was fourteen.

'You woke me up,' she complained.

'I'm sorry,' said Slider humbly.

She was instantly mollified. 'S'all right. I had to get up anyway. What j'want?'

'Just a talk.'

Her eyes narrowed suspiciously. 'What about?'

Slider made a small outwards gesture of his hands. 'Do we have to do it here on the balcony? Can I come in?'

'Have to do what on the balcony? 'Ere, have you come for a freebie?'

'I'm a happily married man. I just want to talk.'

'Most of my customers are happily married men,' she said with unusual acuity. She yawned right back to her fillings, closed down with a smack of the lips, and said, 'I need a coffee.' She turned and went in, leaving the door open – all the invitation he was going to get.

In the tiny, chaotic kitchen she fumbled about for the kettle, shook it to gauge its fullness, and switched it on. She sorted through the dirty crockery for a mug, waved it at him in enquiry, and when he shook his head, shrugged in reply. A woman of few words, was Nichola. She rinsed the mug meagrely under the cold tap, put it down by the kettle, spooned in powdered instant out of an industrial-sized tin, added sugar, and settled down to wait, folding her arms across her chest as women do when comfort is their priority rather than allure.

'So, what's it all about?' she asked, though without much invitation.

'I want to pick your brains,' he said.

'Not a bloody gain,' she said with huge exasperation, rolling her eyes theatrically.

'Come on now, Nichola, I haven't seen you for months.'

She tacked off, easily distracted. 'Why ju always call me that?'

'It's a pretty name.'

She stared at him, trying to fathom whether he was being ironic, or kind, or had some other devious ploy too subtle for her to grasp. In the end she gave it up and said, 'You're a funny bastard, you are.'

He smiled. 'But I'm okay,' he suggested, as if that would have been her next sentence. She only shrugged. 'I looked after you all right when you had that bit of trouble—'

'And you never let me bloody forget it!' She responded again with the disproportionate, withering sarcasm that seemed to be the only mode of communication with girls like her. He supposed it must come from the soap operas, and perhaps the tabloid headlines – a continual artificial outrage whipped up about the most trivial of 'offences'. Slider had always got on well with prostitutes, having cut his teeth on Central Division, which covered Soho, but the younger ones were hard to talk to. Apart from the automatic stroppiness, they seemed to have huge and baffling areas of ignorance about quite basic things, so that at any moment a perfectly ordinary conversation suddenly became the equivalent of discussing the fine detail of a Test cricket match with a middle-aged farmer from Iowa who'd never left his home town.

'So you're all right now?' he pursued. 'You haven't had any more trouble?'

'No, he's buggered off. Much you'd care!' she added, as if afraid she'd been too gracious. 'So what j'want, anyway?'

'Some information.'

'I ain't the bleedin' Yellow Pages.'

'You know the estate and you know lots of people. And you're a clever, noticing sort of person.' He was afraid he might have gone too far with this, but she didn't react. 'You've got what you might call specialist knowledge.'

She tilted her head a little sideways, and smiled. 'You don'alf talk funny,' she said. 'But you got a nice voice. I always said that, din' I? I always said you got a sexy voice.'

She never had said anything of the sort, but he saw she was building a scenario for herself in which she would help him, so he went along with it.

'We were always good friends,' he said. 'And that's what friends do, help each other.'

'Yeah,' she said. The sentiment sounded right to her, and she had no concept of logic. The kettle boiled and clicked off, and she turned away to make the coffee, and then, taking up the mug, said much more pleasantly, 'J'wanna come and sit down? It's a bit of a tip in there, but—'

Given the kitchen, he could imagine. He said, 'Whatever you like. I'm all right here, but—'

'Okay,' she said, settling again to lean against the work surface, folding one arm and propping the other elbow on it so that the mug was within easy reach of her mouth. 'What's it about?'

'There was a man murdered in the park on Monday night,' he began.

'Oh, yeah, someone said,' she agreed. He remembered she didn't read newspapers. Come to think of it, he had no evidence that she *could* read. She had had eleven years of progressive education at a State school, after all. 'I don't know nothing about that,' she said.

'No, of course not. But not long before that, Monday night about eleven, this man had a fight outside the Phoenix with—'

'Eddie Cranston, yeah,' she finished for him.

Slider managed not to jump as the missing surname was provided so easily and casually. 'Oh, you know about the fight?' he said.

'People are talking about it. I never knew it was this bloke what got murdered, though. He give Eddie a black eye.' She grew enthusiastic. 'Eddie's ballistic about it. He fancies himself rotten, and he thinks it spoils his fabulous good looks, know't I mean? That's why he's not been out of the 'ouse since. Lying low until his eye goes down. Plus, he don't like being made a fool of, and this bloke's got the better of him, en't he? I mean, Eddie's picked a fight with this bloke to show 'im who's boss, and he's come off wiv a black eye, and this other bloke's walked away wivout a scratch, right?'

'Well, not exactly,' Slider said. 'The other bloke's dead.'

'Oh, yeah.' Her eyes widened and the mug was arrested on its way to her lips. 'Yeah,' she breathed, 'you're right. You reckon Eddie done him in, then?'

'It's a possibility,' Slider said. 'So tell me about this Eddie Cranston.'

'He's a git,' she said simply. 'He thinks he's God's gift, know't I mean?'

'And is he?'

'What, God's gift? Well, he's good-looking, I give him that,' she said grudgingly. Slider made an enquiring noise and she responded, 'Tall, black hair, suntan. Sharp dresser. He's all right-looking, but he's a total bastard.'

'In what way?'

'Treats you like dirt,' she replied shortly. She sipped her coffee, her eyes over Slider's shoulder, as if the interview was finished.

'So where does he live, this Eddie?' he tried next.

She snorted so hard she did a nose job with the coffee and had to wipe her face on her dressing-gown sleeve. 'Where *doesn't* he live?' she said eventually.

'What does that mean?' Slider asked patiently.

She put the mug down, the better to tackle his ignorance. 'Listen, he's got this scam. He's got women all over the estate, all round Shepherd's Bush.'

'You mean they're working girls, like you?'

'Nah!' Huge withering scorn. 'That'd be too much like hard work for Mr Eddie Bloody Cranston! No, they're all on benefit – most of 'em have got kids – and he just comes round and takes his cut.'

'Why do they give it to him?'

'Why j'think? Cause he's a smooth-talking bastard. They all think he's *their* bloke. It's love, innit? Plus, he'd knock their teeth in if they didn't.'

That covered the bases, Slider thought. 'How do you know about this?'

'I know one of 'em, Karen. She used to be a mate at school. I've told her, I've said you're dead stupid, you are! But she says he's the farver of me kids – well, one of 'em. She says she loves him. I've told her, I've said to her you ain't the only one, you know. I've told her he's got women all over. But it don't make no difference. She thinks it's her he really loves, and he'll give the others up one day and settle down. Gaw!' She rolled her eyes skywards at the stupidity. 'I said to her, I said at least I get paid for it. And I don't have to have'm hanging round afterwards. Quick in an' out and cash in me 'and, and the rest of me time's me own. But *she* pays *him*, the dozy cow. Cuh!'

She drank some more coffee while Slider let this sink in.

'You say he's a sharp dresser,' he said at last. 'But where does the money come from? Taking women's social security doesn't add up to much, even if he has got a lot of them. I suppose he'd have to leave them enough to live on. He couldn't take it all.'

She didn't seem much interested in this. 'Oh, he's got other scams,' she said. 'Bound to.' Evidently she didn't know what they might be. Slider changed tack.

'This bloke he had the fight with, Lenny. Unlucky Lenny, they call him. Do you know him?' She shook her head, her eyes blank and far away. 'Some said he lived with a working girl.'

'I don't know him.'

'Do you know what the fight was about?'

'Nah. I never heard.'

She had plainly grown bored with the whole process and any minute now would yawn and send him away. He said, 'You've been really helpful to me, Nichola. I shan't forget this. Your friend Karen – Karen what, by the way?'

'Karen Peacock. Why?'

'Do you think she'd talk to me? Where does she live? Have you got her address?'

Nikki's face sharpened. 'You barmy? Talk to the cops about Eddie? He'd break every bone in her body if he found out.'

'I'd make sure he didn't find out.'

'She'd never do it,' Nikki said certainly. 'Anyway,' with a look of cunning, 'I don't know where she lives, so I can't tell you.'

'Fair enough,' Slider said peaceably. Nikki's black hole of ignorance was working in his favour now. It simply didn't occur to her that if Karen Peacock was drawing benefit there would be an official record of her whereabouts which Slider could consult. It would save time if Nikki would tell him, but saving time was as nothing weighed against not alienating a useful informant and not having her warn her friend that he was coming.

And when it came to Karen Peacock's safety, he thought Eddie Cranston was less likely to find out he had been asking questions from him than from Nikki herself. When Nikki had been expounding her philosophy of life she had said, 'and I don't have to have'm hanging round afterwards.' Slider was pretty sure the ''m' had been 'him' rather than 'them'. That, plus a certain something in the quality of her scorn for her friend, persuaded him that Nikki knew Eddie Cranston rather more Biblically than she was letting on.

He took his leave and stepped out into the fading evening. He was tired and hungry, but he had got a handle on the case at last, a first step towards identifying Unlucky Lenny. He couldn't get through to social security until the morning, so he was free now to go and get something to eat, and relax for what was left of the evening. He walked back to the station more cheerfully than he had left it. By the time he drove out onto Uxbridge Road he had decided on Alfredo's for his supper, a big bowl of pasta with lots of tomato and garlic in the sauce, and a couple of glasses of Apulian wine. And then home, bath, bed. And the possibility that Joanna would phone from the hotel, after the concert and before sleep. Talking to her in bed was one of the great joys of life – even if she was in a different bed at the time.

CHAPTER FIVE

The Eyes Have It

Hollis appeared in Slider's doorway. 'Edward Cranston,' he read from the printed sheet. 'Age thirty-eight, height five foot eleven, eyes brown, hair brown, mole on right cheekbone. Last known address in Ladbroke Grove four years ago.' He looked up. 'Any money on him still being there?'

'It's not far across the fields from White City,' Slider said. 'A mile, if that.'

Hollis snorted derision. 'As to his record, well, he's not Robbie Williams. Not even top fifty material. All small-time stuff. He's got possession of a controlled substance, possession of stolen goods, dah-di-dah-di-dah. Living off immoral earnings. Drunk and disorderly, affray – five Public Order offences altogether. And one assault and actual. That was his finest hour. Broke the cheekbone of the girl he was living off. Our brothers in conflict at Notting Hill caught her at the hospital when her guard was down and got her to prefer charges. Wanted to run him off their ground. Reckoned he was up to a lot of stuff they couldn't nail him for. But his brief coached him, he pleaded guilty, sobbed contrition, and the judge gave him a suspended, on condition he went through anger management counselling.' Hollis blew out through his scraggy moustache in disgust. 'Where do they dig 'em up from?'

'Did he go?'

'What, guv? Oh, to the classes. No, he ducked out after the first, but Notting Hill reckoned they'd scraped him off their shoe so they weren't too bothered. He's got nothing since the assault, so he's been keeping out o' trouble, or at least out of their hands. Dave Tipper at Notting Hill said if we can find him, we can have him. Joke, unfunny, officers for the use of.'

'Well, if we can find him, we can slap him for breaking the terms of his suspended,' Slider said. 'That'll make things easier.'

'If we can find him.'

'Check with the old address, just in case. Someone there might know. Then look in all the usual places. Most likely he's claiming benefit – you might try there first.'

'If he's offed Unlucky Lenny he's probably done a bunk.'

'Oh, I don't know. These overripe types who fancy themselves often think they can't be caught. He might lie low for a bit, but if he's got good scams set up round here he won't want to abandon them.'

'If he's that cocky, he'll probably turn up at the pub again, once his black eye's gone down.'

'Yes, but that could be four or five days. It strikes me that Sonny Collins probably knows more about Eddie Cranston than he's letting on. I think we might get him in and lean on him, see if he creaks.' Slider frowned in thought a moment. 'Run him through the system, will you, see if he's got any form.'

'What, Collins? Righty-o, guv.'

'Anything will do. Parking tickets, smoking in the lav. And someone can go round and have a chat with Karen Peacock – though if she's as wet as Nikki says she is, she probably won't know anything about Eddie worth knowing.'

It was common wisdom that women preferred to unburden themselves to other women, but Slider had always begged to differ. It was one thing for a female to Tell All to her bosom chum, but in his experience they had a basic animal suspicion of women who were complete strangers, whereas they would spill the most astonishing intimacies to a strange man if he were sympatico enough. Atherton said it was all to do with sex, and proved that women, even more than men, were always potentially on the pull. 'At least men stop for football,' he pointed out.

So Slider didn't send Swilley to interview Karen Peacock. He toyed with the idea of sending Anderson, who was a nice, unthreatening family man, but remembering her penchant for handsome bastards, plumped in the end for Atherton.

'I suppose you mean that for a compliment,' Atherton said.

'It's all to do with sex,' Slider said serenely.

Karen Peacock lived in Evans House, almost opposite the park and a plastic pint glass throw from the Phoenix. Atherton tried not to get too excited about this fact. Nowhere on the estate was *that* far from the Phoenix. He trod up the stairs like a cat avoiding something spilt, and found Karen Peacock in. She was a depressed-looking woman who was probably in her early twenties but looked older because of her draggledness. Her face was pale, her eyes defeated, her hair dyed black with a luminous red streak, which defiant punkery went with the rest of her appearance like liver and custard. She was not more than usually overweight, but everything about her seemed to droop baggily, from her face to her shoulders, her bust, her belly and her clothes, as if they were all despairingly giving up the fight and sinking to the ground. She was dressed in unforgiv- able Lycra leggings and an enormous mauve teeshirt, her bare feet in flip-flops revealing chipped burgundy varnish on the toenails. She had three silver studs in the rim of one ear, and three small children, the middle one of which had obviously been sired by a black man and didn't match the other two. Atherton wondered which one was Cranston's. He supposed the youngest, unless the man was unnaturally forgiving, or merely businesslike.

If Cranston was as tasty as reputation had him, Atherton expected difficulty in getting anything out of one of his women, but when Karen opened the door to him she looked up at him with a mixture of fear and submission, and it only took a moment or two of smiling charm before she invited him in. Soon he found himself sitting on her dreadful sofa in her clean and tidy but dreadful lounge. For the purposes of furthering their relationship he expressed an interest in her children, though unfortunately attention only encouraged the eldest, Bruce, a boy of four, to show off, and their subsequent conver- sation was punctuated by shouts, loud bangs as he whacked furniture with various blunt instruments, and weak pleas from his mother not to put his toys down the toilet or torture his little brothers.

Atherton's charm worked on Karen so well that her submis- sion was soon tinged with a fluttery sort of pleasure rather than fear. She responded to his generous labelling of Cranston as her husband by saying, 'Well, we're not actually married.

Not as such. Really, I'm still married to Vinnie's father – that's my middle one – but Eddie is Eric's father – that's my baby.'

'He's a lovely little boy. Does he look like Eddie?' This line removed the last traces of Karen's reserve. It also prompted an offer for Atherton to hold the baby, but he supposed that was a small price to pay. Baby Eric was placid enough – indeed, almost inanimate, like a large lump of flesh that had been excised from somewhere or other. It sat on Atherton's knee and stared at nothing. He thought of his trousers and prayed its nappy was leakproof.

After this diversion, Atherton brought the conversation back to Eddie. 'But he does live here with you?'

'Well, not as such. You see,' she looked sidelong, almost coyly, at Atherton, 'you get more from the social if you don't live together. Eddie's got his own place.'

'I see. But I expect he's often here.'

'Oh yes,' she said, but her eyes filled with tears. A bit more probing and she spilled it out, that Eddie had other women – well it was only natural, he was so handsome and everything – but it was her he loved really. 'He's told me so, ever so often.' This was the clincher, Atherton mused with a sort of sad disgust. If he said it, it must be so.

'What about this fight he had with Lenny over at the Phoenix?'

'Oh, that was terrible!' she said. 'Lenny give him a black eye. I mean, Eddie! He's got such beautiful eyes.'

Eddie had been with her that evening. He'd dropped in around nine, nine-thirty. He'd come to bring her some things he wanted washing. She did his hand-wash for him, his nice jumpers and that. She'd been putting the kids to bed. She'd made him something to eat – a fry-up, that was what Eddie liked, with baked beans, and then one of them jam roly-polys and custard that you do in the microwave. Eddie had bought her the microwave. He got it from a pal of his, cheap. She used it a lot. It was really useful for warming up the baby's bottles and that.

Where had Eddie been before he visited her? She didn't know. She never asked Eddie where he'd been or where he was going. He didn't like her to ask questions. He just liked her to be ready for him whenever he dropped in. After he'd had his supper he watched telly a bit and then he went. He said he was going over the Phoenix for a drink. That would have been about a quarter past ten. No, he hadn't come back afterwards. He hadn't said he was going to so she didn't expect him. In fact, she hadn't seen him since.

'But you heard about the fight? Do you know what it was about?'

Now for the first time she seemed reluctant to answer. But after a pause, she whispered, 'It was about a woman.'

'That must have been really upsetting for you,' Atherton sympathised. Bruce, the eldest child, was standing behind his mother amusing himself by pulling faces at Atherton. He was using both hands to get some of his effects. Atherton made an effort and shut him out of his consciousness. The application of a little more lard soon eased Karen out of her shell, and her long-buried sense of grievance surfaced.

Eddie, she confessed as much to herself as him, did not just see other women on a casual basis. She wouldn't have minded that – much. After all, men couldn't help themselves, could they? And when he did have women like that, it never meant anything to Eddie. He said so.

What hurt was that he had other women like her, regular, settled women like wives, and at least one of them had children by him.

It must have shocked her when she realised, Atherton crooned. How it must have hurt! To know he had treated her so badly, lied to her, double-crossed her—

Oh, but he still loved her, Karen cried hastily, leaping to the defence of her tormentor in time-honoured fashion. It was just he was so good-looking and everything, women wouldn't leave him alone, and she supposed he'd got trapped and that.

Some natural tears she shed – or at least, her eyes moistened. She blew her nose dismally and he eased her back to the fight outside the Phoenix.

Eddie had found out this Lenny was bothering some of his other women. That's what he had gone over the Phoenix for, 'cause he knew Lenny was going to be there and he wanted to have it out with him. And they'd started arguing, and that Sonny had chucked them out, and then they'd got into a fight outside and Lenny had give Eddie a black eye.

How had Karen found all this out?

Because that cow Carol Ann had told her. She was one of Eddie's women. She claimed to be his real one, but Karen knew better. It was her Eddie loved; Carol Ann was nothing. She was just a slag. But Carol Ann had phoned her up the Tuesday to tell her about the fight and that Eddie had gone to her after, as if that proved anything.

Where did Carol Ann live?

'I don't know,' Karen said crossly, 'and I don't want to know. He doesn't live with *her*. He's got his own place. He told me. Because of the social money.'

'What's Carol Ann's other name?' Atherton asked. But Karen didn't know that either. It was Carol Ann Lying Cowface as far as she was concerned.

'And what about Lenny? Where does he live?'

She had never met Lenny. She'd only heard Eddie talking about him Monday night, that was all. She didn't recollect hearing his name before, but Eddie didn't talk much about his friends or anything. He didn't talk much at all, really.

Atherton could see in his mind's eye the amiable Eddie dropping in for food, sex and washing, taking the first on the settee in front of the telly and the second probably in seconds, a practical thing like blowing his nose. His idea of foreplay was probably, 'Brace yourself!' No, conversation would be way, way down on his list of wants from his woman.

Outside again, and anxiously inspecting his trousers for damp, Atherton wondered how Eddie had known that Lenny would be at the pub that night if he was not, *apud* Sonny Collins, a regular. He also reflected that if Eddie had gone to Carol Ann Cowface after the events of the evening, she would probably know whether he had killed Unlucky Lenny or not. She would probably be required by Eddie to provide his alibi, and she would probably know who Lenny was too. She was an extremely important part of the jigsaw. Unfortunately, like everyone else in this case, she came without the basic courtesy of a surname. He sighed. Like ants, they were, shifting a mountain of sugar grain by single grain.

Sonny Collins was not a happy rabbit. His barely contained rage swirled round the interview room like a tiny tornado in a bottle, and his good eye moved about so much it met up with its partner only rarely, like a frightfully mismatched pair of ball-room dancers.

'Can I get you a cup of tea?' Slider offered daintily.

'I haven't got time for all that,' Collins snarled. 'You asked me to come here, and I've come. I'm a busy man and I haven't got time to mess about. So what do you want?'

'Eddie Cranston,' said Slider.

'What about him?'

'Oh, you know who he is? Last time I spoke to you, you said you didn't know his surname.'

'Maybe I'd forgotten it.'

'And maybe you hadn't. So let's have a bit more co-operation now. Tell me everything you know about him.'

'He comes in my pub. That's it.'

'Where does he live?'

'I dunno.'

'You said he was local.' Sonny shrugged. 'What's he up to, Mr Collins? What's his scam? Where does he get the money to buy his nice clothes?'

Both eyes fixed on Slider for once. 'Is that what you dragged me in here for? I told you I don't know him. All right, I know his name, but that's it. He comes in my pub two-three times a week and I've heard him called by it. Why should I know anything else about him, or any of my customers? I'm a publican, not a bloody lonelyhearts agency.'

Time for the thumbscrews, Slider thought. He held out his hand to Atherton, who gave him, with a nicely judged solemnity, a buff wallet-file, from which Slider extracted a piece of paper, allowing a glimpse of a not inconsiderable wad of other papers within. It was the file on the long-defunct Shepherd's Bush Nick football team (osp) but Collins was not to know that.

'So, you're a publican, are you? For how much longer, I wonder.'

Collins tried not to look as if he was looking at the file. 'What's that supposed to mean?'

'It means that my colleagues in uniform have had their eye on the Phoenix for some time. Drinking after hours is only the least of the things that worry them.'

'Rubbish!' Collins snapped.

'Oh, I don't think so,' Slider said, running his finger down the page in his hand. 'You've been under observation. Dates, times, number and description of people seen drinking in your fine hostelry after closing time *and*,' he tapped the sheet with his fingernail, 'the names and addresses of those who've been apprehended leaving your premises at inappropriate times. Would you be willing to place a small bet on the likelihood that they wouldn't give you up to save their own skins?'

'That's total bollocks,' Collins said calmly; but suddenly he was beginning to sweat. Slider could smell it; and his bald crown was shining. 'If you've got anything on me, charge me. Otherwise—'

Slider shook his head. 'As I said, that's the least of your sins. Observation suggests there's a great deal going on that we'd like to know about.' All this he had from Nicholls, the uniform sergeant in charge of the observation. The file might be bogus, but the suspicions weren't. 'People passing drugs to one another. Illegally imported cigarettes—'

'I don't know anything about that,' Collins interrupted. His voice was still calm, but the tension in his body was almost tangible. Slider was afraid he might blow apart any minute, filling the room with thousands of tiny cogs and springs. 'If people take drugs, I don't know anything about that.'

'Yes,' Slider said with broad sympathy, 'but if it happens on your premises you're still responsible. It's a bugger, isn't it? Now so far we haven't pushed the investigation because, frankly, you're fairly low down on our hit-parade of villains. But you can always be moved up the list—'

'You can't prove anything against me.'

'And,' Slider went on as if he hadn't spoken, 'it wouldn't take a moment to send off this list of after-hours offences to your brewery. Have you got a second career lined up, Mr Collins? Any other job you've always had a secret desire to try out?'

The mobile eye went very still as Sonny Collins indulged in some deep thought. It was staring at the wall over Slider's left shoulder. Because of the angle of his head, the glass eye was staring over his right shoulder. It was unnerving.

'What do you want from me?' Collins asked at last in a low growl.

'Just a little information,' Atherton said. He had been standing all this while. Now he pulled out the chair beside Slider and sat down as if they were all coming to business.

'What, about Eddie Cranston?'

'That'll do for starters,' Atherton agreed. 'What's he up to, Sonny? What's his scam?'

'He's just a poncey little slag,' Collins said with large contempt. 'He hasn't got the balls to get into anything big-time. Listen, he's got a string of women he lives off, takes a cut of their benefit money – that's the kind of toe-rag he is.'

'Yes, we knew that,' Atherton said. 'What else does he get up to?'

Collins seemed to have a little difficulty with moving his lips, as though the next confession was harder. 'He gets hold of a lot of iffy stuff, flogs it off to mugs.'

'Receiving stolen goods?'

'I never said stolen,' Collins said.

'Of course you didn't,' Slider said. 'How could you know?'

'What sort of goods?' Atherton asked.

'Electrical stuff – microwaves, CD players.' He shrugged. 'And a load of other crap. Umbrellas. Toys. Aftershave once. Anything. You know, the sort of gear you get at flood damage sales.'

'Of course. He's a regular little Del Boy, isn't he?' Atherton said. 'Cigarettes?'

'No,' Collins said sharply. 'He's never had cigarettes as long as I've known him.'

'What about drugs?'

The lip curled. 'Him? I told you, he's not got the balls. He's strictly small-time.'

'So what were he and Lenny getting into together?'

The eyes went still again. 'Who's Lenny?'

Slider leaned forward a little. 'Oh, come on, Mr Collins. Unlucky Lenny, the man who had a fight with Eddie at your pub and ended up dead a few yards from your doorstep the very same night? What a short memory you've got.'

'I told you,' Collins said, working up a spurt of anger, 'I don't know him. He's not a regular.'

'But you'd seen him before?'

'No. Never seen him before in my life.'

'Oh, really?' Atherton said. 'But Eddie came to your pub on purpose to meet him. Why was that, if he wasn't a regular?'

Collins stared a moment, and then was suddenly calm, as if

he'd thought of something. 'You'd better ask him. No use asking me, is it?'

'We'll do that. So where does he live?' Slider asked.

'I don't know,' Collins said, and this time he anticipated the protest. 'It's the truth. I don't know. It's somewhere local, that's all I know.'

'Where does Carol Ann live?' Atherton asked, quickly and lightly.

Collins looked surprised. 'Carol Ann? The barmaid at the Boscombe?'

'That one,' Slider confirmed without missing a beat.

'*I* dunno,' Collins said, and it sounded genuine.

'How do you know her?' Atherton countered.

'She's a barmaid,' Collins said as if it were self-evident. 'We all know each other. What's she got to do with it?'

'You're getting confused,' Atherton said. 'I ask the questions, you give the answers, right?'

'All I know about Carol Ann is she works at the Boscombe Arms. If you want to know any more, ask them. But she's straight as far as I know. Is that it now? Have you finished? Only I got work to do.'

'Just for the record, where were you between eleven Tuesday night and eight Wednesday morning?'

He stared thoughtfully. 'I was in the pub clearing up till about a quart' to twelve. Then I locked up and went down the Shamrock Club for a drink. Barman there'll tell you. Liam.'

'And you stayed until when?'

'Must've been about ha' past two, quart' to three. Then I went home. Took a taxi. Got home fourish, give or take.'

'Anyone at home to confirm when you came in?'

'Do me a favour,' he said scornfully. 'I live alone, above the pub. Let me know when they make that illegal. Anything else?'

'That's all for now,' Slider said. 'Thank you very much for your co-operation.'

Atherton stood as Collins stood so that he could look down at him. 'Isn't it much nicer when we're all friends?' he enquired sweetly.

Collins managed to stare at both of them at once. 'I could break you in half with my bare hands,' he told Atherton with horrid confidence. He was wearing a black sports jacket over his usual kit, but still Atherton could see the muscles squirm under his skin-tight vest. He looked like an unusually well-dressed sack of ferrets.

'Well, that was very nice,' Atherton said as they trod upstairs. 'And almost painless.'

'I wonder why he decided to co-operate,' Slider mused.

Atherton gave him a look. 'Because we threatened him. Have you forgotten?'

Slider shook his head. 'That wasn't it. He was frightened all right, but I don't believe he was frightened by anything we could do. The way it looked to me, he decided to give up Eddie Cranston in the hope it would deflect us from something else.'

'Yes, the drug dealing or whatever else he's got going that can lose him his licence. I think you're making it too complicated.'

'Maybe. It's just he didn't seem worried by the suggestion of drugs, either passing in his pub or Eddie being mixed up with. It wasn't that that made him sweat. And I still think he knows Lenny.'

'You think he gave up Eddie to keep us away from his connection with Lenny? But why?'

'Maybe. I don't know. It's just a feeling.'

'We all love your feelings,' Atherton assured him.

'His alibi's all just a bit too pat, isn't it?'

'If it checks out.'

'It'll check out. He wouldn't have offered it otherwise. I wish we'd asked him for it yesterday, before he'd had a chance to get it organised. I don't trust a man with an alibi ready for the asking like that.'

'There's no pleasing some people. Anyway, it doesn't cover the whole night. Maybe Lenny was killed at five am after all.'

'Don't humour me. Anyway, I thought it was Eddie we were after?'

'True, oh king. And now we've got a handle on Carol Ann, which ought to lead us to said Eddie, and that's enough to be grateful for for one morning.' Slider was silent, still in thought. 'We can always get Collins in again later and beat him up some more.'

Now Slider looked at him, amused. 'Funny how when you both stood up, he looked the taller of the two.'

'Those muscles are all for show,' Atherton assured him airily. 'I have the subtle but amazing trained strength of the master of eastern martial arts. My whole body is a lethal weapon.'

'Quite a few women have told me that,' Slider agreed.

CHAPTER SIX

From Err to Paternity

The Boscombe Arms, on the corner of Percy Road and Coningham Close, was a very different sort of pub from the Phoenix: one of those tall, handsome High Victorian efforts, all wood panelling, mirrors and elaborate engraved glass. It attracted a different kind of clientele, did a lot of food, and would have recoiled in horror from the mere suggestion of plastic glasses.

The guv'nor was a youngish, stocky, sharp-eyed man with a taller, older and even sharper-eyed wife who came up behind him like a shadow as soon as she realised he was answering police questions. She didn't say anything, but you could tell her husband was speaking with her in mind.

'Carol Ann Shotter. No, she's not in today – called in sick on Tuesday. Said she had the flu. What's she done?'

'Nothing that we know of. We just want to ask her about a friend of hers. Has she worked here long?'

'Oh, about six, eight months. Nine maybe. She's a good worker. Never given any trouble. She had good references. Used to work in the Elephant in Acton.'

'Why did she leave there?'

'She said she got fed up with the buses, wanted to work nearer home. She only lives in Abdale Road. She wasn't in any trouble,' he assured them earnestly. 'This is a respectable house. We don't have any trouble here, and we don't take on dodgy staff. All my staff are very good people. Can't afford otherwise. We get a nice class of customer in here – lots of money. They wouldn't come in if we had riff-raff behind the bar.'

'So it sounds as if the Eddie–Carol Ann romance might be a recent thing,' Atherton said. 'If Sonny Collins hadn't heard about it, and she's only been working locally for a few months—'

'Maybe. And if she's a fully employed barmaid she isn't one of his benefit babes,' Slider said.

'No wonder Karen Peacock got all uppity about her. Nothing like real superiority to get under a person's skin.'

'It wasn't very superior of her to phone Karen Peacock up just to boast.'

'She probably didn't. I don't gather that Karen is very bright. I expect she phoned with a message from Eddie about his alibi and Karen heard what she expected to.'

'You can be quite psychological when you try, can't you?' Slider said.

The house in Abdale Road to which they had been directed was not one of the done-up-regardless ones. It was not a slum by any means, but it had the tell-tale marks of a rented rather than an owned property – the cheap paint job, the cracked concrete in the front patch, the chipped coping of the garden wall and the missing gate, the gay tussock of grass growing in the roof gutter. Landlord was written all over it. It had heavy but clean nets in the downstairs window, and the upstairs window had its curtains drawn.

'House of sickness,' Atherton observed. 'Is she in bed, or has Eddie gone to ground up there? Or both?'

'Why do you always ask rhetorical questions?'

'Do you think we need back-up?'

'Let's hold our horses. We're just asking questions at this stage. We don't even know he's in there. She might really have the flu.'

'A flu that conveniently started on Tuesday morning. Suppose he panics and runs out the back?'

'He can't get anywhere. All the gardens back onto one another. He'd have to scramble through every garden right down the row and then shin over a ten-foot wall at the end. I think we'd hear him.'

'I love your confidence.'

'It's not mine. I'm looking after it for a friend. Look, if she's his alibi, he's not going to run away, is he? If his story is he never done nuffing and she can prove it, he wants to be found in her house, doesn't he?'

'It's a lot of "ifs".'

'Just knock on the door.'

Atherton still didn't really expect the knock to be answered. He expected the upstairs curtain to twitch, followed by a muffled sound of feet running down the stairs and a rattle of the back door being opened. But after quite a short pause the door opened and a woman stood there with the half enquiring, half suspicious look any normal person wears in the circumstances.

'Miss Shotter?' Slider asked, showing his brief. 'I'm Detective Inspector Slider and this is Detective Sergeant Atherton. Would you mind if we had a little talk with you?'

Carol Ann Shotter was in her late twenties or early thirties. She was a dyed blonde with a good figure, and her face missed being attractive by such mere millimetres that at a quick glance or in a poor light she'd have passed as a bit of a sort. There was a tension about her as her eyes moved quickly from one face to the other, but it was more a readiness for action than fear or guilt. She seemed not nervous, but watchful, expectant.

'What's it about?' she asked, inevitably.

Slider smiled. 'Just a few questions. I'd rather not ask them on the doorstep, if you don't mind. Can we come in?'

She yielded. The house was laid out in classic London Dogleg – stairs straight ahead, narrow passage hooking round them, one room at the front, one at the back, and the back-addition scullery beyond. But it was all on a tiny scale, like a human doll's house. The front room into which she led them was about nine feet square, so that the small sofa, two armchairs and television arranged round the miniature fireplace (blocked in and fitted with a gas fire) took up all the available space, and four people sitting in the four available places could have linked hands for a séance without leaving their seats.

The furniture was old and had been cheap to start with, as had the carpet; and there were no pictures or ornaments to soften the furnished-let look. One of the shallow chimney alcoves had been filled in with shelves, which were stacked not with books, but with videos. The only reading matter in sight was a heap of holiday brochures dropped on the floor at the end of the sofa. The other feature of the room that jumped to Slider's attention was that though the television set was at least five years old, the video player under it was brand new.

Carol Ann Shotter sat down, nervously tugging at her skirt. She had good legs in sheer black tights, Atherton observed, but she was too old by ten years for a mini that short. Perhaps it was professional kit. Her stretchy cotton top emphasised her bust, and she was well made up for a woman at home on sick leave. But the purported flu was not in evidence. Not so much as a sniffle.

'I understand you're Eddie Cranston's girlfriend,' Slider opened, not making it a question.

'I – well – yes, I suppose so,' she said with less than a whole heart. 'I mean—'

'He lives here with you, does he?' She hesitated, and Slider pushed her a little. 'Well, does he or doesn't he? You must know, surely?'

'Well, he sort of does and he sort of doesn't,' she said. 'He's got his own place, but he stays here a lot.'

'I see. He's here now, is he?'

'He's upstairs in bed,' she said. 'He's not well.'

'Oh dear,' Slider said, 'not this awful summer flu? You've got it yourself, haven't you? But no, wait, there's been a miracle cure!'

She looked at him with dislike. 'Are you being funny?'

'Your boss says you phoned in sick on Tuesday, and you've been off since. But here you are, bright as a button, not a soggy tissue in sight.'

She roused herself to fight back. 'What right have you got to go round asking my boss about me? You want to lose me my job?'

'Not at all,' Slider said politely. 'I just wondered if your absence from work could possibly have anything to do with Eddie's little adventure on Monday night?'

'Look,' she said – the first word in the vocabulary of capitulation, 'I don't know what this is about, but Eddie's not done anything.'

'Then there's no reason he shouldn't talk to us, is there?'

'He's ill in bed.'

'Oh come on, love,' Atherton said. 'Do we go up there, or do you get him down? It's up to you.'

She sighed. 'I'll go up and tell him.'

'Just call him down,' Atherton amended.

One more burning look, and she stalked past him to the foot of the stairs and shouted, 'Eddie! Come down here. Come on!'

There was a long pause and then the murmur of a voice from above. Atherton, from his angle, could see a pair of male feet in socks at the top of the stairs.

'Who d'you think? It's the police.'

Another murmur.

'Oh, for God's sake, get down here! I'm sick of this.'

After a hesitation, the feet began to descend, and slowly a pair of black tracksuit bottoms joined them, and then a blue teeshirt with some dark hair peeking out at the neck, and then the face and head of Eddie Cranston, visible at last. He had the dark, ripe good looks and thick, black, swept-back hair of a complete bastard, along with a narcissistic suntan and the obligatory gold jewellery, including a watch so vast and covered in knobs it looked like a mine on a strap. The identifying small mole on the cheekbone was there, along with a fine black eye. Judging by its state nearly three days on, he mustn't have been able to open it at all on Tuesday.

He reached the foot of the stairs and stopped, looking at Slider and Atherton, trying to be the hard man, though it's not easy for a man to appear cool when he's obviously recently lost a fight. Carol Ann plainly felt the same. She stepped aside to give them a clear view, and said in that withering tone women reserve – Slider never understood why – for men they were sure of: 'Look at him. Didn't want anyone to see him with a shiner. I ask you!'

'I think it's a little more serious than that,' Slider said. 'Isn't it, Eddie?'

Eddie's eyes flitted about, and he licked his lips. 'I haven't,' he said faintly, 'done nothing.'

'Where were you on Monday night, Eddie? After you had the fight with Lenny, I mean?'

'He was here,' Carol Ann said quickly, before he could answer. 'He came round here, and he's been here ever since.'

'Yes, I thought that might be the case,' Slider said. 'It's the bit in between we're interested in, though.'

Atherton took it up. 'Between the fight and coming here. The bit where Lenny got stabbed to death. The Lenny you'd just had a fight with, I mean – just to make that quite clear.'

'I never,' Eddie said. 'I never. It wasn't me.' He still tried to strike the defiant pose but his eyes – or eye, to be more precise – was conscious and afraid.

'Why don't you come down to the station with us and tell us all about it?' Slider said.

Eddie pulled himself together. 'Are you arresting me?'

'Well, I could if you like, but don't you think it would be nicer if we did it on a friendly basis?'

'You got nothing on me,' he said.

'Then you've got nothing to worry about, have you?' As Eddie still did not move, Slider added, 'You broke the terms of your suspended. I can nick you for that, if you like, if it'll make you feel happy.'

Eddie swallowed. 'No,' he said. 'All right, I'll go and get my shoes on.'

As he started up the stairs, Slider looked at Atherton and flicked his head, and Atherton went up after him. Turning, Slider found Carol Ann's eyes burning him. 'Just a precaution, in case he tries anything silly,' he explained.

'He's daft enough for that,' she said bitterly. 'Look, he never killed Lenny. He's not the sort. If you knew him, you'd know he's not got the balls to kill anyone.'

'I would like you to come down to the station as well and make a statement,' Slider said.

'No,' she said. 'I'm not getting mixed up.'

'I'm afraid you already are. Come on, love. Better get it over with.'

'I told you,' she said, working herself up and losing her refinement in the process, 'I'm not going down *no* station to make *no* statement, so you can stick that where the sun don't shine!'

'Don't make it hard for yourself,' Slider advised.

'If you want me down that station, you're gonna have to arrest me,' she said with supreme confidence.

He looked across her shoulder into the sitting room. 'That's a nice video you've got there,' he said. 'New, isn't it? Have you got the receipt?'

'No, it was a—' The next word forming was 'present', but before it reached the air understanding came to her. A strong emotion crossed Miss Shotter's face; her nostrils flared and her lips tucked themselves down tightly. A child within range of an expression like that would have known it was likely to be followed by a wallop. 'Oh, my good Gawd,' she said in soft fury. 'The stupid bastard!' She met Slider's not unsympathetic eye and it burst from her. 'I said he was daft: he's a bloody dipstick!' Slider was inclined to agree with her.

Eddie Cranston was sweating freely, and the interview room was filled with the miasma of his body, his cigarettes, and his chain coffee drinking. Interview room coffee came from the vending machine and to Slider's mind smelled like dirty socks. He sometimes wondered if it could be banned under the United Nations protocol on torture.

'Lenny Baxter,' Cranston said, giving them so lightly the piece of information they had been yearning for from the beginning. The spectre of a television appearance retreated from Slider a pace or two.

'Where does he live?'

'I dunno,' Eddie said. 'Somewhere local. He lives with this tart, Tina. That's all I know.'

'How do you know him?'

'Oh, I seen him around.'

'At the Phoenix?'

Eddie shrugged. 'Just around. Everybody knows Lenny.'

If only that were true, Slider thought. 'So what was your beef with him?'

'Look,' Eddie said, 'I never had no problem with him. I hardly knew him. Just seen him around. He was all right as far as I was concerned. I mean, we all got to live, right? But then he started messing with one of my women. I couldn't have that, right? I mean, that was well out of order.'

'Messing with one of your women?'

Eddie Cranston lit another cigarette and leaned back a little in his chair. 'All right, Carol Ann's not my only bird,' he said, as if modesty almost forbade him admitting it. 'I can't help it if women throw themselves at me, can I?'

'You could move out of the way,' Atherton murmured, but only Slider heard him.

'How many women have you got?' Slider asked mildly.

He shrugged. As well ask a sultan for a tally on his harem. 'Oh, quite a few. I get around a bit.'

'You're not married to any of them?'

'Nah! What ju take me for?'

'I wouldn't take you for a king's ransom,' Slider said, but it went past Eddie. 'But some of them have children by you?'

He shrugged. 'Well, it keeps 'em happy. Women like kids.'

'And you get more from the Social Security if they have children,' Slider concluded. 'So in what way was Lenny messing with one of your women? You mean he was having sex with her?'

'Nah!' Eddie said broadly. 'A git like him? Leanne wouldn't touch him with a bargepole. I tell you, my birds are all crazy about me. When you've had the best – forget the rest, right?'

'And besides that,' Slider said, 'to quote a friend of yours, you'd knock their teeth in if they didn't toe the line?'

He looked taken aback. 'What friend? Who said that?'

'Never mind. So if Lenny wasn't poking your woman, what was he doing?'

'He was taking money off her. Been round threatening her to pay up. She didn't want to tell me, but I got it out of her. So, as I say, that was well out of order, wasn't it? I had to give him a smacking, didn't I?'

Eddie was leaning so far back now the two front chair legs were off the ground. His smirk was interrupted only by the need to put a cigarette between his lips. Atherton thought of the draggled Karen Peacock and her three children and his palm itched. He looked pointedly at Eddie's black eye and said, 'Except that it seems Lenny was the one did the smacking, right?'

The chair crashed back to earth, and Eddie scowled. 'He got a lucky punch in, that's all.'

'And having come off worse in the first encounter,' Slider said, 'you followed him and got your revenge by stabbing him through the heart.'

Now he paled, seeing where he had been led. 'I never! I went straight to Carol Ann's.'

'Why do I find that so hard to believe?'

'I never killed him! I swear!'

'What, a hard man like you, whose women have been bothered by a git like Lenny? You had to show him who was boss.'

'Look—'

'You're a big name in the criminal world.'

'No, I—'

'You'd lose your cred if you didn't off him, wouldn't you? I can see that. People would say you'd bottled out. So you had to kill him.'

'No, it's not like that!' Eddie's bubble was well and truly burst. He was almost pleading now. 'Look, it's not me that's the villain. I never done nothing wrong. It was Lenny upsetting my bird. I had to make him leave her alone, that's all.'

'You didn't want him taking money from her, because that's what you do.'

'It's different,' he said, wiping sweat from his upper lip with his forearm. 'Look, Lenny's a runner for a loan shark. Golden Loans in Uxbridge Road. Old Herbie Weedon, he's his boss. He got Leanne into it. Give her a loan against her benefit. You know what the interest is like on them sort of loans! She's getting further and further into debt, and Lenny's going round muscling her—'

'Getting at her money before you can,' Atherton suggested.

'He was frightening her!' Eddie protested. 'You never saw it like I did. Leanne was crying her eyes out. She didn't want to tell me at first, but I got it out of her. She was worried sick about it. So I went after him.'

'How did you know he'd be in the Phoenix that evening?'

'I didn't, not for sure. But he often was. Anyway, he wasn't there when I went in. I had a few pints and waited, and he come in just before closing. So he goes up and talks to Sonny Collins, and I wait till he's finished, and then I goes up to him and says, "You've been messing about with my woman, and I'm not having it." So he tries to pretend he don't know what I'm talking about and we start having a shouting match and Sonny Collins says, "For Gawd's sake take it outside, Lenny," so Lenny legs it for the door and I follow him. And outside I grab him and I say, "You're not getting away that easy," and we start rowing again, and then I lose me rag and throw one at him, only he puts his arm up, and the next minute he's hit me right in the eye.' Eddie paused for breath and put an unconscious hand up to touch the bruise tenderly. 'Gawdamighty, you'd never think it could hurt that much. Otherwise I'd have had him. As it was, I went kind of dizzy for a minute, and while

I'm standing there swearing off a blue streak, waiting for me vision to clear, right, he legs it, the mouldy little coward.'

'Which way?'

'Down past the football ground. Time I could look around, he was out of sight. So I went straight to Carol Ann's.'

'Why did you go there?'

'Well, I got me own place, but she was nearer.' He drooped a bit further. 'I didn't want to walk about looking like that. You never know who might see. If it got out—! And I didn't know how bad me eye was. I didn't know if I ought to go up the Casualty. I thought she could have a look at it.' He looked at them pathetically. 'And I been there ever since. That's it and all about it.'

'Why didn't you go home on Tuesday morning?'

'I told you, I didn't want anyone to see me with an eye like that.'

'Come on, Eddie. You were scared, weren't you? You'd killed him and you were lying low.'

'No, I never!'

'What did you do with the knife, Eddie? A flick-knife, was it?'

'I've never had no flick-knife.'

'Did you make Carol Ann get rid of it for you? It wasn't right to get her involved. That makes her an accessory, you know. She didn't deserve that. But then you're a bit of a bastard when it comes to women, aren't you? You don't care what happens to them as long as you can save your own miserable hide.'

'It wasn't like that! I never killed him! I haven't got a knife!'

'I'm sure you haven't got one now,' Slider said, and with a glance at Atherton, passed the ball over to him.

'Tissue of lies?' Atherton said when they left him.

'Full box of Kleenex,' Slider responded, but he sounded thoughtful.

Swilley, who had been having a go at Carol Ann, met them back in the office. The rest of the team gathered round hopefully. 'Nothing,' she said. 'She's got her story tight in her head and she's sticking to it. She says he arrived on her doorstep about half past eleven Monday night with a black eye, saying he'd been in a fight, and he hasn't left the house since. He was so upset she called in sick to stay home and look after him. She says he's a real baby about hurting himself, like all men. Well, that bit rings true at least.'

'Ta muchly,' said Hollis on behalf of them all.

Swilley ignored him. 'I found out how Karen Peacock knew about it, by the way. So much for Carol Ann phoning her – it was her phoned Carol Ann. She'd heard about the fight and wanted to know if Eddie was all right. Eddie had given her Carol Ann's phone number, the dipstick. Any luck with yours, boss?'

Slider shared the result of the interview with them. 'Trouble is, we haven't got any exact times,' he said. 'The fight took place just about, or just after, closing time, which could mean anything from eleven to twenty past. And he got to Carol Ann's house at about eleven-thirty.'

'Which is five minutes' walk from the Phoenix,' Atherton put in.

'But Lenny was stabbed – we assume – in the park,' Swilley said, 'which means they either went over the South Africa gate, or went round and through the Frithville gate, which has got to be ten minutes' walk. And then another five, probably, back to Abdale Road.'

'It doesn't take long to stab somebody,' Mackay said. 'Even with fifteen minutes' walking, it's still enough time if the fight happened anything up to ten past.'

'But *why* would they go all that way round?' Slider complained. 'If they wanted to go into the park it would make more sense to climb over the gate only yards from where they were standing.'

'Because if they climbed over someone might see them,' Anderson suggested.

'And we know there were no fingermarks on the gate to match Lenny's, so we can assume they didn't go over,' Swilley said.

'The fingerprint evidence doesn't help at all,' Slider said. 'There was nothing clear on either gate, but it doesn't mean some of the smears weren't one of them, or both. But why would they go into the park at all?'

'As I see it, guv,' McLaren said, 'Lenny runs off, climbs the gate to get away, meaning to run through the park and out that way. Cranston follows him, catches him up by the playground, they have another tussle, and he knifes him.'

'Your brain's come unstuck again,' Swilley said impatiently. 'Why would Lenny run away from Eddie? He's already won the fight.'

'All right,' McLaren said comfortably, 'Eddie runs away from Lenny, bunks over the gate in a panic, Lenny follows him to finish him off, corners him, Eddie's got his knife out and – bang.'

'It makes more sense that way,' Hollis agreed.

'Right,' said McLaren, encouraged. 'Then Eddie goes back over the gate and round to Carol Ann's. Five minutes the lot.'

'Why not through the park and out through the Frithville gate?' Atherton asked.

'The way I see it, he wants to get under cover as soon as poss,' McLaren said. 'Why would he go the long way round?'

'Sometimes,' Atherton conceded, 'you almost sound like an intelligent life form, Maurice.'

'I'm still not happy about all this climbing over gates,' Slider said. 'For one thing, there'd be some sign, surely, on Lenny's clothes? And for another, if this was closing time there ought to have been people on the street. *Someone* would have seen them.'

'Maybe they did and just aren't coming forward,' Atherton shrugged.

'And another thing,' Slider said, 'Eddie said he'd seen Lenny in the Phoenix. Why did Sonny Collins say he'd never seen him before?'

'You want a *reason* for Sonny Collins to lie?' Atherton said incredulously.

'And,' Slider went on, 'Eddie said that Collins said "Take it outside, *Lenny*."'

'I refer the hon member to my previous answer.'

'It looks straightforward enough to me, guv,' Hollis said. 'And a right squalid little story it is. Nasty small-time lowlife preying off women. Benefit fraud, loan shark muscle-men. Two bits o' scum squabbling over their miserable pickings like two dogs with a mouldy bone. And it ends like usual with one dead and one in the slammer where he belongs.'

'What a poetic way you have of putting it,' Atherton said.

'The trouble is,' Slider said, 'that we haven't got a shred of proof. Eddie doesn't deny the fight, but that doesn't prove he's the murderer. We've no witness, no weapon, no timetable. All we've got is a motive.'

'That'll do it, nine times out of ten,' Mackay said.

'You know and I know the CPS won't move without a cast-iron case, and so far this one's as sound as a cardboard canoe.'

'But it's a start?' McLaren pleaded.

'It's a start,' Slider allowed kindly.

'It's more than that,' Atherton said. 'We started off this case with a sack of people who all had one eye, no surname and no address. I think we've worked wonders to get this far.'

'Yes, well, now we've got to start finding some evidence,' Slider reminded him.

'What are we going to do with Carol Ann, boss?' Swilley asked. 'I think we'll have to let her go pretty soon. She's coming over all operatic. Dying duck in a thunderstorm.'

'Ah yes, duck *à l'orage*,' said Atherton.

'She can go any time she likes,' Slider said. 'She's here voluntarily. I'd like to search her house though.'

'They've had two days to tidy up.'

'But we might spot what he used as a weapon, or there might be a bloodstain on something. It's surprising what they miss.'

'I don't think she'll agree,' Swilley said doubtfully.

'She will. There's that video recorder, remember.'

CHAPTER SEVEN

Bra-Tangled Spanner

'You'll have to rewrite your TV statement,' Porson said.

Slider's heart sank. 'I was hoping I could get out of that, now we know Eddie's and Lenny's surnames.'

'You don't know Lenny's address.'

'Yes, but we've got a lead on that. His employer's bound to have it.'

'Fair enough. But you said yourself there's got to be witnesses. I agree with you. All this fighting and climbing over gates – someone saw something, that's crystal, but no-one's come forward. Got to shake 'em up. Once the community starts turning a blind ear to crime, you're walking down a thin blue line. I'm not having any part of my ground turned into a no-show area. Nothing emerged from the door-to-door?'

'Not so far.'

'Local TV news, then. That's the ticket. And you're the man. Nice sympathetic face. Not a crumbling old ruin like me.' If it was a joke, he didn't laugh, and Slider thought better of smiling, even sympathetically. Strike the wrong note with Porson and he could take your head off clean as a vole with an earthworm. 'What do you want to do with Cranston?'

'Now we've got his address, I'd like to search his drum. Either he can give permission or I can arrest him, whichever way he wants to play it.'

'Not shouting, is he?'

'Mute as a swan. Seems to have resigned himself.'

'Don't nick him unless you have to. Got enough to do without realms of paperwork.'

'Right, sir,' Slider said, grateful for small mercies.

'All right, Bill,' Porson said, suddenly kind, 'better go and work on that statement of yours, get yourself in the right frame of mind. You'll be doing it over at Hammersmith, of course.'

'Will I?' Slider hadn't expected that.

'They've got a proper press suite all set up. And the press officer wants you there an hour beforehand to prepare you. Check your nose hair, give you electrocution lessons, that sort of thing.' He surveyed his junior. 'Had any lunch yet?'

'No, sir.'

'Thought you looked a bit fagged out. Go and get something to eat, and get your statement drafted. Your mind'll work better on a full stomach.'

Slider, as he trudged off, wasn't sure there'd be room for food with all the butterflies.

Golden Loans occupied one of those dusty-windowed offices above a hardware shop in Uxbridge Road. Access was via an extremely battered door which stood between the hardware shop and the deli next door. The smell of paraffin and salami competed on the air. The door was on the latch and pushed open to reveal a long and steep flight of stairs covered in green marbled lino which sported a collection of muddy footmarks that would have delighted the heart of a Holmes or early Wimsey. Since it hadn't rained in over a week, it was plain that office cleaning was not high on the list of priorities.

At the top of the stairs was a half-glazed door through whose hammered glass it was perfectly possible to see the outline of the high toilet cistern and its dangling chain. No female staff then, Atherton concluded. The passage led back towards the front of the building and another half-glazed door on which the name in gold paint had been partly scratched off so that it now read GOI DEN L AVS. From the Bakelite doorknob hung a cardboard-and-string home-made sign on which was written in irregular capitals KNOCK AND ENTER.

Atherton knocked and entered. The door swung only ninety degrees, stopped by the massive desk which dominated the room. Between the door and the wall to Atherton's right was an empty patch of lino'ed floor about two feet square, but that was the only empty space in the room. There were two small, hard kitchen chairs against the right-hand wall, for customers, presumably – or applicants or supplicants or whatever the correct term was in the loans-to-the-unthrifty biz. The rest of the room was filled with filing cabinets, a large metal stationery cupboard, a table cluttered with paperwork, the huge desk, and the man behind it.

Herbie Weedon was vast and almost shapeless: if it weren't for his head you'd have been hard put to it to swear he was human. He seemed penned behind his desk like something dangerous, for the files and papers which covered the desk had stacked up in interlocking piles like a dry-stone wall, those furthest from him the highest, in teetering columns. He looked dangerous, but to himself more than the world: his blood pressure appeared to be well over into the red zone and almost off the gauge. His nose was spread, bumpy and purple, his eyes sunken and congested, his cheeks an aerial map of tiny red veins. His hair was sparse, as if it had been pushed off his skull by the terrifying forces within; his breathing filled the office, rivalling the traffic sounds from outside. He was like an ancient steam boiler with a jammed safety-valve, ready to blow at any moment. Yet by contrast his pudgy hands were pale and almost dainty, with well-kept nails. One rested on the desk top; the other was occupied with conveying a small thin cigar to and from his mouth. They looked as if they were quite separate entities from the rest of him: milk-white handmaids serving a bloated old sultan.

'Mr Weedon?' Atherton said gently, on the principle that one doesn't shout in an avalanche zone.

'The same,' he wheezed. 'Do for you?' Behind the puffy lids the little dark eyes were as knowing as a pig's. 'Police?'

'Is it that obvious?'

'To me,' Weedon said, pleased with himself. 'When you've been in this business as long as I have . . . I've seen them all come and go. All sorts. Spot a copper a mile off.'

Atherton was upset by this. He knew what coppers looked like: cheap suits, big bottoms, thick-soled shoes. Had his standards slipped so far?

'It's the eyes,' Herbie explained just in time for Atherton's self-esteem. 'Which nick are you from?'

'Shepherd's Bush. Detective Sergeant Atherton.' He showed his brief but one of Weedon's hands waved it away magnanimously.

'Who's The Man up there now? Can't keep track since old

Dickson died. Great bloke was your Mr Dickson. Many a brandy and cigar we had together down at the club. University graduate he was not, but he was what I *call* a copper. There's many a fine degree earned in the great School of Life.'

'It's Mr Porson now,' Atherton said, hoping he wasn't going to throw up. But he knew what Weedon was really saying: *I'm older than you, laddie, and I know important people. I can get things done.* And also, *You and I are on the same side of the law.* If he had ever supposed Golden Loans was a squeaky-clean outfit, he would have revised his opinion after that.

'Porson? No. I don't know him,' Weedon said thoughtfully, accepting a suck of cigar from right-hand maid. 'So what can I do for you this fine day? An advance against your salary? You wouldn't be the first copper to come through that door for that. Shocking badly paid, you blokes. Wouldn't do your job for all the tea in Wigan. Siddown, siddown.' Left-hand maid waved Atherton to a kitchen chair. 'Standing around like that, give me a crick in my neck looking at you. Make yourself comfortable. Smoke?'

'Thanks, I don't,' said Atherton.

'Very wise. I'm giving it up myself.' He began to make a terrible noise and Atherton, who had almost sat down, almost leapt up again, his mind on resuscitation techniques. Then he realised Herbie Weedon was laughing at his own joke. The laugh ended in a racking, phlegmy cough that bounced his whole body, and left-hand maid dashed to his pocket for a handkerchief and tenderly wiped his face.

'I'm interested in an employee of yours,' Atherton said, thinking he'd better get the questions asked before it was too late.

'Oh yes?' gasped Weedon.

'Lenny Baxter.'

The eyes sharpened. The breathing slowed. 'Oh, yes,' said Weedon in a very different tone. 'What's he been up to?'

'He's dead,' Atherton said kindly. 'I rather thought you might have noticed.'

Weedon smiled a little. 'I might have, if he'd died in here. But as it happens, he hasn't worked for me for a couple of months. He was one of my collection agents, but I had to turn him off. He was coming up short.'

'You mean he was stealing the money he was supposed to collect?'

Weedon looked away towards the window and waved his cigar gently. 'Oh, I don't like to use a harsh word like that. He might have lost the money. He might never've *had* the money. It might have been stolen off him. But a collection agent who doesn't deliver I don't need. So I said thank you Lenny and bye-bye.'

'And when was this?'

'Like I said, a couple of months ago.'

'From what I hear, he was still collecting much more recently than that. Like maybe last week or early this week.'

Weedon shook his head, quite unmoved. 'Not for me.'

'Did he collect for other people, then?'

The hands spread in a little gesture. 'He was a freelance, he could work for anyone he liked. I didn't enquire.'

'I thought he was employed by you.'

The little eyes gleamed. 'Self-employed.' Aces over tens. Beat that. All the possible leverage of employment legislation down the tubes.

Atherton had no choice but to become the supplicant. 'So what else was Lenny up to, Mr Weedon? You're a sharp man. You must have an idea.'

Weedon leaned forward a little, and for a moment Atherton thought he was going to come across. But he said only, 'It's a big bad world out there, Mr Atherton, and full of dark deeds. I wouldn't be at all surprised if Lenny Baxter was into something too big for him and it turned round and bit him. He was a cocky sod and he thought he knew it all. But what that thing he was into might have been I can't tell you.'

'You must have a suspicion.'

'Maybe I have. Maybe you have. But if it comes to guessing we can each guess for ourselves. Maybe Lenny Baxter had it coming. That's all I can say.' He blew out smoke and leaned back in his chair. 'Anything else I can do for you this fine day?'

Atherton sighed inwardly. Without some leverage he would not get any more out of this old trouper, and any threats he uttered would have to be well filled to work. No use just hinting Golden Loans was crooked. He acknowledged himself beaten. 'Lenny Baxter's address,' he said.

'That,' Weedon said graciously, 'I can do for you.' Both hands were placed flat on the desk and he began heaving himself up. It was a terrifying process. The vast white-shirted torso melded into a vast black-trousered behind propped on short thick legs as big round the thigh as the average man was round the chest. The colour in the face deepened, the wheezing became a roar. Once up, Weedon clamped his cigar firmly in his teeth and waded round to a filing cabinet to pull out a drawer. At close quarters Atherton could hear a whole extra symphony of breathing sounds resonating within the clogged chest, as if he had a family of meercats living in there.

Weedon returned to his seat and wrote the address down on a slip of paper. Atherton pocketed it and thanked him, and rose to go. At the last minute, as if taking pity on him, Herbie Weedon said, 'Dark deeds, Mr Atherton. It's a jungle out there. Young Lenny thought he knew it all. He thought I was an old fool. But he's dead and I'm alive.'

Only just, was Atherton's uncharitable thought as he went out into the dark passage and shut the door behind him.

The search of Carol Ann's house and of Eddie Cranston's flat in Scotts Road revealed nothing of any interest as far as Lenny Baxter's death was concerned. Cranston's place was a tiny one-bedroom conversion, and looked as though he used it for little more than to get changed in, for it was chaotic and short on conveniences. The kitchen showed no sign of being used for food preparation, and, indeed, there was nothing in the fridge except for eight cans of Stella, a pint carton of milk gone solid, with a 'best before' date of two months ago, and a part-used tub of low-fat spread wearing an interesting blue fur cape under its lid.

The other thing Cranston evidently used his flat for was to store things. Just as it was deficient in home comforts, it was over-endowed in other areas: packs and packs of cigarettes, an unopened boxed dozen of vodka, several boxes of assorted used CDs, a large cardboard box containing about fifty shortie umbrellas, another of shocking-pink nylon fur soft toys with the sort of button eyes on pins that any self-respecting toddler would have out and swallow before you could say 'peritonitis', and three cases of imitation leather wallets from Slovakia. A right little Del Boy he seemed indeed.

It was going to be a whole separate investigation to find out what, if anything, was nicked and what was genuine stock in trade, especially as Cranston didn't seem the sort of man who bothered much with paperwork. Fortunately the search team also found a lump of cannabis resin wrapped in kitchen foil in the bedside cabinet drawer, which was enough to keep Eddie under wraps should he feel like legging it.

All this, plus the result of Atherton's interview with Weedon, Slider learnt when he returned in somewhat of a foul mood from Hammersmith, where he had done his statement and appeal for witnesses before both local TV channels, three local radio channels, four local newspapers and the *Standard*. It would add up, he reckoned, to about one and a half minutes of air time, and had used up nearly three hours of his day. And who knew if it would yield any results?

He stamped up to Porson's room to report, and found it empty, to his surprise. Porson's mac and briefcase were gone. He made his way down to the shop where Sergeant Nicholls was in charge, patiently filling in prisoner report forms. 'Nutty' Nicholls was a handsome Scot from the far north-west, where they speak a pure English, and the accent is soft with the wash of sea and rain. He had some surprising talents. Once at a police charity concert, got up by the egregious area commander Mr Wetherspoon, Nicholls had sung the 'Queen of the Night' aria in a fine, true falsetto and brought the house down.

'Nutty, do you know where Porson is?'

'He's away home,' Nicholls answered.

'*Porson?*' The old man never went home early. Slider wouldn't have been surprised to learn that he never went home at all.

'Went through half an hour ago.'

'I thought he'd have waited for me to do my bit on TV.'

'I think his wife's not very well,' Nicholls said.

'Oh. Hard to think of him having a wife, really.'

'How did it go? Your piece.'

'All right, I suppose. According to that press female over at Hammersmith, anyway.'

'Amanda Odell. Aye, I know her.' He eyed Slider cannily. 'What's eating you, Bill? I know you don't like the press, but they're a necessary evil.'

'It's that Odell female mostly. She's supposed to be one of

us, but she has a completely different set of priorities. We're trying to deal with a murder case, and all she cares about is how I place my hands and whether my tie is sympathetic enough.'

Nicholls shrugged. 'It's her job,'

'There shouldn't be a job like that,' Slider said, the exasperation bursting through at last. 'What kind of a people are we, for God's sake? Everything's judged by appearance. It doesn't matter what people do any more, only what they look like.'

'You're upset, laddie,' Nicholls said wisely. 'You didn't like being in front of the cameras.'

'I hated it,' Slider said. 'I felt exposed and – invaded. I feel as if I need a very long bath.'

'You need a very long drink,' Nicholls corrected. 'I bet you came across just fine, anyway.'

'Well, I tell you, never again! Porson can do it. They don't pay me enough to go through that.'

'When's Joanna coming over?' Nicholls asked, cutting to the chase.

Slider looked at him. 'You think that's what's wrong with me?'

'If I was only seeing Mary once a month I'd be climbing the walls.'

'It's a bastard of a situation,' Slider admitted.

'Aye. Listen, I'm due a break. D'ye want to have a cup of tea and a chin? Two ears, no waiting?'

'No. Thanks, Nutty, but I've got to go and do the search of Lenny Baxter's drum, now we've got the address.'

'No minions?'

'No overtime. It has to be me, as the song says.' He sighed. 'Not that it's likely to yield anything, after all this time.'

'He was living with someone, wasn't he?'

'According to sources.'

'Why didn't she report him missing?'

'Word is she was a tom, so I don't expect "co-operation" and "police" ever come together in her vocabulary.'

'A-huh. Who're you taking with you?'

'Swilley, in case the female's there.'

'Atherton's gone home to the wife, eh?' Nutty smiled.

'I certainly hope so. If the present set-up doesn't curb his wandering spirit we'll have to think seriously about getting him neutered.'

'Well,' said Nutty, going back to his paperwork, 'if you're at a loose end later, I'll have a drink with you when the relief's over.'

'Thanks,' Slider said. 'I might keep you to that.'

'Friendship's the next best thing to love,' Nutty pronounced.

'You've been at the *Reader's Digests* again,' said Slider.

Lenny Baxter's flat was in Coningham Road, the basement floor of a large Victorian house. It had its own entrance via the area steps; the flats on the three floors above were reached by the stairs up to the front door.

'Nice and private for coming and going,' Swilley remarked.

There was no response at the door and no sound from within. It proved surprisingly easy to break in, however, for although there was a deadlock on the front door, it was not engaged.

'I wonder why he didn't lock up properly when he left?' Slider said. 'He was obviously careful – serious locks on the windows.'

'I suppose the woman, whoever she is, was the last to leave and she didn't bother,' Swilley said.

The flat was not large. The passage from the front door ran straight to the back. Off it to the left were the sitting room with the window onto the area and a rather dark bedroom, with a tiny windowless bathroom between them. The passage ended in the kitchen, which had a window onto the rear area. There was no access to the garden, and the area had railing round the top of its wall to prevent – or at least discourage – access from the garden. All the window locks were engaged and there was no sign of a break-in.

The whole flat was a mess: the occupants plainly had not believed in tidying up. Clothes, papers, dirty crockery: whatever was used seemed to be left where it dropped. But gradually through the casual mess emerged something else: the disorder left by a hasty flight. In the bedroom, drawers had been emptied and most of their contents were missing. A pair of black, flimsy nylon panties lay on the floor halfway to the door and half a pair of sheer black stockings was tangled in the crumpled sheets of the unmade bed, mute witnesses to the hasty packing. The dressing table had marks in the dust to show where toiletries had been swept off it wholesale, and a bottle of eyeliner had fallen down into the limbo between it and the skirting-board.

The wardrobe stood open, and there was a suitcase-sized space on the high shelf; one end of the clothes rail was empty, wire hangers were scattered on the floor, and a strappy dress hung askew where it had resisted arrest.

A man's – presumably Lenny's – clothes were still present, on the rail and in drawers, and men's toiletries and an electric razor were still in the bathroom. 'His girlfriend's done a runner,' Swilley concluded.

'And in some panic, by the look of it,' Slider said. The air in the bedroom was strong with her scent. *Paris*, he thought. Yes, there was an atomiser, left behind with a bottle of body moisturiser on the dressing table.

The sitting room smelled of Lenny's French cigarettes.

'He wasn't short of a bob or two,' Swilley observed, noting the hi-fi gear, the very latest wide-screen TV, the new video recorder. 'I suppose that's why he had the window locks. Well, there's nothing for us here by the look of it.'

'That's it,' Slider said. 'The look of it. Just stand still a minute, get an overall picture.'

She obeyed, but after a minute she said, 'What, boss?'

'Someone else has been here. There are things missing.'

'We know that. She's packed and run.'

'Yes, and that's disguising it to an extent. But apart from her frantic scrabbling about, someone else has been through the house. A professional.'

'I don't see it,' Swilley said.

'Remember the bedroom: her dresser drawers are on the floor, but his have been pulled out and left out. Why would she do that? She must know where things are kept. Someone searched his drawers, and a professional starts at the bottom to save wasting time pushing them back in. And in here, the stuff on the lower shelf of that table has been taken out and roughly stacked on the floor. Why? And look, there by the telephone, there's a gap in the mess on the top. Smallish, square – an address book?'

'Maybe,' Swilley said unwillingly.

He looked at her. 'All right, a little bet. Try last number redial. I bet you a tenner it's the speaking clock.'

She didn't accept the bet, which was just as well, because he was right.

'An amateur wouldn't be likely to think of that. We'd better try 1471, but I'll bet that's been blocked too. It'll probably be a public phone box number. These people know what they're doing.'

'But what were they after?'

Slider knew a rhetorical question when he heard one. 'We'd better have a search team in to go over the place, but I doubt if it will yield anything. They'll have taken anything incriminating, and they'll have worn gloves. And we'll have to interview the neighbours, and see if anyone knows who the girl is and where she's likely to be.'

'Boss, if this place was done over by an expert, could it really have been Eddie Cranston? I mean, he comes over as such a plonker.'

'Yes, and if he's only acting the idiot he should be up for an Oscar,' Slider said.

'Carol Ann's no fool, though. Sharp as a packet of needles, that one.'

'But she's got no form.'

'That we know about. Maybe we ought to look into her background. She did shield Eddie.'

Slider gave a tired smile. 'Maybe she's not that bright, after all, then.'

He went for the drink with Nutty. They walked round to the Crown and Sceptre in Melina Road where they served Fuller's, which was worth the extra distance; and, since Nutty didn't want to drink on an empty stomach and Slider didn't know where his next meal was coming from, they ordered toasted cheese sandwiches as well. When they came, Slider noted without surprise that even pub sandwich garnish had succumbed to the cherry tomato mania. He had nothing against cherry tomatoes except that any attempt to cut them shot them off the plate with a velocity that could lay out a gemsbok at fifty paces, and putting them in the mouth whole and biting down was a not entirely pleasant experience that could result in doing the nose trick with tomato seeds.

'It's presentation again,' he said to Nutty. 'Trying to find a new way to make you buy something you've got used to.'

'People like miniatures,' Nutty said. 'God knows why. It's a fad, like those selection boxes of tiny wee Bountys and Mars Bars. Mary's got a friend who collects doll's house furniture. She hasn't a doll's house, you understand. She just thrills to Welsh dressers and Regency chairs small enough to stand on the palm of her hand.' He shook his head in wonder. 'She seems normal enough otherwise. But everybody seems to collect something nowadays.'

'I seem to be shedding rather than collecting,' Slider said. 'Wives, children, homes . . .'

'So what's going to happen with you and Joanna?' Nutty asked, licking the foam from his upper lip. 'I have to tell you, Bill, that's one of the great relationships. Antony and Cleopatra, pork pie and mustard – you two just go together.'

'It's like that when she's back,' Slider smiled. 'Last time – well, not to go into details, but it was like the first time we met. Couldn't keep our hands off each other.'

'Aye, a-huh,' Nutty said wisely, 'but a relationship's not all damp hands, is it? Nice though that is.'

Slider agreed. 'I want her there all the time. I want to do everything with her. Even the shopping – that's how far gone I am! God knows we've got little enough time to be together anyway, with her job and my job.'

'But this new job of hers – it is temporary?'

'She's doing it on a trial basis, but it's a permanent job.' He turned his glass round and round on the bar top. 'I keep thinking, if she stays away, maybe she'll meet someone else.' He looked up, met Nutty's eyes, and shrugged. 'It happens.'

'Maybe you will,' Nutty said.

Slider shook his head. 'I'm starting to think maybe I will have to chuck it in and go over there. I'll have got my twenty-five in at the end of this year.'

'That's only half final salary. You can't live on that.'

'I might be able to find a job where the language isn't a problem. Tourist guide or something. Of course, she'd be travelling, but I'd see more of her there than I will here.'

Nicholls thought it all sounded hopeless. 'You'd miss the Job,' he said unemphatically.

'Like the toothache,' Slider said with a swift smile. 'Still, it helps to pass the time.'

'How did your search go?' Nicholls asked, taking the offered exit from the tender subject. 'Was Baxter's lassie there? Did you find the murder weapon in her underwear drawer?'

'Why should you think that?' Slider asked, startled. He thought of the flimsy knickers, abandoned on the floor. Was Nutty psychic?

'That's where women always keep things. First place your professional burglar looks for the jewellery – you know that.'

'But do you think she did it?'

'Christ, man, don't look at me!' Nutty protested. 'I've not been following yon soap opera. It's just a lifetime's conclusion that women are at the bottom of most things. Are you going off Cranston, then?'

'Cranston leaves a lot of questions unanswered,' Slider admitted. 'It's starting to look more like a professional job, and Cranston doesn't come across as that organised.'

'Well, I hope it is him,' Nicholls said. 'He's a nasty little creep, and from what I've observed, a professional getter-away with things. I don't like freeloaders. Another pint?'

'That sounded like a very pointed juxtaposition,' Slider said. 'It's my round – same again?'

While he was waiting for them to be pulled, his mobile rang. He had to go outside to get the privacy and the quiet to answer it.

'Hullo, Mr S.' It was the husky tones of Tidy Barnet, one of his snouts – though nowadays they were supposed to call them CHIS: Covert Human Intelligence Sources. Some boy wonder destined for great things spent his days in his comfy office at the Yard thinking up things like that.

'Hullo. You got something for me?'

'Seen you on the telly,' said Tidy. 'You was good.'

'You think?'

'Manner born. The wife reckons you could be a pin-up.'

'It can be my second career. I'll need one if I don't get a break soon.'

'Got a bit of gen for you. That Lenny Baxter – lived down Coningham, right?'

'That's right.'

'He was seen outside his house Mundy night, about half eleven, quart' twelve, talking to a pair o' right tasty bastards.'

Slider's pulse quickened. 'Got any names?'

'Nah. My bloke don't know 'em, but he knows the type. Muscle-men for some big wheel. Top-price minders. Baseball caps, shades, leather jackets. Wearing gloves, and it was a warm night. Well nasty. Unlucky Lenny was in over 'is 'ead all right, right?'

'You don't know who killed him, I suppose?'

'Nah. Nobody don't seem to know.' Tidy sounded slightly surprised at this. 'I've 'ad me ear to the ground, but there's nuffink going round.'

'Well, thanks anyway. Keep listening, and thanks for the tip. Oh, by the way, this stuff about the minders – is it good?'

'It's A1, Mr S.'

'You're starting to sound like one of us,' Slider said. Police graded intelligence using the four-by-four system, starting at A1 at the top, for reliable information from a proven source, down to X0 at the bottom, for something gleaned from an alien from outer space.

CHAPTER EIGHT

Bet your Bottom Deux Lards

The main office was full of sunshine, the smell of McLaren's fried egg sandwich and the murmur of voices. Atherton strolled in with a bag of doughnuts for everybody.

'What are you so happy about?' Swilley demanded suspiciously.

'Can't I just have a generous impulse?' He opened the bag under her nose and shook it gently. 'That one's got cream in it. Go on, Norm, you know you want to.'

'Oh, all right. Ta.'

'The woman tempted I, and she fell.'

'Where d'you get 'em?' Anderson asked, edging up and pincering in.

'The baker's under the railway bridge,' Atherton said. He held the bag out to Mackay. 'There's a Scottish girl serving in there. I said to her, "Is that a cream cake or a meringue?" and she said, "Ye're no wrang, it is a cream cake."'

'Your Scotch accent's bollocks,' McLaren said as he was passed by. 'Here, don't I get one?'

'For Chrissakes, you're already eating a sandwich.'

'Well, I can have it for later, can't I?'

'Surely an oeuf's an oeuf?'

McLaren didn't get it. 'I can have it for afters,' he said, finishing his sandwich in one goose-throttling swallow.

'Maurice, I love you, and I want to have your babies,' Atherton said. 'Here, take one, then. And one for little *moi*, and that just leaves one for teacher.'

'Where is he, anyway?' Mackay complained.

'He's gone upstairs to see Mr Porson,' Hollis said.

'Porson's not in,' said McLaren through the sugar sticking to the egg yolk on his lips. 'His old lady's sick. I heard Sergeant Paxo on the dog about it when I come in.'

'What is it, the flu?'

'Dunno. I never heard. But she must be bad for the old Syrup to stop home.'

Slider came in. 'Are we ready to go? Did anyone get me any tea?'

'Over here, guv.'

'What's up with Mr Porson's old lady, guv?'

'Word spreads in here like a virus in a hospital ward. I don't know. I was only just told he hasn't come in this morning. I expect we'll hear later. Let's get on, shall we? Any minute now the SCG will have sickies coming back on duty and they'll want this case back.'

'And we don't want the sceptre of failure stalking us,' Atherton said, quoting Porson. Norma glared at him. 'What? It's affectionate,' he protested.

'Some of you may know,' Slider said loudly, 'that we got a call last night after my TV appearance—' He waited for the outbreak of whistles and catcalls to stop. '—from a lone community-minded member of the public who was passing the Phoenix on his way home on Monday night and saw the fight between Cranston and Baxter. That's the good news. The bad news, from our point of view, is that his account largely agrees with Cranston's. It was between ten and a quarter past eleven, our witness estimates. The men were standing outside arguing when he first noticed them. He was on the other side of the road, approaching from the Bloemfontein Road end, and kept an eye on them in case they came his way.'

'Your nervous type,' said Mackay.

'Sensible,' Swilley corrected.

'Anyway,' Slider continued, 'as he drew nearer there was a scuffle and the taller, darker one reeled away, swearing and clutching his face, apparently hurt. The other one immediately made off, not running but walking fast, down South Africa Road past the football ground towards Bloemfontein Road – which I don't need to tell you is the opposite direction from the park. Our man went past quickly, not wanting to appear too interested, but when he'd put a bit of distance in he looked back to make sure he was safe, and saw the taller one heading for the cut-through by Batman Close.'

There were murmurs of comment, over which Hollis said, 'We're getting witness in today to look at mugshots just to be sure, but the descriptions fit all right. It seems like the goods.'

'And I had a bit of information from one of my snouts last night,' Slider went on, and repeated what Tidy Barnet had said.

'Coningham Road's more or less opposite the end of Bloemfontein Road,' Mackay said, 'so Baxter was probably heading home when he left Cranston.'

'If he was seen alive at a quarter to twelve, that lets Cranston out anyway, doesn't it?' Anderson said. 'His alibi's from half past eleven.'

'Only if you believe it,' Swilley said.

'They could have met again later, we don't know,' Mackay said.

'Let's go through things in order, shall we?' Slider said. 'Lenny Baxter was stabbed to death some time between eleven forty-five Tuesday night and eight o'clock Wednesday morning. That's a fact. His body was found in the children's playground in Hammersmith Park. That's a fact. Eddie Cranston had a fight with him at about ten past eleven. That's a fact.'

'I think we could assume he was killed in the park,' Atherton said. 'The general public may be unobservant, but you can't carry a dead body through the streets like a roll of lino.'

'My own feeling is that he was killed where we found him,' Slider said, 'but we have always to bear the other possibility in mind. It's possible he was taken in a van up to the Frithville gate, though I think someone would have noticed that. No-one's come forward, but of course that doesn't mean it didn't happen.'

'You're not your usual cautious self today, guv,' Atherton complained.

'If he was killed elsewhere, wouldn't that let out Cranston?' Anderson asked.

'Not at all. As Swilley says, we don't know that his alibi is true. And I'm afraid the new evidence that Baxter was seen alive at eleven forty-five doesn't let him out either. We've got a wide leeway on the time of death. We don't know exactly when Lenny was killed. It would be nice to be able to rule Cranston definitely out or definitely in, but life ain't like that, ladies and germs.'

'I just hate having anything Slob Eddie's told us turn out to be true,' Atherton complained.

Slider continued. 'Now, the case against Cranston, such as it is – and let me remind you we don't have any evidence against him – has the merit of simplicity, but it leaves questions unanswered. What did he do with the weapon?'

'No problem there,' Swilley said. 'Even if he really didn't leave Shotter's house between then and the time we found him, it still gave her two full days to get rid of it.'

'Which would make her an accessory and an accomplished liar,' Slider said.

'I've put some enquiries in train about her,' Swilley said. 'She's got no record, but DC Hughes at Acton owes me one. He's going to sniff around the Elephant for me.'

'You conjure up some dainty images,' Atherton said.

'The pub, dickbrain.'

'Second question,' Slider intervened, 'if it was Cranston, why did he go through Lenny's pockets, what did he take, where is it, and why didn't he take the money?'

No-one had any suggestions to offer. After a pause, McLaren said, 'Well, it's still Cranston for me.'

'That's the kiss of death to any theory,' Atherton said.

'You're such a snot,' Swilley snapped, and turned to McLaren. 'Go on, why?'

McLaren blinked in her sudden warmth. 'Well, we've got nothing else. And he did have a fight with him.'

The warmth switched off. 'You've got to lay off those stupid pills, Maurice. Boss, if it wasn't Cranston, what was Lenny doing in the park? Was he meeting somebody? If he was, maybe it was him that used the Frithville gate. We know he went home, and that would be the logical way for him to come back.'

'But where are the bolt-cutters?' Hollis asked. 'And where's the padlock and chain?'

'Most likely the park keeper just forgot it and it never was locked,' Mackay offered.

'To back up the Cranston Is Innocent theory,' Slider went on, 'we've got all these dark hints that Lenny Baxter was mixed up in something bigger than collecting loan repayments from women on benefit.'

'Herbie Weedon got quite apocalyptic about it,' Atherton said.

'Yes, but he wanted to get you off his tail,' said Swilley. 'On the other hand, there's the evidence that Baxter's pad was searched by a professional. They didn't take his goods and chattels so they must have been after something else. Something that would incriminate someone, maybe.'

'And he was chatting to two heavies outside his house,' Anderson said.

'They might just have been friends of his,' Atherton said fairly.

'But someone who wasn't interested in money went through his pockets,' Slider reminded them.

'And that's definitely sinister,' Hollis said. 'Contempt of money is the root of all evil.'

'I've heard that,' Atherton said.

'To me, the single stab wound to the heart always looked more like a professional killing than the result of a drunken fight,' Slider said. 'But even a drunk can get lucky, and we've got to keep open minds. So what lines have we got to follow up?'

'Check on Carol Ann Shotter and keep an eye on Cranston,' Swilley said. 'If he knows he's being watched he might do something stupid.'

'Right.'

'Put pressure on Herbie Weedon about who Lenny might have been annoying,' Mackay said. 'Cranston might not have been the only one of his customers out for his blood.'

'Right.'

'And there's Sonny Collins,' Anderson said. 'He's a loose end, isn't he? Said he didn't know Lenny but according to Cranston called him by name. He and Lenny might have been into something together.'

'Right,' said Slider again. 'We must see what we can find out about Mr Collins. And let's not lose sight of Lenny's missing girlfriend.'

'Yeah, what's the story with that?' Mackay asked. 'She came home, found the pad had been searched, knew Lenny had been offed, panicked and ran?'

'Maybe she came home and surprised them at it,' Swilley said, 'and they snatched her to keep her quiet.'

'Maybe don't feed the bulldog,' Atherton said.

'Either way, we need to find her,' Slider said. 'Ask around, boys and girls. Get your snouts on that, and on who those two heavies were, seen chatting to Lenny outside his house. And keep cracking on with the search for witnesses. Everybody in west London can't be deaf, blind and dumb!'

'Sonny Collins has got no criminal record, guv,' Hollis reported.

'I didn't think he would have,' Slider said. 'Breweries have to be pretty careful.'

'Right. I've had a quiet word with them, and they said they checked him up when he applied. He'd had three other pubs before, and nothing against him. Before that apparently he was in the navy.'

'Oh? How traditional.'

'The brewery didn't know anything about his service record. Didn't check it up, apparently. Do you want me to?'

'Might as well. May give us an insight.'

'They were a bit antsy about me asking about him,' Hollis said. 'I said it was just routine and we had no reason to suspect him of anything. Well, we don't want to ruin his life if he is innocent, do we?'

'You're a regular boy scout. Did they believe you?'

He grinned. 'Would you believe me if you were them?'

'Not if he was him and I'd ever met him,' Slider said.

'But we've covered our arses either way,' Hollis concluded with satisfaction.

'That's the kind of bet I like,' Slider said.

'Are you in tomorrow?' Atherton asked from the doorway.

Slider looked up. 'No.'

'Sunday off? Blimey, is that a two-headed calf I see baying at the blue moon?'

It said a lot for Slider's state of mind that he actually began to turn his head towards the window.

'I'm having the kids,' he said. 'It was arranged ages ago, and if I miss my turn it's hell's own job to set it up again.'

Atherton spread his hands a little. 'You don't have to justify to me. No reason why you should work Sundays.'

But Slider went on, feeling guilty out of habit. 'There's nothing to be achieved by my being here. And they can call me in if they have to.'

'Be sure they will if they want to,' Atherton said.

A detective inspector, whatever agreement he thought had been reached after the Sheehy Report, was expected to be available on a 24/7 basis, as the jargon was. As chief inspectors left and were not replaced, and sergeants like Atherton cannily refused to apply for promotion, inspectors, like Issachar, were the asses couched down between two burdens, inheriting work from both directions. And inspectors were not paid overtime, either, which made them cheaper labour in these budget-conscious days.

'D'you want to come over for a meal with Sue and me tonight?' Atherton asked. 'I'm doing that chicken and rice dish you like.'

Slider hesitated wistfully. Atherton was a noted gourmet and he cooked as good as he tasted. 'I've got all this stuff to finish,' he concluded. 'I don't know how long it's going to take me. Thanks, but I'll grab something on the way home.'

'You'll get ulcers,' Atherton predicted. 'Ah well, you know where I am if you change your mind.'

He left, the office quietened, and Slider sank into his paperwork. Outside on the street Saturday night was winding itself up, and down in the shop they'd be bracing themselves for the influx, later, of drunks and druggies, the combative and the intellectually altered; barmy old gin-dorises wanting a maunder down memory lane, and stinky winos who'd performed their own lobotomies with decades of cheap booze and falling down on their heads; electric-haired conspiracy theorists; smudge-eyed lost teenagers scooped temporarily out of harm's way; morally vacant youths who thought crime was a lifestyle choice. Black eyes, bleeding noses, wandering wits, sullen silences, vicious insults, foul language, an unstaunchable stream of repetitive stupidity masquerading as cool; smell of fear, smell of feet, smell of beer, smell of pee; and vomit, and blood. All the glamour of the eternal cops 'n' robbers story.

In his office, in the pool of his desk light, Slider wrote in silence like a don in his tower. All policemen start in uniform. He knew what it was like down there. And once you've been on the right side of the counter, it changes your mind-set. You

look at things differently. That was how old pros like Herbie
Weedon could spot a copper: the eyes are the window on the
soul, and what's soul if it isn't mind?

He'd gone so far down that he didn't hear the phone until it
had rung four or five times, as subconscious memory told him
as he picked up the receiver.

'Did I interrupt you in the middle of somebody?' Joanna
said.

'That's my line.' Just the sound of her voice made various
parts of him tingle. What was it with her? Most of the blood
in his head packed up and headed south, leaving him wanting
wits but definitely *homo erectus*. 'Is it the interval?'

'We've not started yet. Ages to go. Concerts here don't begin
until nine. The Spanish like to dine first.'

'The Spanish?'

'You get a lot of them in Barcelona,' she reminded him.

'Oh. I'd forgotten. I was thinking of you being in Frankfurt.'

'That was Wednesday. Keep up, Inspector!'

'Duh,' he said obligingly.

'Hey, did I ever tell you the story about the trumpet section
in Frankfurt?'

'You mean with your old orchestra?'

'Yes, the dear old Royal London Philharmonia. We'd been
doing one of those lightning tours, six capitals in seven days,
and we'd all got a bit punch-drunk. Anyway, we were doing
Shostakovich Five, and there's a long, long passage in the third
movement when the trumpets aren't playing. It's second
trumpet's job to count, so Bob Preston, who was playing first,
had sort of drifted off. Not asleep, you understand, but just
totally vacant. You get that way on the road. Anyway, suddenly
he comes to himself, grabs Brian's knee – that's the second
trumpet – and hisses, "Where the fuck are we?" So Brian whis-
pers, "It's all right, Bob, we've got fifteen bars to go." And Bob
grips harder and hisses desperately, "Not that, you dork, which
town!"'

Slider snorted. 'I know the feeling.'

'I know, my darling, I've seen you like it. You shouldn't be
there at this time of night.'

'I've nearly finished.'

'Then what are you going to do?'

'Go home, I suppose.' He heard how glum that sounded and made an effort. 'Atherton did invite me over for dinner, but . . .'

'And you refused? Have you been bungee jumping off short buildings again?'

'Well, he's got Sue now. I don't want to play gooseberry.'

'Jim's a big boy.'

'What?'

'So I've heard. Anyway, he wouldn't ask you if he didn't want you.'

'Oh, well, it's too late now.'

'No it isn't. It's only half past seven.'

'Is it? I thought it was much later than that. Well, maybe I will, then.'

'Yes, do. Pack up and go now. Then I can stop worrying for one night at least that you aren't eating properly.'

'I wish you were here,' he mentioned.

'If I were, eating would be the last thing on your mind.'

'Or any other part of my anatomy. What time do you get in on Monday?'

'Ten-fifty. I suppose you won't be able to meet me.' It was not a question.

'Come straight here and we can have lunch,' he suggested.

'And I suppose if you've got a murder case on we'll have hardly any time together,' she sighed. 'Why can't people hold off from killing each other for two minutes together? Interfering with my love life! I could kill them.'

'It's a pity you couldn't have come tomorrow, when I'm having the day off.'

'Saturdays and Sundays are when they have concerts, dear,' she explained kindly. 'Besides, you'll have the children. Never mind, we'll just have to catch as catch can. I'd better go. This is costing a fortune.'

'Off you go, then. Play well.'

'I always do. Go and get fed.'

'Did you say "come to bed"?'

'As Monica said to Bill, "Close, but no cigar." I'll see you on Monday. Bye.'

Slider replaced the receiver, stretched mightily, stacked his papers together, and got up. Half an hour later he was knocking at the door of Atherton's small house in Kilburn, a gussied-up

Victorian artisan's cottage – or artesian cottage, as Joanna called it, on account of the damp. Here Atherton had always lived the flighty bachelor life, with a rusty black tom called Oedipus who could be trusted to make himself scarce out by the catflap when his master eased prime totty through the front door.

But things were changing. Oedipus had died, gently of old age under the ceanothus, and – unwisely, Slider thought, but probably with some urging from Sue – Atherton had bought not one but two teenage Siameses to fill the gap, on the basis that they would keep each other company while Atherton was out working. However, what Sredni Vashtar and Tiglath Pileser mostly did while Atherton was out was to egg each other on to ever greater feats of vandalism. A couple of mobile shredders was what they were. No toilet roll was safe, and Atherton now had lace curtains in every room.

The other new thing in Atherton's life was Sue Caversham, a violinist friend of Joanna's. She opened the door to him now, a kitten teetering on each shoulder, their tails straight up as though they were suspended by them from the ceiling. Music was throbbing gently behind her, a violin concerto. Slider was getting better at recognising classical music but he couldn't place this one. Modern-ish. Not Tchaik or Mendelssohn or Brahms, anyway.

'Hullo,' she said, and the kits – Tig and Vash as they tended to get called – said 'Mwah' and 'Ftang' respectively. The smell of chicken wafted from the kitchen. 'Jim thought you might come.'

'Joanna rang and broke my concentration,' he confessed, following her in and shutting the door. 'She said you wouldn't mind if I turned up.'

'Of course not.'

'Thanks,' said Slider. 'What is that?'

'The music? Prokofiev. How is she?'

'Okay, as far as I know. She told me a story about Bob Preston.'

'Oh, well, that's all right then. Glass of wine?'

'Thanks.'

'Have a cat,' she said, and scooped Sredni Vashtar from her shoulder to his. The cat purred, kneading bread with a fine pinging of jacket threads, head-butted him affectionately; and then did one of its disconcerting flying-squirrel leaps, kicking off lightly from Slider's shoulder and sailing through the air to land five feet away halfway up the curtains, where it clung, looking back over its shoulder as if waiting for the applause. Sue had missed it, having turned away to pour Slider's wine. At the same moment, Atherton appeared in the door to the kitchen and nodded a greeting.

'I'm glad to hear you're taking the day off tomorrow,' Sue said to Slider, still with her back turned. 'At least that means Jim gets some time off too. I know it's overtime for him, but for a wonder I was free on Wednesday and Thursday, and it's a pain when he has to work on my evenings off. I get so few of them.'

Atherton's face was inscrutable, but as Sue turned back with the glass of wine, he met Slider's eyes over her head.

Slider adjusted seamlessly. 'Yes, I'm sorry about that. Needs must.'

'You're a bleeding slave-driver,' Sue told him genially.

'Dinner won't be five minutes,' Atherton said, disappearing again.

Slider sipped some wine to avoid having to think of anything to say. What was Atherton up to? Or rather, who? Slider had thought all that was behind him. Damn and blast it, what was this self-destructive streak in him? He itched to kick his bagman's well-tailored bags.

'So which Bob Preston story was it?' Sue asked. Her blue eyes were merry and sympathetic, and Slider couldn't help feeling she knew exactly what had just been passing through his mind.

Sod's Law said that if you got an urgent call it would always come at the time when you were least able to obey it. O'Flaherty called Slider when he was heading in exactly the wrong direction with a carful of children. Well, there were actually only two of them, but it felt like a carful when he was trying to have a telephone conversation through one of their routine did-didn't quarrels.

'Issat you, Billy?'

'You rang me. Who did you expect? Jodie Foster?'

'Ah, that's a sexy female,' O'Flaherty breathed. 'Is she there, then?'

'If you've called me just to talk nonsense I'm going to kill you, next spare moment I get.'

'I'm safe then,' said O'Flaherty. 'You'll have forgotten by then. Listen, I've got Billy Cheeseman in here looking for you.'

It took Slider a moment to remember that was One-Eyed Billy's surname. 'Has he got something for me?'

'He might have. He says he wants a meet.'

'Wants a *meet*?' Slider hated that pseudo-cool expression, especially in the hands of a terminally dopey specimen like One-Eyed Billy.

'He won't tell me what it's all about. Says he can only tell you. Seems fidgety, eyes flittin' everywhere like a virgin at a wake.'

'That's not like him,' Slider said. 'He's too daft to be nervous normally. Maybe he has got something. I'll be there as soon as I can.'

'And when'll that be?'

'Half an hour, forty minutes.'

'Sure God, he'll have gone off the boil by then!'

'I can't help it. I'm on the way to drop the kids off at school. I can't tip them out on the dual carriageway, can I? You'll have to hold the fort until I get there.'

As he holstered the telephone his brain wanted to race off and speculate, but he yanked it back. He saw so little of the children, they deserved his full attention. He examined them as he tried discreetly to speed up. Matthew, slumped in the front seat with the aggressive relaxation of adolescence, looked as if he had slept in his clothes. It was an effect he could achieve within minutes of putting them on freshly laundered. The same mysterious alchemy could turn a tidy bedroom into something resembling Dresden, while Matthew had apparently been lying completely immobile on his bed.

Kate was bouncing up and down on the back seat like one of those Furbies on elastic. Her school uniform looked like a fashion statement. Her brown hair was the same heavy, shiny texture as her mother's, and like Irene she wore it short, the better to set off her sweet face and blue eyes. They were his eyes, but otherwise she looked the image of Irene when he had first known her: neat, pretty, self-contained. Any minute now, he thought with a father's pain, she would start on the boy

business, and these days that didn't just mean exchanging sentimental notes and static, breathy kisses. Various scenarios
slouched like rough beasts towards his imagination and he
flinched from them. Would Irene advise her effectively? Would
Ernie Newman, the new step-father, protect her? Could Slider
have, had he and Irene not split up? Children these days were
exposed to so much so early.

He was aware that Kate had asked him a question and was
waiting for an answer.

'What's that, sweetheart?'

'Can I take fencing lessons?' she repeated with the huge,
elderly patience she often assumed when talking to him. She
already had that habitual eye-rolling exasperation that marks
out young womankind. 'At school.'

'I didn't know you were interested in fencing.'

Matthew roused himself from his matutinal torpor. 'She's not.
She just fancies the fencing teacher.'

'I do not!'

'Yes you do. Mr *Brierly*,' Matthew mocked, as though Brierly
were an intrinsically ludicrous name.

'And I suppose you're not in love with your precious Mrs
Wolfton!' Pleased with herself, Kate expanded. 'Oh, Mrs Wolfton,
Matthew's so in *lurve* with you. He wants to *marry* you.'

Matthew blushed richly, bringing his spots into high relief.
He was going to be a nice-looking boy once his skin settled
down – not handsome, any more than Slider himself was, but
just nice-looking. Girls would like him. But at the moment he
was going through the worst period in a man's life: he was a
war zone of rampaging hormones, and his face was the visible
battlefield. Slider wanted to jump in and defend him, but that
would be to hurt his pride. Instead, neutrally, he asked, 'Who's
Mrs Wolfton?'

'Violin teacher,' Matthew muttered.

Kate bounced harder. 'I don't know why you want to learn
stupid old violin. It's so *dorky*.'

'It is not!' Matthew retorted.

'It is. It's stupid. Only a pathetic saddo would play the violin.'

'What about Nigel Kennedy?' Slider said mildly.

'Oh, puh-lease! He's an ancient, boring old saddo! All violin-
ists are nerds!'

'You shut up!' Matthew said with sudden fury, swivelling round to make a menacing face at her. She stuck her tongue out as far as it would go, and then, apparently satisfied, reverted to her normal tones and the previous question.

'So can I, Daddy? Take fencing?'

'What does your mother say?' Slider hedged.

Kate cut to the chase. 'It's *extra*,' she said succinctly.

Slider blenched. This fee business was a minefield, what with male pride, and Ernie's income being twice Slider's. 'Oh. Well, we'll see. I'll talk to Mummy about it.'

'I suppose that means no,' Kate said, but without grief. They had turned into the road where her school was, and her attention was on the other girls being dropped off. 'There's Melanie,' she said suddenly. 'Let me out here, Daddy.'

She ran off, bag over her shoulder, with that strange impervious completeness of little girls, perfect miniature grown-ups as boys never were. In seconds a group of them had their heads together: all alike with their long straight legs and glossy hair, like foals. It tweaked at Slider's heart with the devastating accuracy of a cat pulling a thread out of fine suiting.

He drove off. Now he had just a few minutes to devote to Matthew, and perversely could not think of anything to say. After a moment, however, Matthew spoke, seemingly from the depths of a long train of thought.

'Dad, are you and Joanna – you know?'

'Am I and Joanna what?'

'Well, is she – you know – coming back?'

Matthew was staring straight ahead and his blush, though less violent than before, evidently came from the same cause. There had been more going on earlier, Slider realised, than mere sibling teasing.

'She's coming back today,' he said.

'Yes, but that's just a holiday, isn't it? I mean—' He struggled with his unwillingness to name demons. What Matthew wanted to know was whether her and Slider's relationship would survive the distance now between them.

Slider would have liked to know that too. 'I don't know what's going to happen,' he said. Matthew moved restlessly, thinking he was being fobbed off, and Slider said, 'Really. I just don't know.'

'I like her,' Matthew said, surprising Slider. Matthew was at the age when any expression of affection was exquisite torture. But all was explained as he went on painfully, 'Mum said it wasn't surprising Joanna went, that no-one could live with you, because of your job.' His spots flared anew.

'She didn't say that to you.' Slider knew that much about Irene.

'No, she said it to Ernie, but we heard. Kate and me. We were just coming into the kitchen.'

All was now explained. A great protective sadness rolled over Slider for his son, who loved him, as painfully and perilously as Slider loved him back. He was not like Kate, who skated lightly and scornfully through life. Matthew's world was a mine-field of angst. He expected every step to blow up in his face; he feared for those he loved as much as for himself.

'That's not why Joanna went,' Slider said. 'We didn't quarrel or anything. It was just her job.'

Matthew hunched lower. 'But she might not come back?'

Slider turned into Matthew's school road. 'We'll work some-thing out,' he said. 'Somehow.' He hoped he sounded surer than he felt.

He found a space and pulled in. Matthew reached over to the back seat for his bag and began to get out.

'G'bye then, Dad. Thanks for the lift.'

'Have a good week,' Slider said. 'And – Matthew?' The boy paused and turned his face to his father, with all the troubles of the world on his shoulders. It was a bugger being a teenage boy. Girls had no idea. 'You don't have to take sides,' Slider said. 'Mummy and I are all right now. She didn't mean anything bad.'

'Kate's an idiot,' Matthew said, jumping a stage of logic; but his face had lightened.

'She's just a little girl. She'll grow out of that.'

'I wouldn't bet on it,' Matthew said. He grinned suddenly, letting Slider see for a moment what he would look like in five or six years' time (how that smile would melt the girls!) and then was gone.

As soon as Slider was alone, his mind snapped him instantly from his domestic into his professional persona. When he was engaged with either one, the other always seemed slightly fantastic. Which was real life, he wondered? He knew what Irene thought. Probably all police wives – unless they were in the service themselves – resented the Job. He shoved the thought away and concentrated on finding the fastest route through the morning traffic back to Shepherd's Bush.

CHAPTER NINE

Arctic Role

Billy Cheeseman had not only gone off the boil by the time Slider got back, he had gone off.

'I couldn't keep him,' O'Flaherty said. 'Said he'd to get to work.' He raised his eyes ceilingwards. 'To think I've lived to see the day when Billy One-Eye says he's to get to work. But he's left his mobile number, says you're to ring him. Every man and his dog's got a mobile these days,' he added, shoving the piece of paper across. 'Sure, when you think o' the crap floatin' about the airwaves – and they say no sound ever dies. What they'll make of it all out on Neptune . . .' As if to illustrate the point, he let out a ripping fart, one of his specials, born of last night's Guinness and his wife's famous steak-and-kidney pudding. Some bug-eyed monster would be swivelling his finger round in his antenna over that one in about 4.18 hours' time, thought Slider, heading for his room.

When One-Eyed Billy answered, there was a babble of background noise which Slider identified, with the aid of a Metropolitan train bashing past on the viaduct, as Shepherd's Bush market.

'Hang on a sec,' Billy said, and there was an interval of indeterminate noise, together with the whistling of Billy's breath, and then at last a low, cryptic, 'Hullo?'

'I'm still here.'

'I've gone round the back for a bit of quiet,' Billy explained. 'I'll have to be quick, only Uncle Sam'll be after me.'

'So what have you got for me?'

'Well,' he said, obviously deeply reluctant, 'about this Lenny bloke what got offed in the park. I don't like getting mixed up in it. My young lady wouldn't like it. Dead posh she is. But me dad said I'd got to help you, so I been asking around.'

'Good for you.'

'But you got to promise to keep me out of it, 'cos of my young lady.'

'Keep you out of what? Spit it out, Billy. What've you got?'

'This geezer what I know, knows Lenny,' Billy murmured, and Slider could imagine the hand cupped round the mouthpiece for security. 'Knows what he was into. It was somethink heavy. He's scared shitless, this geezer. He won't come in the nick and talk to you. So it's gotter be a meet.'

'All right. Where and when?'

'It's gotter be off the manor. He's scared someone'll see him.'

Slider sighed. 'This had better be the goods, Billy. If I find you've been wasting my time—'

'It's the goods all right,' Billy said, faintly resentful. 'I'm tryin' twelp, like me dad said. But this bloke's scared for 'is life.'

'All right, so where?' Slider said again. Off the manor? He hoped it wouldn't be anywhere too exotic.

'You know the Dog up the North Pole?'

Slider translated this encryption effortlessly. It was a pub called the Dog and Sportsman (or as Atherton called it, the Dog and Scrotum) on the corner of North Pole Road. It was only surprise that checked him. North Pole Road was about three-quarters of a mile from the White City. If that was 'off the manor', the unknown informant had a very parochial standard of geography.

'Yes. I know it,' he said.

'I'll get him in there,' said Billy. ''Smorning, about eleven. I got to go up Willesden for me uncle, so he won't know. All right?'

'All right,' Slider agreed.

'But you gotter come alone,' Billy said. 'He'll talk to you, 'cos I told him you was straight, but if you bring anyone wiv you he'll scarper.'

'All right, Billy. I'll be there,' Slider said. All told he was getting off lightly. It could have been midnight under the railway bridge in Huddersfield, with all its attendant problems. But if the unknown informant really was scared, wouldn't he have wanted somewhere a bit more private and a lot darker than a pub on a main road at eleven in the morning?

Before heading out for the 'meet', Slider snatched a moment to ring Irene to let her know he had dropped the children off as arranged, otherwise she'd be ringing and accusing him of thoughtlessness and not caring about his children's safety. Materially she was very comfortable with her new man, but he had found that the less she had to worry about at home, the more she sought out a *casus belli* with him. He supposed it used up her spare energy – and Irene was one of those whiplash-thin women who never sit still. It was a pity Ernie Newman had a cleaning-woman: Irene had no Hoovering to do any more to work it off.

'Oh, by the way, Kate was asking me about taking fencing lessons,' he said.

'Fencing?' Irene sounded blank.

A lifetime's knowledge made him familiar with her thought processes. He smiled. 'With swords. Not garden fencing.'

'Oh! Well, I know they do teach girls woodwork these days . . . Fencing? They say it's good for the figure,' Irene dredged up from the wide-ranging sagacities of 'Them'. 'It makes you graceful. As good as ballet, that way.'

'She can hardly be said to *have* a figure yet. Anyway, I just thought I'd warn you, so she didn't take you by surprise.'

'Why, are you against it? It must be all properly supervised or they wouldn't offer it.'

'I'm not against it. Fencing's a big thing in the Met – a lot of coppers do it. But it's Extra.'

'Oh! Well, that's—' She stopped, and Slider divined from the intonation that she had been about to say, 'That's all right, Ernie can afford it,' but caught herself just in time. 'I expect it's just a passing fad,' she said instead. 'You know what she's like.'

'If she's really serious about it . . .'

'We'll see,' Irene said comfortingly. 'She'll probably have forgotten by the time she gets home.'

Which meant, he translated when he had hung up, that if Kate really wanted to take fencing, Ernie would cough up and they would all try not to mention it to Slider. His former marriage had become like a game of bridge, where you had to translate codes to discover the true state of your partner's hand. He thought fencing would be good for Kate, but he simply couldn't afford it on his screw. That was a fact. Now all he had to decide was whether he minded more denying her the pleasure, or letting Ernie Bloody Newman be Father Christmas – again! Life! he thought. Hate it or ignore it, you can't love it.

The Dog and Scrotum was unreconstructed fifties, an arterial road giant too large for its clientele now that they all had more comfort at home and didn't need to seek it outside. In defiance of the national trend it served no food but crisps and pork scratchings, so at the lunchtime session it was the haunt of equally unreconstructed old keffs of the sort who wore a cap indoors and rolled their own cigarettes, plus a sprinkling of undesirables who had been banned from all the other pubs in the area.

The Dog occupied a corner spot, with two doors, one in each street. One-Eyed Billy and his friend were sitting at the table beside the main door, a position in which, on account of the way the door opened, they could see anyone coming through before *they* saw *them*, and could also keep an eye on the subsidiary door onto the side street. This positioning did not escape Slider's notice, and he was very sure it could not have been Billy Cheeseman's idea. His friend, then, had something of the pro about him.

Billy waved Slider over and introduced the other man with a hint of awe. 'This is my mate Everet Boston. Him and me was at school together.'

'Yeah, for one year. Long time ago, Bill,' the other said, as if distancing himself from that happy time. His eyes scanned Slider and darted away to check the rest of the pub again. He was a tall black man who, if he was a contemporary of Billy's, looked a lot younger than he was. He could have passed for mid-twenties, and had an air of flexible slenderness which was belied, on closer inspection, by the power in the arms and chest.

Beside him on the seat was a very fine suede jacket which Slider could smell was new. He wore his hair in four long dreadlocks caught into a bunch behind, his clothes were casual but sharp and expensive, he had the obligatory gold crucifix and chain round his neck, and he sat at an angle with one leg crossed over the other, clasping the ankle with the hand that was not occupied with his smoke. The word 'cool' sprang to mind, and then slunk away, acknowledging its inadequacy. No wonder they were meeting 'up the North Pole'.

'Get you a drink?' Slider asked, mindful of the proprieties.

'Yeah, I'll have a pint, please,' One-Eyed Billy said quickly, happy as if it were a social occasion.

Everet Boston seemed to hesitate a breath, and then said, 'Captain Morgan. Straight up.'

Slider got them, and a tonic water for himself, and when he brought them back to the table, Boston shifted along the banquette to the next table, giving Slider his seat and keeping the clear getaway for himself. He tossed back half the rum without speaking, and then said, 'You wanna know 'bout Lenny Baxter.'

'Anything you can tell me. I'm very grateful to you for coming forward.'

Boston waved the kindness away with a short sweep of the hand. 'I ain't done it for you. Billy ast me an' I owe 'im one. An' there's another reason.' He waved that away too. 'But I shoon't be here. Make it quick, right? An' no *names*,' he added, with a fierce look at Billy. 'You can't say it's me, right?'

'Who are you afraid of?' Slider asked.

Boston shrugged. 'If they find out, I'm brown bread. I ain't tellin' *you*.'

They all watched too much television these days. 'Okay,' Slider said. 'Any way you like it.'

One-Eyed Billy was evidently deeply impressed with his friend. The rum, the dreadlocks, the cryptic utterances, the hint of violence in the air: it all added up to one supercool dude. He beamed with proprietorial pride, so that with Everet's flickering caution and Slider's professional reserve they made a thoroughly mismatched trio.

'I won't quote you,' Slider said. 'Tell me about Lenny Baxter. What was he up to?' To prime the pump he added, 'I know he was in financial trouble. He used to play the ponies up to a year ago, and lost heavily. And he lost his job at Golden Loans because he was fiddling the takings.'

'Yeah, old Lenny was in trouble,' Everet Boston said. 'He was a rotten gambler, man! Never 'ad no common when it come to 'orses. You fink he stopped playing the ponies? But 'e never. He just stopped going to the bettin' shop, right? That's when I got 'im the job, yeah?'

'What job?'

'He wasn't just runnin' for ol' Herbie Weedon,' Boston said, with a scorn in his voice that suggested if Slider didn't know that, he didn't know *nuffin'*, man. 'He was a bookie's runner.'

'Illegal bookmaking,' Slider said, enlightened.

Boston shrugged. "At's right, man. On the street: No tax, no pain, right?'

It was big business these days, Slider knew. If you bet at a betting shop, you paid tax either on your stake or on your winnings. Bet with an illegal bookie and it was all tax-free, as were the bookie's profits. And he would give you credit, which William Hill would not. Of course, it was on his terms, and the exaction of dues and interest on such loans could sometimes be a stressful process, which was why runners had to be big, fit men – like the late lamented Lenny. Like Everet Boston, perhaps?

'Is that what you're into, son?' Slider asked, trying to catch the flitting eyes.

'I ain't no son of *yours*,' Boston said scornfully. Slider was pretty sure he was right.

'But you work for the same boss?'

'What I do is my biz, okay? I'm tellin' you about Lenny.'

'Fair enough,' Slider said. 'How did you know him?'

'I met 'im down the snooker hall down Harlesden High Street. Must be two-three years ago. I fought he was all right, sort of. Guess I didn't know 'im that well,' he added broodingly.

'So who is this boss Lenny was running for?'

Everet shook his head. 'I ain't tellin' you *that*,' he said, as if amazed at the stupidity of the question. 'What ju fink, I'm nuts? You find out for y'self if you wanna know. Look, Lenny was in bovver. He was runnin' for Herbie an' he was runnin' for this other boss. He was suppose' to fix the bets and take the money, that was all, but 'e couldn't keep off the ponies 'imself, right? An' 'e was unlucky. He started owin' more'n he could pay. So he started crossin' the money, usin' Herbie's money to make up what he was short on the bettin' money.'

'And Herbie found out and sacked him?'

'Yeah. Then he was really in the clarts. So he went round some of Herbie's customers, try to get 'em to pay him like before, told 'em he was still workin' for Herbie.'

And one of them was Eddie Cranston's bird and he objected,

sought Lenny out, and got into a fight, Slider thought. But Lenny could look after himself, and the fight was over before it began. So who killed him? Did Eddie go back for a second crack?

He tried a wide shot. 'What was Lenny doing in the park that night?'

'He used to do some business there,' Boston said. 'He used to sell shit an' poppers – maybe white, I dunno – and that was where 'is customers met 'im, right?'

'How did he get in?'

Boston shrugged. 'Froo the gate, man, how should I know? But everyone know that's where 'e is certain times.'

'Was he selling drugs for this same boss?'

'Nah. I don't fink so. He never done the serious stuff, just bhang an' amyl, y'know? I fink it was just like a sideline. I dunno where he got the gear. Lenny, 'e was mixed up in a lot of stuff. He liked to freelance. Maybe that's why he got in trouble.'

Slider felt a certain weariness coming over him. If Lenny Baxter was selling cannabis and amyl nitrate poppers it opened up a whole new cast of potential murderers. Eddie Cranston had a lump of cannabis in his flat. Maybe he had been one of Lenny's customers and knew him, therefore, a little better than he had let on. And if he was a customer, he'd have known where to find Lenny to kill him. The trouble was, so would everyone else.

He struck out again, hoping for shallower water.

'How was Sonny Collins mixed up in it?'

Everet Boston looked surprised, and suddenly frightened. 'How d'you know about Sonny?' Slider got his own back and merely shrugged. 'I don't know what Sonny's into,' Boston said. 'He does some biz for the—' He stopped himself, and went on, 'for the Man. I dunno what, though. Lenny run messages sometimes. We all do. Sonny passed 'em on.' He stopped again. His eyes flickered nervously. 'I don't know nuffink about what Sonny does. The Man keep everything very private. We don't ask an' he don' tell. That way he stay ahead an' we stay alive. You don't wanna get on the wrong side of 'im, I tell you.' He slugged back the rest of the rum and said, 'Look, man, I gotta go. It's dangerous talkin' to you.'

'You think the Man might be watching you?'

'He watches everybody,' Boston said.

'Tell me who he is.'

'You fink I'm mad? I shoon't be here.'

'Yes, why are you here?' Slider asked. 'I'm very grateful, but what made you do it?'

The supercool pose altered subtly as a different Everet peeped through the tightly drawn curtains of street attitude. 'There's this bird Lenny lived with.'

'Tina,' Slider supplied. 'You know her?'

'I knew her before.' Everet looked suddenly ferocious. 'Lenny was a bastard! He was a total ratfuck bastard an' he got what was comin' to 'im. I'd a killed 'im myself if I could a got away wiv it.'

'I suppose you didn't kill him, did you?'

'I jus' told you. Wojer fink, I'm comin' here givin' myself away? You fink I got shit for brains? I come here to help you, and no way you goin' to stick this on me, you bastard copper! I'm gettin' out of here.' He half stood, and glared at Billy. 'Last time I do anyfink for you.'

Slider spread his hands. 'Calm down. Of course I don't think you did it. But it would help if you could tell me where you were that evening, just so we can cross you off the list. Between eleven Monday night and eight Tuesday morning.'

'I was down the Snookerama all night, from about ten till they shut, about one o'clock,' Everet said, head back in a defiant pose. 'Then I went home. If I'd've knew what was goin' down I'd've been there in the park givin' 'em the Mexican Wave while they done it, all right? But I never.'

'I believe you,' Slider said. 'Do you know who did kill him?'

Boston hesitated. 'Lenny, he trouble. He don' play by the rules, right? I reckon he had it comin'. And nobody won't shed no tears for him. Not Tina, that's for sure.'

'Do you know where Tina is now?'

The innocent question seemed to shock Everet. He stared at Slider, his eyes widening. 'I fought she was at 'ome.'

'She's not, and her clothes are gone. Where is she?'

Everet's lips parted, and for a moment Slider thought he was going to get something, but he only licked them and then, as if coming to a sudden decision, got up with a violent move-ment and said, 'I gotta go.'

'If you want to tell me any more,' Slider said desperately,

'you know where to get me. If you give me names, I can protect you.'

'No-one coon't protec' me against the Man,' he said bleakly, and with a sidling speed, like a threatened snake, he headed for the door. At the last minute, he turned to say, 'That night Lenny got done – it wasn't 'is night for dealin' shit.' And then he was gone.

Slider would have liked a moment's silence with his thoughts, but One-Eyed Billy wanted notice and recognition.

'He's brill, innee? Ol' Ev was always a right one. He was always in trouble at school. I got you the goods, didn't I, Mr Slider? You'll tell Dad I helped you like he said I had to?'

'What puzzles me,' Slider said, to Billy since he had to, 'is if he's so scared of his boss finding out he's been talking to me, why meet here in broad daylight?'

Billy looked pleased. 'He told me that. He said anyone can go in a pub, and in daylight you can see people coming. He said if you meet down an alley after dark they know you're up to something.'

'That's very interesting,' Slider said. Stupid, possibly, but interesting. No, to be fair, it was probably true. Maybe Everet Boston really was as cool as he tried to appear. 'What was this Tina to him?' he asked. 'An old girlfriend?'

'I dunno,' Billy said. 'He never mentioned her to me.'

But he obviously cared strongly about her, Slider thought, and he was obviously alarmed that she was missing. He thought of the two heavies outside Lenny's house. Had she been abducted? Or was she fleeing this tiresome Mr Big Everet wouldn't name? At all events, Boston's moment of humanity warmed Slider to him just a degree, while poor old Unlucky Lenny, the victim, was becoming less lovable the more was discovered about him.

As Slider approached his room his nostrils began to twitch, but he was so deep in thought and speculation that he didn't realise what it was he was smelling until he turned in at his open doorway and saw Joanna sitting on his desk swinging her legs. It was her scent, of course. Her face lit up like a pinball machine awarding two thousand bonus points and an extra game, and he was across the room in a Cartlandesque single bound.

When they paused for breath, Atherton said, 'Ahem. Cough

cough.' He was standing by the door into the office, and on the Everet Boston principle had been masked from Slider's view by the open door onto the corridor.

With large portions of Joanna still pressed against him, Slider could afford to be lenient. 'What are you doing here? Come to ask about that career move to the stolen cars unit?'

'I was keeping her entertained until you got back.'

'Well, you can go away now.' He turned back to Joanna. 'It's so good to see you. You look well.'

'She looks more than well,' Atherton said. 'She looks glowing.'

'Are you still there?'

'Apparently,' Atherton said blandly. 'How did your interview with One-Eyed Billy go?'

Slider moaned. 'At a time like this, he wants me to think of work.'

'Shall I go?' Joanna offered helpfully.

'No, no, stay. I don't have any secrets from you.'

'We could go and get some lunch while we talk,' Atherton suggested. 'Joanna's hungry.'

'Of course, you must be. It'll have to be the canteen, though.'

'Okay by me,' Joanna said.

'Has Porson come in?'

'No, he's not coming,' Atherton said as they headed out of the office. 'He phoned in to say he'll be out for a couple of days. I hope it's nothing serious.'

'So do I. He's a funny old duck, but I like him.'

As it was Monday, the canteen had bubble and squeak on.

'They like to keep up these little traditions,' Atherton said, handing Joanna a tray.

'It's quite good,' Slider said. 'It goes with the cold roast pork.'

'And wiz zat, madame,' Atherton hammed, 'Ah recommend ze rock 'ard carrots and ze soggy cauliflowair.'

'Oh brave new world, that has such menus in it,' Joanna said. 'I'll have the cottage pie, please. What?' she protested, catching Atherton's expression. 'I've been living on horse and chips and Wiener schnitzel for weeks.'

'Same for me,' Slider said to the server.

'Chips an' gravy, love?' she offered Joanna. And to Slider, 'No gravy for you, isn't it, sir? Would you like some of the bubble on yours?'

Atherton took a salad. 'I don't know how he does it,' he said as they sought a table. 'One look from his sad-puppy eyes and he has 'em eating out of his hand.'

Joanna batted her eyelashes at Slider. 'I'd eat anything out of your hand. Even cottage pie. Do you know,' she added in a normal voice, 'the worst thing in the world to watch someone eat?'

'McLaren's fried egg sandwiches?'

'Worse than that.'

'*With* tomato ketchup?'

'Worse than that. It's what Brian Harrop – second trumpet in the Phil – used to have at the Clarendon Arms after concerts. A cottage pie sandwich. It's true. A great big wodge of cottage pie, with gravy, between two slices of white Wonderbread. It's something you never forget. Like doing the nose job with porridge.'

'Thank you for sharing that with us,' Atherton said, sliding into a corner seat. 'So, dear old guv o' mine, what about this new lead from One-Eyed Billy? Tell us, Entellus.'

'One-eyed—?' Joanna began, but Atherton stopped her with a quick gesture.

'Not important. Who's the informant?'

'It was a dude called Everet Boston,' Slider said, unloading his tray.

'A *dude*?' they chorused in protest.

'No other word for it,' Slider said. 'A slick, smart, streetwise, slinky-shouldered black with a Willesden accent you could slice and bottle. He was as painfully hip as a hospital waiting list.'

'I'm getting the picture,' Atherton said in disparaging tones.

'Yes,' Slider said, 'but for all his attitude, he wasn't standing behind the door with One-Eyed Billy when they were passing out the brains.'

'Please,' Joanna begged, 'stop with all this one-eyed stuff. It sounds like a black-and-white B film from the fifties.'

'Billy Cheeseman,' Slider elucidated. 'His dad owned a pie and eel shop down the Goldhawk Road.'

Joanna put her head in her hands and whimpered. 'No more! I'm coming over all Jack Warner.'

'I'll talk to Atherton,' Slider said kindly, and between fork-fuls, told what he had heard that morning, adding a swift blocking in of the rest of the case for Joanna's benefit.

'And you didn't bring him in?' Atherton asked when he had finished.

'I'd have needed at least eight wild horses,' Slider said. 'But Billy obviously knows him, and where he lives. If need be we can go and fetch him, but I'd rather not at this stage. He was genuinely scared, and if we want him later in court we'd better cherish him now.'

'You believed all this bollocks about a Moriarty lurking in the shadows?'

'*He* believed he was in danger,' Slider said. 'I said from the beginning it looked more like a gang killing to me.'

'You did,' Atherton allowed.

'If the boss, whoever he was, ordered Lenny's killing for some unspecified crime against the organisation, the same could happen to Everet.'

'So you think it was an execution?' Atherton said.

'How many times do I have to tell you—'

'He doesn't speculate ahead of his data,' Joanna finished for him. 'He likes to keep an open mind. Don't you, beloved?'

'What she said,' Slider nodded.

'The thing that strikes me, as an outsider, as significant,' Joanna said, 'was saying Monday wasn't Lenny's usual night for selling drugs. Which suggests he must have been meeting someone there by arrangement, who, presumably, killed him. So doesn't that rather rule out this other bloke, Eddie Whatsit?'

'Unless he followed him,' Slider said. 'He might have been out looking for him, spotted him on his way to the park and followed.'

'On that basis, it might have been anyone,' Atherton said.

'Quite. But there's also the possibility that Eddie was also working for the boss, whoever he was. We know he's stupid, but he might be useful as a blunt instrument, if he takes orders well.'

'Maybe that's why he stayed indoors for two days. Maybe he was told to lie low,' Joanna said. 'The stuff about being too vain to go out with a black eye sounds a bit thin to me.'

'You've not met him,' Atherton said. 'He's more vain than a blood donor clinic. I can't believe anyone would use him, even as a blunt instrument, if they had any choice. Well,' he concluded, spearing the last quarter tomato, 'it's obvious that Sonny Collins is the man to lean on.'

'I thought you'd had two goes at him,' Joanna said.

'Yes, but now it's time to take the gloves off,' Atherton said. He noted her expression. 'I can spout worse clichés than that in a good cause.'

'You're right,' Slider said. 'We'll get him in again, and this time he stays in until he comes across.'

'I suppose that means you want me to scarper,' Joanna said with barely a sigh. She knew the score.

'I'll try not to be late tonight,' Slider said, 'but you know—'

'I know. Don't worry about me. I'll ring you later and see how you're getting on.'

'What will you do?'

'I'll go and see Sue. Is she at her place or yours?' she asked Atherton.

'Mine, as far as I know,' he said.

'Oh good. I'm longing to see your cats.' She kissed Slider goodbye with her eyes, respecting his dignity. 'Go get 'em, tiger! See you later.'

CHAPTER TEN

Chicken Ticker

This time Sonny Collins came in accompanied by his brief, none other than the famous David Stevens, who represented all the worst villains in west London. Stevens was a small man with a well-lunched figure, smooth hair and a smooth face. He had merry twinkling eyes, the unfailing cheerfulness of one of life's higher earners, and suits so expensive and beautiful they would make a boulevardier faint.

Slider's heart always sank when he saw Stevens turn up with someone he wanted to question. They had crossed swords many times, and Stevens usually came off better. Behind his bonhomie he had a mind like the labyrinth of Knossos, and any argument he put up had more clauses than Santa's family tree; but Slider couldn't help liking the man. He beckoned, and Stevens turned aside willingly to chat with him.

'How can Collins afford your fees?' Slider asked, after they had exchanged the amenities. Stevens only beamed at him. 'Don't tell me the brewery's paying his bills?'

'A famous brewing firm would naturally want to protect its reputation,' Stevens said.

'So it is them?'

'I didn't say that.'

'I can't believe they'd lash out that much on a bloke who runs the Phoenix. Have you seen the Phoenix?'

'No. But I can't believe it either.'

'More likely they'd just sack him if they wanted to keep their hands clean.'

'Much more likely.'

Slider whimpered. 'Five minutes talking to you and I feel like a dog trying to bite its own tail.'

'But where can you get one at this time of day?' Stevens said genially.

'So you aren't going to tell me who's paying you?'

'Not in these trousers.'

'You know we're investigating a very serious crime?'

'Of course. And if my client is suspected of committing a very serious crime I'm sure he would like to hear your evidence.'

'I just want to ask him some questions,' Slider said. 'Why does he feel the need for a high-powered brief? Has he got a guilty conscience?'

'My client has already co-operated with you on two occasions. Taking him from his legitimate business for a third inquisition almost amounts to harassment, and he felt he needed a friend at his side to guide him.'

'I love the way you talk,' Slider marvelled through his frustration. 'I suppose what that means with the peel off is that he's not going to tell me anything?'

'That depends on what you ask him,' Stevens said, obviously enjoying himself hugely.

'I'm glad someone's having fun,' said Slider. 'All right, let's get this over. I wish you'd remember sometimes,' he added as they headed for the interview room, 'that we're supposed to be on the same side.'

'Not we,' Stevens said. 'Only you.' He patted Slider on the shoulder. 'You need a holiday, old son. Cruise in the Caribbean, maybe. I've just come back from one and it's lovely there this time of year.'

Sonny Collins sat almost bursting out of his jacket with subdued power and emotions, but – interestingly to Slider – seemed less at ease with David Stevens beside him than he had seemed without. At every question he looked at the solicitor for instructions on how to answer, which seemed to inhibit him, especially as for the most part the sublimely relaxed Stevens merely twinkled at him.

It was as Slider expected: Collins would tell him nothing.

'Mr Collins,' Slider said patiently, 'we know that you knew Lenny Baxter, so why do you keep denying it?'

'Never seen him before in my life,' Collins repeated.

'You called him by name in the presence of Eddie Cranston.'

'Eddie told you that? He's a lying toe-rag.'

'I agree with you,' Slider said. 'Eddie's scum, but in this case he's telling the truth. You and Lenny Baxter did business together.'

'Prove it.'

'I have a witness who says you did.'

'He's lying too.'

'I don't think so. He worked alongside Lenny.'

'So where is he, then?' Collins said defiantly. 'What's his name?'

Slider put his hands flat on the table. 'Look, Sonny,' he said, 'you know that we've got an ongoing investigation into your little doings. If you don't start co-operating with me—'

Stevens intervened. 'Sounds like the opening phrases of a threat. You will be careful not to threaten my client, won't you?'

Slider tried to ignore him. 'Lenny Baxter was killed, and I think you know a lot more about it than you've said. Who was Lenny working for? Tell me that, and maybe it'll be enough from you for now. We're looking for a murderer. I don't want to clutter up my desk processing you for whatever little games you're mixed up in. Buy yourself some time, Sonny. You can clean up your act before we come after you. Tell me who Lenny was working for, and go back to your pub with an easy mind.'

Collins, sitting up straight as a ramrod, looked scornful. 'Easy mind? What do you know about it? You don't know who you're dealing with.'

'My client has nothing more to say to you,' Stevens intervened smoothly.

'Who, Sonny?' Slider urged. 'Who am I dealing with?'

'You got nothing on me!' Collins said. 'I'm saying nothing. I want it on record. I know nothing and I've said nothing.'

'He must be a pretty big shit if he can put the frighteners on you,' Slider said with interest. 'What can he do to you, Sonny? Lose you your job? I can do that. If you know something and don't tell me, I can have you for obstruction. Maybe perverting the course of justice. You can go down for that. How would you like a spell inside? Plenty of people inside would admire your fine physique. I'm sure you'd make lots of new friends.'

'Do it then. I don't care. It'd be a piece of piss compared with—' He stopped himself, and his good eye swivelled round to Stevens. 'I want out of here!'

'Unless you are intending to charge my client . . . ?' Stevens said on an interrogative note, looking at Slider, who waved a negative hand. 'Then my client is free to go.'

Slider looked sadly at Collins. 'You leave me with no option but to bring forward the investigation into your other activities. Everything's going to come out. All the little bits of business going on at the back door. We've got plenty on you already and if you don't think we'll get the rest you overestimate the loyalty of your customers. You're going to go down, Sonny – and all for want of a name. That's all you have to do, give me the name.'

Collins, already on his feet, paused, clenching his fists down by his sides. It seemed a curiously involuntary gesture. 'You don't know what you're talking about,' he said again. 'If I gave you his name—'

'This interview is over,' Stevens said.

'He'd never know it was you,' Slider said, holding Collins's gaze.

'Over,' Stevens repeated.

'*I'd* know,' Collins said with finality. 'Do what you like, I'm saying nothing.'

It was an odd little emphasis that puzzled Slider.

Atherton sat on the windowsill, backlit by the sunshine like a Dutch old master. 'So he's tacitly admitted that he works for the same boss – or at least, does business with him.'

'But he's too scared to give the name,' Slider said. 'Scared or – something.'

'Something? I'm dazzled by your eloquence.'

Slider frowned. 'There was something odd going on there. Some emotion or concern I couldn't guess at, but it was stronger than the fear of prison.'

'And Everet Boston's scared blue. This man provokes powerful loyalties.'

'Oh, so you believe in the big boss now?'

'Do me a lemon.'

Slider looked worried. 'I'm wondering about David Stevens.'

'Don't. That way lies madness and destruction.'

'But I can't believe Collins would have the money or the know-how to hire him, and if it's not the brewery—'

'Then it's Mr Big retaining him for defence of one of his minions?' Atherton said.

'Shoring up a potentially weak place in the organisation,' Slider concluded. 'But if that's the case then Stevens knows who he is.'

'As I said, that way lies madness,' Atherton repeated. 'Anyway, it's all pure conjecture. You know my feelings about this whole Mr Big story.'

'You think I've got a Moriarty complex.'

'I think small-time crooks like to talk big. If Boston's right about Lenny dealing drugs, it's more than likely he was doing a spot of trade in the park and one of his customers was blasted and did him to avoid having to pay.'

'But then why didn't they take the money?' Slider objected. 'And where's the lock and chain?'

'I think you can get too hung up on the lock and chain. They'll turn up somewhere.'

'They irritate me.'

'Maybe the park keeper's got them.'

'Maybe. I think we'd better have another word with him, at least clear up how Lenny was able to use the park as his office. Tell Mackay to go and fetch him in. He'd better check with the council first to find out where he is. I don't suppose he spends his entire day hanging around the one park.'

The telephone call established that Ken Whalley had not been in to work. It was natural enough, said the woman in the parks department, after such a terrible shock. Two weeks' compassionate leave, they'd given him, the same as you get for a close-family bereavement. They were going to arrange counselling for him, as soon as he phoned in to say he was ready for it. He was at home as far as she knew. She didn't think he had any family or anything, so unless he'd gone away for a holiday . . .

'Found him cowering indoors with the chain on,' Mackay reported when he had brought him in. 'Wouldn't answer the door at first, and even after he'd seen my brief it took me ten minutes to talk him out. He thought I was from the council, come to tell him he'd got the sack.'

'But they've given him leave,' Atherton said. 'Why would they do that if they were going to sack him?'

'I don't think he's very bright,' Mackay said. 'Apparently they offered him counselling and he thought that was something to do with a solicitor. Thought it meant they were taking him to court.'

'What for?'

'Dunno,' Mackay shrugged. 'He's not making much sense.'

When Slider went downstairs he could see why. Ken Whalley had gone downhill since Tuesday. He was unshaven, his hair was a wild bush, and he smelt as if he hadn't washed in as long as he hadn't shaved. He was wearing a pair of black shell-suit bottoms and an indescribably grubby teeshirt, and his bare feet were shoved into flip-flops. His pudgy face seemed to have melted into a shape of woe and the hair sprouted from it in irregular patches like mould. His droopy basset-hound eyes raised themselves to Slider's face in abject misery. He was a bad dog, and he had come to be punished.

'I never meant it to happen. I never meant no harm,' he whined before Slider had spoken. 'I sweartergod, if I'd of knew, I wouldn't never of done it. But when he ast me, I didn't see no harm in it. I never knew what he wanted it for.'

'All right, just calm down and we'll go through it from the beginning,' Slider said.

'Am I gonner lose me job?'

Slider sat opposite him, wishing there were a way to stay upwind of Whalley's miasma; but in a small enclosed space all directions were down. 'Never mind about your job now,' he said with measured sternness. 'This is much more serious than your job. If you're going to stay out of prison, you're going to have to co-operate with me fully, tell me everything.'

'Oh Gawd,' Whalley said faintly. 'What—?'

'No, I ask the questions, you answer. That's the way it's going to be. Do you understand?'

'Yessir,' Whalley said. Being managed seemed to brace him a little, as Slider had guessed it would.

'Now then, how did you first meet Lenny Baxter?'

Whalley licked his lips. 'I never—'

'The truth! You lied to me before. You said you'd never seen him before in your life. But that wasn't true. You knew him very well. That's why you were so shocked when you found him dead.'

'I fought,' Whalley said in the same wisp of a voice, 'I fought I'd get the blame for it.'

'How did you meet him?'

'He come up to me in the park one day. Got chatting. Wanted to know about me routine, locking up and that.'

'And he made you a proposition?'

'Not then. Not right away. I see him in the park a few times. Sometimes he comes over and chats. Then one day he comes in when I was locking up—'

'When was that?'

'Last year. In the summer. I know it was summer 'cos it was a late lock-up. 'Cos it gets dark later in summer,' he added helpfully.

'I understand. Go on. What did Lenny say?'

'He ast me to go for a drink. So I says yes. We went down the Coningham. That's his local, he says. So we goes for a pint.'

'And he made a proposition to you,' Slider asked, hoping to speed matters up a bit. 'What did he want you to do?'

Whalley looked down at his dirty fingernails, coming to the moment of shame.

'He wanted me to borrow him the key.'

'The key?'

'To the Frithville Gardens gate. He said he'd give it back. I said I couldn't, 'cos of opening up in the morning, so he said he'd come the next day after I opened and he'd have it back to me before I had to lock up.'

'And what did he want it for?'

'I dunno,' Whalley said, still looking down.

'I think you do,' Slider said.

'He never said.'

'He wanted to get it copied, didn't he? So he'd have a key of his own. So he could get in and out of the park when he liked. Isn't that right?'

Whalley nodded. 'Maybe. He never said, but – well, what else'd he want it for?'

'Why did he want to get into the park?'

'I dunno. He never said.'

'You do know.' No answer. 'Look at me!' The reluctant eyes lifted, full of fear and guilt. 'What did he want to use the park for?'

'I swear I dunno. It's the honestroof.'

'You must have known he was up to no good. Why did you go along with it?'

'Well, he ast me.'

'You could have said no.'

Whalley looked as though he might cry. 'I was scared,' he admitted. 'He was big. You never saw him. He was a big bloke. I fought he'd do me over if I said no.'

Slider looked at the pathetic lump of putty. Ken Whalley was such a coward you could have held him up through the post.

'So what did he offer you for letting him borrow the key? Was it money?'

'No,' Whalley said. 'I never took no money off him, not a penny, only the drink he bought me.'

Slider detected a note Whalley was probably unaware of. 'Not money. But he did give you something, didn't he? What was it?'

'I can't,' Whalley said, bowing his head. 'I can't say.'

'You will say. What did he give you? Come on, Ken, I can sit here all day if I have to. You're going to tell me. What did he give you in exchange for the key?' Whalley muttered the answer, and Slider couldn't catch it, it was so low. 'What? Say it again. Louder. What did he give you?'

'It was a woman,' Whalley said, and from the slump of his shoulders, it was clear they were coming to the bottom of this sad creature. 'It was this bird he lived with – Tina, he called her. She was gorgeous. A real cracker. Well, I'm – you know. I mean, look at me! I'm no good with women. They don't fancy me. I've never had a proper girlfriend.' Out with the plastic waterweed and the miniature gothic castle, they were down to the gravel now. 'If you wanna know,' he said abjectly, 'I'd never done it. Never in me life. I'd never done – you know – with a woman.'

It was a sad confession, and as a man with plenty of you-know under his belt, Slider pitied him.

'Are you gay, Ken?'

'No! I'm not like that. I like women. Only they don't like me. They laugh at me. And Lenny – he was such a big hand-some sod. He could have all the women he wanted. He treated 'em rough and they loved it. But me . . . He got it out of me, when we had the drink, and he said if I'd do that little favour

for him, he'd set me up with a woman. I mean, set me up like
– have sex with her. He said she'd do anything I wanted. I
thought she'd turn out to be this real dog, you know what I
mean? But he said no, he said, she was gorgeous. And she
was,' he finished simply.

'So when did this meeting with Tina take place?'

'Next night. After he give me the key back he said he'd meet
me at locking-up time and take me to her. I never fought he'd
be there.' He looked at Slider to see if he understood.

'You thought once you'd done your part of the bargain he'd
have no reason to stick to his? You thought he'd stiff you?'

'Yeah. Why wouldn't he? He'd got what he wanted. But he
was there. He played straight with me.' The gratitude was pathetic.
This, Slider saw, was one of Lenny's many holds over Ken
Whalley's loyalty, that he had had the chance to cheat him and
hadn't taken it. 'So he took me to a place – his flat, I suppose it
was – and she was there. This black bird, Tina. A real cracker.
And young and everything. He left me with her and – and we
done it.' He was silent a moment, perhaps reliving the moment.
Then he said, 'After that, I never see him again, not to talk to –
only the once.'

'When was that?'

'About a fortnight ago. He come in the Smuts, where I drink,
and he took me outside and he said, Ken, he said, have you
been talking? And I says no, I swear – which I hadn't. I'd never
mentioned it to a soul. Why would I?'

'To boast about the girl, maybe?'

'What, tell everyone I'd never done it in me life till then?
Anyway, who would I tell? I haven't got any friends,' he said
with simple truth. 'No, I never mentioned it to a soul. Anyway,
he believes me, and he says, you just keep it that way, he says,
'cos he says if I ever say a word to anyone, he'll know, and
he'll get me. He'll beat me up, he says, so's my own mother
won't know me. So I never said nothing.'

'Even after he was dead?' Slider said. 'Why didn't you tell
me the truth when I first spoke to you? There was nothing he
could do to you then.'

'I fought you'd fink I did it. And I fought – all right, he was
dead, but someone else would get me. I mean, he musta been
in it with someone else. Like – a gang or summink.'

He lit a cigarette with fumbling hands. Slider noticed absently that it was a Gitane, unusual choice for a dork like Whalley. Then his attention sharpened.

'Where did you get those cigarettes, Ken?'

'Lenny sold 'em me cheap. I don't usually smoke this kind. I don't like 'em much, but he let me have 'em so cheap it was worth it.'

'Where did he get them from?'

Whalley looked slightly surprised at the question. 'I dunno. Abroad, I s'pose. Maybe that's what he does – import and that.'

'Illegal import,' Slider said. 'Otherwise known as smuggling.'

Whalley looked frightened again. 'I dunno. He never said. I didn't know they was illegal. I just – I just—'

'Oh come on, Ken, you know how that game's played. Don't tell me you didn't know they were smuggled.'

'I never ast him. You didn't know Lenny. You never saw him. You wouldn't ast him questions. You just wouldn't.'

'So what was his game? What did he do in the park? Come on, don't say you don't know.'

'I don't, I swear. I didn't want to know.'

'If he was up to something really bad, like dealing drugs, that makes you an accessory. You can go down for that – jail, Ken. Think of that. Locked up for years with a bunch of big ugly tough bastards like Lenny, only not so kind-hearted. You help me out, tell me what Lenny was up to, and I might be able to keep you out of there.'

'I don't – I didn't – I'd tell you if I could, but I *don't know!*' Whalley wailed in fear.

Slider shook his head and sighed. 'Bad choice, Ken. Seriously bad choice. If you won't help me, I can't help you. I'm not going to put myself out for you. You're going down. Not just accessory to Lenny's game, but accessory to his murder. How does that sound? You're going to prison for a long, long time.'

Whalley turned so white Slider thought he was going to throw up. The cigarette shook in his fingers and fell, rolling off the table into his lap; but he didn't notice. His cowardly heart had tried to do a runner: his eyes fluttered upwards and he slumped into a dead faint, his head hitting the table top with a sound like a judge's gavel.

'I think you went a bit too hard on him, guv,' Mackay said impassively.

Joanna sat up, her short, thick hair madly tousled.

'Wow,' she said. Succinct, but heartfelt.

'Why, thank you, ma'am,' Slider said. 'And wow yourself.'

'Food now,' she pronounced.

'No, no, you stay, I'll go. I've had this planned for days.'

'All right,' she said, settling herself back on the pillows, 'I'll do the sultan bit.'

'Sultana,' he corrected, heading, naked, for the door.

'I know, I'm your currant entanglement.'

'More my raisin d'être,' he said.

He was back soon with the tray: the best pâté de fois from the deli in Turnham Green Road, a ripe and creamy Gorgonzola, crusty French bread, fat Italian olives.

'Wow,' she said again.

'Nothing but the best for my lady.' He kissed her, getting back into bed.

'And what's this? Rocket?'

'Dressed with lemon juice and black pepper, à la Atherton.'

'You really did think this through! And what's in the bottle?' She shifted the cooler sleeve upwards to look at the label, and then turned a deeply impressed look on him. 'Meurseult?'

'Uh-huh,' he said modestly, tearing bread.

'I think I love you,' she said. 'This is not the most practical meal to eat in bed. We're going to have serious crumbs in the sheets.'

'I give you my personal promise to grind them to dust later on.'

'Swank-pot.'

'Pâté first or cheese?'

'Pâté, please. Oh, yum! Pour me some wine, also. Thank you.' Slider lifted his own glass to her. 'To us.'

'To us.' They drank. 'You come very obligingly to the point,' Joanna said; but the phone rang.

'Frolicking bullocks,' said Slider, quite mildly in the circumstances. It was Atherton. 'Good evening, Detective Constable,' Slider said.

'Sorry, guv. Did I catch you in the act?'

'Never mind what I'm up to. Just make it quick.'

'Your wish is my command. They've had a phone call at the office from Herbie Weedon, the Golden Loans geezer. He wants to talk to me. Apparently got something interesting to tell.'

'Good,' said Slider. 'Anything else before I hang up?'

'Slow down a bit. I rang him back and he sounds as nervous as a dog in a Korean restaurant. He said he couldn't talk on the phone. He has to meet me, and he wants it to be now, tonight.'

'Is he serious?'

'I think so. I got the impression when I met him that he's an old pro. He knows which way is up. If he's decided to spill he'll have something worth sticking the bucket under.'

'I wonder why he's changed his mind?'

'I suppose I rang his bell,' Atherton said modestly.

'He could be working for the other side, hoping to find out what you know.'

'I don't think so. That wouldn't frighten him. And he was frightened.'

'All right,' Slider said. 'I'll authorise it. Go and get him while he's hot. But be careful. Don't walk into a trap.'

'Tell your grandmother. I'm the pump, he's the pumpee.'

'I didn't mean that sort of trap.'

'You and your Moriarty complex!'

'I mean it. Be careful. I like your face the way it is.'

'I'm not that sort of girl,' Atherton said, and rang off.

'What was all that about?' Joanna asked, and he told her, and filled her in on the interview with Ken Whalley. 'God, what a sleazy lot,' she said at the end.

'What did you want, glamour? All crime is sleazy,' Slider said, 'and murder's the sleaziest of all.'

'Never mind glamour, you might once in a while investigate some people with nicer habits,' Joanna said. 'This Lenny, lending his girlfriend out like a bicycle!'

'Yes, he's not turning out to be a very lovable chap, our Lenny. Still, he did give Ken Whalley the only happy memory of his life.'

'You men!' Joanna said. 'How can there be any pleasure in having sex with a stranger you'll never see again, knowing they're doing it purely as business? And she probably didn't even get paid!'

'Oh, that'd make it better, would it? If she got paid?'

'Better for her, anyway.'

'And less of this "you men" business.'

'It's a man thing.' She eyed him askance. 'You don't do it, but you understand it.'

'Academically. It's my job to. Are you working up for a quarrel?'

'What, me?' She leaned across and kissed his cheek contritely. 'It's just that the world is too much with us.'

'Late and soon, when you're a detective inspector,' he agreed. 'Have some more wine. Shall I put some music on, to soothe our ruffled breasts?'

'Yes, that'd be nice.'

'I'm getting good at this music business,' he said, getting out of bed. 'When I went over to Atherton's the other day he had the Prokofiev violin concerto on, and I very nearly recognised it.'

'I'm impressed,' she said. When he returned from putting on the CD, she said, 'Have I told you the story about the Jewish lady in New York, who took her son to the Carnegie Hall? She went up to the box office and asked if they had any tickets for the Isaac Stern concert. The ticket man said no, they were sold out weeks ago. So she says, "How much would they have cost if you had any?" and he said, "I'm afraid the cheapest seat was eighty-five dollars." And the lady whacks her kid round the ear and says, "Now will you practise?"'

Slider laughed, easing himself in under the tray. 'D'you want to try the cheese now, or shall we do a little more practising of our own.'

'The night is young,' said Joanna. 'Let's see how we get on.'

It was much later, after both food and practice, when they were lying in each other's arms talking in a desultory way that she said out of a brief and relaxed silence, 'I'm glad we've got this time together, Bill, because there's something important I want to discuss with you.'

His scalp prickled at the words and the tone of her voice. 'Oh yes?' he said helplessly.

'I don't know if you've guessed what it is. Oh, damn it, I suppose I'd better just come to the point.'

Here it comes, he thought, and would have given anything

to put it off. It was another man thing, dislike of this woman thing of always wanting to 'have things out'.

'Go ahead,' he said, bracing himself; and the telephone rang again.

'Oh, bloody Nora,' Joanna said. 'What is it with your telephone? Have you got a symbiotic relationship going with it?'

'Sorry,' he said, reaching for it.

It was Nicholls, and sorry was the first word he said, too. 'Sorry to interrupt your evening in paradise, but we've got an emergency.'

'It had better be good,' Slider said. 'Or rather, it had better be bad.'

'Oh it's bad,' Nicholls assured him. 'Herbie Weedon's dead, and it's not natural causes. Can you come right away?'

'Shit,' said Slider, not for the first time in his career.

CHAPTER ELEVEN

Herbie Brown Bread

'He didn't turn up at the meeting place,' Atherton said, looking unexpectedly pale.

'Which was?'

'Shepherd's Bush station – the Hammersmith and City line. I was supposed to get a ticket and wait somewhere discreetly until he came through the booking hall, then follow him and get on the train with him. It was his usual ride home. Sit or stand next to him and he'd give me the information under cover of the train noise, but not to look at him or appear to know him, and not to react to anything he said.'

'He really was cautious. Where did he go to on the train?'

'Ladbroke Grove station. He lived in Lancaster Road.'

'That's only two stops. He couldn't have had much to tell you.'

'Maybe it wouldn't have taken long. Maybe it was just the name you've been wanting. Anyway, I waited about twenty minutes past the time and then rang his office, but there was no answer. I thought maybe he'd had some business come in or he just thought better of it, so I gave it up, but as I was walking back to the nick – I was still parked in the yard—'

'Of course.'

'—I passed the building and there was a light on in the Golden Loans window. The street door was on the latch so I went up. The office door was unlocked too. And there he was.'

There he was, thought Slider, and he was not a pretty sight. Herbie Weedon was still sitting in his chair behind the vast and cluttered desk, where he had lived so much of his life, and from which he was not parted even in death. When the forensic teams had finished and the mortuary van came for him it was going to be hell's own job getting him out, like prising an enormous crab from its shell.

There had been little struggle: a few papers scuffed to the floor, that was all. Maybe he'd tried to get up: Slider imagined him putting his hands on the desk top, grunting as his breath shortened, trying to push himself to his feet. But they'd have been between him and the door, so even if he got upright, where could he go? No, more likely he'd have tried to talk his way out of it. Not the physical sort, Herbie. He must have talked his way out of – and into – a lot of things in his life.

It didn't work this time. The red and purple face Atherton had described so graphically was congested, the little blood-shot eyes bulged like those of a stuffed toy, and round his neck was a thick iron chain with a padlock hanging from it like a pendant, resting on his chest, as if they'd made him Lord Mayor of some very industrial city. The marks in the swollen flesh of his neck exactly matched the links of the chain. There was no doubt he had been strangled with it.

'Though it probably wouldn't have taken much,' Atherton said. 'He wasn't exactly in peak condition.' He felt not only royally pissed off at having been cheated of the information he was to have had, but ridiculously sorry about Herbie. Ridiculous because Herbie had been an old villain, and there was no doubt he had caused much misery in his time; but there was something about this penned and helpless death that disturbed him. Herbie's eyes were open. He had seen it coming, like the stalled ox awaiting the blunt end of the butcher's axe.

'I wouldn't be at all surprised,' Slider said, interrupting his thoughts, 'if this were the missing lock and chain from the park.'

'Good heavens! Do you think so?' Atherton played up.

'They wanted him found,' Slider said. 'They left the lights on deliberately. And the street door on the latch. I think this – leaving the chain like this – is their idea of a joke. Like leaving Lenny sitting on the swing in the playground. Taunting us.'

'In which case,' Atherton said, 'they'd have to have known he was meeting me, and what he was going to tell me. How would they know that?'

'Not necessarily. They might have seen him as another weak link and the timing was coincidental. On the other hand they might have tapped his phone. Or overheard him. Or got it out of him with threats. Or he might have told someone else what he was going to do, and they grassed him.'

'I can't see him doing that.'

Slider shrugged. 'One thing's for sure, we know there's some powerful business behind it somewhere. Organisation like this doesn't exist unless someone's making a healthy profit.'

'Your Mr Big?'

'It's looking that way.'

'A Mr Big with a sensayuma,' said Atherton, looking again at Herbie Weedon. 'What's work if you can't have a laugh?'

'I could do without it,' Slider said.

Joanna caught up with them again in the canteen for breakfast.

'You look tired.'

'Didn't get any sleep, did we?' Slider said. 'Are you having the full house?'

'Why not?' she said. 'Makes a change from endless bread and jam. What kind of a breakfast is that, I ask you? It's no wonder we always beat them in wars. I mean, Napoleon's Old Guard – *café au lait*, two croissants and a dab of apricot jam; British Grenadiers – porridge, kippers, ham and eggs, sausages, toast and tea. No contest.'

While forking in the big fry-up – or scrambled eggs on toast in Atherton's case – they told her about the new developments.

'So now we know where the lock and chain went,' Slider concluded, 'but not how it got there.'

'Presumably whoever killed Lenny took it away with them,' Joanna said.

'But why?'

'Maybe they were going to strangle him with the chain the same way they killed the old man, and then as it happened they used the knife instead.'

'Then why take the chain away?'

'Forgot they were carrying it, perhaps,' Joanna offered. 'You can do that in the heat of the moment.'

'Or maybe they were going to use it to incriminate some-body,' Atherton said. 'I don't see that the chain and padlock are very important, except that they suggest the same person did both murders. Or at least they were ordered by the same person.'

'What, the big boss?' Joanna said. 'Have you started believing in him now, then?'

'There's been another development,' Atherton said. 'Another witness – of sorts.'

'Why of sorts?'

'She didn't see much.'

A woman working late at the BBC Television Centre had been leaving via the back gate into Frithville Gardens in a taxi at about two o'clock on Tuesday morning and had passed two men walking down the road, in the direction away from the park gates. She hadn't seen them coming out of the park, but they looked suspicious types to her. They were both wearing dark glasses, baseball caps, blouson-type leather jackets and dark trousers, and had given her the impression of being young and of muscular build. One was talking on a mobile phone. The other had something thrust into the front of his jacket. The woman, Elly Fraser, had said he was 'sort of supporting it with his hand as if it was heavy'. It was what had attracted her attention in the first place.

'The chain?' Joanna suggested.

'Might be. The bad news is that she's sure she wouldn't be able to recognise them again. Only got a glimpse – dark glasses etcetera. And they might not be anything to do with it, of course.'

'Or they might,' said Slider, 'especially as Lenny was seen talking to two similar characters earlier that evening. But the chain definitely suggests the two murders are linked. And the unfunny joke in each case was a warning to anyone else who might think of talking. Whoever he is, he's got a tight hold on his people.'

'But was Herbie Weedon one of his people?' Atherton said. 'I definitely got the impression he was an independent operator.'

'Doesn't matter, does it? If he'd ever done any business, if he'd merely rubbed shoulders with this big boss socially, he was going to tell you who he was, so he'd have to be silenced.'

'I wonder why he wanted to tell,' Joanna said.

'Get rid of a rival, maybe. Or pure public-spiritedness.'

'Please!' Atherton protested. 'Not while I'm eating!'

'I'm serious,' Slider said. 'Herbie Weedon was obviously as straight as a pig's tail, but there's villainy and villainy. You often find that people like him resent it when someone a lot worse than them comes clodhopping over their patch and—'

'Giving criminality a bad name?' Joanna finished for him.

'I suspect Herbie stopped at murder,' Slider said, 'and thought other people should too.'

'Well, it's all academic now,' Atherton said. 'And it leaves us an idea short of *Mastermind*.'

'We'll have a look through Herbie's house,' Slider said, 'though I'm not hopeful of finding anything. I tend to agree with you, I don't think he was actually working for them—'

'—and if he was they'll have been there before us, like they were with Lenny.'

'It occurs to me,' Joanna said, 'that if that was a gang punishment killing as you're suggesting, it might explain why they didn't take the money.'

'Then what did they go through his pockets for?' Slider asked.

'His keys,' she said. 'So they could let themselves in at his house.'

'You're brilliant,' Slider said.

'I have my moments,' she said, fluttering her eyelashes at him.

'If I can interrupt the love fest, where does it leave us?' Atherton said. 'Sonny Collins won't talk, and everyone else can't talk.'

'There's Everet Boston,' Slider said. 'We'd better try and get to him before they do.'

'And what about Lenny's girlfriend?' Joanna said. 'She must know something about what was going on.'

'Yes, but it's a case of *cherchez la femme*. She's gone AWOL,' Atherton said.

'But Everet seemed to know her from somewhere,' Slider said. 'I think he's got to be our lead to her as well. He's definitely next in the big black chair.'

'Looks like I won't be seeing much of you,' Joanna said.

'I'm sorry,' Slider said. 'This had to happen just when you manage to get over for a few days.'

'Ah well,' she said philosophically. They scraped back their chairs and got up. 'I'll push off. I've got dirt to scratch and eggs to lay.'

He gave her a grateful look. She would not burden him with her needs, even though she wanted to have a Serious Talk with him and had been twice baulked. 'You're a gentleman,' he told her.

She smiled at the compliment. 'Ring me when you can,' she said, and left them.

'You know what the definition of a gentleman is?' Atherton said conversationally as they headed for the stairs. 'Someone who knows how to play the piano accordion, and doesn't.'

'I wonder why they always play one of those things in the background of films set in Paris.'

'Shorthand,' said Atherton. 'Like onions, berets and bicycles.'

They both had things to keep the mind away from.

Atherton staggered into Slider's room, his hands over his face. 'The shining! The shining!' he moaned.

Slider looked up from the paperchase with bare interest. 'Jack Nicholson. Too easy. And if you've got time to play charades—'

'No, no,' Atherton said, resuming normal service, 'you're way out. It was the light of his countenance that dazzled me.'

'His who?'

'Him what sent me to summon you unto his presence. I am not that light—'

'Now you're getting blasphemous,' Slider warned. '*Who?*'

'Detective Chief Superintendent Palfreyman has descended from the clouds and wishes to bless you.'

'Oh Nora! That's all I needed.'

Palfreyman was the head of the Homicide Advice Team, whose decision it had been in the beginning to leave Lenny Baxter's murder with them rather than give it to the over-stretched SCG. The arrival of the HAT car followed the discovery of a corpse as summer follows the swallow, but Slider was not pleased to be revisited. It was never good news when top brass got interested in what you were doing. They were lucky at Shepherd's Bush to have Porson as their Det Sup, for he was old-fashioned enough to see his job as standing between his men at the sharp end and the demi-gods at Hammersmith – those blessed ones whose exalted rank and sheer weight of salary left them with nothing much to do all day but think of ways to make the working copper's life more burdensome. Their previous Chief, Richard (or 'God') Head, had vaulted from their shoulders clean to the stars, otherwise known as SO19, the firearms unit at Scotland Yard, where he could deploy troops and shout 'Go! Go! Go!' into a radio mike to his heart's content.

'I suppose I'll have to go and see what he wants,' Slider sighed, getting up.

'He's in Porson's room,' Atherton said. 'Better run, lad. And stick a book down inside your trousers!' he called after him. 'The Head's looking batey!'

Actually, Palfreyman was looking, as he always did, superficially genial. He was a tall man in his thirties, quite good-looking, and slim, except for his hips and upper legs, which seemed disproportionately thick. Slider had noticed many times that tall, slim men with fat thighs were often to be found in managerial positions, and that they were generally popular and successful with their peers and seniors, and ineffectual at their jobs. There must be a fat-thigh gene that marked you out for the top-of-the-range Mondeo, the executive swivel chair and the 'Mr So-and-so's in a meeting, can I take a message?' Now he came to think of it, DCS Head had had fat thighs too. The difference was that Head delivered his life-complicating 'initiatives' with a snarl, while Palfreyman did it with a smile. Palfreyman wanted everyone to like him; but that was in any case a function of management style these days. He would vault to the stars just like his predecessor, but not having Head's predilection for kicking down doors, would probably find his resting place in a 'think-tank' or policy unit. It was the third law of thermo-dynamics in the Job that bollock-brains always ended up where they could do the most harm.

'Ah, DI Slider?' he said as Slider appeared in the doorway. 'Come in, close the door. Bill, isn't it? May I call you Bill?'

Slider's lips said yes, yes, yes, but his eyes said no, no no.

'Sit down.' Palfreyman gestured genially, and sat down himself behind Porson's desk. 'Just thought I'd pop in and have a little chat.' He was as conciliatory as an old-fashioned ward sister with an enema in mind. 'See how you're getting on. In Detective Superintendent Porson's absence. That causing any problems, at all?'

'Is there any news from him, sir?' Slider asked. 'Do we know when he's coming back?'

'I'm afraid not. His wife's rather poorly, apparently.'

'*Poorly?*' Slider couldn't help himself. As if The Syrup would stay home just to mix the Lemsip and pass the tissues!

'Not well,' Palfreyman translated kindly, as if Slider perhaps did not know that 'well' and 'poorly' were antonyms. Actually, Slider would have bet a substantial chunk of his dinner money that Palfreyman wouldn't know an antonym if it sat in his lap and peed on him.

'In what way, not well?' Slider asked stonily.

Palfreyman flushed a little. 'I'm not at liberty to say,' he said. 'I didn't come here to answer questions, but to ask them. This big case of yours – there's been a rather serious development, I understand.'

It wasn't a question, so Slider didn't answer it. He knew it was foolish to provoke a demi-god, but he couldn't help it. Palfreyman was so young, and so pointless.

'There's been another death, hasn't there?' Palfreyman went on.

'Yes, sir.'

'It doesn't look good, you know. Not good at all. Do you think they're connected?'

'I think the second victim was killed to stop him giving us information,' Slider said.

'I see. And does that point to any particular individual?'

'I believe we may be dealing with a criminal organisation, and that the first death was a punishment killing.'

'Ah, yes, I see. An organisation, eh? It's a gang thing, then.' He pondered a moment, tapping his fingers on the desk. 'Perhaps you should look into the operations of all the criminal organisations in your area and see if there aren't similarities of method.'

'We have done that,' Slider said patiently, and added in language Palfreyman would understand, 'It's an ongoing process, but to date it has not yielded any significant data.'

The DCS looked happier. 'Ah, clearly you are keeping on top of things. There has been some discussion – I've been talking to Peter Judson—'

'Is the SCG taking the case over, sir?' Slider asked quickly. 'Because if so, I'd sooner they did so now, before I commit any more effort to it.'

'I'm sure you're doing your best,' Palfreyman said. 'But a second death – and connected to the case – it just doesn't look good.'

'Is the SCG taking the case?' Slider insisted.

Palfreyman's eyes slithered away. He disliked directness. Directness never built any empires. Well, actually, directness had built most of the empires in history, but that was in the bad old days, before interactive human resource management residential training seminars had been invented.

'Mr Judson would like to, but the manpower situation is critical at the moment. He has so many men tied up in court, now the terrorist business has gone to the Old Bailey – well, you know how it goes. He just hasn't a man to spare. But if your case is stuck and you can't get any progress on it, we may have to think of bringing in some people from outside the borough. And I don't think I need to tell you how Mr Wetherspoon would feel about that.'

The honour of the school is at stake, Slider. Ten to make and the last man in.

'We have some lines to follow up, sir,' he said. 'I don't think we can say the case is stuck at this point. It's only been a week.'

'But this gang – if it is a gang: there's nothing in records to help?'

'Either they're very new, or they're very good, and they seem to have a powerful hold on their people. But that's the very reason I'd really like to get at them. I don't like new kids on my block throwing their weight around.'

'Very well,' Palfreyman said. 'You go ahead and do what you have to do. Get a quick result on this one, and a lot of people will be very pleased indeed.' By which Slider divined he didn't mean the good burghers of Shepherd's Bush. 'And of course if there's any help I can give in Mr Porson's absence, my door is always open.'

'You're staying here, sir?' Slider said, surprised.

'Oh – well – no. I was speaking metaphorically,' Palfreyman said hastily. Olympians couldn't breathe the air down here for very long. 'But you can always telephone me. You've got my direct line number.'

Slider was on his way out when Palfreyman, having relied so far, as HR guidelines dictated, on the carrot, decided there was no harm in a wave of the stick. 'I'll need to see some concrete progress very soon, though. We're under a lot of pressure over our clear-up figures, and you don't need me to tell you that any murder is a high-profile case, whoever the victim.'

No, Slider thought as he headed downstairs, I don't need you to tell me, so why do you? Obviously, because everyone knew that Slider had so little understanding of the seriousness of murder that he wouldn't exert himself to clear up the case unless he was chivvied – and chivvied, moreover, by an expert who'd been on all the right courses and was a fully qualified chivvier.

He didn't get all the way to his office. On the stairs he encountered WPC Asher who said, 'Oh, sir, they're looking for you in the front shop.'

'No point in looking for me down there when I'm up here, is there?' Slider said reasonably.

Asher's rather hard blue eyes did not soften. She hadn't much sense of humour. 'No, sir, I mean Sergeant Paxman was looking for you. There's a man come in with some information about your case, sir.'

'Thank you,' Slider said meekly, and went. The man waiting for him in the reception area could only be American. It wasn't just the height and the air of having achieved a perfect diet, but above all the immaculateness. He was wearing a blue chambray shirt, open and with half rolled sleeves, over a white teeshirt so gleaming bright it would have had an oncoming motorist flashing his lights in annoyance. His blue jeans managed to look brand new and yet softly worn at the same time; his pale leather desert boots were unscuffed and unmarked and his socks – dead giveaway – were white. Everything was exquisitely clean and perfectly ironed. When the Last Trump sounded and all hearts were opened, the American nation was going to have to give up the secret of laundering to everyone else.

He seemed to be in his thirties, though it was getting harder to tell these days. He had the shining hair and supple tan skin of lifelong good nourishment, and the straight white teeth of expensive orthodontics. He was also wearing, for reasons Slider hoped to discover, a faintly hangdog look.

'I understand you have some information for me, Mr—?'

'Garfield. Tom Garfield. Yes, I have, but – could it be in private?'

'Of course,' Slider said. He led the way into one of the interview rooms.

Garfield looked about with a keen interest that seemed hardly warranted by his drab surroundings; and then explained it when he said, 'This is all new for me. I haven't been inside a British police station before. But it's just like the TV programme. Do you watch *The Bill*?'

'I never seem to get home in time to watch the television,' Slider said. He could have added that what you didn't get on *The Bill* was the smell, but desisted on the grounds that in the present circumstances he was an ambassador for his country. He invited Garfield to sit down and asked, 'What have you got for me?'

'Well, it's a little embarrassing.' Garfield crossed one leg over the other and smiled nervously. 'You see, I don't know whether what I've got is important anyway, and I really don't want to get myself into trouble . . . ?' He added a tempting question mark to the pause so that Slider could leap in with an amnesty.

Slider regarded him solidly. 'Do you know something about the murder of Lenny Baxter?'

'Lord, no, not about the murder. But I did know Lenny. Only slightly. In a business sort of way.'

'Your business with him was not of a legitimate type, I take it?'

The smile became ever more winning. 'There's an expression, "victimless crime"?'

'Mr Garfield, if you know anything that may help us solve this terrible crime you have a duty to – tell me.' He just managed to stop himself using the words 'disclose it'. What was it about talking to well-brought-up Americans that made his vocabulary slip back fifty years?

'And my own little – misdemeanour?' Was Garfield likewise struggling against the word 'peccadillo'?

'I will turn a blind eye to anything I can. It's not in my interests to make life difficult for witnesses.' He had to get him started somehow. 'Why don't you tell me a bit about yourself?'

'Oh. Well, okay. I work at the BBC – you know, at the TV Centre – as an assistant programme editor. I started out in journalism back home, working on a local paper.'

'Where's "back home"?'

'The States. I thought you'd – oh, you mean where exactly. In Springfield, Massachusetts. My folks come from Vermont but we moved there when I graduated from high school. I started out on the *Springfield Messenger*, and then I went over to broadcasting. I moved to Boston, to a radio station there, and then I met a guy from IRN. He was over from London on secondment and I got pretty friendly with him and his wife and, to cut a long story short, they got me in with a news agency – Visnews – in London, and from there I went to the BBC. End of long story,' he added with a nervous laugh.

'So if you work at the Television Centre you must know that we have had enquiries out for the best part of a week for information about Lenny Baxter.'

'Yeah. I kind of—' He shrugged. 'Okay, I hoped someone else would come forward and I wouldn't have to. And, like I said, I didn't know if it was important anyway. I couldn't see how it could be. But then my girlfriend kept on at me, and – well, here I am. You see, they're saying you want to know about Lenny's leather jacket, and it was me that sold it to him.'

He looked at Slider to see what effect this news had. Slider guessed that the leather jacket was not the source of Garfield's embarrassment. In fact, he had a pretty fair idea what it was Garfield didn't want to tell him. He confined himself to raising an eyebrow and saying, 'Where did you get the jacket?'

'From a guy back home. I went back to see my folks at Christmas and I spent a couple of days in Boston, checking out old friends. One of them had these jackets.' He spread his hands ruefully. 'Okay, maybe I should have asked more questions, but Sparky swore they weren't hot and – well, I wanted to believe him.'

'These jackets? How many did he have?'

'A boxful. Maybe about twenty, I don't know. He said they were a discontinued line, but they looked pretty good to me, and the price he wanted for them, I suppose I should have guessed he'd knocked them off. But I knew I could sell 'em over here and make a few bucks. So I took four. I'd have taken more,' he added frankly, 'only I couldn't have got 'em in my baggage.'

'Describe them to me.'

'Oh, you know. You've seen one of them. Three were black leather and one was tan suede, and they all had this tartan lining, but not Scottish tartan, just shades of brown. And the label was Emporio Firenze. That's a top smart label in Boston.

I should have cut the labels out, really, but I didn't want to spoil the jackets.'

'And you sold these jackets to Lenny Baxter?'

He looked embarrassed. 'I thought if I offered them to people at work questions might be asked. Lenny was always selling stuff anyhow, and he said he'd take all four off my hands. I thought it'd be easier that way. I didn't make a whole lot when you come right down to it, but I was kind of regretting I'd bought 'em by then. You've got to have the right kind of contacts if you want to go in for that kind of thing. I mean, it's okay for guys like Sparky and Lenny, but when I offered one to a friend of mine he looked at me as if I was peddling human flesh or something.' He gave Slider an engaging smile. 'I sure have learned my lesson. From now on I buy in a shop or nowhere.'

Slider remained unengaged. 'How did you come to know Lenny?'

This was the question Garfield didn't want asked. A blush spread across his fresh, boyish cheeks. 'Oh – I don't know. I kind of saw him around, you know.'

'Around? I can't think Lenny Baxter moved in the same circles as you.' Garfield didn't speak. Slider decided to put him out of his agony. 'Did you buy something from Lenny, was that it? You said he was always selling stuff. Did you buy something from him that you don't want to tell me about? Maybe a little something to smoke, or a little something to sniff?'

'Hey, listen, I don't do cocaine, okay? I mean, I know a lot of people who do, but I don't touch that stuff.'

'So it was cannabis, was it?' Garfield blushed more richly, but said nothing. 'Look,' Slider said, 'what you say to me on that count is not going to get you prosecuted. It would be pure hearsay, and I am too busy with other matters to take it any further. I just want the facts, okay?'

'Okay,' Garfield said, but he sounded a little resentful. 'But you guys over here are so stiff about it. I mean, my folks used to smoke grass at college, and they didn't think it was so bad. Okay, they didn't exactly *encourage* me to take it up, but I know damn well they still like to toke a little weed just to wind down at the end of the week. There's no harm in it.' He laughed. 'Hell, American TV is such shit you've got to have *something* while you watch it.'

'So how did you meet Lenny?'

'A guy I know put me on to him, when I said I wanted to get hold of some hash. He introduced us at a pub. After that Lenny gave me a mobile number and when I wanted something I gave him a ring and we'd meet somewhere.'

'In the park behind the Television Centre?'

'Yeah, once, but I didn't like it. I was scared stiff someone would see me going in or coming out. I know he did stuff there, but, frankly, I didn't want to meet any of his other customers. Mostly it was in pubs. A different one each time. He was very careful.'

'And was cannabis the only thing you bought from him?'

'Yeah. He was always offering me other stuff – watches, cameras, videos, you know? That's why I offered him the jackets. But I wasn't tempted.'

'Did you meet him alone?'

'Of course. You think I was going to take witnesses along?'

'Was he alone?'

'Sometimes he had his girlfriend with him. Tina. She's gorgeous,' he added with enthusiasm. He seemed to hesitate on the brink of something.

'Yes?' Slider prompted. 'What about Tina?'

'He – Lenny—' He stopped again, with an expression of distaste, and met Slider's eyes with a renewal of the blush. 'She was one of the things he offered me.'

'Did you accept?'

'What do you take me for?' Garfield said angrily. 'For Chrissake! He offered her to me right in front of her, and she's sitting there listening while he tries to tell me what she does, and what I can do to her. It nearly made me throw up.'

'Do you think she was willing to be offered like that?'

'Willing? Poor kid, she looked like a frozen mummy or something, staring at the wall, like she wouldn't dare make a sound or a movement. I don't know what he did to her, but he made her do what he wanted, I know that. Lenny was a bastard, and he deserved what he got, as far as I'm concerned.'

'Why do you think he did it?' Slider asked curiously. 'Just for the money? I suppose he wanted a good lot from you for the pleasure?'

'I never got as far as finding out,' Garfield said with dignity.

'I told him to shut up right away. But as to why he did it – I suppose it must have been the money. I guess he'd sell anything to anyone if the price was right.'

Slider pondered a little. Lenny was a bad gambler and had been mixing up the money he collected, trying to pay his debts. Maybe he was desperate enough for money even to sell his girl-friend. But of course, he had sold her before, hadn't he, to Ken Whalley in exchange for the park keys? And that hardly consti-tuted grave need. Was there something else going on there?

But at least now he knew where the leather jacket came from. Four of them, eh? Probably not important, but where did the others go? And he had confirmation that Lenny sold whaccy baccy, both in the park and elsewhere.

'Tell me,' he said, 'what did you think of Lenny Baxter? Apart from his attitude to his girlfriend.'

'How do you mean?'

'Did you think he was a real hard man? A top-notch crook? The sort no-one could get one over on?'

'He was a crook all right,' Garfield said. He paused, looking back into memory. 'He was a kind of good-looking bastard, the sort who gets women running after them and treats 'em badly. And he was tough all right. He could take care of himself. I mean, I wouldn't have wanted to get into a fight with him.'

'But?'

Garfield hesitated. 'I don't know. It's hard to put into words, but there was a sort of—' He paused again. 'I don't know,' he said, shaking his head at the impossibility of explaining it. 'All I can say is that I wouldn't have been surprised to find out he'd made a really stupid mistake. You got the feeling he had a bit missing, a common sense bit.'

'You mean he was reckless?'

'I don't quite mean that. I don't really know what I mean. It was just a feeling – that he'd trip up one day, and it would be something really stupid that tripped him. I wasn't surprised to find out he'd been murdered.'

Herbie Weedon's house was a nightmare.

'The old geezer must have lived there since Moses was at primary,' McLaren said. 'And he never threw anything away.'

'Papers everywhere,' Mackay supported him. 'It's going to

take for ever to sort through that lot. I mean, you never saw anything like it. It's even stacked up the stairs. You can hardly see the carpet.'

'You wouldn't want to,' McLaren interpolated.

'It was a death-trap, I tell you that, guv. He hadn't had his wiring done since before the war—'

'Hadn't had anything done. Blimey, you should've seen the kitchen!'

'—and with all that paper hanging around—'

'The only clear space is a sort of track leading to the piano.'

'Herbie Weedon played the piano?' Slider said.

'Half the stuff lying about everywhere's piano music,' Mackay said, 'and old song sheets from God knows when, Queen Victoria's time or something. You know, all curly writing and drawings on the front of geezers in penguin suits with big moustaches.'

'A suit with a moustache? That'd save a lot of time,' said Atherton.

There was something faintly disturbing, Slider discovered, about the thought of that mountainous old villain going home at night and playing the piano to himself, all alone in his unreconstructed house with his one social grace.

'Well, I suppose we'll have to go through the motions,' Slider said, 'but I don't believe there'll be anything in the house to help us. These people knew what they were doing, and if Herbie had incriminating documents they'd have taken them away.'

'More likely if he'd had something like that he'd've kept it at the office,' Hollis said reasonably.

'And we know they've been there,' Atherton concluded.

'So where are we going next, guv?' McLaren asked.

'Keep watching Eddie Cranston. I'm not convinced he knows anything – I think he knew Lenny Baxter as a freelance rather than as Mr Big's runner – but you can't be too careful. And keep watching Sonny Collins.'

'If I have to drink any more of his pissy beer—' Mackay began.

'No, your face will be getting too well known by now,' Slider said. 'We'll have to put someone else onto it.'

'Why don't we just do him for something?' Anderson said. 'We must have enough on him to nick him.'

'Yes, but where would that get us? He won't tell us the name of the big man.'

'We could lean on him.'

'Not nearly as hard as the big man leans,' Slider said. 'You saw what happened to Herbie Weedon. Collins is tough, but he's practical. He knows it'd be better to go down for a spell as a martyr than to end up dead. No, our only hope's to watch him and pray he gives us a clue to follow up. Anybody who comes in looking like a courier, we put a tail on.'

'It's all long-term stuff,' Swilley commented. 'No quick result there.'

'Yes, I know, and Mr Wetherspoon doesn't want jam tomorrow. I want all of you to keep asking around. Try and find Lenny's girlfriend, Tina. And look for Lenny's ex-customers, both on the bookie side and the drugs side. I know,' he added to their murmur of protest, 'that it's not easy to get people to incriminate themselves, but all we need is a hint, a start in the right direction. Use your powers of persuasion.'

Atherton followed him back into his office. 'That was it? That was your best Billy Graham-style rouser?'

Slider turned in frustration. 'What kind of a gang is it that no-one knows about? Tidy Barnett's come up with nothing. He's asked everywhere and no-one knows anything.'

'Or they're not saying.'

'Tidy knows everything that happens on the manor, but he can't get any handle on who the two heavies were that were seen talking to Lenny. All he gets from people is that there's a big game going on, but they don't know who's running it. Whoever the top banana is, he seems to be well insulated from the underworld.'

'Well, Lenny Baxter and Everet Boston can't be the only runners. There must be more of them if the business is all that big, and if we pull them in one by one, someone's bound to squeak sooner or later.'

'I'd almost put a bet on Everet squeaking,' Slider said, 'if I could just get hold of him.'

But Boston was not to be found. His address was a flat in Harlesden, but no-one had answered the door, and the locals who were watching it reported no movement in or out. And he had not been to any of his known haunts.

'Maybe we should get a warrant and search Boston's place,' Atherton suggested.

Slider rubbed distractedly at his hair. 'Yes, maybe. I'm just worried that if we show too much interest in him, what happened to Herbie Weedon will happen again.'

'You can't proceed on that basis,' Atherton said reasonably, 'or you'll never do anything. That would be letting them win.'

'If Everet Boston gets offed, they win.'

'Maybe they've done him already,' said Atherton. 'Maybe that's why there's no answer to his door.'

'You're such a comfort to me,' Slider said.

CHAPTER TWELVE

Not Buried But In Turd

One-Eyed Billy was distinctly nervous. He had got himself right up the end of the bar in the British Queen where he could keep his back to the wall and watch the door.

'I don't like it, straight I don't,' he said, and tipped the rest of his pint down his throat in two swallows. Nerves seemed to make him extra thirsty.

Slider nodded to George, the barman, who sidled up and refilled Billy's glass, his eyes darting from face to face from under his Neanderthal brow. George was a short, long-armed, potato-faced bloke who looked as though his descent from the apes had been via a handy short cut. He had worked at the Queen just about for ever, and was invaluable to the management because most people were scared of him; though Slider knew him well enough to know that he was really a gentle, inoffensive man who was very good to his mum and by no means as dumb as he looked.

'Look, Mr Slider,' Billy went on when George had moved away, 'I want to help you. Me dad said I had to help you. But what's going to happen to me? I mean, Ev said he couldn't go home 'cos they were watching his drum. He's frit for his life. I mean, what if they're watching me? What if they see me talking to you?'

'Do you know who they are, Billy?' Slider asked patiently.

'No! Course I don't. I don't work for 'em. I'm straight.'

'Then why should they mind you talking to me?'

'They killed old Herbie Weedon just for talking to you.'

'Obviously Herbie knew something. And we suspect he'd done business with them. Like you said, you don't work for them. Why should they kill you? These are professionals, and believe me, professionals don't go round killing people unless there's a really good reason – from their point of view.'

Well, it sounded good, and Billy seemed to buy it. He lowered a quarter of his pint, wiped the foam off his upper lip with the back of his hand, and seemed a notch calmer.

'Just tell me what Everet said,' Slider urged.

'I told you, he said he couldn't go home 'cos they were watching.'

'Yes, and what else? Did he say where he was? Any clue at all?'

'No, he just said he was laying low for a bit.'

'What could you hear in the background?' Billy looked blank. 'When Ev was talking on the phone, what was going on in the background? People talking? Music? The sound of urinals flushing?'

A long gawp ensued. 'Nah, none of them. Maybe – traffic. No, I'm not sure.'

'All right.' Slider cancelled that line of enquiry. 'What else did he say?'

'Like I told you, he said to tell you to lay off him, 'cos other-wise the Man'd have him rubbed out, an' that he didn't know nothing about Lenny being offed so there was no point in trying to find him. And he said to tell you to find Tina. That's Lenny's bird.'

'Yes, I know.'

'"Find Tina," he said, like that, all urgent. And he said he'd ring me again when he could and see if I'd heard anything from you.'

'Why is he so keen on this Tina?' Slider asked.

'I dunno. He knew her from before, that's all I know. Maybe he fancied her.'

'All right, Billy. Look, if Everet phones you again, tell him to phone me. Take this number, and give it to him, and tell him he *must* phone me, all right? It's really important.'

As Slider got up to leave, George caught his eye with a look of significance. Slider raised an eyebrow and was given an infini-tesimal nod, and a flickering glance sideways. Slider left the pub and loitered casually round the corner into Thorpebank Road, and in a moment or two George appeared at the staff entrance.

'You got something for me, George?' Slider asked.

'Billy's mate Ev Boston,' George said without preamble. He had the enviable ability to speak without moving his lips at all, and the rest of his face was so inexpressive it was like sound issuing from a stone.

'You know him?'

George shrugged, indicating that this was not a deep and abiding friendship. 'I play snooker up the Snookerama in Harlesden High Street. Well, I live up Craven Park, don' I? So I seen him there. He used to come in with this bird Billy's talking about. Tina.'

'When?' Slider asked.

'Not recently. A while back. Couple years.'

'Girlfriend?'

'Nah. She was a lot younger than him.'

'Was Ev working her?'

'Nah, I don't think she was a tom. I think maybe she was a relative. Cousin or something. From the way they talked to each other. That's all I know. Any good?'

'Thanks, George. That is a help.' He slipped a note across to George's ready fingers under cover of the drying-cloth he was holding. As an afterthought he said, 'You don't know anything about this man Ev was working for?'

'Nah. Sorry. I know you got the word out. Whoever he is, he keeps himself private. All I've heard is it's big business.'

'Yes, well, I guessed that. If you do hear anything—'

George gave a curt nod and sidled away. He was not one of Slider's regular informants, but Slider had known him a long time and did not underestimate him, for which George was in a quiet way grateful. This was not the first piece of information George had given him.

Slider called Swilley in. 'I've got a job for you.'

'Now or tomorrow?'

'Oh Nora, is that the time? Well, it's going to take a while. You'd better start in the morning.'

'Okay. D'you want to tell me about it?'

'It's a bit of a long shot anyway,' Slider sighed, and told her about Everet Boston's putative relationship with the missing Tina. 'I want you to go through the records. Start with the toms register, but don't restrict yourself to that if nothing comes up. Try the name Boston. Of course, cousins don't always have the same surname, but it's a chance. And if that doesn't work, just look for any possible connection with Everet. Tina's probably not her real name, which adds to the fun for you. Get onto Everet's old school, get them to look up what his address was when he was there, see if that yields anything. A lot of these Harlesden families live close together. I know it's a tenuous brief, but that's why I want you to do it. Use your intelligence.'

'Thanks,' said Swilley; and then, 'It's that bad, is it?'

'Oh, I don't know,' Slider said. 'We're bound to get a handle on them sooner or later. I'd just prefer it was sooner.'

'You think this Tina's in danger?'

Slider met her eyes. 'Everet thinks she is. And he knows them better than we do.'

Passing the door of Porson's office, Slider saw to his surprise that Porson was there, standing by his desk, reading.

'Sir,' he said.

Porson turned. He looked worn out. 'Just looked in,' he said hoarsely, cleared his throat and tried again. 'Make sure everything's all right. I've been on the dog to Mr Palfreyman, so he's filled me in *vis-à-vis* the status quo. But you don't always hear everything when it's coming down from above rather than up from below.'

And with Palfreyman it had a long way to fall, Slider thought. Porson met his eyes and there was a sudden sympathy between them.

'I expect you've come in for a bit of the brown shower,' Porson said. 'That's usually my job, to intersect it. Act as a sort of umbrella for the pony. Otherwise you lot'd be buried up to your navels and never get anything done.'

'We do appreciate it, sir,' Slider said. Porson looked bleak, and he added, 'It's a lonely job.'

That was going too far. Porson's face tightened and he said briskly, 'So what leads are you following as of this instance?'

Slider gave him a précis. 'It seems at the moment that Everet Boston is our one hope, and he's disappeared. We're watching his house but I can't see him going back there in his present state. What we have got is his mobile number. It's switched off at the moment—'

'He is being careful,' Porson remarked.

'Yes, sir. But he has said he'll phone Billy Cheeseman again and he may phone me. What I'd like is a warrant for the mobile service provider so that if he does use his mobile again they'll pinpoint where he is, and we can pick him up.'

Porson considered a moment, and then said, 'Well, it's a long shot, but this is a bastard of a case. I'll authorise it. Get it typed up and I'll sign it.'

'I've got it here,' Slider said. 'I was going to send it over to Hammersmith, but—'

'Glad I'm useful for something,' Porson barked. He fumbled at his pocket for a pen, then went behind his desk to get one out of a drawer. As he bent over to sign, his rug slipped forward, and he pushed it back with a careless hand. Was it possible to lose weight on your actual skull? Porson straightened up and Slider moved his eyes hastily.

Porson passed over the warrant. He fixed Slider with a steely gaze. 'We haven't got long on this one. It's going to turn into a political problem if we don't break through and they'll have to bring in an SCG from another borough.'

'I've half expected it before now, sir.'

'All right, it's no shame to us. Normally they'd have had it off us from the start. We've only been left holding the bathtub this long because of the manpower situation. But they'll bring in people who don't know the ground, and I'd as soon not have 'em treading mud over my carpet. Mud or worse. Capisky?'

Slider nodded. 'I'll do my best, sir.'

'I know, laddie, I know. You always do. I'm not just breathing down your parade to annoy you. You've got my full support. Any warrants you want, as much overtime as it takes. Whatever you need.'

Slider thanked him. 'Does that mean you're back, sir?'

The old granite face seemed to harden a fraction more. 'No, laddie, I'm not back. I just popped in, like I said. I've got to get back to the hospital.'

Hospital? Slider started to say, 'I hope—' and then realised there was no way to finish that sentence. *I hope it's nothing serious?* But he wouldn't be away from work if it weren't.

Porson seemed to appreciate the reticence. He nodded. 'If you need anything, call me on my mobile. And you can send someone over with anything that wants signing. Come to me, not Mr P.'

'Yes, sir.'

'And keep leaning on every bit of lowlife in the borough. This lot may be well organised, but somewhere out there there's a weak link, and I want us to put our foot through it before they do.'

Joanna opened the door of Atherton's house to him, with a cross-eyed teenage Siamese clinging to her scalp.

'Gosh, you're late,' she said.

'Doesn't that hurt?' Slider asked.

'Like hell,' she assured him mildly. 'I can't detach it until you're inside.'

'Sorry. Shall I do the honours?'

'Yes please – *gently*!'

He lifted it, freed the curved claws from the chunks of hair, and placed it on his own shoulder.

'He jumped on me from the top of the kitchen door as I came through,' Joanna said.

'Which one is it?'

'Vash,' she said. 'But it makes no conceivable difference. They're both bonkers.'

Sredni Vashtar teetered on Slider's shoulder, purring like an engine; then, as his brother's voice was upraised plaintively in the kitchen, scuttered straight down Slider's front and disappeared in two flouncing leaps towards the smell of food. Slider took the cat-free window of opportunity to kiss Joanna.

'Mm, you taste nice,' he said at half-time.

'It's Jim's sherry.'

'No, it's you,' he assured her, and sank back in.

'God, you two!' Sue said, coming in from the kitchen. 'You're like horny teenagers.'

Slider straightened up. 'We haven't seen each other in a while.'

'I haven't seen my gran for years,' Sue said, 'but all she gets is a peck on the beak and a box of Quality Street. Have a bruschetti.'

'Thanks. Isn't that plural?'

'You want waitress service *and* a Linguaphone course?'

'I'll get you a drink,' Joanna said indistinctly, having stuffed the smallest slice whole into her mouth. She went into the kitchen, leaving Slider alone with Sue. She fixed him with a penetrating blue gaze. Tinted contact lenses, Slider thought absently as doom fell on him.

'He wasn't working overtime last week, was he?'

'What do you mean?' Slider said. That was feeble. He'd never been good at this confrontation thing.

'Wednesday and Thursday. Oh, it's all right,' she said, waving away any possible answer he might have been going to give – which from where he was standing was not likely to have arrived until next week some time. 'I won't ask you to perjure yourself. I know the symptoms. That's where you men always get it wrong. You think we're stupid.'

'I don't think you're stupid,' Slider said, which could have meant very nearly anything, so wasn't the height of tact.

'I just thought,' she went on, 'that we'd got all that nonsense over with.'

Slider felt a looming trap. 'Look,' he began, and she flapped a hand to stop him.

'For God's sake don't say anything that starts with "look". Sentences like that lead anywhere and they're always fatal.'

'Sorry.'

'No, I'm sorry,' she said, and Slider saw she was. Sorry and angry and also afraid.

'He really cares about you,' Slider said awkwardly. Doing the old bosom-baring on your own behalf was bad enough, but having to talk girly about a male friend was as easy as eating a sand sandwich.

'I can't keep going through this time after time.'

'Talk to him,' Slider said.

'Talk to him who?' Joanna asked, coming back in with a tumbler of gin-and-tonic. It was a beauty – long and cool, blue with gin, clinking with ice, and with a floating demi-lune of lemon beaded delicately silver on the upper side. Slider wanted to dive in and stay under till the coast was clear.

But Sue rescued him. 'Jim,' she said easily. 'About the case.'

Which showed, Slider thought, that a lady could be a gentleman as well as a bosom friend.

*   *   *

At the table, over a starter of baked goat's cheese and rocket, Atherton said, 'I don't think we're ever going to solve this one. No witnesses, no info. We haven't even got a weapon.'

'What about the old man who was strangled with the chain?' Joanna asked.

'Herbie Weedon? Same story. No-one saw anyone go up. The hardware shop was closed at the time but the deli was still open, but they said they never took any notice of people going in and out of the door to Golden Loans. And why should they?' Atherton finished in frustration. 'People just don't look at each other any more. Everyone wanders round in their own little bubble as if no-one else on the planet exists.'

'But how could the killer know Herbie was going to talk to you?' Joanna asked.

'Maybe his phone was bugged,' Atherton said with a faint shrug. 'He said it wasn't safe to talk on the phone.'

'Is it really that easy to bug someone's phone?' Sue objected. 'Outside of a James Bond film, I mean.'

'Oh, it isn't difficult, if you've got the know-how. The gear exists, and it's very sophisticated and very compact these days. It doesn't even have to be inside the actual phone. They've got radio bugs that are so powerful they can pick up what's said on both sides of a telephone conversation from anywhere in the room.'

'Wouldn't you have found the bugging device if there was one?'

'Not if whoever killed him remembered to remove it,' Atherton said. 'And I suspect they might have.'

'But then,' said Joanna, 'you're talking about a very sophisticated killer. And if the same person who killed Herbie Weedon killed Lenny Baxter—'

'Which we assume is the case because of the lock and chain,' Atherton said.

'—then that means Baxter wasn't killed by one of his drugs customers or his betting customers—'

'Or any other of the assorted lowlife, like Eddie Cranston, that we think he associated with,' Slider concluded.

'But the killer himself needn't have been sophisticated,' Sue said, reaching for the bottle and pouring more Chablis. 'If it was a gang thing, he could be just a crude tool given orders by a sophisticated boss.'

'Not too crude,' Atherton said.

'Everet Boston is smart enough,' Slider said. 'And so is Sonny Collins. The trouble is we just don't have any evidence to point to anyone.'

'Or even a motive?' Sue suggested.

'Murders, very generally, are done for one of two reasons,' Slider said. 'Money, or passion.'

'But in this case, the money was left in the victim's pocket,' Sue said.

'Well, there's money as in wads of folding, and money as in don't jeopardise my business,' Slider said. 'Robbery from the person isn't the only option. What we need is a witness. Some helpful passer-by with a description we can act on. Or, failing that, we could do with laying our hands on someone who knows something from the inside. Like Lenny's girlfriend.'

'Or Everet Boston,' Atherton said, standing up and beginning to clear plates. 'It's a pity you didn't keep hold of him when you had him.'

'Yes, Mr Atherton. Sorry, Mr Atherton,' Slider said.

Sue followed Atherton out of the room with her eyes. 'Do you let him talk to you like that?' she said in mock amazement. 'He's only the cook.'

'You just can't get the staff these days,' Slider apologised.

In the car on the way home, Joanna asked out of the blue, 'Is Jim up to his old tricks again?'

'I don't know,' Slider said. She looked a protest. 'Really, I don't know.'

'Sue seems to think he is.'

'Is that what she said?'

'Not directly. It's just the impression I got.'

'From what?'

'Stop being a detective for a minute. What is wrong with him?'

'If he is up to something – which I don't know that he is – he probably wouldn't think there was anything wrong with him, or it. They're not married.'

She gave him a hostile glance. 'That's beside the point. Either he wants a relationship or he doesn't. He's got to make up his mind.'

'Why? I'm not defending the position, just asking.'

'In a spirit of pure enquiry? All right, because he expects her to have made up her mind. He wants what she's got to offer him, but he doesn't want to give her anything back.'

'I don't know that that's true,' Slider said. 'It's just—' He couldn't phrase it, and fell silent.

At last she prompted. 'It's just what? He doesn't even really try very hard not to get found out. That's insulting.'

'No, it isn't. It's the one hopeful thing, that he *wants* her to find out.'

'So she'll punish him? But she's not his mum. He'd better shape up soon or that'll be that. Can't you talk to him?'

'Not possible,' Slider said firmly. 'But if he should open the subject with me—'

'Yes?'

'I'll tell him he's not Peter Pan,' Slider concluded. 'Good God, there's a parking space!'

'Grab it, quick,' she said, allowing the subject to be changed.

Later, sharing the bathroom basin for tooth-cleaning, she said, 'I understand, really. He doesn't want to stop chasing women because that will be the end of his merry days of youth. And he's afraid of feeling too much for Sue because she can hurt him, where none of his casual dollies could.'

'Are you sure he's that deep?' Slider said. 'Maybe he just can't help it.'

'If that's what you say about your friends, heaven help your enemies,' she said, without heat.

He rinsed his brush and watched the water swirling away down the plughole. He wasn't a bit sleepy now, and as personal problems were the flavour of the moment . . . In for a penny, he thought. Might as well get it over with.

'You wanted to have a serious talk,' he suggested.

She turned back in the bathroom doorway. 'Oh that. No. Not now. I'm not in the mood.'

'Is that good or bad?' he asked tentatively.

'Depends on your point of view.'

'What are you in the mood for?'

'No more talk,' she said. 'Let's just go and have some really rampant sex.'

'There are no two points of view about that,' he said, following her and putting out the light.

During the morning one small piece of comfort in an otherwise unpleasant case arrived on his desk: the PM report on Herbie Weedon suggested that he had not actually choked to death. His neck, which Slider remembered as being about the same width as his head, had been so well-covered that the chain had dug in and restricted his breathing but had not actually stopped it altogether, and none of the delicate bones – the cricoid, hyoid etc – had been fractured. Perhaps, eventually, sufficient force would have been administered to achieve these effects but, in Freddie's opinion, Weedon's heart, which was in a shocking condition anyway, had given out before that happened. Why Slider should find any comfort in the fact that Weedon had died of heart failure rather than being strangled he didn't know, but it seemed just marginally better. Not a ray of sunshine, precisely, but a small one up to them. Herbie had slipped under the net. They had not got him – *he* had got him.

Swilley interrupted his thoughts. 'Guv, have you got a minute?'

'Where would I get one of those?' Slider asked.

Swilley took that for an invitation. 'I think I may have something.'

'Really? That was quick.'

'Well, I don't know if it is anything,' she backpedalled, 'but, look. I didn't find any match for a girl with the name Boston—'

'I didn't really think you would,' Slider said.

'But I got onto Everet Boston's old school, and they put me onto his old form teacher. He remembered Everet very well. A bright lad, but always in trouble. And when Everet's mum was unavailable – which was often, because she was apparently a bad lot – they used to have to call in his auntie, a Mrs Angela Coulsden who lived in Wrottesley Road. That's just round the corner from Furness Road where Everet lived with his mum. So I ran the name Coulsden through the records and came up with a Mary Coulsden, who had two minor busts a couple of years ago, one for underage drinking and one for shoplifting a lipstick from Woolworths. Cautioned for both and nothing recorded against her since.'

'Same address?'

'No,' Swilley said apologetically, 'and the appropriate adult that was sent for was her dad, a Neville Coulsden. But the address was All Souls Avenue, which is only two minutes from Wrottesley Road. They could easily have moved.'

'True.'

'And Mary was the name on his tattoo.'

'Which Doc Cameron says is fairly recent.'

'*And*,' Swilley concluded, as one coming to the fruitiest bit last, 'when the store dick in Woolies nobbled her, she gave a false name to begin with. She called herself Teena Brown – spelt T, double e, n, a. Only gave her real name when they got her down the nick. Which was Mary Christina Coulsden. Maybe she didn't like the name Mary,' she concluded, looking at him hopefully.

'So if she is the same person, she might still be going under the name of Teena Brown,' Slider said. 'Did you—?'

'Yes, I checked, but there are no busts against a Teena Brown, spelt either way. But that doesn't mean anything. She might have been careful, or lucky—'

'Or Lenny Baxter might have been doing everything for her,' Slider concluded. 'Well, it isn't much, but it gives us another line to follow up. Put the word out for a tom using that name, and see if you can find the parents. They might still be at the same address—'

'The father is. He's on the current voters' register.'

'Oh?'

'No mention of Angela, though. He's listed as living alone.'

'All right. Go and see him. If it is the same, maybe the girl's run home; or if she hasn't, he might know where she might go to hole up. Good work, Norma. If this works out there could be a sainthood in it for you.'

She smirked. 'Something like a golden ha-lo?'

'Don't you start,' Slider said.

'For you, Jim,' Hollis called across the room. 'Line two.'

Atherton took it. At first he thought he was getting an obscene phone call: there was nothing but heavy breathing. But when he said 'Hello?' again, there was an instant response.

'Hello, hello, Mr Atherton? Sorry, I thought someone was coming in. It's James Mason here – not the actor of course.'

'I should hope not. Yes, Mr Mason, what can I do for you?'

'I hope maybe it is what I can do for you,' Mason said. 'That leather jacket you brought to show me.'

'Yes? You've had some thoughts on it?'

'Better than that, I've seen its twin. One of my regulars came in this morning to bespeak a new suit. A very nice gentleman, and a very good customer. Appreciates fine cloth and good tailoring just as you do. I showed him that cashmere-mink cloth I showed you, and he said yes right away. Couldn't wait. Of course, there will be enough there for two suits, if you should change your mind—'

'Not at the moment, thanks. What about the leather jacket?'

'Ah, well, he wasn't wearing that himself, of course. A very good dresser, always, and never casual, not in town. Knows the value of matching the outer shell to the inner strength. We are what we wear. No, I don't think I would ever see him in town in a leather jacket. There are places—'

It struck Atherton that Mason was more than usually rambling, and it sounded like nerves. 'So who was wearing it, then?' he asked with a hint of impatience.

'His driver,' Mason said. 'He was waiting outside with the car – there's no parking outside my shop, as you know – and while we were in consultation he came in and said that there was a traffic warden coming, and asked my gentleman if he was ready. My gentleman said he should drive round the block and come back. That was when I noticed the jacket. It was the same quality, the same cut and style, and the lining was the same – that very fine tartan wool in the shades of brown. I couldn't see the label, of course, because he was wearing it.'

'So you don't really know—'

'One moment please, Mr Atherton. There is more. I took my gentleman into the back to consult on the style of the suit – his measurements I have already, of course; those I did not need to take. Later the shop bell rang, and I put my head out just to see who it was. It was the driver come back. I said we would be a few moments longer, and he nodded. But he seemed to feel it warm in the shop, and he slipped the jacket off. That's when I saw the label. It was the same.'

'I see. That's very interesting,' Atherton said. 'Did you say anything to either of them?'

'No, indeed! For one thing, I did not know how important the jacket might be. To be making a fuss for nothing – and for another thing, I should not like to upset a very good customer by asking impertinent questions. Also—'

'Yes?'

'If it is a serious matter, I should not like to do the wrong thing. Perhaps you would not like me to ask anything. So I let it go, and I pondered. And now I have rung you. *Is* it important?'

'I don't know,' Atherton said. 'When I first came to you, it was a question of identifying someone—'

'The dead person, yes.'

'But we know who he was now. On the other hand, we still know very little about him. The jacket might be a lead. If your customer's driver bought it from the same person, it might give us an idea of what he was up to. Do you have the driver's name?'

'Oh, no. I've never made for him,' Mason said simply.

'Then I had better have your customer's name,' Atherton said. 'I notice you've been careful not to let it drop so far.'

Mason hesitated. 'The thing is, my dear sir, that the gentleman is a very good customer of mine, and I should not like him to think I had been talking about him behind his back.'

'I'll be tactful,' Atherton said. 'All I want is the name and address of his driver. He can't object to giving me that, surely?'

'Oh, no. No, no. Of course not. No, any respectable citizen must want to help the police in any way they can, and he is a very respectable citizen.' He sounded deeply doubtful.

'Don't worry, Mr Mason, I'll treat him with kid gloves. What's his name and address?'

'It's Mr Bates. Trevor Bates. And he lives in Aubrey Walk in Holland Park.'

'He's well-to-do, then.'

'Oh yes, indeed.'

'I'm not surprised you don't want to upset him.' He wrote down the full address. 'Telephone number?'

'It's ex-directory,' Mason said unhappily. 'I *really* don't think I can give you that. It would be breaking a confidence.'

'All right,' Atherton said, 'I'll manage. Thank you for telling me this. It might not turn out to be important, but you never know.'

'My pleasure, my pleasure, sir. And if you would like to pop in some time, I should be extremely happy to make you a suit, or a pair of trousers—'

'I'll see what I can do,' Atherton said. Never let it be said that he had broken a tailor's heart.

CHAPTER THIRTEEN

How Grim Was My Valet

All Souls Avenue was a wide road, once respectable but now brought low, blighted by traffic from having become a through route. The terraced houses were shabby, and most had been broken up into flats and rooms. Mr Neville Coulsden had a ground-floor flat in a three-storey house whose front garden had been concreted over and had its fences removed so that cars could be parked on it. A bile-green Fiesta sat inches from his bay window, two of its wheels up on blocks and a confetti of rust all around it. On the other side of the path were several hunks of rusting metal – car innards of some kind, Swilley deduced – and the gay multicoloured gleam of crisp bags and sweet wrappers blown behind and underneath them showed how long they had been there. The top-floor windows of the house were open and the beat, but not the melody, of heavy rock music issued forth past the dirty net curtains, as if someone up there were regularly whacking something springy with a wooden mallet.

Mr Coulsden opened the door to Swilley with a searching look and a rather flinching mouth. Expecting bad news, she thought. Inside his flat the music noise was both worse and better. The slight upper-register jingle perceptible outside, like change rattling in someone's pocket, was here inaudible; but the regular thump was closer and more personal. Transmitted through the fabric of the house as a vibration, it seemed to assail the skin rather than the ears, like a physical threat.

'Won't you sit down? I'm sorry about that,' he said, raising his eyes to the ceiling. He had a mild but musical West Indian accent. 'It don't do no good to hask. They just turn it up even more. Can I make you a cup of tea?'

'No, thank you, nothing for me.'

Coulsden nodded gravely and sat down in the armchair opposite her, but well forward, elbows on thighs so that his hands
hung over the space between his knees. He was a very big man,
tall and bony, with large chalky-nailed hands and a massive
head. He was neatly dressed in grey trousers and a white shirt
open at the neck, a home-knitted sleeveless Fair Isle cardigan
and tartan bedroom slippers. His close-cropped hair was quite
white, so it looked like sheep's wool, and his brown eyes were
appropriately mild, but the overall impression was of a still
strength, quietly contained and waiting – though for what?

The sitting room was tidy and clean, furnished with a hideous
brown brocade three-piece suite with fringe edging, and one or
two pieces of early MFI finished in wood-style veneer. The carpet
was crimson cut-pile, the wallpaper patterned with brown and
cream cabbage roses, the curtains grey with a yellow and turquoise
zigzag motif. Spotless nets shut out the view of the rusting Fiesta
and the migrating mastodons of buses and lorries beyond, and
in front of them, on a small table, stood a fern in a pot, its fronds
trembling to the rhythm of the Garage beat from above.

On the wall in one fireside alcove was a large framed print
of the Sacred Heart of Mary, and on the narrow, low, tiled
mantelpiece over the gas fire a tiny statuette of Pope John Paul
II stood amid a collection of well-polished brass ornaments.
There was a large, elderly television, Swilley noted, but no video
recorder, and no books anywhere, no reading matter at all except
for the *Radio Times* folded open on the set-top. There was an
air of stillness about the flat, into which the disco thump intruded
like an unpleasant menace, like the evil men starting to break
down the door of your hiding place in one of those pursuit
dreams. Stillness and emptiness and the unstoppable thud. How
did he live here? It made Swilley shiver.

'Thank you for letting me come and talk to you, Mr Coulsden,'
she began. And then – she had to ask. It was her job. 'Is Mrs
Coulsden—?'

'My wife is dead,' he said calmly, but the dry old lips trembled again. 'Eighteen monts ago. We'd been married forty-five
years. We married in Kingston the year before we came over.
She was a wonderful woman. Forty-five years and never a cross
word.'

'I'm sorry.'

'You weren't to know,' he said kindly. He looked round the room in a rather lost way. 'It hard without her. I try to keep things nice, the way she did, but I can't get used to it. I keep thinking she going to come in the kitchen door and tell me tea's ready.'

'So you live here alone?'

He inclined his head, and the faintest gleam of humour came into his eyes. 'Doesn't sound like it sometimes, eh? Hall day long they go on like that. Young people! Why don't they go out to work? I wish I went out to work, then I'd get a bit o' peace. I'm retired now.'

'What did you do?'

'Train driver. I drove trains for London Underground. Hit was quieter in the tunnels than it is in here when they playing that stuff.'

'I believe you. Does your daughter come and visit you?'

'Mary? No. I haven't seen her in nearly two years. She used to phone sometimes, but since her mother died, she hasn't phoned me once.'

'Oh dear. Why is that?'

The lines of his face grew stern. 'It that man she live with. That wicked, evil man. I suppose that's what you've come about.'

Bullseye, Swilley thought with relief. They had got the right Mary after all. 'You mean Lenny Baxter?'

'Our Lord forgive me, but I hate that man for what he did to Mary. I saw on the TV he'd been murdered. So he got what he deserved. Just not soon enough.'

'I'm sorry, but I have to ask. What did he do to Mary?'

'Put her feet on the path of evil. Took her from us, and from the Church. Now she living in a state of sin, and if—' He stopped and swallowed, and then asked with a quiet, desperate courage. 'Have you come to tell me something bad happen to her? Is she dead?'

'No – I mean, we don't know anything about her, except that she's not at Lenny Baxter's flat. Some of her clothes are missing and we assume she's gone into hiding. We'd like to find her and we hoped you might know where she is.'

'I don't know anything about her life since she left us. But she in a state of sin. If anything happen to her now—' He shook his head, unable to articulate the awful possibility.

'How did she meet Lenny Baxter?'

'Her cousin Ev introduced them. You know Everet Boston?'

'We have talked to him.'

'That boy always getting into trouble, from the time he could walk. But Angela – my wife – she had a soft spot for him. She thought he was a good boy underneath. Otherwise we wouldn't have let Mary see him.'

'Did they go out together?'

He frowned, evaluating the question. 'No, it wasn't like that. Everet older than Mary. He like a big brother to her. He was round here a lot when he was a boy. His ma – Angela's sister – lived round the corner, but she was a bad mother, so Angela tried to do her best for the boy. Teresa wasn't married, you see. The black sheep of the family.' He looked to see if she disapproved, and she pursed her lips in what she hoped was a noncommittal way. 'She was a bad mother, so I suppose hit no wonder Ev went wrong too. He not a bad boy really, but he got mixed up with bad company.'

'Like Lenny Baxter?'

'I wish to God Ev never introduced Mary to him. Ev used to go down the snooker hall couple of times a week. He always fond of Mary, an' he took her sometimes. We didn't approve of that, but Ev said it was a respectable place. What could we do? If we forbade her to go with her cousin, she might do something worse. And Ev swore he'd look after her. But Lenny Baxter play at the same snooker hall – that how Ev knew him – so of course Mary get to know him.'

'They went out together?'

He bowed his head in assent. 'We think nothing of it at first. But we see a change come over Mary. She wouldn't go to church any more. Then we find she smoking that weed. Lenny Baxter give it to her. I don't know what else he getting her into.' His eyes were distant now, reliving the old misery. 'But she a different girl. Disrespectful to her mother. Paying no heed to her father. It was row, row, all the time.' He focused suddenly on Swilley. 'She not a bad girl, you understand? But she was yong and full of life and she wanted fun, and she got into bad company.'

'Yes, I understand. It happens all the time.'

'I never thought it would happen in my house,' he said sternly.

'Was that when she got into trouble with the law?'

'You know about that?' He seemed pained. Swilley nodded. 'She stole a lipstick. The police were very kind. They know we not that kind of people. They let her off with a warning. But it a terrible shock to Angela and me. We just couldn't understand how she could do such a ting. Then one day she tell us that she moving hout, going to live with Lenny Baxter.' He shook his head slowly, goaded by memory. 'It broke our hearts. Angela was never the same afterwards. We always been churchgoers. After Mary left, Angela wouldn't go to church any more. Said she too ashamed, with a daughter living in sin with a bad man like Lenny Baxter, God forgive him.'

It was odd, Swilley thought, how believers could say 'God forgive him,' as if it meant the exact opposite. 'Do you know what line of work Lenny was in?'

'I don't know what he did at first. But Ev working for this bookmaker – we didn't approve of that, but at least it a job, and Ev did pretty well at it, enough money to dress nicely and buy a car. Hanyway, he got Lenny Baxter into it, working for the same boss.'

'Do you know the name of the boss, or the company?'

He shook his head. 'I wonder sometimes,' he said painfully, 'if it all legitimate. I wonder if they not mixed up with some criminal hactivity.'

It was fortunate he didn't know the half, Swilley thought. 'Is Mary your only child?' she asked.

'Angela and me had tree sons. Much older than Mary. She was our little afterthought, Angela always say.'

Menopause baby, Swilley translated.

'But we loved her all the more because of that. She was a gift from God. That's why we called her Mary.'

'But when she was arrested for shoplifting she gave a different name.'

'Yes. She made up a name. I don't know why she did that. Maybe she was a bit ashamed.'

'Is it possible she's going by that other name again now?'

'I don't know what she doing hany more,' he said with bitter dignity. 'At first she used to phone her mother sometimes. But when Angela died—' He paused, coming with difficulty to perhaps the hardest part. 'She didn't come to her mother's funeral. After that I never hear from her again.'

'What does she do for a living?'

'Nothing that I know of. That man give her money, I suppose.'

So he didn't know about the prostitution, Swilley thought; or knew and wasn't allowing himself to believe it.

'Did you ever meet him?'

'No. She knew better than to bring him here. But Everet talk about him sometimes. Said he very free with his money. Maybe that's what Mary liked about him. He gave her a watch one time – expensive one. Angela and me never wanted for anything, but we couldn't afford loxuries. We thought we'd brought Mary up to know that the things of this world are a snare and a delusion. All our boys turned out straight. Good, hard-working boys, married with families, always paid their way, like we did. But Mary stole a lipstick. It was like she slapped me and her mother in the face. How could a child of ours do such a thing? It was never the same afterwards. It was like something in us died. And then she went away with that man . . .'

He stopped talking, as if it was all too much effort, lowering his head and staring at his hands. Swilley was beginning to get a picture of a lively teenager fretting against the restraints laid on her by staid and elderly parents and the heavy hand of the Church. Yes, if every minor peccadillo – things her contemporaries didn't even think were wrong – was portrayed as a dagger of ingratitude through the heart of her mother *and* the BVM, one could see why she might prefer to hang out with the street-cool Ev and, ultimately, his friends. Every influence in her life other than her parents would be pulling her in a contrary direction. Maybe it just got too much for her.

'Well, we really need to find Mary,' Swilley said, interrupting his reverie. 'Would she perhaps have gone to stay with one of her brothers?'

'I don't think so. She never had much to do with them. They were grown up and left home before she was born.'

'I think we'd better check, just in case. Can you give me their addresses?' He nodded. 'And also, can you give me a recent photograph of Mary?'

'I haven't got a recent one, not since she went away. The last one I have must be two years old at least.'

'That would be better than nothing,' Swilley said.

He got up and went over to the piece of furniture in the corner, a mixture of display shelves, drawers and cupboards usually called, with unconscious irony, a unit. A moment later he came back cradling a photograph in his big palm, which he bestowed on Swilley as if passing over a baby bird.

In front of a grim, modern urban church a stout, bespectacled black woman in a yellow print dress, white hat and handbag beamed at the camera; beside her was a slim young girl, mini-skirted and skinny-jumpered, leaning on her mother's shoulder as if on a lamp-post, legs crossed, other arm outstretched in some obscure gesture. She was remarkably pretty, from what Swilley could tell, but in her age, her clothing, even her pose, she looked like the woman's grandchild rather than daughter.

'You'll let me have it back?' Mr Coulsden asked.

'Yes, of course. Thanks. Now can you think of anywhere at all Mary might have gone? An old friend? Another relative?'

He shook his head. 'She dropped everyone when she went off with that man. Everyone except Everet. If he doesn't know where she is, no-one does.'

A sense of futility came over Swilley. Nothing in this case seemed to lead anywhere. Every little rivulet ran out into the sand. And this place was beginning to get her. Though there was no smell of damp the room struck cold, despite the bright sunshine outside. Cold as a tomb. Swilley wanted to be gone. She knew now what this quiet old man was waiting for.

He showed her to the door, and said suddenly, 'There was a woman. When Mary get to know Lenny Baxter, they went out as a foursome with Ev and a woman called Susan. I remember because when Mary came back one time after she moved out to collect some more of her things, this woman drove her, waited for her outside in the car. She was older, more Everet's age. Did he tell you about her?'

'No.'

'Maybe it nothing then. Just a casual acquaintance.'

'Still, it might be worth checking. Did you get her surname? Can you describe her?'

He shook his head. 'I only caught a glimpse at the door. And I never heard another name. Mary just said, "I've got to go,

Sue's waiting," or "Susan's waiting." And then I remembered
that she'd mentioned her before. That's all.'

Swilley thanked him, shook his cold, old hand, and left. As
she filed between the Fiesta and the rusting junk, she felt his
eyes on her, and resisted the urge to turn back and look. She
didn't think she could bear the sight of him, standing all alone
in his doorway, a dry rock out of the flow of life.

Atherton assured Slider that he needed his company when he
went to interview Mr Bates. 'I'm the one that knows about
schmutter.'

'I'm only going to ask him the name of his driver,' Slider
said. 'I already know the name of his tailor.'

'Well, I promised James Mason I'd take care of him, and it
makes it more natural for me to ask this Bates bloke, since he
and I have a whistle or two in common.'

'Feebler and feebler. Why don't you just admit you want to
see your rival face to face?'

'Rival?'

'You're afraid he's better dressed than you.'

'I have no rival,' Atherton said. 'I am the nonpareil. Anyway,
there's no need for *you* to go at all. Why don't you just admit
you want to see the house?'

'Certainly, if it will make you happy,' Slider said genially.
Architecture was a passion of his – or an interest that would
be a passion if he ever had time to indulge one. 'All right, you
can come with me, if you think you can control yourself.'

'Do what?'

'I don't want you dribbling on this bloke's lapels.'

'Ditto his parquet flooring.'

Aubrey Walk was a posh small street in the posh area of
Campden Hill, which itself was the priciest part of Kensington;
but the house Slider and Atherton found themselves standing
in front of was far beyond expectations. It was detached, a mid-
Victorian villa standing in a small square of ground entirely
surrounded by high walls. The only ingress was through a stout
and high pair of electronically operated gates topped with a
security camera; the ten-foot-high walls were embellished with
revolving spikes and an almost invisible wire which Slider
guessed would trip an alarm if touched.

Through the gates they could see a gravel sweep up to the front door. Doors and windows were all hard shut and there was no sign of life. The upper ones seemed to have blinds pulled down over them. The square, handsome villa had a false parapet around the top of the façade which partly concealed the pitch of the roof, and Slider caught a glimpse of a satellite dish lurking there, together with a cluster of tall and powerful radio aerials and a telephone mast that looked like the upturned fitment from a giant rotisserie. Apart from the electronics and security, the condition of the house alone – the attention to detail, the quality of the paint job, the immaculate state of the gravel – would have been an indicator of the real-estate value, which, added to the location, the size and the detachedness, made it a seven-figure job.

'This bloke must be earning serious biccies,' Atherton remarked.

'Unless he inherited it,' Slider suggested.

'Either way, it makes me like him more.'

'How's that?'

'Because for a really seriously rich man it would be very easy for him to get his clothes from a posh outfitter up in Jermyn Street, or even from Paris or Milan or whatever. And of course,' he added fairly, 'he may do that as well. But he must have real taste and judgement to go to a funny old geezer like James Mason; and taste and judgement like that do not come automatically with the large bank balance.'

'You talk such unreconstructed cobblers sometimes,' Slider said. 'It's quite refreshing.'

On pressing the bell and announcing their business, they had the gate opened for them by some unseen remote hand. The front door did the same ghostly gape just as they reached it, snapping to behind them with a heavy clunk of dropping tumblers, leaving them in a small vestibule. Before them glazed doors gave a view of a beautiful hall of black-and-white marble tiles, pillars, gigantic chandelier, and a splendid staircase. A man was approaching them through the hall, and opened the glazed doors with a slight bow of the head. He was dressed immaculately in a butler's jacket, but he had a security guard's eyes, and there was something definitely un-Gordon Jackson about his build. Hudson over a lifetime of cleaning cutlery never lifted as much metal as this man must have had to, to achieve that boulder-in-a-bag look.

'Mr Bates is expecting you,' he said, and gestured for them to follow him across the hall. All three of them were wearing rubber soles – probably for the same professional reasons – and in the absence of their footfalls Slider could hear through the white silence of air conditioning the very faint whine of a security camera tracking them. Rich man's toys? But a house like this must be something of a target to burglars. And there were one or two fine pieces of furniture in the hall and old paintings on the staircase wall.

They climbed in Indian file on the crimson carpet which ran up the centre of the staircase. On the first floor the man opened a door and admitted them to a room which was rather surprising in its modernity. The floor was of bare, shining pale wood, the walls distempered white – the better, Slider supposed, to show off the modern paintings hung all around in plain polished steel frames. He didn't know anything about modern art, but he could see they were originals and therefore, presumably, valuable. A modern settee covered in scarlet cloth was against one wall, a spiky halogen standard lamp angled over it like a predatory bird. A massive glass coffee table stood before it, and on the other side were two leather-and-steel chairs so determinedly modern it was impossible to think of anyone sitting in them. They looked more like hide-covered Zulu shields bent in the middle.

The windows were completely covered in a thin white material which let in light but kept out the sun (for the sake of the paintings, perhaps?); not in the form of blinds but actually stretched taut and fixed somehow to the window frames themselves, so they were obviously a permanent fixture. It was not unattractive, though Slider thought it claustrophobic; but this was not the sort of room one would linger in anyhow. In the bay of the window was a desk of blonde wood, with a computer terminal standing on it, and the rest of the room was bare but for two enormous parlour palms in brushed-steel pots. The empty space, the blonde wood and the sunken halogen ceiling lights all made it look like a modern art dealer's gallery, and Slider wondered briefly if that was how Mr Trevor Bates made his money.

It was a room for having meetings in, that was all. Or perhaps it was an observation cell? There was no large suspicious mirror, but there were security cameras: three, small and discreet, tucked into the angle between the wall and the ceiling and covering the whole room; and Slider wouldn't have given a tenpenny piece for the chance that there weren't hidden microphones too. He drew Atherton's attention to the cameras with a flick of his eyes, and he nodded slightly. Neither of them was tempted to speak or move around. They stood where they had been left, looking at the pictures; and a few moments later the door opened again and a man came in.

Atherton could tell immediately from the suit that it must be Trevor Bates. He was not above medium height, but carried himself very upright. His body was well muscled but not out of proportion: the sort of figure a tailor would enjoy making for. His face was lean and firm, with a good straight nose, strong chin and prominent cheekbones, a face remarkable enough to have been called good-looking, though it was not conventionally handsome. His skin was pale and curiously clear, stretched lucently over those good bones like an advertisement for inner cleanliness, and decorated with one or two small freckles.

His suit – everything about his dress – was expensive, smart and conventional. The only unusual thing about him was his hair, which was a vigorous, dark red, brushed straight back from his face, and grown – thick, glossy and neatly trimmed – to shoulder length. The effect was startling, and probably it was done deliberately to put the opposition at a disadvantage: it was not what any chief executive would expect to have come walking in at his office door.

'Gentlemen,' Bates said, pausing inside the door and surveying them. Posing so they could look at him? Slider wondered. 'I am Trevor Bates. What can I do for you?'

He walked past them and stopped again, turning to face them so he was now cut out against the diffused light from the window. Good entrance, Slider thought. Definitely theatrical. Bates had what horsemen call 'presence', that indefinable quality that commands your attention and makes you keep looking. And indeed there was something horselike to Slider, the countryman, about that fleshless, clean-cut head and the thick backswept mane of hair. But there was nothing horselike about his eyes: grey, hard and intelligent, a businessman's eyes.

Slider introduced himself and Atherton. Bates nodded but did not ask them to sit down. 'I shan't take much of your time,' Slider said. 'I'm sure you must be a very busy man.' He moved his gaze round the room. 'Wonderful paintings. Is this your line of business – fine art?'

'I collect paintings. Sometimes I sell them.' He had a strong and vibrant voice like an actor's, and a neutral accent which told nothing about where he came from; but he spoke very precisely, as though he had often to talk to people whose English was not their first language. 'Call it investment rather than business. Investment and a hobby.'

'Oh, I see,' Slider said. 'You obviously know how to keep them and display them, so I wondered. What is your line of business, sir, if I may ask?'

Bates made a tiny movement of impatience, which Slider knew he was meant to see. 'Property, mostly. You had something you wanted to ask me?'

'Yes, sir. The name and address of your driver, if you'd be so kind.'

'My—?' Bates looked astonished, his eyebrows making perfect arcs above his eyes; but the eyes themselves were unmoved.

Atherton took over the tale. 'When you went to visit your tailor yesterday morning, the man who was driving your car was wearing a particular leather jacket, and we're rather anxious to ask him where he got it.'

'I hope you're not suggesting he stole it?' Bates said. 'I trust my driver implicitly.'

'No, no, nothing like that,' Atherton said. 'It's just that it is very like the jacket worn by the victim in a case we are investigating, and we hoped that if we could trace the jacket to its source we might find out something more about the victim.'

'Victim? Do you mean he's dead? It's a murder case you're talking about?'

'Yes, that's right,' Slider said. Bates waited with still eyes and Slider supplied the data silently requested. 'Lenny Baxter was the man's name.'

'Oh, yes, I saw something on television about it.'

'Did you know him, sir?' Slider asked.

'No, I've never met him,' Bates said with calm indifference.

'I recognise *you*, though, now I come to study you.' He looked at Slider thoughtfully for a moment and then said, 'Well, I doubt whether the information you want about the jacket will help you. You see, I gave that particular item of clothing to my driver.'

'Did you, sir?'

'Yes, I bought it for myself in a rash moment, but when I got it home I knew it wasn't really me. I very rarely dress casually – I prefer a suit, whatever I'm doing. So I gave it to Thomas.'

'When would that be, sir?'

'About two months ago, perhaps. Does it matter?'

'It may do. Where did you buy the jacket?'

'In the States. I can't remember where exactly.'

'Could you please try?'

'It was somewhere in Boston. A small shop in a side street. I had some time to kill between meetings and wandered in just to amuse myself. I bought the jacket on a whim, almost instantly regretted. I took it home with me but never wore it.'

'Why *did* you buy it?' Atherton put in, with an air of frank, clothesman to clothesman enquiry.

Bates frowned just slightly, as though the question were an impertinence, and then said, 'I liked the smell. There's something about new leather, don't you think?'

'It's the best reason for buying a new car,' Atherton said.

Bates smiled, but did not thaw. 'Quite. Well, gentlemen, if that's all?'

'Almost all,' Slider said apologetically. 'You wouldn't happen to have the receipt, I suppose?'

'I'm sure not. Why?'

'So that we can trace the shop or perhaps the maker. It seems a coincidence that our victim was wearing a jacket just like it—'

'Hardly,' Bates said shortly. 'These things are mass produced, after all.'

'But not in this country. And we have been given to understand that this jacket was not made for export.'

'Even if you're right about that – which, frankly I doubt,' Bates said impatiently, 'America is not exactly inaccessible, is it? Your man probably went there on holiday like thousands of others.'

'I'm sure you're right,' Slider said. 'It's just that we have to check all possible avenues. I'm sorry if it seems pointless to you, but there it is. We have to be thorough.'

Bates gave a perfunctory smile. 'Of course you do. It's your job.'

'Can you remember the name of the shop? Or even the street?'

'I'm sorry.'

'Well, if it should come back to you, perhaps you'd let us know. And if you could just give us the name and address of your driver – Thomas, you said his name was?'

'No, I don't think I can do that. I have a duty to protect my employees—'

'From helping the police?'

'From needless annoyance. I've already told you that I gave the jacket to Thomas. He knows nothing more about it than that.'

'He may have known the victim, Lenny Baxter.'

'Why on earth should he?' Bates said impatiently. 'That's a nonsensical thing to say. Like suggesting that all the people who wear Marks and Spencer shirts must know one another.'

'Nevertheless,' Slider said steadily, 'we would like just to speak to him. I'm sure you can have no reason to want to prevent that?'

The still grey eyes met his for a moment, and then he seemed to shrug faintly. 'Of course, if you insist. His name is Thomas Mark, and he lives in my staff quarters here.'

'May I see him now?'

'He is not in the house at present,' Bates said. 'He is out on business for me. However, if you really feel you need to see him, I can send him down to the police station when he returns.'

'Thank you, sir,' Slider said.

'And now, if you will excuse me,' Bates continued, stretching out his arm in an ushering gesture, 'I am a very busy man, and there is obviously nothing more I can do to help you.'

At the door Slider said, 'If you should find the receipt, sir, or remember the name of the shop—'

'Yes, I'll telephone you.'

Bates opened the door, and the butler type was standing outside, waiting to see them out. How had they arranged that? Slider wondered. Perhaps he had been watching the meeting on camera somewhere nearby.

When they were outside in the street and away from electronic eyes, Atherton turned to him and said, 'Phew! Sent away with a flea in our collective ear.'

'No use in being a high-powered businessman if you can't face down a couple of coppers.'

'Well, the jacket seems to be a dead end,' Atherton said. 'Another dead end, I should say, in a Hampton Court Maze of them.'

'What did you think of him?'

'Mr Bates? Bit of a poser. But sharp. Well, he must be to have done so well for himself, considering there was a time in his life when he must have been called Master Bates.'

'Yes, a handicap for any child. He had a lot of security equipment.'

'So does every house in that bracket.'

'And a security guard for a butler.'

'Better he takes care of himself than gets burgled or done over and wastes our time.'

'True again. Still, I confess to just a teensy touch of curiosity about Mr Bates. You go on back to the factory. I'm going to see a bloke I know in the property world.'

'It's no use setting your heart on that house,' Atherton advised. 'You'll only be disappointed.'

CHAPTER FOURTEEN

Lifestyles of the Rich and Shameless

Ben Tarrant was tall, good-looking, in his early thirties, and an estate agent, but still Slider liked him. He gave Slider an excellent cup of coffee, leaned back comfortably in his swivel chair and said, 'Oh, the Aubrey Walk house? Yes, I know it well. I didn't sell it myself, more's the pity, but I had a look at it for another client of mine. We were outbid, though. Quite handsomely. It's a very nice property. Eight bedrooms, all *en suite*, plus staff bedrooms on the top floor. Four recep, not counting the entrance hall – including a thirty-foot drawing room – and a swimming pool and gymnasium in the basement.'

'So Mr Bates has plenty of money?'

'Oh, yes. He undertook extensive renovations, and put in all the latest security electronics. Heavy stuff.'

'I saw some of them. Why so particular?'

Tarrant shrugged. 'He's a rich man, which makes him a target. And I think it's rather a thing with him, anyway.'

'Privacy?'

'Yes, that, but also the gadget side of it. Boys' toys, you know? You often find your wealthy bachelor goes in for that sort of thing.' He laughed. 'I'm a bit of a hi-fi fanatic myself.'

'So Bates is unmarried?'

'As far as I know. Mind, this is all hearsay – I don't know the man personally. But for a mega-rich guy, his name has never been linked with any famous woman, as far as I know. I mean, he doesn't turn up at gala openings with a Liz Hurley on his arm, as you'd expect.'

'But he does turn up at gala openings?'

'Oh, yes. You'll find pictures in the newspaper morgues,' Tarrant said intelligently. 'How else he takes his pleasure I don't know, but what with his business, the gym and the electronics, I don't suppose he's short of something to do with his time.'

'And what is his business?'

'Oh, I dare say he's got fingers in a lot of pies. When you get to his level, the divisions between one branch of business and another are extremely permeable. But his home branch, from what I understand, is property. Buying and selling. Developing. There's money to be made there if you get the right start. He buys run-down houses and does them up, and he's got a knack for spotting where the next yuppification is going to happen, getting in while the prices are still low and selling when they soar.

'Is Aubrey Walk his permanent home?'

'I think it's his main place, but he's got houses all over the show, here and abroad, and in the US – though he may only be holding them until the price is right to sell. He seems to have a fondness for this area, though. He's got a house in Loftus Road he's just done up. He's a big QPR fan, apparently.'

'I think I know it,' Slider said. 'I've passed a house that's been done up to the nines.'

'Yes, he doesn't cut corners. I think he's got a genuine feel for houses.'

'You seem to admire him,' Slider suggested.

Tarrant shrugged. 'Oh, I don't know the man at all, but I admire anyone who can make a fortune from his own efforts, and of course property's my field so it's close to my heart.'

'So you've never heard anything to his detriment?'

'No, I can't say I have. Why, do you want him to be a villain?'

'Not at all. I was just wondering.'

'Well, he's a businessman, and I suppose there must be areas of all big businesses that are less than snowy white. But I haven't heard anything, that's all I can say.'

'Are you sure it's all right for you to take time out to drive me to the airport?' Joanna asked. 'I don't want to get you into trouble.'

'Oh, I've got minions toiling away at the factory, covering my back,' Slider said.

'Mixed metaphor. It's a tricky one, this one, isn't it?'

'We'll be all right once we get on the M4,' Slider said, threading his way round Hammersmith Broadway.

Joanna smiled. 'I meant the case.'

'Oh. Well, it's not obvious, that's for sure. No blunt instrument covered in fingerprints matching those of the nearest and dearest. The thing that puzzles me most,' he added, 'is that there's no word on the network about it. We've got a lot of good informants between us, but no-one seems to know anything about this particular gang.'

'I suppose they're very well organised,' Joanna suggested.

'Well, we know that. But even if they're well kitted and sophisticated, someone ought at least to have *heard* of them.'

'You'd have thought so.'

'And it's not as if Lenny Baxter was doing anything very high-powered,' Slider added in frustration. 'An illegal bookie's runner doesn't amount to much. If his boss was only a tax-evader, was it worth murdering two people to cover that up?'

'Tip of the iceberg,' Joanna said. 'Maybe the boss had other businesses too, that were worth protecting.'

'I suppose he must have. He certainly put the fear of God up Everet. *And* Sonny Collins, who doesn't look as if he usually had trouble sleeping at night. But that brings us back to the question, why doesn't anyone know who he is?'

'Oh well,' Joanna said, 'you'll crack it. I have every faith in you.'

'It's not faith in me that's needed, it's a few witnesses. But we've still got doors to knock on and reports to filter from the TV appeal. Maybe something'll come up.' He stopped talking while he threaded the needle through the traffic emerging from the Fulham Palace Road and accelerated hard round the corner onto the Great West Road. Then, 'I'm sorry,' he said, 'that we haven't had much time together.'

'Luck of the draw,' she said. 'Couldn't be helped.'

'It was good seeing you, though. It was worth it from my point of view, even for those few hours.'

'Mine too,' she said. She seemed on the verge of saying something else, but did not.

He felt it was time to face trouble. 'About that serious talk you wanted to have.'

She laid a hand on his leg. 'It's all right.'

'We've got half an hour now.' She didn't say anything, and he pushed on bravely, 'Was it the usual? I mean, about us – your job and mine?'

'In a way,' she said. 'But don't worry now. It's not the time and place. It can wait.'

He felt a craven relief, but also a nervous doubt. If it could wait, did that mean she was becoming indifferent, giving up on him? The man in him wanted to put off that sort of 'talk' as long as possible, preferably for ever, while the detective in him wanted to know what was going on. 'I love you, you know,' he said, which was not what he meant to say, but worth a mention anyway.

'I know,' she said. 'I love you too.'

He slipped a sideways glance at her, and she appeared calm and untroubled. Oddly, this did not reassure him. She might look like that if she had got another man and wasn't coming back, just as much as if everything really was all right.

She caught him looking, and turned her face to him. 'Look, you've got this case to think about and I don't want to compete with that. It's something we need to talk through together, but I'd like to have your undivided attention when we do. But really, it can wait.'

One more thing to add to the seething pot, he thought.

Atherton waylaid him when he got back. 'Yon Thomas Mark came in, and guess what?'

'He said his boss had given him the jacket.'

'And?'

'He didn't know Lenny Baxter.'

'You're getting good at this. So that's another dead end.'

'Is it? We're looking for a big boss.'

'And you think Trevor Bates is it?'

'I haven't got as far as that yet. But the jacket bothers me.' They reached his office and he sat down behind his desk while Atherton propped himself as usual on the radiator, folding his long, long legs at the ankle. 'It's just such a coincidence.'

'Is it? I thought he had a good point, about Marks and

Spencer. Yes, I know this jacket isn't mass produced in this country, but we've only got James Mason's opinion that it isn't made for export. And you might just as well say it's a coincidence Bates and I both go to the same tailor, therefore I must be in it with him.'

'All right, fair point. But why did he buy the jacket at all? If, as he says, he never dresses casually—'

'Weak moment. Every man has his off day.' Atherton cocked an eye at his boss. 'What's your idea, then?'

'If – and it *is* a big if at the moment – Trevor Bates is our Moriarty, he wouldn't want it known that several of his employees were connected through these jackets. So maybe said he had given it to Mark to stop the investigation dead in its tracks. To turn it into the dead end you greeted me with.'

'That's a very long shot.'

'I know.'

'He'd have done better to deny all knowledge, surely? And why "several"? Mark and Lenny make two.'

'Everet Boston had a new suede jacket when I interviewed him. I noticed the smell.'

'You didn't mention that before.'

'It didn't connect, being suede and not leather; but it had the same lining, and Tom Garfield said one of the ones he sold Lenny was suede.' He pondered a moment, drumming his fingers softly on the desk top. 'You didn't get any joy from the Americans on Lenny Baxter?'

'The Cultural Legation? No, nobody recognised the mugshot or the tattoo.'

'How are you with them? Are you in?'

'I'm getting on very well with a nice young woman called Karen Phillips. Archivist. We talk books – she collects crime fiction first editions. Why?'

'I didn't want you to be stepping on toes, but if you've got a reasonable in, you might try them again with Trevor Bates, see if he's got any connections there.'

'Why should you think he has?'

'Oh, it's just a hunch, nothing more. We know he goes to the States a lot, and he lives in Holland Park, not far from the Legation building.'

'Pure propinquity, then?'

'Than which nothing propinks better. You could try them with the jacket as well.'

Atherton shrugged. 'You're the boss.'

'Yes, I am, aren't I?' Slider said pleasantly. 'In that case, you might get someone to fetch me a cup of tea – and tell Norma I've got a job for her.'

McLaren stuck his head round the door. 'Guv,' he said urgently. 'It's Everet Boston on the blower.'

'Right. Put him through. You know what to do.'

McLaren nodded and disappeared. Slider's phone rang and he picked it up. 'Slider,' he said.

There was a long, static-creating sigh of breath. 'Wha's happenin', man? Billy said to phone you. You gotter make it quick. It ain't safe.'

'I know,' Slider said. 'They're after you. That's why you've got to help me get them before they get you.'

Everet moaned. 'Oh man, I can't do this, awright? If I talk to you I'm dead, like ol' Herbie Weedon.'

'If they're half as good as you think they are, you haven't got a prayer. I'm your only hope, Ev. You've got to tell me who the boss is.'

'But I don' know. Straight! I'm tellin' you. That was the way he ran it. Hardly nobody never met him. It was all done froo contacts. All I knew, we called him the Needle.'

'Why was that?'

'I dunno. That was what we called him. I dunno what his real name is, and that's the honestroof.'

'So who was your contact?'

'Sonny Collins, o' course. Me an' Lenny bof.'

'Does Sonny know who the boss really is?'

'I dunno. He might. But if he does, he'll never tell you.' He sounded quite sure about that at least. 'It don't matter what you do, he won't talk.'

'Why did they kill Lenny?'

'Lenny, he wasn't a team player. He done fings on the side – stuff for himself. But the Needle like everfing tight, everfing done exactly the way he said, right, and no argument. Control freak, right? That way he reckoned we was all safe. But Lenny don't like to be told. I reckon he was a mistake, and that's why they rubbed him out.'

'Did Lenny know who the Needle is?'

'Maybe. I got him the job 'cos he was short of money, but he was a lot furver in than me. Maybe that's anuvver reason they done him. 'Cos he knew.'

'And Herbie? Why was he killed?'

Everet moaned. 'Oh, man, it was me put the bug in ol' Herbie's office. I was just doin' what I was tol', but I wish I never. He was all right, ol' Herbie.'

'Why did they want him bugged?'

'I reckon he must've knew somefing. Guessed it maybe. He's been around a long time, he knows a fing or two. Or maybe it was 'cos Lenny worked for him, and they knew Lenny was trouble. Like they was gettin' rid of anyone 'at might lead the fuzz to the Needle, you know?' This seemed to remind him of a deeper concern. 'You found Teena yet?'

'Not yet, but we're doing all we can. She's your cousin Mary, isn't she?'

There was a breathy pause, then he said on a failing note, 'Yeah. How d'you find out, man?'

'We're not as dumb as you think.'

'She was a good kid. Lenny ruined her. I fought he really loved her, you know? The bastard.'

'Ev, you've got to help us,' Slider said. 'It's not just you that's in danger, it's Teena as well.'

'Shit, man, I know that. D'you fink I don't know that? I seen what happens to girls wiv 'im. But I dunno where she is. I've been lookin' for her. That's why they're lookin' for me. Listen, I gotta go.'

'Wait a sec,' Slider said quickly. 'Where did you get that suede jacket you had when I saw you?'

'Oh, man! You wanna talk about *cloves* now?'

'It's important. Where did you get it?'

'I bought it off Lenny. He had 'em in the Phoenix one day, four of 'em, going cheap. Shit, man!' His voice changed, and there was an indeterminate scuffling sound from the background. 'I gotta go. For Chrissake find Teena, okay? If they get her – oh, shit!' Another scuffling noise, and the connection was broken.

Slider put down his receiver. He hadn't had a chance to ask about Susan. 'Shit, man,' he said in sincere imitation.

After a bit, McLaren came to the door. 'There's good news and bad news.'

'Isn't there always?'

'The good news is they've pinpointed the origin. The bad news is it's in Soho, and they can't get it down closer than three or four buildings.'

'Soho, eh? If I was running from the Needle I think I'd go a bit further afield,' Slider said.

'Bashy boys like Everet Boston wouldn't go out in the fields,' McLaren said. 'He'd be lost out of London.'

'He wanted to be lost. Well, let's get on with it.'

McLaren followed him out. 'Who's the Needle?' he asked belatedly.

'Your head's running about two minutes slow,' Slider told him.

The most likely candidate out of the possible buildings was one of those narrow brick houses turned into bedsits where toms plied their trade. Slider ruled out the Chinese restaurant. Of the other two buildings one was a hardware shop, with storerooms on the upper floors and a single flat at the top which was occupied, according to the proprietor, by a very nice man who worked as a waiter in Claridges. Slider couldn't see him harbouring Everet Boston; and besides, he was at work and there was no reply at the door. The other building had one of those weird shops on the ground floor that sell candles and tarot packs, joss-sticks and cushion covers decorated with sun and moon motifs, and a selection of daffy books on the occult, obscure eastern religions and feng shui. The upper floors were flats, but of a more decorous and permanent sort. Two elicited no reply and the occupants of the other two seemed respectable and genuinely puzzled.

So with the help of the local lads, they went through the tom house and waded through the ocean of lies, insults, righteous indignation and sheer bullshit, looking for even a square foot of firm ground. Prostitutes were a different breed nowadays from when he had worked Central in the balmy days of his youth, and with the hiving off of vice into a discrete unit the local boys had much less of a relationship with the toms than had been possible in his day. Many of the girls were shockingly young (had they been that young in the past? Maybe his memory was at fault) and many of them were not Londoners, while two at least were drug users. It was hard to tell if they were lying or not, as they would probably lie whatever you asked them. Slider's suspicions coalesced eventually on a tall and spectacularly ugly woman with dyed black hair who was somewhat older than the rest – nearer Everet's age – and had a West London accent you could have sliced and bottled. She also said she didn't know what they were talking about and she'd never heard of no Everet Boston, but when Slider caught her eye as she said it there was a flicker of consciousness there.

He looked permission to his colleagues and took her a little to one side. 'Look, love,' he said confidingly, 'it was me Ev was talking to on his mobile. I want to find him to protect him. I don't know how much he told you, but it's not me he's on the run from. If his ex-boss gets to him before I do, he's in deep trouble, you know what I mean? He was here, wasn't he?'

She looked uncertain, which was enough for him.

'Where's he gone? What scared him off? Did someone come for him?'

'Nah, he fought someone was coming, the tosser, but it was only a customer for one of the girls downstairs,' she said with the usual ripe contempt of a pro for anything in trousers. 'But he went anyway. He said you'd trace his call.'

'So where did he go?'

'I dunno. He never said.'

'Come on, love. It's for his own safety.'

'Straight up, I don't know where he went. And I don't care neither,' she added. 'It's nuffing to do with me.'

Slider sighed and tried again. 'Look, if you know where he's gone, or even where he might be, it'd be better for you to tell me. Don't forget, if I could trace his call, his ex-boss might be able to. He might be round here soon asking the same questions, only he won't be nice about it, d'you know what I mean?'

She looked alarmed. 'Oh, blimey, I told him not to come here! But I had to let him in. He was good to me in the old days. Now what's he gone and done, the silly sod? What's he got me into?'

'Tell me where he's gone. It's the only way to help him.'

'I don't know. That's the trufe. If I knew I'd tell you.'

Slider believed her now. 'Well, you might want to get away from here for a few days. Have you got somewhere you can go?'

'Me sister's,' she said after a moment's thought. 'I can stop wiv her for a bit.'

'All right. But just think for a minute – did Everet ever mention anyone called Susan?'

'I dunno. Maybe.' She shook her head, evidently trying to be helpful now. 'I'm tryna think.'

'Was she a working girl?'

'Susan.' More brow furrowing. 'Wait a minute, was it Susie Mabbot? She run this posh house down Notting Hill, introduction only, you know the sorta thing? Businessmen an' escorts. I never worked for her, but Ev knew her from way back. Maybe that's who you want.'

'I've checked with all the main renting agencies for central London,' Swilley said, 'and there's two that specialise in letting to American service people and embassy staff. One of them – Hughes Garvey – pricked up their ears all right when I mentioned our Mr Bates. He apparently has quite a few nice properties they handle for him on short leases, mostly flats but one or two houses – including that one in Loftus Road, which he's only just given them.'

'And what do they think of him?'

'I didn't get the impression they knew him personally, only that he's a respectable businessman and very astute. Yanks are favoured tenants and letting to them's the top end of the market, so you're looking at nice properties and everything done above board. The US Government's very particular about the way their people behave when they're abroad, so when you let to one of them you've got Washington and the Pentagon standing guarantee.'

'Yes, I see,' said Slider. 'You couldn't want a better reference than that, could you?'

'No, boss,' Swilley said. 'It looks as though Mr Bates is squeaky clean.'

'Yes,' said Slider.

'And the business with the jacket is just coincidence.'

'That's right,' said Slider.

Swilley eyed him. 'All of which convinces you that he must be a villain, right?'

'Right.' Slider smiled ruefully. 'Am I just being perverse?'

'I've known your hunches to come off before,' she said politely.

'But?'

'But just be careful, eh, boss? If this bloke is clean and he finds you've suggested otherwise – well, he doesn't sound the sort to let bygones be bygones. If he hasn't got a tame lawyer up his sleeve I'm a monkey's uncle.'

'Nothing simian about you,' Slider said. 'I wonder who paid for David Stevens to appear at Sonny Collins's elbow?'

'Wondering's free.'

'If we could establish some link between Sonny Collins and Mr Bates . . .' Slider mused. Swilley waited. 'Look, if this bloke's that big, there must be some biographical information about him somewhere. Try the newspaper morgues, *Who's Who* – you know the form. All the usual places. Anything about his past and his private life you can dig out.'

'Okay.'

'I wish we could find the girl. No nibbles on her yet?'

'The usual number, I should think.'

'Nibbles, not nipples.'

'No, we haven't scored with the name Teena Brown, but of course she might have changed it again. You think she's important?'

'I don't know. Maybe. Boston's certainly worried about her, and it may not all be family feeling.'

'Well, we'll keep looking.'

'Right. Meanwhile, Atherton's out being urbane at the Cultural Legation, and Sonny Collins is being watched. Not that I think that will produce anything. If they're as careful as Everet Boston thinks, nothing will be passing through Sonny Collins for the time being. They'll have frozen that bit of the operation.'

'If Collins is the key, why not just get him in and lean on him again?' Swilley suggested.

'It wouldn't do any good. He'd just sit us out. We've got to get more information, something we can really hit him with – something that scares him more than the Needle does.'

'And what might that be, I wonder?' Swilley speculated.

'Maybe it doesn't exist,' Slider admitted.

CHAPTER FIFTEEN

A Time to be Bald and a Time to Dye

'All right, settle down,' Slider said. The sunny spell had broken at last, and outside the windows the sky was a uniform blank off-white, depthless, as though the whole world had been enclosed in Vitrolite. It was still warm though, and the troops had all taken off their jackets, letting loose a faint prickle of male sweat into the air to compete with six different after-shaves and Norma's *Eau de Givenchy*.

'First of all, I've got some sad news. I've been informed by Mr Palfreyman that Mr Porson's wife died in hospital last night.' There was a murmur of comment. 'I know he has the deepest sympathy of every one of us. I think we should send him a card to that effect.'

'I'll do it, boss,' Norma said.

'Thanks. Get everyone to sign it and come to me for his home address. Now, I imagine that means we won't be seeing anything of him for a day or two more, but it would probably cheer him up if we could get a result on this Baxter business, so let's see what we've got.'

Hollis took over. 'Our first suspect was Eddie Cranston, because he'd had a fight with Baxter. But we've got no evidence against him.'

'I think Eddie's too much of a plonker to have done it and not give himself away,' said McLaren.

Swilley performed an introduction. 'Pot – kettle. Kettle – pot.' McLaren made a face at her.

'I can't believe it's Eddie,' Atherton said. 'I think he just stum-bled over the corner of the operation because of his beef with Lenny Baxter. Remember the very first interview with Collins? He didn't mind giving up Eddie's name, while he denied all knowledge of Lenny. He was happy for us to go and investigate Eddie's little games because it led us away from the real danger.'

'Also,' Swilley said, 'his alibi is Carol Anne Shotter and she seems to be completely straight. Not that women haven't lied for men before now—' She waited for the whoops to die down. 'But she comes across all right and everyone I've spoken to who knows her thinks she's honest.'

'All right, let's put Eddie aside,' Slider said. 'Next up is Everet Boston.'

'His alibi checks out as far as it goes,' Hollis said. 'He was definitely in the Snookerama snooker hall – half a dozen witnesses – but nothing to say where he was after one o'clock. He could have got back to the park by about half past, and we don't know for sure exactly when Baxter was killed. And we know he had a motive – some kind of ill-treatment of his cousin Mary, aka Teena Brown.'

'As against that,' Slider said, '*he* came to *us* with information, which he'd hardly have done if he'd offed Lenny. And he's apparently now scared for his life and in hiding.'

'I don't think he did it,' Swilley said. 'What you said is right, boss. He wouldn't have come forward if he had. He came forward because he had a beef against Lenny that he wanted to air. And there's no evidence against him anyway.'

'There's no evidence against anybody,' Anderson pointed out.

'Which makes it more likely that it was a professional killing, punishment by the gang,' Swilley went on, 'which is what Everet said.'

She looked round to gather opinion, realised that no-one was looking at her and swivelled in her seat. Detective Superintendent Porson was standing in the open doorway. The sight of him had frozen the entire room in shock. It was not that he looked utterly drawn and about a thousand years old – anyone might have expected that – but that he was not wearing his wig. His high bald dome was pale and strangely bumpy, and the few wisps of grey hair round the edges seemed only to emphasise the nakedness, as pubic hair contributes to pornography. It was somehow indecent. All these years he had toted the appalling rug about, denied its existence and vented his fury on anyone who so much as looked at it, let alone mentioned it; and now he had simply abandoned it. If he had stood there totally starkers with his dangly bits on parade it could not have caused more consternation.

Slider rallied himself. It was too bad for everyone to be staring at the old boy. He scraped up a voice and said, 'We weren't expecting to see you in here today, sir. We heard the news. I know I speak on behalf of everyone when—'

'None o' that,' Porson said sharply, cutting him off with an imperiously lifted hand. His pink-rimmed eyes swept the room. 'Consider it said. We've got work to do. I've had Mr Palfreyman on the dog, chewing my ear off. He's not as compunctionate as you lot, apparently. He's agitating to take this case away, given I've taken my hand off the steerage. Fulsome apologies and all that, but wouldn't it be better under the circs, de-dah-de-dah. So let's get on with it. I haven't lost my marbles yet. I can still out-copper any bastard with a degree in sociology.' He quelled Atherton's rising comment with a look and nodded to Slider. 'Carry on where you picked up.' And he sat down on a desk at the back of the room, forcing them all to turn their heads away from him.

'All right,' Slider said, and with an effort caught hold of his thread. 'That brings us to Sonny Collins, who on the surface of it looks very tasty. However, he has no criminal form.' He looked at Hollis. 'Have you managed to get anything on his service record?'

'Yes, guv. That was interesting. He was in trouble a few times for fighting, but nothing major. The best bit comes at the end. He was in a shore-based posting in Hong Kong and got in a fight one night outside a bar with a local. The other bloke produced a knife and stabbed him. That's when he lost his eye, apparently. In retaliation Sonny hit him under the chin so hard it broke his neck. Well, all hell let loose as you might expect. There was the civilian police enquiry as well as the naval one, and questions asked right up to the Governor and the diplomatic bag.'

'Be more respectful of the Governor's wife,' Atherton said sternly.

Hollis resumed. 'Anyway, the other bloke was a known troublemaker and already wanted by the Hong Kong police on several other counts. So, given that witnesses saw him get Collins with the knife, and his mates swore Collins wasn't carrying –

which he was known not to – it was brought in self-defence. When Collins came out of hospital he got his discharge on medical grounds and there was no court martial. Otherwise he couldn't have stopped in Hong Kong, o' course.'

'Did he?' Slider asked.

'Opened a tattoo parlour in Kowloon, ran it for a couple of years before coming home and going into the licensed trade. Must've tattooed a few tars in his time there. Maybe he did his own neck. I'm wondering what other services he offered as well as the skin pics.'

'Yes, that might be worth knowing. Any way you can follow it up?'

'I'll have a go,' Hollis said. 'I might be able to trace some of his mates.'

'Okay. Well, Collins is tasty, and he denies knowing Lenny Baxter, though Eddie Cranston was sure enough that Lenny was a regular at the Phoenix to wait for him there; and of course Eddie says Collins called Lenny by name. And there's Everet Boston's statement that Collins was the gang control for both him and Lenny Baxter. Which all looks nice and suspicious.'

'But Collins has got a good alibi,' Anderson said.

'Not for the whole night,' said Mackay.

'For the likeliest bit,' Anderson asserted.

'Yes, what about that alibi?' Slider said.

Atherton looked at him patiently. 'I know you don't like it, but if Collins actually did the killing he's not likely to have arranged himself an alibi up to four o'clock and then gone a-murdering afterwards, is he?'

'And besides,' said Anderson, 'we've got that Elly Fraser bird's statement about the two heavies walking down Frithville Gardens at two o'clock, which is right in the middle of his alibi time.'

'We don't know they were the killers,' Swilley said. 'And don't forget there was a report from one of the residents saying there was no chain on the gate when he came home from the pub just after midnight.'

'Yes, but that's not what he said the first time his door was knocked on,' Mackay pointed out. 'He only came up with that after the telly appeal. Probably just wanted to make himself important. You know how they do.'

'I don't think Sonny Collins actually did the killing,' Slider said to Atherton. 'But I still don't like that alibi.'

'Guv, I think it's genuine,' said Anderson. 'Liam the barman at the Shamrock remembers very well, because he said Sonny Collins hadn't been in for months, and when he did come in, he never stayed that long, just had a couple of drinks to unwind and went away. And Liam was the one called the cab for him, so he knows what time he left. And the cab company confirms the booking, and the driver identified Collins and said he dropped him outside the Phoenix about ten past four.'

'That's exactly what I mean,' Slider said. 'It's all so perfect. He hadn't been to the Shamrock in months, so why suddenly did he go there that particular evening and stay so long, with extra precautions to establish the time he left?' He answered his own question. 'Perhaps because he knew Lenny was going to be eliminated. Maybe he was warned to make sure he was covered.'

He looked round, and saw no absolute resistance to the idea. 'Let's look at the sequence of events,' he continued. 'Lenny goes into the Phoenix, as we're told he often did, and if we believe Everet Boston he had every reason to because Collins was his contact. He goes in just before eleven, let's say to transact some business with Collins or to give or receive a message. He's not expecting to be molested by Eddie Cranston. An argument starts. Collins tells him to take it outside. Eddie tries to make a fight of it but Lenny knows he mustn't get involved with that sort of thing, so he slugs Eddie a good one and instead of following it up, legs it like one John Smith, and heads home.

'We next find him talking to some professional minder types outside his own home at about half past eleven. Shortly after that Sonny Collins pushes off to establish himself an alibi. And later that night Lenny is killed very neatly and efficiently by a single stab wound to the heart by some one or some ones who go through his pockets to remove something but leave his wad of money behind. Later again, Lenny's house is expertly turned over and his girlfriend hastily packs her bags and runs for it – we don't know whether before or after, or whether the people who searched the house also took her with them, either by force or otherwise. Everet is sure they're after the girl – presumably because she knows too much about the outfit, maybe even who the Needle is.'

'Guv,' said Mackay, 'if it was the minders who done Lenny, why didn't they do it when they met him at half eleven? Why wait until later?'

'Well, they wouldn't want to kill him in a public street, would they?' Anderson said.

'They could have taken him inside his house and done it there,' Mackay said.

'Yes,' Slider said. 'That's a point. Any suggestions?'

'Maybe he wasn't due to be done then,' McLaren said. 'Maybe the minders reported back something he'd said, and it was that that made the Needle put the order out on him.'

'Or maybe he'd said something to Sonny and Sonny reported it,' Swilley said. 'And got his orders to get himself an alibi at the same time.'

'Maybe what Sonny reported was the fight with Eddie,' Hollis said.

'That's certainly a possibility,' Slider said. 'According to Everet, Lenny wasn't a team player and that was what the boss objected to. We've got him running for Herbie Weedon and crossing money to fund his gambling habit. We've got him selling dope in the park on the side. And we've got a lot of iffy goods in his flat which he may have been processing outside of his job for the boss. If he was seen as the weak link and likely to bring police attention down on the gang, that would be good reason to get rid of him.'

'They got rid of Herbie Weedon just for wanting to talk to me,' Atherton said. 'And Everet Boston is running for his life. Could it be that the boss is determined to stop us making any connection between the lowlife and him?'

'Maybe what was lifted from Lenny's pocket, apart from his keys, was some kind of paperwork that would link him with the boss or the gang,' said Swilley. 'His betting book, for instance, maybe with a telephone number or something in it. He must have written down the bets somewhere, and we never found anything like that.'

'Yes,' said Slider, 'and there was an inkstain on the inside of his empty pocket. Maybe he habitually carried his betting book in there, along with a Biro, which leaked at some point, as they always do.'

'Brilliant, boss. And we thought something was lifted from beside his telephone at home – which could have been an address book or something similar.'

'But why kill him in the park like that?' Mackay said. 'I mean, it's a public place. Anyone could have seen them.'

'Well, evidently anyone didn't,' Atherton said. 'When you think about it, it's one place they could be sure there'd be nobody around, and it's not overlooked. They've only got to walk up the street and through the gates – no suspicious climbing over because they know Lenny's got the key. And we know nobody notices anyone walking up the street, particularly late at night, because he's been doing business there for years and we've never had word of it. And the woman who *did* see the two heavies walking away didn't think anything about it. She didn't come forward for a week, thinking there was nothing in it.'

'There's people coming and going to the BBC's back door all the time,' Swilley said. 'I suppose that's cover.'

'I've said before,' Slider continued, 'that the way Lenny was left, sitting on the swing, looked like a joke. That and the park chain round Herbie Weedon's neck could point to the boss having a nasty sense of humour.'

Porson spoke up suddenly, surprising them all: they'd forgotten he was there.

'All this is all very well, but it's all supperstition. Maybe, maybe, maybe. You've got no murder weapon, no witnesses, no suspects. If it was a gang killing, it'll have been orders to some hood to carry it out. There'll be nothing to connect the killer with the victim.'

'Except the boss,' Slider said. 'We'd have to trace it back from the boss.'

'Ah yes, the boss. But you don't know who he is. You've got no evidence he even exists, apart from the word of one villain on the run.'

'I think he exists. I think Everet Boston is telling the truth,' Slider said steadily. 'He's got no reason to lie; it makes sense of a lot of things; and he's genuinely scared, both for himself and for his cousin.'

'Well, as it happens,' Porson said, 'I agree with you. But it doesn't get you any further forward. Who is the boss?'

'Everet called him the Needle.'

'And you think it's this Trevor Bates bloke?'

Slider hesitated. 'There's nothing to connect him except the leather jacket, and that could be a coincidence.'

Porson eyed him cannily. 'But you don't think it is?'

'It's just a hunch,' he admitted.

'Well, I'm all for hunches,' Porson said. 'You can't learn hunches at bloody Keele University.'

Palfreyman really had got up his nose, Slider thought. 'Four jackets,' he said aloud. 'Garfield sold Lenny four. He wore one himself, sold one to Everet and one to Thomas Mark. Who had the other one, I wonder? And why did Bates lie about it? To cut us off at the pass? But how much did he know about the jacket's origin? I suppose there's no reason Mark shouldn't have told him, just idly in conversation, that he bought it from Lenny. That would be enough to make him want to stop that line of enquiry.'

But Atherton shook his head. 'You don't know for sure that's where Mark got it, guv. Anyway, Bates apparently makes a fortune out of property. Why would he want to mix himself up with stuff like illegal bookmaking, and small-time crooks like Boston and Baxter? Why would he risk it? It doesn't make sense.'

'A lot of fingers in a lot of pies. Diversification. Running a huge empire. Pulling the threads and manipulating people. Pulling the wool over our eyes.'

'A Moriarty complex, in fact,' Atherton said. 'But we've no evidence at all that he's crooked.' He stopped.

Slider looked at him. 'Something just occurred to you.'

'My contact at the Cultural Legation,' he said, a little unwillingly. 'When I asked her if she knew Trevor Bates, and described him, she said no, but,' he shrugged unwillingly, 'I think she was lying.'

'A hunch, eh?' Slider said innocently.

'It was just a look in her eye. But I'll swear she was straight. Apart from anything else, the Americans are very careful about the people they send over.'

'All right,' Porson said. 'Here's what we do. Sonny Collins is your man. Turn his drum over. Check his phone records. I'll okay the warrants. And go into his past with a tooth-comb. Also this Trevor Bates. Find some connection between them. We can't touch Bates as it is. Until we find out he's not pure as the driven, he's sacrospect. But if we can get anything on him at all, we can look into his financial affairs, check his bank accounts, and I think we'll find enough to start putting pressure on him. There's not one of these entry preeners can stand being put under the microphone. And,' he added on a different note, 'go up and down Frithville Gardens, ask everyone who they saw coming and going. Yes, I know you've asked 'em already, but ask 'em again!' He looked round them, and the animation faded from his face, leaving a bleakness as embarrassingly naked as his head. '*That*'s police work,' he said. 'Ninety-nine per cent perspiration, and one per cent sheer bloody luck. Get on with it.'

Since Sonny Collins lived in the flat above the Phoenix, there was some urgency in getting there with a search team before the pub opened. So when the warrant was forthcoming, Slider and Atherton went round there with half a dozen uniform PCs and Porson's promise that if they found anything at all interesting he would order up a Polsar team to take the place apart.

What they found when they got there was no answer at any door or to the only telephone number they knew. The pub was silent, the curtains were drawn upstairs, and the youth with a ring in his left nostril who acted as barman (cash in hand – no National Insurance, no pain, Slider would bet) was hanging around, knocking at the door and peering up at the flat. As soon as the cars drew up he had it away on his tiny toes. To chase a fleeing man is as instinctive to a copper as to chase rabbits is to a dog, and PC D'Arblay was out of the car before it had come to a complete halt; but chummy had too substantial a lead. He shot down the cut between Evans House and Davis House and was lost to them. Slider consoled D'Arblay as he came panting back that they could find him if they needed him.

'But I expect,' Slider said when their own knockings had gone unanswered, 'he was just trying to report for work.'

'But work there is none,' said Atherton. 'Where's our Sonny? Gone away?'

Slider looked up at the curtained windows and shivered a little in the May warmth. Somewhere nearby – in the park probably – a blackbird was singing, and the chippy in the parade of shops had started frying the first batch of the day. Those were the sounds and smells of life; but the closed curtains gave him a premonition of death.

'All right,' he said. 'Force an entry.'

There was a separate door round the side for the flat. Renker and Coffey burst it in, while the others held the gathering crowd at bay. Inside was a tiny lobby with a locked door into the bar and stairs straight ahead. Slider listened, and then with Atherton at his shoulder started up the stairs.

The flat consisted of a sitting room, bedroom, kitchen and bathroom, all with the unrelieved flat walls and mean proportions of the sixties. It was sparsely furnished, and unexpectedly clean and tidy, the walls painted cream, the floors lino-tiled, everything stowed away in cupboards as if the owner were still at sea and under orders. There was also a spare room which was set up as an office and contained, as well as what was needed to administer a public house, a powerful two-way radio. So that, Slider thought, was how information and orders were passed without bothering British Telecom.

Mr Colin 'Sonny' Collins was in his desperately tidy bedroom, lying naked under a sheet on the hard single bed. On the locker beside the bed was an empty pint glass which seemed to have held water, and empty pill bottle with the label removed, and a bunch of keys with a luggage label attached on which was written in capitals HW. Collins's eyes were closed, his hands folded together on his chest as if he had composed himself with an easy conscience for sleep, but he was dead and cold.

'Pipped at the post,' Atherton said. 'Blast and damn it! So they decided to sacrifice him?'

Or did he sacrifice himself? Slider wondered. He liked that possibility even less.

'But how did they know we were on the way?' Atherton went on. 'You don't think they're bugging us, do you?'

'I hope not,' Slider said. 'But I dare say they're bugging Everet Boston. Mobiles are relatively easy to hack into. He pointed us at Sonny. Don't forget he said he was the control for him and Lenny.'

'So they didn't trust Sonny to keep his mouth shut?'

'Maybe. Maybe he didn't trust himself. Whatever he might have told us, we'll never find it out now.' He looked at the pill bottle – sleepers? Probably. You could force a person to take sleepers by threatening a worse death, but Slider couldn't see Sonny Collins caving in without a fight, and there was no sign of a fight, on him or in the flat. But if he took them voluntarily, what order of loyalty did that suggest? It wasn't nice to think about. 'Maybe the pill bottle's a ruse and we'll find there was a different cause of death,' he said. 'Mustn't pre-empt the post-mortem.'

Atherton nodded. 'What about those keys, left prominently for our attention?'

'I shouldn't be surprised to discover that HW was Herbie Weedon, would you?'

'Not overwhelmingly. We're being led by the nose to the supposition that Sonny killed Herbie.'

'Well, maybe he did,' Slider said. 'Anything's possible.'

Porson looked even more haggard than in the morning. 'This is getting out of hand, God damn it! What the hell is going on? We've already got two murders on our hands and now this! We can't have our ground littered with bodies like Amsterdam after an England away! And not a suspect for any one of the three!'

'I think we're meant to take it as confession and suicide,' Slider said cautiously. 'The keys are the keys to Weedon's office and house. We're meant to assume that Collins did Weedon and then topped himself.'

'Then why no note?'

'Maybe they thought that would look too obvious. This way is more natural-looking – more subtle.'

Porson gave him a ripe and goaded look. 'Subtle? A subtle criminal? This is not Ealing Studios! What are you going to give me next, the cockney char? The tart with the heart of gold?'

Slider withstood the blast. 'They left the keys in case we wanted the evidence. The way I see it, it's an invitation to us to let it go.'

'An invitation?'

'It won't be hard for them to guess we're over-extended – it's all over the papers every week – and here's a way for us to clear up something, get the Brownie points and release some manpower.'

Porson's frown was terrific, but he was following, however unwillingly. 'That still leaves Lenny Baxter.'

'Maybe they're just hoping we'll write that off, let it go by default. After all, we've got no evidence and nothing to link him with anyone.'

'Except Everet Boston.'

'Yes,' said Slider.

'What price his life now?' Porson moved restlessly, the light from the window throwing his head into planes and his face into shocking hollows. How much weight had he lost, for Pete's sake? 'I've put out an all units on friend Boston, but if he keeps using his mobile like the plonker he is, I don't stack any hope on us finding him before they do. But what kind of bloody people are they? This isn't Chicago!' He paced about a bit, thinking. 'Where do we go from here, if it's not a rhysterical question. We've got no concrete evidence on either the Baxter or the Weedon murders,' he continued, 'which is what you'd expect if they're professional. No forensic, no witnesses. And Collins either was or wasn't suicide, and there'll be no evidence there either, you can bet your bottom boots. So unless we can pick up Everet Boston, we've got nothing to connect any of this with the gang or the boss – Needle, or whatever they call him. What a bloody shambles! So what are you working on?'

'Trying to trace the Susan or Susie Mabbot we think may have been the friend of Boston and Baxter, in the hope that she may know where Baxter's girlfriend Teena is.'

'What good will that do if you do find this Teena?' Porson snapped suspiciously.

'She lived with him, so she may know who the two minders were who talked to him that night, and she may have seen who searched the house.'

Porson snorted. 'May and might butter no parsons! I can't see any future in wasting effort trying to find her. If she knew anything they'll have done her as well. You said yourself she might have been lifted when they searched Baxter's gaff. What else?'

'We're trying to find out more about Trevor Bates.'

'But you don't know he is the Needle. You've no reason even to think so, except for that bloody jacket.'

'And the sophisticated electronics equipment and the radio and telephone masts on his house.'

'Anyone could have those.'

'Anyone could, but he *has* got them. I think he's worth looking at.'

'All right. But carefully. We don't want a case against us. What else?'

Slider shrugged. 'Keep slogging on, looking for witnesses.'

'Right,' Porson said gloomily, and turned to stare out of the window. 'Someone saw something. Sometimes it takes months. Sometimes it takes years. Look at the Dando and the Russell murders. But we're not rolling over. I'm not having some bastard smart alec villain treating my manor like his own private playground.'

Death, Slider thought, had suddenly become personal to Porson. 'We'll get him, sir,' he said, which was as near as he could go to offering sympathy.

Porson turned. 'See you bloody do!' he barked, but there was understanding in his red-rimmed eyes.

CHAPTER SIXTEEN

Intimations of Mortality

The search of Collins's house had revealed in the storeroom a vast stock of cigarettes, including Lenny's own favoured brand Gitanes, for which there was no paperwork upstairs in the office, and which it was pounds to peanuts had been brought in illegally from the low-tax continent; ditto various cases of spirits. Evidently Sonny, either on his own behalf or for the Boss, had been used to augment his income by the sale of these private stocks without involving the brewery. Slider wondered if the smuggling was itself another of the gang's operations. With cigarettes retailing at £4.50 a pack here and purchasable for £1.20 in Spain, there was plenty of leeway in between for a healthy profit to be made. Perhaps Sonny's pub was a distribution centre? The brewery was not going to be happy about that.

The brewery had of course been told that Sonny was dead and that the Phoenix was closed while the investigation went on. It was agitating for more information and for a date when it could reopen with a new manager, and the phone calls were coming from progressively further up the hierarchy; to which Slider had responded at last by leaving orders for all such calls to be rerouted direct to Mr Palfreyman. Palfreyman got the big money, let him have the nuisance, Slider thought. He had enough to do without that.

The rest of the search had revealed a very Spartan lifestyle for Mrs Collins's son Colin. The bed was hard and narrow, the floors uncarpeted, the kitchen sparsely stocked. Even the soap in the bathroom was Wright's Coal Tar. Personal possessions were few, with the notable exceptions of an old and beautiful piece of scrimshaw work, and a ship in a bottle which Slider thought might be late eighteenth-century or early nineteenth. But these two rather exquisite esoterica only seemed to sharpen the question of what Sonny spent his money on. There seemed little point in a criminal career if you didn't enjoy yourself with your ill-gotten gains. Maybe he was stashing it away for a comfortable retirement? But the kind of spare living exemplified in the flat did not argue a disposition that craved comfort. Maybe it was just the power he had craved. That at least made sense. But why, then, had he so obligingly killed himself?

One gratifying thing emerged from the search, however. Sonny's clothes were generally few and monotonous, leaning heavily towards the black trousers and teeshirts. Everything was spotlessly clean, beautifully ironed, and squared neatly away in true Bristol fashion. The man even ironed his underpants, Slider discovered, with a sense that it was more than he really needed to know. But hanging in the wardrobe (the first wardrobe he had ever seen in a private house where you could actually push things back and forth along the rail) was a black leather jacket with a rather distinctive tartan wool lining in caramel shades; a jacket new enough to make the wardrobe smell like the inside of a Rolls-Royce.

'The fourth jacket!' Slider had exclaimed happily when they discovered it; at which Atherton had warned him sternly not to jump to conclusions. But it was a perfect match with Lenny Baxter's. It gave Slider great satisfaction to have this small part of the puzzle sorted.

'But it doesn't help,' Atherton pointed out. 'All it proves is that Lenny knew Sonny, and we knew that already.'

'I know,' Slider said, 'but when little things like that trip up the mighty, it makes it all seem worthwhile. Lenny Baxter has four leather jackets and sells one of them to Thomas Mark, driver to the great mogul Trevor Bates—'

'Who we have no reason to suspect is the Needle,' Atherton interpolated.

Slider waved that away. '—and thus provides a link without which no-one would ever have looked in Bates's direction. It's the mad bitch Chance at her most trivial. It's beautiful.'

'So you're determined to believe it's Bates?' Atherton asked.

Slider tapped his chest. 'I feel it. In here. He lied about the jacket, you see. That was his mistake.'

'But you don't *know* Mark got the jacket from Lenny,' Atherton said, frustrated. 'Bates could have bought it in Boston. After all, how did he know it was American if he didn't buy it there himself?'

'I suppose Lenny told Mark and he told Bates.'

Atherton shook his head. 'You're more obsessed with jackets than Spud-u-Like.'

Slider looked at him, amused. 'You're determined it isn't Bates, aren't you? What is it, his suits?'

'I've no feelings about the man either way. I just don't like to see you run ahead of your data. It's not like you.'

'What's a man without a hunch?' Slider said lightly.

'Tall,' said Atherton.

Freddie Cameron telephoned.

'Working on a Saturday?' Slider wondered.

'So are you,' Cameron pointed out. 'Got to catch up with the workload somehow. Besides, we've got builders in, and it offends my delicate sensibilities to watch them spend all day drinking tea and listening to Kiss FM on my penny.'

'What are you having done?'

'We're having the bathroom refitted, God help us. Of course the brunt of it falls on Martha, but what drives me mad is that they could have finished a week ago if they'd just got on with it. If it was me, I'd sooner work hard for a week and have a week off than slop around for a fortnight for the same money. But what do I know?'

'Start taking your work home,' Slider suggested. 'That'd have 'em out in no time.'

'The speed one of them moves, I suspect he's clinically dead anyway,' Cameron said bitterly.

'So what have you got for me?'

'The Collins PM. The report's in the post, but I thought you'd like to know that it was the pills that killed him.'

'That's something, I suppose.'

'It was a short-acting barbiturate, secobarbital. He'd had a large dose – blood levels were 20mg. Death would have oc-curred within about half an hour, from respiratory collapse.'

'Any idea where he might have got hold of it?' Slider asked.

'Well, as you know, old boy, barbiturates haven't been prescribed in this country for twenty years, or in any of the other civilised countries, but they're more or less freely available in places like Mexico and China, so they leech in across the borders onto the illicit market. My personal preference for country of origin in this case would be China. I found remnants of the capsule cases in the stomach, and they were coloured a shade of blue that I've come across before with Chinese drugs. There's a large Chinese population in every major city in the world, and half the cargo ships on the high seas are crewed by Chinese, so distribution's no problem. That's only an opinion, mind; I can't prove it.'

'Your opinion's usually good enough for me.'

'By the way, I didn't find any evidence of force – no bruises or chipped teeth – so it does look like suicide. And, unusually, there was no alcohol in the bloodstream. He did it stone-cold sober in the clear light of morning. Odd, that.'

'It's not just odd, it's creepy,' Slider said.

'Greater love hath no man?' suggested Freddie.

'Yes, but love for what?' said Slider.

The Chinese restaurant Karen Phillips chose for her rendezvous with Atherton was down one of the little side turnings off Holland Park Avenue. It had ground-floor and basement dining rooms, and the latter was low-ceilinged and divided into a multitude of secret little booths by bamboo screens and large palms in pots. The lighting was dim, from low-hanging bulbs shrouded in red paper lanterns, and monotonous Chinese music from a loop tape added to the authentically mysterious atmosphere of an opium den in a *Carry On* film.

Miss Phillips herself, a strikingly pretty young woman with thick, dark, curly hair and innocent brown eyes, was evidently deep into the character of conspirator. She had chosen a booth in the darkest corner and looked round constantly and nervously in a manner guaranteed to draw attention to herself, should anyone actually be watching them. Atherton found this rather endearing. Most of the women he knew were so briskly capable that her ineptitude at intrigue had the attraction of novelty.

'I shouldn't really be here, you see,' she said in a low, thrilling voice. 'I mean, not talking to you like this. Not that we're not allowed to meet people, but there are things we're not supposed to talk about.'

Atherton gestured towards the menu. 'Shall we order lunch and get that out of the way?'

'Well, I don't really want anything to eat,' she said, in faint surprise that he hadn't twigged that.

'Yes, but it would look rather more like a secret meeting if we didn't have any food, wouldn't it?'

'Oh! Yes. You're smart! I guess your training makes you think of things like that.' She smiled self-deprecatingly. 'I'd never make a detective, would I? Or a spy.'

'Oh, I don't know,' he said. 'You've got a distinct advantage to begin with.'

'Why's that?'

'Somehow one never suspects beautiful women of anything underhand.'

To his surprise she withdrew a little. 'Now you're making fun of me.'

He backpedalled. 'Sorry. That sounded a bit patronising. I didn't mean it like that. It's this place going to my head.'

She giggled. 'Yeah, it is kind of goofy, isn't it? I keep expecting Inspector Clouseau to jump out and do a karate chop or something.'

The waitress came and hovered, and they ordered some food, more or less at random, and tea – Karen said she didn't drink at lunchtime. While they were thus engaged some more people came in and took tables: a young man and woman; three giggly twenty-something females; an older woman with two younger ones, mother and daughters who'd been shopping. Another waiter appeared to attend to them. Everything looked like normal enough lunch trade to soothe Karen's nerves, and they chatted easily about books and movies until the food arrived.

When they were alone again, she said, 'So, what did you want to talk to me about?'

'I think you know that,' Atherton said. 'Trevor Bates, of course.'

She looked round with an instinctive, guilty movement to see that no-one was listening. 'I told you, I don't know him.'

Atherton smiled. 'Yes, you told me. But I know that isn't true. And if you didn't want to tell me the truth, why are you here? Have a prawn ball.'

'Look,' she said, leaning forward a little, 'I do want to tell you, but I don't want to get into trouble. Do you promise me no-one will know I've been talking to you?'

'Scout's honour,' said Atherton.

She frowned. 'I'm serious.'

'So am I. This is a very serious matter. Two people have been murdered.'

Now her eyes widened. 'Murdered?' she gasped. 'I didn't know that. I thought it was about—'

'About what?'

She shook her head. 'That's awful. You think he did it? Oh God, that's awful! I kind of guessed he was a bad guy, but I never thought . . . Were they women?' she asked suddenly. 'The people he killed?'

'We don't know that he killed them. And, no, they weren't women. But we have our reasons for suspecting he's involved and we need to know everything we can find out about him. So, tell me, how do you know him?'

'I don't really know him,' she said. She seemed shocked. The prawn ball between her chopsticks slipped out and fell back into her bowl without her noticing. 'I've seen him coming and going, and I know his name. I mean, I know the man I've seen is Trevor Bates because he was signing in one day when I was passing through reception and I heard the security guy call him by his name.'

'So he comes to the legation? Often?'

'I've seen him around a few times. I don't know how often.'

'What is his business there?'

'I can't tell you that.'

'Can't, or won't?' She hesitated, looking down unhappily at her lunch. 'What does a cultural legation do, anyway?'

'Oh, all sorts of stuff,' she said automatically. 'Promoting United States goods and cultural exports, protecting our intellectual property, liaising between artists and governments, dealing with the media and British Government agencies—'

'I see,' said Atherton ironically. 'And what has Trevor Bates to do with all this?'

'He – he provides some kind of goods and services. I can't say what,' she said. Still her eyes were down.

Atherton waited for more, and eventually broke the silence by saying, 'Well, if that's all you've got to tell me, it was a bit of a waste of time meeting, wasn't it? Or was it just an excuse to date me?'

She looked up. 'I said he was a bad man. I don't mean in his business – though he may be a crook for all I know – but I mean in his private activities.'

'Which are?'

'He – he has strange sexual tastes.' It seemed an effort for her to get it out, and Atherton's interest quickened.

'Tell me about it,' he said more gently. 'How do you know? Has he done anything to you? Or said anything?'

'Oh, no! Not me. But there was this girl – she's gone back now. She worked in another department but she and I got friendly. We used to lunch and go to the movies together, that sort of thing.' Atherton nodded, to encourage her, and she went on, with gathering fluency. 'Well, sometimes we talked girl talk, you know the way it goes. And one evening when we went out Mr Bates had been in the building and, I don't remember how it came up, but I said I thought he was good-looking, in a weird kind of way. Kind of charismatic, you know, with all that auburn hair and that pale skin. And a great body. And terrific clothes. Well, Katy – this girl – she looked at me kind of sideways, and said I had to be joking, and she asked if I'd spoken to him. I said no I hadn't, and she said I should keep it that way. "If he comes on to you," she said, "you run a mile. He's bad news," she said.'

'Bad news in what way?' Atherton asked.

She shivered a little, unconsciously. 'Katy said he likes hurting women. She said that's how he gets his kicks. She said he's got this house not far from our place, built like a fortress, with all kinds of creepy security guards and stuff to keep people out. She said he takes women there and does stuff to them and takes movies of it so he can watch it all again later on his own.'

'Had Katy been to his house?'

'I don't know. I guess not.'

'Had he done anything to her?'

'I don't think so.'

'So how did she know about his strange tastes?'

'I don't know. I didn't ask. She just said what I've told you, but she sounded like she knew what she was talking about.' Karen looked apologetic. 'I guess it doesn't sound like so much now I tell it. But I believed her, and if ever I saw him round the building I made sure to stay away from him and not catch his eye, you know? I still believe it. I mean, there must be something wrong about him, or why are you here asking me questions?'

Atherton didn't follow that by-way. 'You said this Katy had gone back? You mean to the States?'

'Yes, about a year ago. Her tour was over – or, wait! No, it wasn't. She went early, now I come to think of it.'

'Do you know why she went early?'

'I never knew anything about it beforehand. One day she just wasn't there and when I asked someone from her office they said she'd gone back. But it does happen. People get moved for all sorts of reasons. Only, later, someone said she'd been sent home under discipline for talking too much.' She looked an appeal at Atherton. 'So you see how important it is that you don't split on me? That's why I didn't say anything when you first asked me. If you get disciplined it ruins your whole career.'

'Well, that was just a waste of time,' Atherton reported, swinging through the door.

'It took you a good long lunch to find that out,' Slider commented.

'I couldn't rush away. She was so worried about anyone guessing she was talking to me, I had to make it look as though we were lunching for pleasure. I had to cover her back.'

'As long as that's all you were covering.'

'Wot, me? I'm not on the pull any more. I've got my hands full with Sue.'

'And Sandra Whitty?'

Atherton eyed him defensively. 'If it's about saying I was working late—'

'My own excuse on many occasions, I know,' said Slider. 'Who am I to complain? It's none of my business anyway.'

'But?'

'I thought you were settled with Sue, that's all.'

'I am. Look, it was just a one-off. I'm not seeing her again. Apart from anything else, she smells faintly of formaldehyde. Very off-putting.'

'So why did you do it?'

Atherton tried for an insouciant smile and almost made it. 'Sheer force of habit. I couldn't help myself.'

'I think we'd better book you in at the vet's,' Slider said gravely.

'I know, I know,' Atherton sighed. 'It takes time to alter the customs of a lifetime, that's all. I'm getting there slowly.'

'But with all that rampant totty out there practically gagging for it—?'

'I have never expressed myself so vulgarly,' Atherton said with dignity. 'Do you want to know what Karen Phillips had to say or not?'

'It'll be charged to expenses, I suppose, so I might as well,' Slider said.

Atherton told him. 'But it's all pure hearsay,' he concluded. 'Even the unknown Katy didn't give a source.'

'Yes,' said Slider. 'It sounds like one of those "everyone knows" rumours. That doesn't mean it isn't true, in some form. But of course we can't use it.'

'I'm glad you acknowledge that much.'

'There's been a development here while you've been hard at it, lunching your socks off.'

'Purely in the line of duty.'

'That goes without saying. Well, my news is that Swilley's been pulling together the various morgue pieces on Bates and there's precious little of it. But one interesting fact did emerge. It seems his background is in electronics.'

Atherton perked up. 'So all that gear in his house wasn't just rich men's toys?'

'He did an electrical engineering degree, then a postgrad in his special area of audio-electronic systems, and then he joined a company called Shenyang.' He looked hopefully at Atherton, but Atherton shook his head. 'No, I hadn't heard of them either,' Slider said, 'but apparently they're a very big name in microelectronics – they're the Sanyo of surveillance devices.'

'Bugs.'

'Not to put too fine a point on it. Much of their work, naturally, is both funded and consumed by the Chinese Government.'

Atherton nodded. 'We all know governments are the biggest buggers of them all. Well, that's a nice pointer, given the bug in Herbie Weedon's office. And the masts on top of Bates's house.'

'That's not all. The capitalist face of Shenyang,' Slider went on, 'is their prestige Shenyang Tower building in Hong Kong. Which was where Trevor Bates worked in the research and development department in those far-off days when he was young – and when, by coincidence, an ex-tar called Colin Collins was running a little tattoo and we-know-not-what-else parlour in Kowloon. Interesting, wouldn't you say?'

'Provocative,' Atherton agreed. 'But *did* they know each other?'

'That's what we're trying to find out. Hollis is tracking down some of Sonny's old service pals, while Swilley is trying to work it from the other end and find someone who knew Bates in those days. That bit's harder. Now that we don't own Hong Kong any more, Shenyang is effectively behind the Great Wall, and getting anything out of the Chinese is like trying to lift paving slabs with a nail file.'

'Still,' said Atherton hopefully.

'Yes,' Slider agreed.

'Well,' Atherton acknowledged generously, 'it looks as if you might have been right about Bates after all. It all begins to add up against him.'

'Even if we prove he knew Collins, it doesn't prove he's the boss we're looking for,' Slider said.

'Now you're just being perverse,' said Atherton.

There was a repeat appeal on the six-thirty regional news programme, for witnesses who saw anyone entering or leaving the park or walking along Frithville Gardens late on the Monday night or early on the Tuesday morning. It was done by the news team themselves, with an OB shot of the street and the park gates to jog sluggish memories, so Slider was not obliged to expose himself again. He watched it on the television in Porson's room, without too much hope that it would yield results. They had pretty well come to the end of the crop from the previous appeal, and nothing had turned up. In a place like Shepherd's Bush, people didn't notice each other much, unless someone was trying to draw attention to himself; and whoever killed Lenny Baxter was too professional to do that.

He was back in his own room, thinking about going home, when the phone rang. Blimey, that's quick, he thought, picking up. 'Slider,' he said.

'It's DI Priestfield here, Harrow Road. You put out an all units on a male IC3, name of Everet Boston? Well, I think we've found him. We've got someone who fits the description and the e-fit you sent out, but there's nothing on him to ID him.'

'Thanks very much for letting me know,' said Slider. 'Keep hold of him, will you, until I get someone over there? I don't want him to go walkabout again.'

'You can take your time. He's not going anywhere,' said Priestfield laconically. 'We fished him out of the Grand Union Canal. He's in the morgue at St Mary's now. He's well dead.'

CHAPTER SEVENTEEN

A L'Eau C'est L'Heure

Slider had to go himself to identify the body of Everet Boston, remembering at the last moment that he was the only one of the team who had met him face to face. Boston had been dispatched efficiently with a blow to the back of the neck, fracturing the cervical spine at the level of the second and third vertebrae – the 'hangman's blow'. A quick death, he thought, for what comfort that was, which was very little. The whole thing sickened him. Gang wars were bad enough when it was pot-headed youths or rival pushers knifing each other in the heat of the moment, but this calculated removal of people merely out of greed, for threatening a livelihood, was disheartening and disgusting.

Back at Harrow Road nick, Priestfield gave him tea and talked him through what they knew, which was virtually nothing, while eyeing him with the interest and sympathy accorded to one visibly on the brink of disaster.

'So what's this now – four?' he asked.

'It doesn't take long to get round on the grapevine, does it?' Slider complained. 'Anyway, this one's on your ground, and I'm no poacher.'

'Thanks,' Priestfield said shortly. 'But it *is* connected with your ongoing, I take it?'

'I wouldn't be a bit surprised,' said Slider wearily. 'I'll give you what we've got, but it's not much. They're all professional hits, and you know what that means.'

'No forensic evidence.'

'Right.'

'And unless you can get to the brains behind it—'

'Right.'

'Ah well,' Priestfield said, 'at least they're not innocent bystanders. It makes me sick when some old keff gets blagged for his pension.' He stretched until his shoulder muscles crackled. 'God, it's been a long day.'

'Are you finished now?'

'Yes, I was only hanging on to see you. The DCI's at the scene and there's nothing for me to do here tonight. I'm going home, see if my dog still recognises me. You can bet the wife won't. You?'

'I haven't got a wife,' said Slider.

'Oh well, you're all right then,' said Priestfield.

Slider thought of the cold empty flat and another tepid take-away meal congealing in its container even as he forked it. 'Yes, I'm all right,' he said.

When he got back to the station, Nicholls warned him that Porson was in. 'Came through looking like a ghost.'

'Say anything?'

'Not a word.'

Slider climbed the stairs and went quietly to the door of Porson's room. It was open, as always, and through it he saw the man himself sitting at his desk, bowed a little forward, hands clasped on the desk-top, staring at nothing. He was so still he might have been asleep, except that his eyes were open.

After a moment, Slider said gently, 'Sir?'

When Porson looked up, Slider realised he had been looking at the framed photograph that always stood on his desk. He also realised that he had never actually seen the photograph, though it was not hard to guess who it was of.

'Did you want something?' Porson said. His voice came out so unused he had to clear his throat.

'I was just going to ask you that,' Slider said.

Porson made a throwaway gesture of one hand. 'Got to be somewhere. Can't settle at home. Keep seeing her out of the corner of my eye. Think I hear her calling me from another room.' He met Slider's eyes with a kind of shyness. 'Maybe that's what gives rise to ghost stories.'

Slider thought of what Nicholls had said, and remembered that someone – was it C.S. Lewis? – had said that a ghost was a person out of his place. To him, of course, Porson's place had always been here. It had been impossible to think of him having a home life – but then it nearly always was with senior brass. By definition they were inhuman. But now Porson's heart and mind were plainly elsewhere, and he was out of place here in his office.

With a visible effort, Porson roused himself. 'Any developments?'

It seemed inhumane to drop it on him; but then Slider thought perhaps it would serve as a useful counter-irritant. 'We've lost Everet Boston.'

'What do you mean, lost him?' Porson asked sharply. 'I didn't know we'd found him.'

'Somebody else found him,' Slider explained, 'floating in the Grand Union Canal.'

'Oh, bloody Nora,' said Porson. 'Go on, then, give it to me.' Slider told him what he knew. 'Well, that's it then!' Porson said with large exasperation. 'Finito. We've got no evidence against anyone, and we've lost every witness we had who might have led us to this so-called big boss. We might as well pack our towels and go.'

Pack our towels? Slider wondered. Was that a Germans-and-deckchair image, or had he caught the tail of 'throw in the towel' as it wandered across his line of vision? He shook the thought away. 'There's still the girl, sir. Lenny Baxter's girlfriend. She might know something about the boss, or at least point us towards someone else in the organisation. If we could find her,' he added fairly.

'If she's still alive,' said Porson. 'What chance they won't have cleared her up like they've cleared up Boston?' Slider didn't answer that. After a moment Porson asked, 'What are you doing to trace her?'

Slider almost shrugged. 'The only lead we've got is the Susan who used to be friends with her and Lenny, who may or may not be Susie Mabbot, who ran a house in Notting Hill.'

'That's not bloody much!'

Slider admitted it. 'We're trying to trace her but we've had no luck so far. And we still might get some witnesses coming forward from the repeat TV appeal tonight.'

Porson hauled a sigh up from his boots. 'Palfreyman's been leaning on me, you know that. And Mr Wetherspoon's leaning on him. Now there's a fourth body—'

'Not on our ground,' Slider said quickly.

'We may get out on a technicality with that one, but three is four too many as it is. They won't leave it with us much longer.'

'How long have we got, sir?' Slider asked.

'The Murder Review Team will be here on Monday, or Tuesday at the latest. If we've got nowhere, they'll bring someone in from outside. Well, I wish them joy of it, that's all. A case like this is a bugger. When you lift the corner of the carpet, you never know what you'll find looking back at you. Do what you can in the time available, Slider, and I'll authorise any overtime you want for your team. If you can get a result, well and good.'

Slider could not hold out the slightest hope that they'd get anywhere by Tuesday morning, so he remained silent. Porson was staring at nothing again, deep in a reverie. Suddenly he came back and said, 'If they take it away I'll have a few days off. Go down and visit my daughter.'

'I didn't know you had a daughter, sir,' Slider said – foolishly, since he hadn't known anything about Porson's life.

'Lives down in Devon. Married, two boys. She's an artist. Paints views for the tourist trade – but good stuff, mind!' he added sharply as if Slider had sniggered. 'None of your tat! She's a real painter. I used to make a joke about it. I used to say to her, "Moira, I may be a superintendent but you're a right Constable."'

Porson making a joke? Slider thought in astonishment. And then, *Moira?* He tried to smile.

Porson went on. 'I'll stay with them for a few days and we can all come up together for the funeral on Friday.'

'If anyone deserves a few days off it's you, sir,' Slider said in a kind of desperation. All this personal revelation was terrifying. He was afraid any minute Porson would ask him to come too.

'So don't beat yourself up, Slider, that's what I'm saying,' Porson concluded in a wholly normal voice. 'If it doesn't come off, let someone else worry about it.'

This was worse than anything, Slider thought. If the old man gave in to the Palfreymans of this world without a struggle, it really would be the end. If the great granite Porson was defeated there was no hope for any of them: the world would crack in two like a saucer and fall into the void.

'But it's *our ground*, sir,' he said, trying to infuse some urgency into the old man.

'Is it?' Porson said. 'I wonder sometimes. I wonder if it's not theirs.' Theirs? Palfreyman's and Wetherspoon's, did he mean? 'Your Lenny Baxters' and your Sonny Collinses',' Porson elucidated. 'Whoever said the meek shall inherit the earth was talking out the back of his head.'

This didn't seem to be the moment to tell him that it was the Lord. Slider kept schtumm.

All the same, someone had to do something, and when he got back to his office he rang his old friend Pauline Smithers. She was now with the National Crime Squad, and he found her still in her office at the West London headquarters.

'Hullo,' she answered him. 'What do you want?'

'That's a very hurtful conclusion to jump to,' Slider said. 'I phoned to say congratulations.'

He had known Pauline Smithers his whole career, ever since he was a probationer in uniform and she had had the stern glamour of five years of seniority over him. There had been a time when something might have started between them, but he had held back through diffidence, and in the end he had married Irene and she had married her career. The gap between them had widened exponentially since that point. He was a detective inspector working seventeen-hour days at a local nick. She was a detective chief superintendent and second in command of a team that had been investigating Internet paedophile rings and had just made a spectacular and widely publicised bust, with a hundred arrests and several lorryloads of porn confiscated.

'I saw you on the telly,' he said. 'You looked very good, Pauly. The grapevine says you're destined for great things.'

'Well, that's what we all thought, but it was splashed in the papers for one day and then forgotten, like everything else. Fifteen minutes of fame, you know? Now we've got to slog it through the courts. A hundred arrests but how many will we get down? Still, it was nice while it lasted.'

'Now don't you let me down,' Slider complained. 'None of

that defeatist talk. You're always bullish and positive. I phoned you for a bit of backbone stiffening, and here you are, *c'est-la-vie*-ing me.'

'Hah! I knew it! You did want something.'

'Well, only a bit. I really did phone to congratulate you, and I should have done it sooner only—'

'You had stuff to do. I know. So what's your problem this time, chum? I don't know but what having a go at yours wouldn't be a nice temporary relief from my own. I'm sick of paedophiles.'

'I bet you are.'

'Sometimes I find myself trembling with rage and wanting to go down to the cells and simply beat them to death. Not good for the soul, that. We've got to keep our objectivity. Like surgeons. We're the last rational people in the whole legal system.'

Slider sighed happily. 'Ah, that's the stuff! Come on, more! Pump it in – I can feel it doing me good already.'

She laughed. 'What do you want, you bastard? I've got stuff to do myself before I can get home to my cot.'

So he told her. Just saying it all out loud helped him to slot the pieces into place. She listened, putting a question now and then, and he imagined her at her desk with the lamp making a puddle of light over her hands, taking notes in her quick, small script. He felt an enormous surge of affection for her, a familiar and comprehensible person in a wild and woolly world.

At the end she said, 'Well, I see why you want this Bates person to turn out to be the Needle, but you really haven't got anything to go on, have you?'

'No, I know. That's where I need you.'

'Oh, is that where?'

Slider missed that one. 'These high-powered people are difficult to get information on. His house is like Fort Knox and I've exhausted the normal routes. But if he's providing some kind of goods or services to the American cultural legation, someone official must know about him.'

'Don't you think that makes it unlikely that he's a criminal?' she asked him kindly.

'What better cover could there be?' he said.

'Yes, but why would he bother?'

'Some people just can't get enough. Look, if he turns out to be pure as the driven, so be it. At least it stops me wasting my time – and I've got little enough of that to waste.'

'All right, I'll see what I can do. But I don't know why you can't just let it go, Bill. After all, there's plenty more criminals where that one came from.'

'Why do you bother catching a hundred paedophiles when there's a hundred thousand more out there? Crime's a Medusa head. Every snake you cut off, another ten spring up. But what's the alternative? You can't let them do it right under your nose without so much as a challenge.'

'All right, I said I'd do it,' Pauline interrupted him.

'Thanks. Right away?'

'By yesterday, if that's soon enough for you.'

'Thanks, Pauly.'

'Is your mobile number still the same? All right then, I'll call you as soon as I know anything. Don't call me, okay?'

'Okay.'

'Okay. How's what's-her-name – your friend?'

'Joanna? Absent.'

'Ah. I smell a story. Well, you can buy me lunch or something and tell me all about it.'

When he had rung off from Pauline, he phoned home to get his answering machine messages – two from Joanna, the second saying she was just going in to play and she'd try again after the concert. He hadn't realised it was so late. He was hungry, too, he discovered. He quite fancied a ruby. Hadn't had one of those for ages. He'd stop on the way home at the Angla Bangla for a nice chicken tikka with saffron rice and a big greasy naan: a thinking man had to keep his energies up.

That decided, he felt more cheerful and embarked on his last task – ringing round his team to get them in tomorrow. Two days. A lot could happen in two days. Even a result wasn't out of the question.

Hollis's quest for people who had known Sonny Collins had led at last to one of those raw new estates built beside the M1 to take the overspill from Northampton. Here he was received on Sunday morning by one Stanley Rice who lived with his wife in retirement at number 5, Meadowview. Despite its name, it looked out at the front only on the houses opposite, across the

Gone Tomorrow227

narrow road and the open-plan front gardens, and at the back on the high wooden fencing that divided the estate from the motorway.

Hollis had driven to Meadowview through Orchard Way and The Glebe, passing such side turnings as Haystacks, Willow Close and Primrose Dene. When he got out of his car and the roar of the traffic hit him, he almost staggered. It thundered past just beyond the flimsy barrier with a noise like a waterfall driving hydro-electric turbines; it battered the air in a way that surely was literally unendurable. It must be like living in the exhaust pit of a rocket launcher. He half expected his nose and ears to start bleeding.

But it was amazing how quickly he got used to it once he was inside the house where, though constant, it was not at killing pitch. It was a mean little house, with low ceilings and tiny rooms, as if built for a smaller race of hominids than your actual *homo erectus*. Hollis came from Manchester, and was reminded of things he had learnt in history lessons about the cramped and gimcrack housing that was run up for factory workers in the nineteenth century. How the wheel turned!

Mr and Mrs Rice had brought with them to their new castle their old furniture, which had been designed with normal-sized houses in mind. With the sofa in place along the only piece of wall long enough to accommodate it, and a footstool in front for Mrs Rice, who suffered from swollen ankles, there was only just room for a person to pass between it and the log-effect electric fire. An armchair placed at either side of the fire made it an obstacle course to get from the door to the far window, under which a gateleg table and two dining chairs filled all the remaining space from wall to wall. There was another window at the front of the room, looking onto the road, and beneath it stood a bookcase and a cupboard with two drawers underneath, which impeded the opening of the door from the tiny entrance hall to the 'living room'.

Every step they took, Hollis reflected, must involve sidling past something or squeezing through some gap. It was depressing. Still, they seemed an immensely cheerful couple and even, to his astonishment, said that this house was much nicer than their old one.

'We've got the hatch through to the kitchen here, for one

thing,' Mr Rice explained, 'so I can talk to Mother while she's in there cooking or whatever, and she can see the television through it, so she doesn't miss things. She likes the soaps, you see, and if they come on when she's washing up or doing the potatoes ... Mustard on the soaps, she is. Aren't you, love?'

Hollis had missed the television. It was behind one of the armchairs, between it and the wall. They would have to push the chair back up against the dining table to be able to see it.

On top of the television was a rather nice model ship, made of wood and ivory.

'I can see you were a naval man,' Hollis said, to get things rolling. 'That model, the painting and everything.' Over the fireplace was a large, cheaply framed reproduction of a three-master in full sail over a rollicking blue sea; while on the narrow, low mantelpiece, the top of the bookcase and the cupboard was a whole collection of ships in bottles, of various sizes and degrees of accomplishment.

'Oh yes,' Mr Rice said, pleased. 'I like my bits and bobs about me. Collect 'em, when I can find 'em. And I've got a lot more stuff upstairs, in the spare bedroom. I make model battleships from kits – the modern ones, you know, not like her.' He gestured towards the three-master. 'Mother laughs at me about my "kid's hobby", but I find it satisfying. She has her knitting, and I have my models, right? Where's the difference?'

'Oh, go on, Stan!' Mrs Rice protested. 'The gentleman doesn't want to know about your silly ships. Would you like a cup of tea, Mr – er? Or coffee?'

'Thanks, that'd be very nice,' said Hollis. 'Coffee, please, if it's no trouble.'

She bustled off and he heard her presently in the tiny kitchen just through the cardboard wall, making kettle-and-cup noises. It was hardly necessary to have a hatch, Hollis reflected. You could have put your hand straight through the wall without half trying. But he supposed if Mr Rice had been a sailor he'd be used to confined spaces and living on top of other people. As to Mrs Rice, women of her generation adapted themselves, in his experience, to absolutely anything.

At Mr Rice's invitation he sat himself in one of the armchairs and chatted inconsequentially until Mrs Rice came back in with a wooden tray on which reposed two cups and saucers of instant coffee made with milk, a sugar bowl, and a plate of mixed biscuits. The china all matched and was decorated with pink and silver roses, and there was a spotless embroidered linen tray cloth underneath. There was something about people like this that made Hollis almost want to cry. He thanked Mrs Rice warmly and admired the china, and she looked pleased, and took herself off with a puzzle book and a Biro to sit at the dining table and give them privacy, or as much of it as was possible at a distance of three feet.

'So, Mr Rice, you knew Colin Collins? Or Sonny Collins, as he was known.'

'Not when I knew him,' Mr Rice said. 'Not Sonny. Never heard him called that. Crafty Collins, we called him. We all had nicknames, o' course. Mine was Speedy. Not that I was fast, or anything – though I was a lot spryer in those days than I am now – but my initials were S.P.D., you see. Stanley Philip David. S.P.D. – Speedy Rice, you see?'

Hollis got it. 'So why was he called Crafty Collins?'

''Cause he *was* crafty,' Mr Rice said promptly, opening pale blue eyes wide. 'I mean, crafty as in handy with his hands, yes, that was one thing. He was what we called an artificer. He could *make* anything *out* of anything. But he was crafty the other way, too. On shipboard, even on a shore base, you live on top of each other, you know, Mr Hollis. And that means you have to get on, you have to trust one another. And if somebody's not honest, it messes up everybody's life. No, he wasn't popular, wasn't Crafty Collins. We knew he'd come to grief sooner or later, and there was no tears shed when he did.'

'Oh, Stan!' Mrs Rice protested, proving she was not as far out of earshot as she was pretending.

Speedy seemed to understand her objection. 'Well, I know it's a terrible thing to lose an eye. But it has to be said he had it coming, if not from one source, then another. A terrible *contentious* man, he was. Always getting into fights. He'd argue about anything. You couldn't say it was raining without he'd pick you up and say it wasn't. He just *wanted* to fight. Needed it, sort of. There are men like that – I've known a few of them.'

He looked enquiringly at Hollis, who nodded and said, 'Yes, I know what you mean.'

'*Thought* you did. After all, the police is a service, just the same as the navy. And men are men all over. And there are some that've just got to be getting their fists out and proving it, even when nobody's said "boo" to them.'

'So how long did you serve with Crafty Collins?'

'Well, let me see. We were two years on the base before he got in his bit of trouble and got discharged, and then it must have been another three years or so he was still there, but as a civilian. Then it was about six months after he left before I was posted back to England, home and beauty. O' course, we weren't *friends*, you understand. I mean, I was a good bit older than him, and I was a petty officer, while he was just a rating. And apart from that, you didn't make friends with Collins. He wasn't a friendly man. Not,' he added thoughtfully, and pausing to sip his coffee, 'that he didn't have a soft spot somewhere. I maintain everyone's got one. And Collins had this bird. We weren't supposed to have pets,' he went on, dismissing Hollis's immediate vision of a girlfriend, 'but on a shore base things are a bit different and blind eyes are turned now and then, if you know what I mean. Anyway, Collins had this little bird in a cage. A finch, I think it was. He bought it off a Chinee – they're big on these little cage birds, the Chinese. Walk through a Chinese section of Hong Kong and you'll see a cage hanging up on every balcony with some canary or whatnot whistling its little heart out.'

'Cruel, I call it,' Mrs Rice put in.

'She's not keen on birds, Mother,' Mr Rice explained for her. 'Give her the creeps.'

'It's not that,' she said. 'I like 'em well enough in the garden, but keeping 'em in cages is not natural. They just sit there hunched up all day and night, like they're in mourning.'

'Fanciful,' Mr Rice explained her to Hollis.

'No I am not,' Mrs Rice defended herself. 'Even when they sing, it's not happy singing. Makes me shiver.'

'I knew a man once had this parrot,' said Mr Rice. 'Or, well, it was a cockateel, to be absolutely accurate—'

Hollis felt they were on a banana skin to unfettered reminiscence, and coughed slightly. 'About Mr Collins?'

'Oh, yes,' said Mr Rice, quite unembarrassed. 'I was saying he had this finch or whatever it was – a little grey bird with a red cap, very smart. Looked like an MP. And, I will say, it whistled a treat. Well, you wouldn't think Crafty would care that much about it. He was built like a bag of boulders, and full of boiling oil, if you know what I mean, and this little bird was only about three inches from head to tail. But he looked after it like a mother. Used to go down the market to get it fresh lettuce and fruit and stuff. He loved that bird, which goes to prove what I've always said, that there's a soft spot in everyone, if you know where to find it.'

'What happened to the bird?' Hollis asked in spite of himself.

'Oh, it died. They don't live long, them sort, even in the wild.'

'And was he upset?'

Speedy gave a snorting laugh. 'I don't suppose there was anyone on the base brave enough or daft enough to ask him. He never showed anything, but I reckon he was upset. He never got another one to replace it, anyway. And I'll tell you something.' He leaned forward a little. 'He gave that bird a Christian burial. Put it in a cigar box and buried it somewhere up on the Peak. I'm the only person that knows that. I saw him put the bird in the box and I saw him leave with the box and come back without it; and later someone told me they'd seen him up there, so I worked it out.' He sat back. 'Nothing as queer as folk, is there?'

It certainly was an interesting, if unilluminating aside on the character of Sonny Collins. 'Tell me about the fight when he lost his eye. What was all that about?'

'Well, I can't tell you officially,' Mr Rice said, settling himself back for the long haul, 'but *un*officially a lot of us knew what was really going on. I told you Collins was crooked, but crookedness doesn't pay when you're practising it on people you live on top of. So he started to look outside, and it wasn't long before he built up contacts with the local people. Well, Hong Kong – you ever been there?'

'No, I haven't,' Hollis said. 'More's the pity.'

Speedy nodded. 'It's a special place, is Hong Kong. I expect it's different now, of course. Pity we ever gave it back, that's what I say—'

'Now, Stan!' Mrs Rice warned.

'I know, I know. Well, as I was saying, Hong Kong is – or was – the best place in the world to set up a bit of business and make a bit of money on the side. Anything you want, they'll get. And when you've got it, there's a stack of people to sell it to – tourists, service people, ex-pats; boats and planes coming in all the time with new customers, all of 'em with money burning a hole in their pockets. So Crafty gets in with a lot of shady characters. This particular one – can't remember what he was called – one of those wing-wang-wong names – he was a right wrong 'un, a real cross-eyed ugly little geezer and as crooked as a dog's hind leg. The local coppers had been after him for years for drug smuggling.'

'Was that what Collins was into with him?'

'I can't tell you as to that, not as a literal fact. But I wouldn't be surprised. Anyway, thieves fall out, as they say, and one night him and this Chinee start arguing, and before Crafty can get a swing at him, he outs with a knife and stabs him right through the eye.' Mrs Rice sucked her teeth in protest. 'The medico said he was lucky to be alive, because a fraction further and it would have gone right into his brain, which is probably what this Chinky was after. But he missed his shot, and Crafty came right back and swung a right hook at him, caught him under the chin and lifted him four feet in the air, so they said that saw it. Flew like a bird. He was dead before he hit the ground. Broken neck, neat as you like. Saved somebody a job, because he'd have been hung sooner or later, the sort he was, sure as eggs are eggs.'

'But Collins wasn't punished for it?'

'Well, it was self-defence, wasn't it? There were enough witnesses, and there he was without an eye and the medico saying he was lucky to be alive. Open-and-shut case. The enquiry cleared him, but he couldn't serve with only one eye, could he?'

'Nelson did,' Hollis couldn't resist.

Mr Rice smiled. 'Nice one! That's one to you! But Collins wasn't no Nelson and the Royal Navy's a bit different now. So he got discharged on medical grounds. Honourable discharge – funny to think of anything Crafty Collins did being called honourable.'

'And then what?'

'Well, everyone thought he'd go home. That's what any of us would've done. But I suppose old Crafty didn't have anything to go back to. No, he stopped on and set himself up in business.'

'A tattoo parlour.'

'That's right. You've done your homework,' said Mr Rice approvingly. 'Well, where there are sailors, you can't go wrong with a tattoo parlour, can you? He learnt how to do it off an old Chinee that was going out of business, and bought his needles and dyes and everything, and there he was. Service people and daft young tourists flocked to him. O' course, tattooing wasn't all he provided 'em with.'

'Now, Stan!'

'Got to tell him, haven't I? That's what he's here for,' Mr Rice said indignantly.

'What else did he supply?' Hollis asked.

'Whatever was wanted. Hashish, cocaine, girls. I dare say he'd find you a watch or camera or pearls if that was all you wanted. But that stuff doesn't pay as well as the other. It wasn't long before he had a very nice stash built up. But o' course that sort of activity attracts attention in the long run. In the end he had to pack up and get out before they clamped down on him, but I reckon he took a good bit back to Blighty when he went. Enough to set up in business.'

But he didn't, Hollis thought. He got a job in the licensed trade. He didn't buy a pub, he got a job as a manager. So what did he do with the stash? Spend it all in one wild debauch? Maybe – except that he didn't seem like the debauching kind.

'Did you,' he asked casually, but with great anticipation, 'ever know a man called Trevor Bates?'

'What, Crafty's friend?' Mr Rice said, little knowing what joy he brought to a policeman's calloused old heart with those three words. 'Well, I didn't know him personally, o' course, but I knew *of* him.'

Thank you, God! Hollis offered inwardly. 'Tell me about him,' he said aloud, settling himself comfortably to listen.

CHAPTER EIGHTEEN

Susie Wrong

'Boss,' said Swilley as he crossed the office on his way back from the loo. He changed direction towards her. She was looking extremely fetching in a skinny powder-blue top that consolidated her assets magnificently. He was about to conclude that Tony was a lucky man when he remembered that Tony was at home alone in his slippers reading the papers while his new wife was here with them, which wasn't so very lucky after all.

'Life's a bitch,' he said.

She raised her eyebrows at him. 'You don't know what I'm going to say, yet.'

'It was a general observation. Go ahead.'

'Well, I hope you'll be pleased. I've found out about Susie Mabbot, and I know now why we had trouble tracing her.'

'Oh?'

'She's dead.'

'Oh, my God, not another one!' Slider sank into the vacant seat at Anderson's desk, next door.

'No, no, it's all right, she's been dead for ages. Before we started.' She spread out the sheets of paper under her hands for him to see, and walked him through it. 'She was pulled out of the river. She was right down at Creekmouth – that's the opposite bank from Plumstead Marshes – but they reckoned she'd gone in a lot further upstream. You know how far bodies can be dragged if the tide's set right. There was nothing on her to identify her, but fortunately one of her girls had reported her missing, and she got matched up as soon as they checked Mispers.'

'And how was she killed?'

'It was a bit strange and nasty,' Swilley said, turning down her mouth. 'I've got the PM notes and the inquest report. Apparently they found a whole lot of tiny holes all over her, only a couple of millimetres deep and so small in diameter they were hardly visible to the naked eye. The pathologist said they looked like the marks left by acupuncture needles.'

Slider frowned. 'Acupuncture's hardly life-threatening. You're not telling me the water rushed in through the holes and drowned her?'

'No, her neck was broken. The pathologist concluded it was some kind of sex game, because there was evidence of penetration, and semen in the vagina, but no sign of force having been applied, apart from the death blow. PM report said her head was probably pulled sharply backwards by someone standing behind her – which of course could be part of it. Naturally once they found out she was a tom they concluded she did it for a client. I mean, being stuck full of needles would be uncomfortable but they do worse things for their money. And then he got carried away and killed her.'

'So if it was a client, I presume they were able to find out which one?'

'No, that's the odd thing. No-one was ever charged. They questioned all the girls, but none of them had anything to say, not even the one who reported her missing. Her evidence says she was worried about Susie being missing because of the nature of their work. Later, with a bit of pushing, she said she knew Susie had a client who was into some weird stuff. Susie had apparently told her she was seeing him that night – the night before she was reported missing – and was apprehensive about it. Here, look, her words: "Susie said this bloke gave her the willies. I said to her, well, don't do it then, and she said it'd be the worse for her if she didn't. She said he wasn't a bloke who took no for an answer."'

'But she never said what it was the bloke did?'

'No. She said she didn't know – Susie never told her.'

'And *no* idea who the bloke was?'

Swilley shook her head. 'They hauled in quite a few of the customers but cleared them all. Well, they had a DNA sample from the semen so they could be fairly sure about it, and most of them were well known to the girls and just ordinary punters. Susie ran an expensive house. They were respectable (ha-ha) businessmen, most of them.'

'I bet that enquiry ruined a few lives,' Slider commented. 'Did the locals suspect anyone, even if he wasn't charged?'

'Nope. Not a clue. I rang Dave Tipper and he asked one of the officers who was on the case. They've never come near to looking at anyone. Of course, they ran the DNA but there was no match on the database. They're now thinking that the killer must have been either a foreign businessman or someone from outside London who visited occasionally and went to Susie for his jollies, went too far and had to dump the body. She was dressed when she was found in the water, so they reckoned he could have got her into a car by "walking" her with her arm over his shoulder and his round her waist, so that if anyone saw they'd think she was just drunk. But apparently no-one did see.'

'Yes, it's amazing how people don't see things,' Slider said. But of course a lot of the time they did see things, and simply wouldn't say. And there was, he knew, a stratum of thought that whatever happened to prostitutes was their own fault.

'So what do you think, boss?' Swilley asked. 'I mean, all this acupuncture business, and Everet's boss being called the Needle – do you think there's something in it?'

'It's certainly very suggestive,' Slider said. 'Whoever this boss is, his people are afraid of him, afraid enough not to grass him, and apparently Susie Mabbot was too afraid of him to refuse sex or to tell anyone his name.'

'But she's dead and it doesn't really get us any further forward, does it?' Swilley said gloomily.

'Oh, it does,' Slider said. 'For a start we've got a DNA profile now, so if ever we do arrest someone we've got something to check against.'

'It's a big if,' Swilley concluded. 'What do you want me to do?'

'Get a picture of Susie Mabbot and take it over to Neville Coulsden, see if he can identify her as the Susan who came to help his daughter move her things. Take one of her in life, if you can. I'd rather not have that poor man faced with a mortuary mugshot.'

'Sure, boss. And if she is the same?'

'One step at a time,' Slider said. 'There's every chance she isn't – or he won't be able to say one way or the other.'

'But *if* she is—?' Swilley insisted.

'Then we know that she knew Everet, who worked for a man called the Needle and might well have introduced her to him.'

'Or vice versa.'

'Whatever. It comes out the same. And as she was killed with those particular marks on her, it is very suggestive that her killer and the Needle are one and the same.'

'But we still don't know who the Needle is,' she pointed out with fatal logic.

'There is just that small thing,' Slider agreed. 'But link by link we're forging a chain.' And eventually, he thought, it might be long enough to trip somebody up.

When Swilley had departed – with a 'publicity' picture of the ex-madam – on her way to Harlesden, Slider took the papers on Susie Mabbot into his own room and went through them again, settling the facts into his head. When he got to the statements of the other girls in the house he slowed, then paused. Then he rummaged amongst the photographs, pulled one out, studied it, and smiled.

'Sassy Palmer, as I live and breathe,' he said. Toms were notorious for using false names, of course, but at the end of every string of aliases, like the crock of gold at the end of a rainbow, was a set of fingerprints and a birth certificate. The employee of Susie Mabbot who described herself as Suzette Las Palma had been pinned down by the patience of the Notting Hill squad as Suzanne "Sassy" Palmer, and Slider knew Sassy. What was more, he knew where to find her. That level of the underworld rarely moved far from its origins, and though Notting Hill came under a different borough, its station and his own were a bare mile apart.

He looked at his watch. This time on Sunday morning she ought to be in bed and asleep after her Saturday night exertions. Just the right time to catch her with her guard down and ask her a few questions.

'Trevor Bates,' said Speedy Rice. 'That was a queer thing, now, the way Crafty Collins took up with him. You wouldn't have thought they had a thing in common. I mean, Crafty, he had enough upstairs. He wasn't stupid by many a long mile. But this Bates bloke, he was college educated and everything. Smart

as a whip. Well, he was an engineer – and I don't mean he was
a greaser,' he added sternly, as if Hollis had expressed doubts.

'Electronics engineer, wasn't he?' Hollis said, to show he was
on the ball.

'That's right. Motherboards and solder, that's as dirty as he
got *his* hands.'

'How did they meet?' Hollis asked.

'Well, as I understand it, this Bates wandered into Crafty's
tattoo parlour because somebody had told him that was where
to go for a spot of the doings, know what I mean? He worked
in one of them tower buildings on the island, you see. Anyway,
him and Collins struck up a what-d'ye-call—?'

'A rapport?' Hollis offered.

'That's the thing. Like love at first sight, kinda thing, only
this was more of an un'oly alliance. They were thick as thieves.
They made quite a team, too. Collins had the brawn – and the
violence – and Bates had the brain. He was a skinny runt of a
feller, was Bates, until Crafty took him in hand. Like the bloke
that gets sand kicked in his face in the advert. Sickly white, too,
and with that red hair – not ginger, but more like Rita Hayworth,
know what I mean?'

'Auburn,' said Mrs Rice, without looking up from the jumbo
EastEnders crossword. Seven letters with two f 's in the middle?
What the blazes was that?

'If that's what it is,' Mr Rice conceded. 'Anyway, Collins
showed him body-building techniques, acted like his personal
trainer, not that they'd invented them in those days. Bates wasn't
half badly built by the time Crafty'd finished with him. No Mr
Atlas, but he looked the goods.'

'And what did Collins get out of the relationship?'

'Well, now,' Mr Rice said thoughtfully, 'as to that, I can tell
you what I think, but it's only my opinion. I remember that little
bird, you see. I think Crafty was fascinated by Bates. I think he
sort of – loved him, in a way.'

'Now, Stan!'

'I don't mean in a queer way, not that,' Mr Rice amended
hastily. 'But he protected him, looked after him just like he did
that little bird. 'Course, he was older than him, Collins was,
older than Bates. Maybe it was like an older brother thing, I
dunno. Anyway, he kept him from being beaten up or killed,

which he quite likely might have been, moving in the sort of circles they moved in. Anyone even looked cross-eyed at him, Crafty'd sort 'em out so's their own mothers'd have to look twice at 'em. On the other side, I reckon it was thanks to Bates that Collins stopped getting followed about by the police.'

'How's that?' Hollis asked.

'Well, Bates tamed him, kind of – taught him to keep his temper, or at least to use his violence a bit more cleverly. Bates was an organiser, and he thought things through the way old Crafty never had. Bash first, think later, that was Crafty. And Bates was clever – inventive, always thinking up new things. Collins was just a doer, know what I mean? Together they could get up to four times as much mischief – and they did, from what I heard. Well, Bates was a bit of a scholar and he got on well with the Chinese – into all the philosophy and Chinese medicine and them eastern therapies and everything. He kind of understood 'em, and they trusted him, so he could do business with 'em without 'em giving him away. That's how Collins made himself a nice fortune without getting caught by the authorities. If you want a solid reason for him liking Bates, that's what he owed him, keeping him out of legal trouble like *he* kept *him* out of physical trouble. But that wasn't what it really was, not to my mind. Bates was that little bird to him. He was his soft spot.'

Mr Rice shook his head slowly, gazing in wonder down the telescope of memory.

'I'll tell you an example,' he went on, 'of how soft Collins could be with this Bates bloke. Have you ever seen him – Collins, I mean?'

'Yes,' said Hollis.

'Well, you might have noticed a tattoo round his neck, a dotted line right round the bottom of his neck.'

'Yes, I've seen that.'

'Well, it was Bates did that to him. I told you he went to Crafty's shop first of all for some of the other things he sold, but the story I heard was he'd never been in a tattoo parlour before and he was fascinated by the needles and the dyes and the stencils and all that. That's how it all started. He might have gone away with his spot of hash and that would've been that. But he hung around to watch Collins working the needle, and kept coming back to watch some more, and they got friendly.'

'Did Bates get a tattoo himself?'

'Oh, no. Squeamish about it, as far as his own white skin went. But couldn't get enough of seeing it done to other people. Well, that's what I heard. Anyway, I was telling you – one day, this is what I heard, he asked Collins, could he have a go using the machine. And Collins let him do one on him. That's how far he'd let this bloke go, because it must've been a big risk, especially round his neck like that.'

'Why that particular tattoo?'

'I heard it was a kind of joke, that it was meant to be like Boris Karloff – you know, the stitches holding his head on?'

'Frankenstein's monster?'

'That's the one! Bates was all brain and Collins was all brawn, like I said, and, what with him only having one eye – well, Bates used to call him that, Frankenstein's monster. Kind of affectionate, I suppose,' he added, but doubtfully.

Hollis thought that from what he had heard so far, it was evidence of Bates's desire to live dangerously. 'So when Collins went back to England, did Bates go too?' he asked.

''Course he did! You couldn't have one without the other. Gammon without spinach that'd be.'

Perhaps, then, Hollis thought, that was where the stash went. Perhaps the faithful Collins used it to set Mr Bates up in business. A capital sum to buy the first old houses to be done up? It was possible – though why would Collins give it all away? Wasn't that taking friendship too far? Most criminals displayed all the loyalty of a tart in a barracks. On the other hand, if they had made the money together, as a partnership, perhaps it was only nominally Collins's, because he had the legitimate business to pass it through: he was the laundry for their joint efforts. And perhaps they shared the profits. There was nothing in Collins's lifestyle to suggest he had money, but maybe that's how he liked to live. It was not impossible that there was a big deposit somewhere they hadn't discovered yet.

Speedy Rice seemed to have come to an end of his recollections. Hollis looked over his notes, thanked him, and asked if he'd be willing to have a statement taken, if anything should come of it.

''Course I will,' he said. 'Got to do our duty, haven't we?'

'I wish everyone thought like that,' Hollis said. He got up to go, thanking Mrs Rice for the coffee and biscuits, at which she beamed with pleasure and said he was welcome, it was nice to have company now and then, and come again.

The company removed itself carefully, stepping over furniture and squeezing through the doorway. Hollis was a thin man and no more than average height, but this place made him feel like the jolly green giant.

Mr Rice had leapt nimbly to his feet and said, 'I'll show him out, Mother, don't you move.' When they got out into the roaring, shuddering street – Hollis could swear the traffic bellow was bouncing off the pavement in lumps – it became clear this courtesy had an ulterior motive.

'I didn't like to say anything in front of the wife,' he told Hollis in a confiding shout, 'but there's some other stuff I could tell you about Collins and Bates.'

'Please do,' Hollis shouted back.

'Well,' said Mr Rice, 'when I said it was like a kind of love, Mother thought I was suggesting they were queer. But it wasn't that. They both had women – lots of 'em. They used to go hunting 'em together. Chinese women, mostly, o' course. There wasn't many of the other sort, and you could get into trouble chasing them.'

'Prostitutes?' Hollis asked.

'I suppose so. There *were* lots of prostitutes, B-girls and dancers, and then all those massage parlours and places that were sort of on the brink.' He made a rocking movement with his hand. 'Could go either way, get me? But there were plenty of women available. I dare say some of them were just poor and needed the money. And maybe some were too scared to say no. They had some funny habits, those two.'

'Such as?'

Mr Rice looked up at him with a sort of stern reluctance. 'It's only hearsay. But there was a lot of talk about Collins and Bates – Collins having been one of ours, you know. The talk was that they liked to hurt women. I'd hesitate to believe that of anybody if I could help it, but I've knocked around the world a bit, and I know what men can be. Even some of the decent lads in our unit, well, they thought Chinese women didn't count the same as white ones.'

'Yes,' said Hollis. 'I've known men like that.'

Speedy nodded, man of the world to man of the world. 'And if you start thinking like that, it's not a big step to thinking no women count.'

'Did both of them get their pleasure that way?' Hollis asked.

'The way I heard it, it was Bates liked to do the hurting, and Collins liked to watch, but he must have been part of it, mustn't he? I dare say he held 'em down or something. Nasty, I call it. People like that – well, I don't know what they deserve.' He paused and then added reflectively, 'So Crafty Collins is dead, is he? There's a lot of 'em gawn, from back then. I go to the reunions, and every time there's another one gawn. The old man with the scythe, you know. And what about afterwards? Collins'll be finding out about that. If there is an afterlife, your sins'll all be looked at pretty bloody close, I reckon. It makes you think, doesn't it?'

'Yes,' said Hollis gravely, 'it makes you think.'

Before Slider could get out of the office, his mobile rang. It was Pauline Smithers, so he sat down again to talk to her.

'Blimey, that's quick,' he said. 'I didn't expect to hear from you for a day or two.'

'Yes, well what I found out I thought you'd better know ASAP,' she said. 'You do like to shove your hand into hornets' nests, don't you, old pal of mine?'

'What have I done now?'

'I hope you haven't done anything. That's why I'm calling you on a Sunday morning when I should be in a deep bath with a glass of Chardonnay.'

'Stop it, you're making me dribble.'

'I'm not fooling, Bill,' she said sternly. 'Do you know what this cultural legation is?'

'Not what it seems?' he hazarded.

'I shouldn't be telling you this, and the person who told me shouldn't have told me, but it's one of those secrets that aren't so secret any more since the end of the Cold War, and in any case I want to stop you hurting yourself.'

'Oh, it's like *that*, is it?' Slider said, enlightened. 'Atherton half thought it might be. He's been chumming up to one of the employees and found her exposition of what the cultural legation did less than convincing.'

'Yes, well, apparently that particular branch specialises in listening, and given that they're willing to share what they hear – or some of it, at any rate – with us, it's one of those situations it's worth turning a blind eye to, as long as no-one does anything that has to be noticed.'

'Like someone drawing attention to himself?' Slider said.

'Never mind himself,' Pauline said. 'I'm thinking of you. If everyone's ignoring everything like billy-oh in the national interest, how grateful do you think they'll be to someone who asks so many questions some of them have to be answered?'

'Oh, Pauly, been there, done that,' he said. 'If I were to tell you how many times I've been threatened—'

'Not by this lot,' she said shortly. 'I know you have to do what you have to do, and in any case, I'm not speaking to you now and this conversation never happened. But for God's sake be careful.'

'I will. I promise. But what about Bates? Did you find out anything about him?'

He almost heard her wince. 'Must you name names? How secure do you think this telephone is? All I know about him is that he supplies some systems and hardware, again with tacit consent – which makes it even more dangerous to mess with him. But I can tell you that according to my source they've got their doubts about him. He's been under investigation for some time. He's got his finger into too many pies, and they think he may be a security risk.'

'Because of the pies, or for some other reason?'

'I don't know specifics. Is there another reason?'

'There may be. That's what I'm trying to find out. Any particular flavour pies mentioned?'

'She didn't say, but I'd guess they were criminal or at least questionable, or why the worry?'

'And are they doing anything about him?'

'Yes, they're going the Al Capone route. The Inland Revenue has got a special investigation team liaising with one of our squads, trying to find out where his money comes from and where it goes to.'

'Ah, yes, softly softly findee monkey,' Slider said bitterly. 'And we've got four corpses and counting.'

'It's no use complaining to me. If you're so keen on him, get some evidence the CPS can't ignore. All I'm saying is be sure you know what you're doing. He doesn't exactly have friends in high places, but high places eat up little chaps like you and me.'

'Yes, okay. I understand. Thanks, Pauly.'

'No sweat. Or not much, anyway. So now you owe me – again!'

'When all this is over I'll take you out for a meal. A real blow-out, okay?'

'When's this lady of yours coming back?'

'Why d'you ask?'

'I'm wondering how she'll feel about you and me and the candlelit dinner.'

'She can come too.'

'Oh. I see.'

He hesitated, and added, 'She may not be coming back at all. This job – she's been trying to tell me something for the last week and not managing it.'

'You think she's found someone else?' Pauline asked with gruff sympathy.

'It's possible,' he admitted painfully. 'I mean, what have I got to offer her?'

'Don't trail your coat. You know what I think of you.' Before Slider, startled, could say 'No, what?' and embarrass them both, she went on quickly, 'If she says she's found someone she prefers, have her certified, that's my advice. And now I've got to go. Take care, Bill.'

'You too,' he said, but he was talking to the air. He sat a moment lost in thought, trying to sort out the strands, to put the personal things aside where they wouldn't interrupt him. Pauline – Joanna – his future, possibly alone. Work was nearly everything, but not quite. It took it out of you – put it back in, too, of course: the pleasure of getting a result; the intellectual satisfaction of sorting out tangles and finding where the truth had been buried, usually at the bottom of a festering pile of profiteroles. But you needed more, you needed the human dimension too, otherwise you became lop-sided. You could end up as twisted as the people you investigated. That was it, wasn't it? Crime was a lop-sidedness They talked about a person being well-balanced, didn't they? Well, how well-balanced could you be doing a thirteen-hour shift and going home to a take-away and a cold bed, day after day? He wanted Joanna, but he needed her too. If she didn't come back – if what she had been trying to tell him was that it was just too hard and she was going to let him go and look elsewhere – could he do the Job without her? Could he ever, now, care for anyone else? He thought he knew the answer to that one, helped to it by kind Pauline. The answer was, not enough.

Forget it for now, he told himself firmly, knotting the whole bundle together and putting it aside. Right now he had more immediate things to think about. And if he didn't get out of the office toot sweet, the phone would ring again and he'd be here all day.

CHAPTER NINETEEN

Déjà Vous

Slider had to knock and ring at the door of the flat just off Portobello Road for a good long time before it opened. Sassy Palmer, in a cotton dressing-gown that was not really man enough for the job, looked at him blankly, then said, 'Oh, fuck me! You again!' and tried to shut the door.

'Don't be like that, Sassy,' Slider said, stopping it with his foot. 'I just want to talk to you.'

'I ain't Sassy to you,' she said irritably. 'Show some respec', for Chrissake. And whut make you think I want to talk to you?'

'Miss Palmer, then,' Slider said placatingly. 'Come on, let me in. You know I'm one of the good guys.'

'You a honky bastard, like all the rest,' she said, but with less heat.

'Better to talk to me than someone else, isn't it? I do respect you, Miss Palmer, I really do. And I'm on your side. I just want some information.'

'Yeah, like that *all* you want!' she said, but she stopped pushing at the door, though she didn't yet abandon it. She seemed to be considering.

He pushed again his main credential. 'If you don't talk to me someone else will come. You don't want a squad of heavy-handed coppers pounding at your door, do you?'

At last she said, 'I ain't alone.'

'You've got a customer with you?'

'At this time o' day?' she said scornfully. 'No, I got my sister stayin' over.'

'I didn't know you had a sister.'

'There a lot you don't know 'bout me. Hanyway, she asleep. Don't you make a noise an' wake her.'

'I won't,' Slider said. Taking this for an invitation he pushed the door again, gently, and she yielded and let him in.

The narrow hall, hardly more than one human wide, had been painted purple by an amateur hand, and an ugly cast-iron chandelier much encrusted with candle wax made the head-room hazardous. Sassy, walking away before him, seemed to fill the space. She was a tall woman, taller than Slider, well-bosomed and slim-hipped, though with a fleshy behind that twitched in what might have been an inviting way under the thin cotton, except that Slider knew she was dog-tired and invi-tation was the last thing on her mind. Her feet were bare except for toe-rings, and silver anklets that clinked at every step. Her hair was grown long and stood out in a great mass round her head and shoulders, too wiry to do anything as pedestrian as hang down.

She led him into the sitting room and flung herself down on the sofa, one foot tucked under her, giving the cotton wrap even more pressing problems to solve. Her eyes were bleared with her interrupted sleep, and one of her long talon fingernails was missing. They were falsies, he supposed, since they were painted black and the short nail on the odd finger was a natural pink. She seemed to like black. One of the walls was painted black – the other three were red, a depressing combination, he thought – and there was a black 'throw' over one of the armchairs. Chairs and sofa were old, probably bought second-hand, and renovated in the cheapest way by hanging a piece of cloth over and tucking the slack into the creases. There were a lot of candles around, and paper flowers, and objects that had been painted with silver paint, or decorated with stuck-on sequins or squares cut from mirror-flex. Everything in the room was cheap and the decoration was home-made, but it was certainly individual. There was a smell in the air which he thought at first was joss-sticks, but realised after a moment was old perfume – hers, presumably – whose brand he knew but couldn't for the moment place.

Sassy yawned mightily, showing the gold cap on one of her front teeth. 'So whut you want, anyhow?' she said uninvitingly. She went to pull her robe together at the front, and noticed the missing nail. 'Shit! How'd I do that?' She pronounced the exple-tive with extra vowels, like an American. Her accent wandered quite a bit, from Harlesden to Harlem, but leaning more towards the latter. When Slider had first known her she had been pretending to be American (that's where she had got the nickname) on the grounds that it was good for trade, and old habits died hard.

'I want to talk to you—' Slider began, then snapped, 'Sassy, pay attention! This is important.'

She looked up resentfully from examination of her fingernail. 'I listening. I don't have to look at you as well.'

'Yes you do. I want to see your face.'

''F you think I gonna lie to you, why you botherin' t' ask me?'

He didn't answer that. 'Until three months ago you used to work in the house run by Susie Mabbot.'

Now he had her attention. 'Shit! Not that again,' she said. Now in her apprehension her accent had come home to London. 'I told 'em everyfing I knew. It's ancient history. What're you draggin' it all up again for?'

'Not that ancient. And I don't think you told quite everything. I don't think any of you girls told quite everything.'

'Listen, Susie was good to us! We was all heart-broken over what happened to her! What d'you think?'

'I know you were. I think you were also scared to death that what happened to her might happen to you. So you did the sensible thing and kept your mouths shut.'

'Yeah, well if we did, we had good reason, didn't we? So what makes it any different now?'

'Like you said, it's ancient history. Over and done with. You're out of the loop, aren't you? So you can talk to me quite safely.'

'I don't want nuffin' to do with it,' she said with finality. And then she added, bethinking herself, 'I don't know nuffin', anyway. I don't know what you're talking about.'

'Yes, you do, Sass, don't say that. This is heavy stuff, and I need your help. You working girls have got enough to worry about without creeps like him. Look what he did to Susie! Don't you want to get revenge for that?'

'I hate him for that,' she said with low anger.

'And now there's another girl in danger. I've got to get him put away.'

'You can't,' Sassy said. 'He's untouchable.'

'No, he's not. We've got his DNA profile. If we can arrest him for anything, we can match it and prove he killed Susie.'

'How d'you get that?' Her eyes widened, her nostrils flared with distaste or distress. 'Not from her?' He nodded. 'After all that time in the water?'

'He miscalculated,' Slider said. 'The river cheated him. The way the tide was she oughtn't to have been found for days, even weeks. She might have gone right down to the sea and never been found. But just by chance she got washed up within hours.'

Sassy wasn't listening to that. She was staring at memory. 'I hate that bastard.'

'He was a customer of Susie's, yes? Why did she keep seeing him? He must have had some powerful hold over her.'

'Money,' Sassy said bitterly. 'He was a rich bastard, and he paid big. Plus she was scared of him. She was scared he'd kill her if she didn't do what he said. I said to her, get away, girl. Jus' get away. But she said he'd find her and kill her.'

'Well, he did kill her,' Slider pointed out.

'Yeah.'

'So you've got to help me.'

'What, an' get myself killed?'

'He can't hurt you if he's inside, can he?'

'He'd find a way. He'd get someone to do it for him. He had people around him. He'd come to the house with a couple of bodyguards, and we'd have to entertain 'em while he was wiv Susie. Bastards!'

'They're just the fleas on a dog,' Slider said. 'They'll go down with him. Help me get him, Sassy. Just give me his name, for a start.'

'I never knew his name,' she said. 'No, straight up, I ain't kidding. Most of the punters didn't use their own names. Susie knew 'em, most of 'em, 'cause a lot of the regulars had accounts. Put it down as business entertainment. But she never told us the real names.'

'So what was this particular man known as?'

'He was Mr Lee. Bruce Lee. I s'pose that was a kind o' joke,' she added. 'Very funny, I don't think.'

'But he wasn't Chinese?'

'Nah, he was English all right. But he'd been out east. That's where he got his funny ideas from. He was into all that Eastern shit, Chinese medicine and—'

'Acupuncture?' Slider suggested.

She had been slipping into it bit by bit, but at this interpolation she started and looked at him with alarm and dislike. 'I told you, I ain't talking. You fink you can trick me into it, you bastard?'

'No, I don't think that. I think you want to help me get back at this bloke, for Susie's sake.'

'An' get myself stuck full o' fuckin' holes?' She started to rise. 'Go fuck yourself,' she said. 'I'm goin' back to bed.'

'Please, Sassy—'

'Don't call me that! You ain't got the right.'

'Miss Palmer, then. Please just talk to me for a bit.'

'I gotta get some sleep. I got a livin' to earn.'

'I'll pay for your time. What do you charge nowadays?'

A little calculation entered the atmosphere. 'A cent'ry, or I go back to bed.'

'I haven't got that much on me,' Slider said. 'I think I've got fifty. I'll give you fifty for an hour of your time. Come on, Sass, fifty pounds an hour's not bad. Only lawyers and accountants get more than that.'

'All right,' she said, flopping back down. Her face was still closed. 'I'll talk to you for fifty, but only 'alf a hour. And I ain't tellin' you anyfin', okay?'

'Blimey, that sounds like a real bargain,' Slider said.

In spite of herself she thawed a little. 'You a funny bastard,' she said.

'I think I must be to go on doing this job. Go on, Sassy, tell me about Susie's special customer.'

It had been going on for a couple of years before Susie's death, Sassy said. He only visited about once a month, but it was pretty regular. They never saw him. He would go straight up the stairs to Susie's private room, while she brought his companions – usually two, and obviously minders – into the lounge for the other girls to entertain.

'What about other customers?' Slider asked.

'Not when he was there. That was the rule. He took the whole house for the whole night. Paid well for it, an' all. That was how Susie got into it in the first place, I s'pose.'

'Do you know how Susie first met him?'

'Nah, I dunno. Maybe someone told him about her. All I know, she said he never went wiv white girls. He only liked black and Chinese. Well, we never had no Chinese girl but there was Susie an' Michelle an' me all black.' She shuddered. 'It could have been me, man,' she said quietly.

'Did Susie have many special customers?'

'Nah, just a couple of others apart from him. She was still gorgeous, but she mostly just done the management an' everyfing.'

And who could blame her, Sassy went on. No sane person would want to earn it on their back if they could make more getting someone else to do it. Not that he should get her wrong. Susie had always been good to the girls, and generous. They all got a bonus when Mr Lee visited, or they did one of them big corporate parties. And Susie kept the customers in order and never let any harm come to the girls. None of that S&M stuff. She said there were other houses they could go to if that was their bag. Which was what made it all the more strange about her and Mr Lee.

And he never had any of the other girls? He never had Sassy?

No, fank God. He didn't like tall girls, Susie said. He only ever had Susie. She didn't say at first what his bag was, but over the months they could see Susie didn't look forward to his visits. She would get quiet and kind of depressed when the day came. Well, not depressed, exactly, but kind of thoughtful. Eventually they all knew she didn't like Mr Lee and wished he wouldn't come, but when Sassy had asked her why she didn't refuse him, she said, 'It wouldn't be wise.' Just that. And she kind of tried to shrug it off and said it wasn't so bad what he did, just creepy.

What did Sassy know about the man?

Not much. Susie said at first he was a rich businessman. Always wore real expensive clothes. But Sassy reckoned his business wasn't legit. Susie hinted as much later on. In any case, why else would she be afraid of him?

Could Sassy describe him?

Like she said, she had never seen him. No, Susie never described him either, 'cept that he had a good body. Oh, and he was very white – his skin. Susie said once, kind of joking, that he must never step out of doors. That was in the middle of a heatwave when they was practically sleeping over in the park. Susie said he lived in the dark like a mushroom. Sassy remembered that because it gave her the creeps. She reckoned it gave Susie the creeps an' all.

No, his goons never talked about him either, not that Sassy ever heard. Well trained. They were real tough guys. You could see it in their eyes. Not cheap-smart tough, like a lot of blokes, all mouth and muscles for show, but the real thing. You wouldn't mess with them guys.

This seemed to be a dead end, and Slider turned to another tack. 'Do you know a man called Everet Boston?'

She answered with barely a pause, but Slider got the impression of wariness in the sudden cock of her attention. 'Yeah, he was a mate of Susie's.'

'A customer?'

'A mate from back home. They used to go out drinking once in a while. It was like her evening off.'

'Did you meet him?'

'Couple o' times. He come in for a freebie once or twice.'

'Did you like him?' Shrug. 'Was the freebie with you?'

'Nah. Another girl.'

'Did he ever bring another man called Lenny Baxter with him?'

'Lenny never come in for it. He wasn't into it much. I see him once or twice when him an' Ev called for Susie to go out. See, she and Ev and Lenny used to make a foursome wiv anover girl. But Susie used to talk about him. Ev thought he was all right, but Susie reckoned he was a wrong 'un.'

'In what way?'

She seemed to have difficulty putting into words. 'He was trouble, she reckoned. Kind of stupid-smart, know what I mean? The kind'd try and be too clever, do somefing stupid, get himself into trouble, and then chuck someone else in it, tryin' to get himself out. She said he'd get Ev into trouble one of these days. She was fond of Ev, Susie was.'

'Was it Susie who introduced Everet to Mr Lee?'

'Ev never met him. No-one never met him. I *told* you that.' She yawned again, gaping like a hippo. Now her acute apprehension had worn off, the sleepiness was returning.

'But Ev did work for him, didn't he?'

'Maybe.'

'You know he did.'

She looked goaded. 'If you know, why d'you ask me?'

'I need confirmation. You know how the game's played, Sassy. Did Susie introduce them?'

'Ev needed the money, and Mr Lee was looking for a smart guy. But they never met. That was the way he done things. Ev would've been contacted by a fird party, all right?'

'A control.'

She shrugged.

He changed tack again. 'Did you ever hear of a man called Trevor Bates?'

'Nah.'

'Are you sure? Think, Sassy.'

'Sure I'm sure. Who is he?'

'I think he might be the big boss Everet worked for. The boss of a criminal ring, a man with the nickname of Needle. Lenny worked for him too. I think he might be the man who killed Susie, and I need your help to pull the two ends together. He's a hard man to pin down.' She was not looking at him, but at her nails again. 'Come on, Sassy,' he said, 'try and help me. There must be something else you can tell me about this Mr Lee. Remember what he did to Susie, and try and help me.'

'Remember? I'd sooner forget!' In her indignation she lost some of her reserve. 'That's what she called him, the Needle. Said it was his nickname from when he was out east, the creep! I'll never forget what she told me. He'd stick them needles in her, one by one, all over, till she look like a porcupine. And then he'd do it. That's what give him his kicks. He couldn't get it up any other way. I hate that bastard.'

'But why did he kill her?'

Sassy paused on the brink a moment, and then lowered her voice and said, 'I'll tell you what I fink, but you must never let on I told you, or I'm dead. Promise me!'

'I promise.'

'Swear it.'

'I swear. Just tell me, Sass.'

'All right. She found something out about him.' She swallowed, and lowered her voice still further, as though she could lessen her guilt that way. 'The week before he came that last time, she told me. She said he told her he'd killed someone by mistake that way, a girl he'd had, only he'd never got found out. He told her while he was doing it, all that needle stuff. You know, to give himself a thrill by scaring her, the filthy bastard! Only she reckoned he might be sorry he'd said it. She was scared. That's when I said to her, get out, girl! Get out while you can. But she said he'd find her, and it'd be the worse for her.' She shook her head in grim wonder. 'How could it be worse? Me, I'd sooner run away an' have a fightin' chance than stand still and wait for it. If she'd only listened to me! But I reckon she was like hypnotised by him, you know? Like one of them snake things.' She made a circling motion with her finger. The allusion escaped Slider.

He tried one last tack. 'What about Ev's cousin?'

'*What* about her?' It was unwarily said, and at once Sassy seemed to realise she had betrayed something. 'I never knew he had a cousin.'

'Then how did you know it was a she and not a he? Come on, Sassy, give me a break! Ev's cousin Mary, or Teena as she called herself, was the fourth in the foursome, Lenny Baxter's girlfriend.'

'You know it all, don't you?' Sassy said sourly.

'So tell me about her.'

'I never met her. She never come in the house. She was just a kid.'

'What did Susie say about her?'

'Oh, she was just a kid,' Sassy said dismissively. She seemed to think of something, and went on more confidingly, 'Susie said she was in over her head with this Lenny character. She was nuts about him – Teena was – but Susie reckoned he'd treat her bad in the end. He was using her, Susie said. And he was a bloke that'd always look after himself, whatever it took, know't I mean?'

This, Slider suspected, was either a smokescreen or a lure, but he didn't know what it was meant to conceal or lead him away from.

'So where is she now?'

'I don't know. How should I know? I ain't seen her since Susie was killed,' Sassy said with emphasis.

Slider noted that she had said before that she had never met her. Was it possible that Sassy knew where Teena Brown was? If so, how could he get her to tell him?

'Look,' he said, 'I think Teena is in trouble. She's disappeared, and I need to find her.' Sassy looked unimpressed. 'I've got to get to her before the Needle does. I think she knows something about him – maybe even who he is – and if he finds her first he might kill her.'

'I told you, I never met her,' Sassy said impatiently. 'I don't know nuffin' about her.' And then, 'Why'n't you asked Ev? She's *his* cousin.'

'I can't ask him. He's dead.'

Evidently she hadn't known that. It was a shock. She stared a long time, perhaps debating whether to ask more, and deciding she didn't want to know. 'I shouldn't a let you in,' she said at last. 'I knew you was trouble. If you've led 'em to me—'

'No, no, I wasn't followed. They're not watching me.'

'You fink they aren't.'

He spread his hands and looked helpless. 'They think I don't know anything. They think I'm harmless. And anyway, why should they bother you? You've never met the Needle. You were just one of the girls. If they were worried about you they'd have done something about you before now, wouldn't they?'

'Yeah, you take chances wiv your own life. I want you out, now.'

She was on her feet. Slider rose too, but slowly. 'One last thing, and then I'll go.'

'Now, I said. I ain't talkin' to you no more.'

'Okay, but you want your money, don't you?' He fumbled in his pocket, as if looking for his wallet, and brought out the inter-view room photos of Colin Collins and Thomas Mark. 'Just look at these while I'm sorting it out, will you. Tell me if they are the men who came with Mr Lee to the house.'

He held them out, and when she didn't take them, flapped them a little, to indicate that he couldn't search efficiently for money without both hands free. So she took them with a shrug, and looked at them. The picture of Collins she rejected with apparent indifference, but at Thomas Mark she nodded and said, 'He was one of 'em. One of his minders. I dunno the uvver bloke.'

Bingo, Slider thought with deep satisfaction. A link at last!

He could have kissed Sassy, had it not been for various hygiene considerations, and the fact that she was bigger than him and could have decked him with one blow. 'I want you to come back to the station with me and make a statement, saying you recognise this man, and where you saw him,' he said.

Sassy recoiled. 'You crazy? I told you you can't let anyone know I've helped you. He'll find out and he'll kill me.'

'No he won't, because we'll have him banged up.'

'I ain't saying nuffin'. You promised me! You swore!'

'I swore I wouldn't tell anyone you told me about him killing another girl,' he reminded her. 'And I won't. All I want is for you to make a statement about this man.' He tapped the photo.

'It's the same fing. I ain't coming.' Her face seemed to crumple. 'Oh Christ,' she said, 'you gonna get me killed. You've led 'em straight to me! I'm dead.'

'If they were following me, you'd be safer at the station than here, wouldn't you? But they aren't. Look, once we've got this man under lock and key, we'll have plenty more evidence against him. I promise I won't use your statement unless I absolutely have to. And it won't have your name on it. Your identity will be protected.' Still she refused, and he allowed a touch of impatience to show. 'I can force you to come, you know. You don't want a big fuss at the door to draw attention to yourself, do you? Come on, Sassy, get it over with. Better me than the local lot. They don't like working girls at Notting Hill.'

'You tellin' me!'

'But you know I'll look after you. Go and get dressed.'

She shrugged at last, and said, 'All right. But I gotter tell my sister where I'm goin'.'

She went out, and down the passage towards a room at the back of the flat. Slider considered the possibility that she might try and escape, but it was the fourth floor, and he knew these death-trap old conversions had no fire escape. Besides, Sassy's real desire was not to go anywhere. Still, he listened carefully for sounds of windows being thrown up, and was just a touch relieved when she reappeared in a short, tight red dress that left everything to be desired, red spike heels and a fake leopardskin jacket. Once a tart, always a tart, he thought with no little affection. He held the front door open for her, and she stalked past him with stunning hauteur.

It was mischievous of him to choose that particular moment to thrust out the small wedge of notes at her.

'I nearly forgot your fifty quid,' he said.

'I don't want your money,' she said scornfully; but she took it all the same.

CHAPTER TWENTY

The Eye of Childhood

The team was assembled in the office. Slider sat on the edge of Anderson's desk.

'There's bound to be a visit from the MRT tomorrow or Tuesday morning at the latest,' he said. 'We'd better get our ducks in a row now, so that we'll have something to present them with.'

'If only they'd called it the Homicide Review Team we could all have had HRT,' Atherton said laconically.

'A lot of people have been suggesting we could do with some extra hormones to pep up our performance,' Slider said.

'I just hope this is worth giving up my Sunday for,' said Atherton. 'I could be at home now with the *Observer*—'

'Make you go blind, that shit,' McLaren warned him cheerfully. The *News of the Screws* was sticking out of his pocket.

'Oh, it's worth it all right,' Slider intervened. 'We've got, at long last, the one thing we've been searching for – a link between Trevor Bates and the Needle. So let's look at the story as a whole.' He checked that he had their attention, and began. 'Colin Collins and Trevor Bates met out in Hong Kong and formed an unholy alliance. Collins had a tattoo parlour and some very shady contacts. Bates had an over-fertile imagination and managerial skills. Together they built up an illegal supply-and-demand business – drugs, girls, whatever. Bates, meanwhile, was developing an obsession with needles and skin; Collins, I suggest, with Bates.'

'Is Collins homosexual?' Atherton asked.

'Certainly not overtly,' Slider said. 'He and Bates shared girls. Let's call it more a fascination – which Bates apparently held for other people, too. Collins was fiercely protective of him, and probably very strongly influenced by him—'

'As those of less nimble minds often are by clever people who take time and trouble with them,' Atherton concluded. 'Well, it makes sense.'

'Fiercely protective and fiercely loyal,' Slider went on. 'They came back to England when Hong Kong started to get too hot. Collins had – and this is all assumption now – quite a bit of money to bring with him. But he took a job, while Bates went on to found a business empire on renovating property.'

He looked at Hollis, who took it up. 'My idea was that maybe Collins gave the money to Bates to get him started.'

'Out of devotion?' Swilley asked with some disbelief. 'I wish I had friends like that.'

'Maybe. Or because he was under his influence, or because Bates was the businessman and could make something of it where Collins couldn't. We don't know that Bates didn't share the proceeds with Collins.'

'And we don't know that he did. Why would Collins go on managing pubs if he had money coming in from Bates?'

'Well,' Hollis said apologetically, 'maybe he liked it. I can't think why anyone would want to own a pub but lots of folk do, because they like the life.'

'Let's not get too poetical,' Atherton said. 'We know that Collins ran two small-time crooks for his boss, and we can assume it was more than two. Maybe the pub was just very good cover.'

'Then why not buy one?' Mackay asked. 'Why risk interference from the brewery?'

'I can think of two reasons,' Hollis said. 'In the first place, running your own pub is a lot more work than managing one. If it *was* only a cover, you wouldn't want it to take up too much of your time. And for a second thing, it'd be much easier to move on if you had to. Changing jobs is easier than selling a pub and buying another one.'

'All right, let's get on,' Slider said. 'We turn now to Susie Mabbot, a tom who ran a high-price house in Notting Hill, catering for rich businessmen. Somehow or other Trevor Bates finds her, or is recommended to her. He has strange sexual tastes which he wants to exercise in strict secrecy.'

'Exercise or exorcise?' Atherton asked.

'He pays her well, she keeps his identity secret – if she knew it at all.'

'I can't see why he'd ever tell her who he was. Presumably he paid her in cash,' said Mackay.

'You'd think so, wouldn't you?' said Slider. 'She calls him Mr Lee. He visits her, in company with two bodyguards, about once a month.'

'Boss, d'you think that's significant?' Swilley asked.

'What, the once a month bit? It's possible. Strange mental urges can run in cycles. I'm not up on all the latest research, but—'

'You don't believe that bollocks about going mad at the full moon?' Mackay protested.

'Linking it to the phase of the moon may well be self-suggestion,' Slider said, 'but it doesn't mean it doesn't happen. However, that's not for us to debate at present. Bates is visiting Susie Mabbot. He mentions he's recruiting – or she brings the subject up, we don't know which – and it results in Everet Boston being taken on by Bates.'

'Boston said he got the job through a friend,' Anderson observed.

Slider nodded. 'Boston and Mabbot were old friends from back home. Boston had another friend, Lenny Baxter, whom he met playing snooker. He introduced Baxter to his cousin Mary, and the four of them – he, Mabbot, Baxter and Mary, who called herself Teena Brown – became friends and went out together. This friendship was broken when three months ago Mr Lee, alias Trevor Bates, murdered Susie Mabbot and dumped her in the river.'

'And if we can arrest him for anything at all,' Swilley said, heartfelt, 'we can cross-match his DNA and get him for that.'

Slider nodded. 'So now we come to Lenny Baxter.'

'Our number one corpse,' said Atherton. 'The first but not the last.'

'Baxter was an unreliable type. He was a prolific villain but a rotten gambler with a taste for the ponies. He was working as a runner for Herbie Weedon's loan firm, but he was short of money, and about a year ago Everet, perhaps with his cousin's welfare in mind, got him taken on by the big boss, whom he only knew as the Needle. But Baxter still kept on his other job with Herbie Weedon. Baxter had gambling debts, and was blacklisted by legal bookies. Getting a job running for an illegal bookmaker must have been like letting Billy Bunter loose in a cake shop. He started placing his own bets as well as the customers', and, when they went down, crossing money collected for Herbie to cover them.'

'And getting himself in a right old two-and-eight,' McLaren concluded.

'Eventually,' Slider went on, 'and here we are in the realm of supposition again, the Needle decided he was too much of a risk and that he should be eliminated. He was conducting business of his own on the side, which included selling drugs in the park. One evening the fiat went forth—'

'I can't see a rich bloke like Bates driving one of them,' McLaren objected. 'He'd have something a bit posher.'

'I see him as more a Beamer type,' Mackay agreed.

'Don't encourage him,' Swilley said witheringly.

'Now here a piece of blind chance intervenes,' said Slider. 'Baxter's going about his normal business when he's waylaid by Eddie Cranston, who's got a beef with him about one of his sidelines – preying on females that Eddie feels are his own legitimate feeding ground. Eddie tries to get into a fight with him, but Lenny knows his boss doesn't like attention drawn to any of his outposts, and makes a getaway. Later he meets with two heavies in a conversation in the street, and later still he's murdered very efficiently in the park, presumably by the two heavies seen walking away from the park down the street at two in the morning, carrying something which I feel we have reason to suspect is the missing lock and chain.'

'Which later turns up round the throat of Herbie Weedon, who was about to tell me something interesting,' Atherton said. 'How did he know, though?'

'We don't know what he knew, but I suspect it was something he gleaned from Lenny Baxter, who doesn't seem to have been the world's most reliable crook. Probably Baxter told him something and he put two and two together out of his vast experience. And the Needle, in the course of clearing up Lenny Baxter's mess, had Boston put a bug in his office and soon found out he was talking to the police in the form of Mr Atherton.' Wolf whistles. 'So Herbie was killed.'

'Which put the wind up Everet Boston and made him run for it,' said McLaren.

'Later again,' Slider said, 'Boston seems on the brink of telling us something, and is murdered.'

'And chucked in the canal,' Hollis mentioned. 'Like Mabbot was chucked in the river.'

'A watery motif,' said Atherton. 'I wonder if he got into the habit of throwing people in the harbour in Hong Kong?'

'And when,' Slider continued, 'it looks as though we are going to lean heavily on Collins, he takes his own life.'

'Why?' Swilley mused. 'Was he afraid he'd break down and start talking? It doesn't seem likely. He was as tough as old boots.'

'I think maybe it all just got too much for him,' Slider said. 'Running one bit of the crime network for his great idol – perhaps stashing away some of the proceeds for his old age – presumably enjoying the odd night out, or in, with Bates, like in the old days – was one thing. But the body count was mounting. Mabbot, Baxter, Weedon, Boston – what next? Maybe he thought Bates was out of control. Disillusion,' he said, looking round his team, 'is a powerful emotion. It can lead to anger or despair. And if in the middle of that he got the idea that Bates didn't trust him any more and was maybe putting him on the list for removal – well, he'd have nothing left to live for.'

'He jumped rather than waited to be pushed?' Atherton said. 'Hm. I suppose it's possible.'

'And there the trail ends,' said Slider.

'But what have we really got against this guy?' Swilley asked. 'He may have killed Mabbot with his own hands but he won't have personally offed the other three. It will have been his minders. And Collins killed himself.'

'It's the old gangland conundrum,' Atherton agreed. 'The bloke with the motive has clean hands and the bloke who actually does it has no connection with the victim.'

Hollis enumerated, holding up his fingers. 'We know he knew Collins in Hong Kong. We know from Ev Boston that the boss was called the Needle. We know from Rice that Bates was fascinated by needles. We know Mabbot's lover and killer was called the Needle. We know one of her killer's bodyguards was Thomas Mark. We know Thomas Mark is Trevor Bates's driver.'

The chain, Slider thought, forged link by link, connecting all the scattered pieces of lives. 'And then there's the whole business of the jackets,' he said aloud.

'Yes, Bates and Mark deny knowing Baxter, but Mark is wearing a jacket identical to one of the four Baxter bought from Tom Garfield. Bates says he bought it and gave it to Mark but can't prove it.'

'And we can't prove he didn't,' Atherton pointed out. 'We can't really prove anything. It's all suggestion. We still don't know who killed Lenny Baxter, even if we think we know who ordered it done.'

'My guess would be that the actual deed was done by Mark and that butler type we saw in his house,' Slider said. 'However well Bates pays and however much he's feared, he's not going to give jobs like that to just anyone. It would have to be done by those closest to him that he trusts the most. And they looked like professionals. So we show their pictures to Elly Fraser and see if she can ID them as the men she saw leaving the park.'

'And if she can't?'

'There's still Susie Mabbot,' Hollis said. 'If we can get him for that on the DNA, it makes the others look more credible. Then they might start rowing for the shore, him and his minders, and shopping each other in the hope of a comfier cell.'

This idea seemed to go down well. There was a murmur of conversation, out of which Swilley spoke up.

'There's still one thing that bothers me.'

'Only one?' said Atherton.

She ignored him. 'If the minders were going to kill Lenny in the park at two in the morning, they must have arranged to meet him there at that time. So why was he there two hours earlier, at midnight? We know the chain was off the gate then, so he must have been in there.'

'We don't *know* the chain was off the gate,' Atherton said. 'A very dodgy witness says it was.'

'He might have been doing a spot of business,' Mackay said. 'Why not?'

'It wasn't his regular night.'

'He wasn't much of a regular guy,' Hollis pointed out.

'But two hours? Hanging around in the park for two hours? And there are no reports of a stream of customers going in and out of the gate.'

'When were there ever?'

'Anyway,' Swilley said, 'I can't believe there'd be that much trade for him on a Monday night, when he wasn't known to be there selling. Maybe for an hour after the pubs closed, but not through to two in the morning.'

'Well, maybe he wasn't there,' McLaren said. 'Maybe he did a bit of biz, then went home and came back at two.'

'Leaving the gate unlocked all that time?'

McLaren shrugged. 'Why not?' Swilley couldn't answer that.

'There is one other loose end,' Slider said. 'Baxter's girlfriend being missing.'

'She's probably in the river too,' Atherton said.

'Some comfort you are,' said Swilley.

'Well, if he's been getting rid of anyone who could finger him, he'd hardly leave her out, would he? She was just as much a threat as Everet and Baxter.'

'She probably wasn't anything to do with it at all,' Mackay said. 'She's just scarpered, and who wouldn't?'

'All right,' Slider said. 'Things to do. We want full statements from Rice about Collins and Bates, and from Neville Coulsden about Mabbot, his daughter, Boston and Baxter. Get Tom Garfield formally to identify Baxter's jacket as one of his. Get Elly Fraser to look at Mark's picture, see if she can identify him.'

'Guv, won't we have to give the Mabbot stuff to Notting Hill? It's their case.'

'First I want to get everything lined up to see if Mr Porson thinks it's enough to get Bates in to answer questions. If he does, we can get the name of his butler bloke and a mugshot to show Sassy Palmer, see if he was the other minder that came in with Mark.'

'If Bates is as bonkers as he sounds,' said Swilley, 'we could probably get him to crack by telling him everything we know about him and Collins.'

'It did cross my mind,' Slider said.

*　　*　　*

Slider was having a very late cheese and pickle sandwich at his desk and working on assembling the paperwork when the phone rang.

'Oh, Mr Slider? It's Andy Barrett – from the Boscombe Arms?'

Slider wrenched his head back into the present. 'Oh, yes. What can I do for you?'

'Well, it's like this.' He sounded a bit furtive. 'There's someone here wants to say something to you, but he's scared of coming into the police station. I wondered if you could pop down and have a word with him?'

'Can't you put him on the phone?'

'It's a bit awkward. You'll see why when you come.'

'All right, I'll send someone down.'

'I don't think he'll talk to anyone else,' Barrett said anxiously. 'Couldn't you come yourself? It's about this Lenny Baxter business,' he added, with the air of speaking without moving his lips.

'All right, I'll try and make time later today,' Slider said unwillingly.

'Oh dear. The thing is, can you come now?'

'Why now?'

'Well, we're closed now, so it's quiet. You'd have a bit of privacy. And – well, it's the wife, you see.' He came to the real reason with a little rush. 'She doesn't like me to get mixed up in anything, and she's out at the moment, so she wouldn't have to know if you came now. Only I know she'd say to leave well alone if she was here, but I don't think that's right, not when it's a case of murder, you know?'

Slider sighed. 'I'll be there in about ten minutes,' he said, abandoning the sandwich. It was stale anyway – yesterday's left-overs, from the taste of it. Not much of a Sunday lunch. Oh, it was a glamorous life in the CID!

The Boscombe had a small snug behind the main bar, and Andy Barrett, having let him in from the street, ushered him in there.

'All right, Bernie, here he is,' Barrett said with a large-lipped, talking-to-idiots emphasis. Passing through the door, Slider saw why. Sitting side by side on the banquette facing the door were Blind Bernie and Mad Sam. 'They've been here since opening,' Barrett added, as though they couldn't hear him. 'I thought there was something on his mind. When it came to closing I didn't realise they were still in here till I'd shut the outside doors. Then he said he had to talk to you.'

'What's all this "he" and "him" malarky?' Blind Bernie said suddenly and angrily. 'I'm not deaf, you know. Nor daft, neither. Is that you, Mr Slider?'

'Yes, it's me. You've got something to tell me, Bernie?'

'Yes, I have,' he said definitely. He turned his face towards the sound of Slider's voice, and then back to where Andy Barrett had last spoken. 'It's for Mr Slider's ears only. I don't want anyone else listening. You clear off and give us a bit of peace, you hear?'

'Now look here,' Barrett said, annoyed. 'You can't talk to me like that in my own pub! I let you stay here on sufferance—'

Slider touched his arm to stop him. Mad Sam, who had been staring about him with his usual vacant expression of goodwill, was growing upset.

'Sufferance, my eye!' Bernie cried. 'Go on, clear off! This is police business.'

'All right,' Barrett said, more to Slider than to Bernie. 'I'll leave you alone. But don't take long. If you aren't out of here by the time the wife gets back we'll all be in the soup.'

Blind Bernie turned his head this way and that, listening. 'Is he gone?' he asked.

Slider sat down opposite them. 'Yes, he's gone. It's just me here now.'

'Is he gone, Sammy?'

'Yes, Dad.'

'Where's my glass? I meant to get him to fill it up again before he went,' Bernie grumbled.

'Drinking out of hours?' Slider said.

'Don't count if I don't pay,' Bernie said promptly. 'I know the law. Ah well, too late now, I suppose.'

During this exchange Slider had been examining the strange pair before him. Bernie was in his sixties, but looked older: a gaunt and grizzled man, sparse white hair mostly concealed under a greasy brown trilby that was never off his head, indoors or out; white whiskers like a horse's; gnarled and blue-veined hands knotted round the end of his old-fashioned white cane, the wooden sort with the crook handle. He always wore the same clothes: a dirty mackintosh that had once been tan, over a grey suit, with a collarless shirt under the jacket and a button-necked vest under the shirt. In the winter he interpolated a pullover and cardigan between the shirt and jacket, and all the layers peeped out from under one another in a stepped *décolletage*. Blind Bernie, the human onion. Slider didn't know why he was blind, whether it was congenital or the result of an illness or accident. There was no sign of it on his face. His eyes were rather small and round and pale blue, and the lack of focus gave him a vacant look, just like his son's. Otherwise they appeared normal, except that the pupils were rather too large and dark which, for some reason Slider could not fathom, gave him the faint look of a budgerigar.

Mad Sam must now be nearly forty, though he looked younger until you studied his face closely. He was hardly taller than his father, but round where Bernie was gaunt; a chubby fellow with a rolling gait and the unlined cherubic face of a choirboy. His hair was thin now, though still dark, and his eyes were blue and round, his expression amiable and harmless. He dribbled slightly from time to time, when his mind, distracted by the necessity to think about something hard, was forced to let go of his jaw to compensate. He always wore the same greenish old tweed overcoat, buttoned up and with a yellow muffler filling in the neckline, winter and summer alike. Slider had no idea what he wore underneath it and was not eager to make the discovery. The two lived together and managed somehow, had done so since Sam's mother died thirty years ago. They spent most of their lives walking about the streets, Bernie's hand on Sam's shoulder: Sam leading, Bernie directing; Sam describing, Bernie explaining.

They lived, as Slider had known but dismissed from his thoughts, in Frithville Gardens – about halfway up, on the right – in the ground-floor maisonette of a two-storey terrace house conversion.

'I'll buy you a pint afterwards,' Slider said to Bernie now. 'And something for Sam,' he added, smiling at the lad (it was impossible not to think of him as a lad, despite the deeply grooved fine creases round his eyes).

'No beer for him,' Bernie said sharply. 'He's not to have alcohol.

It's not good for boys.' He had never lost his slight northern accent, and from talking almost exclusively to his dad, Sam had it too.

'I don't like beer,' Sam said easily, in his rather childish voice. 'I don't want beer, Dad.'

'You'd better not,' said Bernie. 'Orangeade's good enough for him, Mr Slider, when he's done telling you what he saw.'

'If it's something important, I can do better than orangeade,' Slider said. 'How about a Coca-Cola?'

Sam's eyes lit up. 'I like that, I do. Can I have Coca-Cola, Dad?'

'It's too good for you,' Bernie grumbled automatically, 'but if Mr Slider wants to waste his money . . .'

'So what's all this about?' said Slider. 'Something to do with that nasty business in the park, is it?'

'Nasty,' said Sam.

'He saw something,' Bernie said. 'That night, the night it happened. Someone coming out of the park.'

'Why didn't you come to me with this before?' Slider asked.

Bernie spread his hands. 'I didn't want to get mixed up in it,' he said defensively. 'Don't hold it against me, Mr Slider. You know what people are like. They want to put me and him in a home. Any chance they'd get to say I was a bad father, they'd use it to put us in a home. If I was to get mixed up with the police . . . Always after us, the social people, ever since Betty died.'

Sam was looking at him in alarm. 'Dad, Dad!'

'Take him away, they would, and then what'd happen to me? Him in the asylum and me in an old folks' home, and we'd never see each other again.'

'Don't let 'em, Dad,' Sam said. 'Don't let 'em take me away.' He began to rock a little.

Slider intervened hastily. 'They won't take you away. Don't you worry, Sammy. They wouldn't punish you for doing your duty, coming forward and helping the police. That's the right thing to do. That's good.'

'Oh, you don't know,' Bernie moaned. 'Any excuse, that's what they want. They'd blame me for taking the lad to a pub. Bad influence, that's what they'd say I was.'

'Well, they won't say that because they won't know,' Slider

said firmly. 'I shan't tell 'em. And they can't touch you for taking Sam to a pub. He's over eighteen. It's perfectly legal.'

Sam looked at him across the table, blue eyes as round as an owl's. 'I don't want to leave me dad. I love me dad.'

'You won't have to, don't worry. I'll make it all right, Sam. Just tell me what it was you saw.'

He didn't understand the question, and only stared, a drop of drool elongating at his mouth corner.

Bernie, recovering himself, took up the questioning. Slider saw him pinch the back of Sam's hand sharply. 'You ready to tell, Sammy? Like we talked about? That night we were down the Red Lion, and we got talking to Mrs Wheeler, and we walked home late? That was the night of that trouble in the park,' he added to Slider. 'I may be blind, but the lad isn't – and he's not daft either, whatever people say. He doesn't know much, but what he knows, he knows. He told me right there and then what he saw, but I was afraid of the fuss and bother, and the social people saying I couldn't look after him.'

'All right,' Slider said soothingly, 'just start at the beginning. You were coming home from the pub. What time would that be?'

'It'd be half eleven easy 'fore we left the Red Lion,' Bernie answered. 'Mrs Wheeler'd tell you, and Sid Field, the barman. And then twenty minutes or so to walk home. Near on midnight it must have been. We was just coming up to our front gate when Sammy says, "There's a lady," he says. "Coming out of the park."'

Sam's face suddenly illuminated, as though someone had just switched him on. He bounced a little in his seat with pleasure at understanding something. 'That's right, that's right!' he said excitedly. 'A lady, I saw a lady. She came out of the park.'

'Was the gate open or closed, Sam?' Slider asked, not from a need to know but to focus him on the memory.

'Closed, it was closed. She closed it behind her. I saw her. She didn't see me, though. She was too upset. She just ran by. She didn't look at us.'

'How do you know she was upset?'

'She was hurrying along and all like hunched up. And she was crying,' Sam said. 'I was sorry for her. She was a pretty lady.'

'Can you describe her to me?' Slider said. 'What did she look like?'

'She was pretty,' Sam said. 'And she smelt nice.'

'What was she wearing?'

'She had a dress on, a nice blue one, like Oxford and Cambridge.'

'Light blue,' Bernie translated. 'The boat race. We're Cambridge, but he always calls it Oxford and Cambridge. He thinks it's the same thing.'

'What else, Sammy?'

'She was a black lady,' Sam said helpfully.

'If you saw her again, would you recognise her?'

Sam nodded his head. 'I would. I would know her. I would.' Then his mouth turned down. 'Because of the nasty thing.'

'What nasty thing was that?'

Sam looked at his father. 'I don't have to say, do I, Dad? I don't like saying it.'

'Aye, you must,' Bernie said. 'Like I told you, you've got to say it to Mr Slider, and you've not got to get upset, or they'll come and take us away and put us in a home. Now get on and tell what the lady did.'

Sam's lip trembled, and his eyes were moist. He rocked again, gently. 'She had something in her hand, something nasty. I saw when she went past. It was all covered in blood. It was nasty.'

'Was it a knife?' Slider asked. Sam nodded, near to tears. 'All right, Sammy, go on.'

'Go on, son,' Bernie encouraged. 'Tell what she did.'

'She threw it away,' Sam said. 'In the house with the weeds, down the area. She went across the road and threw it in there. And then she ran all the way down the street and turned the corner that way.' He made a gesture of turning right.

'I understand,' Slider said. 'Is that all?'

Sam nodded.

'That's all,' Bernie said. 'But when we heard about the murder, I couldn't decide whether to say anything or not. You won't let them hold it against me, will you, Mr Slider? I know I'm old, but we manage all right. We look after each other. If they split us up, I don't know what would become of the boy.'

'I won't let it make any trouble for you,' Slider said, with more conviction than he felt. It wasn't that anything they had done or not done was reason for institutionalising either of them; but Bernie knew with the instinct of self-preservation that in their situation you did not draw attention to yourself. Journalists might get hold of the story and decide to splash it for 'human interest'; or simply being in court might direct official eyes in their direction. And then questions would be asked, and appalling things done to them for their own good. A social worker would only have to smell them to know they ought to be put in a home; and God knew what the inside of the maisonette was like.

'That man was killed,' Sam said suddenly and confidingly. 'I know, I heard it. I saw our street and our park on the telly. That man was killed with a knife, a sharp knife, a pointy knife, and there was all blood and he fell down dead. Bang!' It was sudden and loud and made Slider jump, which in turn made Sam flinch. He was getting too excited.

'Never mind about that,' Bernie said sharply. 'You sit still and be quiet or I'll give you what-for.' And to Slider, 'I don't like him watching telly. It's not good for the lad, but they have it on sometimes when we're down the pub. He saw you on the telly, Mr Slider—'

'I saw you on the telly, Mr Slider,' Sam nodded.

'He's not daft, whatever people say. He wanted to tell you about the lady and the knife—'

'It was a sharp knife, all covered in blood! It was nasty!'

'But I was afraid. I told him to forget about it, but then my conscience wasn't easy.'

'Well, you did the right thing, Bernie, and I'm grateful to you. To both of you. And I'll make sure there's a little something for you both to say thank you.'

'Oh, no, that wouldn't be right,' Bernie said gravely. 'Not a reward for doing your duty.'

'I'd like to give you something anyway. There's nothing wrong with that. You didn't do it for the money, so it's quite all right.'

'Well,' said Bernie, but less doubtfully.

'Now I want you both to come with me to the station, and we'll take down what Sam saw in writing, to make it all official. And then I'd like you, Sam, to sit and look at some pictures and tell me if any of them look like the lady you saw. Can you do that?'

Sam looked sly. 'Can I have a Coca-Cola if I do?'

'You can have the back of my hand if you don't do as you're told,' Bernie said fiercely, and Sam collapsed like a pricked balloon. You could have blown Bernie away with a puff of wind, and Sam was twice his weight at least; but in the minds of both of them Sam was still nine years old and in short trousers.

CHAPTER TWENTY-ONE

Content – Liable To Settle

'The house with the weeds,' Mad Sam had said, and Slider, having been up and down Frithville Gardens often enough in the past week, had no difficulty in identifying it. One house on the left-hand side going up (the side opposite to where Blind Bernie and Mad Sam lived) had been empty for some time and was boarded up and semi-derelict. Weeds had sprung up with mongrel vigour from the small patch of earth on the side of the area, ragwort and grass was sprouting from cracks in the steps and windowsills, and the gutters were gay with buddleia so that the house looked as if it was wearing an Ascot hat.

Atherton looked with distaste down the area, which was choked not just with weeds but with rubbish, carelessly discarded tins, bottles and fast-food boxes, and the inevitable skeleton of a pushchair. The rate of attrition of children's buggies was so abnormally high, he thought, it was something to bear in mind when looking for shares to invest in.

McLaren was equally unimpressed. 'You want me to go down there?'

'Well, I'm not trousered for it,' Atherton said.

'And there's got to be some advantage to my higher rank,' Slider added. 'If it's not that, I can't think what else it can be.'

'You're breaking his heart,' Atherton warned. 'Come on, Maurice, you're the one who'll feel most at home among all those KFC cartons.' He nudged McLaren towards the steps. 'Be careful, though. There might be rats.'

'Not at this time of day,' Slider intervened. 'Get on with it.'

McLaren donned his gloves and descended gingerly. It was fifteen minutes before he straightened up and said, 'I think I've got something.'

'I wouldn't be a bit surprised,' Atherton murmured.

McLaren was clambering back up. He displayed his booty: a paperknife in the shape of a stiletto, sharply pointed and narrow, double-edged, and with a blade about five and a half or six inches long.

'Probably a souvenir of Toledo,' Atherton commented.

'It's still got blood on it,' McLaren noted happily.

'And with any luck,' Slider said, 'fingermarks.'

'It'll take time to get it processed and get a match on either,' Atherton observed.

'Doesn't matter,' Slider said. 'Mad Sam picked her photo out without the slightest hesitation.'

'Mary Coulsden, aka Teena Brown,' McLaren said with satisfaction. 'Well, at least we know we've *got* her prints on record, so we've got something to match the fingermarks with, when we get 'em back.'

'But if Teena killed Lenny, what does that do to our lovely house of cards?' said Atherton. 'Doesn't it all come tumbling down?'

'No, no,' Slider said distractedly, 'it all makes perfect sense.'

'All we've got to do, of course, is find her,' Atherton mentioned.

'I think,' said Slider, 'that I know where she is.'

Sassy Palmer was dressed this time when she opened the door – not in the red dress but in a pair of mauve Lycra leggings and a tight, low-cut top of ocelot-printed cotton.

'Not a-bloody-gain,' she said with enormous, theatrical exasperation. 'I already spent half me Sunday down the cop shop. Can't you buggers leave me alone?' She eyed Atherton professionally and slipped abruptly into her Harlem persona. 'How you doin', honey? I hain't seen you befo'.'

'I'm sorry to have to bother you again,' Slider said, slipping his foot into position, 'but I'd like a word with your sister.'

'My—?' Sassy's eyes narrowed as she recollected. 'She's not here. She's gone.'

'Oh, I don't think so,' Slider said.

'Yeah,' Sassy assured him earnestly. 'She was only stoppin' over the one night. She lives up – up Birmingham,' she added inventively.

Slider looked at her sadly and kindly. 'The game's up, Sassy. I know Teena's here. I smelt her scent when I was here before. She wears *Paris* and yours is *My Sin*. Come on, love. We've got the evidence now, and we have to take her in. But you know I'll be gentle with her. Better me than somebody else.'

'You always say that,' Sassy complained, but she seemed near to tears.

'You've been a good friend to her,' Slider said, laying a hand on her wrist. 'Come on, be a good girl and let's get this over with.'

She seemed to consider resisting, but then to realise it was pointless. She did not, however, *let* them in: Slider had to push her gently out of the way, understanding that it was her way of salving her conscience.

They could see through the open door that the kitchen and living room were empty. Atherton looked in one bedroom, Slider in the other. There was a sharp cry and a scuffle, and Slider reversed hastily and ran to help Atherton, who was holding Teena Brown by both wrists while she screamed at him in a mixture of anger and fear.

She was wearing a white teeshirt and a pair of pink pedal-pushers, and her pretty face was drawn and exhausted with fear and distress. 'Let me go! Let me go!' she cried. 'I ain't done nothing! You don't understand!'

'Yes, I do,' Slider said. 'Calm down, Teena. Stop struggling – you'll only hurt yourself. I know what's been going on. I know you killed Lenny, and I know why. It's all over now.'

She stared at him a moment and then burst into tears, and feeling the struggle leave her, Atherton released her so she could sit down heavily on the bed behind her and sob into her hands. Behind Slider, Sassy was swearing softly and continuously under her breath, but she made no move to intervene.

Slider had hardly ever been sorrier than when he began, 'Mary Christina Coulsden, otherwise known as Teena Brown, I arrest you for the murder of Lenny Baxter. You do not need to say anything . . .'

'Hullo. Am I disturbing you?'

Slider looked up sharply. Joanna was standing in the doorway of his office, her overnight bag slung over one shoulder, her handbag over the other. It took him a moment of wondering what was strange about her – apart from her actual presence here – before realising that she did not have her fiddle case in her hand. It didn't look natural, somehow.

'I got tired of having my phone messages ignored,' she added, seeing his brain was still catching up, 'and since I haven't got any work to do until Wednesday morning I thought I'd hop on a plane and come and see how you're doing.' She cocked an eyebrow at him. 'Say something, even if it's only "bleh".'

'Joanna,' he said.

'Well, that's a start. At least you recognise me.' She crossed the room and he stood up hastily, sending a plastic dispenser cup tumbling to the floor, where it bounced hollowly but fortunately drily. Then his arms were round her, and she was pressing against him, warm and real and full of the usual interesting bumps.

When he released her she smiled and pushed him gently backwards and said, 'Sit. You look fit to fall down.'

'I feel it. What time is it?'

'Nearly seven. When did you last go home?'

He thought. 'Saturday night,' he said.

'You do realise it's Monday night? No wonder you're tired.'

'Everything's happening,' he said. 'We've made an arrest on one murder and we're about to make an arrest on another, and what with one thing and another—'

'Yes, I get the picture. That accounts for why you haven't picked up your messages.'

'You could have called me on my mobile,' he said.

'I'd have loved to,' she said drily, 'but it's turned off.'

'Oh yes,' he said vaguely, 'I did that to stop it ringing.'

'That'll do it,' she agreed. 'Have you eaten anything?'

'Not for – oh, years and years,' he said, managing to smile.

'Come and eat, then. You can spare the time for that. Even Wellington took time out at Waterloo for a snack.'

'Station buffets can be handy.'

'They haven't knocked the cheek out of you then,' she noted, taking his hand and tugging, gently but insistently, like a child.

The canteen was quiet, and they took a corner table well out of earshot of anyone else. 'You're right, of course,' he said, unloading his tray. 'I'm famished.'

'And the brain needs food to operate properly,' Joanna said. He'd chosen the all-day breakfast, heavy on the beans; she had a piece of quiche and some salad. She wasn't really hungry, but knew he wouldn't eat if she didn't. She talked inconsequentially while he stifled the first urgent pangs; then, when his fork-work slowed below warp speed, he told her about the case, and about Mary Coulsden.

She had always admired her cousin Everet, the slick, streetwise, ineffably sophisticated yet kind cousin Ev, her hero and icon of naughtiness. When he had introduced her to Lenny Baxter, she was predisposed to like him, as she would have liked anyone Ev recommended to her. But Lenny was handsome and well-built, smartly dressed, appeared to have money, and was generous with it. He had an air of edgy dangerousness that was missing from the more familiar Ev, which thrilled her; and he had charm, too, something that of course could not be known to anyone who had only ever met him dead.

She fell instantly into infatuation with him, and after only a few dates was ready to move out from her parents' home and into his.

'She was finding life at home too stifling anyway,' Slider said. 'A lively youngster with old parents, and church-going parents at that. All children want to rebel at some point.'

'I bet you never did,' Joanna said.

'I grew my hair long in 1968,' he mentioned.

'*Ruat coelum!*' she said, but he didn't understand her pronunciation. 'Go on.'

'Well, things seemed all right at first for her with Lenny. She found him exciting, she liked spending money, smoking and drinking, and going about with him and his wicked friends to the sort of places she knew her parents would disapprove of. She was in love with him and thought he was in love with her. The first shock was in the course of a drunken party when he proposed to share her with two of his friends. She was drunk too, and rather excited by the wickedness, and went along with it, but the next morning she felt bad about it. She told Lenny she would never do anything like that again. Lenny told her not to be so narrow-minded and that it was just a piece of fun – and Lenny, after all, must know best.'

'Yes, I can see how it would have gone,' she said. 'I bet he made fun of her parents' religion.'

'How did you know?'

'Figures. Religion isn't cool these days.'

Not long after the incident at the party, Lenny told her he wanted to 'lend' her to Ken Whalley in return for the key to the park.

'She argued about that one; but he pressed her, saying old Ken was harmless and it would all be over in seconds. Then he was offended and said he'd thought she loved him and why wouldn't she do this one little thing for him. In the end he wore her down, and she did it.'

'What a bastard,' Joanna said.

'Yes. Of course, she began to realise in the end that he *was* a bastard, and to guess that he didn't really love her. But if ever she got close to rebelling he'd charm her back again and tell her he loved her and buy her a present.' He shook his head at it. 'I've noticed time and again that women don't seem to care how badly a man behaves, as long as he *says* he loves her. And vice versa – they'll leave a good and loving man because he doesn't use the words often enough.'

'We're so shallow and fickle,' Joanna said, and he managed a troubled smile.

'Sorry. All generalisations are false—'

'Including that one,' she finished for him.

So the truth was that Teena, who had first been mentioned to Slider as the tom Lenny lived with, was not a prostitute in the proper sense. It was all at Lenny's instigation, sometimes for money – as time went on and his affairs became more involved, always for money – but there was another motive which Teena, from her innocent upbringing, only ever sensed and never clearly understood. Lenny *liked* lending her; he liked having her in company, and he liked to watch other men having her. She didn't like it, felt besmirched and humiliated by it, but Lenny's hold over her was absolute. She quickly learnt about his temper, and that the air of dangerousness which had thrilled her – and still did – was in fact the leading edge of a real violence. So out of fear and infatuation she stayed with him. Life was at least more exciting with him, and where else, after all, could she go? Certainly not back home. Lenny offered her soft drugs, and she relied on them more as time went on to soften the edges of her world and lend an air of unreality to the things her childhood conscience still told her were wrong.

She had no idea he was in money trouble, though she knew he spent freely and was losing money on the horses. Still his 'business' interests seemed so wide and varied she assumed they would cover his lifestyle. But as his money troubles got worse, and he got himself into more of a muddle, his temper grew worse and she grew more afraid of him. Sometimes now she wanted to get away from him, but the one time she had hinted at leaving him he had grabbed her by the neck and said if she ran away he would find her and kill her. It was what men like him said, and not all of them meant it, but she believed it. Who would take the risk that he didn't? It was what accounted, said Slider, for so much abuse of women.

Then one day Lenny told Teena that the boss – the Needle himself – had seen her and fancied her.

'How?' Joanna asked. 'I mean, where did he see her?'

'In the Phoenix. There were CCTV cameras in there. We thought they were just for ordinary pub security, but of course they'd been put in by – or at least at the order of – Needle Bates, who liked to spy on his employees. Lenny had taken Teena in there several times. She is very pretty, of course; and it might have occurred to Bates that being under Lenny's thumb she'd be compliant about his strange ways; and also, of course, he could be sure Lenny wouldn't object.'

'What a sweetheart,' said Joanna.

'Which?'

'Both.'

'Yes, Lenny wasn't exactly above his company. Well, anyway, what he didn't know was that Teena knew something about the Needle's proclivities, having heard it from Susie Mabbot during one of those ladies' loo confessions when they were out in four-some with Lenny and Everet. Susie made light of it, but Teena could see she hated it and feared the Needle. And of course Susie was now dead, and Teena had her suspicions about who had killed her. The evidence about all the tiny holes had not been generally released, but that only gave her imagination room to run riot. So she refused point-blank to do what she was told. First Lenny argued and cajoled – this was so important to his career, he would get into trouble if she didn't do it, et cetera. Then he smacked her around a bit – but carefully, so as not to damage the goods – and told her if she didn't obey, Bates would kill him, but not before *he* killed *her*.'

'Poor kid.'

'Yes. Anyway, then things all came to a head at the same time. This is speculation, but I think Bates had decided to get rid of Lenny, partly because he was unreliable, and partly as a way to get Teena for himself. Lenny must have been dragging his feet about "lending" her, hoping to talk or bully Teena into it. Teena, meanwhile, had worked herself up into a pitch of terror. Lenny had told her he was going to force her to do as she was told and be nice to the boss, and she couldn't see any way out. She apparently tried to get Everet to help her but he didn't understand or didn't believe what she was trying to tell him.'

'Everet didn't know about the Needle killing Susie?'

'Not then. It was only afterwards he began to put two and two together with his buried suspicions and make ten.'

On that Monday night, Teena had been out to the all-night supermarket and on her way back saw Lenny outside the flat, talking to two of the Needle's men. She assumed they were arranging her fate between them, and that it was imminent. She concealed herself and watched. When they went away and Lenny went into the flat, she rang him on her mobile and told him that she had something important to tell him and he must meet her in the park.'

'Why there?'

'She knew the flat was bugged. Lenny had told her. It was one of the conditions of employment. And she knew, of course, that Lenny did his own business in the park so it must be private there.'

'And what was she going to tell him in the park?'

'She wanted to plead with him one last time. Her idea was that they should both run away and start a new life somewhere else.'

'How traditional.'

'But when she'd seen him leave the flat, she dashed in and grabbed the paperknife from beside the telephone, in case he wouldn't listen to reason. She'd got to the point when she felt it was him or her. And,' Slider added thoughtfully, 'she probably wasn't far wrong.'

Joanna reached across the table and laid her hand over his, and he chafed her fingers as he spoke, as if it comforted him.

'So she followed him to the park, to the children's playground where he used to conduct his business. She said when she saw his face, she knew straight away that it wasn't any good, and she just walked up to him and stabbed him before he could guess what she was up to, and before she lost her nerve. I thought that single blow straight to the heart was professional,' he said, 'but it turns out it was just lucky. One of my many misjudgements.'

He must have gone down like a felled horse, he thought: a dreadful thing, and yet giving small, slight Teena a terrifying sense of power. Then horror overcame her, and she ran for it; ran sobbing back the way she had come, a murderess now, and still afraid for her life; too upset to notice Blind Bernie and Mad Sam – though if she had noticed them she probably would have ignored them.

'They were street furniture, practically,' Slider said. 'And anyway, who would think of them as witnesses? Not the CPS,' he added, 'that's for sure.'

Finding herself still clutching the bloody weapon, she flung it away as she passed the empty house. Later she had thought that was the wrong thing to have done, but it was not surprising if she hadn't been able to think clearly at a moment like that. She thought that the Needle's men would be after her, and she certainly feared them more than the police. She went back to the flat, packed a bag in jittering terror, and left.

'She didn't know where to go. She thought of Everet, but didn't know how far he could be trusted. He still worked for the Needle, and suppose he just gave her up to him? She couldn't go home to her parents – certainly not now she'd killed a man. In the end she thought of Sassy Palmer, whom she'd met at Susie's house and knew had been a friend of Susie's.'

'Always trust a girlfriend when you're in trouble,' Joanna said. 'How did you know she was there?'

'I guessed. Sassy said she had never met Everet's cousin, but she knew the word "cousin" was female in this case. And she said she had met Lenny with Everet when they called for Susie to go out as a foursome, but not Teena. Why would they have left Teena outside? So if she had met Teena and was lying about it, there must be a reason. And finally I realised I had smelt her scent in Sassy's house – *Paris*. I'd smelt it first in Lenny's flat.'

'God bless your nose,' Joanna said. 'You're so clever.'

'No, I'm slow, too slow. There were indications I ought to have picked up. Right at the beginning, Freddie Cameron said there was a fresh pint of beer in Lenny's stomach. That ought to have told me he was killed earlier than two in the morning.' He paused, thinking. 'Funny thing, Nutty said to me that there was a woman at the bottom of most things. There were enough hints I should have picked up. If I'd got onto the true line earlier two lives might have been saved.'

'I doubt it,' she said, but he only shook his head, unable to be comforted by her. She knew this mood of his after a serious case. It was reaction to the tremendous mental effort and the awful responsibility. 'You're tired,' she said. 'When are you finishing tonight?'

He looked a little blank, and then dragged in a sigh. 'I hadn't even thought about going home, but now you're here . . .' The food was making him sleepy now. 'Give me another half hour at the desk, and then we'll go home together.'

In the car, going home, he told her the rest of the story: conjecture still, but he hoped capable of proof. Bates's goons had gone to the park later, at the time previously arranged, the time for which Sonny Collins would have fixed his alibi according to orders. Finding Baxter dead, they had gone through his pockets for the keys to the flat, for any form of identification and, perhaps, for his betting-book.

'I imagine they rang the boss for instructions and Bates told them to sit the corpse on the swing as a kind of joke. It's too depressing to think of them having that sort of sense of humour for themselves.'

'What about the chain – why did they take that away?'

'I don't know. Maybe they picked it up on the way in with the intention of using it on Lenny, and then took it with them without thinking. Or maybe the boss told them to keep it for some other purpose. I don't know how devious his mind really is.

'After that it was a matter of clearing up behind them. Back to Lenny's flat to remove anything that might incriminate anyone.

'And, presumably, to take Teena. But Teena was gone. Bates must have been furious.'

Then the other strands of Lenny's life had to be unpicked. Herbie Weedon, his other employer, was bugged. When it looked as though he was going to be a nuisance, he was eliminated.

'Or perhaps he wasn't supposed to die, only to be frightened. But his heart gave out.'

And then Everet Boston, at last worried for his cousin and tending to put two and two together and to talk too much – Everet had to be silenced. But he had already revealed the importance of Sonny Collins in the network. So now Sonny was a danger.

'Did Sonny jump or was he pushed?' Slider wondered, waiting for the traffic lights to change. 'The thing I'd most like to know, and never will, is what was in his mind when he took the pills.' Maybe he wasn't up to all the bodies. To get rid of Lenny he might have seen as essential, but one murder was leading to another, and where would it end? And doing nothing might – was this the final betrayal? – lead to his being murdered himself, if Bates, who seemed to be getting more and more paranoid, decided he couldn't trust him. Maybe the Needle he had known and loved in Hong Kong was mutating into something even he couldn't contemplate. To live with the knowledge of his evil, or to give him up, were equally unthinkable alternatives. The only other way out was the Big Sleep.

Slider was silent until they moved off again, and then he said, 'The most extraordinary thing of all was the sheer chance of it. Bates was so careful. If it hadn't been for the leather jacket, we never would have looked at him at all. And the Phoenix was just a little outpost of the empire. The whole towering structure of Bates's world, built up piece by piece over the years, was made to totter through the frailty of Lenny Baxter, and one American amateur smuggler.'

'Will you get him – Bates? For the other murders?'

'I think so. We'll get him for Susie Mabbot; and Teena can identify the two men she saw talking to Lenny outside the house. We know one is Thomas Mark, and we think the other is Bates's butler. Once we've got them tied in, and tied in with his visits to Susie Mabbot's, I think they'll give him up to save themselves.'

'And what about Teena?'

'Her fingermarks are on the paperknife along with Lenny's blood, which supports her confession, so we probably won't have to call on Mad Sam, which is a blessing. It's enough to convict her, but she'll turn Queen's evidence against Bates and get off with a reduced sentence for manslaughter, I should think. Well,' he added wearily, 'it's out of my hands now. Susie Mabbot was Notting Hill's case anyway, and the NCS has already got an enquiry in train on Bates. They'll take the whole thing over.'

'Including Teena Brown?'

'I should think so.'

'But it will be good for you, won't it? I mean, you got a result.'

He gave a tired smile. 'Oh, I should think I might get a commendation.'

'As much as that?'

'I'm glad you're here,' he said. 'How long can you stay?'

'If I get up at the crack of dawn, until Wednesday morning. That was our turning, by the way. You've gone past it. You really are tired, aren't you?'

'Bashed,' he said, indicating right at the next corner.

'But you got him,' she said encouragingly.

'They'll get him,' he corrected. 'We got her. Poor weeping thing.'

After some satisfying lovemaking and a hot bath, he found himself irrationally wide awake again, so he opened a bottle of wine while she put some music on and they got into bed to enjoy them.

'So what's going on with Sue and Jim?' she asked.

'Oh, I think they're all right,' he said.

'What about his wandering eye?'

'I think it's ceased to wander, really. He's discovered he doesn't really want to. It was just force of habit.'

'Fine excuse.'

'We had a bit of a chat earlier on. He was going home this evening to apologise and make everything right.' He looked at her sideways. 'Do you think she'll forgive him?'

'She'll have to,' Joanna said. 'They can't split up now they have two cats between them, can they?'

'No. Divorce is hell on pets – turns them into feline delinquents.'

He felt her come to it, an almost physical sensation, like an indrawn breath. 'And what about us?'

'*What* about us?' he gave the question back. 'You've been gearing up to say something to me, I know. You held off because of my case, but I can't hide behind that for ever. Maybe it'd be best to get it out and get it over with.' She was still silent, and he went on, 'Say something to stop me babbling. Can't you tell I'm scared to death?'

She gave him a strange look. 'Scared of what?'

Over the edge in a barrel. 'That you want to end it. That you've found someone else.'

'After the proofs of love I've just given you?'

'You might just have been being kind,' he said; but he almost grinned with huge relief. It wasn't that. He could tell. There was no-one else. Maybe she was just going to revive the question of his going to Amsterdam, a much less scary possibility. 'Go on, out with it. What did you want to talk about?'

'I'm going to tell you something,' she said in a rather strained voice, 'and you have to be very careful what you say in reply, because if you get it wrong it'll kill me. Are you ready?'

'As ready as I'll ever be.'

'All right then. Here it is.' She swivelled to face him so that she could watch his expression. 'I'm pregnant.'

He said absolutely nothing. His brain could not get to grips with it.

'Well, I suppose that's better than saying the wrong thing,' she said. She looked at him wryly. 'You hadn't guessed that's what it was? Some bloody detective you are!'

'How?' was all he managed to say.

'What do you mean, how? Didn't they do human reproduction in biology?'

'Not when I was at school. I suppose I mean when, really. On what occasion.'

'When I came back in February, as far as I can make out.' She looked a little conscious. 'I don't remember missing a pill, but when I got back to Amsterdam I found I must have.' She gave a lop-sided smile. 'It wasn't deliberate, I promise you, but – well, they say there's no such thing as an accident, don't they? Maybe subconsciously – look, I'm doing all the talking. You still haven't said anything. About it. About being pleased. Or not.'

'I'm pleased,' he said, taking her hand. February? She was three months gravid, then. The child was well on the way. His child, his-and-hers child. And what did he think about that? Children, to him, were Kate and Matthew. He'd been a father already, he'd done that bit, and he wouldn't have been normal if he didn't think, however fleetingly, of broken nights and nappies, responsibility and expense, and the curtailment of freedom children brought.

But it was only fleeting. Her dear face was close, and though she was trying to make light of it he could see her apprehension. *If you say the wrong thing it will kill me.* She had been alone with the pregnancy for nearly three months, alone and wondering, hoping for the best and fearing the worst, afraid to tell him in case he was not delighted.

Well, she should not be alone with it any more. He was delighted. A child, her child, their child, was already started and on its way, and the least it deserved was for them both to be wholeheartedly glad about it. It should not come into the world with any remembered coolness to blight it, no unwelcoming word, like the bad fairy's gift, to come back to haunt it.

'You really didn't guess?' she said, watching his thoughts flit about his face, and – more importantly – the slowly dawning smile.

'Not a bit. Call me dumb.'

'Dumb. But you really are pleased? I mean, I know it wasn't planned, and the situation is—'

He stopped her with a kiss. 'I'm dumb with bliss. It wasn't what I expected, but how could I not want our child?'

She almost sagged with relief. 'Bless you for that. I've made a complete mess of this. I should have told you weeks ago. I just didn't know how to.'

'I understand,' he said. Matthew and Kate and – well, call him X. Him or her. He felt a surge of wild excitement grasp his loins. Their child would be special. What would Kate and Matthew think about it? He must make sure they never felt set aside for the new one. He would have to talk seriously to Irene to make sure she said the right things too. And what the hell was he thinking about Irene for at a moment like this?

'But what will you do now?' he asked. 'I mean, you're over there and I'm over here. We'll have a schizophrenic baby.'

'What would you think about my coming back?'

'What about the job?'

'I was only doing it on trial. I'd have to give it up, of course. Try and subsist on casual work, whatever I could pick up over here. For as long as I could work. I could keep going almost up to the day. And after the baby's born—'

'We'll manage,' he said.

'It'll be tight.'

'It'll be all right. Money's the least of it.'

'Oh brave man! You just wait.'

'I mean it,' he said. 'I know about babies and expense, remember. People expect too much, that's what makes the problems. You can always manage, if you have to.' He lifted her hand and kissed it. 'There is just one thing.'

'Oh?' she said suspiciously.

'One small proviso.'

'I smell a rat,' she said.

'Well, I think I'm entitled to one demand. After all, you did trick me into this—'

'You bastard!'

'Nail on head, as usual,' he said. 'I'm an old-fashioned sort of bloke, as well you know.'

'Hidebound,' she agreed. 'Practically ossified.'

'And if we're going to have a baby, I'm afraid I must insist on our doing it properly.' She looked at him. 'Will you marry me? And I warn you, it's one of those "Nonne" questions.'

'What questions?'

'Questions that expect the answer "yes".'

'Oh, those!'

The phone rang. They looked at each other and then burst out laughing. Slider picked it up.

'I thought you were still at work,' Atherton said.

'What are you ringing me here for, then?'

'I thought you'd like to know the result of your advised plan of action. You know, bottle of wine, nice meal, soft lights, heart-to-heart talk?'

'How did it go?'

'Well, apart from the cats going mad around us, very well. She forgave me.'

'I thought she would. And?'

'She still loves me.'

'Wise woman. And?'

'Brace yourself for a shock. I asked her to marry me.' Slider began to smile, slowly. Into his silence, Atherton spoke again. 'Are you there? Did you hear what I said? I said, we're going to get married.'

'Now there's a coincidence,' said Slider.

Dear Departed

In loving memory of Geoffrey Knighton –
Hero, reluctant soldier, teacher, writer,
critic and friend.

"Life's race well run, life's work well done."

CHAPTER ONE

open.guv.ok

There is nothing quite like knocking on a strange door for getting a policeman's adrenaline going. Slider stood in the hotel corridor, listening to the white noise of the air-conditioning and the interesting tattoo of his own heartbeat, and wondering if he was about to die.

His mouth was so dry he had to pause a moment and manufacture some spit. The kevlar vest under his shirt made him feel hot and awkward, and the tape holding the wire to his flesh was making him itch. He'd had to borrow a jacket from a larger colleague to conceal the fact that he was protected. He looked, and felt, overweight and stupid.

In front of him was an ordinary, typical hotel door, and behind the door was an extraordinary, untypical man, who, moreover, might well be armed, and had amply proved his willingness to kill. Robert Bates, alias The Needle, was being brought to book at last. He had been the subject of ongoing investigations by various CO departments of Scotland Yard, not to mention – because nobody ever did – MI5 and MI6.

Slider's path had crossed with his during the investigation of a murder, which, it turned out most disappointingly, Bates didn't do. However, Slider had turned up a number of things Bates did do, including the undoubted murder of a prostitute whom Bates had used, tortured, and then dispatched. Because of the involvement of higher authorities, Slider had been warned off Bates, but such disappointments were commonplace in a copper's life. Sooner or later, he had reasoned, The Needle would get his come-uppance. Then two days ago he had been summoned to the office of the area supremo, Commander Wetherspoon.

'Ah, Slider,' Wetherspoon said, tilting his head back so that he could look down his nose at him, 'someone here who wants to speak to you, Chief Superintendent Ormerod of the Serious Crime Group Liaison Team.'

Ormerod was a large and serious man, who towered over Slider and would have made two of him in bulk, and at least ten in conscious supremacy. He had a handsome, authoritative face, eyes like steel traps, and the smell of power came off him like an aura. This man was from the far, far end of policing, the place of hard deals done behind closed doors, of anonymous corridors, terse telephone calls, operations with code names and briefings with senior ministers where the senior ministers behaved quite meekly. It was as different from Slider's place on the street as the Cabinet Room of Number 10 was from the checkout at Tesco's. Slider felt faint just breathing Ormerod's aftershave; and when Ormerod smiled, it was even more frightening than when he didn't.

Ormerod smiled. 'Ah, Inspector Slider. Bill, isn't it? I'm glad to meet you. I won't waste time. Trevor Bates. You did some smart work on that case. I'm sorry you had to take a back seat, but very large things were at stake.'

'I understand, sir,' Slider said, since something seemed to be required.

'We've got to the point now where we're ready to arrest him, and we want you to be the one to do it.'

'Me, sir?' Slider couldn't help it, though it made him sound like Billy Bunter.

'Thought you'd like to be in on it,' Ormerod said. 'Sort of thanks for all your hard work.'

'Consolation prize,' Wetherspoon put in, and Slider was glad to see him quelled with a single look from Ormerod. Anyone who could quell Wetherspoon was a Big Monkey indeed.

'Also,' Ormerod said, 'we think you could be useful to us.'

Ormerod explained. Bates was a high-powered criminal, and as sharp and cunning as a lorry full of foxes. It would be impossible to arrest him in his home, which was better defended than Fort Knox, and pretty hard anywhere else if he saw them coming. Bates often went armed, and usually had armed bodyguards around him.

However, the day after tomorrow he was attending a business conference in a hotel in Birmingham, and staying overnight, and was unlikely to be armed in such a place, especially as they had taken pains to fall back from him over the past few weeks and let him relax. He would not be expecting trouble, and though he would have an 'assistant' with him, for which read bodyguard, he would probably not be taking very heavy precautions.

'All the same, we can't take him in any of the public rooms, in case his goon gets rattled and starts loosing off,' Ormerod said. 'So we have to arrest him in his room at the end of the day. But we don't want to go kicking the door in and provoking a shoot-out. We need someone to distract him. That's where you come in. He knows you, you've spoken to him before, and he's not afraid of you.'

With the rind taken off, what Ormerod was saying was that Bates thought Slider was a pathetic dickhead whom he'd already outsmarted once. He would therefore be more likely to open the door to him. Bates was also tricky, smart and strong, and had an unhealthy liking for torture, knives and needles. And guns. The words 'tethered' and 'goat' had wandered through Slider's mind, looking for something to link up with.

Which was why Slider now regarded that anonymous hotel door with trepidation. If Bates opened it at all, it might be simply to shoot him, and he didn't want to die. His pulse rate notched up another level as he raised his hand and rapped hard on it. The team was all behind him, he reminded himself. They had watched Bates to his room, watched the 'assistant' to his adjoining one, and were waiting just out of sight, listening to everything that came over Slider's wire, ready for his signal. He hoped the wire was still working. He hoped they weren't being deafened by his heartbeat.

He knocked again. Bates's voice – Slider recognised it, with a shiver - called out irritably from within. 'Who is it?'

Slider gulped. 'Detective Inspector Slider, sir, Shepherd's Bush. Could I have a word, do you think?'

'*What?*' Bates said incredulously. 'Slider, did you say?' His voice came again from just behind the door, and Slider guessed he was being examined through the peephole. He held up his brief. 'I know you,' Bates said. 'What are you doing here? What the hell do you want?'

'I'd like to have a word with you, sir,' Slider said stolidly, Mr Plod to the core. 'I'd like to ask you a few questions.'

There was a click and a rattle, and Slider's stomach went over the edge of a cliff as the door was flung open and he waited for the hot flash and burn of a bullet or a knife in the guts. The kevlar was a comfort but it didn't cover everything.

But he didn't die. Bates stood there, lean, weirdly attractive, with his pale, translucent skin, clear grey eyes and backswept, shoulder-length fox red hair. He was still in his suit – three piece, exquisitely cut – but he had removed his tie and opened the top button of his shirt.

'What the *devil*?' he said, and looked Slider up and down with amused contempt. 'You came asking me questions once before about some pathetic trivia or other. A leather jacket, wasn't it?'

'It's a little bit more serious this time, sir, I'm sorry to say,' Slider plodded. 'Can I come in? I don't think you want to discuss your private business in the corridor.'

'I don't intend to discuss my private business with you at all,' he said. 'What the devil are you doing here anyway? Do your superiors know you've come bothering me?'

'I don't need permission from anyone when I'm following up a case,' Slider said, hoping he would take this to mean he was mavericking. Bates had not shut the door on him, apparently fascinated by the absurdity of this idiot policeman following him all the way to Birmingham. Ormerod had read him right: arrogance would be his downfall. Slider took the opportunity to walk past him into the room, noting with huge relief that there was no-one else in it. The goon was still in his adjoining room, the door of which was over to the left. One shout from Bates and he would come busting in, probably with a gun. Slider was not out of the woods yet.

'I didn't give you permission to come in,' Bates said, sounding annoyed now.

'This won't take long, sir,' Slider said. His voice shook slightly, but it probably didn't matter. Bates would expect him to be nervous of a powerful man like him. 'And it is rather important.'

'More lost clothing? Or is it a lost dog this time?' Bates sneered; but he walked away from the door, and it swung closed with a soft click. Slider cleared his throat, which was the signal. Nearly there now. Just a few seconds more. The team would be creeping towards the two doors, pass keys in hand.

Slider turned towards Bates, so that Bates had his back to the door. Triumph was beginning to sing in his veins along with the adrenaline, a heady mixture. He felt drunk and reckless with it, and knew it was a dangerous state of mind.

'It's a bit more interesting than that,' he said, and the change of his tone brought alertness into the hard grey eyes. Slider saw the nostrils widen as though Bates were scenting like an animal for danger. 'It's to do with a certain prostitute called Susie Mabbot. I'm sure you remember her, even among your many conquests.'

'I don't know any prostitutes. How dare you suggest it?' Bates said, advancing grimly. Slider backed a step to encourage him.

'You used to know poor Susie, in the Biblical sense, anyway. Then one day you got carried away and killed her. Stuck her full of needles, had her, broke her neck, and chucked her in the Thames.'

'You're mad!' Bates said. Outside the team slipped the pass card into the magnetic lock and it gave a faint but unmistakable clunk. Bates's eyes flew wide as he realised the trap. He yelled, 'Norman!' and his small but rock hard fist shot out at Slider's face.

Without the adrenaline he'd have been felled, but all those flight-or-fight impulses he had been resisting in the last five minutes came to his aid now. He jerked his head aside so fast that he ricked his neck and the fist shot past his head, grazing his left ear. In the same motion, Slider ducked in low and flung himself at Bates, grabbing him round the middle, and Bates, thrown off balance by the missed punch, was just unstable enough to stagger backwards and go down, hitting the floor with Slider on top of him as the rest of the team burst in through the two doors simultaneously.

From the next room there was thumping, crashing and shouting as the bodyguard put up a vigorous resistance. For a moment Bates writhed viciously, but then he suddenly seemed to see the futility, or perhaps the indignity of it, and became still. With his teeth bared, he hissed at Slider, 'You'll regret this. I'll see you regret this, you pathetic moron. You don't know what you're meddling with. You're in over your depth. You're nobody!'

'Well, at least I'm not a murderer,' Slider said. He knew he ought not to provoke the man, but he couldn't help it. That fist had taken skin off his ear, and his neck hurt.

'You can't prove a thing against me,' Bates said, utterly assured.

'Oh yes I can,' Slider said blithely. 'Poor old Susie got washed up. We found her.'

It was impossible for Bates to pale, but his eyes widened slightly. 'You found her?'

'Yup. Got the body, got the semen, got the DNA. You're nicked, mate.'

A policeman's life, he thought afterwards, holds few moments so beautiful as seeing an arrogant, vicious, self-satisfied criminal crumple in the face of what he knows is the inevitable. Slider got to his feet, and as Bates began to struggle up, he began his victory chant.

'Trevor Bates, I arrest you for the murder of Susan Mabbot. You do not have to say anything, but it may harm your defence . . .'

Bates wasn't listening. He stared at Slider as though burning his image into his brain. 'I'll get you for this,' he said.

'. . . anything you later rely on in court,' Slider finished. And suddenly he felt very tired, as all the adrenaline got bored with this part of the proceedings and went off somewhere else to look for a fight.

It is an immutable law, formulated by the eminent philosopher Professor Sod, that you will always wake up early on your day off. It was six a.m. when the alarm in Slider's head went off. He woke in his customary violent fashion, with a grunt. He rarely managed a controlled re-entry: usually he hit consciousness like a man being thrown out of a moving car.

Joanna wasn't there. He listened for a moment, then got up and padded into the kitchen. She was standing by the sink drinking water, staring out of the window into the small oblong of rough grass and blackberry brambles she called a garden. Since her pregnancy had begun to show, she had stopped wandering about in the nude. In an access of modesty she had taken to wearing a loose white muslin dress by way of a

dressing-gown. As it was almost but not quite completely transparent, it was far more erotic than nakedness, but Slider hadn't
told her that. He just hoped that she didn't answer the door in
it when he wasn't there. The postman didn't look as though his
heart would take it.

He slipped his arms round her from behind and rested his
chin on her shoulder. 'All right?' he murmured.

'Hmm,' she confirmed.

'Couldn't sleep?'

'Not since half past four. Why are you up, anyway? We were
going to lie in and cuddle.'

'Hard to do when you're in the kitchen,' he pointed out. 'Shall
we go back to bed?'

He felt her hesitate, and knew what was coming.

'I'm hungry.'

'You're always hungry. It's just your hormones.'

'My hormones and I go everywhere together. Why don't the
three of us have breakfast? It's such a beautiful morning, too
good to waste lying in bed.'

He detached himself from her back. 'I thought pregnant
women were supposed to feel extra sexy,' he complained.

'You've got to fuel the engine,' she said.

She fried bacon and tomatoes and made toast while he got
a shave out of the way, and then they ate and talked.

'Fried tomatoes are definitely a seventh-day thing,' Slider
said. Joanna had a theory that God had done all His very best
creations on Sunday, when He was at leisure. A large amount
of food seemed to get into her list: toasted cheese, raspberries,
the smell of coffee.

'It's such a long time since we did this,' she said happily. 'I
don't even remember when you last had a day off.'

He had only known since May that Joanna was pregnant.
She had given up her job with the orchestra in Amsterdam and
was back home permanently, looking for work for the next few
months. With the baby due in November, she could work until
about the end of September – if she could get the dates. She'd
had no luck so far. Still, it gave her a chance to look for a place
for them to live. Her tiny flat had one bedroom, one sitting
room, a small kitchen and a breathe-by-numbers bathroom –
adequate for them but tight for them plus baby.

Being an old-fashioned kind of a bloke, he was determined they should get married before the baby was born. And before they got married they had to announce everything to their respective families, something which work had made impossible for him. But now, with the debriefing and writing up of the Bates case done at last, he had two days off. Tomorrow he and Joanna were going to spend the day with his father – his only relly – and today they were going down to Eastbourne to see her parents. Slider had never yet met them, and was nervous.

'What if they don't like me?' he asked.

She was good at catching on. 'They'll like you. Why wouldn't they?'

'Debauching their daughter, for one. Getting you pregnant before marrying you.'

'My sister Alison was born only six months after the Aged Ps married.'

'Really?'

'Mum mellowed one night when Sophie and I took her out for a drink for her birthday, and confessed. She was a bit shocked the next day when she remembered. She swore us to secrecy, so don't say anything. Apparently the others don't know.'

'Except for Alison, presumably.'

'I wouldn't even be sure of that. She may not have put two and two together. She was always good at ignoring inconvenient facts.'

Slider reached for the marmalade. 'Tell me them again. I haven't got them straight.'

'Doesn't matter. You aren't going to meet them all.'

'You know me. I like to do my homework.'

'All right. Alison's the eldest, then the three boys, Peter, Tim and George.'

'They're in Australia?'

'No, only Tim and George. They all emigrated together but Peter came back.'

'Oh, yes, I remember now.'

'Then Louisa and Bobby, then me, then the twins that died, then Sophie.'

'What a crowd. It must have been nice, growing up with so many people around you.'

'I'm sure you got a lot more attention,' said Joanna.

'But you don't have much backup when you're an only child. No insurance. When Mum died there was only me and Dad, and when he goes . . .'

She reached across and squeezed his hand. 'You'll still have a wife, an ex-wife and at least three children.'

He began to smile. 'At least? What are you trying to tell me?'

She looked casual. 'Oh, well, I just thought if you're going to fork out all that money for a marriage licence, you might as well get your money's worth.'

He inspected her expression and was thinking they might go back to bed after all, when the phone rang. Joanna met his eyes. 'Oh, no,' she said, looking a question and a doubt.

He felt a foreboding. 'It couldn't be. They wouldn't. Not on my day off.' But he knew they could and would. Detective inspectors had to be available for duty at all times, and since they didn't get paid overtime it was easier on the budget to call them rather than someone who did.

He got up and trudged out to the narrow hall (Never get a pram in here, he thought distractedly) and picked up the phone. It was Nicholls, one of the uniformed sergeants at Shepherd's Bush police station. 'Are you up and dressed?'

'This had better be important,' Slider growled.

'Sorry, Bill. I know it's your day off and I hate to do it to you, but it's a murder.'

'Oh, for God's sake!'

'Came in on a 999 call. Female, stabbed to death in Paddenswick Park. Looks as though the Park Killer's struck again.'

'Why can't Carver's lot catch it?'

'They're knee deep in that drugs and prostitution ring. The boss says you're it. I'm sorry, mate.'

'Bloody Nora, can't people leave off killing each other for two minutes together?' Out of the corner of his eye he saw that Joanna had come out into the hall. At these words she turned away, and the cast of her shoulders was eloquent. 'All right, on my way.'

Joanna was in the bedroom. She looked up when he came in and forestalled his speech. 'I gathered.'

'I'm sorry,' he said.

'I know. Can't be helped.'

He could tell by her terseness that she was upset, and he didn't blame her. 'You'll explain to your parents?'

'Don't worry about it.'

'Will you still go?'

'No point. I'll call it off,' she said shortly, passing him in the doorway.

He rang Atherton – DS Jim Atherton, his bagman – and got him on his mobile at the scene.

'You don't need to hurry. Porson's got everything under control.'

'Hell's bells. What's he doing there?'

'He was in the office when I arrived at a quarter to eight. I don't think he'd been home.'

Porson, their Det Sup, had recently been widowed. Slider wondered whether he was finding home without his wife hard to cope with.

'The shout came in about a quarter past eight,' Atherton went on, 'and he grabbed the team and shot over here. He's already whistled up extra uniform to take statements, and the SOCO van's on the way.'

'So what does he need me for?' Slider asked resentfully.

'I expect it's lurve,' Atherton said. 'Gotta go – he's beckoning.'

So it was away with the cords and chambray shirt, hello workday suit and Teflon tie. Blast and damn, Slider thought. Any murder meant a period of intensive work and long hours, but a serial murderer could tie you down for months. If it was the Park Killer, there was no knowing when he'd get a day off again.

The traffic had built up by the time Slider left the house, and he had plenty of leisure to reflect as he crawled along Bath Road. The Park Killer had 'struck' – as the newspapers liked to put it – twice before, but not on Slider's ground. The first time had been in Gunnersbury Park, the second only a month ago in Acton Park. On that – admittedly meagre – basis it looked as though he was moving eastwards, which left room for a couple more possible incidents in Shepherd's Bush before he reached Holland Park and became Notting Hill's problem. Slider wondered what could be done to hasten that happy day. The very thought of a serial killer made him miserable. The idea that any human being could be so utterly self-absorbed that he would kill someone at random simply as a means of self-advertisement was deeply depressing.

It was part, he thought, as he inched forward towards a traffic light that only stayed green for thirty seconds every five minutes, of the modern cult of celebrity. To get on the telly, to get in the papers, was the ultimate ambition for a wide swathe of the deeply stupid. And the newspapers didn't help. This present bozo had killed two people, and already he had a media sobriquet. No wonder he had killed again so soon. He had a public to satisfy now. He was a performer.

To be a celebrity act, of course, you had to have a trademark, and the Park Killer's bag was to kill in broad daylight in a public place full of passers-by – people walking dogs, people going to work, people jogging, roller-blading, bicycling. The newspapers had been full of wonder (which the killer probably read as admiration) as to how he had managed not to be seen. Paddenswick Park fitted this MO. It lay between Goldhawk Road to the north and King Street to the south, and was not only a cut-through but was well used by the local population for matutinal exercise and dog-emptying. Morning rush hour was the PK's time of choice. If nothing else, Slider reflected, it slowed down the police trying to get to the scene.

By the time he reached the area, he had plumbed the depths. To add to the stupid senselessness of every murder, in this case there would be all the problems involved in liaising with the Ealing squad – how they would enjoy having to share with him the fact that they had got nowhere! – not to mention dealing with the inevitable media circus. It looked as though it would be a close-run thing whether he would get to marry Joanna or draw his pension first.

The park and a large section of Paddenswick Road, which ran down its east side, were cordoned off. Atherton was standing in the RV area behind the blue-and-white tape; he came over and moved it for Slider to drive through. Within the area were several marked police cars, Atherton's and the department wheels and the large white van belonging to the scene-of-crime officers. Inside the park gates he could see that all the people who had been on the spot when the police arrived had been corralled, with a mixture of CID and uniform taking their basic details.

Though Slider kept a low media profile, some of the reporters recognised him and shouted out to him from where they were being kept at bay beyond the cordon. They only had one question, of course. 'Is it the Park Killer?' 'Do you think it's the Park Killer?' A nod from him and they'd dash off, click together their Lego stock phrases, and every paper and bulletin would have the same headline: PARK KILLER STRIKES AGAIN. Slider ignored them.

'What it is to be a star,' said Atherton.

'Me or him?' Slider asked suspiciously.

'Me, of course,' said Atherton. He was elegantly suited, as always, and his straight fair hair, which he wore cut short these days, had just the subtlest hint of a fashionable spikiness about it, making him look even more dangerous to women. That sort of subtlety you had to pay upwards of forty quid for. Slider, who had used the same back-street barber for twenty years and now paid a princely nine quid a go, felt shabby and rumpled beside him. With his height and slimness Atherton sometimes looked more like a male model than a policeman. He was also, however, looking distinctly underslept about the eyes.

'On the tiles again last night?' Slider enquired. 'Let me see, it was that new PC, wasn't it? Collins?'

'Yvonne. She's new to the area and doesn't know anybody,' Atherton said, with dignity. 'I was just making friends.'

'A wild night of friend-making really takes it out of you,' Slider said.

'Crabby this morning,' Atherton observed. 'Bad luck about your day off. McLaren's gone in search of coffee and bacon sarnies,' he added coaxingly.

'I had breakfast,' Slider said. 'I still don't know what I'm doing here, if Porson's in charge.'

'Looks as though you're about to find out,' said Atherton, gesturing with his head.

Slider turned and caught Detective Superintendent Fred 'The Syrup' Porson's eye on him across the little groups of coppers and witnesses. Porson was tall and bony and reared above the mass of humanity like a dolmen, his knobbly slap gleaming in the sun. It was still a shock to Slider to see old Syrup's bald pate. He had earned his sobriquet through years of wearing a deeply unconvincing wig, but he had abandoned it the day his wife died. Slider was forced to the unlikely conclusion that it was Betty Porson (who had been quite an elegant little person) who had encouraged the sporting of the rug. The nickname had been in existence too long to die; now it had to be applied ironically.

Slider liked Porson. He was a good policeman and a loyal senior, and if he used language like a man in boxing gloves trying to thread a needle, well, it was a small price to pay not to be commanded by a twenty-something career kangaroo with a degree in Applied Pillockry.

The Syrup was signalling something with his eyebrows. Porson's eyebrows were considerable growths. They could have declared UDI from the rest of his face and become a republic. Slider obeyed the summons.

'Sorry about your day off,' Porson said briefly. 'I've got things initialated for you, but you'll have to take over from here. I've got a Forward Strategy Planning Meeting at Hammersmith.' His tone revealed what he thought of strategic planning meetings. These days, holding meetings seemed to be all the senior ranks did – hence, perhaps, old Syrup's eagerness to sniff the gunpowder this morning. 'Gallon was the first uniform on the spot – he'll fill you in on the commensurate part. I've got people taking statements from everyone who was still here when we got here, and SOCO's just gone in. All right?'

'Yes, sir,' Slider said. 'But—'

Porson raised a large, knuckly hand in anticipation of Slider's objection. 'A word in your shell-like,' he said, turning aside. Slider turned with him, and Porson resumed, in a lower voice: 'Look here, this might be the Park Killer or it might not. It could be, from the look of appearances, but I want it either way. The SCG's had to send most of its personal to help out the Anti-terrorist Squad, so Peter Judson's down to two men and a performing dog, and they're up to their navels.' The Serious Crime Group had first refusal of all murders. 'So it'll probably be left with us, at least for the present time being. If we can clear this one, it's going to do us a lot of *bon*. Definite flower in our caps.'

Slider wasn't sure he wanted anything in his cap. 'If it is a serial, there's Ealing to consider,' he said.

Porson looked triumphant. 'That's the beauty of it. They've not managed to get anywhere with it. We get the gen from them, and *we* clear it, see? Who's a pretty boy *then*?' Something of Slider's inner scepticism must have showed, because Porson lowered his voice even more, and practically climbed into his ear. 'Look here,' he said, 'I'm not trying to blow sunshine up your skirt. The bottom end is that I'm being considered for promotion. I've not got long to go. If I can retire a rank higher it makes a big difference to my pension.' His faded, red-rimmed eyes met Slider's without flinching. 'I've given my life to the Job. I think I deserve it.' Slider thought so too, but it wasn't his place to say so. 'But you know as well as I do what flavour goes down with the upper escalons these days,' Porson went on. 'We're not young and sexy. Dinosaurs, they call us, coppers like you and me. But a big-profile clear-up, that's just an incontroversial fact. They can't ignore that.'

Slider noted that Porson didn't say, 'Do this for me and I'll see you all right.' He had always been loyal to his troops and simply assumed that they knew it. Slider admired him for it. So he waved goodbye to his time off and did not sigh. 'I'll do my best, sir,' he said.

'I know you will, laddie. I know you will.' Porson was so moved he came within an inch of clapping Slider on the shoulder, changed the gesture at the last moment, tried to scratch his non-existent wig, and ended up rubbing his nose vigorously, clearing his throat with a percussive violence that would have stunned a starling at ten paces.

Slider decided to take advantage of the emotional moment. 'Any chance you can get me a replacement for Anderson, sir?' he asked. DC Anderson of Slider's team had been snatched by the National Crime Squad on a long-term secondment, leaving him a warm body short.

'I'll see what I can do,' Porson said, 'but don't hold your horses. You know what the situation is *vis-à-vis* recruitment.'

Slider returned to Atherton. 'All right,' he said, 'tell me about it. Where's the *corpus*, then?'

'In the bushes,' said Atherton.

On the Paddenswick Road side, the park was bounded by a low wall topped with spiked iron railings, the whole combination about nine feet high. An iron gate let on to a wide concreted path, which ran straight for twenty feet and then branched to give north–south and east–west walks, plus a curving circumference route round the northern end of the park that was popular with runners. The whole park was pleasantly landscaped, mostly grassy with a few large trees and one or two formal flower-beds beside the paths, filled now with the tidy summer bedders beloved of municipal gardeners – bright red geraniums, multicoloured pansies, edgings of blue and white lobelia and alyssum.

It was all open space, not at all murderer territory, except for a stretch of vigorous shrubbery of rhododendrons, spotted laurels, winter viburnum and other such serviceable bushes, plus a few spindly trees of the birch and rowan sort. The shrubbery ran north to south, bordered on the east by the railings and on the west by the north–south path, which ran down to the gate opposite the tube station. And here, it seemed, among the sooty leaves, the murderer had lurked, and attacked.

PC Gallon, as promised, filled Slider in.

'It was a bloke walking his dog that found the body, sir, just after eight o'clock. A Mr Chapman, first name Michael, lives in Atwood Road?' Gallon was young enough to have the routine Estuary Query at the end of his sentences, but in this case he wanted to know if Slider knew where that was. Slider nodded.

'Well, he had his dog on one of those leads that reels out, and it went into the bushes there. He didn't notice till the dog starts barking and making a hell of a fuss. So he tries to reel it in, but it won't come, and he reckons the lead's caught up on the bushes or something, so he goes in after it, and there she is.'

'Was it him who phoned Emergency?'

'No, sir. Chapman comes out of the bushes and stops the first person he sees, bloke called David Hatherley who's walking through on his way to work, and he calls 999 on his mobile. Call was logged at eight twelve.'

'All right. Let's have a look,' Slider said.

Here, in this short stretch of path inside the gate and before the junction, the bushes grew close together, presenting an unbroken green wall of foliage. 'Here's where Chapman went in,' said Atherton. 'And presumably where the killer dragged the victim in.'

There were scuffmarks in the chipped bark mulch that had been spread under the shrubs to keep the weeds down. Some bark had spilled over onto the path, and there were two deep parallel grooves disappearing like tram lines into the shrubbery.

'You'd have thought there'd have been more damage to the bushes,' Slider complained. 'There's a few leaves on the ground, but no broken twigs or branches.'

'I suppose they just bent and whipped back,' Atherton said. 'There's better access for us round the other side. That's the way SOCO's gone in.'

They walked the few yards to the junction and turned left down the north–south path. On this side of the shrubbery the growth was less vigorous, and about twenty feet along there was a good two- to three-foot gap between two of the bushes. The crime-scene manager, Bob Bailey, met them there. He was a tall, lean man with wiry fair hair and a stiff moustache that Slider always thought must be hell on his wife. The scene-of-crime officers were civilians who worked out of headquarters at Hammersmith. In the course of things Slider and Bailey had a lot of contact and got on pretty well.

'The doc's been and gone, sir,' Bailey greeted him. 'Pronounced at eight twenty-nine.'

'Dr Prawalha? That was nippy.'

'Well, he only lives round the corner,' Bailey explained. 'We've nearly finished with the photographs and the measuring. Then you can come in and have a look.'

The modern trend was towards excluding even the senior investigating officer from the crime scene, and they were working on a 3D laser video camera that would create a digital version of the scene you could walk through on computer screen without ever getting near the real thing. But Slider had to see for himself. It was not self-glorification or thrill-seeking, it was just the way he was. There was so much he could glean from his own senses that he knew would not be the same in virtual reality. Bailey knew his preference, and since Slider was both polite and careful, he tolerated it. Not that he could do anything else, given that Slider seriously outranked him, but there was good grace and bad grace.

'There won't be much to be got from this bark,' Slider observed. 'No footmarks.'

'No, sir. And blood patterns will be hard to spot. It's either brown bark or dark green leaves. And everyone and his dog could have been in here. I hate outdoor scenes.'

'At least it's not raining,' Slider said, to comfort him. 'Well, let me know when I can come in. I'll go and talk to the witness.'

Michael Chapman didn't have much to add to the story as told by Gallon. His dog, a small, jolly-looking terrier, was lying down on the path now, chin on paws, thoroughly bored. Chapman was obviously still upset. He was in his late fifties, Slider guessed, well dressed and neatly coiffed, with a worn look to his face that seemed to predate the present shock. Early and reluctant retiree, perhaps?

'Yes, I do walk Buster here most mornings,' he said, in answer to Slider's question. 'I take him out later for two or three longer walks, but I generally do the first turn here. I only live just down the road, you see, so it's convenient.'

'So, as a regular park user, have you seen this girl before?'

'I'm not sure,' he said reluctantly. 'I might have. I can't really say. There are so many people exercising here in the mornings, jogging and so on. I don't really notice them. Anyway, I didn't really get much of a look at her in there,' he said, with a jerk of his head towards the bushes. 'Not to see her face.' A thought came to him, and his eyes widened in appeal. 'You won't make me go and look again?'

'No, sir,' Slider said reassuringly. 'You went in just there, I understand?'

'Yes, that's right. Between those two laurels.'

'Did you notice those marks in the ground?'

'Well, no. I didn't really notice anything, except that Buster was barking his head off and wouldn't come back.'

'Did you touch the body at all? To see if she was still alive?'

'No!' he said vehemently; and then looked worried. 'Should I have? As soon as I saw her I was sure she must be dead. I didn't want to go any nearer. I just wanted to get Buster out.'

'Did Buster touch the body?'

'Not to my knowledge. When I got in there he was jumping and barking but not actually touching her. She was lying on her back and her eyes were open and there was all that – all that blood – on her – on her T-shirt.' He swallowed hard, screwing up his eyes as if to force the vision away. 'I dragged Buster out the same way we went in, and then I saw that gentleman talking on his mobile phone and asked him to call the police.'

The phone owner, David Hatherley, was a different kettle of fish from the shocked and patient Chapman. He was a tall, vigorous, expensively suited young Turk, annoyed at being kept from his turkery by bumbling officialdom. He turned on Slider as he approached, scanned him for authority, and demanded hotly, 'Look here, how much longer am I going to be kept hanging around? Some of us have work to do, you know.'

'Yes, I do know, sir. We are doing our work at the moment,' Slider said.

The nostrils flared with exasperation. 'Well, I can't help you. I know nothing about it. I was just walking past when that idiot tried to grab my phone, and then started babbling about dead bodies. I had to interrupt a very important business call to dial 999.'

'It was very public-spirited of you, sir,' Slider said soothingly.

Hatherley seemed to suspect irony and snorted. 'So can I go now? Your man's taken down every damned detail from me, address, telephone, right down to my shoe size. You don't seem to realise, every minute I stand here I'm losing money.'

Slider had used those minutes to look over Hatherley's clothes, his face and hands, his manner. There was nothing there for them. 'Yes, you can go. Thank you very much for your help, Mr Hatherley. We might be contacting you again.'

When he had gone, Atherton said, 'He can't be our man, not in an Armani suit.'

'No,' Slider said. 'I think he just happened by at the wrong moment. Like Chapman. But with Chapman, he was actually on the scene, so we'd better get fingerprints and a buccal swab from him for elimination purposes.'

'What about the dog?' Atherton said merrily. 'Should we get his DNA as well?'

'I'm glad you're finding this entertaining,' Slider said.

The photographer was coming towards them. Old Sid had retired – not before time given his increasing misanthropy, which was ratcheted upwards by every scene he captured for posterity. The new man was David Archer, young, enthusiastic but with a nephew-like shy deference towards Slider and most of his team. He was a rather delicate-looking creature, so handsome he was almost pretty, and didn't look robust enough to cope with the things he had to photograph; but he was so passionate about his equipment and the wonderful things modern digital technology could do that Slider suspected the subject of his work didn't impinge much on him.

'Bob asked me to tell you you can go in now, sir,' he said to Slider.

'Finished your work?'

'Yes, I'm going back to the van to have a look at it, but I'll be on hand in case there's anything more when the forensic biologist arrives.'

'Do something for me,' Slider said. 'Take a long, slow pan around with your video camera at the crowd. All the onlookers. Try not to be obvious about it. Keep as far back as you can and do it on the zoom. Everyone who's hanging around the scene. I want their faces.'

'Yes, sir,' Archer said. He was too polite to ask, but there was a question in his eyes.

Slider took pity on him. 'I wouldn't be surprised if the murderer came back for a look. He'd want to see who found her, what their reaction was, how baffled we were. That'd be part of the fun. He might be here right now, enjoying himself watching us running round after him.'

'I'll get what you want, sir, don't worry,' Archer said. 'Would you like me to make a series of stills, so you can have them to study?'

'Good idea. Thanks.'

'He wouldn't hang about all covered in blood, surely?' Atherton said, when Archer had left them.

'No, but he probably wore a protective garment, which he might have discarded somewhere before coming back.'

'He might even live locally,' Atherton went along with it. 'Went home and changed and came back.'

'You do think of them,' Slider complained. They walked back to the gap in the shrubbery and clothed up, and then, conducted by Bailey, walked along the stepping boards that had been laid to make a safe path into the scene within the shrubbery.

The rhododendrons were massive specimens, some of them ten or fifteen feet high. They grew their leaves where the light reached them, so on the back side they presented bare trunks

and branches. What looked from the path like dense vegeta-
tion was in fact a series of hollow caves. With the thick mulch
of bark on the ground, there was nothing to mar the uniformity of dark brown except the odd piece of litter. Blown in by
the wind? It didn't seem likely, inside the shrubbery. Left by
kids playing, more like – or by someone hiding, lurking? Slider
noted a cigarette packet (B&H), a torn strip of a Walkers crisps
bag, and two wrappers from chocolate bars: one Picnic and
one Double Decker.

'We'll have those,' he said to Bailey. 'There'll probably be
some cigarette ends, as well.'

'There are,' Bailey confirmed. 'Quite a lot scattered about.'

'Take them all,' Slider said. Smokers were so used to throwing
away the butt when they'd finished that they did it automatically,
either not knowing, or forgetting, that DNA could be recovered
from the saliva on them.

'Thank God there's no such thing as a non-smoking murderer,'
said Atherton.

In the heart of all this brown, in a clear space, lay the body.
It was a young woman, dressed for jogging in knee-length black
Lycra shorts, a sleeveless white shirt, trainers and short white
socks. She was slim and fit-looking, with lightly tanned skin, and
shortish, tousled blonde hair that gave Slider an unpleasant tug
because it reminded him of Joanna's. It was a shade lighter, though.
Joanna's was more bronze. The sunlight filtering through the
leaves touched it here and there and made it gleam like true
coin.

She was lying on her back, one arm flung out, the other
resting beside her body. Her face was very pretty, heart-shaped
with a short, straight nose and full lips, parted to show good
teeth. Her skin was smooth and lightly tanned, her hands well
kept with short, unvarnished nails. She had small gold studs in
her ears and a thin gold chain round her neck on which hung
a gold disc – a St Christopher, he supposed. Around her waist
was a sort of utility belt of elasticated webbing, on which was
hung a plastic water-bottle on the right, a CD Walkman on the
left, and a small zip purse in the middle. The headset was
hanging round her neck, the cord loose, pulled out from the
Walkman socket. He noted that the Walkman had been switched
off.

The warmth of the day was lifting a pleasant, woody smell from the bark chippings and birds were singing near and far off in the park. Broken by the gently moving leaves of a birch tree, sunshine was dappling the ground and the girl. She might have stretched out for a rest to gaze up at the patch of clear blue sky above, except that her T-shirt was spatched and blotted with blood.

'Multiple stab wounds,' Atherton said, breaking the silence. 'Would that qualify as a "frenzied attack"?' It was what police reports and the media always called it, a cliché there seemed no escaping. Atherton used it consciously, knowing Slider hated it.

The bark was scuffed in the immediate area, though not as much as Slider would have expected it to be. He hunkered down close to the victim, and now he could smell the clean odours of her shampoo and body lotion, and under them the reek of blood. There were defence cuts on her forearms and the palms of her hands, the blood resting in them, hardly smeared at all. There was definitely blood on the bark immediately around and under the body, but it was impossible to see how much, or to discern any spread patterns.

'Is there blood anywhere else?' he asked Bailey.

'We haven't found any so far, but it's impossible to be sure without close examination,' Bailey said. 'All I can say is that it looks as though all the action happened in this spot.'

Atherton, looking over Slider's shoulder, said, 'What's that grey mark on the T-shirt? Sort of greyish-brown, a smudge?'

'I think it's a footmark – or a toemark, at least,' Slider said. 'He turned her over with his foot. She was lying face down and he turned her over. It's the sort of dirty mark that could be left by a shoe.'

'I suppose he wanted to check she was dead.'

'We might possibly get a partial sole pattern from it,' Slider said.

'Yes, sir,' said Bailey. 'We have photographed it.'

Slider stood up and looked back towards the north side of the shrubbery. 'I don't understand why he dragged her in that way. Much easier the way we came in.'

On both his previous outings, the Park Killer had dragged his victim under cover, once into a shrubbery and once into a rose garden, stabbed her to death, and escaped the scene without anyone's seeing or hearing anything. Speed had to have been of the essence. Probably that was why he had not robbed or molested either of his victims. It was getting away with murder that interested him, it seemed.

Atherton considered. 'The bushes give better cover on that side. If he'd lurked on the more open side, someone might have seen him.'

'I suppose,' Slider said. He looked around to fix the scene in his mind, and then again down at the body. She was out jogging, listening to her music, perhaps thinking about the rest of her day. He looked at her pretty face, all animation gone, her softly muddled hair, the yielding shape of her body against the earth, still warm and pliant, but pointlessly so now. He imagined the killer turning her over with his foot, thought how it would have felt, heavy and soft. In his country boyhood he had handled dead rabbits and knew that limpness. A dull anger filled him. Partly it was because she had reminded him fleetingly of Joanna, and he felt newly vulnerable about her. But the anger was for this girl as well, and especially. When she had got up and dressed in the morning, she had not planned to die this day.

The world was not safe. There were people in it who would do this hideous, hateful thing. Life, which was so strong and tenacious and filled you tight to the skin when you were young, could be taken from you so easily, slip away through a hole in you like a mist dissolving. The solid reality that you walked on was in fact no more than a thin sheet of ice, through which you might fall at any moment into the black water of oblivion beneath.

Everything this girl had, had been taken from her in the name of conceit. All Slider could do was to find the killer and hope to see him punished. He was glad now that Porson wanted it. It was his case now. He would find the killer. The really depressing thing was that even cornered, caught, accused, charged, tried and sentenced, the murderer would probably never really see the enormity of what he had done. What had they done to themselves as a society to have bred a person who would kill to get his name in the papers?

He pulled his mind back to the scene. 'I wonder why there's no blood on the footmark. You'd have thought with all this stabbing going on he'd have stepped in at least some of it, especially as he wouldn't have been able to see it.'

'Just lucky, I suppose,' Atherton said. 'Our first problem is going to be identifying her.'

'Yes,' Slider said. 'People don't go out jogging with their passport and driving licence in their pockets.'

'People don't go out jogging with pockets,' said Atherton.

CHAPTER TWO

Close Enough for Jazz

The CID room was quiet, with most of the troops still at the scene, helping with the search for blood, bloodstained clothing, and a murder weapon. Speed was of the essence. There was constant pressure on the police to reopen a cordoned-off area.

Slider was in his room making a start on the paperwork when the gorgeous DC Kathleen Swilley, always known as 'Norma' on account of her machismo in the field, came in. She was an expert in martial arts, could kick the eyebrows off a fly at five paces, and bring a man to his knees by use of just a forefinger and thumb. Or, indeed, without them, Slider reflected.

'Nothing so far, boss,' she said. 'Everyone in the park's had a preliminary interview and they're starting on the bystanders. And I've put in an enquiry to the traffic department about any parked car or MTI activity for this morning. The SOCOs are still going over the ground looking for more blood. The body's been taken away now.'

'Is that the deceased's effects?'

'Yeah. No help with her ID, though.' She put them down on the desk and went through them with him. The little purse on the victim's belt contained nothing but a Kleenex tissue and a set of door keys – one Yale and one deadlock – on a ring whose tag was one of those articulated metal fish. That, and her gold medallion, were the only personal items they had to go on.

'We got some good lifts off the Walkman,' Swilley said. 'Presumably the victim's. We're waiting for her tenprint to compare. I've run them through records but there's no previous.'

The medallion turned out not to be St Christopher after all, but St Anthony. 'An unusual choice,' Slider commented. 'It may help to confirm her identity once we know it.'

'Ditto for the door keys,' said Swilley. 'So what's a St Anthony medal for, boss?'

'He's patron saint of the poor and afflicted, I think,' Slider said. 'And lost things. And travellers.'

'I thought that was St Christopher?'

'It's not exclusive. And some people think St Christopher didn't exist.'

'The things you know,' Swilley marvelled.

Slider sighed. 'What I don't know is how to ID our victim without trawling through the neighbourhood with a mugshot. And I really hate doing that when the only mugshot I've got is taken from the corpse.'

'It's early yet. Someone may miss her and come forward,' Swilley said. 'The report of the murder's going to be in all the noon bulletins. If someone hasn't turned up to work . . .'

While Slider was contemplating this slender possibility, Atherton came in, back from the scene. 'No clothes or knives as yet,' he reported. 'There were eight cigarette ends in that part of the shrubbery, but most of them are obviously not fresh.'

'He might have staked out the area beforehand,' Slider said. 'Keep them all until we see what else we get, before having them DNA tested.' There was always the budget to consider.

Atherton resumed. 'Mackay and McLaren are on their way back with the first stack of statements to go through, and the photographs have arrived. Hollis is putting them up on the whiteboard with the stuff we got from Ealing.' He looked at Slider's desk. 'Is that her Walkman?'

Slider smiled slightly. 'It would hardly be mine, now, would it? I'm a dinosaur, didn't you know?'

Atherton blinked, but let it pass. 'What was she listening to?' he asked.

'She wasn't listening to anything, if you remember. It was turned off and the headset was unplugged.'

'It probably came unplugged in the struggle,' Norma said.

'Yes, but it does seem odd to me—' Slider began, but Atherton interrupted him. He had picked up the evidence bag containing the CD.

'Ah, now, look at this! This isn't a commercial CD – it's a demo disc. This could be something. It might give us a lead on who she is.'

'How come?' Swilley asked.

Atherton was always glad of an opportunity to impress her. Since he had got his new haircut, he had shown a renewed interest in Swilley, even though she was now married to the man she had lived with for years. Atherton, who was not one to let logic spoil a good prejudice, insisted that the husband didn't exist – despite the fact that Slider had been at the wedding. He said nobody would really marry a man named Tony Allnutt. And anyway, even if he did exist, Norma would surely be regretting her folly by now, and be ready for Atherton's sophistication and non-joke surname.

'When a band makes a demo CD,' he said, 'they don't go on sale, they're distributed to the A and R people at record companies and to promoters and festival organisers and so on, which would cut down the field anyway. But this is even better. You see, the label's not printed, it's hand-written, and there's nothing on it but the band's name, the studio name and the recording date. That suggests that it's a master, or a band copy – something only a very few people would have. It would mean that our victim was closely connected with the band, or just possibly the recording team.'

'What's the date on it?' Slider asked.

'Monday,' said Atherton. 'That makes it even more likely that she was with the band. It's probably a first impression, given to them to approve before the final mixing. After mixing it would be a couple of weeks for the copies for distribution to be ready. This may be the master, or one of as few as half a dozen prints.'

'Well, that's good news,' Slider said. To have got a handle on the ID this early was a bonus. 'I thought we were going to have to house-to-house the whole of west London.'

'What band is it?' Swilley asked, trying to see over Atherton's shoulder.

'Baroque Solid,' Atherton said, passing it over to her.

She wrinkled her nose at the name. 'Never heard of them.'

But Slider looked enlightened. 'I've heard Joanna talk about them. I think they were mentioned in the paper last week, weren't they?'

'Only in the arts section,' Atherton said. 'They're new and hot and they do fusion music – classical meets jazz. I saw them doing a foyer performance at the National Theatre – Satie and Stockhausen and a bit of Bartók. I thought they were pretty good, but it's an unusual taste, and without the right breaks that sort of thing can die the death. But they did a Purcell Room concert last week and got good reviews, so it looks as though they might be taking off.'

'Fusion music? It sounds dire,' Swilley said.

'It takes a bit of listening to. I expect you like Abba and Fleetwood Mac,' Atherton said kindly.

'Anyway, it's a stupid name,' she retaliated. 'If they mess up, everyone'll be calling them Baroque Bottom.'

Atherton's eyes gleamed. 'Now, I've always thought *you* had a—'

Slider intervened hastily. 'How do we get in contact with these people?'

'There's bound to be a website address for the band. Let's have a look.'

They went through into the CID room, where the computer sat in a corner, its screen-saver trekking through an endless brick maze, turning left and right at the dead ends with the strangely fluid jerk of a goldfish. Slider brought up the search engine and tapped in the band's name, but as soon as the site began to load Atherton was breathing down his neck in his eagerness. 'She's probably one of the musicians,' he said. 'I seem to remember there was a pretty female amongst them.'

She wasn't, though, and Slider was faintly and ridiculously relieved, as though it would have been a threat to Joanna if she had been. There were photographs of the eight members of Baroque Solid on the website, and though they were all in the right age group and four of them were female, none of the four sufficiently resembled the victim even to be worth wondering about.

'So what now?' Slider asked. Atherton was much more *au fait* with the music world than he was, in spite of Joanna.

'Go and see them. The victim must be closely involved with the band. There's the snail-mail address at the bottom. It's only just down the road in Barons Court.'

'Don't beg. You've got the job,' Slider said, handing him the disc.

'Everyone hates a volunteer,' Swilley said coolly, as Atherton bounded away.

Joanna came in to the office just before six, bringing two jam doughnuts in a bag from the good baker in Shepherd's Bush Road.

'Peace offering,' she said.

'Peace offering for what?'

'I think I was less than gracious this morning.'

'You were disappointed,' he excused her.

'So were you.'

'I'm used to it by now.'

'Well, I'd better get used to it too, if I'm going to be a policeman's wife. With the emphasis on "if".'

'Oh, Jo, I'm sorr—'

'Joke,' she assured him. 'Officers' wives for the use of. And talking of officers' wives, where's Jim?'

'Did you have doughnuts for him, too?' Slider asked innocently.

'Absolutely not,' she said grimly. 'I was talking to Sue today.'

'It's not his fault she changed her mind about marrying him,' Slider said.

'Isn't it?' Sue Caversham, Joanna's friend and colleague, had been Atherton's girlfriend, putting up with a great deal from him while he adjusted to the alien idea of monogamy. It was hard for a lifelong hound to give up the chase. On the very evening Slider discovered that Joanna was pregnant and proposed to her, Atherton was proposing to Sue. Slider couldn't have been more surprised – or thought he couldn't, until a month later Sue changed her mind. She had said she couldn't marry Atherton after all, a row ensued, and they had broken up.

'She was naturally doubtful about the leopard's changing his spots,' Joanna went on. 'All she needed was a bit of reassurance, and everything would have been all right. But what does he do? Bawls her out and then rushes off and starts dating other women like an amphetamine James Bond.'

The door between Slider's room and the CID room was open, as usual, and he felt this was not the place for this discussion. He turned her gracefully by saying, 'It looks as though the victim might have had something to do with that band you were talking about the other week, Baroque Solid.'

She allowed herself to be turned. 'Oh, no, don't say one of them's been killed! They're so talented.'

Would that make it worse? Slider wondered. From the outside, perhaps – talent being a rarity. But from the inside – everyone's life is precious to them. He said, 'No, she wasn't one of the musicians. We had a look at the website and there were photos of them. But she must have been close to them in some way.' A thought crossed his mind. Classical music was a small world and everybody tended to know everybody else. 'Would you be willing to have a look at the mugshot, to see if perhaps you know her? It would save a lot of time if you could give us a name.'

'You don't know who she is?' Joanna said, and then, mind working rapidly, she got it. 'Of course, she was out jogging and didn't have a handbag or anything with her. All right, I'll have a look.' She put out her hand, but then a thought came to her and she faltered. 'It's not – she's not—?'

'No,' he said, 'not disfigured or anything.'

'Only dead,' Joanna finished wryly. She took the photo, looked carefully, and passed it back. 'No, I don't know her. Poor girl, she's so young and pretty. What a monstrous thing to do.'

Monstrous, Slider thought. Yes, that was a good word for it.

'Well,' Joanna said, 'I'd better not disturb you any longer. I suppose you'll be late tonight?'

'I'm afraid so,' said Slider. 'They're doing the post mortem at seven and I want to go to that.'

'The fun you have!'

He came round the desk to kiss her goodbye and escort her out. 'Did you have a proper lunch?'

'Yes, Mother. I had a very nice tomatoey pasta and a salad in Pizza Express, in between estate agents. I bet you didn't have anything.'

'I've got two doughnuts now,' Slider said.

She eyed him with sympathy. 'I'm going to go home and make a casserole that won't spoil for long, slow cooking. So whatever time you get home—'

'I'll try not to be too late.'

*   *   *

The murder made the BBC's *Six o'Clock News*, though there was so much else going on it only got a short mention. Slider and Hollis went along to Ron Carver's room to watch – Carver, fortunately, having gone home. There had always been rivalry between Slider's firm and Carver's, though Slider did all he could to discourage it. But DI Carver had been born with a grudge and was never happy unless he was nurturing some fancied slight to himself. The fact was that he always had the best of everything, more men, more overtime allowance, more consideration. Even a television. The overlords having decided that the department ought to have a TV set, it was put in Carver's room as a matter of course; and when Slider asked for one as well he was told that there was no sense in having two – one for everybody was quite sufficient. Of course, Carver was a mason, everybody knew that. Atherton said that was just paranoia on Slider's part, but as Slider said, *you*'d be paranoid if everyone was plotting against you.

The murder came in fourth, behind the oil crisis, the Middle East peace talks, and the prime minister's visit to Washington.

'A young woman was stabbed to death in a park in west London this morning, in what appears to be another attack by the so-called Park Killer,' said the studio announcer.

There followed a quick resumé of the previous cases, with background footage of the other two parks involved, and then a brief moving camera shot of the Paddenswick scene from earlier in the day: the blue and white tape, the policemen on guard duty, and a shot of a SOCO on hands and knees examining the bark at the edge of the shrubbery. Then it jumped straight into the next item, about a riot in an asylum seekers' camp in Australia's Northern Territory.

'Short and not sweet,' Slider said.

'They'll probably do a bit more on the local news,' said Hollis, and they settled in to wait.

The local news had it as lead item.

'Nothing like a murder on your own patch,' said Hollis. 'Local boy makes good sort o' thing. Or local girl makes corpse.'

The bulletin had almost identical film to the main news, but obviously taken from a minutely different camera angle. 'Good use of the licence fee money,' said Slider. 'Send two complete teams from different offices in the same building.'

'Everyone knows local telly's a job creation scheme,' Hollis said. 'I mean, look at the presenter bird. Who else'd employ her?'

London News also billed it as the Park Killer Strikes Again and précis'd the two previous outings, but they varied the approach with some of their beloved on-the-scene vox pops. There were short clips of local residents saying it was shocking, and you didn't feel safe on your own streets any more. Then one young woman said she would never walk through Paddenswick Park again, and another said she always walked through the park and saw no reason to change now.

Finally the reporter, who looked about fifteen, faced camera and, with lavish hand gestures, said, 'Police are asking anyone who may have seen anything unusual to come forward. They are pertickerly asking anyone who was in the park between seven forty-five a.m. and eight fifteen a.m. this morning to come forward and identify themselves so that they can be eliminated from enquiries.' And then it was back to the studio.

'Did you ask for that?' said Hollis, his pale green eyes bulging alarmingly.

'Not me,' Slider said. 'Someone did, though.' He did not need to say more. The press liaison unit was at headquarters at Hammersmith, close to the source of godhead. It took its orders straight from the fount, and it would not occur to anyone to let the blokes at the sharp end know what was decided.

'We'll have to man the phones tonight,' Hollis observed.

'And I've got a post to go to,' said Slider.

'I'll get on it, guv,' Hollis said kindly. 'We probably won't need more than a couple. I don't expect there'll be many calls tonight anyway.'

'You mean, because the Beeb didn't feature it prominently?'

Hollis looked pitying at his ignorance. 'No, guv. Because there's a footy match on tonight. World Cup. England v. East Moldavia. Nobody's going to miss the one tie we might win.'

The address for Baroque Solid was Gunterstone Road, a ground-floor flat in one of those big three-storeys-plus-basement terrace houses that abound all over Hammersmith and North Kensington. A new sticker had been put above the bell saying, 'Baroque Solid – Music Fusion'. This was the strapline from the website, too, and Atherton thought it neat and punchy. It was not until his third visit at half past seven that he got a reply to his ring.

The door was opened by a young woman in jeans, black T-shirt and a loose chambray shirt worn open.

'Is this the office for Baroque Solid?' he asked, glimpsing behind her what was obviously a residential and not a business space.

'Well, yes, it is,' she said, as though there were a good deal of doubt about it. He showed his warrant card, and she relaxed a little – a novel reaction in Atherton's experience. Most people tensed up when they realised their visitor was Lily Law. She said, 'You see, it's where I and Joni and Tab live, but it's also the band's headquarters. At the moment, anyway. Until we get really, really famous.' And she laughed to avert the hubris. 'Would you like to come in?'

She led him into the big front room on the left of the entrance passage. At the far end with the bay window, there were bare floorboards, a semi-circle of hard chairs and music stands set on some kind of specialised rubber mat, and against the wall an impressive bank of sound equipment. At this, the door end, there was an office desk, a filing cabinet, a computer on a stand, and a table covered with papers.

'This is the beating heart of the operation,' she said, with an ironic wave of the hand. 'We're really just getting started. But we had our first proper concert last week, on the South Bank.'

'Yes, I know,' Atherton said. 'In the Purcell Room.'

'Oh, were you there?' she asked, with about equal parts of surprise and pleasure.

'No, but I read the reviews. And I've heard you before, in a foyer performance.'

'Are you into music?'

It was an expression he loathed, but it was sweetened a little for coming from her lips. When she had opened the door to him, he had thought her quite plain, with her straight brown hair and unmade-up face. But now at closer quarters and inspection, he was finding her unnervingly attractive. The hair, for instance – brushed straight back and cut about shoulder length – was a silky waterfall, and the word 'brown' didn't begin to cover the fabulous complexity of natural tints in it, from shining chestnut to amber and toffee, shot through with gleams of ink and pure set-on-fire copper. Her eyes were large and expressive and hazel, and makeup, he thought, would only have diminished their luminosity. Her mouth was wide and generous, and when she smiled she showed teeth so beautiful he wanted to kiss them. To find someone's teeth erotic must mean he was in a bad way; but so 'twas. He couldn't take his eyes from her.

'I love music,' he answered her belatedly. 'But I'm afraid that's not why I'm here.'

'Oh dear, I hope we're not in trouble,' she said. 'I'm sorry, I didn't catch your name.'

'Atherton. Detective Sergeant Atherton, Shepherd's Bush.' And then, to his own surprise, he added, 'Jim,' and held out his hand.

She took it. Hers was warm and dry and strong. A hand of ability. He wondered if she was a violinist. 'I'm Marion,' she said. 'Marion Davies.'

It was an oddly old-fashioned name, Marion. He wondered if she had older parents. But its plainness appealed to him. It suddenly seemed the essence of femininity.

'I play second fiddle,' she went on.

The words 'second fiddle' immediately brought Sue to his mind; one of those instant and uncontrollable associations. She lurked in his mind all the time anyway, though he kept his mental eyes firmly turned away from her.

'You haven't got a mark,' he said to Marion Davies, looking at her neck.

From the background of his thoughts of Sue, he had spoken too intimately. She blushed, and her skin was so delicate and clear he could actually see the blood racing up the corpuscles like BMW drivers up the M1. 'I've been lucky. But I've always used a pad,' she said.

He pulled himself together, and said, 'The reason I'm here is that we have come by one of your demo discs in unusual circumstances, and I wondered if you could give me an idea of who was likely to have had one.' He handed over the disc in its bag, and she took it, looking a little bewildered.

'Unusual circumstances?' she said. And then, 'I can't think how you got hold of this. We haven't sent them out yet. I mean, this isn't even a finished disc. We're going back to the studio on Friday to do the mixing.'

'I was hoping that was the case,' Atherton said. 'So how many other copies like this were there and who had them?'

'Well, it was just us in the band. Eight of us. Though I don't know if they made any for the studio people. It's a small independent studio in Goldhawk Mews,' she added, looking up at him.

'Yes, I know.' They must have longed to call themselves Goldhawk Studios, but as that name was already taken, they had gone with Mews Studios, which was a bit like chewing rubber.

'There's Mike, Mike Ardeel. He owns the studio. And there's Tony and Phil, the sound engineers.'

'And that's all? No-one else you can think of who might have had one.'

'No,' she said; and then, 'Oh, of course Chattie had one.'

'Chattie?'

'It's short for Charlotte.' She smiled. 'How cool is that? I love it! Chattie Cornfeld. She's our PR person, and – well, she does all sorts of things for us.'

'Can you describe her to me?'

'She's not in trouble, is she?' Marion asked, looking concerned, but only as worried as a speeding fine, perhaps, or a parking ticket. Atherton didn't speak, only gave her a stolid silence into which to insert her answer. 'Well,' said Marion, 'she's about my height, short blonde hair – very pretty.' She looked at him enquiringly, to see if that was enough.

'Does she wear a gold medallion round her neck?'

Now, belatedly, real worry entered. 'Yes, it's a St Anthony medal. She got it in Tuscany last year. She loves it. Why? What's happened?' She looked down at the disc in its transparent evidence bag. 'Why have you got it all wrapped up like this?'

Atherton said, 'I'm going to ask you to look at a picture and tell me if you think it's her.'

She could tell from the kindly way he said it. 'Oh, my God, what's happened? She's been hurt.'

Atherton said nothing, only offered her the mugshot. She looked at it for a moment, and then nodded. He saw her throat move as she tried to swallow. 'She's dead, isn't she?' she managed to say.

'I'm sorry,' said Atherton. He was having to restrain himself from clasping her to the manly booz. She might have some irritating verbal habits, but she was as cute as all-get-out.

'What happened? Was it an accident?'

'No,' he said. 'I'm sorry. It wasn't an accident.'

Her eyes widened. 'You don't mean – she was *murdered*?'

'Yes, I'm afraid so.'

She had paled, and her lips moved soundlessly a few times before she was able to say, 'But who did it? Who would do such a thing?'

'I'm afraid from early appearances it seems to have been a random killing.'

'Oh, my God,' she said again. She swayed a little, and Atherton put out a hand to catch her elbow, and used it to guide her to a seat. 'When?' she asked.

'Early this morning. She was attacked while she was out jogging.'

'Oh, my God,' she said again. 'I can't believe it. Not Chattie.'

Normally Atherton felt restless while this sort of thing was going on, but this time he waited patiently, allowing her to cope with the shock and disbelief. After a bit he said, 'I'm sorry, but I need to ask you a few questions about her. You see, as she was out jogging when it happened, there was no form of identification on her, apart from this disc. That's why we had to come to you. You obviously knew her quite well.'

She straightened her shoulders to do her duty, though her eyes were still unfocused with shock. 'Well, yes. She's been involved with the band practically from the beginning.'

'Is she a musician?'

'Oh, no. Well, she studied music but she doesn't play. She has this really cool company called Solutions. She does all sorts of office-consultancy services to small businesses, the sort of things they haven't got the time or the skills to do for themselves. Like, for us she does the PR and advertising, and she advises us about everything, even pensions and what we can claim off tax. She knows *everything*, honestly. She's so clever. And she does all the IT stuff. She designed our website, and she found the guy to do the actual build.'

'Was she the one who designed the strapline – the one you have over your doorbell?'

'Do you like it?' She was brightening as she talked, the fact of the death slipping out of her mind with the ease of self-defence. Humankind cannot bear too much reality. Unconsciously she slipped into the present tense again. 'She's really brilliant at things like that. I mean, words are really her thing. It was her that thought up our name, Baroque Solid. I mean, cool, or what? Because that's what jazz fans used to say about really cool jazz in the old days, in the fifties or whatever. They used to say it was "solid". So it's a kind of cute name, don't you think?'

Atherton did think, had thought a long time back, and rather wished that this divine creature had some of the dear departed's skill with words. 'Was she actually at the recording session on Monday?' he asked.

'She wouldn't have missed it. It was her idea. She set it up and booked the studio and everything. She was going to do all the PR for it, and she'd already worked out the list of people to send the demo disc to. I dropped the band copy round to her yesterday evening so that she could listen to it before the mixing session on Friday. We couldn't have that without her. She was always our best critic.' Reality came back and smacked her round the ear. Her lips trembled. 'But she won't be there now, will she? I can't believe she's dead. I only saw her yesterday.'

'You saw her yesterday?' Atherton asked. 'What time would that be?'

'Well, I picked up the copies of the disc from the studio at about six o'clock and took one round to her house straight away, because she lives nearest. Then I dropped the boys' and Trish's off, and brought the others back here for Joni and Tab and me.'

'You actually saw her when you called at her house?'

'Oh, yes. Well, she'd just got in. She was still in the hall in her business suit sorting the mail when I rang the bell, hadn't even put her briefcase away. We had a bit of a chat but she seemed in a hurry, and she said she had to get changed to go out, so I said, "See you on Friday," and that was that.'

'So you left at what time?'

'Half past six, maybe. I wasn't there long.'

'And did you see her later? Or speak to her?'

'Well, no.' There were tears in her eyes now.

'Do you know where she was going that evening?'

'No, she didn't say and I didn't ask. She seemed a bit – well, preoccupied.'

'I don't suppose it matters,' Atherton said. He had asked out of habit. If she was the victim of a random killing it didn't matter where she had been or with whom. 'Well, you've been very helpful in identifying her for us. It's saved us a lot of time. And now I wonder if you could give me her address?'

'Oh, yes, of course,' she said, rather hopelessly, and then pulled herself together. 'I've got one of her invoices here. She worked from home.'

Across the top of the invoice in large, heavy, raised type was the name 'SOLUTIONS' in caps. Under it in slightly smaller caps it said, 'OFFICE CONSULTANCY FOR SMALL BUSINESS AND SELF-EMPLOYED'. And under that, in yet smaller type, in italics, upper and lower, '*PR and IT Solutions and Much More*'.

The address was Wingate Road, a two-minute walk, if that, from the park gates.

Marion Davies showed him out, and at the door he turned back and said, 'By the way, just one more question.'

'Yes?' She raised her large, tear-polished eyes to him.

'Are you doing anything tonight?'

CHAPTER THREE

Pas de Lieu, Rhône, Que Nous

Slider always felt that Freddie Cameron, the forensic pathologist, was out of place against the backdrop of the mortuary of
a modern steel-glass-and-concrete hospital. There was something quintessentially old-fashioned and gentlemanly about him,
with his good suit, bow-tie and polished brogues (he always
changed from black shoes to brown at the beginning of Henley
week). He belonged with Victorian architecture and solid values.
He was marble, not corian; leather, not plastic; solid mahogany,
not veneered furniture board.

He was also looking seriously overworked. His eyes were
red-rimmed and dark-bagged.

'Been making a night of it?' Slider enquired politely.

'You might say. Hannah had her baby last night – or, rather,
early this morning – and since Andy's abroad, Martha and I
stayed with her all through. It was a harrowing experience, I
can tell you.'

'Why couldn't Andy get leave?' Freddie's son-in-law was a
high-earning oil-rig engineer.

'The baby's three weeks early. He's on his way now, but he
was in some God-forsaken backwater of Kazakhstan, and it'll
take him twenty-four hours to get home.' He sighed a profoundly
weary sigh. 'I'm at the age when I need my zeds. To be fair,
Martha did say at one point I should go home and leave it to
her, but I couldn't do that.'

'Of course not.' Slider knew that Hannah was Freddie's
favourite daughter.

Cameron met his eyes. 'It looked a bit touch-and-go at one
point,' he said, and the starkness of his expression underlined
the English understatement of the words.

'She's all right now?'

'Both all right. Another boy. They're going to call it Seth, poor little blighter. Mind you, if it had been a girl it would have been Daisy. Where do they get these names from? So I left Martha there at about half past six this morning, dashed home for a shower and a shave and was out doing my list at half past eight. It never seems to get any shorter. I could do without extras from you, thank you very much.'

'Sorry. Not my idea of fun either,' said Slider. 'It was good of you to fit me in.'

'Oh, I'd sooner get it out of the way. Don't want to be like a proctologist and get behind in my work.'

'Is this your last?'

'Yes, thank God. I might be home by nine with a bit of luck. I laugh at a mere twelve-hour day.'

The morgue attendants came in with the trolley and Cameron received the park corpse with the air of a long-haul passenger facing the fourth airline meal of the flight. 'What is it with you and parks anyway, dear boy?' he enquired of Slider. 'Some kind of symbiotic relationship?'

'I could do without it,' Slider said. 'And I hate a serial.'

'The Park Killer must have read what a good job you did on the Baxter case,' said Cameron. 'Deep down, they all want to be caught, you know. Subconscious desire for a father's discipline.'

'Are you qualified to practise psychiatry?' Slider asked coldly.

'Not me, old bean. I'm a corpse-cutter from way back. Got an ID on this one?'

'Atherton's working on it as we speak.'

'Good. I hate to think of a pretty young thing like this going unclaimed.' He stared a moment at the face. 'When you think what went into the making of this work of art, it makes me mad as hell that someone could destroy it so lightly. I think that's why I became a forensic pathologist.'

'You told me it was because dead men don't sue,' Slider objected.

'There is that,' Freddie agreed. 'Well, let's see what we've got.'

The TV image of the lonely pathologist toiling away in solitude was the stuff of fiction. What with Cameron's assistants, his students, the morgue attendants, the identifying officer, the photographer, the evidence officer, the investigating officer, his bagman, old Uncle Tom Cobbley and all, there was always a crowd around the table. With the new tables that constantly drew the fluids away from underneath, there was little or no smell. But Freddie handed round the Trebors out of old habit. With so many onlookers, the miasma of peppermint could have felled a horse.

Cameron pressed the recording pedal under the table with his foot whenever he murmured his commentary; in between he whistled softly, a habit he had developed in the early days to distract him from distress. The 'Songs for Swingin' Carvers' selection today was 'April in Paris'.

'Subject is female, aged about twenty-eight or -nine, height five feet six, well nourished, appears fit and well muscled, no apparent signs of disease or drug dependency.'

McLaren, as evidence officer, received the clothes as they were removed and examined, and bagged them. Cameron examined the T-shirt, bent to look at the wounds, and at last said to Slider, 'Tell me, old chum, was there anything that struck you as odd about our friend here?'

'I did think there wasn't as much blood as I'd have expected,' Slider said tentatively.

'Give that man a coconut. For a frenzied attack . . .' Everyone says it, Slider thought resignedly '. . . there doesn't seem to be very much damage. One, two three, four, five wounds in front and one in the back, but all except one are quite superficial. You see here, and here, the blade has hardly penetrated at all. This is the only deep wound, this one in the back. You can see from the pattern of flow on the skin and the T-shirt that most of the blood comes from here.'

'Perhaps he couldn't get near enough,' Slider said, but immediately thought of the objection to that. The Park Killer had to be quick. His victim had to be grabbed, overpowered and killed within seconds. He couldn't afford a lot of dancing about and light wounding, with her screaming her head off and passers-by coming to investigate.

'Another thing,' Cameron said. 'Look at the way the blood has run from this wound in the back. Look at the flow pattern. What does it tell you?'

Slider saw it now. The lines of blood ran from the wound sideways around the victim's ribs towards the front. 'She was lying down.'

'Correct.'

'So he knocked her down first and stabbed her when she was prone?'

'Cowardly,' Freddie acknowledged.

After the wounds had been photographed, Cameron took a blood sample from the femoral artery, and then began his delicate butchery, laying open the body from chin to pubic bone. Slider found an excuse to turn his head away at the first stroke of the scalpel. From this morning's sweet domesticity to the ugliness and stupidity of murder was too large a stride all at once. This young body and pretty face had so recently housed a hopeful life that he didn't like to see it mutilated, even though it was now surplus to requirements. Once the first cut had been made, however, experience and professionalism took over. Laid open, it was not a person any more. He was always all right once the first cut had been made.

'You see,' Cameron said to Slider, 'even the one deep wound doesn't touch any of the important organs. I wouldn't have thought it would be a fatal blow.'

'You mean she bled to death? Or died of shock?'

Cameron shook his head doubtfully. 'It wasn't exsanguination. And shock? Unless there's any congenital heart defect . . .'

He removed the heart to a separate table and cut it open carefully. 'A nice, clean, healthy heart – just what you'd hope for in a young jogger. No sign of disease. No infarction. Let's have a look at the brain.'

It was the part Slider disliked most. He hummed inside his head as Cameron deployed the electric saw, breathing shallowly not to smell the barbecue reek of burning bone. Cameron removed the top of the skull, then ligated and lifted out the brain, which he sliced like a large, pallid loaf. 'No sign of anything here. I'll take a section to examine under the microscope, but it all looks nice and normal. I think we can rule out heart disease or stroke.'

'So what killed her, then?'

Cameron turned a frank if rather bistred gaze on him. 'You tell me, chum.'

'Only if you hand over your pay packet.'

'Fat chance,' Freddie grinned. A forensic pathologist earned about three times what a detective inspector did. 'All right, then, let's see. She didn't put up much of a struggle. No broken fingernails, no skin or blood under them – she didn't scratch her assailant. Also – now, look here. Sandra, do you mind if I borrow your body for a moment?'

His assistant, used to these demonstrations, stood back from the table and waited. He walked behind her, put his left arm round her shoulders and positioned his left hand in front of her mouth, but without actually touching it, of course. 'I grab my victim from behind, covering her mouth to stop her screaming. Probably use my right hand, like this, to get her by the upper arm. And I drag her backwards by her arm and jaw—'

'Into the bushes, right,' Slider finished for him.

'But,' Cameron said, 'there's no bruising to the face or arms. No bruising anywhere on the body.'

'Well, that's – odd,' said Slider.

'There's more. Thank you, Sandra.' Freddie released her and continued. 'I knock her down without leaving a mark. Well, I suppose that's possible, if I caught her off-balance, or simply threw her down. I stab her in the back – the first wound, deep, but not disabling. But she doesn't scrabble away from me on hands and knees, or try to get up, she just lies there.'

'Too shocked, too frightened to move?'

'Perhaps,' Freddie allowed, though without great belief.

'Then he turned her over with his foot – or with the help of his foot,' Slider said, 'and stabbed her in the front.'

'Very lightly,' Freddie amended. 'Restrained, wouldn't you say?'

'Not much like the Park Killer on his other outings.'

'And when did she get the defence wounds on her arms and hands?' said Cameron. Sandra was about to speak but he silenced her with a glance.

Slider thought. 'I can't work it out.'

'I'll tell you when she got them,' said Cameron, with an actor's timing. 'After death. The cuts on the arms and hands are all post-mortem wounds.'

'You're sure?' Slider said – but surprise makes you say foolish things.

'Of course,' Freddie said. 'They aren't even very convincing – in the wrong place and at the wrong angles. I've seen enough of the real thing to know. So what we have here, old chum, is . . . ?' He paused invitingly.

Slider filled in the space. 'A set-up.'

'*Exactement*,' said Freddie. 'It was only meant to look like a frenzied attack.'

'Someone killed her and tried to made it look like the Park Killer's work?'

'Not terribly like. It was someone either not very bright or not very *au fait* with our methods, if they thought it would fool us for more than a few hours.'

'I knew there was something wrong with it from the start,' Slider said resentfully. 'The marks on the ground: there were two long grooves going into the bushes, but if you were dragged in still on your feet, there'd be a lot of scuffing and digging as you tried to get a toehold and resist. This looked like the heel-marks of a corpse being dragged.'

'Done afterwards, you think, to add verisimilitude . . .'

'. . . to an otherwise unconvincing narrative,' Slider finished. 'But if she wasn't stabbed to death and didn't bleed to death, what killed her?'

'Well, it is just possible that she died of fright, but it's a very outside possibility. In an old, frail person it might be plausible, but a fit young person tends to be more tenacious of life. I think, old boy, that we may have to wander down the primrose paths of toxicology,' Cameron concluded, with a sigh. 'She looks a little cyanotic to me – wouldn't you say, Sandra? And the lungs are too dark and show some congestion. I think she may have died of respiratory collapse due to an overdose of a depressant drug.'

'You mean – he poisoned her, and then when she was dead stabbed her for effect?'

'No, only the defence wounds were post-mortem. Certainly the main wound in the back was pre-mortem. Those in front have bled so little they might almost be *syn*-mortem, if such an expression were allowable. Of course, the killer might well have thought she *was* dead by then. She was probably so deep down, she was hardly breathing.'

Slider shook his head at the scenario that was opening up. 'So what was the poison?'

'Ah, that I can't tell you,' said Freddie. 'I'll send off a blood sample to the toxicology lab, but you know what they're like.'

'Yes, four to six weeks to get a result. You'll have to help me out, Freddie.'

'Well, there are the antidepressant drugs. Many of the tricyclic and tetracyclic drugs have an anticholinergic action that depresses the brainstem, which would lead to respiratory failure, but the trouble there would be that you'd need a pretty high dose. The sedatives, the benzodiazepines, are more likely culprits, and they leave no particular post-mortem appearances – though you might expect convulsions with a severe overdose, and there's no sign she convulsed. And then,' he added, with a faintly reluctant air, 'there are the barbiturates, though they're harder for the layman to come by. A high dose of one of the short-acting or ultra-short-acting barbiturates like thiopentone or hexobarbitone would produce rapid unconsciousness and death within ten or fifteen minutes.'

Slider met Cameron's eyes, and saw in them the memory of an old case of some years back, the Anne-Marie Austin case, where such a drug had been used. It had come at a bad time for Slider and had almost tipped him over into a breakdown, as Cameron knew very well. First another body in the park, now another death by short-acting barbiturate? Was he to be forced to relive his past like a police version of *Groundhog Day*? On the good side, he'd get to meet Joanna again; on the bad side, he'd keep finding himself still married to Irene. He brought his errant mind back to the problem in hand.

'But,' he said, 'if you want to poison somebody, you do it privately indoors. Why would you do it out in a public park in broad daylight with all the likelihood of being interrupted? And how do you get someone out jogging in the park to take poison anyway?'

'That,' said Cameron, 'I gladly leave to you.'

He rang Joanna to tell her he was on his way home.

'What do you think about James?' she asked, as soon as she heard his voice.

To his credit, he caught on. 'Do all women do that?'

'Do what?'

'Think about babies' names all the time.'

'I don't do it all the time. Anyway, you ought to know.' He'd had two children with his ex-wife Irene.

'Too long ago,' he said. 'Don't remember.'

'Well? What about James?'

'It might not be a boy.'

'Of course it will be. First time out – you want the teapot *with* the spout, don't you?'

'If you say so. But James Slider sounds like badly fitting false teeth.'

She sighed. 'True.'

'Freddie Cameron's new grandson is called Seth.'

'Flaming Nora,' Joanna said. 'Seth Slider's even worse.'

'I wasn't suggesting it.'

'No votes for anything with an *s* in it. When will you be home?'

'Before you can say psephologically sesquipedalian.'

At least he had missed the evening rush hour. Traffic on the Uxbridge Road was down to tolerable levels, mostly people going out for the evening, pottering between traffic light and traffic light, off to the pub, to restaurants, to visit friends, to pick up a takeaway. Real life. None of them had spent the day pondering over a corpse.

Atherton phoned him with the identification when he was at the East Acton Lane lights. 'Did your witness give you a next of kin?' he asked.

'No, she didn't know. But she's sure deceased wasn't married and didn't live with anyone, and I tried the home telephone number and there was an answering machine on. I tried her mobile number, too, but it was switched off.'

'Odd that she didn't have it with her,' Slider said. 'Young businesspeople are usually wedded to them.'

'Maybe she wanted a bit of peace and quiet,' Atherton said. 'Or maybe the killer nicked it. How was the post?'

'Interesting,' Slider said. He told Atherton Cameron's findings.

'Oh,' said Atherton. 'Well, that's – interesting.'

'Is that the best you can come up with?'

'I'm trying. It puts a whole new complexion on things. If it wasn't a random killing, we're back with the who-saw-her-last and what-enemies-did-she-have routines.'

'Did you get any of that from your Marion Davies type?'

'I didn't ask, not knowing it was needed. She did say she saw the victim yesterday at around six p.m. and she was all right then. Just about to go out for the evening.'

'With whom?'

'As I said, I didn't ask. But I've arranged to see her again, so I can ask then.'

'See her again? What for?'

'What for?' Atherton repeated derisively. 'She's a bit of a sort, that's what for.'

'Oh,' said Slider. The lights changed and he moved off and turned left down Stanley Gardens, which perhaps prevented him saying something he'd later regret.

'Well, I've got the victim's address, anyway,' Atherton said. 'Do you want to look at the house tonight?'

'No. If she lived alone, tomorrow will do. Just put someone on the door. The media are still putting it out as the Park Killer, so the real villain will think he's getting away with it. And I'm less than five minutes from home.'

'Lucky man.'

Slider thought he sounded a little wistful, and said, 'Joanna's made a casserole. Do you want to—?'

'Thanks, but no. I've got a date,' Atherton said breezily.

'Fine. Well, don't let me keep you.'

He rang off, reflecting that it was just as well Atherton had refused, given that he was not Joanna's favourite person at the moment. Besides, he really wanted to be alone with her this evening, to enjoy the peace and comfort of her company and whatever was simmering in the slow oven. Plus a bottle of good, hearty red. He wondered who Atherton had a date with, but as he was turning the last corner before home he didn't wonder very much. There's no place like home, he thought, because in fact home isn't a place, it's people. There is no place, only us. And a bottle of Saint-Joseph.

Porson was there when Slider arrived in the morning, as if he had never been home. He was stamping about his room like a man looking for a cat to kick. Top-brass meetings at Hammersmith always did nasty things to his blood pressure. Under the harsh neon light of his room his head had a strangely bumpy look, like a bag full of knuckles. Bubbles of frustration trying to escape, perhaps?

'You were off pretty sharpish last night,' he snapped at Slider.

'I went to the post mortem. Cameron put it on the end of his list.'

'Oh. You could have let me know.'

'I left a message on your voice-mail, sir.'

'Oh,' said Porson again. 'I always forget about that bloody thing. Whatever happened to a piece of paper on your desk?'

Before he could think of anything else to complain about, Slider told him of the discoveries of the day before. His pacing slowed as he listened.

'Not bad for a start,' he said grudgingly, when Slider had finished. And then, 'Good thought of Atherton's to get the ID that way. He's a smart lad.' That was not always a compliment in the Job, but this time Porson meant it.

'Yes, sir,' said Slider. 'I presume we'll be keeping the ID under wraps for the time being?'

'Until we've informed the next of kin, at any rate.'

'Also,' Slider added, 'it might help us to let the villain think we've bought the Park Killer scenario?'

Porson frowned. 'Yes, that's a bit of a queer thing, isn't it, what Cameron's saying?'

'Of course,' Slider said, 'we don't know whether the drugging was meant to kill her, or only subdue her so she'd be easier to stab.'

Porson pondered. 'Doesn't make much difference, does it? Whoever gave her the drug was the killer, one way or the other. But you're sure in your own mind it wasn't the Park Killer?'

'It isn't his MO,' Slider said. 'As far as we can be sure from only two previous cases.'

'Right. He could have changed his pattern, I suppose.'

'But I think it's unlikely. The stab wounds were mostly superficial and not given with any force.'

'Not a frenzied attack, then.'

'No, sir. A slow and deliberate attack.'

'Well,' said Porson, gripping and bending a plastic ruler between his large hands, 'that's good news in its way.'

'Yes, sir. I hate a serial.'

'We all do, laddie, we all do. But what I meant was, while I was over at Hammersmith yesterday, I took the chance to have a talk with Mr Palfreyman about this.' Palfreyman was head of the Homicide Advice Team, the demigod with the power to say who would investigate any particular murder. 'As we know, the SCG's lost most of its men and they're struggling under a backlash of work. So there wasn't much chance of them taking on the case. On the other hand, Mr Palfreyman wasn't happy about leaving us to pedal our own Canute, so his idea was to form a new temporary dedicated Park Killer squad with some of us and some of Ealing's boys and girls, under his own personal regis.'

Slider looked his horror at the idea. Porson was so moved at the thought of it that he bent the ruler too far and one end slipped from his grasp. It flew whirling across the room like a rogue helicopter blade, hit the wall and fell with a clatter. Porson hardly flinched.

'Yes,' he said, 'so it's not bad at all if we can tell him convincively that it *wasn't* the Park Killer, you see.'

Slider saw. The special squad was a mind-watering idea, and given that it was Palfreyman's brainchild, which he had presumably seen as a path to glory, he wasn't going to be happy about giving it up.

'I'm satisfied in my own mind it wasn't,' he said firmly.

'So am I,' said Porson. 'The Park Killer's a stab-and-go raging nutter. He's not going to pussyfoot about with narcrotics, hang about having a fag while he waits for his victim to lie down for a kip. You can't teach an old leopard new stripes. So I think you can take it as read that we'll be keeping this one at home, Slider. I'll say what needs to be said to Mr Palfreyman.'

'Yes, sir,' Slider said. And, 'Thank you.'

Porson raised his eyebrows, and his deeply sunken eyes took the opportunity to flash fire. 'I don't know what you're thanking me for. You don't know yet what sort of a case this is going to be. It could turn out to be a sticker, and all eyes are going to be on you now to pull the chestnuts out of the fan in double-quick time.'

'All eyes' meaning Mr Palfreyman's, Slider thought. Well, he'd been threatened with top-brass disapproval all his career. 'I can live with that, sir,' he said. 'By the way, did you have a chance to ask about extra help?'

'Yes, I did. They're sending someone over this morning who's been on a roving brief, so they're more or less spare.'

'Roving brief?'

'Some diversity programme follow-up survey,' Porson said, with an absolute absence of expression. These were dangerous waters, Watson.

'Oh,' said Slider.

'Only one body,' Porson went on, 'but it's better than nothing.'

'Right, sir,' said Slider. He hoped it would prove so. Some young go-getter who'd stepped straight from Hendon into a political-statistical job might well prove to be more of a liability than otherwise.

'So we have a whole new game on, boys and girls,' Slider addressed the troops, who were slumped over their tables in attitudes that would have made a chiropractor weep. Hollis was removing relevant stuff, now become irrelevant, about the Park Killer from the whiteboard. Atherton was writing up his report on the information he'd got from Marion Davies. Swilley was in a corner talking quietly to the coroner's officer, a new man who'd never met her before, who looked as though he couldn't believe his luck and was right about that. McLaren was bracing himself for the rigours of the day by eating Toast Topper straight from the tin with a plastic spoon, using his left hand to alternate mouthfuls from a small box of microwave chips. Slider wished he could get rid of that microwave oven, but its use was probably guaranteed under the Geneva Convention, not to say EU employment law.

He continued. 'It's back to basics, find out everything we can about deceased, who had a grudge against her, who had a reason to kill her.'

'It still could be a random killing, though, couldn't it?' Mackay called.

'It could,' Slider said fairly, 'but I think it's unlikely.'

'Only, it's a funny sort of way to off someone if you know them,' he persisted. 'I mean, if you wanted to poison them, you'd put something in their food or drink at home, wouldn't you? Where you could make sure she was dead, and clear up after yourself, without being interrupted.'

McLaren did a hasty swallow that would have challenged a

boa constrictor and said, 'Yeah, I'm with Andy on that, guv. Most likely to me is that it's a copy-cat Park Killer, only he's not got the balls just to grab and stab, he's got to drug her first.' He looked round defensively. 'Well, I can see that. That makes sense.'

'Only to you and a moron,' said Swilley, who had sent her disappointed swain away and rejoined the group. 'Honestly, Maurice, if brains were money you'd need a mortgage for a cup of tea. How's a complete stranger clutching a big knife going to get her to swallow drugs while she's out jogging and then hang around until she feels sleepy?'

'Well, whoever did it's got to get over that problem,' Mackay said.

'Yeah, why's she going to do that for anyone?' McLaren put in resentfully.

'Guv, do we know how the drug was administered?' Hollis asked, like a breath of sanity.

'Doc Cameron says for the quickest reaction it should have been injected. I left him going over the skin with a magnifying glass. If it was administered orally, it would take quicker effect in liquid than solid form. Something may emerge from the stomach contents.'

'God, I hope not,' Atherton said.

'Maybe the murderer put something in her water-bottle,' said Mackay.

'He'd have had to have access to her house to do that,' Slider said. 'But we'll have the contents checked anyway.'

'How quickly would it take effect?' Swilley asked.

'We won't know that until we know what it was and how it was given. But for the method to work at all it would have to be pretty quick. Meanwhile, whether it was a murder by someone who had a grudge against her—'

'Or whether we go with the dim bulbs' theory,' Swilley inserted under her breath.

'—or it was a random killing,' Slider went on, 'much of the work is still the same. We carry on searching for a weapon, for blood marks, for clothing. Get her telephone statements and check all the numbers she rang, see if there was anything un-toward going on. Ask the neighbours about any comings and goings or people hanging about. Follow up anything on the statements we've already taken. Start doorstepping the street, anyone who overlooks the park, the shops along Paddenswick Road, the streets on the other side of the park too.'

'What about the pub, guv?' Mackay asked.

This was the Wellington, which years ago had been called the George and Two Dragons, because it was run by a little man called George Benson who was henpecked by both his wife and mother-in-law. It was on Paddenswick Road and opposite the park railings, hardly more than a few yards from the park gate.

'Yes, good point. Someone had better call in there today.'

'I could go. I know the landlord pretty well,' Mackay said.

'All right.'

'And there's a different crowd in at night from lunch-time,' Mackay added quickly.

'True,' said Slider. 'All right, you can do an evening visit as well. You'd better have some help.' McLaren perked up no end at that, sat up straight and tried to look reliable. 'See if one of the uniforms is willing. Plain clothes, of course.' He thought. 'Not Renker: he'd still look like a copper if he was stark naked. Willans has got his hands full. See if D'Arblay's up for it. He's a nice, confiding lad. People open up for him.'

'Right-oh, guv.'

Swilley spoke up. 'There's the tube station, boss. The killer might have made his getaway that way. We ought to have someone on there at the same time of the morning. And maybe some leaflets to hand out.'

'Good thought. You can arrange that,' said Slider. 'All right, anything to follow up in the statements so far?' There were negatives all round. 'Anything come in on the telephone last night?'

'Just the usual attention-seekers and Daft Dorises,' Hollis said. 'Apparently there were strange lights in the sky over the park Tuesday night.'

'There are strange lights in the sky over the park every night,' Slider said. 'It's on the flight path to Heathrow.'

Wingate Road, where the victim had lived, was just off the main road, but surprisingly was a little haven of quiet. It was a short street with a pub at one end, a nice, small, old-fashioned-looking hostelry called the Anchor. It was obvious from the state of the pub and the houses that the street had been gentrified. Everything was in a condition of cherished middle-class repair, and the parked cars were rust-free and mostly under three years old.

The terraced houses dated from the 1850s, earlier than adjacent streets: two storeys plus semi-basement, square stuccoed fronts, the pitch of the roof hidden by a ruled-off parapet, the age given away only by the lovely proportion of the tall sash windows, each divided into nine small panes. At some point all the residents had been seized by a common urge to paint their stucco in a dusty pastel shade. The effect was delightful, like a tube of Refreshers.

'That's it,' Atherton said, indicating a house of pale hyacinth blue. 'Gloriosky! There's a parking space. I wonder if one of these is her car?'

'Didn't you ask what's-her-name – Marion Davies? You were there long enough.'

'She wouldn't have known, anyway,' Atherton said. 'Women never cease to amaze me. When you think of the hours they spend rabbiting to each other about shopping and hairdressers, and they don't even know what sort of car each other drives.'

Slider parked the car, pulled two pairs of gloves from the box in the dash compartment, and got out.

'Did you bring the key?' Atherton demanded.

'Yes, dear,' Slider said patiently.

Inside the house, the long hall was cool and dim, a pleasure after the heat of the day, and it smelt beautifully clean, with an undertone of furniture polish. The staircase rose up straight ahead, the handrail a shining snake of wood, smoothed and rubbed to a rich patina by a hundred and fifty years of hands. Though the house looked small from the street, it went back a long way, and the ceilings were lofty, eleven or twelve feet high, Slider thought. It was a wonderful house, built with the fine proportions and attention to detail that were characteristic of the age: the skirtings, the panelled doors and brass door-furniture, the decorated cornices and ceiling roses, the handsome fireplaces.

'Looks as if she made a decent living from this company of hers,' Atherton said.

'Or maybe she just had good taste,' Slider said. There was nothing expensive about the furnishings, but the simplicity with which everything was arranged made it look good. The floors had been stripped and polished, and there were a few rugs here and there for comfort; modern furniture, plain walls and curtains, and no clutter.

There were two rooms on this floor. At the front, with the bay window, was the drawing room. The sofa and two armchairs were in coarse off-white material, grouped round a heavy glass coffee-table. Against the walls were hi-fi equipment, television and video, and a range of bookshelves. There were no pictures on the walls, just two four-foot-by-two framed posters. One was a movie poster for *Casablanca*. 'That must be worth a bit,' Atherton remarked. The other advertised a Festival Hall concert by the London Symphony Orchestra, with a date from the 1950s. Boult and Curzon, Slider noticed. Frivolity was limited to a number of large plants in big floor pots, their leaves glossily polished. The room was so big it was a little too bare for Slider's taste, but there was no denying it was stylish.

The rear room was slightly smaller, square and fitted out as an office, with the usual equipment. Here, too, everything was neat, tidy, clean and dusted. There was a big engagements diary and a red address book on the desk, which Slider noted for removal; and a small pile of unopened mail. Postmarks suggested it was yesterday's. Presumably, then, it had arrived before she had gone out for her morning jog. She had picked it up and put it in here to be looked at when she got back. But she never got back.

'Everything in here will have to be gone through,' Slider said, with a wave that included the filing cabinets and the contents of the in- and out-trays. 'We need to know what sort of business she was doing, and with whom.'

This floor of the house was slightly above ground level, and stairs at the back of the hall led down to the semi-basement, with a landing halfway down with a lavatory and a door to the garden. The basement had been knocked into one long, large room with the original stone-flagged floor, fitted out as kitchen and eating area.

'Nice-looking kitchen,' Atherton said. 'All that slate and black granite must have cost a bob or two. She didn't stint herself.'

They went back up to the hall, intending to take a quick look round upstairs before getting down to a proper search, but as they were walking towards the front door, a shadow appeared behind its glass and the bell rang.

'Now what?' Atherton said.

Slider was ahead of him so he was the one to open the door. There, grinning engagingly, stood a very pretty young black woman in a bottle green trouser suit, with her hair plaited in windrows and tipped with green beads.

''Allo, guv,' she chirped. 'I was told to report to you.'

CHAPTER FOUR

Brother, Can You Spare Me a Paradigm?

Slider stared like a man who'd just been hit on the head with a large fish. 'Hart?' he said.

'Hollis fought you might need help. S'prised to see me?'

'Surprised doesn't begin to cover it,' Slider said. 'Don't tell me you're the extra body Mr Porson wangled?'

DC Tony Hart nodded. Slider stepped back to let her in. Behind him, he heard Atherton say, 'Extra body's the *mot juste.*'

'I ain't 'alf glad to be 'ere, I can tell you,' Hart went on. 'I'm sick of being the token black, token woman on all these special squads. I mean, it's all bollocks, innit? I told Mr Wevverspoon I wanted to get back operational, but he said I was too valuable to waste on police work.' She opened her eyes wide. 'I mean, straight, guv, can you believe it?'

'I believe six worse things than that every day before breakfast,' Slider said.

'I've been on this Diversity Advice Follow-up Team for three months now, wiv this bunch o' total tossers who've never been on the street in their lives. The acronym says it all. Honestly, not one of 'em noticed what it was.'

'Well, I'm glad to have you with us, Hart,' Slider said, skipping over that bit. Of all the firms in all the cop shops in all the Met, he thought, she had to walk into his. The last time she had worked with them, she had had a torrid fling with Atherton. Joanna, however, had opined that Hart had actually only chased Atherton because she really fancied him, Slider – a deeply unsettling thought. Whichever way round it was, complications like those he didn't need, especially given Atherton's currently over-stimulated state. Hart was too juicy by half to expose him to.

Hart turned her attention to Atherton now, and said lightly, 'Wotcher, Jim. I like the barnet. Cool or what?'

'Best not to encourage him,' Slider said kindly. 'He's on the loose again.'

'I can take care'v meself,' Hart said.

'Has Hollis filled you in on the story so far?'

'Sort of. The vic was drugged and stabbed in the park, to make it look like the Park Killer struck again.'

'Don't call her the vic. She's not a theatre.'

'All right,' Hart said agreeably. 'So what we doin'?'

'Looking round the house. What we need immediately is a photograph of the victim we can use with the public, and any information about next of kin. There'll be a full team in later to do the serious search. Of course you needn't ignore anything interesting or unusual if it jumps up and bites you. You'd better come upstairs with me and have a look at the bedrooms. Atherton, you can start going through the office.'

Upstairs, on the next floor, there were two bedrooms and a large bathroom, which, given the age of the house, must have originally been another bedroom. The floors were stripped and varnished all through, and echoed to their footsteps.

'Bit chilly,' Hart remarked. 'I like a nice bit o' Wilton meself.'

Slider thought it would be unwelcoming in winter, though at the moment it was pleasantly cool. The bathroom was done in a retro style, with a free-standing claw-footed bath, high-level cistern and old-fashioned pedestal basin. An odd place to make a stand for heritage. Of all rooms, surely the bathroom was the one in which you most wanted clinical modernity.

Of the bedrooms, the one at the back was the smaller. It was unfurnished, and being used for storage. There were several removers' cartons, still sealed up, presumably never having been unpacked since she moved in. There were also a number of ordinary cardboard boxes containing a variety of odds and ends – clothes, shoes, board games and jigsaw puzzles, sports equipment, ornaments, crockery, and one full of dolls and soft toys.

'It's like she brought everyfing wiv her when she left home,' Hart said. 'Look, there's pairs o' bally shoes in here, must be all of 'em goin' back to when she was five. An' about a thousand china horses. This is the sort o' stuff you leave cluttering up your mum and dad's house until they get mad and chuck it out.'

Yes, Slider thought, she was right. It was a good insight. 'Hell of a lot of sorting through to do,' he said.

'Oh, I dunno, guv,' Hart said comfortingly. 'If she's never unpacked it, it prob'ly never had anything to do with her present life. I wonder why she brought it wiv her, though.'

'Maybe her parents divorced and the family house was sold,' Slider suggested.

Hart grinned. 'Yeah, but most of us would still make our mums take all this crap to her new house. There's people all over the country've got their cupboards stuffed full of their grown-up kids' junk, while their kids swank about bein' all minimalist in warehouse conversions wiv no storage.'

The larger, front room was evidently her bedroom. A king-size bed, neatly made; an extensive range of built-in wardrobes; an oak chest, probably Jacobean, under the window; a beautiful secretaire, probably Regency.

Hart had a look in the wardrobes. '*Well* nice,' she said, in emphatic understatement. 'Some top gear in here. Gucci and Karen Millen. Manolo shoes, even. Oh, and look at this pink suede skirt! Viv Westwood. I'm drooling, boss.'

'Just don't get DNA on the goods,' Slider warned. 'She did keep everything tidy, didn't she?'

'It's like one of them adverts for fitted bedrooms,' Hart said. 'Or that makeover programme – you know – where they turn out your messiest room and make you chuck stuff away. It looks about like this when they let the people back in. I've always thought they should do a revisit a week later. Nobody keeps their clothes like this. What was she, an alien from another planet?'

Slider headed for the secretaire. 'This is for us. This'll be where she kept her personal papers.'

'An' there's a photo,' Hart said. It was framed and standing on top of the secretaire, next to a small vase containing a single rose, whose petals were beginning to fall.

Slider picked up the photo and turned it to the light. The girl in the picture was smiling with radiant happiness, her face sharing the space inside the frame with that of a very nice bay horse.

Hart came close and looked too. 'Pretty. Nice face.'

'The girl's not bad, either.'

Hart slung a sideways glance at him. 'Bally an' horses. She was someone's little princess, wasn't she? Will it do?'

'We could screen out the horse,' Slider said, 'but she was in her late twenties, and she only looks about seventeen or eighteen in this.' He looked round. 'Strange that this is the only photo. Most people have scads of them.'

'The only one on display,' Hart corrected.

The top part of the secretaire held lots of documents and letters. 'We'll have to take all this stuff back to the office and go through it,' Slider said.

In the drawer, along with various unremarkable odds and ends, was a number of Boots' developer's envelopes full of photographs. Slider and Hart looked through them, spread some out on the bed. There were holiday pictures and snaps of parties, outings, picnics, weddings and christenings. Young, good-looking faces were everywhere, laughing, mugging, drinking, having a good time. There was nothing that looked like a family shot – all the principals were young. Chattie herself appeared in very few of them – she must have been the one holding the camera – but when she did appear she seemed generally to have a champagne glass in her hand and her arm draped round a young man, and she was always laughing. Those fine, well-kept teeth shone out, the eyes disappeared into slits of hilarity, and everyone seemed to be looking at her, crowding round her as if she were the life of the group.

'Definitely a princess,' Hart observed, and it did not seem an entirely complimentary judgement.

Slider, though, was fascinated by her face. 'I'd like to have known her.'

'You'd nevera kept up, guv. She liked to 'ave it large, by the look of her,' Hart said. 'Any of these any good for us?'

'We'll take them back and have a look. She seems to be laughing too much in most of them,' Slider said, with a hint of sadness. 'Let's look upstairs.'

There was another staircase, much plainer and narrower, going up into the roof space, into what must originally have been the servant's bedroom. Given that one of the main bedrooms was being used for storage, Slider would have expected more boxes up there, but it was furnished with a divan, fitted dressing table and wardrobe and a tiny shower-room-and-loo carved out of a corner. It was also, in contrast to the rest of the house, perilously untidy, with clothes and shoes and bags spread over every surface, used mugs and plates on the floor, apple cores in the fireplace. A vast array of makeup and face and body unguents in clogged and dribbling bottles choked the dressing table, smeared tissues lying where they had been thrown at the wastepaper basket and missed. Where any bare surface showed it was thick with dust, and there was a stale smell in the room, which was being baked to well-risen perfection by the heat under the roof.

'Oh, I love what she's done up here,' said Hart. 'Very post-modern.'

'Interesting,' said Slider. 'A complete personality change when you come up these stairs.'

'This is the attic she had in her picture,' Hart said.

'Eh?'

'Oscar Wilde. I knew there was something wrong wiv a person who kept her wardrobe that tidy. This is where her evil alter-ego had its 'orrible outlet.'

'Or,' Slider said, throwing cold water, 'she had a lodger.'

'Oh, yeah,' said Hart. 'There is that possibility.'

But apart from clothes and shoes and toiletries, there were no personal effects or documents in the drawers and cupboards. 'Not a permanent lodger, then,' Slider concluded.

'Maybe a friend who lived out of town and needed a place to crash during the week,' Hart suggested.

They descended again. Hearing their footsteps Atherton came out into the hall and said, 'I've found a safe.'

Hart assumed a breathless excitement. 'Hidden be'ind an ancestral portrait?'

Atherton gave her a quelling look. 'One of us doing that sort of thing is enough. No, it's sunk into the floor under the desk well. There's a ring in the floorboards that lifts up a square section and the door to the safe is underneath.'

Slider went and looked. 'Nice. Just hidden enough—'

'But not too tasty,' Hart concluded. ''Ow we gonna get in?'

'Manufacturer,' Slider said, and regarded her expression. 'Did you think we were going to blow it open with *plastique*? You really have got out of touch with reality.'

'I'm desperate for excitement,' she admitted. 'I feel as if I've been in a meeting for two years.'

'Meanwhile,' Atherton said patiently, 'I've found one or two things. Her passport – nothing much there, a few trips to the States, well spaced, probably holidays. Of course, European trips don't get stamped now, more's the pity.'

'We found holiday snaps upstairs,' said Hart. 'She liked to par-*tay*.'

'And I've found her bank statements. She had two accounts, one with a local NatWest for the business. Her personal account – this is the interesting bit – is with Coutts.'

'Coutts?' Hart said. 'That's the nobby bank, in't it? The Queen's got one of them.'

'That's right,' Atherton said. 'But you don't have to be a nob. Anyone can have a Coutts account – anyone with assets of a quarter of a million.'

Hart's eyes widened satisfactorily. 'Is that straight?'

'So what are you suggesting?' Slider asked.

'I wasn't suggesting anything. I was just making observations,' Atherton said.

'No, you weren't,' said Slider.

'All right, then. I'm suggesting she must have had some other form of income than this business of hers, because the amounts going in and out of *that* account wouldn't buy her one of Coutts's paperclips.'

'This house must be worth a bit,' Slider said.

'I agree, but that doesn't change the question, does it? Where did she get the money to buy the house?'

'Is there a mortgage?'

'There's a monthly direct debit to Cheltenham and Gloucester, but working back from the amount it could only cover a mortgage of around a hundred thousand, which is about the most the business would support. This house must be worth four times that.'

'Inherited wealth, then, or rich parents?' Slider said. He thought of the photograph with the horse; he thought of the taste of the furnishings and decoration; he thought of the whole look of the body, the good skin, glossy hair, fine teeth. Someone's little princess, as Hart had said. 'If there was inherited wealth it might have something to do with the murder.'

'That's what I was thinking,' Atherton said. 'Given that all murders come down to sex or money. But the other possibility is that she had some kind of more lucrative sideline we haven't come across.'

'I don't like what you're suggesting,' Slider said uneasily.

'I don't either,' Atherton replied airily.

The Wellington was doing a roaring trade. Not only was it the closest the public could get to the goings-on in the park, but you could actually see quite a lot from the windows. The landlord had made the best of the situation. His 'pub grub' sign now sported a hand-written addition: 'We make KILLER sarnies!'

'You got to make a quid where you can, haven't you?' he excused himself, without shame, to Mackay. He added, with convoluted logic, 'I mean, if my pub had been a couple o' yards closer to the park gates, you lot would've closed me down for the duration, wouldn't you?'

Mackay wouldn't be drawn. 'Have a look at these, will you?'

'Is that her – the victim?' The landlord shook his head over the pictures – they were using cropped versions of the horse photo and a wedding snap where Chattie was in the line-up. 'No, I can't say I know her. Doesn't ring any bells.' He handed them back. 'We don't get the young crowd in here much. It's an old-fashioned kind of a pub. We get nice, steady regulars, local people, and the sandwich trade at lunch-time. Nothing here for youngsters. They mostly go down the Crown, now it's been done up and made all modern.'

Mackay reflected wryly that they, Slider's firm, had stopped going there for the very same reason.

Everyone was talking about the murder; everyone had something to say about the Park Killer. You couldn't chuck a brick in there without hitting an expert forensic psychologist. D'Arblay, with his nice wholesome face and gentle manner, was talking to some of the older customers, who clucked and ooohed in slow horror over the murder like broody hens, and found a perverse thrill in contemplation of the photos. 'That nice young thing!' 'Who could do a thing like that to such a pretty girl?'

The star of the show, however, was an old man who, it turned out, had actually spoken to the victim. He recognised her at once from the photos and said, 'It's that girl I see in the mornings when I'm walking the dog!'

He lived in Dalling Road, up the Brackenbury end, and mornings he took the old dog out, just round the streets, down Dalling, up Wingate, along Goldhawk as far as Brackenbury and back round. He used to take the dog to the park, but he was getting on now, the dog was, and round the streets was enough for him with his hips. Had Arthur Itis in his hips, the dog had. Well, oo 'adn't? He never knew dogs could get it, though. Got a lot of yuman diseases, dogs did. What come of living with yumans, he supposed. Anyway, quite often he'd see this young lady setting off in her PT gear, and she'd smile and say hello.

'Normally they wouldn't give you the time o' day, young people,' he said, with a sniff. 'Look at you as if you was dirt – if they don't barge right through you, just as if you wasn't there. Never think we fought two world wars for the likes of them.'

D'Arblay guessed his age to be about sixty-five, which meant he wouldn't have fought in one war, never mind two, but he listened patiently. You never knew what you might find out if you kept your ears open and your mouth shut – that was what Mr Slider (something of a hero to D'Arblay) said.

'What time of day would that be?' he asked.

'Ooh, lessee, about a quart' past seven, give or take, time I get round there. We don't walk fast, the dog an' me. And she'd be coming out, down her steps, or I'd pass her going down the street. I see her most days, and she always give me a "good morning", and she'd say "nice day" or something like that. She walked nice, with her head up, not slouching along like some of 'em. Always smiling. Lovely smile, she had,' he said sentimentally, as though she had been a childhood sweetheart. 'Sort that makes you feel good to be alive, know what I mean? I can't believe anyone would kill her.' He sighed, drained off his pint, and smacked his lips hopefully, with a sideways glance at D'Arblay. D'Arblay only looked blank. The old man sighed again and said, 'Not a bit like that other one. Nasty piece of work, she was. Wouldn't give you the drippings off her nose, that one, never mind a smile.'

'What other one is that?' D'Arblay asked.

The old man feigned deafness, staring into his empty glass. D'Arblay fetched him another pint, and the old man perked up at once.

'Very nice of you. Very civil. Cheers!' He drank off half the bounty, wiped his lips, and said, 'That other one, I seen her going in and out now and then, different times o' day. Sometimes with my young lady, but sometimes not. 'Ad 'er own key.'

'What did she look like?' D'Arblay asked. They had all been briefed about the top-floor room. If he could get a lead on the lodger, or whatever she was, it would please Slider.

'Scrawny,' said the old man. 'Bag o' bones. Dyed hair – black – cut all messy, you know the way they do. Studs everywhere. She looked like she'd been up'olstered. And that 'orrible makeup, like Drackerler's mother, and black nail varnish. Skirts up to 'ere, no brassière and them thin little tops so you could see all she'd got.' He shook his head in condemnation. 'The other one was a lady, but this bit, well, she looked like a tart, there's no other word for it. And never a smile. You know the way they look, girls like that. Sullen, I'd call it. Like everyone was out to do 'em down. Most of 'em don't know what 'ardship is. And we fought a war for the likes of them.'

D'Arblay asked him a few more questions, but he didn't seem to have anything more to add, and D'Arblay left him to it, telling his story again to a fresh group who gathered round to marvel at someone who had actually Known The Victim.

The description of the Sinister Lodger went down well back at the factory.

'And it gives us a handle on her morning routine,' Slider said. 'The jog was evidently her usual daily round, so the killer may have known about it.'

Swilley had gained a small piece of information at the tube station. The paper-seller there had recognised the photo of Chattie and said that he saw her every morning. The station entrance, where he had his stand, was opposite the south gate of the park and he would see her come out of the park, 'in her tracksuit or whatever', and cross the road to buy the *Guardian* and the *Telegraph*. Round about eight o'clock, that'd be. Then she'd stick one under her arm, open the other, and start reading it as she walked back the way she'd come. He, too, described her as a 'really nice young woman, always ready with a smile and a bit of chat; friendly, you know? Not like some of them, just throw the money at you.'

'But she didn't have the newspapers with her,' Atherton said. 'It looks as though she was killed before she went down to the station, so a little before eight o'clock.'

'Unless the killer took the papers away with him,' Swilley said.

'Why would he do that?'

'Suppose they got covered with blood?'

'Well, that wouldn't matter, as long as it was her blood,' Atherton pointed out.

'If the murderer was bright enough to realise that.'

'So,' Slider said, 'she leaves home about a quarter past seven, runs around the park for half an hour or so, then on her way to the station to buy her paper meets the murderer.'

Of the incoming reports following the appeal, the most promising were of a man running out of the Paddenswick gate, and of a man on a bicycle riding very fast out of the King Street gate. The latter had almost knocked down the informant, a Mrs Beryl Rose, who was walking to the tube station on her way to work. He hadn't even looked round to see if he'd hurt her, though she'd shouted at him angrily. He'd just pedalled straight into the traffic, nearly causing an accident, weaving wildly round the cars and vans and shooting off down King Street towards Chiswick. This report was corroborated by two people, one of whom had stopped to ask Mrs Rose if she was all right, and exchanged a few words with her about the menace of people who rode bikes on the pavement, and why didn't They do something about it. The time given was variously just after eight, five past eight and ten past eight. The man was described as young, white, probably tall, probably fair, wearing black skin-tight cycling shorts, a lightweight blue windcheater jacket and a cycling helmet.

'Why would he be wearing a jacket on a hot day?' Hart asked, and answered herself, 'To cover up bloodstains maybe?'

The most promising thing about the description was that
Mrs Rose said he had a sports bag strapped to the carrier
behind the saddle. A bag of some kind would seem to be an
essential for removing the weapon and any bloodstained
clothing from the scene. On the other hand, the other two
witnesses to Bicycle Man had not noticed the bag, so it was
only Mrs Rose's word.

Running Man had also been fingered by three people, inde-
pendently of each other. He was young, black, wearing baggy
fawn chino pants, a loose grey hooded jacket over a black
T-shirt, and trainers. He had raced 'like the wind' out of the
park gate and up Paddenswick Road towards the Seven Stars.
A further witness had seen him 'run madly' across the road
at the Seven Stars, dodging the traffic filtering round the
double roundabout there, and disappear up Askew Road. The
time given was about eight o'clock, just before eight o'clock,
and five or ten to eight. Against Running Man was the fact
that none of the witnesses said he'd been carrying a bag,
though one witness thought he had been carrying a mobile
phone.

Probably they would turn out to be nothing, but both Running
Man and Bicycle Man would have to be looked into. A media
appeal was planned, asking them to come forward and get
themselves eliminated from the inquiry. If Bicycle Man were
innocent, there was good hope that he would turn up; but
young black men in gangsta gear were generally suspicious of
the police, and Slider was afraid that he would continue a thorn
in their side for some time.

Porson got back from Hammersmith and scooped up Slider on
his way upstairs. Slider scurried in his wake, feeling like Alice.
Porson's legs were long, and he moved at a terrific rate, like
an ostrich, his summer coat flapping around and behind him
like shabby plumage. In the winter he wore a tent-like green
ex-army overcoat, but his summer tegument was a beige mac.
It had once been expensive, and had flaps and capes and
pockets and buttons everywhere.

Reaching his room he barked, 'Close the door,' over his
shoulder, shucked off his coat, threw it at the old-fashioned
elk stand in the corner, and seemed slightly soothed when it

caught and stayed. 'Well,' he said, 'I've done it. It wasn't easy. Mr Palfreyman wasn't best pleased, and I had to do a bit of fancy footwork, but I've got us the case *and* the budget. But we've got to get on with it. We can only have the extra uniform for a week. Have you got anything yet?'

Slider told him about Running Man and Bicycle Man. 'Of course, they may not turn out to be anything. What we really need to do is find people who saw the victim in the park that morning, but we're hampered because we can't issue a mugshot through the media until we've informed the next of kin.'

'And you don't know who they are?'

'We're going through her papers now, hoping to find out. It's a vicious circle, really – if we could publish her picture, we'd have all sorts of friends and family coming forward.'

Porson looked gloomy. 'Got to respect the susceptitivities of the great GP,' he said, without conviction. 'If someone finds out about it the wrong way, they'll start screaming bloody murder.' Then his frustration burst forth. 'Everyone wants to sue these days. Nation of crybabies, that's what we are now. Everything you do, you have to look over your shoulder all the time in case a writ's coming flying at you.'

Slider murmured something sympathetic, and Porson stared at him, flame-eyed, working up to something.

'Fact is, I'm sick of all this pussyfooting PC malarkey. They tie both your hands, won't let you talk to anyone in case it upsets them, and then wonder why your clear-up rate's down. I'm thinking of pulling the plug after this case, promotion or not.'

'Oh, no, sir, don't do that,' Slider said.

Porson snorted. 'Miss me, would you?' he enquired ironically.

'Yes,' Slider said sturdily. 'We all would. A good super is hard to come by, more especially these days. Everybody admires and respects you, sir.'

Porson looked surprised. Then he turned away to stare out of his window and spoke with his back to Slider. 'Fact is,' he said again, and with the awkwardness of one unused to making personal confessions, 'I'm afraid of losing my edge.'

'No, sir,' Slider protested, but Porson held up his hand in his traffic-stopping gesture.

'It's true. When Betty died . . .' A long pause. 'When you suffer a bereavement, you run the gambit of emotions. I expected that. Says it in all the books. Denial, anger and so forth, blah-de-blah.' He waved away the psychotalk with a large hand gesture. 'But now I'm through all that, I just feel tired. As if I can't be bothered.'

Slider said, 'That's one of them. One of the reactions. You'll come through that, too.'

Porson said nothing. He cleared his throat thunderously, then fumbled a handkerchief out of his trouser pocket and blew his nose. He began to turn and Slider was afraid of what he was going to see – the trace of tears? A tremulous, confiding Syrup? He wasn't sure he could handle that.

Porson showed him a face like a badly hewn statue, and eyes that gleamed like steel rivets under scowling brows.

'So bloody well get on with it, then! Thirty-six hours on and you haven't even got a next of kin? I've stuck my neck out to get this case, and if you make me look like dick over it, I may be leaving, but you can kiss your bollocks goodbye, clear?'

'Yes, sir,' said Slider. He almost smiled with relief. Abuse from above made him feel more comfortable. It was his normal medium.

Atherton and Hart were seated at one desk, heads close together, going through the victim's diary and address book, cross checking them with each other and with other documents taken from the filing cabinet.

'The trouble is,' Atherton said, when Slider delivered Porson's gee-up, 'though she tends to write in business appointments with proper names, with the personal ones she uses a lot of initials and codes.'

'How do you know those are the personal ones?'

'Well, I'm guessing, of course, but it tends to be the evening engagements. There's one on Tuesday night – "JS 8pm". Her business engagements check out against the clients on file, and she keeps a time sheet for each, showing when and for how long she either worked for them or was with them on their premises. Expenses too. All very businesslike.'

'But then there's all this "DC 10 TFQ" stuff,' Hart put in.

'That's in here for Tuesday. I'm trying to run down the initials through the address book, but I'm not having much luck. There's definitely no-one under Q. DC 10's an aeroplane, and TFQ sounds like an airport terminal. Maybe she was meeting someone off a plane – ha ha.'

'If she was, she was spending the afternoon with them. There are two business appointments for the afternoon, both crossed out. We checked, and she cancelled them on Monday. So Tuesday is a mystery,' Atherton said. 'Apart from Marion saying she saw her at a quarter past six, we can't place her at all for that last day.'

'Marion!' Hart snorted, but very quietly.

'What about next of kin?' Slider pressed his own urgent need.

'People don't put their mums and dads in their address book,' Hart said. 'I mean, they know *their* addresses, don't they? There's nothing under Cornfeld, anyway. I tell you what, though, guv,' she added, lifting a confiding face, 'there's a lot of blokes' addresses in here, and quite a lot of just blokes' names and telephone numbers. I reckon she had a right merry old time on the quiet. Out most nights by the look of it.'

'The credit-card statements bear that out,' Atherton said. 'Quite a few donations to charities – I'm making a list of them. But lots of jollies, too – restaurants, theatres, cinema tickets, big food and drink bills. She didn't stint on enjoying herself.'

'Well, she was a good-looking bird, why not?' Hart said. 'If she had a lot o' boyfriends, what of it? This is the twenty-first century. Women are just as entitled to enjoy themselves as men.'

She had turned her head as she said that last bit, and she and Atherton looked into each other's eyes.

'I hate to interrupt this episode of *Oprah*,' Slider said, 'but could you concentrate on the problem in hand? Have you looked for a birth certificate?'

'Yes, but we haven't found one,' Atherton said. 'It's possible it's in the safe. Any word on when that's going to be opened?'

Slider shook his head. 'Some time tomorrow is the best I can get out of them.'

The phone on Atherton's desk rang and he answered it. 'No, he's here.' He handed it over. 'For you, the front shop.'

It was Sergeant Paxman, who was manning the front desk. 'Someone here to see you, about the Cornfeld case.'

'On my way,' said Slider.

CHAPTER FIVE

Get Thee to a Mummery

The public access to the police station was a square room with the big, high desk across one side and a bench running round the other three. On the bench were two rather hopeless-looking young males with chronic sniffs and terminally baggy trousers, and, sitting as far away from them as possible, a middle-aged woman, neatly dressed though in cheap clothes, with a large shopping bag on her knee. She had grey hair with a few blonde highlights, done in the eternal short, rolled perm of the Decent Working Classes, and her face was tidily made up with blue eyeshadow and pink lipstick. She and her kind were the backbone of the country and Slider hoped it was her he was down here to see, and not one of the sullen youths.

Paxman pointed her out discreetly. 'Says she knows Cornfeld.'

'How did she know the name? We haven't released it yet.'

'She didn't. She says she thinks she knows deceased, wants to be sure.'

'What's her name?'

'Hammick. Maureen. Mrs,' said Paxman.

Slider resisted the urge to say, 'Lot. A. Thanks,' and went out to accost the woman. 'Mrs Hammick? I'm Detective Inspector Slider. I believe you wanted to talk to me.' She lifted suffering eyes, and he said, 'Would you like to come somewhere a bit more private?' and led her through into one of the interview rooms. He chose No. 1, which was marginally less repulsive than No. 2. They both smelt of sweaty feet, but someone had thrown up in No. 2 yesterday and it took time for the vomit stink to fade completely.

As soon as the door closed behind them she said, 'It's about Chattie – Chattie Cornfeld. Someone said – they said she was – that she's been murdered. Is it true?'

'Where did you hear that?' he asked neutrally.

'A neighbour of mine was in the Wellington lunch-time and she said there were policemen there showing a picture of Chattie and asking if anyone knew her. She recognised her because she's been with me when I've met Chattie in the street. But I thought maybe she'd made a mistake. I mean, she doesn't know her well. So I thought I'd – but it *isn't* her, is it?'

She looked at him with appeal, but not much hope. Silently Slider held out the photos. The woman took them, and her hand began to tremble. 'You took this one from her bedroom,' she said, as if that clinched it. 'You've been to the house.' She looked up at him. 'She's dead, then? She's the one – the Park Killer's latest victim?'

Slider nodded, reflecting how even at times of great emotion people couldn't help talking like the tabloids. 'Would you like to sit down?' he asked gently. He pulled out the chair from under the table and she sat, blindly, her eyes fixed on the empty air, her hands moving in slow distress, massaging the handle of her shopping basket. Slider took the seat opposite, and was glad to see that, though deeply affected, she was not crying or heading for hysterics. A sensible, level-headed woman – could be a good witness, if she had anything to tell.

'How do you know her?' he asked, after a respectful moment.

'I clean for her,' said Mrs Hammick.

Well, that accounted for the immaculateness of the house, anyway, Slider thought, because if this woman wasn't a thorough cleaner he'd eat his feather duster.

'I work for Merry Maids agency in Brook Green. They'll give you a reference, if you want. But we're more like friends now, really, and I do other bits of things for her as well, not through the agency – pick up her dry-cleaning, wait in for the plumber, that sort of thing. Well, I've got the key anyway, and I only live in Greenside Road, just across the road from Wingate.'

'So you know her quite well?'

'We're *friends*,' she said, with a little, desperate emphasis, as though that would change things, make the bad news not to be. 'It's not like with my other clients. I hardly see them, and most of them I wouldn't care if I never saw. But she works from home, so from the beginning she was often there when I came to do my work, and she's such a nice, friendly, cheery person we got on right away. She'd come up when I was halfway through my time and say, "Come on, Maureen, come and have a cup of tea and a good old chinwag,' and down I'd go to the kitchen and we'd have a chat over a cuppa. After a bit, I never bothered about how much time I spent there. I just did whatever she wanted doing, and if it took me over my time the agency was paying me, well, so be it. But she was a real lady, she always gave me a Christmas present and something on my birthday – "For all the little extras you do for me, Maureen," she'd say. And I'd tell her, "You don't have to give me anything for that, I'm your friend." But she did, anyway. There's nothing I wouldn't do for her.'

Slider felt there was more and waited in silence. She looked down at her hands, and said, 'Last year when I had my divorce, I wouldn't have got through it if it hadn't been for her. I mean, just someone to talk to, yes, and she always had time for me; but apart from that she gave me advice, helped me with the papers and made phone calls for me. I mean, she was a person that just knew what to *do* about things, you know what I mean? I don't know what I'd have done without her.'

'How long have you known her?' Slider asked.

'I've been cleaning for her for three years, ever since she moved into that house. But it feels like a lot longer.' She looked up. 'She was a lovely person, ever so kind. Just last week, Friday, when I came in, she had this visitor, a poor lad with terrible acne. I could hardly look at him, poor soul, but the way she was looking at him and listening to him, giving him all her attention, you'd think there was nothing wrong with him at all. And then there's an old lady down the street she visits, spends hours down there talking to her – not a relative or anything, just to cheer her up. She was always cheerful, always smiling, full of jokes. And she worked so hard at that business of hers, all the hours God sent. She said, "Maureen, I'm going to make good, and it's going to be all on my own efforts." I admire that, people who do that. I can't stand freeloaders, people who expect you to carry them – like that sister of hers.'

'Sister?'

Mrs Hammick's mouth turned down in disapproval. 'That Jassy. You couldn't want a bigger contrast between two people.' She looked at him questioningly. 'You've been to the house? You've seen that room of hers?'

Slider was enlightened. 'The top-floor room.'

'That's it.'

'The sister lives there?'

'No, not now. She'd like to, but Chattie put her foot down – which is rare enough, because she's *too* kind, if anything, and people take advantage. Jassy walks all over her, and she'd have the shirt off Chattie's back if she could, in a minute. She lived with Chattie for about six months and it nearly drove her mad. Never cleaned up after herself, wore Chattie's clothes and spoiled 'em, brought people home without asking – not nice people. She was supposed to be putting up just for a week or two until she got her own place, but it was weeks and then months and I thought she was going to be a permanent fixture, only Chattie finally had enough and told her she had to go. But Jassy still regards that room as hers, and she's got a key to the house, so she comes and goes and sleeps there when she feels like it – when she has a row with her boyfriend, I expect. Or she wants to cadge money off her sister.'

'I gather you don't like her.'

'Jassy? She's one of them that thinks the world owes them a living. Never done an honest day's work in her life, lives on the dole and doesn't even try to get a job. Borrows money and never pays it back, takes Chattie's things without asking, and then complains that Chattie doesn't do enough for her. *And* she hangs around with a nasty rough lot. That boyfriend of hers – well, if he's not a criminal, I don't know! He's a coloured, you know.' She looked at Slider to see his reaction. 'I've got nothing against them as such, but I'm sure as I stand here that Darren's up to no good. He's got a shifty look in his eye, and once when Jassy brought him back to the house I found him snooping about where he'd no business. Casing the joint, that's what you call it, isn't it?'

'Did anything go missing?'

'Not that I heard, but that doesn't mean he wasn't thinking about it. I wouldn't put it past Jassy either. Just this Monday I caught her sneaking around the house. I'd just popped in with some croissants for Chattie – I get them at a bakery near a lady I do on a Monday afternoon, and Chattie likes them specially, so I often get her some and drop them round for her Tuesday breakfast. I was just walking down the hall when Jassy pops up the stairs from the kitchen, and as soon as she sees me she looks guilty. Gives a little jump, you know, and says, "Oh, it's you, what are you doing here?" or something like that. I said, "Chattie knows I'm here. I wonder if the same could be said for you," and she said, "I was just passing and I thought I'd drop in and see my sister. I just went down to the kitchen to make myself a coffee." And I thought, Yes, very likely, but I didn't say anything. I just stood there, and she sort of sulked off. I had a good look round, I can tell you, but I never saw anything missing. Interrupted her in time, that's what I think.'

'Did you say anything to Chattie about it?'

'No, Chattie's too soft-hearted. It wouldn't have done any good. She's so honest herself, she can't believe anyone else is different – though she did see through that Darren in the end and told Jassy not to bring him any more. But Jassy – well, you've seen that room of hers. I said to Chattie, in the end, I said, "I'm sorry, but I'm just not going to clean up in there any more. I'll do anything for you," I said, "but I'm not cleaning up after that little madam." And Chattie said she didn't blame me and she'd tell Jassy to clean it herself. But of course she never did. I always say, you can tell a lot about a person from the way they leave their house, and that Jassy's room is filthy and nasty, just like her.'

'Is she thin, black hair, lots of studs?'

'You've seen her, then?'

'No, someone described her. Said she had makeup like Dracula's mother.'

Mrs Hammick gave a grim sort of smile. 'That's good! Dracula's mother. Yes, black lipstick and purple eyeshadow and stuff like that. She's pretty enough underneath, though not a candle to Chattie in my opinion, but she makes herself look as ugly as she can. It's like she's spitting in your eye, you know?'

'Do you know her full name, and where she lives?'

'Her name's Jasmine – she hates it, that's why she calls herself Jassy – and her surname's different from Chattie's. Her mum and dad got divorced and her mum got remarried. She's called Jassy Whitelaw, and she lives somewhere down south of the river, Clapham, I think. Her address'll be in Chattie's book – the red address book on her desk.'

'Yes, we have that. Do you know Darren's surname and address?'

'Well, the address is same as Jassy's – they live together. But his surname . . .' She thought a moment, shaking her head slowly. 'I think it might be Brown. Darren Brown. Or Biggs? Or Bates? No, Brown,' she said firmly; then paused. 'Or was it Barnes? Yes, I think that was it. Darren Barnes.'

'And would you know who Chattie's next of kin would be?'

'Ooh, I'm not sure. I suppose it would be her mother, with her being divorced as well. Chattie's never mentioned her father to me, so I don't know whether she still sees him or anything, but she talked a lot about her mum. She's a writer – quite a famous one. Stella Smart – have you heard of her?'

The name was vaguely familiar to Slider, as something seen in passing, on a shelf in Smith's. 'I think so. She writes romances, doesn't she?'

Mrs Hammick looked quite stern. 'Not romances, they're ever so much better than that. They're like those Aga sagas of Joanna Trollope's – good, long books you can get your teeth into, about real people. I've read quite a few of them now, from the library, and they're ever so good. Anyway, Chattie goes to see her and her mum phones her up, so I know *they* get on all right, so I should think she'd be her next of kin,' she concluded, as though it were something elective. 'But as to her address – well, I know it's in Hertfordshire somewhere, near Hemel Hempstead I think she said, but I don't know exactly.'

'I'm sure we can find it out, now we know who she is. If it isn't in the address book, the publishers will be able to tell us.'

'Yes, that's right,' said Mrs Hammick, looking despondent now, as her elation left her and she remembered why she was there in the first place. 'It'll be a terrible shock to her, poor lady. What a shocking, dreadful thing to happen to someone like Chattie. If it was Jassy, now, you could understand it, the sort of people she mixes with. I've often said she'd come to a bad end one day.'

'You've been very helpful,' Slider said. 'One more thing perhaps you can tell me – did Chattie have a boyfriend?'

Mrs Hammick pursed her lips. 'Well, she had a lot of menfriends, but not what you'd call a boyfriend, not one special person. She was always going out, meals and things, and it was generally with a man, but it was all casual, if you know what I mean. It seemed to suit her that way,' she added sadly. 'I sometimes said to her, wouldn't she like to get married and settle down, but she always said she was happy as she was. "I haven't got room in my life for another man," she said. "I'm too busy making my way in the world," she said. I said she didn't want to leave it too late, if she wanted to have kiddies, but she said she wasn't interested in that. I think maybe it was to do with her mum and dad getting divorced. It was a real pity, but I always thought she'd meet someone one day and then she'd change her mind pretty quick. I used to say to her, "You won't feel that way when you meet the right man." But now she never will, of course,' she remembered, and had to fumble in her handbag for a handkerchief.

'Did you ever meet any of them?' Slider asked. 'Did they come to the house?'

'Oh, yes, sometimes. She had them to stay over sometimes. Well, she was a healthy girl with normal urges,' Mrs Hammick defended her. 'I met one once, when he was still in the kitchen when I arrived to do my cleaning. Very nice young man he seemed, but I didn't linger, only to say hello, because he wasn't dressed yet which made it awkward. But usually they were gone by the time I got there. Well, people go off to work so early these days, don't they?'

'Can you remember any of their names? Was there one she was seeing more of recently?'

'I don't know,' she said thoughtfully. 'She did talk to me about her menfriends, told me funny stories about them. But I can't remember her mentioning anyone special, not lately.'

'Did she seem unhappy recently?'

'Oh, no, she was just like usual. But now you mention it, the last few days she might have been a bit more – I don't know – thoughtful than before. I mean, she was always cheerful when she spoke to me, but I caught her now and then with a frown on her face, when she didn't know I was looking.'

'She was worried about something?'

'I wouldn't say worried, exactly. More as if she was thinking something out. Just – well, thoughtful.' She came back to the word by default.

Slider took her contact details and thanked her for coming forward, and warned her that the house was now off limits and that she shouldn't try to go in. 'In fact, if you have the keys with you, it would be better to let me have them, for safety's sake.'

'They're in my purse,' Mrs Hammick said, rummaged it out of her bag and handed over the Yale and deadlock keys on an unmarked ring. At the last moment her hand lingered on them before she dropped them into Slider's waiting palm. It seemed to have struck her all at once. 'I suppose I shan't ever need them again. I can't believe she's dead. I just can't believe it.' She shook her head slowly.

Like the man who fell off the Cairo ferry, Slider thought, she was in denial.

When he got back to his office, Atherton came in and said, 'Mr Porson wants you urgently.'

'Is there another way?' Slider said wearily.

'What did your witness want?'

'She wasn't a witness, just the victim's cleaner.' He gave him a brief outline of the interview. 'Said Chattie was a really nice person, the sort who'd do anything for you.'

'Helpful.'

'Also that she had lots of boyfriends, but not one special one.'

'We sort of deduced that from her diary and address book.'

'Got any further with her Tuesday meetings?'

'No, we've pretty well drawn a blank. DC 10, TFQ and JS remain mysteries. We can't place her at all that day.'

'I wonder if that's significant?'

'Anything could be, and hardly anything ever is,' Atherton said. 'I was thinking of going home now, if you don't mind. See what a little R and R can do for the deductive powers. Or in my case, a lot of R and R.'

'Going out tonight?' Slider said, and then, hating himself for it, 'Hart, is it?'

'Hart?'

'You seemed to be getting on rather well.'

'She's just a colleague,' Atherton said. 'No, I'm seeing Marion Davies again.'

'Two nights running sounds serious. And boffing a witness? I'm surprised at you.'

'Considering that's how you met Joanna,' Atherton said, and didn't need to finish the sentence. 'Anyway, she's not a witness. Just a friend, like your cleaner.'

'You don't know that.'

Atherton smiled delicately. 'Then I'm going the best way about finding out.'

Slider got up from his desk and waved him away. 'Go. I've got Mr Porson waiting for me.'

'I won't offer to swap,' said Atherton.

Porson wasted no words. 'Right, I hear from Hemel police they've informed the mother.'

'What about the father?'

'The mother says the victim had no contact with him, and she doesn't know where he is. So we can go on air with the photo. They've sent us over a studio portrait the mother came up with, better quality than what we've got, so we'll go with that.'

Slider looked at his watch. 'It's too late to get it on the *Six o'Clock News.*'

'Time you entered the twenty-first century,' Porson admonished. 'Hemel sent the photo electronically to the Beeb at the same time as us, and they're going on with that, and a plain studio statement. "Police have named the victim" blah-de-blah. But they want a live body for the ten o'clock, so you've got to go and record something.'

Slider's heart sank. 'Me, sir?' He hated being on screen.

'The camera loves you, Slider,' Porson said, straight-faced. 'They'll be filming it in the publicity suite. Get yourself over to Hammersmith quick as you like. You know what to say?'

'We're still sticking with the Park Killer?'

'We'll leave it run a bit longer,' Porson said. 'Don't say it was him, just that first impressions point that way, you know the score. Noncommittal. The publicity woman, Amanda Odell, will run through it with you. Ask for witnesses to come forward. And for anyone who was in the park to get himself crossed off the list.'

'Especially Bicycle Man and Running Man,' Slider said.

'Right.'

'What about manning the phones tonight?'

'I'll see to that. You get yourself to Hammersmith. Go. They're waiting for you.'

Get thee to a mummery, thought Slider, trudging away.

*   *   *

'You're early,' Joanna said, when he let himself in.

'It's nearly nine o'clock,' Slider said. 'You call that early?'

'I wasn't really expecting you until later.'

'Does that mean there's nothing to eat?'

'We can go out if you like,' she said, and then, seeing from his face how well that went down, 'or I could pop out and get some fish and chips.'

'Now you're talking,' he said, brightening. 'But what about you – haven't you eaten?'

'Only a snack. I could find space for fish and chips,' she said. 'Anyway, we're celebrating.'

'We are?'

'I've got some good news. Really good news. I had a phone call today.'

'Huh, that's nothing. I get those every day.'

'Stop clowning, this is important. I've been booked for some sessions.'

'Oh. Good for you. What sessions?'

'It's the soundtrack for the new James Bond film. Nine sessions, at Watford, tomorrow, Saturday and Sunday.'

'Tomorrow? That's short notice.'

'Well, obviously I wasn't the first choice,' she said. 'I'm subbing for some poor sap who's fallen ill and who's going to miss out on all the goodies. She'll be kicking herself, because film sessions pay top dollar, and it doesn't end there. They're going to make a CD of the music later, which will be more sessions; and Ronnie said there's some talk of taking it on the road as a concert promotion.'

'Ronnie?'

'Ronnie Barrett, the fixer. The soundtrack and the CD will all be on the one contract, so it'll be the same people for both, but he likes me so he says he'll try and get me the concerts as well.' She beamed. 'Lots of lovely work and lots of lovely money. Aren't you pleased?'

'Of course I am. Delighted for you. But – three lots of three sessions? On consecutive days? Isn't that too much for you, in—'

'"In my delicate condition"? My dear Inspector, you can't say things like that any more,' she laughed. He saw that it was not so much the money she was so happy about as the work.

She had missed being in the loop, missed the company, the music and the sense of importance it gave her, the shape it gave to her life. How would she cope when the baby came? And if, after her maternity absence, she couldn't get any more work at all, what then?

'Borrowing trouble are your two middle names,' as his mother would have said. Deal with that when and if it arose.

'I just want you to take care of yourself,' he said at last.

She stepped closer and put her arms round his waist. 'I will. I'll be sitting down all the time, remember.' She kissed him. 'I promise I'll eat proper meals and rest in the breaks. And I won't even have to drive. Pete Thomas lives in Hammersmith and he's going to pick me up, and we'll share petrol money.'

'Okay.' He felt the hardness of her belly pressing against him. 'I love you,' he said.

'I love you, too.' She kissed him again. 'I'll go and get the fish and chips now, shall I, while you change?'

'All right. We can eat them in front of the telly and you can criticise my performance.'

'You're on the telly again? My dear, this house is just full of artistes!'

The day dawned sunny, but the sunshine and the blue sky both had a watery, unstable look. Slider shoved his mac into the car, returned to kiss Joanna again – she was practising, from a book of 'studies' that looked like black hairy caterpillars crawling up and down the staves – and set off for Hemel Hempstead. Before he was within striking distance, loose, wet grey clouds came up, and sharp rain began to hit the windscreeen.

Stella Smart's address was Owl Cottage, The Dene, and it was just outside the town – he had got directions from the Hemel police. He imagined a country lane and a cob cottage with a crooked roof and small, deep windows burdened with creeper. And Stella Smart he thought would either be artistic-Bohemian with pre-Raphaelite dresses, gypsy hair and clashing bangles, or celebrity-glamorous with lots of makeup and gold costume jewellery.

He stopped in Hemel on his way to buy one of her books in Smith's. He picked up *Long Summer Days*, which seemed to be the most recent paperback – there were lots of copies of it, anyway – and pulled into a lay-by to thumb through it. It seemed to be about a nice vicar's wife of the jam-making, sensible-shoe kind, who thought her husband was being unfaithful to her. There was a lot of villagey stuff about WI meetings and cricket clubs, and a lot of drinking went on – people seemed to be always propping up the bar in the village pub, or downing G-and-Ts in each other's kitchens. He was about to throw it aside and drive on when the word 'nipple' caught his eye and he found himself in the middle of a torrid love scene between Mrs Vicar and a young man, an artist and newcomer to the village. So, he thought, what would you call that, then? An Aga-bonker? A surplice-ripper? The Bohemian image of Stella Smart now seemed the more appropriate.

It was a surprise all ways up, therefore, when The Dene turned out to be a road on a dinky new estate of little Lego houses of yellow brick, with pink-tiled roofs that looked mysteriously as if they were made of Plasticine. To an eye used to London's Victorian stock, they looked impossibly small, as if they had been built to house the garden gnomes that decorated so many of the front gardens. Owl Cottage was a corner house, just as new, boxy and Legoland as the rest, and the door was opened to him by a small, neat woman in a plain dark blue linen suit over a white blouse, with tidy hair and makeup, who might have been just off to work in a solicitor's or estate agent's office.

'Mrs Smart?' he asked, though he knew it was her from the blind look of grief that had settled into her face. Perhaps he ought to have said Miss Smart, if it was her writing name. He wasn't sure of the etiquette. If she hadn't remarried she was probably Mrs Cornfeld. 'I'm Inspector Slider.' He proffered his brief, but she didn't look at it.

'They said you were coming,' she said; and then, with an air of pulling herself together, 'You'd better come in. You're getting wet.'

She backed off to let him into the hall – necessary because it was only as wide as the door and hardly any longer. She held out her hand for his mac. He struggled out of it, elbows bumping the walls, and she hung it on top of the others on the coat pegs. 'Come in,' she said, and led him through a glass-panelled door which gave directly onto a through-lounge-cum-dining room ending in French windows onto the garden. The room was not, to begin with, spacious in this gnome-sized house; but the cramped effect was heightened by the fact that all the furniture in it had been made for a different class of house altogether. Old, fine and lovingly polished, it crowded the narrow space: a huge bookcase to the right, giving the impression of having to duck its head under the low ceiling, a lovely chiffonier on the left, a large brocade chesterfield and two Queen Anne armchairs beyond, lamps and wine tables forced in somehow, and in the dining room section a mahogany table with William IV chairs and a wonderful high Edwardian sideboard, which between them meant holding your breath and sidling if you wanted to get past to the garden. There were paintings on the wall, a mixture of watercolours and small oils, and on the surfaces delicate pieces of porcelain and two lovely clocks. Presumably some necessity had brought Stella Smart to this inappropriate setting.

'You'd like some coffee,' she said, and it was hardly a question, so he didn't answer it. 'Do sit down.'

She waved him to the chesterfield and went out through a door between the two sections of the room, which presumably led to the kitchen and stairs. The smell of fresh coffee sneaked in before the door closed again, relieving him of the fear that he might have to drink instant. Evidently she had everything ready for him, for before his look-round had had a chance to do more than note the similar-looking row of hardbacks in the bookcase, which were presumably her own, and no photographs anywhere (a family trait?) she came back in with a tray. She was keeping up standards: delicately embroidered tray-cloth, bone china decorated with tiny forget-me-nots, coffee in a china jug to match, and a plate of what looked like home-made shortcake.

She took an armchair catty-corner to him and put the tray down on the small table between them. 'How do you take it?'

'Black, please. No sugar.'

She poured, passed, handed him the shortcake, and he waited in silence while she did these things. She was marking her territory, giving herself the upper hand by these small rituals, which was as it should be. He studied her as she poured her own coffee. She was in her fifties, he thought, and well preserved rather than young for her age. Her hair was fair-going-grey; she was small and slight – thin, almost – with a bony nose and sharp chin. He could not see much resemblance in her to Chattie. He would not have called her pretty or even handsome, though there was something in the direct look of her brown eyes when she lifted them at last that was attractive. They were pinkish now, and the lids still swollen from crying, but at other times he thought she would have been able to do things with them that would have fetched most men.

She sat back now with her cup and sipped, looking at him steadily, not initiating anything. He gave it time, trying his coffee – very good – and the biscuit.

'Good shortcake,' he commented. 'Did you make it yourself?'

'Yes,' she said.

He waited, but she offered nothing more. He set down his cup and said, 'I am very sorry for your loss.'

'Thank you,' she said.

'And I'm sorry to have to bother you at a time like this, but I would like to talk to you about your daughter.'

'Why?' she said.

He had not expected that. 'Because I need to know as much about her as possible,' he said.

'But if she was murdered by the Park Killer,' said Stella Smart, 'he would have picked her simply because she was there, not for any other reason. How can knowing about her help you find him?' The eyes were like policeman's eyes, he saw now: they not only looked, but saw. He had never met an author before. He supposed that noticing and deducing would be part of a writer's trade too. An interesting new thought to come back to.

'You're very quick,' he said. 'I had better tell you at once that we don't think she was one of the Park Killer's victims.'

'Why not?'

'There were discrepancies in the method. I don't want to go into that with you. But we think the murderer was trying to make it look like the Park Killer's work.'

'I saw the news last night. It gave the impression—'

'Yes. We thought it might help us to let the murderer think we were fooled. But I believe she was killed by someone who knew her.'

She examined his face. 'You must have ruled me out, if you're telling me this.'

He had, in the first few moments. 'I can see what she meant to you.'

Now she moved her eyes away, breaking contact. She could observe other people, but could not have her own feelings observed. 'She was everything to me. She was all I had.'

'What about . . . ?' He glanced towards the bookcase.

'My work?' she said, with a sour twist of her mouth. 'Yes, I used to think it mattered a great deal. But that was while I still had Chattie. Now I can see it's just a handful of dust.'

'Tell me about her,' he invited.

Her eyes became remote as she looked into the past. She sipped at her coffee. He saw as she put the cup back in the saucer that there was a slight tremor in her hands, and now he looked more closely, there were broken veins in the cheeks and on the nose that the careful makeup only just didn't conceal. He wondered if she was a drinker.

She said, 'She was a happy baby, with a wonderful chuckle. She walked and talked very early, and then she was running about and chattering all day long. That was when we nick-named her Chattie. Everyone loved her. And she was clever, too, and musical. Did well at school, won a scholarship at eleven, sang in all the school choirs, took up the cello. After school she went to the Royal College, and I thought she'd be a musician, but she didn't feel she had sufficient talent, though I thought she was wrong about that. Anyway, when she finished college she got a job instead. She worked for Regina Stein, the big music agency, for two years, and for a record company for another year, and then she decided to set up on her own.'

'Solutions,' Slider suggested.

Stella Smart's mouth turned down a little. 'Yes, that's what she called it. I said she should have called it Dogsbodies.'

'You didn't approve?'

'It wasn't a matter of not approving. I thought she was wasting her talents and that she would never make a living out of it.'

'Did you quarrel about it?'

'No,' she said. 'We never quarrelled. You couldn't quarrel with Chattie. She was too good-tempered.'

'How did the idea of Solutions come to her?'

'Oh, it was something she came across in America, and she liked the idea of the variety it would give her. She never wanted

to do a routine nine-to-five job. She helped a couple of musician friends to set up websites, and taught herself about that
side of the business that way. She thought she'd have all sorts
of clients, but with her background a lot of them have turned
out to be musicians and, of course, they never seem to have
any money. She has a struggle to get them to pay. And much
of what she does is menial office work. It's been four years,
and she's still only scratching a living. All that intelligence and
energy and talent, and she's doing people's filing and writing
their letters.'

She sounded angry and frustrated. Definitely a *casus belli*
here, Slider thought.

'How has she managed for money, these four years?' Slider
asked. 'Did she have any other job, or source of income?'

'How could she?' she said sharply. 'It took up all her time.'

'Was there family money?'

'No,' Stella Smart snapped. 'Apart from some furniture and
things left to me by my mother, I have only what I earn from
my books, and that, believe me, is no fortune. You see,' with a
gesture of the hand, 'what I am reduced to.'

'Did you help her out with money?'

'She wanted to do it all herself, with no help from anybody.'

'What about her father?'

'Chattie has nothing to do with her father. She feels the same
way about him as I do. She hasn't seen him for years.'

'It's just that she seemed to live quite a lavish lifestyle,' Slider
said delicately. 'Lots of restaurants and theatres, nice holidays
and so on.'

She looked at him with a faint, triumphant smile. 'A woman
can always enjoy those things without having money, if she
knows how to attract men. Chattie never lacked for male
company.'

'Did you ever visit her house?' he asked.

'She lived in some ghastly slum in Hammersmith – all she
could afford. She never invited me there and I never wanted
to go. We met in Town, or she came here.'

Slider wondered now whether the mother had really known
anything about her daughter's life. Chattie might have had lots
of dates, but she spent her own money as well; and the house
was no slum. Either the mother was dissembling for some

reason, or Chattie had kept secrets from her. He tried another tack. 'She was your only child?'

'Yes.'

'I thought there was a sister, or step-sister?'

The face became stony. 'Half-sister. Jassy is not my child, and I have nothing to do with her.' Slider kept looking at her expectantly, and after a pause she sighed and said, 'I had better tell you the story, or you won't leave it alone. I met Chattie's father at some ghastly party or other. We had an affair. He divorced his first wife for me. Later he met Jassy's mother and had an affair with her, and left me for her. So I suppose you could say I was served right.' Slider wouldn't have dared. 'There was a child from the first wife, too, another daughter, Ruth. So there are three half-sisters; but none of them grew up together.'

'Presumably Chattie had some contact with them?'

'None, as far as I know, with Ruth. She's a lot older, a different generation. They had nothing in common. And Chattie never liked Jassy. She disapproved of her.'

'But from what I've heard, Jassy lived with her for a while.'

'Chattie's too soft a touch. She never says no to anyone. Jassy leeched off her. The girl is a slut with no morals – just like her mother. Mother and daughter, they're like those ghastly underwater things with suckers that simply attach themselves and live by draining the victim's blood. I've never been beholden to anyone, and I'm proud of Chattie for making her own way and owing nothing to anyone.'

There was a great deal of food for thought here, and a lot of seething emotions under this Noddy roof, but he wasn't sure where it was getting him.

'I have to ask you this,' he said. 'Do you know of anyone who would have wanted to harm your daughter?'

'No,' she said decidedly. 'Everyone loved her. She hadn't an enemy in the world.'

'What about jealousy as a motive?'

'Lovers, you mean? I don't believe that. She had a light touch. Yes, she always had men around her, but I don't think she ever cared deeply for any of them. It was just fun – on both sides. She knew how to handle them. She learned that from me.'

'Do you know of anything she might have been mixed up

in, any business interests she had other than Solutions, any money troubles?'

'No, not at all.' She looked at him shrewdly. 'I take it that not everyone agrees with your assessment that it was not the Park Killer?'

Slider was startled. 'I'm sorry?'

'At first, when you came in, you said "we" all along, but then you said, "*I* believe she was killed by someone who knew her."'

'That's very observant of you,' he said.

'People are my livelihood – how they look and what they say. If I did not observe, I couldn't write.' She looked around her, with the air of someone suddenly waking up; the animation drained from her face, and the blind, grieving look returned. Talking with him, she had forgotten, deep down where it counted, that they were talking about her daughter's murder. Now she had reminded herself. 'What does it matter, anyway?' she said dully. 'Find her killer, don't find him. She's dead, and she won't be coming back.'

He took his leave. As he struggled into his mac, the book fell out of his pocket, and he picked it up and hesitated a moment, wondering whether it would please her if he asked her to sign it. But she looked at it, and when she met his eyes he saw that it would not be a good idea.

'What did you bring that for? *Long Summer Days*. My latest success,' she said, with bitter irony. 'It's waste paper. Throw it in the nearest bin. My daughter's dead, my lovely, smiling daughter. It makes me sick to think I ever cared about anything else.'

CHAPTER SIX

Summer Daze

The rain had cleared away, and the pavements were steaming in a Bangkok sort of way as Slider parked the car. His wet mac was making the car smell like old dogs, so he carried it in with him to dry out indoors. It must be hell on the tubes today, he reflected.

Stuff had bred on his desk in his absence, as usual. There was the preliminary report from Bob Bailey, and he pulled it out to read it first. There was nothing new. They had not found any blood other than that in the immediate vicinity of the body, which suggested the killing had taken place at that spot and without a struggle – but he already knew that. It also meant that the killer had not tracked the blood around and probably did not have much on his clothes; but Slider pinned his faith on a belief that you could not stab someone without getting blood on you somewhere. Blood from the bark next to the body had been sent off for DNA profiling and to be tested against the victim's. Sweet wrappers and cigarette ends were being held pending instructions.

On another piece of paper was a message asking him to call Freddie Cameron. He dialled, and just as Cameron answered Atherton appeared in his doorway with a question on his lips. Slider held up a hand. 'Freddie. What's new?'

'Ah, back from the jungle so soon? They told me you were in the wilds of Herefordshire this morning.'

'Hertfordshire.'

'A distinction without a difference. Well, old chum, I thought you'd like to know my official findings in advance of the written copy. It's pretty much what we discussed at the post. In my opinion death was due to respiratory collapse, caused by a toxic substance at present unknown.'

'So the stabbing had nothing to do with it?'

'The wounds aren't severe enough to cause death, and in any case wouldn't account for the cyanosis and congestion. If she was conscious when it was going on, it might have contributed to shock, but she would have died anyway.' He heard Slider's silence and added, 'My view, considering the blood patterns, is that she was probably unconscious when the blows were struck.'

'Thanks,' said Slider

'Does it occur to you,' Cameron said kindly, 'that you're too sensitive for this job?'

'Pots and kettles, Freddie. What else?'

'I found no puncture wound such as would be left by injection, and the stomach contents revealed no solid matter.'

'Jogging on an empty stomach? Not the recommended way.'

'What I meant was there were no tablet or capsule residues. But yes, you're right, no eggs and B, no toast, no porage. Just a quantity of liquid. I've sent a sample off to the tox lab, along with blood, kidney, liver and vitreous humour –'

'Sounds like a mixed grill.'

'– but from here on we just have to wait. Those tox boys are in a different time zone from the rest of us.'

'So she drank the poison?'

'It would seem so.'

'But how would she be induced to take it?' Slider mused.

'Not my province, thank God,' said Freddie.

'That never stops you having an opinion,' Slider said. 'How quickly would she lose consciousness?'

'Depends what the drug was and how much was administered. But liquid would pass quickly into the small intestine and be rapidly absorbed from there. With one of the ultra-short-acting barbiturates she could be unconscious within a few minutes and dead minutes after that. And,' he added, 'it would have had to be quick, wouldn't it, from the murderer's point of view? Anything taking longer than a few minutes to induce unconsciousness would risk the victim calling for help or running away.'

'It's a good job she was stabbed, otherwise it could be suicide and we'd be even more hampered. I wonder the killer didn't think of that.'

'This strikes me as a very stupid killer.'

'We'll have to have the contents of the water-bottle tested, just to be sure.'

'Done and done.'

'All right, assuming she was drugged with a short-acting barbiturate, where would the murderer get the stuff?'

'It's not prescribed in this country and you can't buy it legally. But there are lots of illegal pharmaceutical drugs about if you know where to go. You can buy them on the Internet these days. Or you can smuggle them in from places like Mexico or Hong Kong where they are prescribed. Or steal them from a hospital or warehouse. The field of possibilities' – Slider imagined him waving a hand – 'is enormous.'

'Thank you so much,' he said drily.

'Don't mention it,' Freddie assured him. 'As to the weapon, I'd say it was a very sharp, narrow, single-edged blade about seven inches long, with a cross-guard only on the cutting edge. So it could be a combat knife or a kitchen knife. I've drawn you a picture of the sort of profile. You'll have the written report later today, when I've checked it for spelling mistakes. The man who invented the spellchecker should be shot. I'll send it over in the bag.'

'Thanks, Freddie.'

Slider rang off, and turned to Atherton.

'She drank it?' Atherton said.

'Apparently.'

'In a bottle marked "Poison", I suppose. Very Alice in Wonderland.'

'Someone might have spiked her water-bottle.'

'But that would mean access to her house that morning. I can't believe she'd fill her water-bottle up in advance, the day before. What did you get from the mater?'

'Not much, except a ferment of emotions revolving round the daughter and the divorce, which was obviously acrimonious. And that there was no family money or private income. But,' he added, with slight reluctance, because he could see this moving in a direction he didn't like, 'she evidently thought Chattie was living hand-to-mouth on the shaky proceeds of her business. She'd never seen the house, for a start. They always met elsewhere. She thought it was a slum and Chattie was ashamed of it.'

'Sounds as if our Chattie had something to hide from Mummy,' Atherton said. 'I wonder what?'

Slider said, to distract him, 'And there's another half-sister somewhere. Stella Smart was the second wife of three. But apparently there wasn't any contact between them. I suppose we'll have to talk to her, but it's not priority.'

'Always nice to have more things to check up on,' Atherton said. 'In the meantime, there was quite a response from last night's appeal. About a dozen people who were in the park and want to be crossed off. One or two possible sightings that are worth following up. And a man who says he saw Chattie on Tuesday evening in the Anchor – that's the pub at the end of her road.'

'Good! Get on to that one.'

'I was going to do it myself,' Atherton said, with a slight question mark.

'Yes, go. What else?'

'Oddly, a lot of people phoned up just to say they knew her and liked her. I've never known anything like that before. It was a bit Jill Dando-ish.'

'So – what then? There's an undertone in your voice.'

'I suppose I'm just being perverse, but when everyone says a person is an angel, I can't help wondering if there's a con going on. And given that she had a lifestyle above her station, and concealed it from her mum, I'm wondering more than ever what she was up to.'

'You're thinking drugs,' Slider said flatly.

'Well, they always do jump to mind,' Atherton said, not watching his feet. 'Or, given the prevalence of the man-motif, high-priced prostitution.'

'We've no reason to think either of those things,' Slider snapped. 'Let's not jump to conclusions, shall we?'

Atherton raised his eyebrows. 'Sorry. Have I stepped on a corn?'

Slider drew a deep breath. The image of her, softly limp like a dead hare, and her rough-cut gold hair, so like Joanna's, called to him for pity and vengeance. He said, managing a fair imitation of lightness, 'It's your mental health I'm worried about. This job makes you too cynical if you're not careful.'

'I shall try to nurture a rosy outlook,' Atherton said, but he gave Slider an odd look as he left. Or Slider thought he did. Maybe it was just his paranoia again.

Joanna phoned. 'Just breaking for lunch.'

'It's not that time already, is it?'

'Half past twelve, ol' guv of mine.'

'Flaming Nora, where does the time go? How was the session?'

'Oh, brill. Lots of old friends. It's basically a scratch Royal London Philharmonia, like the one we used to cobble together for concerts in Croydon in the dear distant days of double booking.'

'Good. So you've someone to lunch with?'

'Lots of someones. God, it's good to be back!' The words burst out of her, and he understood the depth of the feelings she had been hiding from him. She needed her work, as he needed his.

'What's the music like?'

'Oh, you know. You've seen the films. Bang, crash, wallop, car chase, speedboat chase – dum-diddle-um-dum, dum-dum-dum. Lots of dots for us. It's hard work, but it's great being with real professionals. All these guys could do it standing on their heads – or, at least, they let you think they could. That's showmanship. What do you think of Charlie?'

He had to be quick on his feet for that one. 'Charles Slider? It sounds like a senior officer in the Salvation Army.'

'That's odd – you know, it does,' she said wonderingly. 'But I didn't say Charles, I said Charlie.'

'You can't christen a child Charlie. You have to start with Charles – and we said nothing with an s in it.'

'Sebastian,' she said. 'Septimus. It's like something out of Monty Python – six seditious Sadducees from Caesarea.'

'Keep thinking, Butch,' he advised. 'That's what you're good at.'

'Gotta go. The guys are waiting.'

'See they keep waiting,' he warned, and she was gone.

As he replaced the handset, McLaren came in with a cup of tea for him – or, rather, half a cup of tea and half a saucer of tea. 'Sorry, guv, I slopped a bit,' he said. Slider hastily cleared a space for him to set it down.

'How's it going?' Slider asked. It was rare to find McLaren with his mouth empty and it seemed a shame to waste the opportunity.

'Not bad,' he said. 'We're getting through 'em. Funny lot of calls we've had, from people saying they liked her. Like if they said what a nice person she was, we'd let her off being dead.'

'Character references,' Slider said, charmed not so much by the flight of fancy, but that McLaren had had it. 'Atherton told me.'

'We've had two people say they saw her jogging, both sound all right. But no help on the murder. She was just jogging round the track, the circular one, with a few other people.'

'With them?'

'Not with them, as such. Just, there were a few going round.'

'Nobody saw her near the shrubbery?'

'Not yet. But,' McLaren went on, 'it's looking good for my idea, the copycat murder.' His head took on a defiant tilt as he said it. 'We've had another four reports about Running Man. A lot of people saw him legging it out of the park, and three of them reckon he was clutching a mobile phone in his germans. And given that the vic's is missing, I reckon that makes him tasty.'

'Don't call her the vic. This is not America,' said Slider, fighting another losing battle.

'All right,' McLaren said equably. 'So whajjer reckon, guv? Shall I follow it up? We know he went off up Askew Road. We could start canvassing up there, see who else saw him, spread the search area, see if he dumped anything.'

Slider considered. He had to be flexible enough to consider that McLaren might be right, even though he was McLaren. 'I need you here for the moment. See how it goes today. If it's still looking good later we may put out a specific appeal on him tonight. Have you got a good description?'

'Yeah, as to height and clothes and probable age. We haven't got a witness who saw his face close up – yet.' He gave Slider a hopeful look, like a dog in the presence of chocolate.

'All right, well, keep on the follow-up for now, but you can ask specifically about him. And you can recontact anyone who was in the park at the right time. If you find anyone who saw his face, get 'em in and try for a photofit. But – McLaren!' He called him back as he swung happily away. 'Don't push. Don't put ideas into people's heads.'

McLaren looked wounded. 'Guv!' he protested. 'It's me!'

'That's why I said it.'

PC Yvonne Collins stuck her head round Slider's door. 'Sir, there's a man in Lycra shorts downstairs for you.'

'Funny, I didn't order one of those,' Slider said.

She sniggered. It was a point up to her that she had a sense of humour; and she wasn't a bad-looking young woman, but there was the hardness in her face that women police always developed, which made Slider wonder why Atherton had gone after her – unless it was purely instinctive, like a dog chasing rabbits.

'It's the bloke you appealed for on the telly, sir, the bloke on the bike.'

'Oh, right. I'll come down.'

Her duty done, she allowed herself a personal question. 'Is Jim Atherton around, sir?'

It sounded rather wistful. Slider felt he ought to warn her off, but what could he say? Anyway, he didn't want to get caught in the fall-out from Atherton's trouser department.

'No, he's out interviewing a witness.'

'Oh,' she said, and seemed not to know what to do with the information. Well, she wasn't his problem, he thought gratefully, as he brushed past her and went off down the corridor, leaving her standing there like a spare dinner at a conference banquet. Which, sadly, was pretty much what she was, he reflected.

'I'm Phil Yerbury,' said Bicycle Man. He was dressed in the skin-tight Lycra shorts and matching vest, and was carrying his helmet, one of the sporty ones with the point to the back and a lightning flash design on the side. He was tall and fair, but tanned, so that his body hair showed up white against his brown skin. A tuft of it poked out shyly from each armpit like a chinchilla rabbit scenting the air. He was very lean and his legs were admirably muscled, the tendons behind the knee standing out sharply like freshly chiselled relief, the calf muscles seeming to squirm impatiently under the tight skin, as if they would go off on their own and get cycling again if their owner stood there talking for much longer.

A wave of heat and a smell of sweat came off him, but it was fresh sweat and not absolutely unpleasant. His face was lean and firm and missed being handsome by so little that you might not notice it in all that healthy tannedness.

'I think I may be the person you were appealing for on the telly last night,' he said, 'but if I am, I don't know why. I haven't done anything.' And in what looked like a nervous movement he pulled the water-bottle from its holster on his belt, and slugged back a good gulp.

'You did the right thing by coming in,' Slider said, putting warmth into his voice. 'Would you like to sit down?'

'I hope this isn't going to take long,' he said. 'I'm working, and I don't want to get behind schedule.'

'Can't you call it your lunch-hour?'

'I don't take a lunch-break,' he said with barely suppressed scorn. 'I'm self-employed. There's terrific competition in the bicycle-courier world, you know. You can't afford to slack.'

He still hadn't sat down, so Slider perched on the edge of the table. 'It shouldn't take long,' he said. 'Were you in Paddenswick Park on Wednesday morning at around eight o'clock?'

'Yes. Well, I cut through it, because the traffic was slow on Paddenswick Road. But I don't know anything about this woman who was murdered. I've never met her or even heard of her in my life.' The eyes were wide and nervous.

'Witnesses say you rode very fast out of the park into King Street, so fast you almost knocked a woman over, and dashed into the traffic without looking, almost causing an accident.'

Relief and annoyance chased each other across his face. 'Is that what it's about? I didn't nearly knock her over, I didn't touch her. I'm an excellent cyclist. I know exactly how narrow a gap I can get through. She only had to stand still. And of course I didn't join the traffic without looking. I wouldn't last a day in this job if I did things like that. There was no near accident. I knew exactly what I was doing.'

His professional pride had been touched, Slider saw, and it was so important to him that he had forgotten there was a murder in the background. This, he thought, was not their man – unless he was a fabulously good actor.

'Why were you in such a hurry?' he asked.

'I was working. I told you, there's huge competition—'

'At that time of day?'

Yerbury looked scornful. 'I start at seven. It's the busiest time, seven thirty to eight thirty. Modern business doesn't slouch in at half past nine any more, not if it wants to survive. It's a competitive world out there.'

'I see. Well, Mr Yerbury, if you'd like to write down your name, address and telephone number for me—'

'But what do you want them for? You can't think I had anything to do with it. You can't think I'm the Park Killer?'

'Actually,' Slider said, 'I've just been thinking that being a bicycle courier would be a wonderful way for the Park Killer to get about and cover his tracks.'

Yerbury's eyes bulged in horror. 'But I—' His mouth remained open, but no further words got out.

'Just sit down here and write your name and address,' Slider said kindly. 'It's routine, that's all. We have to check everything and everyone, you must see that. And write where you were immediately before and immediately after your ride through the park. I presume you were in transit from one firm to another. If they can vouch for you, I don't expect we'll need to bother you again.'

He sat, and took up the biro laid waiting for him, and applied himself to the pad. His hand shook at first, but writing calmed him down. 'I was delivering to a printing firm in King Street,' he said. 'I don't know their phone number offhand, but you can get it from Directory Enquiries.'

'You have a bag of some sort on your bicycle, I suppose?'

'Not a bag, a box. A plastic carrier – like a cooler box, only with a locking lid,' he said, not pausing in his writing. So much for the witness's accuracy. It was amazing how much people got wrong. Or perhaps what was amazing was how much the layman expected them to get right. If juries only knew.

Yerbury finished writing and looked up at Slider. 'Am I done now?'

'Yes, you're done. Unless there's anything you can tell me that might help with the investigation. A young woman was brutally stabbed to death in the park just about the time you rode through. Did you see anything, anyone, unusual?'

'I was riding fast,' he said, but apologetically now. 'I mean,

I pass people in a flash. Obviously I didn't see anyone killing anybody. Whereabouts in the park did it happen?'

'In the shrubbery.'

'Well, I wouldn't be able to see in there.'

'You rode past it,' Slider said, not making it a question or a challenge.

His eyes went past Slider's as he thought back. 'There were a couple of people on the path by the shrubbery, standing talking. I had to dodge round them. I don't suppose that was anything?'

'Anything might be anything. What were they like?'

'I don't know. I was past in a flash, I only got an impression. Just two joggers stopped for a chat, I suppose.'

'Why did you think they were joggers?'

He screwed up his face in effort, but said, 'I really don't know. It was just a flash as I went past. I think one of them had one of those hooded tops that joggers wear.'

'Colour?'

'I really don't know.'

'Was it red?'

'I don't think so. A neutral colour or a dark colour perhaps. I don't think it was anything obvious like red.'

'Hood up or down?'

'Well, up,' he said after a fractional pause, 'otherwise I wouldn't have known it was hooded, would I?'

'Were they male or female?'

'I think the one facing my way was a woman. Maybe with fair hair? The one with the hood was taller, so I suppose it was a man. But I can't say anything for sure. It's just an impression. I was going too fast, and thinking about other things.'

'And whereabouts were they standing?'

'On the path by the shrubbery, the path that goes down to the station and King Street.'

'So you came in at the Paddenswick Gate, turned left at the junction of the path, and *then* you saw them?'

'That's right.'

That was on the side of the shrubbery where the SOCOs had gone in, not on the side where Mr Chapman's dog had disappeared. If the people Yerbury had seen were Chattie and the killer, it was more suggestion that the grooves in the bark were faked.

'All right,' Slider said. 'Thank you. You've been most co-operative. And if anything else occurs to you that might help us, or you find you can remember more about the people you saw, you will contact me at once?'

'Well, yes,' he said, rising and exuding relief along with the sweat, 'but really, I don't think there's anything more I can tell you. I just happened to be there at the time. I didn't even know the woman.'

Slider saw him out, and went back to his room, pondering. Yerbury's story held together, and Slider did not feel he was their man. A policeman has to go on instinct a lot of the time, or the work would never get done. On the other hand, it was looking better for McLaren's copycat-killer theory. Running Man had been wearing a hooded sweat top – a hoodie, the young people called it. And if Yerbury had seen two people talking on the path by the shrubbery, someone else would have, too. At that time of day, with so many people around, someone would have.

A sunny afternoon was shaping up after the morning's rain. The air seemed washed, the trees moved about as if refreshed, and happy, trotting dogs had a whole lot of new scent-marking to do. The Anchor had its door set open, and a pleasant murmur of voices drifted out. Atherton went in and waited a moment for his eyes to adjust from the brightness outside. It was a nice, ordinary, old-fashioned pub, with no music, no games machines, no décor, and a fireplace in the corner that bore all the marks of having a real fire in the winter. People were sitting around tables eating, drinking and conversing – a nice mix of ages, but all responsible adults. The sight of decent English people not bothering each other was a lovely thing, he thought – a sort of poetry.

He went up to the bar, and the barman approached him with an expectant face, polishing a glass without looking. 'Help you, sir?'

'I'm looking for a Mr Fosdyke,' Atherton said.

'That's me. Reggie Fosdyke. I'm the landlord.' He was a round man with a round, red face. He was bald over the top of his head, and had a close-clipped white beard – got his head on upside-down, Atherton thought automatically. He was smiling genially but he had the cold and noticing eyes of a London licensee and they went over Atherton like a scanner. 'From the police?' he concluded.

'You rang saying you had information for us,' Atherton said.

'Right it is. Come up the end of the bar, bit of privacy,' said Fosdyke. 'Drink?'

'Not for me, thanks. I'm on duty.'

'Oh, come on! I know coppers. Anyway, it looks bad you sitting there without a drink. I'd as soon the rest of the bar didn't know you were the Bill. Nosy bastards, some of them – especially that lot up the end. What do you drink? Gin and tonic, is it?'

Atherton assumed this was a calculation rather than a wild guess. The man was good. 'Thanks.'

'On the house,' Fosdyke said. 'If anyone asks, you're my new accountant.'

He mixed the drink, excused himself to refill someone's pint, and came back to Atherton. 'Sorry about that. The girl's on her lunch.' At that moment a young woman came in from the back, wiping her lips, and he said to her sharply, 'Finished? About time. Look after the bar, will you? I'm having ten minutes talking business here. Right, then.' He settled himself, elbows on the bar, arms folded, head approached confidentially towards Atherton's. 'You wanted to know about Tuesday night?'

'Yes. I had a message that you had seen Miss Cornfeld in here.'

'Is that her name? Chattie, she was called, that's all I know. Nickname or something. She lives in this road. I dunno the number. But,' he caught himself up with a short laugh, 'you know that. Why am I telling you? You got the house sealed off and about a million coppers in and out. Searching it, are you? What you looking for?'

'You saw Chattie in here on Tuesday,' Atherton prompted evenly.

Fosdyke tapped the side of his nose and winked. 'Right. Fair enough. Well, she comes in a lot, does our Chattie. What a nice girl, eh? Always full of it, having a laugh – and jokes? She knew a million of 'em. Said it was hanging about with musicians – they're always telling jokes. Mind you,' he said sternly, as if Atherton had made an adverse suggestion, 'she was a nice girl. A real lady, if you know what I mean. She could tell a joke, right, that was, well, a bit blue – funny as hell – and it'd be just on the line, but she'd never cross it. She knew exactly how far to go, know what I mean?'

'Tuesday night?' Atherton suggested.

Fosdyke was offended. 'I'm just filling in the background for you. You in a hurry?'

'Not at all,' Atherton said soothingly. 'I'm enjoying my drink. Please go on.'

'Well, Tuesday night,' Fosdyke resumed, with a little huffiness, 'she came in about five past seven. The bloke was waiting for her. He came in about five to, so I reckon they'd arranged to meet at seven.'

But the diary entry was 'JS 8pm', Atherton thought.

'Can you describe the man?'

'Yeah. He was, what, about twenty-five or so – looked younger than her. Kind of roundish, babyish face. About medium height, had very dark hair, straight, kind of flopped in his eyes – kept pushing it back, you know?' He made a graphic gesture of swiping his forehead clear. 'I don't know how he could stand it. It'd drive me barmy, having hair in me eyes all the time.'

Atherton resisted the urge to glance at his bald top. 'You didn't catch a name, I suppose?'

'Well, I think it was Toby,' Fosdyke said. 'Only when she came in, she said, "Hello, Tobes." Or I think that was what she said.'

Toby, Atherton thought. One of the musicians in the band, the oboist, was called Toby Harkness; and from what he remembered from the photographs on the website, he had a young face and dark hair. It was not in the diary, so it was a casual meeting. He must have called her up – on the missing mobile, perhaps – and said meet me in the Anchor. Why hadn't he gone to the house, though? Maybe he'd rung from the pub – come on down for a drink.

'Did they seem on friendly terms?'

'Oh, yes. She got up on the stool next to him and kissed him hello.'

'On the cheek or the mouth?'

'On the cheek. And then she sort of ruffled his hair – a bit mumsy, like. As if he was her kid brother. He didn't like that – sort of jerked his head away. But they were friends all right. Known each other for ages, I'd've said.'

'How long did they stay?'

'Not long. Had a drink, then she up and leaves, about a quart' to eight, give or take.'

'He didn't leave with her?'

'No, he sits there looking a bit glum, and I goes up and asks him if he wants another, and he sort of shakes himself and says, no, he's off. And he gets up and goes.'

'Did they quarrel?'

'Well, I wasn't hanging over 'em listening. I was serving, and it was a busy time – lot of office workers call in on their way home. Seven to eight's a busy time. But I don't think they quarrelled. I never saw anything of that. And when she goes, she seems friendly towards him, and, like, kisses him again. No, I wouldn't say they quarrelled. But,' he added, with the air of having saved this until last, 'they were talking seriously. You didn't often see Chattie without she was laughing, and I didn't see her laugh with this Toby bloke.'

'Had you seen her with him before?'

'Yeah, I reckon I had, once or twice, but not recently. Mind you, she often came in with a man and it wasn't often the same one twice.' He dropped a ghastly wink. 'Well, why not?' he asked broadly. 'Nice, pretty girl like that, full of beans, why shouldn't she play the field? I know I would, if I had her opportunities.' A thought seemed to strike him. He looked almost bewildered. 'Doesn't seem possible she's gone. What sort of a bastard would do that to a pretty girl? I know what I'd do to him if I caught him.'

'So Chattie left at about a quarter to eight? And you didn't see her again?'

'No,' he said, with a sentimental sigh. 'I never laid eyes on her again. If I'd known then what I know now . . .'

He left it hanging, and Atherton couldn't imagine how the sentence could be ended. More interesting was this serious talk with Toby, probably Toby Harkness, which she left for the date with JS. Had she told Toby whom she was going to meet? Had she told him what was on her mind? The cleaner had said she was thoughtful the last few days, now Fosdyke said she had a serious conversation for once in her life. If she'd had some business with JS that went wrong, was it possible that he had killed her the next day? He felt there was some investigating to be done around Baroque Solid's members, which was a happy thought for him.

CHAPTER SEVEN

A Tree Grew in Brixton

It was lucky for credibility that the call came in to someone
other than McLaren. Witnesses were suggestible at the best of
times, and his keenness had led him astray on previous occasions. But it was Hollis who came to Slider to say, 'We've had
another witness, guv, who saw the victim talking to someone
in a hoodie on that bit of path.'

'Let's be accurate. We don't know that it was the victim,'
Slider said.

Hollis smirked under his appalling moustache. 'We do now.
This bloke was walking past and saw her. He recognised her
from the photo on the news.'

'How sure is he?'

'He sounds okay,' Hollis answered the question behind the
question. 'Sensible enough. And he described her hair and
clothes and general height and build, which I don't think he
could have got from the telly.'

'Did he see the face of the man?'

'No, guv,' Hollis said regretfully. 'Bloke had his back to him.
He says he had his hands in his pockets and the hood up and
was sort of hunched. Looked furtive, witness says, made sure
to keep his face hidden as he went past. But he says he was
slim and a bit taller than the victim.'

'Wearing?'

'Well, the hoodie, like he said – grey, he thought. But he
wasn't sure what else he was wearing. Thought it might be a
tracksuit bottom and trainers.'

'Running Man was wearing chinos,' Slider reminded him.

Hollis shrugged. 'Get him in and get a full statement from him.
Try and test his memory about the victim, see if he remembers

the CD Walkman or the water-bottle. Was she holding anything? Did he see her expression? Was she talking or listening? Anything to substantiate his identification of her.'

'Right you are,' said Hollis. 'He's on his way now. Pity he didn't see the man's face, but at least it fits with what Yerbury said. It was the same part of the path. So it looks as if we can chuck the random killing idea. I can't see a savvy bird like her going into the shrubbery with a stranger if she wasn't forced.'

'*If* the person she was talking to was the killer,' Slider said. 'He might just have been someone asking for a light.'

'No, guv,' Hollis said, 'there was more to it than that. This witness saw them standing together for more than a minute before he passed them. He was coming from the station end and he saw them when he came round the bend of the path. And when he turned right to go out the Paddenswick gate, he thinks they'd gone.'

'Both of them?'

Hollis's large, gooseberry eyes widened as he nodded to the implication. 'Both of them. So where could they have gone except into the shrubbery?'

On leaving the pub, Atherton decided to pop in at the house to see what was going on. It was only sense, as he was right there on the spot; nothing to do with the fact that Hart was among the searchers. PC Renker was on the door, and nodded to him as he trod up the steps.

'Sounds as though there's a bit of excitement down there, sir,' he said, gesturing with his head over his shoulder. 'I wouldn't be surprised if they hadn't found something.'

The raised voices were coming from the basement. Atherton went down the stairs and Hart turned as he entered, and said, 'Wotcha, Jim. Is that good timing or what?'

'Judging by your enormous grin, you've found something,' Atherton said. There were two other people there, a woman called Viv Preston, borrowed from the SOC team, and WPC Coffey, who was blonde, hard as an acid drop, and had had a sense-of-humour bypass when she joined the Job.

'First time I come down here,' said Hart, 'I said to myself, "Blimey! Top kitchen! I bet this cost a bob or two." And now I think I know where the bobs came from.'

She gestured to Coffey's position by the furthest cabinet. The door of the wall-mounted cupboard was open, and on the worktop below were some tins of tomatoes and soup evidently removed from it.

'Go on, 'ave a look,' Hart invited.

Atherton went across. Inside the cupboard a few tins still remained, and tucked behind them, peeking out coyly, was a ziplock plastic bag containing a white powder.

'Cocaine?' he said. It was the sort of thing to thrill a sad copper's heart. Everything suddenly became much more explicable when drugs entered the equation.

'And not just a single wrap, either,' Hart said happily. 'It's not even a party-sized bag. There must be something like a hundred grams in there, enough to sell to a lot of friends for a nice profit.' She almost chortled. 'Little Princess Perfect turns out to be a naughty girl after all.'

'I did feel all along she was too good to be true,' Atherton said. 'But the boss won't be pleased. He's taken a shine to her.' He turned to Viv Preston. 'Can you take a photograph of its position?'

'I already have,' she said. 'You can take it out now.'

He gloved up, and carefully withdrew the package. 'Of course,' he said, holding it up by one corner and estimating the weight, 'we don't know until we test it. Might be bicarb for all we know.'

'Yeah,' said Hart ripely. 'And my arse is an apricot. Anyone want to bet it ain't charlie?' No-one did.

It was cocaine. They had field kits at the station for all the common drugs: a presumptive test and a confession could save a lot of time and money in possession cases.

'Well,' said Atherton, lounging against the door jamb of the CID room, 'it certainly helps to explain how she could afford the high life, and the house.'

Looking round the room, Slider saw how cheered everyone was by this find, which seemed likely to explain so much. He, on the other hand, felt his heart sink, and realised that he had become attached already to the pretty, clear-skinned girl called Chattie, the smiling, always cheerful girl, who was nice to old men and paper-sellers. Perhaps she wasn't Princess

Perfect, as Hart had dubbed her, but an awful lot of people had liked her. He didn't want her to be a coke-head and a drug-dealer.

Atherton must have divined his thoughts, because he said, 'A lot of people don't regard cocaine as a dangerous drug, and don't think it ought to be illegal. To them, snorting it or even selling it wouldn't seem like a crime.'

'Yeah, celebs do it all the time,' Hart said, belatedly catching on. 'They talk about it openly, and they don't even get, whacher-callit, *déclassés*.'

But she'd be *déclassée* with me, Slider thought. 'What about fingerprints?'

'There were a couple of nice ones on the plastic bag,' Atherton said. 'They're comparing them now with the victim's tenprint. Luckily people don't generally bother to glove up when they're handling their own little baggie of joy.'

'Boss,' said Hart, 'I've just thought: what if the killer was her supplier? That would make sense of why she went into the bushes with him. Say she was scoring a bit o' charlie to sell to her friends, she wouldn't want to do that in full view of the joggers and jigglers.'

'Yes,' said Slider, but uneasily. He could see the images, of the man in the hooded top talking to Chattie by the shrub-bery, of the man in the hooded top running away 'like the wind' from the park; and in between he could construct a scenario of the two of them in the shrubbery talking, a quarrel – over money, perhaps; the flash of a knife, the urgent flight. What didn't sing to him was the notion of a drug-dealer calculatedly sedating his victim before stabbing her. 'If it was a real stabbing,' he said, 'it would play like panto. As it is – why would he drug her and then go in for a bit of light wounding?'

Swilley said, 'That's right. I can't see a drug-dealer being squeamish about putting the knife in.'

'With all due respect to Dr Cameron,' Atherton said, 'we don't know that she did die of a drug overdose. Not till the tox report comes back.'

Swilley looked at him pityingly. 'That's when you know you've got to get out more – when you start trying to make the evidence fit your theory.'

'It's not evidence, only the doc's opinion,' Atherton said.

'Freddie Cameron's opinion *is* evidence,' Slider said.

'Leaving aside the method of killing,' Hollis put in, 'her line of business would be ideal for dealing coke. She moved around a lot, met lots of musoes and showbiz types.'

'Yeah, she was giving 'em all sorts of services – why not that? And maybe a bit of the other an' all,' McLaren said, with relish.

Slider controlled himself. 'Well, let's remember that this is all conjecture. We've no evidence yet that she did anything untoward. What else have we got?'

'Still haven't found her mobile, guv,' Hart said. 'We found her handbag in her bedroom, but it wasn't in there, and we pretty well covered the house. I reckon she must have had it with her and the killer took it.'

'Which would fit with the drug-dealer idea,' Mackay said. 'If she was murdered for personal reasons, why would the killer have it away with her phone?'

'Well, we know it's switched off,' Slider said. 'We can put the provider company on alert and as soon as it's switched on again we can get a fix on it. So, we're actively looking for Running Man?'

'Yes, guv,' McLaren said. 'Asking everyone about him. Is there gonna be another TV appeal tonight?'

'On the local news only,' Slider said. 'The main news has lost interest. Too much else going on with the Middle East crisis and the cabinet split. And yes, I will make sure that they ask about Running Man. But let's remember we don't know that he has anything to do with it, or even that he is the same man who was seen talking to her.'

This caveat went down with the assembled troops like a barbed-wire sandwich.

'So let's consider the possibility that it was a murder for personal reasons,' he went on. He looked at Atherton. 'What about the man who saw her in the pub on Tuesday evening?'

Atherton told the tale. 'The description he gave fits Toby Harkness, who was one of the members of the band Baroque Solid, so I thought that would be a good place to start.'

'How come you didn't latch onto it before, Jim? You've been spending enough time with the band,' said Hart.

'Maybe if you'd had your mind on the job when you were on the job,' Swilley began dangerously.

Slider intervened. 'All right, Toby Harkness. Maybe there was some sort of history between them.'

'Or maybe she was just selling him charlie,' Hart said. 'It don't sound romantic. Ruffling a bloke's hair in public is a quick way to lose his interest. They hate that – don't they, Jim? Buggers up fifty quid's wurf of blow-drying.'

'But,' Hollis said, being the voice of sanity, 'I thought her date for Tuesday night was with a JS?'

'True,' Atherton said, 'and so I thought—'

'Wasn't one of the band called Jasper something?' McLaren asked. 'I remember thinking what a poncey name it was, just what you'd expect for a Beethoven freak.'

'That's right,' Hart said. 'There was a Jasper. What was his other name? I can't remember.'

'It was Stalybrass,' said Atherton. 'I thought I'd go and see him, and Toby.'

Hollis looked considering. 'If she was seeing both of them at the same time, that might cause jealousy—'

'And a motive for murder,' Hart finished for him. 'If they knew about each other.'

'Oddly enough,' Atherton said, 'that had occurred to me.'

'Well, you're the obvious man for the job,' Slider said, 'since you're so well in with the band. But can you see them separately without the other knowing? Don't they all live together?'

'No, Mark Falconer, the cellist, shares a flat with the clarinet, Chaz Barnes. But Jasper Stalybrass and Toby Harkness each have their own flats,' Atherton said.

'It woulda been hairy dating both of 'em if they'd lived together,' Hart observed. 'I'd a given the vic plus ten for balls.'

'I can tell you've never studied anatomy,' Atherton said kindly.

McLaren had been looking impatient, and now burst in with, 'All this love and jealousy guff makes me tired. We've got a bloody great bag of charlie out of her gaff, and she was a high spender. What more do you want?'

Slider could have told him, but at that moment the telephone in his room rang and he left them to it while he went and answered it. When he returned the discerning might have noticed a quiet smile of satisfaction on his face, but the discerning weren't looking.

'That was Viv Preston,' he said. 'She's run the fingerprints from the cocaine bag against the victim's tenprint. They don't match. Nothing like.'

'Oh, pants,' Hart said. 'Another good theory bites the dust.'

'No, hang on,' Mackay said. 'Just because there's someone else's prints on the bag, doesn't mean it wasn't still hers. I mean, what was the stuff doing there anyway? Look, maybe it was one of her boyfriends left it there for her – didn't that cleaner say she had a lot of people in and out? She had to get the stuff from somewhere. Someone might have dropped it there for her to pick up. Just because her prints weren't on it doesn't mean they weren't going to be, see what I mean?'

'Or maybe she was just careful,' McLaren said. 'Smart bird like her, she might always have used gloves.'

'So who was she meeting in the shrubbery, then, in your theory?' Slider asked.

'Someone she was selling to,' McLaren suggested shamelessly.

'Nice try,' Slider said. The mention of the cleaner had triggered something in his mind. 'But I think I've got a better theory. Mrs Hammick said she saw Chattie's sister Jassy in the house on Monday, coming up from the kitchen and looking furtive and guilty. She also said that Jassy mixed with a rough lot.'

'Yeah,' said Hart, 'I've seen the mess she made of her bedroom. Drugs do fit better with the stud-queen image than with Princess Perfect,' she admitted.

'I think perhaps it's time we had a talk with Jassy,' Slider said.

'Me for that,' Hart said. 'Remember, her boyfriend's black. She's more likely to trust me than one of you white boys. Where's she live, boss?'

'Clapham, I think. Ferndale Road,' Slider said, from memory. 'The number will be in the address book.'

Hart raised her eyebrows. 'Then you'd definitely better send me. Ferndale Road's not Clapham, it's Brixton.'

'There's a lot of fuss about Brixton,' Atherton said. 'It's just Shepherd's Bush having it large.'

'They'd be on you like a flock of piranhas,' Hart discouraged him. 'There's another thing, guv,' she went on. 'Jassy's boyfriend's black and Running Man was black.'

'There's more than one black person in Shepherd's Bush,' Slider mentioned.

'Yeah, but if she wasn't dragged into the shrubbery by force, which we know she wasn't, it had to be someone she knew, di'nt it? This way, you've got the personal motive and the drugs motive together in one person.'

Slider sighed. 'Since I can't seem to stop you jumping to conclusions, I suppose I'd better go with you and keep a hand on the rein. What?' he answered her look. 'You didn't think I was going to let you go there alone, did you?'

'I'm a big girl,' Hart complained.

'That's why I'm going with you,' said Slider.

Atherton was right, there was a lot of fuss over nothing made about Brixton. Though there was a greater preponderance of black faces, white people still lived there perfectly peacefully and went about unmolested. Nobody even glanced sideways at Slider as he walked with Hart from the throbbing heart of Brixton down Ferndale Road. As with most communities, the vast majority of people of all shades just wanted to get on with their lives without bothering or being bothered by their neighbours, and the small element that did want to cause trouble was as disliked by the majority as anything else that made their environment unpleasant.

Still, there was a certain healthy tension in Slider's muscles, because they had looked up Jassy's boyfriend before they left. Darren Barnes – as it had turned out to be – was well known to the police, having been pulled in numerous times for possession, possession with intent, social-security fraud, once for affray (that was a brawl outside a pub) and once for malicious wounding. He was not one of the big racketeers, just a small-time distributor of recreational substances, and Mick Dangerfield at Brixton nick had told Slider that he seemed to try to avoid trouble on the whole, and lived a reasonably comfortable lifestyle on the proceeds of his dealing and multiple claims on the state's purse, plus, probably, other minor scams they hadn't caught up with yet. But, Dangerfield had warned, he was also known to go tooled up, and apart from the malicious wounding charge was thought to have used a blade on other occasions when the victim had not been willing to tell his side of the story to the police. Barnes was also inclined to be political, which made him more trouble than it was worth to take all the way, and accounted for his numerous warnings rather than charges. He had gone to court after the malicious wounding, but the judge had decided there was probably equal fault on both sides and had given him a suspended. The other time he had made an appearance before the beak was for the social-security fraud, where the sentence was generally community service. Barnes had been sent to help out at a youth club for black youngsters in Clapham which, Dangerfield said wryly, had proved right up his particular boulevard as it enabled him to extend his customer base clear into the next borough.

So, thought Slider, the drugs and the knife were all present and correct, which was one up – two up – to McLaren; and while it was comforting to think that Darren usually tried to avoid trouble, there was always danger when you cornered a fox in its own lair. And if Darren Barnes had been both Running Man and Talking-to-Chattie Man, there might be enough at stake to make him reckless.

There was a beautiful London plane growing outside the house, which was the only nice thing about it. The house itself was tall and run down, and obviously divided into flats or rooms. The front door stood open, and the steps up to it were cracked and chipped and had lost their handrail. Inside the door was a passage floored with worn and dirty brown linoleum, the walls painted brown up to dado-level and cream above. The usual litter of electricity bills addressed to long-departed tenants, handbills and junk mail lay on the floor beside and behind the door. From somewhere above the relentless beat of rap music shook the air, which was cold inside the dark hall and smelt of feet, sweat, junk food and the rich undertone of ganja.

'Just like home,' Hart said, straight-faced, noticing Slider's nostrils twitch. 'So, which flat is it?'

'Number six,' Slider said. There were two doors off the hall, and stairs straight ahead. 'Let's assume these are flats one and two.'

'Let's,' Hart humoured him.

On the next floor there were three doors, behind one of which a baby was crying monotonously. The stairs that went on up were much narrower, and the thumping music came from the door at the top.

'That's gotta be six,' Hart said.

'No worries about creeping up on them,' Slider said.

They went on up. It was quite dark at the top, and the sheer volume of the music seemed somehow threatening. Slider began to feel vulnerable. With only a small landing and the steep narrow stairs behind them, they would be an easy target for whoever opened the door. If they opened it. He glanced at Hart, who seemed cheeringly unperturbed, took a deep breath and thumped long and hard with the side of his fist on the door. He was so sure there would be no answer that he almost fell back down the stairs in surprise when the door was flung open and someone said, 'Dow?'

Despite the crepuscular gloom, Slider recognised Jassy Whitelaw at once from the descriptions. She evidently recognised the Bill when she saw it, too, for alarm widened her eyes, and she said, 'Shit!' and tried to slam the door. Hart inserted her body and Slider his foot in the path of it, and between them they forced it, and her, back.

'Iss all right, girlfrien', it ain't grief for you,' Hart said soothingly. 'We jus' wanna talk.' She was exaggerating her accent for purposes of winning trust. Slider still had no idea whether it was deliberate or instinctive.

'Better let us in, Jassy, so we can talk where it's private,' he said. 'You don't want to talk out here where anyone can see you.' They inched her backwards until Slider could close the door behind them, preventing her from trying to bolt. 'He's not here, then, your boyfriend?' he deduced. When Jassy had said, 'Dow?' she had not been offering Slider a glass of port. It was the Londoner's pronunciation of 'Dal', which was the Londoner's abbreviation of 'Darren'. She had been expecting him back, otherwise she might not have opened the door at all.

Her way forward blocked, Jassy turned and ran. The short, dark hall led into a large, lighter room with a sash window straight ahead and the shadow of an old-fashioned iron fire escape outside. They caught her while she was still trying to heave the part-open window further up. Like most old sashes it had not only warped but had been so often and so badly painted that there was no chance of it gliding effortlessly as it had been originally designed to do.

'Don't be daft, girl,' Hart said, pulling her round. 'You jus' makin' trouble for yo'self. We gotta talk to you some time. No sense puttin' it off. You wanna sit here and talk nice, or you wan' us to take you down the station? 'Sup to you.'

Seeing she had the situation under control, Slider sought out the source of the brain-pulping beat and turned it off. Hart was coaxing Jassy backwards towards a sofa, and he had his first good look at her. She was thin – not just slim but last-chicken-in-the-shop bony – and it was emphasised by the skimpy dress she wore, sleeveless, low-necked and nearly back-less, which left her collarbones, shoulder-blades and spine sticking out and clearly visible under her sallow skin. There was clearly no room under the dress for anything by way of underwear, and her hip bones and ribs and nipples were outlined seamlessly by the clinging pink knitted cotton. The skirt was short, above her bony knees; her feet were bare, with matching pink varnish on the nails; her bony arms ended in nervous hands with bitten fingernails.

But it was above the neck that she was truly remarkable. Her hair was coke-black and cut in haphazard spikes. She looked like a cartoon character who has touched a live wire, except that the spikes were not symmetrical. Her face was very white, her eyeshadow and lipstick a very dark near-black red, her eyes a mass of thick, black mascara. She had four rings around the rim of one ear and three round the other and black shiny studs in the lobes, a stud in her nose and one between her lower lip and her chin, two rings in one eyebrow and a row of studs in the other.

She had done everything she could to make herself look disagreeable; but someone else – presumably the absent Darren – had still done more. Her eyes were red with crying and her mascara had smeared clownishly below them. Under the white foundation her face had a bumpy look with which Slider, like other policemen, was sadly all too familiar. She had a large bruise on her right cheekbone, a cut on the left side of her mouth, which was swollen, and a bruise on her left cheekbone, which had spread round the eye. Three blows, he thought, with sad expertise. A right-handed assailant: hit the left side first, then a backhander to the right (the cut was probably caused by a ring), then the left again. It was the carelessly callous assault of accustomedness. And yet still she expected him back and opened the door to him.

'Did Darren do this to you?' Slider asked, injecting fatherly tenderness into his voice.

'None of your bloody business,' she muttered.

'You don't have to take that, you know, Jassy. No-one's got the right to hit you.'

'What do you want?' she asked irritably, but with a shade of weariness, as if she'd heard it all before.

'Just to talk to you.'

'I've got nothing to say. Not to Fascist lackeys like you.' She glanced at Hart. 'What're *you* doing this job for? You're the worst sort, sucking up to the enemy. Haven't you got any loyalty?'

'Just sit down, Jassy,' Slider said firmly, 'and let's get this over with.'

'Who d'you think you're talking to? You can't order me about in my own home. Get out of here and leave me alone. I'm not talking.'

'I'm trying to make this friendly,' Slider said, 'but I'm not going to waste my time. Either you talk to us here, or I'll arrest you and you can talk at the station. It's up to you.'

'Arrest me?' she said, with a fair attempt at lip-curling contempt. 'What for?'

Hart took it up. 'We got some very nice lifts off that bag o' charlie hidden in Chattie's house. We gonna find out they're yours soon as we print you.' Jassy's face registered dismay for a telling moment. 'You know how it goes, girl. Own up and you get some credit. Make us work for it and you don' get nuffin'. Plus, this is your chance to tell your side o' the story. What's it gonna be?'

Slider thought she was overdoing it a little, but it played like vaudeville with Jassy, in her, presumably, overwrought state.

'Bastard,' she said, but it didn't seem to be directed towards either of them. She sat down heavily on the sofa, and tears began to well up in her eyes. She tried to sniff them back, and said, in an unsteady voice, 'You got any fags? He cleaned me out, the bastard.'

Silently, Hart produced a pack and handed one over, and Jassy reached across to the coffee table for a box of matches. While she was lighting it, Slider took a quick and covert glance round at the room. It was sparsely furnished, but in a way that suggested this was a style choice rather than lack of money. The stereo system racked along one wall would have cost thousands, and there was a large, new plasma-screen TV on an expensive corner unit. The floor was stripped and polished – which must make life miserable for the people underneath, he thought, given the kind and volume of the music Jassy seemed to prefer – and the black leather sofa and chairs were top of the range, and still smelt new. Whatever Jassy was doing here in Brixton, it wasn't slumming – unless of the cultural sort. Though her language was not elegant, her accent was out of its place.

'So where's Darren?' Slider asked at last.

She shrugged, without looking at him.

'He hit you, and then he took off?' Another shrug. 'What did he hit you for?' No answer. 'Was it about the cocaine in Chattie's house?'

She fidgeted a bit, but didn't answer. One arm was folded across her waist, the elbow of the other resting on it so that her hand was by her face, handy for concealing it, and for smoking and nail-biting which she did alternately. She stared away from them, out of the window, which, being at the back of the house, had no view of the lovely tree, only the no-escape fire escape and the backs of other buildings.

Slider tried again. 'Did you know that your sister Chattie was dead?' he said, hoping that either way it might shock a response out of her.

It worked, though it was not the reaction he had expected. She looked at him balefully for an instant. 'Oh, for Christ's sake, what d'you think this is all about?' There was a breath of a pause, and then resentment burst the banks. 'It's all her fault, stupid cow! She always had everything she wanted, always, and I never had anything!' And then she cried – not tears of grief and mourning, but what, in Slider's experience, were always the most sincere and heartfelt of all, the tears of self-pity.

CHAPTER EIGHT

Snow White and the Severn Dork

There was a residual reluctance to overcome, but Hart worked on Jassy with sympathy and sisterly solidarity. 'Look at your face. I wu'nt take that from no-one, girl. He ain't got the right to knock you aroun'.'

'We had a row,' Jassy confessed, wiping tears and kohl from under her eyes with a Kleenex.

'About the bag o' white at yo' sister's house, was it?' Jassy did not answer this. Hart leaned forward a little and said earnestly, 'Listen, grassing up a mate's one fing, I know that, but this is different. This is serious. You don't want to do time for that bastard, do you? After what he did? He ain't wurf it, girl. I mean, that's yo' fingerprints on the bag, ennit, an' we know you was there. We got a witness.'

'That cow of a cleaner, Maureen or whatever her name is,' Jassy said viciously. 'Always poking her nose in. Who does she think she is?'

Hart tossed Slider a quick look, and he took up the thread. 'Jassy, I want you to understand this is something much more serious and important than the bag of cocaine. Now, if you help us by telling us everything you know, you won't get into trouble for that. But if you won't help us, then we'll have no option but to arrest you. That was a very large quantity of snow in that bag. It's not just possession. We're talking jail here.'

She stared at his stern face, and then at Hart's sympathetic one, and sighed. 'I never wanted to do it in the first place,' she said. 'I mean, that's Darren's business. I didn't want to know.'

Happy to live off the proceeds, though, weren't you? Slider

could see the thought in Hart's eyes, but fortunately Jassy didn't.

'So he made you hide the bag in Chattie's house? Why was that?'

'*I* don't know.'

Slider looked at Hart. 'I don't think this qualifies as co-operation. I think we'd better continue this down at the station.'

'Yeah,' said Hart. 'You can't be nice to some people.'

Jassy stirred indignantly. 'Look, I don't know. He just said to take it there and put it in the cupboard behind the tins of tomatoes. I thought he needed a safe place to stash it, that's all. I know some of your lot have had their eye on him. Maybe he had a tip-off or something that he was going to get turned over.'

'He didn't give a reason and you didn't ask for one? You just hid a bloody great bag o' white in your sister's house, no questions asked?'

She gave a sulky shrug. 'Why should I care about her? She's never done anything for me.'

'But Darren obviously knew his way about her kitchen all right, if he knew what was in that cupboard,' said Slider. 'How well did he know your sister?'

'Look, if you're suggesting there was something going on between them—'

'I didn't suggest anything, but it's interesting that you jump to that conclusion,' said Slider, with an air of intellectual enquiry.

Hart lowered the tone judiciously. 'Was he bonking her, love?'

'No!'

'So it was a business relationship?'

'I don't know, and I don't care,' Jassy said. 'I hid the charlie for him, that's all. Then Wednesday night he tells me to go and get it. But when I get to the house there's a copper on the door.'

Atherton got that done just in time, Slider thought.

'So I came home and told Darren and he was furious. He just went off at me, as if it was my fault. I told him it was nothing to do with me, but he said the coke must have been found and I couldn't have hidden it properly, and he shouted at me and then he hit me and then he took off and I haven't seen him since.' She drew a breath, and added, 'I don't care if I never see him again, either, the bastard. It wasn't my fault. I put it where he told me to. He'd got no right to hit me.'

'You're right there,' Hart said warmly. Jassy turned minutely towards her and away from Slider, responding, he saw, to female sympathy. Hart was good, he thought. 'So where was Dow Wensday morning, Jass? Did he go out early?'

'I don't know,' she said. 'I wasn't here. I went to see my mum Tuesday night and stayed over. But he wasn't here either. He went up to Manchester to see some mates on Tuesday. That's why I went to see Mum. He didn't get home until about eight o'clock Wednesday night, and then he told me to go over to Chattie's and get the coke.'

'How come he's got mates in Manchester?' Hart asked.

'He went to college there. Not for long – they chucked him out for selling weed.' She smiled slightly as she said it – a proud smile for the rebel without a cause.

'D'you think that's where he's gone now?'

'I don't know. It might be.'

'You haven't tried to find him? Rung round your friends?'

'Why should I, after what he did? I never want to see him again. I hope he rots in hell, the bastard.'

'Can you give us the name and address of these mates?'

She came down off her high horse, belatedly alarmed. 'What d'you want that for?'

'We'd like a word with him about that charlie – and we can do him for assault on you at the same time, if you like,' said Hart.

But Jassy looked uneasy. 'He's got some funny mates up there, hard men. I don't want to get mixed up with it. I mean, they'd be pissed off if they thought I'd put the coppers on their tail. They could be serious trouble.'

'We won't tell them it was you told us,' Hart said. 'There's lots of ways we could've found it out.' Jassy still looked uncertain, and Hart allowed a little toughness to creep into her voice. 'In return for a bit of leeway on your prints being on that bag of coke.'

'I've told you about that. It wasn't mine.'

'Yeah, but he's put you right in it. You don't wanna go down, just protectin' him. Do yo'self a favour. You don't owe him nuffin'. Give us a name, girlfrien'. No-one won't know you said anyfing. 'At's a promise.'

Jassy sighed, and said, 'I know one of 'em's Dave O'Brien.

I don't know his address but his phone number's around some-where. Will that do?'

'Yeah, that's good, girl,' Hart said. 'You get that for us, an' that's a lot o' Brownie points for you.'

Jassy got up and said, 'If you find Darren, make sure he falls down a flight of stairs or something.' She found the number on a pad by the telephone and handed it to Hart with an air of having finished all transactions.

But Slider said, 'So when did you find out your sister was dead?'

She turned to him, wariness creeping into her expression and posture. 'Eh?'

'When you went to her house on Wednesday night and saw the policeman on duty, you didn't know then she was dead?'

'Well, of course I didn't. I thought it was to do with the coke. That's why I had the fight with Darren.' She said it with the exaggerated exasperation of the age.

'So when did you find out?'

Jassy sat down. 'If you must know, my mum phoned me up about it last night. She saw it on the telly, on the news.'

'Don't you watch the news on television?'

'No, why should I? It's a load of rubbish. Capitalist indoctrin-ation. All those TV companies are tools of the establishment.'

'That's a big TV set you've got,' Hart remarked.

'It's Darren's. He watches the sport on it.' It was said with a roll of the eyes.

'You don't seem very sorry that she's dead.'

Resentment flared. 'Why should I be? She was only my half-sister. Anyway, she wouldn't care if it was me. She always thought she was a cut above everyone else. Her mum is a stuck-up bitch. She called my mum all the names under the sun for stealing my dad from her, but she'd done just the same, so who was she to give herself airs? The first time I went to her house for tea when I was a kid, she went on and on about table manners and had I washed my hands and was I allowed to eat like that at home. I wasn't good enough for her. I mean, I was just a little kid! You don't take it out on a little kid like that, do you? And Chattie was just like her – thought she was oh-so-posh, looked down on me and my friends, all holier-than-thou every time I wanted to do a line of charlie or a couple of tabs of E or whatever. The fuss she made when I smoked a bit of weed in her precious house! You'd have thought I'd been spraying anthrax around. I said to her, everybody does it, and she said, I don't, and I said, well, that doesn't surprise me because you're just bloody perfect, everybody knows that. Her and her stupid little piddling business, and all that crap about doing it on her own and not taking anything from anybody! That was aimed at me, that charming little remark. All very well for someone who's always had everything they wanted, all very fine and nice. She made me sick, she was so bloody pious, sitting in her ivory tower and telling me I had no right to draw social security, as if it was a crime. I said to her, I know my rights, and she made some smart-mouth remark about not knowing my duty. Duty! Yeah, duty to the forces of global capitalism, I said. Never mind the third-world poor, grind them in the dust, as long as you've got your share! She was such a hypocrite. I mean, she only had that house in the first place because our dad gave her the money for it. So much for not taking anything from anybody.'

'Is your dad well off?'

She shrugged again. 'All I know is, he's never given me anything.'

'Are he and your mum still together?'

'You've got to be joking!' she said, with a toss of her head. 'He scarpered the moment I turned up. Cleared off and left Mum to it. I was just glad he'd done the same to Chattie and her snobby mum. Her and her stupid books! My mum got one out of the library once. She said it was rubbish.'

'Sounds like you've really got some issues wiv your sister,' Hart said sympathetically.

'She always had everything,' Jassy cried, with a fresh burst of self-pity. 'She's pretty, she's brainy, and everybody always takes her side, because she sucks up to them. Everything she does turns out right, she always had tons of boyfriends, and now she's got that house and she hangs around with celebs in that potty job of hers, and her life's just bloody perfect! All I've got is this crummy place, and Darren. And now,' she reached the peak and tumbled over, 'Darren's hit me and gone off and I don't know where he is or when he's coming back!'

She began to cry again, and Hart handed her another Kleenex and met Slider's eye over her bent head. The resentment was fresh and hot and there was plenty of material here for motive. And the absent Darren, Hart's look said as clearly as words, was more than a bit tasty.

Baroque Solid were not playing together on Friday evening. Marion and Trish had outside work, playing at Milton Keynes, and the others were about their normal social rounds – or normal-ish, considering the shock they had all sustained. Atherton eventually tracked Jasper Stalybrass down in a pub in Islington, which was filled with well-scrubbed, well-dressed young people spending large amounts of money on designer beers (the men), which they drank out of the bottle, and bizarre cocktails (the women) that came laden with fruity bits and twisty glass straws. Stalybrass was tall and handsome and was evidently being the life and soul of the group of laughing people he was in company with. It was a delicate manoeuvre to cut him out from his adoring fans.

Atherton's experience, backed up by what he had learned from Joanna and Sue, was that horn-players were often men with enormous charm and cold, cold hearts, so he started off with a mild prejudice against him, especially as he had found him telling jokes and laughing heartily. But once he had him alone in a quiet corner, he fell victim himself to the charm, especially as it was allied to a sharp mind, a straightforward delivery, and an obviously genuine shock and sadness about Chattie.

'God, it's hard to believe,' he said. 'I keep forgetting for a time, and then remembering all over again. It was a hell of a blow, I can tell you. I mean, everybody liked Chattie. Who in the world would want to kill her?' He put his hand up to scratch his eyebrow in an almost boyish gesture of hiding his tears. He cleared his throat, and then said, 'But I was forgetting – it was this Park Killer, wasn't it? So that means he picked her at random. God, what a terrible, awful chance. You never think it could happen to anyone you know, do you?'

'I imagine the whole band is very upset,' Atherton said neutrally.

'Upset? That doesn't come near it. We were back at the

studio today to do the final mix on our CD, but we all just sat around and talked about Chattie. We hadn't got the heart to get on with it. Mike Ardeel – the studio boss? – he was really cut up. He said in the circumstances he'd give us another session and wouldn't charge us for the wasted one, and usually he's red hot on money – has to be, in a small operation – so that shows you. But really, none of us could think about doing it right then. It would have been too weird. The last time most of us saw her was in that studio on Monday. The girls were all in tears. I nearly was myself.'

'You knew her quite well,' Atherton said, as a statement rather than a question.

'Yes,' Stalybrass said. He eyed Atherton for an instant, as if working out how much he already knew, and then said, 'Well, I suppose it doesn't matter if it comes out now. She and I were very close. We'd been having a thing for about a year.'

'You were lovers?'

'Yes,' he said. 'But I don't want you to get the wrong idea about it. We weren't in love or planning to live together or anything like that. It was all very light-hearted. We liked each other very much but we were just good friends, with sex added, that was all. Chattie was a great girl – a real pal, if you know what I mean. One of those rare women who can meet men on their own terms and be proper friends without dragging in all that female baggage and emotional trappings. We met when we felt like it, made love when we felt like it, lived our own lives and had no obligations to each other beyond having a lot of fun.'

'Was that the way she was in general?'

'Well, I can't speak for every corner of her life, but from what she said to me it was. She liked men and she enjoyed sex but I don't think she'd ever felt seriously about anyone. She told me that she'd never been in love, and never expected to be. She said to me more than once, "There's no room in my life for another man."'

Atherton noted that, the same words she had used to Mrs Hammick. Another man? So who was the first? 'Had she had a bad love affair and been hurt, or something?'

'Not that I ever heard. She just liked to keep emotions at a distance,' Stalybrass went on. 'Well, it suited me, because I've been through a bad divorce, and it suited her, and it was nobody's business but ours, was it?'

'So she may have been seeing other men as well as you?'

Atherton was amused to notice that he didn't like that question. For all his vaunted independence, he didn't want to think of Chattie in someone else's bed. 'She may have been,' he said lightly. 'I suppose I ought even to say that it was likely. She was very attractive and she liked men, so why wouldn't she? But I would never have asked her, and if I had, she certainly wouldn't have answered. She was quite a private person in many ways.' He smiled faintly. 'I've seen her and Marion having those girls' heart-to-hearts they all go in for and, believe me, it was Marion doing the telling and Chattie doing the listening. She would never have given away *her* inmost secrets.'

Touché, thought Atherton. So it was all round the band, then, that he had seen Marion two nights running? He had managed not to come face to face with Marion's flatmates yet, by bedding her at his place and leaving her at her door afterwards, but evidently there were no secrets kept within the group. Or, perhaps, not within the female half of it.

Down to business. 'Did you have a date with her on Tuesday night?' he asked.

'Yes. How did you know that?'

'It was in her diary. "JS 8pm". It seemed likely that JS was Jasper Stalybrass.'

'JS could have been anyone, but in fact it was me. I've nothing to hide. We went to see the new Woody Allen film, and then we went back to my place, but she didn't stay long. She said she had a lot to do the next day and wanted to get up early.'

'Did she usually stay the night?'

'More often than not, but not invariably. Sometimes we went back to her place instead, and then I generally stayed the night, unless I had something early the next day.'

'Did she say what it was she had to do?'

'No, we didn't talk about business. But she did seem a bit preoccupied – not as forthcoming as usual.'

'Was she worried about something?'

'I wouldn't say worried exactly. She just seemed to have her mind on other things. She was perfectly cheerful when she did talk, and she laughed her head off at the film. No, not worried or unhappy, just busy, I think.'

'Do you know what she had been doing earlier that day?'

'No. She'd been working, I presume, but she didn't say and I didn't ask.'

'It didn't come up in the course of conversation?'

'No, we mostly talked about the band and the CD and music in general. She never did speak much about her other clients, unless they were friends of ours. And even then – well, she was discreet, I suppose. Which was quite right.'

'Of course,' Atherton said. 'It's just that there was an entry in her diary for that day which we haven't been able to work out. It said, "DC 10 TFQ". Does that mean anything to you?'

He shook his head slowly. 'No, I'm afraid not. I've no idea what that means.'

Atherton tried another angle. 'You said about your relationship with her, "It doesn't matter if it comes out now." Were you keeping it a secret?'

'It wasn't really a relationship in the sense—'

'Okay, take that as read, but was it a secret you were seeing each other?'

'Yes, it was – but not for any sinister reason,' Stalybrass said, and he gave a charming, confiding smile which Atherton tried to resist, but with difficulty. 'You see, though Chattie never took any relationship seriously, it didn't always follow from the other side, if you get what I mean. She'd been out a couple of time with Toby – Toby Harkness, our oboe-player – and he'd fallen desperately in love with her. He just couldn't understand that she didn't feel the same. Poor old Toby's a bit intense, and he had a sheltered upbringing – in Bristol, to make it worse. To him, the fact that she'd been to bed with him meant she loved him and they were going to get married. Once she found he wasn't singing from the same hymn sheet she tried to disengage from him but it was difficult. In the normal course of events she would just have refused to see him or talk to him any more. But, of course, with Tobe she couldn't do that, because of everything she was doing for the band. She'd be seeing him in the course of things several times a week, so she had to try to let him down gently. And part of that was not letting on to anyone that she and I were seeing each other, because it would just about have killed old Tobes, and if any of the others had known it would have got back to him. So I'd be grateful if you didn't let on about this to anyone.'

Atherton promised nothing. 'Did you know she saw Toby on Tuesday evening, before she met you?'

He raised an eyebrow, but didn't look unduly concerned. 'No, I didn't. Where was that?'

'In the pub at the end of her road.'

'The Anchor? Oh, well, I expect he was just trying to get her to go back with him, and she was telling him kindly it was no go.'

'So she was still sleeping with him?' Atherton tried. He had to wonder whether Chattie had not been a manipulative little minx.

'Oh, no, it had only been a couple of times, and it was all over as far as she was concerned. But I'm not altogether sure she was right about handling him with kid gloves,' he added thoughtfully. 'I mean, I know Toby's an emotional sort, and all oboe players are a bit mad anyway, but he just wasn't capable of believing there'd been nothing in it, and a short, sharp shock might have been better for him in the long run.' His expression changed and he said bleakly, 'Well, he's had that now, hasn't he? Couldn't be any shorter or sharper. I suppose old Tobes will be able to go to his grave believing she loved him really. Oh, God, I just can't believe – I mean, I was making love to her on Tuesday night and just a few hours later—' He chewed his lip, staring away from Atherton while he tried to keep control.

Much as Atherton would have liked to resist, he felt honesty in this man, and real affection for the dear departed. Whatever he was, he didn't think he was First Murderer.

'You said, "All oboe-players are a bit mad"?' he queried.

'Well, it's playing with a double reed, you see – causes huge pressure on the frontal lobes. They all go a bit barmy in the end.' Stalybrass smiled and added, 'It's a musicians' joke, that's all. Well, some of them are peculiar but, then, to a horn-player, anyone who wants to play any other instrument seems peculiar.'

Atherton had heard about oboists being mad from another source – well, from Sue, not to mince matters. He shied away from the thought of her. 'How has Toby reacted to Chattie's death?'

'Well, he was devastated, like the rest of us. Maybe a bit more so, given that he thought she was the one true love of his life. And he tends to be a bit intense anyway, does Tobe. Artistic temperament. He was just sunk in depression at the studio this morning – hardly said a word to anyone.'

'Is he the jealous kind?' Atherton asked. 'Did you keep your affair with Chattie secret from him not to hurt his feelings, or from fear of what he might do?'

'Fear of what he might do?' Stalybrass looked puzzled.

'You see, we aren't making this public at the moment, but we don't think it was the Park Killer who did it. We think it was someone who knew her.'

Now Stalybrass looked alarmed. 'Oh, good Lord, you aren't thinking Toby did it? He would never do anything like that. Not old Tobes. He's a bit emotional and, as I said, he's had a rather sheltered upbringing, so he didn't understand Chattie the way we would.'

Atherton liked the touch of the little slipped-in 'we' – men of the world like you and me, he meant.

'But he would never hurt a fly. Wouldn't have the guts, apart from anything else. I mean, if you knew the man – well, it's laughable to think of him stabbing anyone. He's really a bit of a dork. And he's soft – even lets wasps out of the window rather than killing them. He's just not capable of murder.'

He stopped talking and looked pleadingly at Atherton. Atherton said nothing for a moment. In the eyes opposite he had seen a flash of knowledge, the sudden realisation that the unthinkable was possible. 'A bit emotional'? Toby had been 'desperately in love' and now the woman he wanted would not see him. Atherton thought of the kiss on the cheek and the hair-ruffling at the last interview. A man in that situation might decide that if he couldn't have her, no-one else should. A man rejected and humiliated and not taken seriously might find that a mixture of anger in with his grief was enough to stiffen the sinews and summon up the blood.

After a moment, Stalybrass said thoughtfully, 'Killed by someone who knew her, eh?'

Atherton nodded. 'So, you see, we need to find out all we can about her and her life.'

Stalybrass seemed relieved by this, as though it were letting

Toby off the hook. 'Well, I'll tell you everything I know. I was pretty close to her.'

'Let me get you another drink,' said Atherton.

It was late by the time Slider got back to the office, but an enquiry at the desk told him that Porson was still on the premises. O'Flaherty, the uniformed sergeant who passed on the news, did it with a sad shake of the head. 'Got no home to go to,' he said. 'Or, at least, not one he wants to be in, wit' the missus gone. I wouldn't be surprised if he was headin' for a crack-up.'

Slider climbed up to the eyrie, remembering, unwelcomely, a previous boss, Det. Sup. Barrington, who had killed himself shortly after Slider had refused an invitation to dinner with him. In the fridge there had been the dinner for two he would have cooked, and nothing else. The loneliness of Barrington's life as revealed had haunted Slider – not that the Syrup was strictly comparable, for Barrington had had no family and was, in any case, seriously bonkers; but if Porson had asked Slider back, he probably would have gone.

Fortunately there was no chance of that. Porson was reading and taking notes at his desk when Slider tapped politely on the open door, and he looked up with work- and insomnia-reddened eyes, keeping his finger on his place to indicate he was busy and this should be kept short. Slider dredged up his précis lessons from school and gave Porson a short version of what they had learned from Jassy Whitelaw.

'So you want to alert the Manchester police and get them to go and give this O'Brien a tug, see if Barnes is there?'

'We've got the phone number. We can get the address from that. And we've got a photograph of Barnes from his flat we can send them.'

Porson considered. 'But you don't know that that's where he's gone. It was only because the girlfriend said that was where he was on Tuesday and Wednesday.' Give the old boy credit, he could fillet a story at the first telling. 'You don't even know that's where he was on Wednesday, either,' Porson continued. 'It's only what he told her. I don't suppose their relationship was based on trust and veracitude.'

'It didn't seem that way,' Slider agreed.

'In fact, he could be anywhere in the country. Or out of it.'

'Yes, sir. But the only lead we've got is this friend in Manchester, and I'd like to get hold of Darren Barnes before the trail gets cold.'

'I don't doubt you would, but when it comes down to it we've no evidence that Barnes had anything to do with the murder.'

'No, sir, but we've got the cocaine against him, and it's a large amount.'

'Fair enough,' Porson acknowledged. 'On that basis you can ask Manchester nicely in the morning and they'll do it when they've got a minute. But you can't go getting them out of bed and telling them to drop everything. Nor,' he anticipated Slider's next appeal, 'can you flash Barnes's picture round the country with a request to apprehend if seen. I'm sorry, Slider, but until you get a bit more to link him to the murder, it's softly softly. Check with his known associates and family, if any, ask Brixton for help, but you can't go demanding favours of other forces without a bit more to go on.'

'I understand, sir.'

Porson raised an eyebrow. 'It's late,' he said. 'Get off home to your woman, laddie. Leave burning the oil at both ends to the likes of me, without one.'

Slider took himself away before he did the unforgivable and offered sympathy. He went back down to his own room to collect his mac (was it really only this morning that he stood outside Stella Smart's door in the rain?) and rang Joanna's mobile. She answered him at once, to the background sound of a car's engine and radio.

'I'm on my way home,' she said defensively. 'We didn't even stop for a drink.'

'I was just going to say that to you. Have you eaten?'

'Before the last session. What about you?'

'Some time last year, I think,' he said. 'I'll stop at that all-night deli in Turnham Green and pick up something.'

'Get enough for two,' she said. 'I'll join you in a spot of supper. I'm hungry again.'

'You're always hungry.'

'This is where we came in,' Joanna said. 'See you soon.'

He had only just got down to his car when she phoned him back.

'I've just had Jim call me,' she said. 'He said he didn't want to call you in case you were still with a witness.'

'You sound as though you didn't believe him.'

'He sounded weasely. He sort of invited himself to supper.'

'How did that happen? I thought you hated him.'

'No, I don't hate him. I'm very sad about him and Sue. Besides, I can't kick his behind unless we're face to face, can I?'

'Perhaps not even then.'

'You know what I mean. Anyway, he said he had something to tell you and he sounded excited, and I was about to say can't it wait for the morning when he asked if we'd had supper and I – sort of – found myself saying come and join us.'

Slider sighed. 'I can't take these late nights like you young-sters. I need my sleep.'

'Better get used to going without,' she warned.

'Don't remind me,' he shuddered. 'So, I'm getting enough supper for three now, am I?'

'Yes, but Jim said he'd bring wine.'

'Small mercies, I suppose,' said Slider.

It was an odd sensation to have the door of Joanna's flat opened to him by Atherton. 'I've just got here,' he said. 'Joanna's getting the plates and glasses out. Is that the nosh?'

He held out his hand for the paper sack in which the deli, aiming for an American look, had taken to packing its wares. In the background there was a clashing sound from the kitchen. Slider handed over the bag and said, 'What was so important it couldn't wait for tomorrow, anyway?'

Atherton raised an eyebrow. 'Am I unwelcome? I didn't think I needed an excuse to have supper with my oldest friend.'

'Oldest is how I feel,' Slider said, but he left the question unanswered. 'Can you two manage between you? I want to wash my hands and face and take my tie off.'

When Slider joined them in the sitting room, they were chat-ting in what seemed a perfectly friendly way, so he assumed that whatever bones Joanna had had to pick with Atherton, she had buried them for the time being. The food had been laid out on the gate-leg table. There was French bread, two kinds of pâté, a thoroughly degenerate piece of Brie that really ought to have been wearing a corset, a large bunch of red grapes, and three slices of the deli's own cheesecake. Atherton's hand was visible in the fact that the lettuce, green pepper and vine tomatoes he had bought had been assembled in one dish as a salad, with dressing: Joanna would have dumped them on the table separate and undressed for picking at. And the wine Atherton had brought was two bottles of beaujolais – Regnié, one Slider didn't know.

'So, what was the news you were so excited about?' Slider asked, as they began. The French bread had been warmed, he discovered – Atherton again.

'Did you tell him I was excited?' Atherton asked.

'Get on with it,' said Joanna. 'Spinning it out like that.'

'All right, here it is – I know who Chattie's father is. Ever heard of Cornfeld Chemicals?'

'I thought it was Cornfield,' Slider said. 'There's that logo of theirs—'

'Oh, yes, I know it,' Joanna said. 'I saw something in the paper about them a couple of weeks ago – didn't read it, because I wasn't interested, but I noticed the logo: the oval thingy with the picture of a field of waving corn on it.'

'That's the one,' said Slider. 'Always reminded me of Ovaltine. I could never fathom what it had to do with chemicals.'

'*I* always read it as "Cornfed Chemicals",' Joanna said. 'You know, like "cornfed beef".'

'You see a picture of a cornfield and read the word underneath and naturally you think the name is Cornfield,' Slider reasoned.

'Oy,' said Atherton. 'You're spoiling my effect. When I say, "Ever heard of Cornfeld Chemicals?" you're supposed to gasp in wonder, not witter on about etymology.'

'What's insects got to do with it?' Joanna said.

'No, that's lepidometry,' Slider said.

'I'll take my ball away and go home,' Atherton warned.

'All right,' Slider said kindly. 'Are you telling us that Chattie Cornfeld had something to do with Cornfeld Chemicals?'

'I'm telling you,' Atherton said with dignity, 'that her father *is* Cornfeld Chemicals. He owns the thing. He started it, he runs it, he is the chairman and chief exec rolled into one.' He used his hands as a balance. 'Dad – Cornfeld Chemicals. Cornfeld Chemicals – Dad. Am I getting the idea across now?'

'You mean,' Joanna said gravely, 'she was *that* Cornfeld.'

'At last,' Atherton sighed, and topped up the glasses. 'Well, at least I've established that we've all heard of the company, even if we didn't pronounce its name right.'

'Heard of it, yes,' said Joanna. 'It's not exactly a household name but one comes across it. One knows it exists.'

'Those of us who are able to read further through the paper than the health and beauty hints,' said Atherton, risking his life, 'are aware that it is a small company, which nevertheless does some important research in its pharmaceutical division and has come up with some cracking new drugs from time to time. Coprylon, for one, which is used to treat epilepsy. And Nuskin, a sterile artificial skin used post-operatively.'

'But Chattie's mother said she didn't have anything to do with her father,' Slider said. 'How did his owning a chemicals company affect her?'

'I shall tell you,' said Atherton, magnificently. 'I had a very interesting talk with Jasper Stalybrass, who knew her pretty well.'

'The horn-player?' Joanna said. 'I know him. I've played with him on gigs over the years.'

'What did you think of him?' Atherton asked.

'A bit full of himself, like most horn-players, but okay. A good player. And good company.' She caught Atherton's look and realised what was wanted. 'I think he's all right, for what my opinion's worth. He came across as an honest bloke and I've never heard anything against him.'

'That's what I thought,' Atherton said. 'Anyway, he's been having a sort of affair with Chattie.'

'"Sort of"?' Slider queried, spreading duck pâté thickly over buttered bread. 'How can you sort of have an affair?'

'Be accurate, I said having a sort of affair.'

'All right, what's a "sort of" affair when it's at home?'

'He said it was like being good friends with sex added, but with no intention of getting any further entangled than they were.'

'You needn't say it as if it sounds like heaven,' Joanna said, with an edge.

Slider flung her a silencing glance and said, 'Okay, go on.'

'Well, over that time, they exchanged life stories, and he knew quite a bit about the Cornfeld ménage. Bolstered by a few dates out of *Who's Who*, I'm now in a position to give you...' He paused and then announced in American movie tones '... The Cornfeld Story: The Early Years.'

'Get on with it,' said Slider.

'Our story opens,' Atherton obliged, but in the same voice, 'in the small Midwest town of Enfield, Middlesex, England.'

CHAPTER NINE

Toby or Not Toby?

Chattie's father had been christened Heinrich. His parents had come over from Germany in 1936 when he was a year old and, having decided to settle permanently in England, they had changed his name to Henry.

The Cornfelds didn't have much money, but Henry was a bright child and ambitious, and he had supplemented his basic education with self-help and library books. His bent and his passion were both for the sciences. When he left school at fifteen he got a job as a laboratory assistant in a private school where, although the pay was poor, he could continue to breathe the fumes, so to speak. When he was twenty his father died, and his mother gave him the proceeds of the life assurance policy so that he could set up his own business.

'I got all this out of a morgue article – one of a series about self-made men,' Atherton said. 'Henry started in a small way with what he knew, supplying chemicals to school labs, and built up from there. Soon he was supplying university and hospital labs too, as a middle man, and then he started the manufacturing side. The thing really took off in the sixties, and he branched out into pharmaceuticals, where the rewards are so much greater.'

'The risks, too,' said Slider.

'Right. But he had the core business to fall back on, to fund the experimental stuff. Anyway, by the time he met Chattie's mother he was well entrenched and pretty well off.'

'So there was family money after all. But what about wife number one?' Slider asked, prompted by his tidy mind.

'I only got the bare facts about her from *Who's Who*. Name, Mary Rogers. He married her in 1960 when he was twenty-five and struggling, but by the time he divorced her he was rich and important and being invited places, so one can deduce that she didn't fit in any more.'

'So he ditched her,' Joanna said indignantly. It was amazing, Slider thought, how they always take the woman's part, even when it's a strange woman they've never met and never will.

'Presumably,' said Atherton. 'There was one daughter from the marriage, a girl called Ruth, born in 1962. He married Stella Smart in 1974. Chattie told Stalybrass that her father gave the first Mrs C the family semi in Enfield while he moved to a more upscale place in Hemel Hempstead with Mrs C number two, which was where Chattie was born in 1975.'

'And the third wife?'

'Ah, that's where all the acid creeps in. Apparently Stella Smart discovered that he was bonking his secretary and went completely spare. Considering she'd snatched him from wife number one, she shouldn't have been too surprised, but – according to Jasper, who gathered it from Chattie, who must have gathered it from her mother – she couldn't stand being superseded by a mere secretary. It was a cliché too far for her, and humiliating to have her husband prefer a common typist. So she confronted him, forced the issue and insisted on a divorce.'

'Now, why do you find that incredible?' Joanna asked. 'I can tell from your voice you think she ought to have kept her mouth shut and put up with it.'

'What I think or don't think has nothing to do with it,' Atherton said. 'But I suppose most women would want to hold on to the meal ticket, if he wasn't agitating to leave.'

'Most women? You really are a—'

'Can we get back to the story, please,' Slider said quickly. 'You two can fight later. I want to hear the end before I fall asleep.'

Atherton resumed. 'So, acrimonious divorce, and Daddy Cornfeld flew the coop and married the secretary. But it seems he was very attached to Chattie, who was a bright child and very clever, and he kept contact with her, and had her to stay in the even smarter house in High Wycombe he could now afford. And in spite of everything that Stella could do to turn her against him, Chattie remained very fond of her father, and was – so Jasper says – intensely proud of him. She was especially proud that he had started with nothing and worked his way up through his own efforts.'

'Ah,' said Slider, 'I'm beginning to understand something Jassy said.'

'About Chattie wanting to succeed in her business without help?' Atherton asked. 'Yes, I got that from Jasper, too. It was a bit of a theme with our Chattie. He said she was so keen to do it alone like him that she never told people whose daughter she was. Afraid people might do her favours on his account. It was a bit of a pillow-confession to Jasper, and she made him swear secrecy.'

'Yes, Mrs Hammick said she never talked about her father,' Slider remembered.

'She might also have been afraid people would tap her for money if they knew she had a rich dad,' Atherton said.

'Don't be cynical. But, look here,' Slider said, 'Jassy called Chattie a hypocrite because in fact she *did* receive money from her father. She said that Chattie was given lots of things while she, Jassy, got nothing.'

Atherton nodded. 'Yes, Jassy came up quite a bit in the conversation. Jasper had no time for her – called her a self-pitying little parasite and an inveterate ligger. He had a brush or two with her at Chattie's house. She was always borrowing, and when that wasn't enough she stole. Found her going through his wallet one day. He said Chattie was far too lenient with her. As to Chattie having everything and Jassy nothing, it seems that the bone of contention from Jassy's point of view was that Daddy Cornfeld gave each of them a lump sum when she reached seventeen. Chattie used hers to buy a one-bedroom flat in an up-and-coming part of Shepherd's Bush, which she sold in 1998 for a big profit. A very smart buy – it tripled in value. This happened to be just the time when Jassy was given her lump sum, so to start with she got it into her head that she hadn't been given as much as Chattie.'

'But—' Joanna began indignantly.

'I know,' Atherton anticipated, 'but with a chip as large as Jassy's, there's no room for logic or common sense. Anyway, Jassy blued her lump sum on a fancy sports car, which she wrapped round a lamp-post soon afterwards, having omitted to get insurance for it. Daddy sorted out the fine for driving without, but he was so furious with her he wouldn't give her the money to replace it, so Jassy was left with nothing but a feeling of resentment and a determination to get as much out of teacher's-pet Chattie as she could.'

There was a silence when he stopped talking. Joanna refilled the wine glasses and took some grapes. 'So,' she said at last, 'it explains how she got the house.'

'But not how she funded the lifestyle,' Atherton said. 'The income from her business wasn't enough. So we come back to the question: where did she get the rest of the money from? Did she deal coke? Did she accept "presents" from her many menfriends?'

'Code language for prostitution, I gather,' said Joanna.

'There are numerous other possibilities we haven't uncovered yet,' Slider said. 'It's all very interesting, but I'm not sure it gets us much further forrard. The question we come back to is who killed her, and why?'

Atherton called on Toby Harkness early on Saturday morning, to be sure of catching him in. He had a flat in Aynhoe Road, just off Brook Green, one of six in a small block that had been put up where a large house had been demolished in the council-vandalism days of the seventies. The block was showing its age, with cracks in the concrete facing, several slipped tiles on the roof and the windows in dire need of replacement. It was often a problem with such places, that they tended to be occupied either by the young or the old, neither of which groups was ever keen on spending money on communal upkeep.

There was an entry-phone, and Atherton buzzed long and hard, then waited, listening to a blackbird in a nearby plane tree trying to pretend this was countryside. He was about to ring again when there was a click and a rusty voice said, 'Who is it?'

'I'm Detective Sergeant Atherton from Shepherd's Bush police station. I'd like to have a little chat with you about Miss Cornfeld. Would you let me in, please, sir?'

There was a pause, and then the voice said, 'I don't—' and broke off in a bout of coughing.

'Press the buzzer, please, sir,' Atherton said. 'I can't discuss things through the intercom like this.'

There were some amplified clicks and bumps, and then the buzzer went off, and Atherton pushed the door. There were three flats to a floor, and Harkness's was upstairs. When he reached the top of the flight Atherton saw him at the door to his flat, holding it open. He was naked from the waist up, showing a rather undeveloped white torso, with a few dark, flat moles scattered here and there, and a hairless chest, hunched round at the moment as if its owner was feeling the cold. Below the waist he was crammed into a pair of tight jeans that looked rather the worse for wear, as if he hadn't been out of them for a few days. His feet were bare, his toenails dirty, and he stood on one leg and used the right foot to scratch the top of the left. His face was unshaven and bleary, his eyes red, his dark hair standing up in a mad bush, and even from the distance of six feet Atherton could smell the booze coming off him in waves.

'Mr Harkness?' Atherton said, not because he was in any doubt, but to get things moving.

'Yes,' he said. 'But I don't—' He broke off, and a sweat suddenly sheened his face, which had turned greenish white. 'Oh, God,' he said, hunching, and put his hand up to his mouth.

'Bathroom, quick,' Atherton barked, and caught the door as Harkness turned and fled. Atherton stepped in and shut the door behind him as the sounds of retching came from somewhere out of sight. The door opened straight into the living room, with the kitchen immediately on the right, and the bedroom and bathroom presumably down a small passage that led off beyond the kitchen. There was parquet flooring in the area just inside the door, which disappeared under fawn carpeting in the living room area, but it was neglected, very scratched and bereft of polish, yea, these many years, if Atherton was any expert. The air smelt stale, even leaving aside the fact that Harkness was evidently a smoker. A quick glance into the kitchen revealed a chaos of young epic proportions, with used plates and mugs piled everywhere along with fragments of food and empty takeaway cartons, some of which looked as though they needed carbon dating. The tiles on the floor were stained with food and grease and liberally sprinkled with crumbs, and the peel of a satsuma and a lone chip lay near the gas stove, mutely begging lenience.

The living room was likewise a mess of clothes, books and papers, used crockery and more empty food cartons, empty beer cans and overflowing ashtrays. The curtains were still drawn over the window, but inefficiently, so that sunlight was streaming in through a foot-wide gap and heating up the composite smells towards combustion point. Atherton went across, drew them back and fought the window open – the metal frame had warped – before he expired from lack of oxygen.

In the bathroom the sounds of vomiting had been super-seded by a lengthy micturition, then flushing, and now the trickle and splash of water being, he hoped, dashed on the face. Harkness reappeared at last, wiping his mouth, the hair round his face damp, missed drops and dribbles running down his chest.

'Sorry about that,' he croaked. He coughed long and hard, then resumed in a sort of gruff mumble, his eyes never meeting Atherton's, 'Bit of a heavy night last night. You know. Trying to cope. Not doing very well,' he added, with a deprecatory half-smile, which did not seem to know what to do with itself and wandered off his face as he looked around the room as if searching for something. 'Time is it?'

'It's a quarter to nine,' Atherton said. 'I'm sorry to call on you so early but I wanted to catch you before you went out. I wasn't sure if you were working today.'

'Not today,' Harkness mumbled. 'Maybe never work again.' He wandered into the living room and slumped on the sofa, his hands hanging uselessly between his legs.

Fried to the tonsils last night, Atherton thought. Slept on the sofa – passed out, rather – and still not fully sober. 'If I make you some coffee, do you think you'll keep it down?'

'Yeah. Thanks,' Harkness said, staring at the floor.

Atherton left him, and went, reluctantly, into the festering kitchen, where he unearthed and filled the kettle and switched it on. While he waited for it to boil, he tried to calculate from the debris how many days were represented by it. Chattie had been killed on Wednesday morning and Harkness would have heard about it, at the earliest, on Wednesday evening, if Marion had rung round straight away, or Thursday morning if not. Two and a half days at most. But the plates, mugs and cardboard cartons had been accumulating here for a lot longer than that. Either Harkness was congenitally untidy, or he had had something serious and depressing on his mind for the best part of two weeks. Atherton knew which option he'd like to go for.

He found instant coffee in a cupboard, washed a mug and spoon and, finding no tea towel he'd be willing to touch without protective clothing, sighed and dried them on his clean handkerchief. In the fridge there were horrors beyond description. Bung a fork of lightning through that lot, he thought, and you could start evolution all over again. There was a cardboard carton of milk but the contents were completely solid to the external touch so he didn't even bother to open it. Black would be better for him, anyway.

When he returned to the living room, Harkness was sitting in the same position but had recovered enough to light a cigarette, and the smoke was curling up into the bars of sunlight and wavering when it hit the air from the window.

'Coffee,' Atherton said, putting the mug down on the edge of the coffee-table in front of him.

'Thanks,' Harkness said. 'I'm sorry about . . .' He waved his hand, presumably to indicate the vomiting. 'Had a load on last night.'

'Just drink, was it?'

'Eh?'

'Or did you mix it? Speed, charlie, any little recreational helpers?'

'Drugs, you mean? No, I don't do drugs,' he said, and the indifference of his voice convinced. If Chattie had been selling, it was not to Toby Harkness.

'You've been depressed,' Atherton suggested, moving out of the way of the smoke, which always seemed to seek him out like a friendly cat when he was in the vicinity of a smoker.

'Yeah,' said Harkness, sinking lower in his seat, his chin slumping towards his chest. 'Well, you know. Christ, she's dead. What d'you think?'

'You were depressed before that, though. You've been unhappy for quite a while.'

Even this minimal sympathy brought tears to Harkness's eyes.

God, he was young, Atherton thought. The slight chubbiness of his face was a boy's, his self-obsession was a student's. He had no curiosity about Atherton or why he was here; he was thinking about his own sorrows, and as he thought, the tears oozed out and down his unshaven cheeks.

'I loved her. I would have died for her, she knew that.' He had a very slight Bristol accent, a rolling over of the vowels, which made him sound even younger than he was. 'But she kept pushing me away. And then she said she wouldn't see me again, except for business. How could I live like that, seeing her but never being allowed to touch her?'

'You and Chattie had an affair, didn't you?' Atherton said, as kindly as he could, given that everything about this young man irritated him. Harkness stubbed out his cigarette and, still breathing out the last mouthful of smoke, reached for another one and put it between his lips. Atherton watched him in amazement. How could he smoke when he depended on his lungs for his livelihood?

'It wasn't an affair. We were in love,' Harkness said. 'The first time I saw her, the first time I played with Baroque, I knew then. She was so lovely. The most beautiful girl I'd ever seen. I didn't believe at first anything could happen. I mean, not with me. I've never been very good with girls. I didn't dare ask her for ages. But I could see she was attracted to me. She always came over and talked to me. When we were in a group, she always sat by me, and was nice to me and made me laugh.'

Sorry for you, Atherton thought. Saw you were shy and tried to bring you out of yourself. He remembered Slider saying once that it was funny how often shy people turned out to be terribly conceited underneath. Harkness saw Chattie's kindness and took it for appreciation of his own fine worth.

'Then it sort of happened one day. We were doing a gig down in Hastings, at the White Rock, and we all stayed overnight, at this weird bed-and-breakfast place – all except Jasper, who stayed with a friend. Well, we had some drinks in Trish's room, and then went to bed. Chattie's room and mine were both on the top floor, and we went up the stairs together. We got to the top landing. She was laughing and suddenly it came over me in a wave and I just grabbed her

and kissed her. And she kissed me back. And then, I don't
know, we were, like, swept away by passion. We went into her
room and—'

He stopped, gazing down a long corridor at memory, his lips
parting in remembered rapture.

'It was wonderful,' he resumed at last. 'And the next day,
when we went back to London, I went to her house and we
made love all night. I told her I loved her. We talked about
marriage. I told her I wanted to spend the rest of my life with
her.'

I bet she was pleased to hear that, Atherton thought.

'It was wonderful at first. I didn't get to see as much of her
as I wanted, because she was often working, and I was too, and
it was hard to get our schedules together. But when we did get
together it was wonderful. Only she wanted me to keep it a
secret. She said it would upset the band if anyone knew about
us. I didn't see that. But she said there was a, like, dynamic,
about the group, and her and me being together would disturb
it. So I went along with it. Well, I thought, they'll know all right
when we get married.' He stopped and drew on his cigarette.

'Did she say she would marry you?' Atherton asked.

He scowled. 'Yes, she did,' he said defiantly. 'Afterwards she
said she never had, but I know what I know. I just don't know
what went wrong. I wanted to see her more often, that's all.
She said she couldn't manage it. She was busy. I said why didn't
we move in together, and then we could see each other all the
time? But she said no, and then she got cross with me for asking.
I said, I love you, and she said, I never asked you to. I mean,
what sort of a thing is that to say?'

'Terrible,' Atherton said, shaking his head sympathetically.

'I said, "I know you love me, why are you treating me like
this?" She said she couldn't see me any more. She said I was
too intense. "Well," I said, "if you love someone, you are intense,
aren't you?" I started to think she was seeing someone else,
but she said she wasn't – and, anyway, if she was too busy to
see me, how could she have had time for anyone else?'

What a plonker, Atherton thought with amazement.

'I told her I'd kill myself if she refused to see me again.
She got angry about that, and said it was blackmail, and I
said it wasn't, it was just that I loved her. How can love be

blackmail? Anyway, she said it would be a wicked waste of my talent if I were to kill myself. She said I was the best oboist she'd ever known. That's how I knew she still did love me, really. She wouldn't have said that if she didn't. I just don't understand why she broke it off.' He paused, smoking hard and slowly. His face darkened as he stared through the smoke at nothing. 'At the end, the last time I saw her, she said if I didn't leave her alone, she wouldn't see me or talk to me at all, not even at the band. She said she'd stop coming to any of the band things.' The tears that had subsided welled up again.

'This was in the pub, the Anchor, on Tuesday night?'

'Yeah,' he said, not interested in how Atherton knew. 'I'd been phoning her all day, but she was out, and when I tried her mobile it was on voice-mail. She always answered her mobile normally, so I knew she was avoiding me. So I sat in my car at the end of her road where I could see the house, so I'd know when she got home. And when she did, I rang her again and said I had to see her. I said I'd meet her in the Anchor. I told her if she wouldn't see me I'd cut my throat.'

'What did she say when you said that?'

'She just said, "No, you won't." But she sounded worried. Anyway, she said she'd see me for five minutes, at seven o'clock. When she came in, she was all smiling and lovely and so nice to me, just like she used to be, and I thought we could patch things up. She'd said five minutes but it was at least half an hour, so she must have been enjoying my company, mustn't she? But then she said this was the last time she'd see me alone, that she was serious, that there could be nothing more between us, that I must really leave her alone or she'd drop the band altogether and it'd be my fault. I couldn't believe it. So then I asked her, is there somebody else? And she looked surprised a bit, and then she said there was, and she laughed. She *laughed*!' He choked on his smoke. 'I almost hated her then.'

'Almost?' Atherton urged, but gently. This was promising stuff. But Harkness said no more. He smoked and brooded. 'Do you know who it was she was seeing?' he asked at last.

'Yeah,' said Harkness, his voice so low it almost went off the scale. 'I didn't then, but I found out. After she left the pub, I went back to my car, but I didn't drive away. I stayed watching her house. I was thinking I'd maybe give her time to calm down and then I'd go and talk to her again. But then after a bit I saw him arrive. He knocked at the door and she let him in and a minute later they both came out and walked off together. Arm in arm. And when she let him in, she kissed him. So then I knew.'

'Who was it?'

'*Jasper.*' It was almost a sob. 'How could she prefer him to me? I mean, he's nothing. He's just a horn-player. And he's never serious about anything. He wouldn't marry her. He was always having different girls, one-night stands. I knew he'd only end up hurting her. He'd break her heart. I couldn't stand that.'

Atherton almost held his breath. 'You couldn't stand to let her get hurt. So what did you do?'

'What *could* I do?' he said.

'Yes, what? A brave man would want to save her from that, at any price. Even if it meant—' He left a tempting space but Harkness did not respond. 'The thought of her having her heart broken by someone like Jasper – well, if it was me, I don't know what I'd do. It would be the worst thing of all. Worse even than—'

This time it worked. 'Yeah,' Harkness said. 'I thought that, too. I thought even death would be better than that.' He sighed tremulously, wiped his nose on the back of his hand, reached for another cigarette.

'So what did you do?' Atherton urged.

'I waited for ages, but they didn't come back. So I went home and got drunk.' He looked around him incuriously. 'I've been drunk pretty well ever since.'

'The next morning,' Atherton said, 'what did you do?'

'Do?' he said vaguely.

'You'd had all night to think it over, about you and Chattie and that man. You decided you had to do something – something drastic to save her.'

Now Harkness looked at him, his eyes widening slightly. 'What do you mean?'

'You thought it would be better, if you couldn't have her, that no-one should have her. You knew she went running in the park every day. You thought it would be the best thing for her as well as for you if she was at peace.'

He had cottoned on now. 'You think I killed her?'

'You had such good reason,' Atherton said soothingly.

'It was the Park Killer,' he said. 'It was in all the papers. It was a frenzied attack, like the other ones, those other girls he killed.'

'And where were you at eight o'clock that morning?'

'I was here, at home. I was in bed asleep. I didn't get up until nearly ten. I didn't know anything about it until Marion phoned me that night. How could you think I'd kill her? I loved her.'

'Love is sometimes the strongest reason. And you did say just now you thought death would be better.'

He stared a moment, and then said, 'No, I meant *my* death. I thought I'd sooner be dead than see her with Jasper.'

And yet, of course, Atherton thought, Chattie's death would yield the same result, with the added advantage of his being around to mourn her properly. And a man in bed, alone, has no witness to his alibi.

The CID room was full, with the firm at their desks and the extra bods from uniform they had been loaned lining the walls. Most people had plastic cups of coffee from the machine or styrofoam cups of something better from the sandwich shop by the market, and one or two had bacon rolls by way of breakfast from the same source. McLaren had two. Some were reading papers. The sun was shining away maddeningly outside the window, eager to remind everyone that it was Saturday, when ordinary mortals washed the car, had a pint down the local and watched the footy.

There was a low buzz of chat. Hart had pulled up a chair to Atherton's desk. 'So what happened about that bird you were dating, then?' she asked. 'Sue? I thought you two were serious. Some said you were gonna get married.'

'Which some was that?' Atherton asked, his nostrils flaring as he tried to work out what her perfume was.

'Oh, stuff gets around,' Hart said airily. 'So, what happened?'

'She dumped me,' Atherton said, going for the sympathy vote. He looked full into Hart's eyes with a tragic air. 'Hell of a shock to the system, I can tell you. First knock-back since I joined this firm, not counting Norma.'

'What are you saying about me?' Swilley said sharply, catching her name. She had been trying not to eavesdrop, but Atherton had meant her to hear that bit.

'He says you wouldn't have 'im, Norm,' Hart said cheerfully.

'I'd rather be the love-toy of a Greek army battalion,' said Swilley, going back to her paper.

'Actually,' Atherton said loftily, 'Ms Swilley doesn't have what I want in a woman.'

'What's that?' said Hart. 'Low standards?'

'God, you're funny,' Atherton said. 'So, what are you doing tonight?'

'Don't tell me you've got no date?'

'I thought I'd give you first refusal. How would you like to have rampant sex at my place?'

'Well, I dunno,' Hart said, pondering. 'I really ought to get home. I've got a banana going black. I shouldn't leave it alone for too long.'

McLaren called across, 'Oy, Jim, I should watch it if I was you. Yvonne Collins is after your blood.'

'I don't know how he's got the energy,' Mackay said wonderingly. 'I mean, he's not as young as he was. Must be the Viagra.'

'Here,' said McLaren, 'did you hear about the load of Viagra got nicked? They're looking for a hardened criminal.'

There were groans. 'Old one, Maurice!'

'Got whiskers on it.'

But McLaren looked round grinning anyway, pleased with himself.

'Who's Yvonne Collins?' Hart asked.

'Don't tell me you haven't heard about her?' Mackay said. 'She hadn't been here five minutes before—'

Slider walked in at that point. 'There's so much gossip in here, you should all have dryers on your heads,' he said. 'Can we settle down, please? There's a lot to get through.'

Quiet descended, and between them Slider and Atherton reported the new information gained from Jasper, Jassy and Toby.

At the end of it, Swilley said, 'So it looks as if we've got two possible directions. There's Darren Barnes and the coke connection, and there's Toby Harkness and the jealousy bit.'

'Harkness is barely a suspect,' Atherton said. 'All we've got against him is motive.'

'And no alibi,' Mackay reminded them.

'Most of the world's got no alibi,' Slider said. 'However, it is such a good motive that I think we ought to look into his background, in case he has any record of violence; and see if we can get a look round his house, to see if there are any bloodstained clothes or knives. But at the moment, Darren Barnes looks a lot more tasty.'

'Right,' said Mackay, 'and the drugs thing makes more sense. The way I see it, Barnes and the victim are in business together. He supplies her with a big bag of white. Gets his girlfriend to drop it at the house. Meets her on Wednesday to collect the cash. Only she's not got it for some reason, or she tries to stiff him, or they have a row about something else, I dunno. Anyway, he offs her and has it away on his tiny toes. Only he doesn't want to leave all that good charlie going to waste at the victim's house. So he goes back home that night and tells his girlfriend to go and see if it's still there – he can't go, you see, in case the place is being watched. She comes back saying it's no go, there's a copper on the door, and he takes fright, belts her one for good luck and scarpers, and he hasn't been seen since.'

He looked round for approval at the end of this narrative, and Slider could see there was plenty of assent in the faces round the wall. It was the sort of simple tale they could all appreciate. They had seen it a dozen times before – fallings out among drug-dealers were about the commonest cause of death on the streets.

'So, do you reckon his girlfriend was in on it?' McLaren asked Mackay.

'No, the way I reckon, he couldn't have got her to go back there if she'd known anything about it. When he got home he must have realised she didn't know her sister was dead yet, so it was worth a try to get the charlie back – especially if the reason he killed her was that she hadn't paid him for it.'

'But why wouldn't he have gone straight round there after killing her?' Hollis asked. 'That would have been the safest time. He could have taken her door keys and let himself in.'

'Maybe he had blood on him,' Mackay said.

'Or maybe he had to establish an alibi,' McLaren put in.

'Some alibi, that no-one knows about,' someone at the back muttered.

'Maybe he just didn't think of it,' Swilley said. 'He doesn't sound as if he was a practised killer. He probably couldn't think of anything but putting as much distance as possible between him and the park.'

'It's a nice scenario,' Slider said, 'but you're forgetting one thing.'

His eye caught that of Hart, and she continued for him, as if he had asked for suggestions. 'She wasn't stabbed to death.'

'In Doc Cameron's opinion,' Atherton said.

'And if she was drugged,' Hart continued, unchecked, 'then it was premeditated, not the result of a sudden quarrel.'

'Right,' said Slider.

'But, boss,' Hart went on, 'even if it was premeditated, it don't mean it couldn't've been Darren. Maybe he didn't trust her, or she was threatening to cut 'im out, or shop 'im. There could've been a stack o' reasons why he'd want her dead. Maybe even Jassy was in on it. We know she was wicked jealous of Chattie, plus she thought she'd been hard done by. She could've got Darren to kill Chattie for her.'

'Why would he agree?'

'Because he's on her side. And there'd be money to come, maybe.'

'Why did he hit her, then?' Swilley asked.

'To make it look as if she wasn't in on it,' Hart suggested. 'She's staying put, and the police are bound to come and interview her. It takes the suspicion off her.'

'And puts it smack on him. She was pretty quick to finger him, by all accounts,' said Swilley.

'Maybe she got scared,' Hart said.

'This is all very well,' Slider said, 'but if Darren did kill Chattie for whatever reason – and I admit he sounds stupid enough to try to fake the Park Killer MO and think it would fool us – where did he get the barbiturates from?'

They all seemed to think this was a foolish question. 'He's in the biz, boss,' Hart answered for them, at last. 'He'd know where to lay his hands on the right tackle. Blimey, you can get drugs, guns and explosives on the Internet wiv a credit card these days.'

'Hmm,' said Slider. 'Well, I agree with you at least that Darren is the best suspect we've got, and that efforts should be put into finding him.' He looked across at Hollis. 'Follow up the Manchester lead, and find out from Brixton who his associates were and get after them. I leave that to you. And the other thing we must keep on with,' he addressed the room at large, 'is identifying Running Man, and finding someone who saw the face of the man seen talking to Chattie by the shrubbery – we'll call him Standing Man. Also, if Chattie really was selling drugs, she must have had customers. Find them, if they exist. Follow up on Toby Harkness. What else?'

'Find out where Chattie was on Tuesday?' Swilley suggested.

'Yeah, and what this DC 10 malarkey is,' said Hart. 'That's bugging me.'

'Well, it may or may not be important where she was on Tuesday, but I agree we ought to know. Try her friends and contacts, see if it makes sense to any of them.'

'If only the killer would use her mobile,' Swilley said wistfully.

'If the wooden horse of Troy had foaled, horses today would be cheaper to feed,' Atherton said.

'Eh?' said Swilley.

'It's the epitome of pointless speculation.'

'I wish you came with sub-titles,' she complained.

CHAPTER TEN

Outrageous Fortune

As Slider was about to return to his own office, Porson appeared at its communicating door with the CID room, and beckoned. 'A word,' he said.

Slider gave him one. 'Sir.' Obedient to Porson's gesture, he shut the door behind him.

'I've had one Henry Cornfeld on the dog. The *grand fromage* of Cornfeld Chemicals. Business typhoon, baron of industry, what you will. VIP.'

'Ah,' said Slider.

'You didn't tell me the victim was one of *those* Cornfelds.'

'We've only just worked that out, sir. The mother was not entirely frank with us. She didn't let on who he was, and told us Chattie had nothing to do with her father. She said she didn't know where he was living.'

Porson waved all that away. 'He wasn't best pleased we hadn't told him.'

'*I*'m surprised he didn't contact us himself. He must have seen it on the news,' Slider countered.

'Ah, well, he's been out of the country for a week. Just back from the States this morning on the red-eye, and various members of his staff all thought one of the others had told him. Carpetings all round.'

'It's a bit much blaming us, then,' Slider complained.

'Oh, don't worry, I told him the circs, identification-wise, and he understood. He's not a raging ecomaniac out to see heads roll. Upset, more than anything, that he was out of the country. Says if he'd had any inclination anything would happen to her blah-di-blah. As if he could have stopped it – but that's a father's paternal feelings for you. Anyway, he wants someone to go and talk to him, and you're it.'

'Has he got anything useful to tell us?'

Porson rolled his eyes. 'I don't know. I didn't give him the first degree over the phone.'

'It's just that there's a lot to do and I don't want to waste time hand-holding. If that's all he wants, we can send him a PC. Preferably a female one.'

'No *bon*, Slider. You're the persona gratis,' Porson said. 'You don't have to be all day about it. Look on it as thinking time. Little trip out into the country, lovely weather for it. And you never know, he might have a tale to tell.'

Slider thought, on the contrary, that he did know. Henry Cornfeld didn't need to have a tale to tell. Like the congenial dustman, he had friends in high places.

It certainly was a lovely day, and as he headed out on the A41 Slider thought what a pity it was that Joanna was working. Her company in the car and a pub lunch – even if a snatched one – would make it all worth while. The Cornfeld mansion was in a village called Frithsden, not far from Hemel Hempstead. So Henry had returned to Stella Smart country in his ripe years, Slider thought.

He wondered at the magnate's coming down to the country after an absence of a week rather than powering his way through his office finding dereliction on all sides. And, Slider reflected, he hadn't threatened Porson or thrown his weight around. He obviously hadn't been to the right school of tycoon paranoia.

The country round Frithsden was lovely: rolling hills, deep lanes, trees, hedges, beech woods. There were fields of green wheat and fields of brown cows – it somehow comforted Slider to see that farming still went on, even so close to London – and the froth of elder dripped petals onto the kex and moon daisies in the lush verges. God, England was beautiful! he thought. It took him three passes through the village (with a longing look at an ancient village pub with chairs and tables set outside) before he found the almost hidden entrance, because trailers of traveller's joy had hung down and roadside grasses, bartsia and mallow had grown up to cover the nameplate. But

apart from this obscurity, there were no other security measures, no cameras and electronic gates but just an open, if narrow,
driveway bending round some mature rhododendrons to the
out-of-sight house.

The house turned out to be mid-Victorian church gothic, and
charmingly appropriate, Slider thought, for a self-made mogul,
given that it had probably originally been built for one such.
An ancient yellow Labrador was lying in the sun outside the
arched oak front door, and banged its tail on the gravel in
welcome as Slider got out of the car, but indicated that it was
far too fat and old to get up. Slider stooped and scratched its
head, noting that the front door stood open, and wondering
again at the lack of security. No-one was in sight, so he lifted
and dropped the cast-iron knocker, which must have weighed
ten pounds, then spotted a bell almost hidden by the wisteria
and rang that.

A young woman appeared, clacking down the decorated tiles
of the hall on impractical high heels. She had a fine figure well
displayed by her tight toreador pants and sleeveless, low-cut
top, dyed blonde hair and a lot of gold jewellery.

'Detective Inspector Slider?' she said. 'I'm Kylie, Mr Cornfeld's
companion.'

At last, thought Slider, a cliché I can recognise. She even
said, 'Would you like to come this way?' and walked off with
a wiggling rump. Slider repressed the Carry On response and
followed her into the cool, lofty hall.

'He's in the morning room,' she said, showing Slider through
an open door. The room was large and light and airy, with a
twelve-foot-high ceiling and fine pieces of furniture thoughtfully
placed and gleaming with care. There was a vast Victorian-
mediaeval stone fireplace, and in the hearth an arrangement of
blue and white delphiniums in a Chinese vase was spitting
petals onto the glazed tiles. Cornfeld was sitting at a small table
by open French windows onto a garden, reading one of a stack
of newspapers.

'Can I get you coffee or anything?' Kylie asked.

'No, thank you very much,' Slider said.

She beamed and withdrew, and Cornfeld stood up and came
across to shake his hand. He was not a tall man, and though
not fat he had an elderly thickness through his body – Slider

had worked out that he was sixty-eight – but his movements were easy and alert, and there was firmness in the lines of his face and the grip of his hand. This was a man in his power, not ready yet to babble of green fields, even if he liked inhabiting them. His face was tanned, his white hair thick and elegantly cut. Despite being at home he was dressed in a suit of admirable cut and beautiful cloth, the style a nicely judged balance of modernity and dignity; but his tie was black, and he did not smile, though Slider guessed that charm would always have been one of his tools in securing his advantage in the world. And there was something in his eyes that Slider recognised, the blankness, the almost wandering look of shock.

'Thank you for coming,' said Cornfeld. 'I suppose you think it's a great nuisance, when you are so busy, to trek all the way out here just to see me. But I had to see you myself, and hear for myself what's been happening.' His voice was strong, the accent neutral, the delivery rather clipped, as though he expected words to do an efficient job like everyone else. But as he said the next word, his voice thickened and wavered, and Slider saw that he was close to tears. 'Chattie – was my favourite child. I know one isn't supposed to have favourites, but she was always the pick of the bunch. So bright, so quick, so clever. I need to know – I need very badly to know – who has done this thing.'

He drew Slider to a chair at the table, and sat himself, folding his hands and pointing his face and his attention straight at him. So, Slider thought resignedly, it is just hand-holding. There was a strong resemblance between Chattie and her father. He had only seen Chattie dead, of course, but the shape of the face was the same, the nose, the chin; there were the blue eyes, too, and he could imagine that the thick wavy hair had once been gold. In Cornfeld *père* he could see what Chattie might have had in life, the sharp intelligence, the firm resolve. He wished again, strongly, that he had known her, and resented less the time he was being forced to give to her progenitor.

Assembling his thoughts into order, he told Cornfeld about the manner of Chattie's death, and what they had found out so far. Only once did Cornfeld turn his face away and pass his hand over his eyes; otherwise he listened with an almost audible whirring of the mental motor. At the end of his exposition,

Slider asked the usual question, 'Do you know of anyone who might have wanted to hurt your daughter?'

'No,' he said at once. 'I think she was universally beloved, or as nearly so as anyone ever is. She was a happy, friendly, funny girl, warm-hearted and generous. Too generous, at times. I can't think what grudge anyone could have against her. If it had been the work of a madman, a serial killer, it would have made more sense to me.'

'I'm sorry to ask this, but what about your business – rivals and so on? Could somebody have been striking at you through her?'

He shook his head slowly. 'Naturally, I've been thinking about that.' The idea seemed to agitate him and he became less coherent than before. 'But there's nothing – I can't imagine – there's no situation I can think of where this would make sense. And surely, if I were the real target, something would have been said – some note, phone call, threat? Why kill her to get at me, and then not be sure I knew? No, it doesn't make sense.' He passed his hand over his eyes again, and said, 'It is something I have thought about over the years. Not in terms of business rivalry, but simply money – kidnap, you know. But I am not so fabulously wealthy, and I've never indulged any of the children, or encouraged them to think they had expecta-tions. I don't believe the younger two even spoke about being my daughters. The parting with their respective mothers,' he added, 'was not friendly. I suppose by now you know things like that?'

Slider nodded.

'Marriage has always been a toll on my time and energy, which I could ill spare from my business,' Cornfeld said. 'Thank God for modern times! Now I don't need to marry them. I can have all the female company I want without repercussions.'

At that moment they were interrupted by another female entering the room – a very different proposition, this one, from Kylie. She was a very elderly lady, with such a look of frailty Slider almost expected the light to shine through her: thin as a rail, a halo of silver-white hair like spindrift around her face, cheekbones you could cut yourself on. She was dressed in an expensive knitted two-piece of brown jersey over a white lace blouse, high-collared with a cameo brooch at the throat, and glossy brown court shoes. But despite the thinness and age, her eyes were bright and her gait steady.

Cornfeld rose at the sight of her. 'Inspector Slider, my mother,' he said.

Mrs Cornfeld inclined her head. 'Inspector.' And then, to her son, 'I came to tell you there is a telephone call from Brussels. Kylie is speaking on the other line.'

'Ah!' Cornfeld turned to Slider. 'I must take this. It's a very important call. I'm sorry.'

'I will entertain the inspector while you are away,' said Mrs Cornfeld. There was no German accent after all these years, only a certain precision about the consonants and a purity of the vowel sounds that might betray a foreign origin. 'Go, my dear. They are waiting on the line. Hurry.'

Slider thought, with an inward smile, that, like his own father, she had not got used to the cheapness of international calls these days. Cornfeld went out, and Mrs Cornfeld walked across to the table by the window and allowed Slider to pull out a chair for her. When she was seated she waved him graciously to his own chair and said, 'It will be a long call. It is the European drugs regulatory authority. We have something quite new coming out. When Henry went away to America he was so excited about it, he looked ten years younger. Now, today, he hardly cares. This has been a great blow to him, a great blow. I would not be surprised if he gave up and retired now, though a week ago he was fit to go on fifteen years more. But this has taken the heart out of him. I truly believe Chattie was the only thing he ever loved, apart from his business. He has always been a driven man; she was his one human weakness. It was I who gave her the nickname Chattie, did you know that?'

'No, I didn't.'

'Henry would not tell you that. Men never know any of the important things in life, only the serious ones.' She looked at him intently. 'I suppose *you* must be interested in minutiae, however, because of your job. It must make you a uniquely satisfying companion for a woman. Are you married?'

He disliked personal questions, but it was impossible to snub such a venerable lady. 'I am – engaged.'

'How nice. I hope you will be very happy. Henry has not been fortunate in his wives, but then, did he deserve to be?

Now he does not think of marriage again. It is better as it is. You have seen Kylie?' The eyes were cataloguing him. 'I can see your thoughts. But, really, she is a dear creature. Like the hedgehog of legend, she knows one thing. I like her very much, and Henry cannot hurt her because she knows exactly what he wants her for.'

Slider could not think of anything to say, and cleared his throat noncommittally.

'Am I being indiscreet?' she said. 'But surely that must be a boon to you, when people tell you what they ought not.'

Slider would not look at his watch, but there was a clock on a table behind the old lady and he allowed his eyes to slip quickly there and back. Not so quickly, however, that she did not note his change of focus.

'You must be very busy,' she said coolly.

'I'm sorry. I didn't mean to be rude.'

'No, no, I understand. And you should be busy, trying to find out who killed my Chattie,' Mrs Cornfeld said, and a world of grief came into her face. 'At my age, one gets used to losing people. Almost everyone I ever cared for has died. But I don't think I can ever get over her death. Do you have any idea who killed her?'

'Not yet. We have some leads to follow, but nothing definite. We think it must have been someone who knew her.'

'Yes, I suppose that is the case with most murders.'

'Were you and Chattie very close?' Slider asked. Might as well make the best of it, he thought. 'Did you see her often?'

'Oh, yes. I loved her dearly and she was very attentive. Once a week at least. We had wonderful conversations. I truly believe she told me everything. She had an unhappy childhood in many ways, but I hope I was able to be an element of stability in it.'

'Tell me about that,' Slider invited.

She looked at him consideringly. 'I go a little way further back first. So that you understand Henry a little.'

Slider settled in for the long haul.

'First, Henry married Mary. She was the daughter of friends of ours in Enfield, a nice girl but plain, and five years older than him. She was thirty by then and "on the shelf" – that horrid phrase. This was – oh – 1960, I suppose. Girls then still did not have careers. They went to school, sometimes they had a little job for a year or two, and then they got married. So Mary was – what shall I say? – not useless, exactly, but surplus to requirements.'

'And Henry felt sorry for her?'

The almost transparent eyebrows shot up. 'Sorry for her? Certainly not. He was engaged in building up his business – going through a crucial stage, trying to set up the manufacturing side. It meant much work, long hours, many difficulties, living on his nerves. He had no time for feelings, for sentiment.'

'So why did he marry her?'

She looked faintly triumphant at having forced him to ask. 'He wanted a housekeeper. He was too busy to cook his own meals and wash his own clothes, and he was not making enough yet to be able to employ servants. The only practical solution was to marry. Also, if he married, he would be able to have sex when he wanted it, without payment and without risk. Do I shock you? No, of course not. You understand the world. So, Mary was available, with the added advantage that she wouldn't have to be wooed. Henry had no time then for wooing. All he had to do with Mary was to ask.'

'Didn't you try to dissuade him?'

'Good heavens, why should I? Mary was no worse off as his wife than living at home with her parents. She was probably happy at first, relieved not to be a spinster. But Henry was not home much, and when he was, I doubt he ever talked to her. She was thrilled when she found she was to have a baby. Henry was not. He was taken aback. It was nuisance and expense. His home comforts were disrupted. And then it turned out to be a girl, not even a son he could leave his business to.'

'That was Ruth?'

She nodded. 'Poor child, she had the misfortune to be just like her mother – plain and dull. Henry could never be interested in her. And as his business grew, he began to move in different circles. Mary was no longer a suitable wife. He needed a hostess, someone who would sparkle in company. At a reception one day he met Stella, and thought how smart and clever she was. So he left Mary and married Stella.'

'And Ruth?'

'He did what he thought was right by her. He paid for her to go to a very good boarding school. He wanted her to have an education and the possibility of a career. And in case the career didn't work out, he thought it would give her polish so she could make a good marriage. But polish didn't take on her. It only taught her to be resentful, seeing what all the other girls had. For a dull girl, she has a surprising capacity for anger – the slow, smouldering sort. Henry left Mary enough to live on, and a perfectly good house, but Ruth saw the way he lived with Stella, the parties, the important guests, the clothes – Stella was always a clothes horse – and thought she and her mother had been hard done-by.'

'Did Ruth make a good marriage?'

'Better than she might have expected. Henry practically arranged it. A young man called David Cockerell who was up and coming in the company. Ruth thought he was the bee's knees – handsome, charming, bound to get ahead. Besides, she'd have done anything to get out of working for a living, which she thought degrading. She'd obeyed Henry's wishes and studied chemistry at school, but she hadn't the intellect to go far. She ended up as an assistant in a hospital pharmacy – couldn't pass the exams to become a pharmacist herself. So David came as a saviour to her. As for David, he thought Ruth would be a good handle on Henry's wealth. And Henry thought David might be a right-hand man for him, take the place of a son in the business. But he soon discovered David's limitations. He was handsome and charming, but nothing more – though he's done well enough for himself on charm alone. But he let Henry down very badly. I suppose he felt he wasn't being appreciated enough, or advancing in the company quckly enough, because he went off and joined GCC – the Global Chemical Company – where he could have a big desk and an expense account and a pension fund. Henry was furious and for a time he wouldn't have David in the house, which of course spoiled things as far as Ruth was concerned. I patched things up, for appearances' sake. God knows, at this distance, why we care about such things, but I did, though I don't think I ever made much difference to the way Ruth felt. To be fair to David, I think he really does admire Henry. They get on all right when David visits him on business. But Ruth only sees the difference in their lifestyle and Henry's. And so we come to Stella and Chattie,' she said, with a twink-ling look at Slider. 'You see, you needed to know the state of play at the time.'

'You must tell the story in your own way,' Slider said neutrally.

'Be sure that I shall,' said Mrs Cornfeld. 'You are a good listener, young man, and I don't have many opportunities to talk without interruption.'

Slider had not been called 'young man' for a long time. 'Please continue,' he said.

'Well, Henry and Stella were happy at first, being very social together and having dinner parties and being important. Stella was happy when her picture was in the paper, and she thought all the new contacts she was making would advance her writing career. Have you read any of her books?'

'I flicked through one,' Slider said, not sure whether he was supposed to admire them or not.

Not, it turned out. 'That is all you need to do. All surface and no substance – nothing of worth in them from beginning to end – like Stella herself. But they might have gone on being more or less contented if she had not found herself pregnant. Unlike Mary she was furious. She had never wanted children and it threatened to ruin her carefully planned life as well as her figure. Henry was moderately pleased, however. He thought he was fond of Stella, and he was more secure now, better off, so he didn't fear the financial consequences. He thought he might quite like to have a son to boast about to his business acquaintances. But of course it was another girl.' She sighed, but it was a sigh of pleasure this time.

'Chattie was a pure delight from the beginning. She seemed born to smile. Henry adored her, and almost forgot he had wanted a boy, especially when she turned out clever as well as pretty. She had a very masculine grasp of intellectual things – and quite a way with machinery too. He taught her to drive when she was only twelve, on a disused airfield. Anyway, things were very happy for a while. But the business was going through another expansion, and Henry was away from home a lot, and Stella didn't like being left behind. She was from an old county family, and she felt she had lifted Henry up to a better social class by marrying him. When she didn't get her share of the parties and being in the papers, she resented it. The last straw was when he went to a reception at 10 Downing Street as a Giant of Industry, or some such nonsense, and she found out that he could have taken her with him. Shortly after that she found that he was having an affair with his secretary and she threw him out; but that was only the excuse. It was Downing Street that did it. She never forgave him for that.'

'And he married the secretary?' Slider said, to get her along.

'Susan Hatter, her name was. He wouldn't have married her, except that she got herself pregnant and he was in the news quite a lot and he thought it would look bad. It was another daughter, of course – Jasmine. Oh, that girl!' She gave an exasperated roll of the eyes. 'He bought a house in High Wycombe and installed Susan there with the child, and by now he could afford staff so it didn't matter that Susan hadn't the first idea of how to run a house or host a dinner party.'

'And what about Stella and Chattie?'

'Stella kept the house – the houses Henry leaves scattered behind him! – and Henry paid her alimony, of course, so she ought to have been all right. But all right was not what Stella thought she was owed. She would have kept Chattie away from Henry if she could, to punish him, but he had visitation rights. And of course he was rich, and Stella loved money. So Chattie went to visit. She loved her father obsessively, and was heartbroken when he left. She'd have been about five or six. He had her to stay whenever he could, and visited her at school, and they were always the best of friends. He arranged her education, and as she grew up she became very like a son to him, with her cleverness and her masculine mind and her determination. They were very close.

'Well, the marriage to Susan was always a mistake and it didn't last, though he was away so much it didn't seem necessary for him to divorce her at once. When the time came, he took charge of everything. Susan didn't want a divorce at all, but she was a very weak-minded woman and easy to bamboozle. He sold the High Wycombe house and bought this one, and moved Susan and Jassy into a small house in St Albans, gave them enough to live on, and forgot about them.'

'And Chattie?'

'Oh, he went on seeing Chattie. When he bought this place I came to live here to run it for him, so it was easier, because we could pretend to Stella she was coming to see me rather than him. Once Chattie was eighteen she could do as she liked, though she pretended for her mother's sake she never saw Henry.

Poor Stella fell on very hard times. She had always been fond of gambling, and after Henry went, she turned to it for solace, I suppose. She was a hard drinker, too, and she liked the high life, and expensive clothes, and when she found she couldn't afford it all, she had to attach herself to really very unsatisfactory men to make up the difference. In the end, Henry refused to pay her debts, so she had to sell the house and move into a horrid little box and pay them off. It's another thing she'll never forgive him for.'

'She told me she had always paid her own way in life,' Slider said.

Mrs Cornfeld chuckled. 'Yes, Stella would like everyone to believe she owed Henry nothing and he owed her everything. She's a woman who lives in a world of make-believe. What she wants to be true, is true.'

It explained a lot, Slider thought. 'And Chattie went to music college,' he said.

'Yes. That was a disappointment to Henry. He liked music but couldn't see it as a career. But when she finished college she decided she didn't have the talent to go to the top, and she didn't want to be second-rate – which was an attitude he *could* understand. So she did an apprenticeship in the commercial side of the music business, thinking she might be an agent. And then she had the idea for her own business.'

'Was he pleased about that?'

'Oh, yes, on the whole. He didn't see that it would ever amount to anything, but he thought the experience could be applied to some other field later on. He assumed she would not be content with a small business, though I think he may have misunderstood her there. Chattie cared about other things than money and success. Anyway, he encouraged her and believed in her. He was only sorry she wouldn't let him give her money to set it up. She said, "You built up your business from nothing, and so will I." I pointed out to her that in fact I had given Henry two thousand pounds to set up; and she said that he had given her a hundred thousand when she was seventeen, so it came to the same thing.'

'Did he never give anything to the other girls?'

'He gave Ruth a lump sum when she was married. And he gave Jassy money all the time. She's a bad lot, that one. The

Lord knows how she gets through so much money. Apart from the car she ruined, I don't know what she spends it on. Drugs, I suppose. After the car, Henry told her no more, enough is enough. But I suspect that cheques get posted off every week or so, after one of her impassioned phone calls. The difference from Chattie could not be greater. She invested the money Henry gave her in property and shares and turned it to good account. He was so proud of her.'

'You mentioned drugs?'

The face became stern. 'Jassy turned up here one day very much the worse for wear. I was shocked. Young people getting drunk now and then is natural, I can understand it, but not this other thing. Thank God Henry wasn't here. I sent her away, told her never to come here like that again.'

'Does Chattie take drugs?'

'No,' Mrs Cornfeld said, shocked. 'She hates them as I do. She hardly even drinks, just wine with meals. She says she hates the feeling of not being in control.'

'We found a large quantity of cocaine in her house. More than one person would take. The sort of quantity a person might have if they were supplying it to others.'

She stared a moment, and then laughed. 'Oh, ludicrous! You thought my Chattie was a drug-dealer? No, no, put it out of your head. If there were drugs in the house, it was Jassy or one of her friends who put them there. I know Chattie's mind on the subject. You see . . .' she hesitated, and then went on in a low voice '. . . You see, there was a time when Stella was smoking marijuana. I think she may have tried other things as well. It was when Chattie was, oh, fourteen or fifteen, and away at school. Sometimes she came home and found Stella the worse for wear, and it shocked her very much. But she never told Henry, so please do not you, either. Poor child, so many secrets she had to keep, holding her tongue when her mother abused her father, keeping her mother's exploits from her father. Chattie knew about the other men, you see, Stella's other men, and if Henry had found out, he could have stopped her alimony. So Chattie was caught between two hard places, poor child.'

'Did Chattie never want to get married?'

'It was the thing that made me most sad, that Chattie would never fall in love. I suppose, after her mother's behaviour, and seeing how her father had gone on, one wife after another and then all the women he has had since, she felt that marriage could never work. And she loved Henry so much. When Henry asked her if there was anyone, she always said, "Only you, Papa." She couldn't take young men seriously. They had to match up to her father and, of course, they never did. I think,' she added, with a world of sadness, 'she would have found someone one day, when she was older, maybe when Henry was dead. But now she never will have the chance. She was a girl with so much love to give, and no-one to give it to – not the right one, anyway. Maybe that's why she was so patient with Jassy. Too much love to keep to herself.' She turned her head away towards the garden, where birds were making cheerful noises in the bushes and trees. 'Who could kill such a girl? So much life, so much love, all gone. Snuffed out. It shouldn't be so easy.'

Slider left a small silence for her, and then said, 'There is one more thing I'd like to ask you, if you don't think it an impertinence.'

She sighed, and turned her head back, ready to do her duty. 'What is it? About money, I suppose?'

'Why do you think that?' Slider was intrigued.

'It is the obvious thing. Henry is a rich man. You want to know how he leaves his estate.'

'Well, yes. In case there might be a motive that way for removing Chattie.'

'Removing! Such a word! But Henry has never told anyone, not even me, who he means to leave things to. He says he doesn't want anyone to have reason to wish him dead.'

'Has he made a will?'

'I don't know. If he has, he keeps it secret.' She gave a snort of laughter. 'Perhaps all will go to Kylie.'

'I believe Cornfeld Chemicals is a public company. Do any of the family hold shares?'

'Oh, yes. When we floated, I and each of the children had ten per cent, and Henry kept twenty. That way the family kept overall control. That was before David left to join GCC, of course, otherwise he would never have given Ruth any. When that happened Henry bought another share, just to be on the safe side. Of course, I always let Henry exercise my vote. He knows what's best for the company. I would not think of anything else – unless it was a matter of principle, but since I brought him up, I should hope his principles are the same as mine.'

Slider smiled at her little joke, and at that moment the willowy Kylie reappeared, with a professional smile that was at war with her attempt to convey heartfelt regret.

'Oh, Inspector Slider, Mr Cornfeld is very sorry, but his call has taken longer than he expected, and now he has to go straight out to a meeting. He sends his regrets, and his thanks for your time in coming here.'

'Oh, really, how deplorable not to come himself. And I was just saying that I brought him up!' Mrs Cornfeld said lightly. 'Kylie dear, you must tell him when you see him that I am very cross with him. Now, Inspector, won't you stay for lunch with me, to make your long journey worthwhile?'

Slider was already on his feet. 'You are most kind, ma'am, but I really have to get back.'

'Yes, of course, what was I thinking? I have enjoyed so much talking to you that I was forgetting.' The light went out of her face and her eyes became bleak. 'You have important work to do. You must find who did this thing. I only wish that there was still capital punishment in this country. I am not a vindictive person, but I would like whoever did this to Chattie to die,' she said seriously. 'I would like very much that they should die.'

CHAPTER ELEVEN

Barn to be Wild

'Exciting things have happened here while you've been away,' Atherton said, sitting catty-corner to Slider at the canteen table, his legs elegantly crossed, his fingers drumming lightly on the table top in a way that told Slider it was not random but the accompaniment to some music going on inside his head. Joanna did it too, on the dashboard, when he was driving. Atherton was one of those rare individuals blessed with perfect pitch. Joanna said perfect pitch was when you got the viola into the skip first throw.

Slider had given Atherton the précis of Mrs Cornfeld's exposition. Now he was forking in a hasty shepherd's pie and beans (no chips, no gravy) by way of lunch, and wondering what he would have got at the Cornfeld house. A delicate consommé, *foie gras*, roast duck and green peas? He sighed and swallowed. The meat in the shepherd's pie tasted of gravy browning and the potato had that slippery, embarrassed texture of instant mash that knows it isn't fooling anybody.

'Exciting things always happen in places where I'm not,' he said. 'I ought to hire myself out to bored people not to be anywhere near them.'

'I'm sure there's a flaw in your reasoning somewhere,' Atherton said. 'And how can you eat that stuff?'

'I've seen the alternatives. Get on with it – what happened?'

'Oh, right. A bloke came in, who not only had seen Running Man but had seen his face. Name of Alan Maltby. He was just about to turn in at the park gates on his way to the station – his usual route going to work – when Running Man shot out and he had to sidestep sharply not to get knocked down.'

'Why hasn't he come forward before?' Slider asked.

'I asked him that. He seemed quite indignant. Said he works on weekdays. Now it's Saturday he's come straight in to tell us and all he gets is abuse. He's got a good mind to turn round and walk right out again – which is about all the good mind he's got in my opinion.'

'You didn't tell him that?'

'What do you take me for? Anyway, for a brief but telling moment, Running Man's face is inches from his and he gets a really good goosy at the famous phizog – so good that he's prepared to sit in on a photofit.'

'Blimey, our luck has changed,' Slider said, pushing his plate aside. 'Shove my pud over, will you?'

'You're not serious?'

'What? I like jelly and blancmange.'

'You've got retarded tastebuds, that's your trouble. Anyway, you might not say that when you've heard all.'

'Might not say what?'

'That our luck has changed.'

'Oh, Nora, what now?'

'Well, friend Maltby had a good look at chummy's face, as I said. Said he was sweating, eyes popping, every sign of agitation, so we all got terribly excited. And he was holding a mobile phone, the same sort of Motorola as Chattie's, though Maltby didn't see any blood or a knife. But when he had okayed the photofit, we compared it with the photo of Darren we got from Jassy, and there was no resemblance. And when we showed the photo of Darren to Maltby, he was confident it wasn't the same man.'

'You had to tell me that. You had to spoil my afters. And it was pink blancmange as well – my favourite.'

'Look, it needn't be as bad as that. After all, Darren could still be the murderer. It could still have been him who was standing talking to Chattie. We don't know that that person and Running Man were the same.'

'I've been telling everyone that from the beginning,' Slider said, frustrated. 'Now you *want* them to be different?'

Atherton waved a large hand blandly. 'Or they could be the same and Running Man is the murderer and Darren's a red herring.'

'No luck with finding Darren yet, I suppose?'

'No. We're trawling around his usual haunts and associates, but no-one's admitting seeing him. Manchester actually sent someone round to the mate's house, Dave O'Brien—'

'That was quick.'

'But Darren wasn't there and they think he hasn't been. They believed O'Brien, and I suppose they ought to know,' Atherton said, with deep scepticism. 'They've promised to keep an eye out for him, but they didn't think we had a good enough case against him for them to make it a priority.'

'Nor have we,' Slider said. 'Oh, well, at least we've got a photofit of Running Man to work with. Get that circulated, will you, and I'll see what Porson says about banging it on the telly tonight.'

Hart appeared, weaving between the tables towards them.

'Boss, they've just rung from the house. The man's turned up to open the safe.'

'At last,' Atherton said. 'I'm sure we could have got someone out of the Scrubs to blow it for us quicker than this.'

'You live in a dream world,' Slider told him, getting to his feet. His lunch slipped about in his stomach, threatening to cause trouble.

'You're going over there?' Atherton asked.

'I wouldn't miss it. You coming?'

'Can I come, boss?' Hart asked.

'It's not a party. Go and get on with your work,' Slider said sternly, but she only grinned and shrugged.

'Wurf a try,' she said.

'You just can't intimidate some people,' Slider complained to Atherton as all three headed for the exit.

'When you've worked on the DAFT squad for three months, there's nuffing more they can do to you,' Hart chirped.

The man from Acme Safes ('How traditional,' Atherton had murmured) was waiting for them at the house, and fidgeting about being kept waiting.

'You kept us waiting long enough,' Atherton reminded him.

'There's a lot of calls on my time,' he said, with imperishable dignity. He was a small, rounded sort of man in very clean overalls with ACME over the pocket and very shiny shoes on his rather small feet, on which he teetered a little like a teacher at a 1950s prep school. His hair was so neat and shiny it looked painted on. 'By rights I shouldn't be here now,' he said sternly. 'This is supposed to be my Saturday off.'

'We are rather a special case,' Atherton said, though Slider had flung him a look that said leave it alone.

'Oh, I know, I know,' Acme man sneered. 'You people think you're so important just because you go around investigating murders. Well, other people have important jobs too, you know. Opening safes is skilled work.'

Slider gave Atherton a slight kick to stop him retorting, and said, 'Please carry on, Mr – er.'

'Pickett's my name,' said the Acme man, and Slider could see now why he had need of so much dignity. PC Gallon, who was in attendance, made a snorting noise, but when they all looked at him his face was rigid and his eyes fixed on the distance, though his cheeks looked suspiciously hollow.

The safe contained one or two pieces of jewellery, cheque-books, birth certificate, house deeds and other documents, and a great quantity of share certificates. Atherton sat down at her desk with them and leafed through, his eyebrows going up and his lips pursed in a soundless whistle.

'This is quite a portfolio,' he said. 'I think we know now where she got the money from to support her lifestyle. I wonder if she did her own buying and selling or if she had an adviser?'

'Her grandmother says she was given a hundred thousand when she was seventeen, which she invested in shares and property,' Slider said.

'But only eighty thousand went on the flat she bought, according to Jasper.'

'So she presumably put twenty thousand into shares. Quite a lump sum.'

'Yes, and at the beginning of the biggest bull run in history. With the right transactions she could have increased that ten or twentyfold. I'd like to take these back to the office and work out what sort of an income they would generate. Enough to keep a girl in goodies, anyway.'

'A lot of them must be Cornfeld Chemicals,' Slider said. 'Granny said she was given ten per cent at the float.'

'Yes. I don't know what the shares are at at the moment. I'll have a look when we get back. I've got a paper in my desk.'

'Might be an idea to find out if there are any other big share-holders, outside the family,' Slider said.

Atherton gave him a sharp look. 'You think it could have been to do with money, or the business?'

'I don't know. But it never hurts to have a few facts to hand.' He was examining the rest of the papers. 'Ah,' he said, 'now here's something.' He held it up, a long, narrow envelope of the sort that only lawyers ever used.

'Her will?' Atherton said eagerly.

'It ain't chopped liver,' said Slider. 'Now we might find out who had a motive for her death.'

'Only if they knew about it,' Atherton said. 'It's usually you warning me not to jump to conclusions.' He waited impatiently while Slider read down the pages. 'Well?'

'Interesting,' said Slider. 'If her nearest and dearest did know about this, there'd have been a few who'd be pissed off with her, but whether it would make grounds for murder is debatable. She's left everything to charity.'

'Really?'

'A very conventional mixture of medical, educational, third world and environmental,' Slider said. 'Well, well. Unless our basic charities have got more ruthless chief execs than hitherto realised, I think we can rule out inheritance as a motive.'

Atherton's afternoon with the newspaper and a calculator resulted in the conclusion that her portfolio was worth about three quarters of a million, and averaging out the yields would have brought her an income of around thirty thousand a year. Not a fortune, but, as he said, enough as a supplementary income to buy nice clothes and theatre tickets and restaurant meals, and to support her generosity to various charities.

His call to Companies House brought further interesting news. 'I thought you said that Daddy Cornfeld gave each of the children ten per cent?' he said to Slider.

'That's what Granny said.'

'Jassy's name doesn't appear on the list.'

'Really? I suppose she must have sold them.'

'If she did, it must have been a while ago. I checked back five years.'

'I'm not surprised, though. Given what we know about her,

I suspect Jassy would have sold anything that wasn't nailed down.'

'Yes,' said Atherton, 'and it's probably another cause of her resentment. She must be kicking herself. The Cornfeld shares have gone up a lot in recent years, and the current yield is five point two per cent. That's partly because of the recent slight downturn in share price, which has affected the whole sector – the whole market, in fact – but the yield–price ratio has always been good.'

'What did Horace say, Winnie?'

'The share has always produced good income as well as capital growth,' Atherton translated.

'It sounded better the other way. Well, I don't know that it gets us any further forward. Chattie certainly had money to leave, but if anyone knew about her will, they'd know they weren't going to get anything.'

'And if they didn't know – who might think they would benefit?'

'Jassy?' Slider hazarded.

'Possibly,' Atherton said. 'She'd been given enough by Chattie over the years. She might think big sis would have cut her in for something and she's selfish enough to be cold-hearted about it. And that brings us back to Darren.'

'The Absent.'

'And now that we know Running Man was not Darren,' Atherton said, 'either Darren was Standing Man and he did it, or Running Man did it – or,' he added, suddenly thinking of something, 'Running Man was a friend of Darren's and they were in it together.'

'Or,' Slider reminded him, 'it was someone else.'

'Yes, there is that,' Atherton said, subsiding. 'Well, I don't know. What now?'

'We carry on, what else?'

'I think I should keep an eye on Toby,' Atherton said. 'The band's playing tonight at the Jazz Barn, and I think I ought to go along and maybe have a word with him.'

Slider eyed him. 'Oh, you think that, do you? It wouldn't have anything to do with Marion Whatsername, would it?'

'Of course she'll be there,' Atherton said. 'Naturally. But I go there for the music anyway. It's a pretty hot scene.'

'Hot scene?' Slider wrinkled his nose at the expression.

'Hot scene – cool jazz,' said Atherton.

'And where is the Jazz Barn?'

'Newport Pagnell.'

Slider suppressed a smile. 'Oh, well, I definitely think you should go, then.'

'There's nothing wrong with Newport Pagnell,' Atherton said loftily. 'I'll have you know it's where they make Aston Martins.'

'Did I say anything?'

'I know the look.'

'I hope you don't expect me to write this up as overtime for you? You'll have to conduct your love life on your own time, like everybody else.'

'All right.' Atherton sighed. 'But if I have a pop at Toby afterwards?'

'Be my guest. But the answer's still no.'

'Oh, this is nice,' Slider said. He and Joanna were lying in bed spoonwise, her back to his front, his arms round her and his hands cupped over her bulge.

'Mmm,' she agreed.

'What a pity you have to go to work.'

'There are two ways to look at that.'

'I know, lots of nice money. But it is Sunday.'

'Extra fee, Sunday,' she said. She squirmed a little, to get even more comfortable, her buttocks nudging into his groin, which began to have thoughts of its own.

'You're enjoying working, aren't you?' he said.

'God, yes! It's wonderful to be back, after all those weeks with nothing. Though I suppose I'd better get used to idleness. There's no guarantee anything else is going to come in after this.'

'Mm. But if it does – well – you'll have to stop eventually, won't you?'

'When the baby comes, of course,' she said; and then, 'Is that what you're worried about? That I shan't be able to live without music when junior makes his appearance?'

'I didn't say I was worried about anything.'

'I know all your tones of voice by now.'

'It's pitiful to be so transparent.'

'No, it's not,' she said, kissing his arm, all she could reach of him. 'It's endearing.'

'I don't want to be endearing. I want to be exciting, challenging, dynamic and overwhelmingly sexy.'

She revolved eelishly in his arms to present her frontside to his body and her lips to his. 'Well, you're already all of those, honeybun.'

'*Honeybun?*'

'Tiger, then. God, it's hard work getting you to make love to me!'

'Oh, is that what? You only had to ask.'

A satisfactory period later, when she was lying damply in his arms with her head on his chest, he said, 'But seriously.'

'Seriously?'

'About this working business.'

'There's no deflecting you, is there?' she murmured. 'Seriously – I am fully cognised of the demands of the situation. And I'm pretty sure holding our child in my arms is going to come out tops over cradling a fiddle under my chin.'

'Only "pretty sure"?'

'I've never done it before, so how can I be certain? But the one is life and the other's a job. So be at peace, my love.'

'What a pity you've got to go to work,' he said, kissing the top of her head.

Ten minutes later she got up, and an hour after that she was gone. Slider felt at a loss. He had said he wasn't coming in, there being nothing on that someone else couldn't do, but he wasn't used to having time off. He finished the main section of the paper, and then telephoned Atherton.

The phone rang for a long time, and then a voice answered, 'Hello?' – a mumbling, sleepy and definitely female voice.

'Hello,' he said kindly. 'I was expecting a baritone, not a soprano.'

'Wha'?' the voice said, then coughed, and said, 'Did you want Jim? I think he's in the shower.'

'He'll be an hour or two, then,' Slider said. Atherton took washing very seriously. 'Can you ask him to ring—?'

'Hello?' It was Atherton's voice this time. He had evidently snatched the receiver from her.

'I see you didn't waste your efforts last night,' said Slider.

'Wait a minute, I'll take it in the kitchen.' The line went dead, and a moment later opened again. 'I forgot to tell her

not to answer the phone. I wasn't expecting any calls. Why
aren't you asleep at this time of a Sunday?'

'It's a quarter past nine,' Slider observed.

'Civilised people don't get up until eleven on Sunday.'

'Well, that accounts for it, then. Was that Marion Davies?'

'Yes,' said Atherton. He didn't say, 'if it's any of your business,' but the implication was there in his voice.

'So how did it go last night? The interview with Toby,' he
added, when the silence warned him he had been misunderstood.

'We all went for a drink at the Sow and Pigs after the concert,
but I managed to get him on his own for a bit, and put some
pressure on him. I think there may be something there after
all. He was definitely edgy, and a bit more leverage could get
him to cough. If only we had any direct evidence. You can't
lever someone effectively if all you've got is no alibi and a
motive. I wonder if we could justify having a look round his
flat? If we could find a hoodie or a bloodstain or a knife—'

'Yes, *if*. I don't think we could get a warrant on that basis.
See if he'll let you have a voluntary look round to begin with,
and we'll go from there.'

'Okay. You're not coming in?'

'I'm going to have a day off if it kills me.'

'Pity Joanna's working.'

'Oddly enough, that sentiment had occurred to me.'

It was another lovely day. He improved the shining hour
by telephoning his ex-wife Irene, had a shy chat with his son
Matthew, mostly about football, and a long listen to his
daughter Kate, who wanted to have her navel pierced – 'no'
was about the only word he managed to get in – and after
doing the washing up, balancing his chequebook, contemplating without enthusiasm washing some shirts and wondering
fruitlessly about Atherton and Marion Davies, he finally settled
down on a chair in the garden with the paper and a gin and
tonic. Atavistic memories of a more leisured life asserted
themselves, and he was beginning to relax and think that being
alone for once in his life was rather pleasant, when the phone
rang. It was Atherton, and he sounded disturbed, which was
in itself disturbing.

'I think you'd better come,' he said. 'We've got trouble.'

*   *   *

When Marion had departed to her own devices, Atherton had decided that it would be a shame to let up the pressure on Toby Harkness now, when he had got him nicely simmering, and went round to his flat to have a little chat with him and see how amenable he was to having his place searched.

His ringing on the entryphone bell was not answered, but he could see Toby's car in its parking slot, so he rang and rang again. Probably dead drunk last night, Atherton thought, and still unconscious. Eventually there were footsteps on the stairs and a tall young woman appeared, dressed in leggings and a vast T-shirt and with her hair sleep-tangled. She mouthed something at Atherton from behind the glass doors and he held up his warrant card. At that, she fumbled the door open, and said, 'Is it Toby you want? I could hear you buzzing him. I live next door.'

'His car's here, so I assumed he was in,' said Atherton.

She looked at him from under her fringe. 'Only,' she said breathlessly, 'I think he might be in trouble. He's been a bit strange these last few days. I mean, usually he's ever so friendly but when I've seen him recently he's just brushed past me as if he didn't see me. And then last night—'

'Just a minute – your name?'

'It's Manda – Amanda Hare.'

'All right. What happened last night?'

'Oh, well, you see he came in late and I think he had someone with him because I could hear him talking. Those walls are ever so thin. And then he put music on, really loud, which is not like him, and I was trying to get to sleep so I banged on the wall, but it didn't stop. And then I heard something like furniture being moved about, sort of thumps and bangs, and a lot of shouting. And then the music stopped and it all went quiet. And since then, nothing.'

'Do you think he went out again?'

'I didn't hear him go out. Anyway, like you said, his car's there.'

'True,' said Atherton, and then something occurred to him. Toby hadn't had his car with him last night. Jasper had given him a lift both ways. He stepped back, looked up and down the road and spotted Jasper's Toyota MR2 parked a few yards away. Something cold walked up his spine. He had said that Toby was edgy last night, but perhaps 'on the edge' was a better description. What if Atherton's pressure had pushed him over?

'I think I'd better go up and see if he's all right. I don't suppose you have the key to his flat, by any chance?'

'No, sorry,' Manda said. 'Are you going to break the door in?' she asked hopefully.

Was he? Atherton pondered briefly the fact that he hadn't any justification for it, except the copper's instinct that was making the hair on the back of his neck stand up like someone in a crowd trying to see the parade. 'We'll see,' he said.

She followed him up the stairs. 'Stay behind me,' he said as he thumped on the door and called out. There was no response. 'Did you hear anything?' he asked sharply, turning to Miss Hare, who was wide-eyed with excitement.

'I don't know.'

'I thought I heard someone call out for help. Very faintly. There, again. Did you hear that?'

'Yeah, yeah, I think so,' she said, her eyes so wide now he was afraid they'd fall out of their sockets. Thank God for suggestible females, he thought, took a step back and kicked.

The Yale gave at the third blow – or, rather, the wood around the Yale, being of the normal standard used in modern building, crumbled like Madeira cake. The door swung back and hit the wall behind with a bang that made Manda Hare squeak. Atherton, adrenaline in place, took in the scene with a single scorching glance. The same mess and muddle, the same smell of frowst, tobacco and stale food, but with something else added that made his stomach sink and his adrenaline rise yet further – the smell of blood.

Toby was sitting on an upright chair at the far end of the living room, naked to the waist, his hands dangling between his knees. The curtains were drawn and his pale face and body gleamed weirdly in the dimness. On the carpet in front of him was sprawled a male figure Atherton had no difficulty in identifying as Jasper, by the clothes he had been wearing last night. He was immobile, and there was a dark stain underneath and around him on the fawn carpet. The blood had evidently soaked through and had run along underneath because it had appeared in an interesting flow across the exposed parquet inside the door, dark, in the gloom, like oil.

Manda made a muffled sound. She had managed to cram the fingers of both her hands into her mouth and her eyes were fixed and bulging dangerously. Atherton moved slightly to block her view of the scene.

'Don't look,' he said. He spoke firmly but calmly. 'Go back to your own flat and dial 999. Tell them to send police and an ambulance. Go and do it now, there's a good girl. Go on. Hurry.'

She went, dragging her eyes away like pulling off a plaster. Atherton turned to the scene again. His nerves were singing with tension and played again and again the image of Toby leaping into sudden action, springing from the chair and across the room like a pale cat. Where was the knife? There must be a knife. It was so hard to see in this twilight. Yes, there it was, on the floor, half under Toby's chair where he must have dropped it. Could he get to it before Toby did? Make a rush for it, or try creeping up? The muscles of his stomach seemed to twitch with their own memory of harm. God, he hated knives!

The cautious approach, he decided, trying to breathe evenly. He spoke quietly and began to edge forward. 'Toby. Toby. Are you all right? Toby, can you hear me?' There was no response. He reached into his pocket carefully for his handkerchief as he advanced. Though Toby's muscles seemed genuinely relaxed, a madman could feign this state of shock and leap into lethal action at the last moment. Atherton's adrenaline peaked as he stooped and secured the knife with the handkerchief, expecting the sudden violent movement; and then subsided with a rush as Toby remained motionless. Sweat was standing cold all down his back, and his legs were trembling. He drew a few deep breaths and backed off a step or two.

The next most important thing, having got the knife, was to check the status of the victim. Jasper was face down and limp, and Atherton thought he was probably dead, but on squatting (keeping his eyes on Toby) and applying two fingers to his neck, he found a faint pulse. Thank God for that! If he survived, he could be a witness to what happened, because Toby didn't look as if he would ever speak again.

But just as he thought that, Toby spoke. 'He defiled her,' he said. The sound of his voice coming out of that still figure made Atherton jump

'What?' he said involuntarily.

'That's why I killed her. I had to do it. And then I killed him. You can only wash away things like that in blood.'

Atherton almost held his breath. 'You killed her?'

'She's mine now,' Toby said, in that same dead, toneless voice. 'She's mine for ever.' And then he drew a great shuddering sigh, put his head into his hands, his elbows resting on his knees, and began to rock.

Slider met him at the hospital, at the entrance to the emergency unit. As they walked through, Atherton filled him in.

'They're both being looked at now. Toby still seems completely out of it. There was a lot of blood on him and plenty of it round the walls, so I don't know if it was a fight and they're both wounded, or all the blood is from Jasper. God, it's a mess,' he finished bitterly.

'It's not your fault,' Slider said.

'Well, maybe it is. I was pushing Toby last night, and Jasper had already told me he was unstable.'

'He only said all oboe-players are mad. And you know that's an orchestra joke, like viola-players being thick.'

'But I knew he was on the edge. That's the very reason I went after him.'

'Stop beating yourself up. It doesn't help. We've got a job to do and we do it.'

They sat on moulded chairs in the corridor until a young doctor with seventy-two-hour-week eyes came out to them.

'Right,' he said. 'Jasper Stalybrass is stable for the moment, but he's lost an awful lot of blood. There is some internal bleeding into the chest cavity and in the abdomen so we have to send him up to theatre to see what's going on.'

'Will he survive?' Slider asked.

'It depends on what we find up in theatre. From observations here I think a lung may have been punctured, but that's survivable. It depends where the rest of the bleeding is coming from. However, he's young and healthy so he ought to have a pretty good chance. He'll be very weak for some time, and there's always a danger of complications, but as long as we don't find anything too bad up there, he should make a full recovery.'

It was as near as you could get to an opinion from a doctor, these days. They were all so scared of being sued. 'What about Toby Harkness?'

'Ah, yes. Well, there was so much blood on him we thought he'd been wounded too, but when we cleaned him up we didn't find any injuries. The blood must have been all the other man's. So he's not physically hurt, but he's very disturbed. We had to sedate him in order to examine him, and we've got him under restraints at the moment, pending a psych consult.'

'Can I talk to either of them?'

'Well . . .' he hesitated '. . . I know it's important for you to know what happened. You can talk to Jasper Stalybrass very briefly before he goes up. Two minutes only. And you can see Toby Harkness, but I don't think you'll get much out of him. As I said, he's very disturbed – and, frankly, we don't want him made more so, so if he becomes agitated I'll have to ask you to leave.'

'I understand. I'll be careful. By the way – about the clothes?'

'Yes, it's all right, I know the drill. They're all being bagged and listed and you can take them away whenever you like.'

Jasper Stalybrass was lying on a trolley under a sheet than which he was not less white. His eyes were closed, the lids delicately blue, his skin with the transparent, waxy look of extreme blood loss. He barely seemed to be breathing. Slider warned Atherton back with a look, and said, 'Mr Stalybrass. Are you awake?'

He hardly expected a response, but the eyes slowly opened.

'I'm Detective Inspector Slider,' he said. 'Can you tell me what happened?'

Stalybrass tried to speak, licked his lips feebly, and then said, in a breath of a voice, 'I drove him home. Went in. For a drink. Sat down. He went – kitchen. Came back – stabbed me. In the back.'

He stopped, panting shallowly. Slider nodded, holding his eyes. 'I understand. Take your time.'

He resumed. 'He was raving. I tried – struggled – get the knife.'

He closed his eyes and Slider waited. The nurse, who had been standing back, came to his elbow. 'We've got to get him up to theatre,' she said quietly.

'I know. Just one minute more.'

Stalybrass opened his eyes again. 'He kept – stabbing me. Raving – about Chattie. Me and Chattie.'

He stopped again. The nurse said, 'Sir—'

Stalybrass held Slider's gaze with feeble urgency. 'There's more,' he said.

'Go on, I'm listening,' Slider said. 'What is it?'

'He said – said *he killed her*,' Stalybrass finished. 'Because of her and me.'

Slider nodded calmly. 'I understand. Well, don't worry about it now. We've got him safe. You just concentrate on getting well. We'll talk to you again later, when you've been taken care of.'

He stood back and Stalybrass was wheeled out. Slider met Atherton's eyes. 'So,' he said, 'your plan last night worked.'

'At a price,' said Atherton.

CHAPTER TWELVE

Absit, O Men

They saw Toby briefly in the emergency room where he was being guarded by a uniformed policeman – it was Ridpath, from Hammersmith, who looked at them curiously, but said only, 'He hasn't said anything, sir.' Toby was lying on the examination bed, his eyes closed, the restraint straps round his body. A nurse was also in attendance.

'Can we talk to him?' Slider asked her.

'You can try,' the nurse said, 'but I don't know if he'll answer. Try not to agitate him.'

Slider approached the bedside. 'Toby, can you hear me?'

The eyes opened. They looked unfocused, wandered a little like those of a new baby. Slider could feel Atherton's tension like heat radiation behind him. 'Toby, I'm Detective Inspector Slider. Can you tell me what happened?' No answer. 'Back at your flat. Jasper came in with you—'

A shudder ran visibly through Toby Harkness, through his body and up his face.

'Did you do something to him?'

'I couldn't bear it,' Toby said, and his face drew into an exaggerated mask of tragedy. '*He'd had her.* Defiled her. I had to kill them both. Better that way.' And he began to cry, weak, tearless sobs, more like the whimpering of a puppy than any expression of humanity.

'Toby,' Slider said, ever more gently, 'are you saying that you killed Chattie?'

Toby moaned, and began rolling his head back and forth slowly on the flat pillow. The moans grew rhythmic, and louder.

The nurse touched Slider's arm. 'I think you'd better leave him alone now.'

Slider obeyed, seeing that he wouldn't get any more sense out of him anyway. He paused on the way out to say to Ridpath, 'Stay with him and write down anything he says. I'll arrange for you to be relieved by one of ours.'

'Thank you, sir.'

Outside in the corridor, Atherton said, 'Well, I don't think that would stand up as a confession, but he did say it to me *and* to Jasper. Assuming Jasper survives. But you heard Jasper say it. I wish he'd confessed to me in front of the neighbour, but I'd already sent her to call an ambulance, damnit.'

'Settle down,' Slider said. 'Toby's not going anywhere, not for a long time. And if he confessed to killing Chattie in a fit of remorse, he'll probably say it again, many times over.'

Atherton looked at him carefully. 'There's something in your tone of voice. A confession and a second attempted killing, what more do you want? With a similar sort of knife. It was a kitchen knife, which is what Doc Cameron thought Chattie was attacked with. A Sabatier, if you want to be picky. Might even be the same one. God, if we could get a bit of Chattie's DNA from it—'

'If,' said Slider. 'Don't get too excited. Confession is as confession does.'

'What does that mean?'

'Toby said he killed Chattie because Jasper had defiled her. Presumably in a rush of blood to the head. But he attacks Jasper *three days afterwards*.'

'That's not much of an objection,' said Atherton. 'He's a coward. Stabbing a female's one thing, stabbing a man taller than him's another. Took him time to get his bottle up.'

'False confessions aren't unknown,' Slider said. 'Especially from young men in emotional turmoil.'

'Going after Jasper had to wait until he was drunk enough and the opportunity presented itself.'

'It could be his way to make himself important to Chattie in retrospect, so to speak, when he knows he wasn't important to her in life.'

'If it was a false confession, then it was my fault for pushing him so hard last night,' Atherton said.

'Oh, we're back there, are we? All right, if you want to punish yourself, think of all the extra work it's going to cause us.'

'What does that matter, if it gets us our man?'

'Attaboy. You can go back to the scene and direct the search of the flat, see if you can find anything useful to back up your theory.'

'Ugh. The thought of searching that flat. You haven't seen it.'

'You've described it to me. I thought you wanted to be punished?' said Slider.

There was no point in thinking about a day off now. Slider went back to his office to begin the procedures surrounding this new event, the back of his mind occupied with wondering whether Atherton was culpable in any way, whether he could have known how close to snapping Toby Harkness was. But you have to trust your men. By all accounts Toby had been sinking further into the mire all on his own. Did he kill Chattie? Motive, no alibi, and now a confession. Slider would have been happier about it if she really had been stabbed to death. There was something about that drugging and fake stabbing that didn't fit with jealous rage. But, then, jealousy often did smoulder rather than blaze, sickening its host: the slow, brooding burn. And someone had said that Toby wouldn't hurt a fly. So maybe the only way he could kill her was to subdue her first. If the prime purpose in his mind was that she had to die, he might have plotted how reasonably he could do it. But where did he get the drug from? If he only knew about Chattie and Jasper on Tuesday night and killed her on Wednesday morning, he would either have had to have the drug to hand anyway (in which case, why?) or have put in an amazingly hard night's work between eight p.m. Tuesday and eight a.m. Wednesday.

Of course, they couldn't be sure he hadn't known about Chattie and Jasper for much longer. He said he had only found out that night, but he could have been lying. A lot would depend on what he said when they were finally able to interview him properly. And what, if anything, Atherton found at the flat. The time lapse between Chattie's murder and the search reduced the chance there would be anything to find; but blood was a persistent little chap, and, as the poet had it, would out.

The phone rang. He picked it up, and a female voice that sounded faintly familiar said, 'Oh. I wanted to speak to Jim. Jim Atherton. Is he there?'

'I'm afraid not. I'm Detective Inspector Slider. Can I help you?'

'Oh. Um. I'm not sure. You're his boss, aren't you?'

He had placed the voice now. A mental association with tousled hair and gummy eyes went with it. 'It's Marion Davies, isn't it?'

'Yes, that's right.' A pause, and then the words in a rush: 'I heard about Toby and Jasper. God, it's terrible! I mean, what's going on? What's happening to us?'

He assumed these were rhetorical questions. 'How did you hear about it?'

'Manda – Toby's next door neighbour – phoned and told me. I tried ringing the hospital but they wouldn't tell me anything. Is Jasper – is he— ?'

'He's not dead. The last I heard he was going up to surgery but there's a good chance he'll recover.'

'Oh, thank God for that. But did Toby really stab him? I mean – Toby! I always thought he was such a, you know, weakling. A mummy's boy. I can't imagine him stabbing anyone. And why Jasper? I always thought they were friends.'

'I'm sorry,' Slider said, 'I can't go into it with you at this stage.'

'I suppose not,' she said, and she sounded despondent. 'But it's so terrible. I can't see how the band can carry on after this. It's like a sort of curse on us, ever since Chattie . . .' Her voice trailed off.

'I'm sorry,' Slider said, who had a mass of work to do. 'But is there anything I can help you with?'

'Yeah,' said Marion, seeming to pull herself together. 'Would you give Jim a message from me? Would you tell him – well, not to come round any more?'

'Isn't that something you ought to tell him yourself?' Slider said, suppressing impatience.

'Oh, I know, but I really can't. I don't want to talk to him. I mean, he's a nice bloke and everything, and I don't want to hurt him, but, well, he's been sort of hanging around me, wanting to see me every night, and honestly, I can't. I mean, it's not going anywhere and, well, we haven't, like, got anything in common, have we? Apart from him looking into Chattie's murder and, well, that's not something you can build on. To be frank, it kind of gives me the willies now, especially with what's just happened to Tobe and Jasper. I mean, I know it's not Jim's fault, but he brings it all back to me, like he's a sort of jinx or something – well, I don't mean that, really, but seeing him again now would be, like, so *ghoulish*.'

Slider had made several efforts to stem this flow, and only his early indoctrination with good manners prevented him from putting the phone down on her. Now as she drew breath he got in quickly with, 'I really don't feel I can—'

But she was off again, and this time, though what she said was short, it was devastating. 'Apart from anything else, well, he's just too *old* for me.'

Slider reeled, but managed to pounce on the pause before it got away again. 'I'm sorry, but I really can't undertake to pass on personal messages of that sort. You'll have to talk to him yourself. Ring him at home tonight.'

She sighed. 'If I leave it that long he'll be round my flat again. Can't you just tell him I don't want to see him?'

'I'm sorry,' Slider said firmly. 'I have to go now, there's a call on the other line.' And he put the phone down. Now his head was occupied with unwelcome bits of knowledge like the worst sort of squatter. He didn't want to be on the inside of Atherton's love life, and it was a damn cheek of the girl to think he was going to be her go-between, especially as she was in bed with Atherton this very morning, and presumably they hadn't only been discussing counterpoint or fingering techniques. It was one thing to think she must be a flighty little madam to bed someone on such short acquaintance and then chuck him out equally quickly, but quite another to be forced to wonder whether Atherton had been making a fool of himself and whether it might have clouded his judgement about Harkness. And, oh dear, oh dear, too old? Atherton, the boy wonder, the serial bird-puller, the Peter Pan of sexual frolic, who was forced to fight the totty off to get a moment's peace – Atherton being knocked back because he was *too old*?

He hadn't got time to think about this, damnit! He shook his head violently, stood up, stretched until his muscles cracked, then sat down again and resumed his work.

The day wasn't over yet.

'It's a bit of a mess,' Porson said, quite mildly, considering.

Nicholls, ringing up to Slider from downstairs to say Porson had arrived, had reported the old boy seemed almost glad to be called in. 'Sundays are hell when you're on your own.' Perhaps that accounted for the mildness.

'Now we've got another two sets of doting parents breathing down our heels – and Harkness senior turns out to be a junior minister in the Arts Department, whatever it's called these days, whose wife is pally with the PM's wife. The last thing we need at this junction is political ramplications.'

Did he mean complications, ramifications or implications, Slider wondered. In any case, he certainly didn't want any of them. 'No, sir,' he said.

'He's busting everybody's guts wanting to know what his son's accused of and when he can move him to a private facility.'

'It looks as though Jasper Stalybrass is going to recover,' Slider offered his own small comfort.

'Yes, that brings it down to attempted murder, or GBH, assault with a deadly, depending on how hard Stalybrass or his parents want to press it. I wouldn't be surprised to learn *his* dad's best friends with the Attorney General and plays golf with the Lord Chief Justice. But what about this other thing? This confession?'

'We haven't been able to interview him yet. He's still under sedation and considered too unstable.'

'Yes, and his father's agitating to get a solicitor in there, which'll shove another spanner in the spokes,' Porson said gloomily. 'If we ask him anything it'll be "questioning while non compost mental", and the case'll collapse and we'll be hung up to dry. What did you think of it – the confession?' he asked abruptly.

'It makes sense, and Harkness hasn't got an alibi for the time in question, and he's certainly been behaving in a disturbed manner since the death.'

'But?' Porson asked sharply.

'It's just a gut feeling, sir. It doesn't feel right to me. But I have to admit I've nothing to base it on. On the other hand, we've no direct evidence against Harkness, apart from the confession.'

Porson sighed. 'Yes, and they won't go on that alone, these days. Mind you, if the lad's gone doo-lally, he'll probably be locked up anyway and that'll be that, though it won't help our clear-up figures. Well, keep an open mind. See if we can find anything to back it up. The knife gone off to the lab?'

'Yes, sir, and we've fast-tracked it. That should mean a result by tomorrow afternoon.'

'Right. Meanwhile, what to tell the press? I suppose we'll have to let them have the assault. It's public knowledge anyway by now. But given it was a stabbing they'll add two and two and make him the Park Killer and Daddy Harkness will never believe we didn't tell them he was. Then the Shah will really hit the Spam. We'll have top brass all over us and writs flying about like doodlebugs.'

'I can't see that we can help that, sir. Even if we don't tell them anything, there's bound to be speculation, given his relationship with the girl.'

'Yes, and the next thing I'll have Daddy Cornfeld round my neck as well. We'll just have to cover our arses and hope for the best. So we'll say Harkness is being questioned about the assault on Stalybrass, which they can't argue about, and so far we have no reason to believe – no, we can't say that, in case it goes the other way – no evidence that there is any connection with the Cornfeld murder.'

'Do you want me to do it?' Slider asked unwillingly.

'No,' Porson said, with a deeper sigh. 'I'd better do it myself. Having an MP involved raises the stakes. No offence, Slider, but we don't want them saying we sent the monkey when it should have been the organ grinder.'

Now how, Slider thought, as he trudged back to his office, could he think I'd take offence at that?

Slider got off the phone from the umpteenth trying conversation to find Hart hovering in the doorway.

'They called from downstairs, guv. There's a woman come in about the murder, something to do with Running Man. She was asking for you, but d'you want me to do it? I know you're busy.'

'No, I'll go,' said Slider. 'I don't suppose it's important, but anything to get away from this desk for ten minutes.'

'I bet you haven't had any lunch,' she said, eyeing him like a mother hen about to start clucking.

'You can't bet with me about that. I know the answer,' he said, heading for the door.

She was not so easily put off. 'D'you want me to get you something? A roll or something?'

He tried to ignore her and hurry on, but his stomach caught his foot by the scruff, so to speak, and he halted involuntarily. 'On a Sunday?' he said.

'There's that place under the railway arch the cabbies go to. That's always open.' She saw she had him by the hearts and minds, and added seductively, 'I could get you a sausage sarnie or a bacon sarnie.'

He practically salivated. 'Well, it's a thought. Do you mind?'

'Course not. Whatjer fancy?'

'Sausage, then.

'Wiv tomato sauce?'

He capitulated. 'Of course. Two rounds.' Might as well go for broke. 'And make sure it's butter, not marge.'

'Yeah, I remember.'

'Thanks, Hart.'

She beamed as if he were doing her the favour, not vice versa.

Downstairs in the front shop there was only one person waiting: a young West Indian woman, in her late twenties, he calculated, with a plump, pretty face, plaited hair and a figure that strained at every seam of her tight Lycra mini-skirted dress. With bosoms and buttocks like those, he thought, she'd take a long time to pass you in the street. Her legs were bare and her knobbly feet, thrust into high-heeled strappy sandals, evidently resented it and were trying to escape through the gaps. She wore hoop earrings, bangles, and a multitude of gold chains round her neck, and she clutched on her lap an enormous shoulder-bag (why did young women these days all go around with these near-haversacks for handbags? What the heck did they need to carry with them all the time?) He noted with interest that she was sweating, despite its being reasonably cool in there, and was extremely nervous. Her brow was furrowed, her hands massaged nervously at her bag strap, she chewed at her lower lip.

When she saw Slider she did not wait for him to speak but got immediately to her feet, and said, 'Are you the man round here?'

'I'm Detective Inspector Slider. I'm in charge of the investigation. What can I do for you?'

'I got to talk to you,' she said. 'It's important.' She had a Shepherd's Bush accent with nothing of the West Indies in it other than the husky timbre. Born and bred, he concluded.

'What's your name?' he asked.

'Lizzie Proctor,' she said. Her eyes flitted about anxiously. 'Look, I can't talk here. You got somewhere we can go?'

Slider conducted her into the nearest interview room, and was interested to note that she looked about her as one to whom this was a new experience. 'It's a bit primitive, I'm afraid, but it's private,' he said. 'Would you like to sit down, Miss Proctor?'

She seemed pleased with the formality, and brushed her skirt under her as she sat down with a little fluttery movement of femininity.

'Now, what's it about?'

She paused a moment, evidently on the brink of some leap, and then said, 'It's about me bruvver. Look, you've not got to let on it was me told you. He'd just about kill me if he knew I was here. But I begged him and begged him to come. I said to him, if Dad was alive he'd make you. I mean, he's just making it worse, innee, making you all look for him? But he never done nuffing,' she said, looking up urgently into Slider's face. 'He's a good boy, and I swear my Bible oaf he never done nuffing.'

'What's your brother's name?' Slider asked, hoping for enlightenment.

She hesitated. 'Look, I'll be straight wiv you. I mean, it don't matter me telling you because you'll find out anyway. He's got a record. That's partly why he won't come in. He's shit scared of the p'lice. But it's only little stuff, and he's going straight now. He's tried so hard, he really has, and me and Mum's so proud of him, and then this has to 'appen and spoil it all.' Her eyes filled with tears.

Slider tried again, patiently. 'Just tell me what he's done.'

'That's the 'ole fing, he's never done nuffing!' she cried, as if he were being wilfully stupid. 'He just happened to be there, that's all, just by chance, and he doesn't know nuffing about it. He never even knew this woman, this Chattie Cornfeld. You got to believe me.'

'Your brother was in the park at the time of the murder?' Slider said.

'That's what I've been *telling* you,' she said, wiping a tear from her eye with a forefinger. 'You been putting it out on the news about wanting to talk to him, and that was bad enough, but at least it could have been anybody. But then you put out a picture of him last night and that did it. He's gone into hiding now and he says he daren't go back to work on Monday, and if he loses that job I just know he'll turn bad. He thinks nobody trusts him.'

Running Man, Slider thought. So that was what it was all about. 'All right,' he said soothingly, 'just tell me from the beginning about – what's his name?'

'Dennis,' she said automatically, without noticing she'd given it away. 'You see, he was always a bit of a live wire, and when Dad died he sort of got into bad company at school, the way kids do, and he done a bit of shoplifting. We didn't know at first, Mum and me, but I was a bit worried because he was out all hours, and he didn't talk to me like he did before. I mean, he was a cheeky little devil, but him and me got on all right, you know what I mean? He told me things.'

She seemed to want a reply at this point so he said, 'Yes, I understand.'

'But now he was never home, and when he came in he'd just rush past wivout saying anyfing and go straight to his room an' shut the door. So I started to get worried. I mean, he was never a bad kid, but they dare each other and egg each other on, kids do. That's all it was to him, just a dare. But he got caught and warned, I don't know how many times, and the first we heard about it was when he was arrested proper, and that one went to court. Well, he only got a suspended, but that was enough. It broke me mum's heart. She always fought the world of Denny. She told him, she said if Dad was alive he'd beat you black and blue for it. And Denny promised he'd never do it again.'

'And did he?'

'He never shoplifted – I don't fink he did, anyway – but when he left school he got in wiv another lot and started smoking weed. Well, 'cause he was hanging about on the streets he got stopped and searched a few times by the – by policemen,' she corrected politely, 'and one time he had some weed on him and he got done for possession. When Mum found out about that one she burst into tears, and Denny was really frit then.

He'd never seen Mum cry before. So then he said he really would turn over a new leaf if we'd help him. Well, me and Mum helped him get this job, and he really has been trying hard, only it's not easy. His mates are always on at him. But I said, Den, you stick to it. You're doin' great, and never mind what them bastards say, excuse my French. And then *this* has to 'appen!' She cried again, what seemed like tears of frustration, and fumbled in her bag for a tissue. 'He's been in such a state since you started asking on the telly for him, and I told him to come in and clear it up, but he wouldn't. He said you coppers have got it in for him, and that you hate blacks, and that you'd fit him up for something. I said, don't be daft, but he said you'd never believe him 'cause he was black an' he's got a record. And the longer he left it, the worse it was. And then that picture was on the telly last night, and now he finks everyone finks he's a murderer!'

'So what was he doing in the park?' Slider asked, trying to keep a grip on the thread.

'He was going to work, of course. He always goes frough the park, it's the quickest way. And the only reason he was running was he didn't wanner be late. I mean, he's a good boy, and just because he's running you make him out to be a murderer and ruin his life.'

'We only ever wanted him to come forward so that we could eliminate him from our enquiries,' Slider said soothingly.

'Well, that's what I *told* him, but he doesn't trust coppers. But it's all right now, in't it? You do believe me?'

Slider believed her. Everything about her was patently honest, and she was trying to do her best by her brother. It did not, of course, mean that the brother had not lied to her.

'We'll have to check into it, just as a matter of routine. If you'd like to write down for me your name, address and telephone number, the time Dennis left home that morning, and the name and address of Dennis's employer, so that we can check with them what time he arrived that morning—'

'If you go asking his boss stuff about him like that,' she said bitterly, 'he'll lose his job and that'll be that.'

'I promise you we'll make it very clear we're just eliminating everyone who was in the park.'

She only shook her head slowly, her face profoundly troubled.

'Denny'll never forgive me. He'll find out I told you and he'll fink I shopped him.'

'I won't say anything about your visit here.' She was still unconvinced, and he didn't want to threaten her, so he said, 'You were right about one thing – the longer it went on the worse it looked for your brother. Now, if we can get this cleared up quickly everything can go back to normal. If you say he didn't know Chattie Cornfeld—'

'He *didn't*. I swear to you. He told me so and I know when he's lying and he wasn't lying then. He doesn't know any white birds.'

'Right. So all we have to do is check with his employer what time he got in that morning, and we're done.' He pushed the pad and pen at her temptingly. 'Sooner the better. Let's get it over with, eh?'

She sighed, reached for the pen, and began to write in an unpractised, loopy hand.

'Where is your brother now?' he asked.

'He's staying with a mate. He's scared to come home.'

'This friend he's staying with, it isn't Darren, is it, by any chance?' Slider said casually.

'No, it's Baz, I fink. Baz King,' she said, still writing. 'That's his best mate. I dunno where he lives, though. I fink it's somewhere in Acton but I dunno the address.'

'But he does know Darren? Darren Barnes?'

'I dunno,' she said. 'I don't fink so. I never heard him talk about him. Who is he?' He showed her the photo of Darren. She looked carefully and shook her head. 'No, I don't know him. Why ju wanna know?' Then her eyes widened. 'He's somfing to do wiv the murder, innee? That's why you're asking did Denny know him. You still fink Denny's in on it.' Tears rose again to her eyes and her lips quivered with anger and self-pity. 'You said you believed me!'

'I do believe you,' Slider said. 'You must understand that we have to check everything and everyone, even those people we believe with all our hearts. It's just our job.'

The use of the word 'hearts' got to her, but she was not quite ready to give up her pique. 'Denny's a good boy. I wish I'd never come,' she said, in hurt tones.

'I'm very grateful to you that you did,' Slider said. 'The more quickly we can get these little things cleared up, the sooner we can get after the real villains.'

She sniffed back her tears and seemed mollified. When she had finished writing, Slider asked her if she had a photograph of Dennis, and she produced one from a little folder in her bag. 'Can I keep this, for the time being? I'll let you have it back in a day or two.'

He ushered her out with full old-fashioned gallantry. 'Thank you again,' he said at the door. 'Mind the steps, now. Good afternoon.'

He watched her descent to the street with amazement, hardly able to believe she could walk on those tiny spike heels. It was something like seeing a huge water-filled balloon balance on a golf tee. As he turned to go back in, Hart arrived at the foot of the steps with a paper bag in her hand, and watched the departing form with raised eyebrows.

'Blimey,' she said. 'I bet she'd make a cracking tight-rope walker.'

'Is that my sandwich?' Slider said, practically snatching it from her. He was so hungry he could have eaten straight through the paper. 'How much do I owe you?'

'You can pay next time,' she said airily.

He gave her a stern look. That sort of thing had to be nipped in the bud. 'How much do I owe you?'

'Oh, well, you can't blame me for trying,' she said. 'You're not married yet.' And she changed the subject quickly. 'Who was that lady I saw you with just now? That was the one who came in, was it?'

'It was Running Man's sister, and she says he didn't do it, but was too scared to come forward because he doesn't trust the police and he's got a minor record.'

'Just the way you predicted, guv,' she said. 'So, do we cross him off?'

'Not just yet,' he said. 'He's run away and gone into hiding with a friend, which might be excessive caution for a man who really hasn't done anything. And we don't know that he didn't know Darren. He used to smoke weed and got done once for possession, according to his sister, so he may have bought something from Darren at some point. We'll have to look into him a bit more closely before we eliminate him.' He passed over the sheet of paper. 'Check with his employer what time he arrived that morning, then we can work out if he had time to do anything between leaving home and getting to work other than getting there. Run his record, see if the sister's told us everything. See if you can find any connection between him and Darren. Show this photo to Mrs Hammick, see if she remembers him ever coming to the house. And try to find this Baz King he's supposed to be staying with, lives somewhere in Acton.'

'D'you want me to go round and roust him out when I've found it?'

'Definitely not. I don't want him flushed out and running. We'll leave him be until we find out whether there's anything in it.'

They reached his door and she eyed the greasy bag in his hand. 'Want me to get you a tea to go with that?'

He hesitated long enough to feel he ought to discourage her from mothering him, but the thought of tea won by a couple of lengths.

'Yes, thanks,' he said. He heard his phone begin to ring and with an inward sigh pushed into his office to answer it, wondering if he'd get to the sausage sandwiches before they grew hair.

CHAPTER THIRTEEN

The Silence of the Labs

Baz King also turned out to have a record – for possession, carrying an offensive weapon, shoplifting and a couple of TDAs – which made it easy to find out where he lived. So if it became necessary to collar Dennis Proctor they could be there in a jiffy. But it seemed less and less likely they would need to. The owner of the small printing shop on the corner of Becklow and Askew Roads, a Mr Badcock, who had the honour to be his employer, was not best pleased at first at being tracked down and bothered on a Sunday afternoon when there was an international on telly; but when he heard that the cause was eliminating Dennis from enquiries he straightened his shoulders and got down to it. Dennis was a good boy, he said, and he was glad to be helping him overcome his unfortunate beginnings. He firmly believed that Dennis had been influenced by a bad lot and that underneath he had the right instincts, inculcated by his late father (who had been a friend of Mr Badcock – they had worked together at one time at the Gillette works on the Great West Road) and upheld by his mother and sister who were decent people.

What time had Dennis arrived at work on Wednesday? Wednesday, Wednesday – oh, yes, wait a minute, that was the morning he was late. He'd been late once or twice before, and Mr Badcock had warned him very sternly about it, so that lad had really been making an effort. How late? Well, not by much. He'd arrived out of breath from running at five past, and Mr Badcock had forgiven him because he'd obviously run so hard to make it on time he couldn't speak for about five minutes. Mr Badcock had advised him to start out earlier in the morning, and set him to work. How did he seem that day? Oh, just his usual self: cheery – a bit cheeky, if you want to know, but that was youngsters, these days, and there was no harm in him. You'd to keep after them, none of them had an idea of hard work, but Dennis was no worse than the rest in that department, a bit better if truth be told because he was interested in the business. Had quite a little flair for setting things out – artistic, you might say. How had he been the rest of the week? Well, now you come to mention it, he was a bit absent-minded on Saturday, and he dashed off on the dot of five without tidying up, which Mr Badcock was going to have to talk to him about. But Wednesday, no, Wednesday he'd been fine.

'You've been a big help,' Hart said. 'There's just one more question – can you remember what he was wearing on Wednesday when he came in?'

'Well,' Mr Badcock said slowly as he thought, 'well, now – no, I can't say that I do. They all dress much the same, don't they, these lads, baggy pants and a T-shirt? Always clean, though, Dennis, I'll say that for him. Spotless, really. I expect that's his mother's influence. But I can't remember exactly what he had on, what colour or anything. I wouldn't really notice, you see.'

'Do you remember if he was wearing a grey top with a hood?'

'No, no, I'm sorry, I can't say. I believe he *has* worn one of those but whether it was Wednesday or any other day . . .' He laughed. 'I have a job to remember what I've got on without looking. Typical man, my wife says.'

'So you see, boss,' Hart said to Slider later, 'it looks as though Dennis may not be our man. For one thing, if he'd just done a murder he wouldn't've been likely to seem just like his usual cheery cheeky self – unless he's a total psychopath. Also, his mum says he left home for work on Wednesday at ten to eight. They live in the flats in Rivercourt Road and that's a mile as the crow flies, a bit more allowing for corners and that. Well, you can do a mile in fifteen minutes at a brisk walk, and he was running like the clappers, but even so—'

'Yes,' said Slider. 'Hardly time to fit in a murder on the way.'

'Unless they're all lying.'

'There's always that,' Slider said. 'But it seems more likely that he dawdled along with his head in the clouds and then realised he was going to be late and dashed the last bit.'

'Yeah,' said Hart. 'Also, McLaren took the photo of him round

Mrs Hammick's, and she said she's never seen him. It don't prove Chattie didn't know him, but it's all on the same side. It's a pity the old geezer can't remember what he was wearing. If he didn't have the hoodie on, that'd mean he'd chucked it on the way, which would be a help, but—' She shrugged.

'Hmm,' said Slider, pondering. 'Well, I think we'd better go round to his friend's house and get him, ask him a few questions, get a voluntary buccal swab from him for elimination purposes, and then take him home. Tell him he's not wanted for anything and there's nothing to worry about. Make sure he believes that. If he really is innocent, I don't want to lose him his job and ruin his life; and if we find evidence against him later, it'll be easier to pick him up if he's going about his normal daily business than if he's on the run.'

'Yeah, boss, good one. Who's going?'

'I think you should do it – you look nice and unthreatening. Take McLaren with you in case he panics, but tell him to keep his mouth shut. We want to reassure this boy, not frighten him.'

'Understood. I'll make 'im stand behind me,' Hart said.

She turned to go, and in the doorway passed Atherton, just coming in. He answered her enquiring look with a shake of the head. To Slider he amplified, 'Nothing. No blood anywhere except in the living room where he attacked Jasper. No traces on any clothes or shoes, nothing down the drains. No evidence at all. It's all on the knife, now. If they don't find Chattie's DNA on that, we've got nothing but his confession. Haven't you heard from them yet?'

'They only had it this morning, give them a chance.'

'God, is it still Sunday? It feels like a week. That flat! I don't know why we have prisons. Making someone live in that would be punishment enough.'

'To you, not to them,' Slider said. He could see Atherton was depressed. He said, 'The hospital phoned to say that Stalybrass is making progress. There were some internal injuries but nothing life-threatening, though they had to remove his spleen. They've got him patched up and it's a matter of rest and recuperation now.'

'That's not all it's a matter of,' Atherton said. 'Remember, I've been there.'

'Well, yes, of course, I know that—'

'But do you? You seem to be taking it very lightly.'

'I'm just trying to reassure you. Don't bite my head off.'

Atherton sighed and rubbed the back of his neck. 'Yes, sorry. I'm tired, that's all. I think I'll knock off now, if you've nothing else urgent for me.'

Slider nodded, and then, unwillingly – but compassion demanded he didn't let his friend walk into it unprepared, 'Have you got plans for tonight?'

Atherton clearly didn't know how to take it. Was he going to be quizzed on his love-life or was it an invitation to supper? 'Um, well, nothing definite.'

'Were you meaning to see Marion Davies?' Slider asked, hating it.

'Nothing planned, but I thought I might call in and see if she's all right. It must have been a big shock for her. Why?'

'So she hasn't phoned you?'

'No. What is all this about?'

'Have you checked your answer machine at home?'

'For God's sake!'

Slider gave in. 'She phoned here, asking for you, and when I said you were out she asked me to give you a message. I made it clear I don't do that sort of thing, but if she hasn't phoned you – well, I don't want you to . . .' He hesitated, looking for the right words.

'Make a fool of myself?' Atherton said, with a sour smile. 'What was the message? From your face I gather it was thanks but no thanks.'

'She doesn't want to see you again. I'm sorry,' Slider added awkwardly. 'I didn't want to get in the middle of this.'

'No, it's all right. I'm sorry you got let in for it.' Atherton wandered across the room and sat down on the windowsill. He stared at his feet, still kneading his neck muscles. The angled sunlight picked out the planes of his face and Slider realised the boy wonder was showing signs of wear.

Atherton looked up suddenly, and gave Slider a rueful smile. 'Can I tell you something? I find I'm actually not too disappointed. I think I went a bit off the rails with her.'

Slider nodded, not to indicate agreement, which would have been tactless, though true, but to show he was listening.

'She's a gorgeous girl, and I couldn't resist her. But – God, she's so young! I mean, not so much in years but – her *mind*. She doesn't know *anything*! How can someone educated be so ignorant? History, geography, literature, current events – all closed books to her. Half of what I said to her went straight over her head. And she wasn't even curious; she didn't care, she didn't even seem to *know* how ignorant she was.' He paused. 'And I hated the way she talked. All that "you know" and "sort of" and "like". All we had together was bed.'

'Well, that's always been enough for you in the past,' Slider couldn't help saying.

'Mm,' said Atherton; and then, 'Can I tell you something else?'

'Is it going to hurt?'

'Eh?'

'Don't tell me anything that's got body fluids in it. I'm squeamish.'

Atherton acknowledged the hit with a movement of his hand and a tired smile. 'I'll keep it basic. I was just going to say that even bed wasn't that great. Not that there's anything wrong with her. She is gorgeous. But it just seemed – oh, I don't know – odd. When I woke up in the morning and she was there, it seemed so weird I jumped straight up and went and showered.' The pause was so long that Slider didn't think he was going to finish, though he had guessed what it was. 'It seemed weird because she wasn't Sue,' he said at last.

Slider kept silence. When people tell you their troubles they rarely want your advice, though the human urge is always to give it. And he didn't want to get into the position of agony aunt to Atherton, who was not only his friend but his colleague and subordinate, which complicated things. Atherton was staring at his feet again, his thoughts far away. At last he said, in a low voice, 'I miss her.'

Despite his noble resolve, Slider found he had said, 'Why don't you ring her?' before he could stop himself. He cursed inwardly.

Atherton looked up, the steel coming back into his face. 'She dumped me, if you remember. She was the dump-er, I was the dump-ee. I am not going to extend my rear for a second kicking, thank you.'

There was an awkward silence (and serve him right, Slider chastised himself, for opening his mouth), and then Atherton rose from the windowsill and said, 'I'll get off home, then, if that's all right?'

'Yes, okay. Nothing that can't wait until tomorrow.' He hesitated and then added, 'Do you want to come round later for supper, when Jo gets home?'

'No, thanks all the same. I might have an early night. I'll just clear my desk and be off.'

He went away into the CID room. Slider returned to his work. A short time later he heard the phone ringing through there, but it stopped quite quickly so Slider assumed someone had picked it up. A few minutes more, and Atherton appeared in the doorway. 'News,' he said.

'Good or bad?'

'Depends on your viewpoint. We've found Darren. He didn't get very far from Brixton, home and beauty. He's been staying with a friend in Coldharbour Lane, about five minutes from Ferndale Road. He and the friend went out in the friend's car this morning to get some more supplies, and got stopped for running a red light: the car's rather conspicuous, death's-head paint job, no silencer and no tax disc.'

'Dumb,' said Slider.

'And it gets dumber. The friend pulls over, and as soon as he stops, Darren's out and running for it. Of course, that's a hare to a greyhound as far as the Brixton officers are concerned. Suspicion circuits engage, they go after him and bring him down running. He manages to break loose and lands a punch on one of them. He gets nicked for assaulting a police officer, while the friend meanwhile takes the opportunity and scarpers.'

'A tale for our time.'

'The patrol takes him in, he refuses to give his name and has no ID on him, but the custody officer recognises him from the picture we circulated, takes his tenprint and runs it to confirm. So Darren is now sitting in a cell in Brixton nick waiting for us to go and interview him.'

'Well, that sounds like good news. Where's the bad news bit?'

'I only said it depended on your viewpoint. It's bad news for Darren.'

Slider stood up. 'I'd better get over there. This Sunday never seems to end.'

'I'll come with you,' said Atherton.

'I thought you were going home?'

'When all that awaits me is the cold hearth and the empty chair? I'll take a sweating villain any time.'

Darren was sweating. He was also sullen. There was a bump on his forehead, presumably where he had hit the pavement after the rugger tackle that brought him down. But he hadn't the look of a junkie, for which Slider was grateful. There might be more frustrating jobs than having to interview the chemically altered, but he hadn't come across one yet. Darren looked well fed and strong, he didn't twitch, his eyes didn't wander – on the contrary, they glared with full resentment and purpose. He looked like a dangerous animal. His hair hung round his head in matted dreadlocks, and he wore a tuft of beard between his lower lip and his chin. There were rings in his ears and eyebrows and a tattoo of a rearing cobra on one forearm – which must have been a bit of a handicap to a criminal wanting to avoid identification. He bared his teeth when Slider and Atherton came in.

'Darren Barnes?' Slider said. The reply was a profanity. 'Give it up, son,' Slider said. 'We know who you are. We want to ask you some questions. Don't make things worse for yourself.'

'What you want?' he snarled.

'I want to know about you and Chattie Cornfeld,' Slider said. He pushed a packet of cigarettes across the table. 'Smoke?'

Darren took one automatically, and then the action seemed to give him pause. He stared at Slider with sudden fear. In a moment of telepathy, Slider saw that the small piece of kindliness had made him realise this was something grave. It was like the consideration of the executioner. Darren, Slider concluded, was not as thick as he looked.

Darren lit the cigarette and dragged the smoke down. His eyes flitted once to Atherton, who was being a self-effacing stork, standing a little back from the table, but then returned to Slider as if drawn by strings.

'Let me help you along a bit,' Slider said. 'I'd hate you to waste your time denying things that are established beyond any doubt. A large stash of cocaine was found in Chattie's house, hidden there by you. This, as I'm sure you know, is too large an amount for a mere possession charge. This is dealing, and you know what that means.'

'You can't prove it's mine,' Darren said, his voice husky with smoke and fear.

'Don't be stupid, of course we can,' Slider said, in an offhand way.

Darren clenched his fist. 'Don't call me stupid!' he shouted, his eyes glaring.

'On the contrary, I don't think you're stupid at all, Darren,' Slider said calmly. 'You've done some stupid things, but you're not such a fool you think you can get away with them. How well did you know Chattie?'

'She's my bird's sister, that's all.'

'You knew her house well enough to know where to hide the charlie, didn't you?'

'I stayed there wiv Jass sometimes.'

'Were you and Chattie closer than that? Were you selling her stuff?'

'Fuck off.'

'That's no answer. Did you sleep with her, Darren?'

His nostrils flared. 'That snotty slag? I'd sooner shag a dog.'

'She turned you down, did she? That must have made you angry.'

'I never asked her. I told you, I wouldn't touch her wiv a bargepole. I just—'

'You just used her house to hide your stash until the heat was off,' Slider supplied. 'Well, we know that bit. What I don't understand is why you killed her.'

Sweat jumped out of his pores almost visibly. 'I never! I never! Get outa here, you pig bastard! You ain't gonna stick that on me. I know what you're like, you fucking pigs.'

'But you were seen, Darren. You were seen talking to her in the park that morning, just before she died, right on the spot where we found her body.'

He stared for a moment, and then something quite visibly came to him. His mouth hung open for a moment as he thought something out, and then his hands relaxed. 'It wunt me. I gotta nalibi.'

'An alibi for what?' Slider asked.

'You never saw me in the park that morning. I was in Manchester.'

'Yes, so we were told. Unfortunately, your mate Dave didn't back you up. He said he'd not seen you in weeks. So I'm afraid that won't help you.'

'Not Dave. I wunt wiv Dave.' He looked at them triumphantly. 'I was in the nick.'

'Nice try, Darren, but not very convincing. We asked our colleagues in Manchester about you and they hadn't seen you either.'

'Yeah, well, they din't know it was me.' He grinned. 'I borrowed me mate's credit card. I went to see a bird I know down Moss Side, but we had a row so I dumped her and went and got legless. The coppers picked me up and shoved me in a lockup overnight and let me go in the morning. I told 'em I was Trevor Wishart. Well, he ain't got a record. You ask 'em. That's where I was Tuesd'y night.'

'We will ask them,' Slider warned, 'so you'd better not be wasting our time.'

'I never killed her,' he said with growing confidence. 'I hated her, but so what? She was nuffing, just a piece o' snobby trash. I wouldn't waste my time killing her.'

'So why did you run?' Slider said. 'You took off Wednesday night and you've been in hiding since. What was all that about?'

The self-satisfied grin faded and he looked sullen again. He shrugged, and smoked.

'The cocaine in Chattie's house? Was that why you ran?'

He muttered something, avoiding eyes.

'You're not such a big man after all, are you, Darren? You're just a chicken-shit little dealer, and we've been wasting our time on you. Brave enough to hit a woman, and leave her to take the fall, but that's as high as you go, isn't it?'

Darren threw him a quick glance, in which anger gleamed, but he held his tongue.

'Or *was* it just about the cocaine?' Slider said musingly. 'Maybe you wanted Chattie dead. Maybe she'd crossed you. Maybe it was about the money. Was it the money? She was pretty well off, wasn't she? If she was dead, maybe her money would go to her sister, your girlfriend.'

'There wasn't nuffing comin' to Jass from that cow. She told her, she leavin' everfing to charity, the stupid bitch!' He said it with deep contempt not unmingled with wonder that anyone could be so mad.

'Revenge, then. That's a good enough reason to want her dead. But you hadn't got the bottle to do it. So you got someone to do it for you – is that the way it was?'

'If I kill someone I do it myself, man,' Darren snarled. 'I don't need no-one to do my dirty work for me.'

'Oh, really? So what sort of work does Dennis do for you?' He slapped down the photograph of Dennis and shoved it across the table in one movement, his eyes on Darren's face.

But Darren looked at the picture with complete blankness. 'Who this piece o' shit little kid? I don' mix wiv the kiddie league. An' who the fuck is Dennis?'

Slider believed him. The whole Darren edifice had crumbled at a touch. He was not their man. He found space in his mind for relief that it looked as though Chattie was cleared of any suspicion of dealing drugs. But mostly he felt a weary anger that they had had to waste so much time and so many resources in trying to find this graceless, worthless crook. If the Manchester alibi stood, and he believed it would, at least they could still get him for the cocaine and for striking a police officer. That ought to add up to a spell inside for master Darren.

In the car on the way back to Shepherd's Bush he was silent, deep in thought. A phone call from Brixton to Moss Side had confirmed that a Trevor Wishart had been held drunk and incapable overnight on Tuesday, and a photograph of Darren sent through was identified as the same man. So Darren had not killed Chattie, however else he was connected with the case – and Slider was afraid it was turning out to be not at all. So much of police work was like that, following trails that petered out in the sand, unpicking lies that had nothing to do with anything and need never have been told.

But it left them with their work to do all over again. Running Man was a washout – it was impossible to believe now that Dennis Proctor had had anything to do with it, and it was very plain that Darren did not know him. And it seemed equally indisputable that Standing Man was not either of them. So who was he? Was he the murderer or had he merely stopped to ask the time or something? Was he Toby Harkness?

Atherton must have been thinking along similar lines, because he said now, 'So we're left with Toby.'

'If he was Standing Man, where are the clothes?'

'Yes, there weren't any tracksuit or jogging-type clothes in the flat at all. And in fact from what I know of him from his colleagues, he wasn't the exercise type – which is confirmed by his chubby, under-muscled bod.'

'Which is not to say he couldn't have bought them for the purpose,' Slider said, 'and chucked them away afterwards.'

'The knife, the knife,' Atherton muttered. 'It's all on the knife. I hope the lab gets on with it!'

'Does it occur to you,' Slider said, a mile further on, 'that there's no reason to think he'd use the same knife? He could equally have bought a new knife for the purpose, and thrown that away afterwards.'

'You do have these lovely thoughts,' Atherton complained, hunching deeper into his seat.

As they trudged upstairs from the yard, Slider realised he was hungry again. His late lunch seemed a long time ago. 'What about some nosh?' he asked Atherton. 'I don't think I can wait until Joanna gets home. Are you hungry?'

'Starving. I didn't get any lunch.'

'Oh, the glamour of police work! I'm just going to tidy my desk, and then I've had it for the day. How about a ruby? There won't be much else open around here this time of a Sunday.'

'Okay, I'm game.'

They reached the door of the CID room, just as Wendell, one of the loaners from uniform, came off the phone. He turned to Slider, his excitement palpable, and Slider had a sinking feeling that Sunday had a few surprises left up its sleeve, and the chances of a curry were receding faster than a prime minister's hairline.

'What is it, lad?' he asked. 'Break it to me gently. I'm in a fragile state.'

'Someone's found some clothes, sir. Looks as if it could be what we're looking for.'

Monday was rubbish collection day in Ashchurch Grove, a side-street that cut off a bend of Askew Road, running between it and Goldhawk Road. The residents were accustomed to putting out their rubbish on Sunday night, because the bin men came early in the morning. Not that they were strictly bin men round there, since they would only pick up black plastic sacks.

Mrs Emerald O'Connor, who was elderly and rather wispy about the chin, nevertheless looked braced by the shock of her discovery rather than upset. Slider supposed that anyone who had lived through the war would be hard to shake; and besides, what old people like her often suffered from most was loneliness and boredom. Here was something new and different in her life, and something, moreover, which made her the centre of attention to all these nice young policemen.

She didn't waste a moment, and was off into a tirade about the garbage situation like an over-eager runner getting off the blocks before the gun fired. 'It's the cats, mostly. You can't keep a cat away from rubbish, not when it's only in a sack. You can see them hanging round on Sunday nights, dozens of 'em, just waiting for people to put the sacks out, and the minute the door's closed they're down there clawing the bags open. And then it's stuff everywhere, bones and packets of this and that and – well, I wouldn't like to say what! And people put their stuff out far too early. Sunday night, it's supposed to be, but I see them bringing it out Sunday morning, even Saturday. Some of 'em put a bag out any old day they like, just to get it out of the house, never mind anyone else's convenience! Oh, no. And there it sits, spreading rubbish about because of the cats, and smelling like the Dear knows what. And all because the bin men won't empty a bin! Have you ever heard the like? What's a bin man for if he won't lift a bin? Too dainty, that's what they are. Afraid of hurting themselves! So we all have to suffer. It'll be rats next, you mark my words. Where I lived before we had them, rats as big as cats, dirty things! And with all the food these restaurants throw out, it's a wonder we haven't all been bitten to death in our beds. It's a crime and a sin to waste food, that's what I've always said, but that one across the road throws out enough food to feed the five thousand every morning. And people passing by see the bags out and they just dump stuff on top. It's nothing but a temptation to bad habits and dirtiness.'

Shorn of the by-way perambulations, what her story amounted to was that she had brought her meagre black sack of rubbish ('Two sacks is supposed to be the maximum, but what some of them bring out – well, you'd think it was the whole contents of the house. It's a wonder they've anything left in there!') down the front garden to leave it in the approved spot by the front gate. As she put it down, she noticed that someone had thrown a plastic carrier bag of rubbish over her hedge into her garden, something that happened not infrequently. She went to retrieve it and put it with the black sack for the bin men to take the next morning.

'And I picked it up carefully, I can tell you, because you never know what's in them things. Broken glass, needles, anything – and worse. But this one was squashy, like something soft, and one of the cats must have clawed at it because it was ripped down the side, like you see it. And naturally I have a look to see what's in there, and I can see it's something grey, and a dark stain on it. Well, of course, then I remembered that nasty business in the park with the poor girl that was murdered, and I remembered it said in the paper that the police were looking for bloodstained clothing. It must have been the smell of the blood that made the cats go after it. Nasty things, cats. I don't like 'em. Dogs, now – I always had a dog, up until a few years ago when my old Dandy died, and I didn't feel I could cope with starting again with a puppy, not at my age, but I often wish I had, because a dog's company, now, not like a cat, stand-offy creatures they are . . .'

She babbled like a running brook as they examined the immediate area. It was plainly only too easy to walk along with a carrier bag in your hand and simply lob it gently over a suitable fence or hedge when no-one was looking. And dumping rubbish in this way was clearly such a commonplace thing that even had someone seen you they would probably not remark it or remember it. Mrs O'Connor had no idea when the bag had been left there. She hadn't noticed it at all until she brought the rubbish down. It could have been there all week, or it could have been left this morning. She simply couldn't say.

The bag proved to contain a grey hoodie with bloodstains on its front – smears, Slider thought, that looked as though the knife might have been cleaned on it – and a pair of latex surgical gloves, also bloodied.

'Well,' said Slider, with satisfaction, 'we've got him now. He must be an amateur to have thrown out the gloves like this. Even if we couldn't get any DNA off the hoodie, we'd certainly find some cells inside the gloves. Thank heaven for the stupidity of criminals.'

'If it was Toby, I can see him being clever enough to think of wearing gloves and daft enough to dump them like this,' Atherton said. 'Definitely not firing on all cylinders. Well, this is better than a poke in the eye.'

'It's the best,' Slider said, much cheered. 'We get Chattie's DNA out of the bloodstain and the murderer's from the gloves or the clothing, and we're home and dry.'

'More work for the lab. Can we fast-track this stuff as well?'

'Oh, definitely. If there was anything faster than fast track, I'd even pay for that.'

CHAPTER FOURTEEN

Aisle Altar Hymn

There are many sacrifices made on the altar of Hymen, but it probably doesn't matter as long as one is sure of the discretion of the spouse. And Slider had good reason, in his own opinion, for telling Joanna about Atherton's romantic difficulties. He didn't tell her that Marion Davies had rejected him, only what Atherton had said about finding he was unhappy with someone who wasn't Sue.

They were having boiled eggs for breakfast (folic acid in the yolks, prevents spina bifida, he thought automatically. Childbirth had become much more complicated since his son and daughter by his first marriage had been conceived). Joanna sat across the table from him, the sunshine in her tumbled bronze hair, the shadow of her breasts under her muslin robe both disturbing and comforting. She looked tired, he thought. Three long days of hard work were too much for her in her— He caught himself up, smiling inwardly. Women throughout space and time had worked long and hard in that condition and never thought twice about it. But there was such a fuss made these days about pregnancy that it was hard not to fall in with it. Joanna had more than once complained that the medical profession seemed to regard it as some kind of serious illness.

Joanna sipped her tea as he told her about Atherton, then put down her mug and said, 'I can see you want me to say something about it but I'm not sure what. He's missing Sue. I'm not surprised. They were very good together – better than I think he was ever willing to admit.'

Slider thought that was unfair. 'He did offer to marry her.'

She gave a faint smile. 'The ultimate sacrifice. How generous.'

'You know I don't think that,' he said, hurt.

'But I think you do – subconsciously. It's atavistic. For centuries men have regarded marriage as a trap in which the only beneficiaries are women, and you can't change that mindset in a minute.'

'Well, let's not forget that it was Sue who rejected him, and not vice versa.'

'I know, and I could kick her.'

'I thought you wanted to kick him?'

'Oh, yes, that too,' she said, as if she were not contradicting herself. The workings of a woman's mind were deep and mysterious, he thought. He remembered the old adage, that having female hormones was like drinking twenty-five cans of lager: you can't talk rationally or drive properly.

'He was an ass to take a huff and not pursue her,' Joanna went on. 'I mean, that's traditional too, isn't it, saying no the first time just to test your suitor's resolve? Read Jane Austen – and I know Jim has, so he ought to have recognised it. But, then, she was an idiot not to realise how fragile he is.'

'Fragile?' Slider exploded.

'Psychologically. Those serial womanisers always are. Low self-image. It's only by numerical conquest they can reassure themselves of their worth.'

'I think he just likes sex,' Slider suggested mildly.

She grinned. 'Who doesn't? But you must admit he was a bit crazy, the way he had to have anything that moved. But of course,' she went on, buttering more toast, 'Sue's fragile too. She had a rotten relationship with a man who knocked her about, and it's made it hard for her to trust. Jim ought to know *that.*'

'You do make things complicated,' he complained.

'*I* do?'

'You women. Why can't two people just like each other and get on with it?'

'Darling, you're so sweet,' she cooed.

'Well, *we*'re all right.'

'We're exceptional people. Intelligent, well adjusted.' She eyed him. 'What is it you want me to do? Talk to Sue? Talk to Jim?'

'I'm not sure that we ought to get involved. They're both adults, after all.'

'As the bird with the broken wing said, that's a matter of a pinion. But it's always difficult,' she added, 'with people who get to their age without being married. It takes adjustment and compromise for two people to live together, and the older you are, the more set in your ways, and the harder it is to change.'

'Hm,' said Slider.

'If I get a chance, I'll talk to Sue. And Jim, if the opportunity arises.'

'All right, but don't say I told you to. I'm having a hard enough time with this case without hurt feelings intruding.'

'Yes, it was awful about poor Jasper. It's terrible when it happens to someone you know. Is he going to be all right, do you know?'

'Probably yes. Physically, anyway.'

Joanna knew he was thinking of Atherton, who had been stabbed in the course of an investigation a couple of years back and had taken a long time to recover his nerve – if, indeed, he had recovered it completely even now.

She said, 'A few people last night said they weren't hugely surprised that Toby went off the rails, because he's been in the balance for ages, only surprised about the level of violence. I didn't know him, but Stef Beaton, the clarinettist, said he's known Toby for years, and thought he was barmy. He had a total obsession with a girl some years ago and ended up practically stalking her. Her father had to warn him off in the end.'

'Pity we didn't know that earlier. So people were talking about the incident already last night?'

'Goss gets round the music world like grass through a goose. I was first told about it at lunchtime. It's a terrible shame for Baroque Solid as well, because I can't see how they can survive the loss of two of their members at this stage – not to mention the shock of what happened. If they were established, they could recruit replacements, but it will all be too personal and delicately balanced at the moment. And they were so talented. It's a great loss.'

Slider nodded absently. 'Did the gossip mention that Toby confessed to having killed Chattie Cornfeld?'

'No,' she said. 'Did he really? There was some loose talk that maybe he had done it – you know the way people speculate – but not that he'd confessed. But that's good, isn't it, from your point of view?'

'Yes,' said Slider, 'if he really did do it. He's so disturbed, it's possible it was a false confession.'

'Oh. But why do you think he didn't do it? I mean, passionate jealousy, a woman who'd rejected him, a rival – it makes sense, especially given this near-stalking thing in the past.'

'Well, of course, I didn't know about that. He had no police record.'

'No, the girl's father sorted it out. It does add a bit of flavour to the confession, though, doesn't it?'

'Yes,' said Slider.

'And doesn't trying to kill Jasper tend to prove it?'

'I'm keeping an open mind about it,' Slider said, 'but I can't help feeling if he was going to do it he'd have done them both more or less at the same time, not waited three days before attacking Jasper.'

'Maybe he didn't have an opportunity before.'

'But he saw him every day.'

'In company with the others, presumably. Maybe he couldn't get him alone before.'

'Hmm.'

'You're not convinced.'

'I wish I were. It just doesn't feel quite right to me. But I'd be happy to be convinced, if only we had some evidence apart from motive.'

'And a confession,' she reminded him. 'And if Toby didn't do it, who did?'

'Ah, that's the problem. We've eliminated the other suspects.'

'Maybe you'll find some more.'

'Thanks.'

There wasn't much to do but wait for the lab reports. Hart had managed to persuade Dennis Proctor to go home, and a phone call to the print shop found that he had gone in to work that morning, which was good. Toby Harkness had been moved to a secure psychiatric bed, and Swilley had been to see him, but was unable to get anything useful from him.

'He's completely out of it, boss,' she said. 'He doesn't respond to questions, just sits rocking himself and staring at nothing. The shrink reckons it could be weeks before he comes back to planet Earth. If he really is off his kadooba,' she added glumly, 'even if we did have enough evidence against him, we'd never get him for it. It'd be diminished responsibility and a nice comfy bed in a psych hospital.'

'What's the news on Jasper?'

'The hospital says he's "comfortable".' She grimaced. 'I love the words they use. I should think that's the last thing he is. But it looks as if he'll recover all right. They said he can be interviewed this afternoon.'

'Right, Hart can do that.'

Swilley was leaving, and turned back to say, 'Toby's parents were flapping round this morning, making threatening noises. I couldn't make out what they thought we were guilty of. I suppose it's just habit with that sort of people, to try and do us down. I mean, there's no doubt he just about filleted poor old Jasper. Literally red-handed. But they're looking for something to complain about, so I thought I'd better warn you.'

Slider spent the time going through all the evidence again, trying to spot an anomaly, panning witness statements for previously unnoticed nuggets, studying the photos taken of the crowd at the scene in the hope of recognising a face.

It was late morning when the lab rang. The labs were all private now, with the police buying their services out of budget, and Tufnell – Tufty – Arceneaux had become head of the biology section under the new regime. Biology basically meant the human body, but the vast majority of their work now was DNA testing, for, with improvement in techniques, DNA could be retrieved from an amazing number of sources and from amazingly small samples. The old blood groups were as dead as phrenology, and it wouldn't be long before fingerprinting went the same way.

Tufty was a huge man with a huge voice, though his new responsibilities and being in the private sector had slightly muted him. It unnerved him to think of the police being 'customers'. But he and Slider were old friends, and in their palmy days, when Slider had been at Central, had enjoyed many a frolic, which always with Tufty involved ingesting large amounts of food and alcohol. Since Tufty had about twice the body mass of Slider, it was always Slider who had come off worse in these encounters.

'Bill! How are you, old fruitbat?' Tufty cried.

'Struggling along. How are you?'

'Fine, fine! Full of juice.'

'How's the family?' Tufty had two sons of whom he was immensely proud.

'Young Rupe's got a new girlfriend. She's a vegetarian,' Tufty mourned.

'Oh, bad luck,' said Slider. 'Are her parents cousins?'

'Wouldn't be surprised. But Triss is doing very well. He's up for a part in what they call a Major Motion Picture. Queer phrase. Always makes me think of an endoscopic examination of the large bowel.'

Slider laughed. 'And how come you never hear about a minor motion picture? Or a minor best-seller, come to that.'

'Beats me. But anyway, Triss reckons he's got a very good chance, and it could be the breakthrough for him. One of those frightfully English pictures, set in the thirties, something about upper-class spies. He's very excited that someone called Ewan McGregor is going to be in it. I thought he was a footballer,' Tufty complained.

'The world is leaving you behind,' Slider sympathised.

'Ah, well, I never go to the flicks these days. Put me in a dark, warm place after a day's work and I either want to sleep or roger something. Or both.'

'But not necessarily in that order.'

'Not sure, these days. Anyway, talking of a day's work—'

'You've got a result on the knife for me?' Slider said hopefully.

'Pulled out all the stops, old bean. I hope you appreciate the fabulous velocity of our efforts, because you're not going to appreciate much else. There's only one sort of DNA on the knife, and it matches the sample you sent us of – let me see, sample number dum-de-dum-de-dum, here it is – Jasper Stalybrass. That's a nice old-fashioned name. I hope he lives to pass it on.'

'It seems probable,' Slider said.

'You sound glum, chum.'

'You've just told me I've got no evidence. Sometimes I wish I'd never left the uniformed division.'

'Ah, life isn't the same without a lump of wood down your trousers,' Tufty sympathised cheerily. 'Never mind, you'll get him some other way, whoever he is.'

'I didn't entirely believe it *was* him.'

'Well, what are you complaining about, then?'

'Just life in general. What about the clothing I sent you, the jacket and the gloves?'

'Plenty of stuff there for me to play with,' Tufty said. 'Blood, of course – presumably the victim's? What's the name – Charlotte Cornfeld? That's who you want us to match it to?'

'Yes, and Freddie sent you a swab and blood sample for that.'

'Yup, all in order. Then there's the wearer of said jacket and gloves, and we've got skin cells, sweat, dandruff and loose hair to work on there. No trouble at all. We'll get a nice profile out of that lot for you.'

'How long?'

'Fast track?'

'Top priority.'

'Thirty-six hours is the absolutely fastest we can do it,' Tufty said. Slider left him a pause, knowing him of old, and after a beat he continued, 'For you, maybe an hour or so sooner.'

'Thanks, Tufty. The ASAPer the better.'

'Well, after all, guv, it doesn't prove it wasn't Toby,' Hart said. 'It just doesn't prove it was.'

'I know that,' said Slider. 'We can only hope the lab tests come back with something. In the meantime, we have to try to find some other evidence.'

'How about we try all the people who've said they were in the park at the time with a photo of Toby?' Swilley suggested.

'The one on the website's a good one,' Hart said. 'We could use that.'

'Fine. And I want someone to follow up on this story that Harkness stalked another girl. Talk to his colleagues and friends, if any.'

'Jim's got the in on that little lot,' said Swilley.

Slider caught Atherton's horrified look and said, 'I think after the Toby-Jasper incident they may want a fresh face. You can do it, Norma. We know he didn't have a record, but there may have been more than one incident. Probably best not to bother his parents—'

'In spades,' Swilley agreed fervently.

'In any case, they'd probably deny it. But get everything you can, and especially if he became violent at any time, even if it was only a punch-up.'

'Righty-oh, boss.'

'And,' Slider said to the whole group, 'we have to consider the possibility that it wasn't Toby, hard though I know that is for you all to bear. We have to find some other lines to follow up, in the eventuality.'

'Well, like Jim always says,' said Hart, 'it always comes down to two motives – sex or money.'

Atherton gave her an ironic bow from across the room. 'So if Toby is sex, who's money?'

'Darren said Jassy knew about the will,' said Hart. 'So it can't be her.'

'There might have been other money that would've come to her if Chattie was dead,' Mackay said. 'What about other relatives? Did Granny have anything to leave? What about her old man?'

Swilley damped his fire. 'But Darren and Jassy have both got alibis.'

'An alibi's made for breaking,' McLaren said almost absently, as he licked the last melted chocolate off the inside of a Twix wrapper.

'Oh, and what does that mean, Food-face?'

McLaren obviously hadn't got as far as working out a meaning for his words. His expression went blank for a moment with effort, and then he said, 'Doesn't say she might not've got someone else to do the hit for her.'

'She hasn't got any money. How would she pay a hit man? They like to be paid up front, you know,' Swilley told him kindly.

'Darren had all that coke. He must have money. He could've given it her.'

'If we've got to look for a contract killer,' Hart said, 'we really are in the clarts.'

'It's too daft a killing for a contract killer,' Slider said. 'Let's not lose sight of the fact that whoever did it, they were dumb enough to try to make it look like the Park Killer's work, and to believe we wouldn't see through it. It's an amateur killing; a planned killing; a cowardly killing.'

'Which sounds,' Swilley said, meeting his eyes, 'more like money than sex.' He nodded agreement to her, but said nothing.

'Well, maybe it's something to do with her dad's business after all,' Hart said. 'Only what? If someone was trying to get at him, you'd think he'd know it.'

'Not blackmail,' said Atherton. 'But how about revenge? He loved her, and a businessman who's successful must have trodden on somebody's toes on the way up.'

'He upset enough people in his family,' Hollis said.

'That's certainly a line to follow up,' Slider said. 'Get on to your contacts on the papers, get everything you can from their morgues on Henry Cornfeld.'

'And keep hoping it turns out it was Toby after all,' said Hollis, 'because we lose the extra bodies tomorrow.'

It seemed strange to have enough time for lunch again. His body was so unused to being fed at the right time that he couldn't manage more than a few mouthfuls of the canteen liver and bacon, mash and peas, and, aware that he was being stared at by some of the uniform relief also lunching, he abandoned the effort and took a cup of tea back to his office. There he sat brooding over the photographs of Chattie, wrung by her smile, trying to make her tell him what had happened. Little Princess Perfect, Hart had called her spitefully, but she had turned out to be pretty nice after all. She had had enough income to have been idle like Jassy, but she had preferred to set up her own business and work hard at it to prove she could make it alone, as her father had done. She was her father's favourite child. Her grandmother had adored her. She had had lots of lovers. Toby had been obsessed with her, Jasper a long-time admirer. Any number of people had come forward to say how much they liked her, how she was kind and cheerful and funny. Yet someone had killed her. Someone – presumably someone she knew – had beckoned her into the shrubbery for a private talk, and she had gone without a struggle, drunk poison and died. It was bizarre. But there had to be a reason. Passion, jealousy, money, what?

Something to do with her father's business? He remembered Joanna saying she had seen something in the paper recently about Cornfeld Chemicals, though she couldn't remember what, not having been interested in the story.

He rang Tufty Arceneaux.

'What is it this time? Asking me again won't get your results any sooner, y'know.'

'It's not that,' Slider said. 'You play the market a bit, don't you, Tufty?'

'Have to, old fruit, now I own shares in this place.'

'Seriously – you always have, haven't you? Do you have someone who advises you? Someone who understands the City, knows what's going on?'

'You mean not just a broker but a chap who knows. Finger on the pulse, head in the bucket, sort of thing?'

'That sort of thing.'

'Fellow you want is Colin Jenkins. Old drinking buddy of mine from way back. Used to be City editor of one of the broadsheets, still knows everybody in the Square Mile. If Colin doesn't know about it, it ain't happening. Want me to give him a bell?'

'Would you? If he's willing, ask him to ring me. I need a bit of information.'

'Willco.'

'Oh, and, Tufty?'

'Still here, old cork.'

'Tell him it needs to be done discreetly.'

'Oh, it'll be discreet all right. Old Col's so discreet, if he had an affair, even he wouldn't know about it.'

The call came through about fifteen minutes later. Colin Jenkins had a rich-toned voice and an old-fashioned accent that would have done well in Tufty's son's new movie. Think Dennis Price playing a senior civil servant, Slider mused to himself.

'Tufty says you need information and that it's in a good cause,' he said.

'Yes. I'd rather not say too much about my thought processes at the moment, but—'

'Tufty's word's good enough for me. What can I do for you?'

'Cornfeld Chemicals,' Slider said. 'What can you tell me about them?'

'Ah,' said Jenkins. 'Well, now, it's a good little company, if anything slightly undervalued. Used to be a family business before it was floated and the family are still large shareholders. The founder, Henry Cornfeld, is the chief executive and chairman of the board, but he knows his business. I'd say it was a sound investment. If you get hold of any shares I'd hang on to them.'

'Yes, I see. But weren't they in the news a few weeks ago? Someone told me they saw them mentioned in the papers, but can't remember what the story was.'

'Oh, yes – there were rumours about a takeover, but I don't think anything came of it in the end. There was a piece in the *Telegraph* City pages – perhaps that's where you saw it.'

'Takeover by whom?' Slider asked. Jenkins was having a good effect on his grammar.

'As I remember, GCC was sniffing around them – Global Chemicals – but I don't think it ever got as far as an offer. Just speculative stuff.'

'Why would they want them?'

'Well, Global's about number three in the pecking order, after Astra and Glaxo, so the thinking would be that an acquisition or two would allow them to punch the same weight,' said Jenkins. 'It's the main preoccupation of these very large companies. Rather like the eighteenth-century obsession with the balance of power. If France has Austria, Britain has to have Russia, you know the sort of thing.'

'I see. So there wasn't anything . . .' Slider paused, feeling for the right words . . . 'Contentious about it? Anything odd or underhand?'

'Not that I know of. Look here, would you like me to do a little sleuthing and come back to you? I'm speaking at present without the full facts.'

'Would you do that? I'd be most grateful.'

'No trouble at all. Anyone in particular you have your eye on?'

'No,' said Slider, frowning. 'I don't think so. I'm just grasping at shadows, really.'

'This is to do with Cornfeld's daughter being killed, is it?' Jenkins asked, with an air of lowering his voice and speaking without moving his lips.

'Yes,' Slider said, 'but I'd be obliged if—'

'Oh, quite, quite. Consider it under the hat. Keeping secrets is second nature in my line of business.'

'So Tufty told me,' Slider smiled, 'only he said it was a secret.'

*   *   *

Hart came back from her interview with Jasper a little less gung-ho than she had left for it. 'I'm beginning to think you could be right, guv,' she said, leaning on his door jamb and folding her arms under her bust to disturbing effect.

'Wonders will never cease,' Slider said, keeping his eyes elsewhere. 'Right about anything in particular, or just in general?'

'Particular. Well, you know I already think you're a total planet-brain,' she grinned. 'That's not a secret.'

'Is that a compliment or not?'

'Yeah. Brain the size of a planet.'

'I see. Well, what's the particular?'

'I talked to old Jasper. He's flat on his back and weak as water, but he was quite clear about what happened. I fought it would upset him to talk about it, but he seemed to want to, so I let him go on about it for as long as he liked. Anyway, he was quite clear old Tobes said he killed Chattie but – this is the duff bit – he said he stabbed her to death. He didn't say anything about any drugging first. Just went on about plunging the knife in and seeing her blood. So I'm thinking maybe you're right.'

Slider, with his often unwelcome trait of seeing both sides of everything, now found himself playing devil's advocate. 'Toby was very disturbed by then. A raving man doesn't give detailed accounts. And the plunging-and-blood bit would have been the part he really cared about, and so the only part worth talking about.'

'Yeah,' she said, somewhat comforted. 'I can see that. He wants to come out king of the jungle, the stalking tiger, not the weak-kneed wally who can't stab a girl unless she's unconscious.'

'Still,' said Slider, 'it doesn't help the case against him. And it's just what a man *would* say, making a false confession on the basis of what he's read in the papers.'

Hart opened her mouth and shut it again, then gave him a bright smile and took herself away. Now she thinks you're irrational, Slider told himself.

Jenkins was evidently enough intrigued to make Slider's enquiry his first priority, for he telephoned again later in the afternoon.

'Good of you to call back so soon,' he said.

'Oh, not at all. I assumed it was a matter of some urgency. Well, the *Telegraph* article was a piece of speculation, based on a rumour that Cornfeld himself was thinking of retiring. He *is* nearly seventy, and though he seems hale enough there was some talk, or rumour, of a heart condition, and a desire on his part to enjoy the sunsets or take up watercolours or something of the sort, before it was too late. Of course, if he did retire, it would mean a big change in the company, seeing as he really does run everything himself – and the old boy's very autocratic. Iron hand in the iron glove, so to speak.'

'Would his retirement mean the company failing?' Slider asked, on the tail of an idea.

'Oh, no. The business itself is pretty sound. But there would be an upheaval and inevitably some reorganisation. And given that GCC was thought to be looking for acquisitions, the article speculated that Cornfeld might be a suitable target.' Jenkins hesitated, and added, 'My chum on the *Telegraph* said that he heard a definite rumour that GCC *was* looking at Cornfeld, but it was all hush-hush, of course, and he couldn't reveal his source, but he says to tell you that you can take it as read that there was something in it. But he hasn't heard anything since, so he's assuming that the idea has gone away or been shelved.'

'Why would they go off the idea?'

'Oh, any number of reasons. I don't think it's because there's anything wrong with Cornfeld itself. It may be that Global is thinking, given Henry C's age, they could just wait until he dies and then pick the place up more cheaply in the aftermath. Or they might be looking at another company to buy. Or someone at Global might have been kite-flying, and it was never more than an idle thought.'

'But there was nothing – sinister about it? I mean, if it had gone ahead, would anybody stand to lose?'

'No, not really. Certainly all the shareholders would be likely to do well out of it. Global would offer them a good price, so they could cash in and do as they pleased with all that lovely lolly. Apart from the dividend, shares have no actual value until you sell them, you know. And given that Cornfeld is quite a tight ship, there wouldn't be likely to be many redundancies, so the employees would be happy. They'd probably expect better peripheral benefits from the larger parent company. The only difference would be that the Cornfeld name would probably be dropped – Global don't go in for that Glaxo Smith Kline Beecham business – but I can't see that anyone would do murder to preserve the company name,' he concluded shrewdly, 'which I suppose is what you're trying to get at.'

'That's the sort of thing I'm wondering,' Slider admitted.

'No, I can't see any reason anyone would be against it,' Jenkins said. 'And especially why anyone would kill the Cornfeld girl over it. I'm assuming she was a shareholder?'

'She was. She held ten per cent.'

'Really? That's quite a lot. But not enough for her to block the deal, so that can't be it.'

'Who could block the deal?'

'Well, Henry himself, I suppose. As I said, he's an autocrat. If he was against it, the board would go with him and not recommend it to the shareholders. But I can't see why anyone would want to block it. It's what they call nowadays a win-win situation.'

'Well, thank you,' Slider said. 'You've been most helpful. Just one more thing.' A thought had occurred to him. 'I'm a complete ignoramus when it comes to shares and stock markets and so on, so forgive me if it seems a stupid question to you—'

'No, no,' Jenkins murmured, impelled by his native politeness.

'But why would it have to be hush-hush if GCC did want to buy Cornfeld Chemicals?'

'Oh, well, because an impending offer by a big company like Global could affect the share price, and the FSA would be down like a ton of bricks on anything that looked like price-rigging or insider-dealing. My chum on the City desk had to go through the paper's lawyers for a pretty rigorous combing even to write what he did, which was a very innocent appraisal of the company and didn't mention Global by name. If Global really were going to make an offer the preliminaries would all be conducted very secretly, and the principals would have to be very careful what they said and who they said it to.'

'Thank you,' Slider said. 'I'm most grateful.'

'My pleasure. If I hear anything more, I'll be sure to let you know.'

Slider put down the telephone absently, and began to search through his papers for the transcript of his interview with Mrs Cornfeld senior. Yes, there it was. Cornfeld's eldest daughter

Ruth had married a David Cockerell, who had won opprobrium from his father-in-law by leaving the family firm and going to GCC. Was he, Slider wondered, still there? That was definitely something worth finding out. Possibly there was nothing in it – and, as Jenkins had said, what reason would anyone have to kill Chattie over the supposed acquisition, which in any case hadn't come to anything?

But, as he ought to have realised before, or at least connected in his mind, David Cockerell's initials were DC. And wasn't it possible that 'DC10' meant David Cockerell, ten o'clock? If she had had a meeting with her brother-in-law on the last day of her life, it was possible he might know something of interest about her circumstances, or her state of mind – if not her death.

CHAPTER FIFTEEN

Who Thrilled Cock Robin?

The Global Chemical Company had its London office in Northumberland Avenue. Slider knew it, one of those huge anonymous buildings, part of a long block lining the street that always reminded him of the Hauptmanised part of Paris. Northumberland Avenue, just off Trafalgar Square. Trafalgar Square. He wrote the words down and stared at them. DC10 TFQ. But Trafalgar Square would be TS as initials. Yet someone jotting down a note while talking on the phone would not necessarily use strict logic, but write down what the mind picked out as significant. TF for Tra-Falgar. And though Square began with an S, the Q was the most significant letter in it. It was eccentric, but it was not unbelievable. Idiosyncratic, rather, was the word. And the whole point of a mnemonic was that it triggered a response in your own brain, not anyone else's.

He went to the door of his room, beckoned Atherton in, and tried it out on him.

'Trafalgar Square? Well, it's possible, I suppose. When I do that sort of thing in my diary I do a little square for Square, and a circle with a dot in it for Circus. We all have our own methods. Why would she meet her brother-in-law in Trafalgar Square?'

'Because his office is in Northumberland Avenue.'

'Yes, but I meant why would she meet him at all?'

'Because his company, GCC, was thinking about taking over Cornfeld Chemicals, and she was a large shareholder.'

'You think?'

'Well, I'd like to find out. Shall we go and see him?'

Atherton looked doubtful. 'Shouldn't we wait for the results on the clothes to come back? We'll look like fools if it turns out that Toby did it after all – which is still the most likely scenario.'

'I'd sooner try to keep ahead of the game than waste a day if Toby's innocent. And I'm curious, anyway. I didn't think there was any contact between those two parts of the family.'

'Curiosity I'm always willing to indulge,' said Atherton. 'Why not? Let's go.'

The GCC building was very old-fashioned inside. A lofty reception hall was lined with polished stone – granite, Slider thought – and at the far end was a wide, dark wooden desk behind which two elderly porters stood, wearing heavy navy uniforms and flat caps reminiscent of the defunct GLC. Was there such a thing as a GLC Surplus Store? Slider wouldn't have been at all surprised. There was a bank of lifts to one side and polished stone steps going up at the side of them, and in all the expanse of floor space there was not one potted plant, leather chair, glass coffee table or magazine. This was a stern, no-nonsense reception hall of the old school, where you stated your business and were admitted, or were firmly ejected with the coldest of cold eyes.

One of the porters examined both Slider's and Atherton's warrant card with almost offensive thoroughness, while the other telephoned 'upstairs', and carried on an inaudible conversation without ever taking his eyes from the visitors. At last he replaced the receiver, wrote laboriously in a visitors' book, produced two clip-on visitors' badges, and said, 'Seventh floor. You'll be met at the lift. Make sure you bring the badges back when you leave. They're numbered,' he concluded menacingly. Both porters watched Slider and Atherton walk to the lift with an air of being prepared to bring them down with a flying tackle if they veered towards the stairs. Neither of them had smiled at any time during the transaction.

Inside the lift, Atherton said, 'Whew! I thought there was going to be a blood test and a retinal scan before we got in.'

The lift was panelled on two sides, but mirrored, behind a decorative grille, on the third. Slider cast his eyes towards it and said, without moving his lips, 'Careful what you say. We may be being watched.'

Atherton smirked, but rode in silence the rest of the way.

Outside the lift doors was a corridor panelled in light oak, with grey carpet on the floor, filled with expensive silence. Whatever was going on behind the closed doors leading off it, no sound penetrated. A woman was waiting for them, a top-of-the-range middle-aged secretary in a fawn suit, silk blouse, knotted silk scarf round the neck, pearl earrings, and large, careful hair in a short bob held off the face with a velvet Alice band. It was like stepping back in time, Slider thought.

She didn't smile, either. 'I'm Mr Cockerell's personal assistant,' she said in a voice so cut-glass you could have sipped single malt from it in a gentlemen's club. 'Follow me, please.'

She led them down the corridor to an anonymous oak door in the oak wall, which led into what was obviously her room, for there was a desk with papers on it, a typewriter (really!) and a computer, filing cabinets and cupboards. It was windowless, which Slider thought horribly claustrophobic. She walked straight across to the door on the far side, tapped on it and opened it, saying, 'Detective Inspector Slider and Detective Sergeant Atherton, sir,' stepped aside to usher them through, and closed the door noiselessly behind them.

The room beyond was a different animal altogether. It was much larger, to begin with, and it had windows all along the far wall, though they were covered with venetian blinds and let in little natural light. The walls were wood-panelled, there was concealed lighting round the edges of the ceiling, and the carpet was thick and plush and blackberry-coloured. There was no office paraphernalia, only a vast oak desk, a sofa, coffee-table, and several chairs. On the left-hand wall was a unit, cupboards along the base, further cupboards up each side, and shelves across the middle, containing a few tooled-back leather-bound books and some photographs in heavy silver frames. The desk had on it only four telephones and a blotter. This was a man, said the office, so powerful he did not have to *appear* to work. Two of the chairs were pulled up to the near side of the desk, and Slider and Atherton trudged towards them, which was hard work given the depth of pile on the carpet. The man seated in a large, padded, leather executive chair on the other side, rose to welcome them.

He was a surprise to Slider too. He appeared to be about fifty, tall and well-built, immaculately suited and extremely good-looking. His thick dark hair was swept back from a lightly tanned face with even features, a straight nose, dark eyes and a firm chin with a slight cleft in it. The surprise, for this place, was that he was smiling. His teeth were white and even – perhaps a thought too white. Slider's rapid process of instant summing up had said here was a man who had relied on his looks and charm all his life, with the corollary that he didn't have many other abilities. He was aware that this was probably unfair, and also probably a reaction from all the stern inhospitality they had met up until this point. He summoned up a smile of his own, pushed away his judgement and prepared to meet the man with an open mind.

'David Cockerell,' said the man, extending his hand. His handshake was efficient, neither too hard nor too limp, and brief without being surly. Professional, Slider thought. 'How can I help you? Please sit down.'

Slider sat. 'I'd like to talk to you about your sister-in-law, Charlotte Cornfeld.'

The smile widened just a little. 'I suppose I was half expecting this,' said Cockerell. 'You fellows have to be thorough, I know that. But I'm afraid I won't be able to help you. I really didn't have much to do with Chattie. That was her nickname, by the way. You knew that?' Slider nodded. 'Can I offer you a drink?' As he said it, he crossed to the unit and opened one of the upper cupboards, which proved to contain decanters and glasses. 'Whisky, sherry, gin and tonic? Not too early, is it? The sun's over the yard-arm somewhere in the world, that's what I always say.' He laughed, a purely functional laugh that had nothing to do with humour but was a social signal: I'm a good guy, you're good guys, let's all be good guys together.

Slider smiled. 'I'm afraid we can't, but please don't let that stop you.'

'No! Really? I thought that was all bushwah, about you people not being allowed to drink on duty. Surely a small one?'

'I'm afraid not, but thank you,' Slider said.

Cockerell hesitated about the glasses, and then decided against solo drinking, closed the door and returned to the desk. He sat, folded his hands together, and placed them on the desk in front of him. 'So, what can I tell you?'

'What was your relationship with Miss Cornfeld?' Slider asked.

'Well, I can't say I really had one. The family wasn't all that close, you know. The occasional dutiful Christmas gathering, and that was that.' He looked straight at Slider, like a man about to reveal something painful. 'My wife and her father do not get on, I'm sorry to say, and so we aren't at the old man's house very often. I believe he and Chattie were very fond of each other, though.'

'Did Chattie visit you and your wife at home?'

'No, I don't think Chattie's ever been to our house. We only ever met at Frithsden – my father-in-law's house – and not very often there, as I've said. Ruth, my wife, doesn't approve of the way her father lives. His personal life. I don't know if you know . . . ?' A delicate pause and lift of the eyebrows.

'You mean Kylie?'

'Ah, you have seen her.' Cockerell leaned back with a faint man-to-man smile. 'She's one of a string of similar lovelies. In my humble opinion, the old man's entitled to take his pleasure where he likes at his age, but Ruth doesn't agree. So we don't visit very often.'

'So when did you last see Chattie?' Slider asked, still as if going through the motions.

Cockerell was quite relaxed. 'Oh, well, let me think. I suppose it must have been last Christmas. Did we go there at Christmas? Oh, yes, I remember there was some disaster in the kitchen and dinner was terribly late.' He smiled. 'One needs these signposts to remember one Christmas from another.'

'So you haven't seen her at all for six months?' Atherton asked, picking up the minute pause Slider left for him. They had worked together for so long they knew each other's rhythms without having to think about it.

'No, I suppose I haven't,' said Cockerell.

'Then last week's meeting must have been about something out of the ordinary,' said Atherton.

Cockerell's smile remained behind, like the Cheshire Cat's, though the rest of his face had abandoned it. 'I'm sorry?' he said.

'Your meeting last Tuesday with Chattie,' Slider took over. 'It was obviously important, as it was so unprecedented.'

Cockerell blinked rapidly several times, and cocked his head slightly. 'I'm afraid I don't follow you. I didn't have any meeting with Chattie last week. Or indeed any week.'

It was well done; it was very natural. But having had the interrogation split, Cockerell did not now know who to look at, and when he looked at Atherton, Slider looked at his hands. The truth, like blood, will out. Cockerell had his face and voice under control, but Slider had seen the small, convulsive clasp of the hands. He relaxed, and felt Atherton beside him feel it.

'Please, Mr Cockerell, don't waste time. We know that you had a meeting with Chattie at ten o'clock on Tuesday morning. Now it may have been – I expect it was – a perfectly innocent meeting, but as it happened on the last day of her life, we have to ask about it. You do see that?'

'I'm sorry, but you're mistaken,' Cockerell said. 'I had no meeting with Chattie. Why should I? And now I'm afraid I shall have to ask you to leave.' He half stood, admitting, though he was not aware of it, defeat.

Slider did not move. 'It is pointless to deny it. We know that you met her – in Trafalgar Square.' He waited a beat, and then said, gently, 'We have the evidence. If you won't tell us about it, we're bound to become suspicious.'

Cockerell, still in his half-risen crouch, seemed to consider. Then he sat down, slowly, leaned back in his chair and swivelled a little, passed a hand over his mouth in thought, and then said, 'Look.'

The word of capitulation. Slider looked.

'Look,' said Cockerell, 'I did meet her, but it has to be kept a secret. It – it wasn't exactly improper, but if it was known that we met, it could be thought that something was going on, that we were colluding. You've got to promise me this won't get out. There could be consequences. Serious consequences. It could ruin the whole deal, and a lot of jobs depend on it.'

'The deal – you mean the takeover?' Slider said. 'The takeover of Cornfeld Chemicals by GCC?'

His eyebrows shot up. 'You know about it?'

'It was in the papers,' Slider reminded him.

'Speculation only, several weeks ago. But we killed that. What made you think we were still interested?'

'We have our sources,' Slider said, 'just as you do. You are still interested, aren't you?'

'Well, yes. But that's not for public consumption. You see why Chattie and I had to keep the meeting secret. The way we were placed, if the reporters had got hold of the fact that we'd been seen together, it would have been disastrous.'

'And what was the purpose of the meeting?' Slider asked.

Cockerell hesitated. 'I wanted to find out how Henry felt about it. Chattie's the person closest to him in the world. I knew she'd know.'

'Why couldn't you ask him yourself?'

'I'm in negotiation with him. He's not going to tell me the truth, is he? That's not the way these things work. He takes a position and I take a position. We try not to give away anything to one another. And Henry's a master at the game.'

'So you thought you might cheat a little and ask Chattie what his real position was?' Atherton asked.

'That's right. But it wasn't really cheating. Just – trying to get an edge.'

'But it was a little shady, so you kept it a deep, dark secret,' Atherton led him on. 'Did your wife know about the meeting?'

'Yes, she knew, and Lucinda knew – my secretary.' In the heat of the moment he had forgotten to call her personal assistant. Lucky she wasn't listening. 'But they're both sound as bells. They would never tell a soul. I don't know how the hell you found out,' he complained. 'I would never have thought Chattie would be indiscreet.'

'You said you were afraid of being seen together,' Slider said blandly.

'Oh, so that was it, was it? Well, that was damnable bad luck. We took such precautions.'

'And what was the result of your meeting?' Slider asked. 'Did Chattie tell you how her father felt about the deal?'

'No, she didn't,' he said. He frowned angrily at the memory. 'She refused. I didn't get anything useful out of her at all, so it was really a waste of time.' He engaged Slider's eyes and tried for lightness after the frowns. 'So, you see, there's no need to report it to anyone. Nothing improper happened, but if it was known we had met, people would assume, and rumours would spread.'

'Was anything else discussed between you?' Slider asked. 'You see, you were one of the last people to see her alive. Did she say anything that might help us? Did she talk of any worries she had? Did she tell you who else she was going to meet that day?'

'No,' he said. 'Nothing else was discussed. The meeting was very short. I wish I could help you,' he said, with a look of sincerity, 'but I knew nothing about her life and she didn't say anything about it then. I've no idea who killed her or why.'

Slider stood up. 'Well, thank you, sir,' he said. 'You've cleared up one little mystery for us. We're most grateful.'

Cockerell was all beams now. 'Oh, not at all, not at all. Glad to help. Anything else I can do for you, don't hesitate to ask.'

He was coming round the desk to usher them out. Slider veered across to the wall unit to look at the photographs on his way out. 'Your family?' he asked.

'Yes, that's my wife, and our son and two daughters.'

Granny Cornfeld was right, Slider thought – they did look dull. But the wife, Ruth, looked faintly familiar to Slider, though he couldn't place her. Perhaps there'd been a photo of her in Frithsden House?

They were shown back to the lift, rode down in silence, handed in their badges to the two Cerberuses, and made their way out of the heavy swing doors into the early-evening sunlight.

'He's lying,' Slider said.

'Yup,' Atherton concurred. 'But why?'

There was a pub at the end of the street, its doors open on the pavement and, for a wonder, no piped music inside. 'Pint?' said Slider.

'Hm. Okay. Might help the little grey cells.'

It was cool and dark inside, one of those *faux*-traditional places with bare floorboards, dark wood everywhere, tall barrels for tables, the ceiling painted an authentic smoke-dimmed dirty cream. They ordered two pints of Director's, and Slider led the way to a couple of stools pulled up to one of the barrel tables just by the open door.

'All right,' said Atherton, having taken the top third off his pint. 'Cockerell's story.'

'It makes sense in its own terms. I just don't feel that's all there was to it. Both Jasper and Marion said Chattie was pre-occupied that evening.'

'Wouldn't she be disturbed by Cockerell trying to pump her about the old man's feelings on the takeover?'

Slider shook his head. 'I'm not sure. If it was just Cockerell saying, is he pro or con, and her saying, mind your own business, would she really be that bothered? It surely wouldn't have been news to her – at least, judging by what Granny Cornfeld said – that he wasn't quite pukka.'

'Well,' Atherton said, as one stretching a point, 'you could be right. But she could have been preoccupied about anything – her business, her love-life, the state of the economy.'

'Of course. But what did she do with the rest of the day? She cancelled her appointments, but she must have been out of the house, because Marion Davies said she was just sorting the mail when she called round at a quarter past six, still in her business suit. So where was she, and with whom?'

'What's your theory?'

'I haven't got one,' Slider admitted, taking a long swallow. 'I'm just working out the pattern. Cockerell said something to her, she was disturbed by it, she – perhaps – went and saw somebody else about it, and the next day she was murdered.'

'You think Cockerell did it?' Atherton said. 'That's a very large size in assumptions. Although,' he allowed, 'I didn't like him, and he did seem to be just dumb enough to do the murder that way. And, perhaps more to the point, he's a senior executive in a drugs company that manufactures ultra-short-acting barbiturates.'

'It does?'

'I do my homework,' said Atherton. 'If anyone could work out how to get access to them, he could. But for all you know, he's got an alibi.'

'That's why we're sitting here – to catch his secretary on her way to the tube.'

'How do you know she goes home by tube?'

'I saw a tube ticket sticking out of one of the front pockets of her handbag.'

'Blimey, the eyes of the sleuth! What if she doesn't come this way to the station?'

'Then we're stuffed,' said Slider patiently, 'but at least we've had a pint.'

'The man's a genius.'

'Keep your eyes peeled.'

Atherton turned his stool so they were both facing the street; and indeed, half an hour later, the big hair and the suit went past, with the addition of a fine leather shoulderbag and a rolled umbrella by way of accessories. Atherton and Slider left their seats and went after her. A little hampered by not knowing her surname, they fell in one on either side of her and almost got clobbered by the umbrella as her natural reactions were set off by being bracketed.

'I'm sorry to startle you,' Slider said. 'We just wanted a quiet word.'

'I thought you were bag-snatchers,' she said, very much annoyed. 'What are you doing here?'

'We've been waiting for you.'

She faced them, glaring. 'This is ridiculous. If you wanted to speak to me, why didn't you do it at the office?'

'I rather wanted to speak to you privately,' said Slider.

'Without Mr Cockerell knowing? I see. And why should you imagine for a moment that I would betray my employer to you?'

'Betray?' Atherton said. 'Now there's an interesting word for you to have used.'

'Betray his trust,' she said witheringly, 'by talking about him behind his back.'

'Oh, come on,' he coaxed. 'You don't *like* working for him. He's a jumped-up little turkey cock. You've got ten times his brains and character. And he called you his secretary.'

Her lips twitched, but she kept her countenance. 'Nothing would induce me to say anything behind his back that I would not say to his face.'

'Fine, then tell him to his face tomorrow. For now, come and have a drink – a gin and tonic to brace you for the tube journey home.'

Slider could only look on in admiration as Atherton worked his magic, and then followed them back to the pub like a younger brother tagging along. This time they took seats away from the door, round the corner. Lucinda Gaines-Harris, for such was her name, accepted the offer of a gin and tonic, and while Atherton chatted her up, Slider observed with interest her struggle to keep her face disapproving and not to show that she was rather enjoying the adventure of something that didn't happen every day or to everyone.

'I bet he's tried to get off with you,' Atherton said, with almost girlfriendish sympathy.

'Why do you say that?'

'I know the type. It must be galling for you. Where did you go to university?'

'Cambridge. Chemistry,' she said, flattered that he had guessed she was a graduate.

'So how did you end up here?'

'It was the best I could do,' she said. 'I get paid more this way than I could as a lowly researcher or a lab-rat, and I have my mother to support. Of course, if I were a man, I could go up the executive ladder. But I don't have back-scratching privileges, so that's out.' She had loosened up enough to swig back her G-and-T like a man, and Slider hastened to get her another before the mood was broken. When he returned with it, she said, 'I hope you aren't thinking of getting me drunk, because it won't work.'

'Absolutely not,' Atherton said. 'I bet you could drink me under the table. I was just being hospitable.'

'So, what do you want to know?' she asked, apparently abandoning pleasure for business. She glanced at a gold watch on a slim wrist. 'I can't be too long, because of Mother.'

Atherton got down to it. 'On Wednesday last week, what time did he get to the office?'

'Eight,' she said. 'He's always in at eight, when he's in the office. Of course, sometimes he goes to other offices, or to meetings elsewhere, or to one of the plants. But when he's here, he's in at eight.'

'Did you actually *see* him at eight that morning?'

'Oh, yes, certainly. In fact, he was already at his desk when I came in at eight.'

'When he comes and goes, does he have to go through your office?'

'No, there's another door to the corridor through his bathroom, which leads off his office. But in the morning he usually comes in through my office and I give him the mail and any messages.'

'I see.' Well, that knocked him out from being First Murderer, said Atherton's glance to Slider. Only Superman could have got from the park to the office, with a change of clothes thrown in, in the maximum possible allowance of ten minutes. Pity, really. It would have been nice to de-smug him. 'And can you cast your mind back to the day before, to last Tuesday? He said that you knew he had an appointment to meet Miss Cornfeld.'

'Yes. Well, he pretty well had to tell me, because I'd have to cover for his absence if anyone called.'

'Did he tell you what the meeting was about?'

'I'm not sure if I should tell you that.'

'He told us it was about the takeover – wanting her to find out how her father stood on it,' said Slider.

She looked relieved. 'Oh, well, that's what he told me, too. But it had to be a secret meeting. Rather dangerous if anyone found out and suspected collusion.'

'The meeting was at ten o'clock?'

'Yes. He left at five to. He said he was meeting her in Trafalgar Square.'

'Isn't that rather public for a private meeting?'

'That's what I said, but he said it was safer in the open because you could see people approaching – they couldn't creep up on you and overhear. I think he saw that in some spy film or other,' she added, with a sneer.

'And what time did he come back?'

'It was about ten to eleven.'

Slider was surprised. 'He told us it was only a brief meeting.'

She shrugged. 'I don't know about that. I suppose he may have gone somewhere else afterwards. All I know is that I heard him come in at that time. He went in through the bathroom and banged the door very noisily. I went straight in to give him his messages and he was stamping about in an absolute temper.'

'What about?'

'I don't know. I said, "Is everything all right?" and he said, "Not now, Lucinda. Leave me alone. I'll buzz when I want you." So I put the messages down on his desk and went out. When he buzzed for me I went in and he was quite calm again, and he didn't mention anything about it, so naturally I didn't ask. It wasn't my business.'

'So you've no idea what put him in a temper?'

'None at all.' She hesitated. 'All I can tell you is that when I went in – the first time – I heard him mutter something like,

"Thank God there's a few days left" or "There's still a few days" – I can't swear to the exact words. But he never mentioned it again.'

'How did he react when he heard about Miss Cornfeld's death?'

'I'm not sure when he did first hear. I heard about it on Thursday evening on the news, when the name was first given. The next morning at the office I said something to him about how dreadful it was, and he seemed already to know then, because he said, "Yes, it's tragic," or something like that.'

'Did he seem very upset?'

She thought. 'Yes, I'd say he was. He was very quiet and thoughtful all morning, quite absent-minded. Brooding, almost, you might say. In the afternoon he went off to the plant in Bedford so I didn't see him again that day.'

'The plant – is that where the drugs are manufactured?'

'Some of them. Bedford's the secure plant for the restricted pharmaceuticals. It's only a small place.'

'Does he go there often?'

'Oh, from time to time. He was there last Monday, as it happens, but that was unusual. It was for the opening of the new lab block. Some local bigwig cutting the ribbon, and the press were there, and there were drinks and so on afterwards, with the Health Minister looking in.'

'A big do like that, that date must have been known well beforehand,' Slider said, the germ of an idea twitching in the depths of his brain.

'Of course,' she said. 'To get a cabinet minister you have to book months ahead.'

'Did you go with him?'

'Certainly not. A frightful waste of time, those things, but useful publicity, I suppose, which is why he had to go. In any case, his wife was there if he wanted his hand holding. I'm not obliged to do it, thank God. Oh, look at the time. Is there anything else, because I really ought to get going? Mother frets if I'm more than half an hour late.'

'Just one last question,' Slider said. 'The proposed acquisition of Cornfeld Chemicals. Is there anything – odd or unusual about it?'

'I don't think so. In what way?'

'I don't know,' Slider said ruefully. 'That's what I'm trying to find out.'

'Well, I haven't heard anything. It's all still very secret – has to be, until the offer's made public, or the shares would go haywire. But as far as I know, it's a simple purchase.'

'Thanks,' said Slider, and stood up to pull out her chair for her as she made getting-up movements.

She gathered her belongings, and at the last moment paused and said to Slider, 'You think she was killed because of something to do with the takeover?'

'I don't know,' he said. 'But all murders come down to money or passion in the end, don't they?'

'I don't know anything about it,' she said, 'and I hate gossip, but I suppose it is murder after all, so I ought to tell you. There was talk a couple of years ago that there was something between him and that girl.'

'He had an affair with Chattie?'

'I don't think it amounted to that. Just a brief fling. For a few weeks there were a lot of phone calls, and he went off for long lunches without saying where he was going, and – well, all the signs of an affair. He's had them before – and since – so I know the symptoms. It may not even have *been* her. I mean, the calls were, but maybe not the lunches and so on. I don't know. It was just what the rumours said. But if it was her, there's been nothing since. The calls stopped, and as far as I know he hasn't seen her until that meeting last week. So you see,' she looked from one to the other, 'it might not have been the takeover at all. I just thought you ought to know.'

They thanked her again, and escorted her to the door. When she had walked away, Atherton said, 'For someone who didn't want to betray her boss, she certainly let her hair down.'

'Chattie, an affair with Cockerell?' Slider mourned. 'I can't believe it.'

'Rather a lapse of taste,' Atherton agreed. 'But we know she liked to have it large, and he's not without his attractions. I fancy even Miss Gaines-Harris has yearned for a slice of that particular beefcake at some time in the past – and didn't get one, which is why she's so ready to shop him.'

'Stop with the psychology. You're making me dizzy.'

'Seriously, when I said I bet he made a pass at you, she didn't say he did and she didn't say he didn't. So I reckon he didn't. Hell hath no fury, et cetera. Anyway,' he went on, 'at least if Chattie did have a fling, it was a brief one. Presumably she fell in a weak moment and got out of it as quickly as possible.'

'I'm not comforted,' said Slider.

CHAPTER SIXTEEN

Can't Say Y

'It's me!' Slider called as he let himself into the narrow hall.

'Hi! I'm in the kitchen,' Joanna called back.

It was every man's dream, he supposed, to come home from work and find his beloved safely in the kitchen. He extended his sensitive nostrils and identified onions, garlic – tomatoes – some kind of herb. After a day of sensual deprivation he fancied something rich and tasty. And a good meal, too. He picked up his mail, which she had left for him in a pile on the edge of the hall table and went to find her.

She was at the stove, stirring a pot. Hallelujah! It was going to be Bolognese sauce.

'Yum,' he said, kissing the back of her neck.

'Me, or dinner?'

'Both. Always,' he said, opening envelopes. Bill, begging letter, you have been preselected to own one of our platinum credit cards (where were they going to go after platinum – titanium? Green kryptonite?), bill, bill . . .

'I'm doing a proper *ragù*, with chicken livers,' she said, 'since I have time. Do you want it over short pasta, spaghetti, or baked in the oven?'

'It would break Garibaldi's heart if we had it over anything but spaghetti.'

'Why Garibaldi?'

'Wasn't he the father of modern Italy?'

'Dunno,' she said. 'All I know is he made the biscuits run on time.'

He wasn't listening. He was reading the letter he'd just opened. He frowned. 'What's this about a scan?'

She turned and craned her neck to read it, and then snatched it from his hand. 'Don't read my letters!'

'It was in my pile,' he protested.

'Since when have you been "Dear Ms Marshall"?'

'I didn't read that bit. I opened it without looking. I assumed you'd sorted my stuff out from yours.'

'You've no right to read my letters.' Her face was a little flushed, though that might have been the heat of the stove.

He looked at her carefully. 'Jo, what is it? It says you're refusing to have a scan.'

'It's none of your business,' she said, stuffing the letter into her pocket with an angry, careless gesture.

'Well, it is, really,' he said gently, not to annoy her. 'It's my baby too.'

'You're not the one who has to carry it and bear it and feed it. Ultimately it's my responsibility.'

'I can't help being a man,' he said. 'I know you have the hardest part, but we're having this baby together, and it's my responsibility too. You both are. Why are you refusing a scan?'

She turned her face away, pretending to be concentrating on the sauce. 'They don't like it, you know. Babies. They try to get away from it. You can see on the monitor. I went with a friend a couple of times, and you can see the babies hate it.'

'But it doesn't harm them, does it?'

'How do we know? It doesn't do any immediate, obvious damage, but who knows what it's really doing to them?'

He took her arms and turned her to him, against resistance. 'Darling,' he said, 'what's wrong? What's really the problem? Surely this scan business is simply routine? Why are you so against it?'

'People managed perfectly well in the old days. My mother had ten children without ultrasound, or any of the other horrible machines they rig you up to these days.'

'People in the old days had their legs cut off without anaesthetic,' he said. 'What's the real reason?'

'You haven't thought it through. They scan to find out if the baby's defective.'

'Yes. Isn't that a good thing?'

She met his eyes with resolution. 'And if it is defective? You know what comes next. They offer you an abortion. Are you prepared to take that decision? Because I'm not. I hate abortion. I would *never* have an abortion. But what if they say the child's terribly damaged in some way, so that it wouldn't die, but live on in some terrible condition?'

He didn't answer for a moment. No, he hadn't thought about that before, and now he did, he saw the gravity of it. To choose life or death, death or tormented life, for your own child? And how much worse for the mother, with the child actually growing inside her, part of her in the way it could never be for the father?

'There are other reasons,' he said. 'They could find something that could be corrected in the womb. It could save the child from being born with a defect.'

'Do you think that makes it easier?'

He saw then that she was really afraid, and close to tears. He pulled her against him and held her close, cradling her head, and she pressed in, needing his strength.

'Darling,' he said, 'don't worry. There's nothing wrong with our baby. Everything will be all right. It's going to be healthy and normal.'

'You don't know that,' she said, muffled by her chest.

'I believe it,' he said firmly.

She pulled her head up and laughed, shakily. 'Oh, religion!'

'Well, what else is there at a time like this?' he reasoned.

'Don't you realise, you jughead,' she said kindly, 'that I'm not a sweet young thing any more? I'm what they call an elderly primipara. Biologically I'm an old lady doing what only young girls should do. It's an extremely risky business.'

'Rubbish,' he said. 'Women of your age and older have babies every day of the week – first babies,' he anticipated her interruption. 'You're perfectly healthy and so am I. Why should anything go wrong?'

'Things do.'

'Not as often as they don't, by a very long chalk. You're falling a victim to the very thing you despise: haven't you said how wrong it was that doctors treat pregnancy as a serious illness?'

'They do. That's what this is all about.'

'They try to, but you don't have to listen. You don't have to let them get to you. You're not ill, you're doing something natural that nearly every woman on the planet does at some point.'

'Easy for you to say.'

He put her back a little to look at her seriously. 'Do you really think that?'

'No,' she said, after a pause. 'No, not really. I know you love me.'

'It's a bit more than that,' he said. 'I think your sauce is sticking.'

'Blast,' she said, and twisted out of his arms to stir it. He saw she had relaxed a little, given him a little of the burden to carry, and he was glad. 'So what about this scan?' she asked, in a small voice, her back to him.

'I think you should have it,' he said, after consideration. 'Not because I think there's anything wrong with the baby, but because if you don't they'll keep on bugging you about it and drive you nuts. But if you really don't want to have it, then I'll support you. I'll write to them and tell them *we* don't want it, and that if they send you any more letters about it I'll come round and reprogram their computer with a very large axe.'

She laughed, turning her head to look at him adoringly. 'My hero! What would I do without you? D'you want to go and get changed? I'm going to put the water on so we're looking at fifteen minutes to eating.'

She said no more about it that evening, and he thought she had put it from her mind for the time being. But in bed, when they had made love and she was lying in his arms and he was drifting comfortably into sleep, she said suddenly out of the dark, 'If I have the scan, and there's something wrong, what then?'

'If that happened, we'd face it together and decide together. But it's not going to happen. So don't even think about it. Never trouble trouble till trouble troubles you.'

She turned on her side then, into her sleep position, and he turned too so that she could burrow into him backwards. He folded his hands round her, one on her breast and one on her belly, and felt her fall instantly into sleep like someone tumbling off a cliff. He held her, wakeful now, thinking of the two lives that lay in his arms; and from there to a whole range of preoccupations, his thoughts knitting and spreading an invisible web into the darkness, stretching wider and wider, thinning and growing more tenuous as the world turned through the short summer night towards dawn. When the first bird sang tentatively outside in the blackness, he slept.

Cornfeld Chemicals had its headquarters in Hemel Hempstead, a neat, new-looking low-rise block set in nicely landscaped surroundings on the edge of the town. Slider was received by Henry Cornfeld at nine o'clock in an office that was as different as it could be from his son-in-law's. It was small, lit from unshaded windows, cluttered with the business of business, and devoid of the accoutrements of glamour and power.

Cornfeld himself seemed to have aged since Slider saw him last. His movements were less brisk, his face seemed to have sagged; even his hair did not spring from his forehead in so lively a fashion. But his mind still gripped. He offered Slider a chair and coffee, seated himself and said, 'Have you found out yet who killed my child?'

'Not yet, sir, but there are promising lines we are following up.'

'That sounds like a stock answer,' he said. 'Haven't you anything better for me than that? I am her father. I love her.'

'I'm sorry. It sounds hackneyed, but it is the truth. We don't know yet, but I think we are getting there. I can't be more specific than that at the moment.'

'But you promise you will tell me, as soon as you know.' His eyes became piercing. 'The moment you know.'

'If you promise you won't take the law into your own hands,' said Slider.

He sat back a little and spread his hands. 'I am an old man. What can I do?'

Neither had promised the other anything, and they both knew it.

'You have some more questions for me?' said Cornfeld.

'Yes, sir. I don't know whether they have any relevance or not, but I'm feeling my way at present. I wanted to ask you about the proposed takeover of your company by GCC.'

'Oh, you know about that?'

'Is it supposed to be a secret?'

'It's not meant to be public knowledge yet. However, these things always do get about, no-one knows how. Everyone swears they haven't told a soul, but somehow people know.'

'So it is still going on?'

'Oh, yes. I have been in negotiation for many weeks now. These things take time.'

'And how do you feel about it? Are you for it?'

He looked surprised. 'Certainly, or I should not be in negotiation.'

'Then – you've always been in favour? Forgive me, but has Chattie's death made any difference to your attitude?'

'No,' he said. 'From the beginning, when Global first contacted me, I felt it was the right thing to do. I am old, and it is time to pass on the baton. It was a good opportunity for me to leave my responsibilities behind while doing my best for my employees and the shareholders. The only difference Chattie's death has made is that it has forced me to realise how old and tired I really am. I want to be done with it now.' Steel entered his face again as he added, 'But I shall drive a hard bargain, you may be sure. I'm not too old and tired for that.' He eyed Slider. 'You seem puzzled.'

'It isn't quite fitting in with what I was thinking.'

'You thought I was unwilling to sell, and that killing Chattie was supposed to take the heart out of me and make me agree to it?'

'You're very shrewd,' Slider said. 'It was one of the lines I was working along. But obviously that's not it.'

'No,' said Cornfeld. He looked bleak. 'It's true that I don't want to go on now, but that hasn't affected this deal in any way. Mine is a healthy, profitable company, with a proud history. We have done valuable work in our time, and produced some important benefits for the human community. I can look back on my life with pride – though this tragedy takes away the joy.'

'That brings me to another question,' Slider said. 'Your mother mentioned, when I was talking to her at your house last week, that you have a new drug that's about to come out, and that you are very excited about it. Can you tell me about that?'

The animation came back. 'Yes, indeed! We have been working on it for a long time, and we've just completed the two years of statutory trials. All we have to do now is to secure the approval of the various regulatory bodies, and we can launch it on the world!'

'And what is it? What does it do?'

'It is something quite tremendous,' he said, his eyes bright. He leaned forward across the desk to emphasise the excitement. 'It is a treatment for acne.'

'Acne?' Slider said.

Cornfeld smiled and shook his head. 'I can tell you don't understand. Well, why should you? One can see you have never suffered from it. You think I'm talking about a few teenage spots. You have no idea of its ravages. You don't know how many millions of lives are ruined by this disease. You can't imagine how many billions of pounds are spent year after year on remedies that don't work, or don't work well enough, or have hideous side effects. Our product, Codermatol, works. It *really* works! It will benefit more people than you can imagine, allow them to come out of the shadows and live full lives. It is one of the most exciting and important breakthroughs of the last twenty years, the most important, I believe, that I have ever been personally involved in.'

'I see,' Slider said.

'*Do* you?'

'I take your word for it, sir. You convince me. And this new drug – this is part of the sale, I take it? It goes with the company.'

'Yes,' said Cornfeld. 'Naturally. That is partly why I am demanding such a high price. GCC knows that once it goes on the market, the share price will jump, so that must be reflected in the offer.'

'And have you any idea when the deal will be concluded?'

'Soon,' he said. 'Very soon. I anticipate the announcement will be made at the end of this week. I am only hanging on to receive the regulatory approval. I want that to come to me, as the crowning moment of my business life. Then I shall go. I shall take the money, and Kylie, and go abroad. I haven't had a holiday in years. I intend,' he said, with a look that dared Slider to mock, 'to make a very expensive fool of myself in all the smartest resorts and casinos in the world. I intend to go out in a blaze of glory.'

Slider didn't mock. He hoped very much that the old man would enjoy it; but he felt it was a hollow ambition and was afraid Cornfeld would find it a disappointment – and, moreover, that he knew it would be, even now at the planning stage.

*   *   *

Slider stood at the door of the CID room, looking round the bent heads.

Hart noticed him. 'You're back,' she said.

'Plus ten for observation. Who had the list of Chattie's telephone calls?'

'Andy,' she said. 'Shall I get it for you?' She jumped up and went across to Mackay's desk.

Slider wandered off into his room. Atherton followed him there. 'I know that look,' he said. 'Did Daddy Cornfeld say something interesting?'

'He's *for* the takeover,' Slider said. 'He always was. Killing Chattie didn't make any difference to his decision. He's been in negotiation for weeks.'

'Another damn fine theory hits the dust,' said Atherton, scratching the back of his head. 'So what does that leave us with?'

'There's something burrowing away at the back of my mind,' said Slider.

'Yes, I know, I just had that feeling,' Atherton said, but Slider, frowning in thought, didn't hear.

Mackay came in with the list. 'You wanted this, guv? I was just getting a coffee.'

'Yes, give it here.' Slider sat at his desk and ran a finger up the list. Mackay had written against the numbers who the subscribers were. 'Here it is,' Slider said, tapping the paper. 'She phoned Cockerell on his mobile on the Monday before she died. Why didn't you mention this?'

'Well, guv, once I found he was a family member – you said anything unusual. I didn't think that counted.'

'Hm. I suppose so.'

Atherton leaned over and looked. 'You were expecting to find that call?'

'It was a hunch,' Slider said. 'Don't you see? *She* made the appointment with *him*.'

'And you can deduce that from the mere fact of a telephone number?' Atherton marvelled.

'Don't get cute. Why else would she call him?'

'Maybe she called him about something else, and he used the opportunity to make the appointment. Why would he pretend he made the running?' Atherton countered.

'Because whatever she wanted to see him for, he didn't want us to know about. We knew he was lying. This is what he was lying about.'

'Ah. Even so, where does that get us?'

'I don't know yet. I have to think.' He waved them away.

Mackay said kindly, 'Shall I get you a cuppa, guv?'

'Yes, that'll help. Thanks.' He turned to Atherton. 'Can you bring me the list you had of the drugs GCC makes?'

'Okay. Anything I should know about?'

'You'll know when I know,' said Slider.

Mackay was a long time getting the tea. He came in at last, saying, 'Sorry, guv. I got waylaid, and then there was a queue.'

'Thanks,' Slider said absently, with the look that told Mackay he probably wouldn't remember it was there until it was well cold. 'Can you do something for me? Track down Mrs Hammick and get her to come in. I want to ask her something. Don't alarm her.'

'Sure,' said Mackay. Slider's head went down again. 'Don't forget your tea, guv. I've put it just here for you.'

'Mm,' said Slider.

Despite anything Mackay could do, Mrs Hammick arrived in Slider's office in a state of tension; though she still had enough self-possession to look round very sharply, and with an absorbent capacity that would have given her a real edge in the CID.

'Thank you for coming in,' Slider said. 'I hope it wasn't too inconvenient. There was something I wanted to ask you.'

'Oh, no, it's all right. I don't mind. I do a lady in Devonport Road Tuesday afternoons, so it's only a step.' She looked at the mess of things on Slider's desk as though it could tell her something. 'I've never been in a police station before, not the upstairs bit, but it's just like you see on *The Bill*, isn't it? Have you found out who killed poor Chattie?'

'We're getting there,' said Slider. 'Mrs Hammick—'

'Maureen, please,' she said, as though this were a social visit.

He smiled distractedly. 'There's something you said to me when I last spoke to you – when you so helpfully came in to the station to tell us you knew Chattie.' She nodded. 'I can't remember exactly what it was, but you were telling me how kind she was—'

'Oh, yes, there never was anyone so kind. Gave loads of money to charity, you know, and always ready to listen to your troubles.'

'Yes, of course, but I think you said that when you were there one day she was talking to a young man with acne.'

'Oh, yes,' she said promptly. 'That was not long before – before that dreadful day. Was it Monday? Let me think. No, Monday was the day I caught Jassy in there, the little tramp, up to no good. I'd only just popped in with the croissants, and a good job I did, as it turns out. No, it must have been the Friday, because it was when I was there cleaning. Yes, that's right. He rang the bell and I was nearest so I went and let him in. Poor young man! Nice-looking, he would have been, if it wasn't for the horrible spots.'

'Do you know if he had an appointment to see her?'

'Well, I think he must have, because as I opened the door, Chattie came out of her office behind me and she said, "Oh, you must be . . ." whatever his name was, and he said yes and she said, "Come in, then," and took him into her office.'

'So you think it was a business call?'

'I suppose so. She didn't seem to know him. I mean, if it was social, she wouldn't have had to ask, would she?'

'No, that's true. Did you hear what they talked about?'

She looked offended. 'Are you suggesting I eavesdrop?'

'Not at all. I'm sure you would never do anything like that. I just thought you might have caught a few words inadvertently when passing the door that would give you an idea of the general subject,' Slider said delicately.

'Well,' she said, giving herself away completely, 'I *was* cleaning the hall at the time, while they were having their meeting, which is how I knew how kind she was being to him, because whenever I went past the door, she was looking at him and listening to him so attentively, poor young man, like the kind person she was. But as to what he was saying, no, I can't say I heard anything that would help you.' Something occurred to her, and she looked alarmed. 'You don't think he was the murderer?'

'No, not at all.'

'Oh, well, that's a relief. I'd hate to think I'd been feeling sorry for him, let alone talking to him, if he was a murderer.'

'You talked to him?'

'Well, I happened to be in the hall when they finished their meeting, and as Chattie and him got to the door of her room, the phone rang, so I said to her, "You take your call, dear, I'll see the young man out." Which I did.'

'And you talked to him?' Slider was not hopeful, given that she had only had the length of the hall to work in. 'What did you find out?'

'Find out?' she bristled.

'I know you were only passing the time of day,' Slider soothed her, 'but did you find out his name, or where he came from?'

'As to his name, Chattie did say it when she saw him at the door, as I said, but what it was I can't remember.' She screwed up her brow. 'Was it Bill something? Or John? Quite a plain name, I think it was. No, I can't remember.'

'If it does come to you—'

'Oh, yes, of course, I'll let you know. But as to where he came from, well, he worked in Boots, that I did find out.'

'Boots?'

'Of course, it might have been one of the other chemists. You see, as I was showing him out, I asked him was Chattie going to do some work for him, because she was very good and very efficient, and he'd not be sorry he'd come to her. Just to help her business along, you understand. I always said that sort of thing when I had the chance.'

'Very good of you.'

'Well, she was good to me. Anyway, the young man said no, that wasn't why he'd come, and I asked him what line of business he was in, and he said he was a chemist. And I thought what a shame it was he should work in a shop all day surrounded by all those medicines and everything, and not be able to do anything about his face, poor man. But I didn't say it aloud, of course.'

'Of course not.'

'And in any case I wouldn't have had the chance, because he was obviously in a hurry, because that's all he did say – "I'm a chemist," he said, and the next minute he was opening the door himself before I had a chance to and he said good morning, really quick, and away he went. Not running, but hurrying as fast as he could walk.' She paused and looked at Slider, head slightly cocked, waiting for his reaction.

'Thank you,' he said. 'You've been very helpful.'

'Is that all you wanted to know?'

'Yes, that was it. If you should remember the young man's name, or if you remember anything you might have heard of their conversation, even a single word, you'll let me know?'

'Of course I will. But I don't promise anything. I wasn't really listening, you know. But if I recall his name . . .' She thought of something. 'It wasn't in her diary?'

'No,' said Slider.

'Oh. Maybe a last-minute thing, then. She always wrote appointments in her diary, but if he just rang on the off-chance and said, "Can I come round?" maybe she wouldn't write it down.'

'I'm sure that was it,' said Slider.

It was lunchtime when Tufnell Arceneaux called.

'You're not going to like this,' he said, his roar muted with sympathy.

'I've been expecting bad news,' Slider said. 'Tell me the worst. The blood on the hoodie isn't Chattie's. It isn't even human blood. It's the wrong clothes, this is the wrong case, and I'm in the wrong job.'

'Dear me, you are depressed,' Tufty said. 'Time I took you out on the spree and showed you how to get the hang of life.'

'Every time I go out with you I get the hangover of life.'

'That's because you lack practice. No skill is acquired without dedicated, repeated practice.'

'Tell me what you've got to tell me and let me crawl away and die in peace.'

'Well, it's not as bad as all that. The blood on the grey top *is* human blood and the DNA profile matches that of your victim, so you've got the right clothes. There was also some of her blood on the outside of the gloves. On the inside of the gloves we found sweat containing skin cells, which we were able to profile. There was also a longish dark hair inside the hood, though there was no bulb to it so we could only get mitochondrial DNA from the shaft, but there were also skin cells inside the hood from the scalp, which we were able to process, to determine that the wearer of the grey top and the wearer of the gloves were the same person.'

'And?'

'It wasn't your suspect.'

'Toby Harkness?'

'That's the feller. Only he wasn't the feller. I didn't even need to do a comparison. It wasn't any feller at all.'

'What do you mean?'

'DNA, my old banana, is a wonderful thing, but as you know, all the profiles in the world won't help a smidge unless you've got something to compare them with. About the only useful thing you can learn from unmatched DNA is the sex – or, not to be invidious, the gender – of the person concerned.'

'You're saying the murderer was a woman?'

'Now, now, don't put words into my mouth. I'm saying the wearer of the grey top and the gloves was a woman.'

'Are you sure?'

'I'll pretend you didn't say that,' Tufty said kindly. 'I know you're under a lot of strain. X marks the spot, old bean. Or, rather, XX. If it was a man, there'd have been a Y – if not a wherefore.'

Slider gave a gasping laugh. 'Tufty, I love you and I want to have your babies.'

'You don't know how many times I've heard that today,' Tufty said gravely.

'Well, well,' said Porson. 'So your hunch was justified. You thought it wasn't Harkness, didn't you?'

'It was the manner of the killing. It didn't look like a passionate frenzy.'

'No,' Porson said thoughtfully, walking up and down the space between his desk and the window. 'Now you mention it, the MO was daft enough, it could only be a woman.'

Slider concealed a smile. It was lucky that remark would never get beyond these four walls.

'So, what have we got in the woman-suspect department? Henry Cornfeld left enough chaos behind him in his personal life.'

'Yes, there are two ex-wives still alive and two other daughters.'

'Not to mention, presumably, a scad of mistresses and outworn dolly birds. But then they'd surely try to murder him, not his daughter.'

'And there are possibilities in Chattie's life – jealous rivals, perhaps.'

'I suppose,' Porson said, pausing to tap his fingers on his desk – shave and a haircut, two bits, 'I suppose the Brixton daughter is the best bet. She's a bit of a loose canyon.'

'Jassy and her mother are alibis for each other,' said Slider, 'and there's nothing to suggest the mother's anything but honest.'

'When it comes to protecting her own daughter, though,' Porson said wisely. 'It's best to take no chances. Better have a look at that alibi.'

'We could get a sample from her and check it against the DNA on the gloves.'

Porson tapped again, frowning. 'Better get some sort of idea first. All this testing is expensive. Any other lines to follow up?'

'Yes, there's something I've been thinking my way through, but there's a link missing in the chain.'

Porson nodded, eyebrows raised, receptive; but Slider didn't want to go through it yet, for fear of dislodging something delicate. He hadn't completely worked it out himself. When he didn't speak, Porson went on, 'By the way, how is Hart working out?'

'She's good, and she fits in well,' Slider said.

'But?'

'Oh, no buts.'

'You sounded a bit muted. Not chucking bokays about.'

'Only that I didn't see the point, as she's temporary.'

'Ah, well, that was rather the point. I was sounding out Mr Wetherspoon, and it looks as though Anderson might be kept on for another six months.'

'Oh, no!'

'Oh, yes, I'm afraid. Which would leave you two men down, seeing as you were a man short before Anderson got requisitioned. I told Mr Wetherspoon it wasn't acceptable, and he agreed with me. In a way.'

'In a way?'

'Said yes, but didn't offer any suggestions. I suppose everybody's ear'oling him for more staff, and he's only got so many bodies to go round. But then I heard a rumour that Hart might want to stay with us.'

He may look like something escaped from Mount Rushmore, Slider thought, but there wasn't much escaped him, one way and another. 'I think she'd jump at the chance, sir,' he said.

'In that case—'

Porson's phone rang. He lifted a finger – the conversational pause button – and picked up the receiver. 'Yes? Yes, he's here. Yes. All right, put her through.' He held out the receiver to Slider. 'Your Mrs Haddock wants a word. Says it's urgent.'

Slider took it. 'Slider here.'

'Oh, Mr Slider? It's Maureen Hammick. I thought you'd want to know straight away, seeing as you said it was important. I've remembered that young man's name, that came to see Chattie on the Friday. It was Simpson. Bill Simpson. I knew it was something plain. And I've been worrying my brain about it while I've been Hoovering, and it suddenly came to me, because there used to be an actor called Bill Simpson, didn't there? Or was that Bill Sikes?' she tripped herself, troubled. 'No, wait a minute, that was Oliver Reed, wasn't it?'

'Oliver Twist,' said Slider, unable to help himself.

'Yes, that's right. Nasty piece of work, he was, a drunk and a bully.'

Slider managed to stop himself asking if she meant Oliver Reed or Bill Sikes, and asked instead, 'The young man who visited Chattie was called Bill Simpson? Are you quite sure?'

'Yes, absolutely positive. I remember now. When I opened the door she came out behind me in the hall and said, "You must be Bill Simpson?" and he said, "That's right," and she took him straight into her room. Seemed very nervous, he did, but maybe it was just his spots, poor thing, knowing what he looked like. But she was wonderful with him, put him right at his ease, and the way she smiled at him and paid him attention, you'd never know he wasn't Pierce Brosnan.'

'Thank you very much,' Slider said, anxious to stem the flow. 'You've been wonderfully helpful, Mrs Hammick.' He near as damnit said Haddock. Porson was catching. 'Thank you and goodbye.'

He handed the receiver back to Porson, who dumped it, and said, 'Oliver Twist?'

Slider made a never-mind gesture. 'Mrs Haddock – Hammick – has just given me what I hope is the last link in the chain.'

'Well, go to it,' Porson said. 'Sic, boy. Let me know if it works out.'

Slider went, blessing Porson's restraint and trust in him in not asking him for an immediate exposition.

CHAPTER SEVENTEEN

Cloaca and Dagger

Hart came to his door. 'You wanted me, sir?'

'Yes, a little job for you. I want you to find out if GCC has an employee called Bill Simpson. They must have a central personnel department.'

'Human resources, guv,' she said. 'You ain't allowed to call it personnel any more.'

'He's a chemist, so he'll probably work in one of the labs.'

'In this country?'

'Of course in this country. I'm not asking you to trawl the world. It'll probably be in south-east England, so if the personnel lists are divided by region, try that first. If you find him, I want his name, address and telephone.'

'Okey-doke. Anyfing else?'

'Yes, send Atherton in.'

To Atherton he said, 'You're good at financial stuff. I want you to find out who bought Jassy's shares. Is that a possibility?'

'If they were bought as a block, it's easy,' he said. 'Anyone who buys more than three per cent of a company's shares has to make a special declaration to the registrar. If they were bought by a number of people it will be more difficult. It'll be a matter of comparing all the transactions at the time and tracking them down.'

'Okay, see what you can do.'

Atherton hesitated. 'Can I know what, yet?'

'Soon,' said Slider.

Atherton was back first, and he looked at Slider with what was almost admiration. 'Bingo,' he said. 'Jassy's shares were bought in a block – or, rather, ownership was transferred. One presumes she got payment for them. They were transferred to an offshore holding company in Guernsey, called Mobius Holdings. And the owners and sole directors of Mobius are David and Ruth Cockerell.'

'Ah,' said Slider.

'How did you know?'

'I didn't know, I wanted to find out. I suppose she got into money trouble and approached him.'

'She seems to have begged from everyone else.'

'Yes. It might have been one of those times when the usual sources had got fed up and cut her off for a time. And he took the opportunity to get his hands on some more shares.'

'I wonder what he paid her for them?' Atherton mused. 'Be interesting to know if it was market value. I'd take a bet it wasn't. She may think she's smart, but Jassy's got the brains of a glass of water. So, that makes the Cockerells together the biggest shareholder after old man Henry, with twenty per cent between them. What's your thinking?'

'That timing is everything,' said Slider. 'But we've still got to find out what the meeting with Chattie was really about. Ah, this could be the missing link.'

Hart had appeared at the door. 'She doesn't look a bit like an ape,' Atherton said.

'Wossup?' she said, looking from one to the other. 'Have I missed anuvver racist remark?'

'Have you got it?' Slider asked, seeing badinage in his colleagues' eyes.

'Yeah, boss. Bill Simpson. Research chemist. Works at the unit at Bedford. But I've found out something more. He's been off work for a week.'

'Has he, indeed? You interest me strangely.'

'Yeah. He phoned in sick on Friday week past, and he hasn't been in since. Said he had the 'flu. The person I spoke to at Bedford said he'd been looking a bit queer for a day or two before, so they weren't surprised he'd gone sick.'

'I wonder if anyone's heard of him since?' Slider said thoughtfully.

'D'you want me to ask 'em?'

'No, I don't want to alert anyone. I'll go round and see him. Where does he live?'

'Luton,' said Hart.

'Well, I suppose somebody has to,' said Atherton. 'I hope you don't want me to come with you.'

'Can I come, guv?' Hart said. 'I ain't picky.'

'No,' Slider said. 'I'll take Swilley. If I'm right, this could take sensitive handling.' He got up and went briskly through to the CID room.

Hart and Atherton looked at each other. 'Well, that's two of us he's insulted at one go.'

Bill Simpson lived in a flat in a glum new block in one of the less appealing parts of Luton. Swilley was a good companion, and rode with Slider in silence all the way, where a lesser mortal would have troubled him with questions. Only when they got out of the car did she say, 'How d'you want to work it, boss?'

'If I'm right, he's holed up and terrified, so he probably wouldn't open the door to me. I want you to knock and get us in. Reassure him.'

'Am I police?'

'Oh, yes. I don't think it's anyone in authority he's afraid of.'

'Right you are.'

The block was long and narrow rather than square, and four storeys high. Simpson's flat was on the top floor, and the lifts weren't working. They walked up the stairs, which smelt faintly of urine, but at least weren't littered with abandoned needles. Glum, but not that rough, fortunately, Slider concluded. When they reached the door, Slider stood back out of sight and Swilley positioned herself in front of the peephole and knocked and rang. After a while she put her ear to the door, and whispered to Slider, 'There's someone in there. I can hear him moving about.'

'Try again, and call out to him,' Slider whispered back.

She knocked again and called, 'Mr Simpson? Could you open the door, please, sir? It's the police, and we want to talk to you.'

As Slider had hoped, the female voice gave the occupant hope. Swilley saw the shadow on the peephole, held up her warrant card, and smiled.

'What do you want?' came a muffled voice from within.

'Just to talk to you,' Swilley said. 'It's not trouble for you, I promise you.'

'Let me see your ID,' the voice said. 'Put it through the letterbox.'

Slider nodded, and Swilley obeyed.

Eventually the voice said, 'All right, it looks genuine. What do you want?'

'I can't talk out here. Please open the door. No-one's going to hurt you. We just want to ask you a few questions.'

'We?' There was quick alarm. 'Who's we?'

'I've got my boss, Inspector Slider, with me. He's really nice, honest.'

She moved aside and Slider moved out to where he could be seen, and held up his brief as well. That, too, had to be pushed through the letterbox before Simpson would consent to open the door a crack, with the chain on. Slider smiled gently at the portion of a face that appeared, and said, 'I know you're frightened, Mr Simpson. We're here to help you, but you must tell us what it's all about. Please let me in. I promise you, you're not in trouble, and no-one's going to hurt you.'

'You don't know,' the voice quavered, and the red-rimmed eyes filled with tears. 'They killed her, and they'll come for me next.'

'We'll protect you. Please open the door.'

He seemed convinced at last, or perhaps was simply too desperate for someone to talk to to resist. The door closed, the chain rattled off, and then it was opened again with great caution. Slider thought he was still expecting the sudden rush, the door kicked in and himself grabbed, so he stood quite still, until Simpson had examined his appearance fully. As to Simpson, he was unshaven, haggard, and exhausted-looking. His hair was matted and tousled, his eyes bloodshot and haunted, and his face was ravaged by that cruellest of diseases, adult acne. Slider found himself remembering Barrington again, his tortured former boss, who had ended up with a gun barrel in his mouth and half his head on the kitchen wall. Barrington's face had been scarred like a moonscape from acne. A huge pity washed through him.

'Don't be afraid,' he said again.

Simpson's lips quivered. He was close to breaking. 'They must have known I overheard them,' he said, almost in a whisper. 'They killed her. It was my fault for going to her, getting her involved. I should have gone to her father, but he was out of the country, and I was afraid to wait. It was my fault she was murdered.'

'No, no, it wasn't,' said Slider, edging in gently past him, Swilley following.

'They killed her and they'll come for me next. You've got to help me.'

'I will help you,' Slider said soothingly. 'Just tell me exactly what it was you overheard.'

Atherton put the phone down. 'The cock o' the walk's not come in to work. Skulking at home with a stomach bug, apparently.'

'It may be true,' Slider said. 'Fear does go to people's stomachs sometimes.'

'You think he knows what we – what you suspect?'

'His secretary may have told him we pumped her,' Slider said. 'I felt at the time she was suffering from a crisis of loyalties. Or he may just be worried because we turned up at all. He didn't strike me as a man of great resolution or great intellect.'

'He struck me as a pillock,' said Atherton.

'That's what I said. Well, it's good that he's at home. We can kill two birds with one stone.'

'We?'

'You can come this time,' Slider said. 'I may need you. I don't know quite how the conversation's going to go.'

'He needs me,' Atherton observed to the air, in a quavering voice.

'Stop clowning, and let's get going,' said Slider.

Cockerell's house was in a village called Buckland Common, in the green and delicious edges of the Chiltern Hills. It was modern, large, set in an acre or so of manicured lawn, and built in the presently fashionable mock-Tudor style, whose vernacular involved stuck-on beams, diamond-pane windows, gables, long sloping roofs, and fancy tile hanging, but omitted any chimneys. There was also a tennis court and a deeply authentic Tudor detached double garage. Given its size, position and acreage, Slider reckoned it would probably market at about a million and a half, which hardly put the Cockerells in the poor and needy bracket. Ruth's resentment of her father's wealth was obviously comparative.

It was she who opened the door. Slider recognised her from the photograph in Cockerell's office. She was of medium height, slender, with dark hair in a hairdresser's arrangement; she wore slacks and a short-sleeved jumper of expensive but dull knitwear; her face was expertly made-up, which went a long way to concealing that she was plain; but her expression was sullen and, at the sight of Slider and Atherton, became also alert and wary.

'We've come to see your husband, Mrs Cockerell,' Slider said.

'Well, you can't,' she snapped. 'He's ill.'

'I'm afraid I shall have to insist. It's very important. Will you tell him we're here, please?'

Calculations flitted about behind her eyes, but at last she stepped back and let them in. 'I'll tell him, but I don't know if he'll come,' she said ungraciously, and left them standing in the hall while she went upstairs.

Slider looked quickly around. The interior was different from both Henry's and Chattie's, in that everything was modern and expensive, but conventional, arranged without flair or taste. It was the wealthy man's equivalent of a room display in a Courts' showroom. The nearest room on the left was the living room, on the right a dining room. The house smelt of furniture polish and new carpet, and was silent, not even a ticking clock anywhere, only the sound of birdsong coming faintly from the garden, struggling through the Tudor double-glazing.

In the living room, on the floor beside one of the sofas, was an expensive crocodile handbag. Slider gave Atherton a sharp look and quick jerk of the head. Atherton went in and picked it up, looked through it quickly. He held up a mobile phone, one of the new tiny Motorolas that would fit into the top pocket of a man's shirt. The same sort that Chattie had had. 'Just one. Switched on,' he said.

Slider nodded and Atherton came back to his side. 'Must be upstairs,' Slider said quietly. 'Probably in one of her drawers.' And he remembered Nutty Nicholls saying once that women always kept things of value, or things they wanted to hide, in their underwear drawer.

Slider took out his own mobile, tapped in the number of Atherton's, and replaced it in his pocket. Then they waited in silence until footsteps came back down the carpeted stairs, and David Cockerell appeared, looking much less *soigné* than the last time, in a pair of grey flannel bags, a blue checked shirt open at the neck, and carpet slippers. Slider had a deep horror of men's carpet slippers and an instinctive suspicion of anyone who would wear them. Cockerell was looking ill enough for his excuse to be true, but interestingly he did not seem to be worried by Slider's and Atherton's presence, only annoyed.

'I don't know what's so urgent that you couldn't wait until I was back at the office,' he opened proceedings. 'I'm not well, as my wife told you.'

'Yes, I'm sorry to hear that,' Slider said. 'But it's rather important. I have some things I want to talk to you about. Shall we sit down and be comfortable?'

'You're very free with my hospitality,' said Cockerell, with weak indignation.

'It might take a while,' Slider said. 'As you're not well, I thought you ought to sit down, but we'll talk standing up if you like.'

Put like that, Cockerell had to submit. He led the way into the living room. Slider almost held his breath over whether Mrs C would come with them, but it seemed she did not want to be left out of anything – or perhaps needed to know what they knew – and she followed them in. They all took seats, and under cover of the general sitting down, Slider pushed the send button on his phone. Atherton's mobile rang.

Slider and Atherton both reached for their phones. It had become a universal gesture, these days. Even Cockerell looked about for his own, and Ruth made a half-rise gesture towards her handbag before Atherton said, 'It's me,' and answered it. Slider pressed the end button on his and returned it to his pocket. Atherton spoke a word or two into his phone, then rose and said to the company, 'Excuse me. I'll just take this outside,' and left the room.

Mrs Cockerell completed the movement towards her handbag, took it back with her to her seat, extracted a packet of cigarettes and lit one, without offering them to anyone else.

'Well,' Cockerell said impatiently to Slider, 'what have you got to say to me? It had better be important.'

'I think it is. You see, someone told me a story today, which I hadn't heard before. It was very interesting. It seems that many years ago an Australian doctor discovered that ulcers weren't caused by an excess of acid in the stomach, as everyone had always thought, but by a bacterium.'

'*Helicobacter pyloris*,' Cockerell said impatiently. 'Everyone knows that.'

'Yes, I suppose most people do know it now. But the thing was, they didn't then. This doctor did all sorts of tests and controlled experiments, and he proved conclusively that it was the bacterium that was to blame, and that you could eliminate it and cure the ulcers with a simple dose of antibiotic. Well, you'd think everyone would be delighted, and I suppose his patients were. But when the doctor tried to go public with his findings, things got rather nasty. The Australian medical profession and the drugs companies banded together to rubbish his ideas and prevent him publishing his findings. They condemned him as a quack and a lunatic. Because, you see, they had been making a fortune for years out of selling antacids to ulcer sufferers, and this doctor's research was going to kill off the golden goose.'

'What the devil has all this rigmarole got to do with me?' Cockerell said testily, but there was consciousness in his eyes. Ruth Cockerell was watching Slider like a cat at a mouse-hole, her whole face and body intent and alert. Only one hand moved, lifting the cigarette to her mouth and away.

'I'm getting to that,' Slider said. 'Just let me finish my story my own way, if you will, or I shall lose my thread. Anyway, this doctor's life was made such a misery that he lost his practice, and he was hounded out of the country. He went to America, where eventually he managed to convince people that he wasn't mad, and his findings were published, and gradually the right treatment began to be offered to ulcer sufferers. Though I believe there are still some doctors who won't believe it and go on prescribing antacids and special diets. And the thing is that it was more than twenty years ago that this doctor first tried to get his ideas into the public forum. Twenty years! Doesn't that astonish you?' His audience didn't answer. 'You see, it hadn't occurred to me before,' Slider said pleasantly, 'but of course there's more money to be made out of cures that don't work than cures that do, because the sufferers keep having to come back for more, and they will do anything and pay anything for relief. And this is especially true with common, non-life-threatening ailments which are, nevertheless, extremely unpleasant to put up with, like ulcers. And like acne.'

Ruth's expression did not change, and her body language gave nothing away, but Cockerell's shoulders seemed to slump a little, and he drew a breath like a sigh, as of one caught at last. Still, he seemed prepared to play the end game.

'I still don't see what this has to do with me.'

'Oh, I think you do, but I'm happy to spell it out for you. On Monday fortnight past, you were at the plant in Bedford for the opening of the new block. You were both there, in fact,' he said, gathering Ruth with his eyes. 'But you were not together the whole time. There was a rather good and rather liquid lunch, and just after it you separated for a very basic reason, and you, Mr Cockerell, went to the gents' lavatory with one of your fellow directors.'

'Is this really necessary?' Cockerell said, with great scorn.

'Yes, it is. Because while you were in there, perhaps fuelled by the champagne, you talked with rather too much frankness about Cornfeld's new drug, Codermatol. But in fact, you were not alone. Someone was in one of the stalls and, without intending to, overheard what you said.'

Cockerell looked startled. He stared at Slider in a strained way. Interesting, Slider thought: Simpson's fears were quite unfounded. Cockerell had not known he was overheard, or, therefore, who had overheard him.

Slider went on: 'GCC makes a huge amount of money from selling acne treatments, none of which is really more than a palliative. But Codermatol really works. Obviously if it came out, it would kill off GCC's golden goose, just as the Australian doctor's findings about the *Helicobacter* would have. That was why GCC was so eager to buy Cornfeld Chemicals – so that it could suppress the new drug and make sure it never came on the market.'

'That's preposterous!' Cockerell said. 'It's total rubbish.'

'It's exactly what you said in the washroom that you were going to do. You had been in the forefront of the negotiations with Henry Cornfeld. You had to make him believe that you were interested in the new drug, and you had to make the offer for his company high enough to convince him that you were, because you knew that if *he* knew you never meant to let it reach the market, he would never have let you take over the company.

'Of course, you had no idea your plot had been uncovered until Chattie telephoned you on Monday last week. The person who overheard you had gone to her with the story, in the absence abroad of her father, knowing her reputation for liberal thinking and charitable actions.'

Ruth snorted at that point, apparently overcome by the praise of the deceased. Slider glanced at her curiously. She changed it to a cough, stubbed out her cigarette and lit another.

'You arranged to meet her on Tuesday, in the hope that you could persuade her to go along with the plot. Did you offer her money? I've been wondering what inducements you used. Well,' he dismissed the question with a wave of his hand as it was obvious it would not be answered, 'it doesn't matter. She refused absolutely to go along with it, and warned you, moreover, that she was going to tell her father as soon as he got back from the States exactly what was going on. And she knew, as you did, that Henry Cornfeld was a man of principle, in this if not in his private life, and that he was immensely proud of Codermatol. He would not allow you to bury it. The sale would not go through – and you had so much to lose, hadn't you, Mr Cockerell?'

Atherton came back in at that moment, and by nothing more than a blink told Slider that he had been successful. Slider felt a huge rush of relief. They were on the right track. A hideous embarrassment and a writ like a Rottweiler to the goolies were going to be avoided.

'Sorry,' Atherton said, sitting down. 'Have I missed much?'

'We were just about to calculate what Mr Cockerell stood to lose if the Cornfeld acquisition didn't go through,' said Slider. 'To begin with there were the shares in Cornfeld Chemicals. Mrs Cockerell's ten per cent, which had been given to her, and the ten per cent you bought very cheaply from Jassy would both show a very nice profit and net you a huge lump sum. And then there was your job at GCC, the promotion, share options and golden eggs you could expect from a company whose continued prosperity you had assured. So Chattie had to be stopped. You were heard to say, when you got back from the meeting with her, thank God there were a few days left – which meant, of course, before Henry Cornfeld came home. Once she'd had a chance to tell him, all would be lost. She said she was going to wait and tell him face to face. But what if she changed her mind and telephoned him in the States? It wasn't safe to take the chance. And the next morning, Chattie was murdered.'

Cockerell made a strangled sound, and his eyes flew wide open. 'Good God! You don't think—? You can't possibly think *I* killed her? I'm not a murderer! I could never do a thing like that.' He stared at them wildly. Ruth was keeping very still, her whole body outlined in tension, still watching and waiting, but poised for sudden action. 'Come on!' Cockerell pleaded, almost groaned. 'I wouldn't hurt her, let alone kill her. I admit I felt a moment's relief when I heard she was dead, because – well, you were right about the other thing, and she was going to ruin it for all of us, the stupid girl. I said to her, you stand to gain as much as the rest of us. Everybody wins, you, me, your father, everyone. But she wouldn't listen. Went all pious and ethical on me, talking about the sufferings of millions. I said to her, it's only bloody acne, not cancer of the liver, but she wouldn't budge. I could have throttled her – oh, God, I don't mean that! That's just a figure of speech! Look, I know what we were doing about suppressing the drug was unethical, and I'm owning up to it, but murder's something different. I could never kill anyone, never. And certainly not for something like this. It's fantastic!'

Fascinating, Slider thought: he doesn't even think about his alibi. He wants to convince me that he *wouldn't* do it, rather than that he *couldn't*. He still wants to be a nice guy, despite all his greedy, sleazy plottings.

Still, he let him writhe a little bit longer before saying, 'As a matter of fact, I know you didn't do it.'

'You – you do?' Cockerell was sweating now, and licked his lips, looking at Slider in a slightly dazed way as he heard these words.

'What time did you leave for work that morning, sir?'

'That – that morning? I don't remember. But – wait – I was in the Northumberland Avenue office that day, wasn't I? So I would have left at half past six. I always leave at half past six, to be in at eight.'

'You were in the office by eight o'clock?'

'Yes. I mean, I don't remember exactly, but I must have been. I'd remember if I were late. My secretary—' he began to add, with a flash of inspiration.

'Yes, she says you were there at eight. And Chattie was killed somewhere around eight o'clock. So we know you couldn't have done it. Actually,' he added conversationally, 'I believe you when you say you wouldn't kill anyone just for money. But there is someone I think would.' He didn't look at Ruth. He kept his eyes on Cockerell as he said, 'When you went home that night, the day you met Chattie up in Town, you were angry. You told your wife all about it, how that damned girl was going to ruin things for everybody.'

'Yes, I suppose I did,' Cockerell said, pulling out a handkerchief to wipe his face, not following where this was going.

Slider turned to Ruth. 'You look very fit, Mrs Cockerell. Do you like to keep in trim – go jogging, go to a gym, anything like that?'

Her face was immobile. 'No,' she said. 'I don't.'

Cockerell, the dope, said, 'Yes, you do, darling. You're always exercising – I'm very proud of my wife's figure,' the poor goop went on, evidently pleased at this less threatening line of questioning. 'She goes out running most mornings.'

'Is that so?' Slider said, with interest. 'So you'll have jogging clothes, then. Training shoes, tracksuits, that sort of thing.'

Mrs Cockerell only glared, her face so tense he could see the muscles of her jaw writhing under the skin, but she didn't answer him.

'I don't suppose,' he said gently, 'that you have an alibi for that morning, Mrs Cockerell?'

Cockerell stared at him in astonishment, and then gave his wife a quick, flashing glance. He opened his mouth to protest to Slider, but nothing emerged. A look of great sickness came over him, sickness and knowledge at the same time, and from the same source.

'Mrs Cockerell?' Slider pressed her.

'I was out running,' she answered, unclenching her jaws for just long enough to get the words out.

'How long had you been planning it? That's what I've been wondering,' Slider said, as if ruminatively. 'A long time, I would imagine. She'd been a thorn in your side for years – well, all her life, really. Your mother abandoned for her mother, and treated so badly in comparison with Stella Smart. And then the usurper's brat turns out to be pretty and clever and everybody loves her, while you – what do you get? Nothing! Your father dotes on Chattie, but he's got no time for you.' Mrs Cockerell's face was undergoing a reaction while he spoke, a look of boiling fury clenching it until he thought her teeth would shatter. 'And then, to crown it all, there were the rumours that she'd had an affair with your husband.'

'No!' Cockerell cried. 'That's not true. Good God, what are you saying?' He looked at Slider, seeming genuinely appalled. 'How can you say such a thing? There was nothing like that between us. We were friends, that's all.' He looked at his wife. 'I swear it was innocent! I never – we never—!'

'Shut up, you idiot!' Mrs Cockerell hissed. 'Don't you see what he's doing? For God's sake, shut up!'

Slider resumed, looking from one to the other with apparent sympathy. 'Well, in practical terms, it doesn't really matter whether it happened or not. The fact was there were rumours. Had you brooded over it, Mrs Cockerell? Thought about murdering her, stroked and cherished the idea of it until it became a possibility, and then an inevitability? Until it was just a matter of how, and when. After all, you wanted her dead, but you didn't want to get caught. And then the Park Killer turned up, practically on Chattie's doorstep.'

'No,' Cockerell moaned. 'Oh, no!'

'Shut *up*, David!'

'The Park Killer kills joggers,' Slider continued to Ruth, not looking at him, 'and you know Chattie goes running every day in the park. But Chattie's younger than you, and she's strong. You don't think you'll be able just to stab her to death, the way the Park Killer does. You need some way to render her helpless first.'

Now the first chink appeared in Ruth's armour. She hadn't known he knew that, that the false stabbing had been detected. Her eyes widened and her nostrils flared, but she closed her lips tightly, as if to prevent anything escaping.

'You'd worked in a hospital pharmacy, so you knew what you needed. And you knew you'd have the chance to get hold of it at the opening of the new building at Bedford, which you were going to attend with your husband. They made the right sort of drugs there, and you knew your way around. No-one would ever wonder at your presence. You took what you needed, and then it was just a matter of waiting for the right opportunity. But when David came home and told you he had met Chattie that day, and what she had said, you knew you couldn't wait any longer. It would have to be done right away. You couldn't let her rob you again of what was your due. Kill her, be revenged for everything, and, as a bonus, break your father's heart, the way he had broken yours and your mother's. She deserved to die, she had to die.'

'Stop it!' Cockerell said. 'I order you to stop it! Get out of my house! I won't have you say those things to my wife!' He jumped to his feet, but Atherton was up too, and stood between him and Slider.

'Sit down, sir,' Atherton said. He could be amazingly menacing when he wanted to, Slider thought absently. 'Just sit. It has to be done. Sit down.'

Suddenly Ruth spoke, quite calmly. 'Yes, sit down, David. Don't make a fuss. This is all nonsense anyway. I didn't do it and they can't prove I did.'

'I'm afraid we can,' Slider said, with infinite, deadly kindness. He flickered a glance at Atherton, a signal between them. Somewhere upstairs, but just audibly, a telephone started to ring. Again Cockerell, the businessman, made the automatic gesture of looking for his mobile, but neither Slider nor Atherton moved. They were looking at Ruth. She looked faintly puzzled at first, and then her jaw dropped a little as understanding came to her.

'You know what that is, don't you?' Slider said. 'That's Chattie's mobile ringing. She had the same sort of mobile as you, the new, very dinky, pocket-sized Motorola. She dropped it while you were killing her, and you picked it up automatically, assuming it was yours. Perfectly understandable, one of those things one does without thinking – like stubbing out a cigarette. How long was it after you got home that you realised you had two mobiles in your pocket, yours and Chattie's?'

Ruth Cockerell gave an inarticulate cry of rage, leaped out of her chair and flung herself at Slider. 'I'll kill you!' she screamed, as she tried to claw his face.

Atherton jumped, and between them, though with difficulty, they managed to subdue her, until she fell back into an armchair, hunched and panting. Cockerell remained motionless all through, his hands clasped together in his lap, his head turned away and his fixed eyes staring at nothing, at disaster and ruin.

'I'm glad I killed her,' Mrs Cockerell shrieked. She punched the upholstered arm of the chair repeatedly. 'She deserved it, the greedy, evil, man-grabbing little bitch. She deserved to die. She had everything, everything she ever wanted, she stole my father and my home, and still she had to have my husband and my money as well. I killed her and I'd kill her again if I could. Do what you like! You can't touch me for it. I hate you all!'

Cockerell moaned softly, closing his eyes, as if that would make it all go away. Slider stood over her, in case she tried to make a run for it, and said, 'Ruth Cockerell, I arrest you for the murder of Charlotte Cornfeld. You do not have to say anything . . .'

The firm's celebratory drink had to wait until Wednesday evening. They went to the Boscombe Arms, having had to abandon the Crown since it modernised itself, and Joanna joined them there. Everybody was hungry, and once they had settled themselves comfortably in the snug, Swilley was sent to operate her charm on Andy Barrett, the landlord, for the provision of snacks, which came in the end in the form of packets of crisps, pork pies and some hastily knocked together cheese and pickle sandwiches.

'A feast fit for a king,' Joanna said, observing McLaren savaging a sandwich with faint wonder. The sandwich didn't have a chance.

Swilley swung the plate her way. 'Have something,' she said, 'before Maurice scoffs the lot.'

It was the first time Joanna had been to one of these dos. She sat on the banquette beside Slider, and felt all the pleasure of being his woman, accepted, not exactly one of the group but a welcome honorary member. Pints were sunk, conversation blossomed, the noise level grew. She answered friendly questions from Swilley about her pregnancy and from Hollis about their plans for finding somewhere else to live. At one point Slider put his arm round her casually to balance himself as he leaned over for a piece of pork pie, and then left it there, warm and heavy and comfortable. She tried not to be aware of Hart watching the action, but noted in spite of herself that Hart looked at Slider a great deal more than she ever looked at Atherton. She saw Atherton watching her and Slider together, too, when he wasn't swapping barbed badinage with Swilley. She wondered whether he wished he had Sue there, as Bill had her.

'And there's something else to celebrate,' Hart said loudly, to catch attention. The noise level fell a notch as everyone looked at her. 'Least, *I* think it's good news,' Hart went on, looking round the group, but allowing her eyes to come to rest at last on Slider. Well, Joanna told herself, that's natural. He is the boss, and the heart of the group: she appreciated so much more, now, for having witnessed the drink-up, how that was true.

'Go on, then, Tone,' McLaren invited, gathering the crumbs from the otherwise empty sandwich plate with a wetted forefinger. 'Tell us.'

'Mr Porson's had a word wiv Mr Wevverspoon, and I'm not going back to the DAFT squad. I'm wiv you permanently. How about that?'

She beamed, and so did everyone else, and there were thumps of congratulation on her back and a tickly kiss on her cheek from Hollis's appalling moustache. Atherton took advantage of the precedent and said, 'Jolly good,' and kissed her too, only on the mouth. She let him, to a chorus of oy-oys, and even gave a show of wriggling her shoulders and lifting one foot behind in a Hollywood manner, but as soon as they broke apart she looked inevitably at Slider for his reaction. Joanna glanced up at him and saw he was smiling indulgently, and laughed at herself for a fool. There was nothing in that smile but fatherliness.

All the same, she thought, there's too much attention being paid to that girl, and she said, loudly enough to attract attention, 'I still don't know the end of the story. Who's going to tell it?'

'Go on, boss,' Hart urged, giving him her full attention. 'I think there's different bits all of us're wondering about.'

So Slider told the tale.

'The effect of theatricals on a weak mind,' he concluded, when he got to the bit about Chattie's mobile. 'I had the feeling that a parade of scientific evidence wouldn't move her – especially as we hadn't actually matched her DNA at that point to the stuff found on the clothes – but the entirely superficial ringing of the mobile got through her guard.'

'How did you know she had it?' Joanna asked.

'I didn't,' said Slider. 'But we couldn't find it anywhere, so it seemed likely that the murderer had taken it away, and when we checked and found Ruth's mobile was the same model, it seemed even more likely.'

'She might have thrown it away.'

'She might have, but if she had, I felt it was likely someone else would have found it, and either they'd have handed it in, if they were honest, or turned it on, if they weren't. As soon as it was turned on, we'd be able to trace the signal. It never was, so it was a matter of Atherton slipping upstairs while I talked to them and seeing if he could find it.'

'It was in the drawer of her bedside table,' Atherton said, 'along with her pearls and her pills. Very traditional.'

'As to the actual murder,' Slider went on, 'Ruth had the perfect excuse to accost Chattie in the park, and persuade her to go into the shrubbery to talk. Chattie would believe it was about the suppression of the Codermatol again, and the secrecy, and Ruth wearing the hood of her top up would make sense and not make her suspicious.'

'You guessed from the beginning it was someone she knew, didn't you, boss,' Swilley said, 'because the CD Walkman had been turned off and she'd taken the earphones off. They were hanging round her neck. She wouldn't go to that trouble to talk to a stranger stopping to ask her for a light, or something.'

'The knife was an ordinary kitchen knife,' Slider went on, 'of the sort of which Ruth has a set in her kitchen. We'll test them all for blood, of course. It's surprising how often you can get enough even from a knife that's been washed several times. She'd have done better – from the Murderer's Manual point of view – to discard it with the clothes and replace it with a new one, but I suppose she didn't like the waste of the idea. She'd been brought up frugally. She wiped it on the grey top before she chucked it. Her biggest mistake, of course, was discarding the jacket and gloves so close to the scene. Otherwise we might never have found them.'

'Yes, why did she?' Joanna asked.

Atherton answered. 'Because she wanted to have a look at the scene of her crime, and admire the way she'd misdirected us.'

'I guessed it when I saw the map in my mind's eye. Ashchurch Grove makes a sort of D shape with Askew Road, Askew Road being the curved bit. When she left the park she went off up Askew Road, presumably heading back for her car; but then she passed the end of Ashchurch Grove and I suppose its direction tempted her and curiosity overcame her. There was no hue and cry after her, so she felt safe and thought she'd stroll back from a different direction and have a good laugh at how she'd fooled us. But she didn't quite like to bring the bloodstained clothes back, so she dropped them, in their carrier bag, over the fence of one of the gardens. There were bags of rubbish everywhere, so why should one more be noticed?'

'And in any case, she'd worn gloves, so no-one could bring it back to her – so she thought,' said Atherton.

'How do you know that's what she did? Did she tell you?' Joanna asked.

'No, I told her,' Slider said. 'At the very beginning, when I still thought it was the Park Killer, I had the faces in the crowd round the scene photographed, because it's amazing how often they will come back to see. Curiosity, I suppose. A very basic human instinct.'

'And she was there?'

'She was there,' Slider said. 'When I saw her photo in her husband's office, I thought she looked familiar. I'd spent so long staring at those damned crowd photos, her face had lodged in my brain.'

'One thing I don't understand,' Joanna said. 'How did she get Chattie to take the poison?'

'I worked that out,' Slider said, 'when I remembered something Bicycle Man, Phil Yerbury, did when he came in to be interviewed. Ruth was a runner too, so she knew the pattern.

What's the first thing a runner or a jogger or whatever does when they stop for any reason?'

Joanna had followed him. 'Take a drink of water?'

'Right. And they don't just sip, they chuck it back in a couple of huge gulps. All Ruth had to do, as Chattie was feeling for her bottle, was to say, "Here, have some of mine." A little Lucozade or something in it to disguise any bitterness and – wallop.'

'Clever,' said Joanna.

'If she'd refused, Ruth would just have had to stab her cold, but it was worth a try. And evidently it worked. Chattie was so kind-hearted she probably wouldn't have refused what seemed like a friendly gesture, especially as I imagine Ruth had not been particularly friendly before. Maybe Ruth said it was a special energy drink or something. Anyway, she swallowed enough to put her into a coma within minutes.'

'And you still don't know what it was?'

'It doesn't matter, really. The tox lab will come back to us in its own good time, but we've got enough evidence to be going on with.' Even as he said it, a slight doubt was niggling the back of his mind. They could link Ruth to the stabbing, but in Freddie Cameron's opinion it wasn't the stabbing that killed Chattie. Unless they could link the drug to Ruth as well, a clever brief might still get her off. His brain began to worry over the possibility, and he pulled it back. Not here, not now.

'Anyone want another pint?' Hollis asked.

The order was taken, and under cover of the conversation that broke out around it, Slider said to Joanna, 'Well, we've got her, anyway, and a better example of where greed and self-pity can lead you, you wouldn't need to find. Her husband's a broken man. Poor Bill Simpson has been scared out of his wits, and still feels guilty about Chattie's death—'

'But at least the acne cure won't be suppressed. He'll be glad about that.'

'I hope it won't.' He sighed. 'So many lives ruined. Things done that can't be undone.'

'Now, don't start that again,' she said. 'You always get depressed at the end of a case. Think positive: you avenged Chattie.'

'But that doesn't bring her back,' said Slider. 'And I only ever saw her dead. I wish I'd known her. I think she was a genuinely good and kind person.'

'Unless she really did have an affair with this Cockerell person,' she teased him gently.

'Of course she didn't. It would have been a deplorable lapse of taste on her part. Cockerell admitted that he fancied her, and tried to get off with her, but she talked him out of it, and they just had a few lunches together and some long heart-to-hearts and became friends.'

'Well, of course, he would say that,' said Atherton, leaning over to put a full pint in front of each of them.

'It was the truth,' Slider said indignantly. 'Why would she want to bonk that slippery cheese?'

'He was the big cheese,' said Atherton.

'No. Sorry. I just don't buy it. Tread softly, for you tread on my dreams. Chattie was a princess.'

His arm was round Joanna and he gave her a squeeze as he said it. She smiled, and then yawned, and said, 'Last pint, then I must get home to bed. I can't take these late nights any more.'

'You musicians have got no stamina,' Atherton said. 'We intend to make the night hideous with our carousings – don't we?' he added to Hart, who had moved round to join them.

'Yeah, what he said,' she agreed, leaning on him. 'So, all over bar the shouting, eh, guv?'

'Yes, thank God,' Slider said. He lifted his pint to his lips, and inside his head, made a silent valediction to Chattie, whom he had never known, but was close to loving.

Swilley called over heads, 'Boss, there's a phone call for you. Urgent.'

'Flaming Nora,' Slider said, 'are they even going to pursue me to the pub?' He struggled up from the velvet embrace of the banquette, edged out from behind the loaded table, and went over to the bar.

The landlord put the phone down in front of him. 'I've put it through to here,' he explained. 'They said it was urgent.'

'Thanks, Andy.' Slider wearily picked up the receiver, expecting trouble. It was not a premonition, just that most urgent phone calls were trouble, of one sort or another.

It was Porson. 'Ah, glad I caught you there, Slider. Just had a bell from Chief Superintendent Ormerod. He thought you ought to know. Put you on your guard, at least.'

'What is it, sir?'

'It's about Bates, Trevor Bates, that last case of yours. Bit of a shambles, red faces all round. Seems they were moving him to the maximum-security remand facility at Woodhill when the van was held up. He must have managed to communicate with some of his people on the outside. That's what comes of treating 'em soft, all those phone calls and private sessions with dodgy briefs.'

'I don't understand,' Slider said. 'You mean the Needle's escaped?'

'Yes, laddie,' Porson said, with deep regret. 'He's escaped. Clean as a whistle. They haven't got a clue where he is now, and given that he wasn't best pleased with you, Ormerod thought you ought to be alerted, in case he came after you. Unlikely, maybe, but even so . . .'

'*Bloody* Nora,' Slider said, with deep feeling and, in fairness, some justification.